FAVORITE TALES OF
SHOLOM ALEICHEM

FAVORITE TALES OF
SHOLOM ALEICHEM

Translated by
Julius and Frances Butwin

Illustrations by Ben Shahn

Avenel Books
New York

*SHORT
STORIES*

This book was previously published in separate volumes
under the titles:
The Old Country: Collected Stories of Sholom Aleichem Copyright MCMXLVI
by Crown Publishers, Inc.
Tevye's Daughters Copyright MCMXLIX by The Children of Sholom Aleichem
and Crown Publishers, Inc.

Copyright © 1983 by Crown Publishers, Inc.

This 1983 edition is published by Avenel Books, distributed by Crown Publishers, Inc.,
by arrangement with Crown Publishers, Inc.

Manufactured in the United States of America

ISBN: 0-517-412942

h g f e d c b a

DEC 10 '83

For My Parents
Gershon and Sonia Mazo

CONTENTS

Introduction

Publisher's note: Favorite Tales of Sholom Aleichem *brings together in one volume the stories that first appeared in* The Old Country, *translated by Julius and Frances Butwin, and in* Tevye's Daughters, *translated by Frances Butwin. The introduction to these collected tales is comprised of Frances Butwin's foreword to* The Old Country *and her introduction to* Tevye's Daughters, *altered slightly, with her permission, to bring them into accord with this omnibus volume of the stories.*

Years ago when Sholom Aleichem came to New York, Mark Twain was among the first to visit him. "I wanted to meet you," he said, "because I understand that I am the American Sholom Aleichem." History does not record the answer of the man who is called variously "the Jewish Mark Twain," "the Jewish Dickens," "the modern Heine."

There should be an end to these comparisons. Sholom Aleichem was none of these things. He was like no one else. He was unique, a genius whose writings are the perfect expression of a people, their mind, their heart, their wit and above all their special idiom.

Sholom Aleichem—"Peace be with you"—is the pen name of Solomon Rabinowitz, who was born in Pereyeslav in the Ukraine in 1859. One of the first modern writers to use Yiddish as a literary language, he wrote some three hundred short stories, five novels, and many plays. Driven into exile by the devastating pogroms of 1903 and 1905, he settled eventually in New York, where he died in 1916.

The work of translating these stories was a delight and a challenge at the same time. Often what was entirely right and simple and flavorsome in Yiddish completely missed fire when translated literally. Some stories just could not be transplanted and had to be abandoned. Sometimes we had to use translators' license with the exact wording. This we did in *A Page from the Song of Songs* and to some extent in *The Enchanted Tailor*, stories which depend a great deal on mood and atmosphere. Others that were carried forward by action and incident like *The Miracle of Hashono Rabo* and *The Convoy* follow the original almost word for word. In a few stories we left out passages that seemed to us irrelevant or outdated. This we did in *The Fiddle* where we omitted an elaborate description of the informer, and in *The Lottery Ticket* where a whole digression occurs that has no bearing on the story. We never tampered with the main flow of the story, and we never changed the substance of a beginning or an ending. A number of words which occur over and over and which have no equivalent in English were retained in the original Yiddish. Those are words descriptive of occupations like *melamed* and *shochet* and others which are almost self-explanatory in their context. Chief among these words is *shlimazl* which means literally a person of little luck.

The choice of stories was for the main part our own. We selected those that appealed to us most and those we thought would appeal to the English reader. Some we rejected for a definite reason, because of some special problem of translation as in the monologues which depend almost entirely on the teller's idiom, or when the story turned on some phrase that was completely untranslatable. Some of the stories seemed to us to be outdated, though there were surprisingly few of those. Others centered about a complicated religious ritual which would have needed a whole essay to explain. In many cases, we chose among several stories similar in type.

One of the most wonderful and at the same time the most maddening things about these stories is the utter simplicity of their language. You ask yourself over and over, how can such a limited vocabulary be such a perfect instrument for expression? It isn't the fact that it portrays a simple people. Compared to the people of a Steinbeck or a Hemingway, these are virtuosos of the intellect. Words are their chief weapon, their joy and their ornament. But it isn't the variety of words at their command so much as the way they are put together that makes their speech distinctive—the way a phrase is chopped off or inverted or repeated with slight variations. It is like spoken Yiddish which depends for its drama on the inflection of the voice, on a pause, a raised eyebrow or a shrug of the shoulder. These things are difficult to transmit into another language, but when you feel that you've succeeded you experience the real thrill of creation.

While the language is simple, it is often violent and earthy. We had to compromise with this earthiness. Take just the small matter of the Yiddish curse. There are as many types of curses as there are people cursing, but the hardest to explain is the mother cursing her child. The child may be crying because he is hungry. The mother bursts out, "Eat, eat, eat. All you want to do is eat. May the worms eat you. May the earth open up and swallow you alive." This mother loves her child; she is only pouring out the bitterness that's in her heart in the only way she knows. But in translation she sounds like a monster. When the wayward son-in-law Menachem Mendel comes home for Passover and his mother-in-law and his wife shower curses on his head he is not offended. He knows his wife is happy to see him because as soon as she is through cursing, she bursts into tears.

We encountered our greatest problem in working on the Tevye stories. They are all in the first person and they all depend for their effect on Tevye's manner of expressing himself. In fact, they *are* Tevye. Tevye is the perfect *shlimazl* and also the perfect *kasril*, the man whom nothing in life can down. He considers himself a man of great learning and erudition—that is what makes his life bearable— and his speech is practically a series of Hebrew quotations from the Holy Books, most of which are, of course, misquotations, hilariously funny to the reader who could understand them, but otherwise meaningless. The problem was not only how to untangle these misquotations, but also how to render mistakes in one language within another language into a third language. We simply had to omit many passages. In others we used Biblical diction to approximate the Hebrew. Of course, some of the pungency and flavor of this most delightful and most completely realized of all of Sholom Aleichem's characters was lost in translation.

I would like to emphasize that throughout his work we made no attempt to be academic or perfectionist. These stories are not for the Hebraist or the Yiddish scholar. They are not especially for those who can read and enjoy the original. Rather, they are intended for the many Jews and non-Jews who, through a barrier of language, have had no access to the work of the most interesting and most beloved of Yiddish writers. They are intended for the general reader to whom they may open a new field of human experience.

Both of us came from the Old Country, I more recently than my husband, but it was he who had the deeper sense of identification with the past. He was brought to America at the age of one from Walkowisk in Lithuanian Russia. For forty years—that is, all of his life—he lived in a middle-sized city in Mid-America. He walked its streets as a native, he knew its buildings and people, its history and politics intimately. The tempo of his life suited him. And yet his roots were elsewhere. He used to say that he knew the geography of Walkowisk as well as that of St. Paul. Here was his grandfather's mill, there the Long Street, here the *cheder* where his father used to teach as a young man. And that mill, that street, that *cheder* could just as well have been in Kasrilevka or Verebivka, in Boiberik or Haschavata. For all of those towns, real or mythical, in White Russia or the Ukraine, in Galicia or Lithuania, belong to the same country to which our parents and grandparents referred when they spoke of *in der heim,* or home.

One Sunday in November 1945, which turned out to be the last day of his life, my husband was talking about his grandparents. He told how his grandfather used to take him walking by the river; how he loved watching his grandmother roll out the thin yellow sheets of dough for noodles. He said, "For me they were the ideal grandparents." And I think that in a restricted but no less real sense the life they represented was to him an ideal life. He was aware of its limitations, its misery and hardship, but he also understood its dignity, its warmth, and most particularly its humor. He was a product of all these things. And it gave him rare pleasure to be able through these translations to interpret that life to his contemporaries.

These stories are intended for those to whom the Old Country is only a name remembered from childhood and for those to whom it represents a whole complex of emotions, of words and pictures, of smells and sounds, for which they have no common frame of reference. If we have succeeded in bringing Sholom Aleichem to Americans, if we have helped clarify and sharpen only a few of those sounds and smells and pictures, if we have lit up only a corner of that vast and wonderful country of the heart we call the Old Country, our work has been well worth doing.

"The Holy One, blessed be He," quotes Tevye the Dairyman, *"wished to grant merit to Israel"*; and in his own fashion he interprets this to mean: The Lord wanted to be good to Tevye, so He blessed him with seven daughters. And what kind of daughters? Meek, ugly, sickly creatures? No! Beauties—everyone of them— fine, well-grown girls, charming and good-tempered, healthy and high-spirited—like young pine trees! But that was as far as the Lord went in His bounty. He granted to Tevye neither money nor luck. And what good are beautiful and gifted daughters if you have neither money nor luck to go along with them? "If they had been ill-tempered and ugly as scarecrows," remarks Tevye ruefully, "it would have been better for them and certainly healthier for me." But then there would have been no Tevye the Dairyman as we know him, no chronicle of Tevye's daughters, as Sholom Aleichem planned and developed it, for the honor and enrichment of Yiddish literature.

That Sholom Aleichem planned the stories of Tevye's daughters as a single chronicle, there can be no doubt. A single theme runs through them all, and the style is identical. But he wrote each one as a separate narrative, with Tevye himself doing the narrating, addressing himself to Sholom Aleichem whom he meets from time to time over a period of fifteen to twenty years—sometimes in the woods near Boiberik, sometimes in Boiberik or on a train to Yehupetz. Each story has the same form; it is enclosed in a capsule, very much like a typical Yiddish letter. Tevye usually begins by greeting his old friend Sholom Aleichem, whom he has not seen for a long time; he goes on to recapitulate something of what went on before, picks up his story from there, and ends finally with farewells and good wishes, and a promise of more to come at some future meeting. This form is peculiarly suited to Tevye's rambling and informal style of narrative, and because we wished to preserve it and also to indicate the lapse of time between the stories, or chapters, we scattered them through the book instead of presenting them in a solid block.

In spite of the fact that these stories are separated by intervals of time and that each one presents a complete incident with its own climax and denouement, taken together they have the unity of a novel. On the surface, this novel is a family chronicle whose theme is the timeless and never-resolved conflict between the younger and older generations. Examined more closely, however, it is something more than a family saga. It is a story of social conflict laid at a precise turn of history—the last days of Tsarist Russia. With the accession of Nicholas II, the government of the Tsars had reached its final peak of intrigue and corruption. This was the last stage in its battle for survival. There was wide political unrest throughout the country, culminating in the revolutionary struggle of 1905-6, whose failure was followed by counter-revolution and a general disillusionment among the masses of people.

The political events of those years are reflected both directly and indirectly in the tragedies of Tevye's daughters. And we must also remember that along with the political conflict, which made its direct impact on the Jews in the form of economic and civic oppression and bloody pogroms, went the ferment within Jewry itself—the breaking up of old paternalistic molds, the influx of new movements: Zionism, the *Haskalah*, the Bund, the spread of secular learning and the revolt against narrow religious sectarianism. In the midst of this vortex, Tevye and his wife Golde represent the comparatively peaceful, patriarchal way of life; while their daughters are acted upon by, and in turn react violently to, the sweeping new currents.

But Tevye himself is not a static figure either. He is deeply religious, but he is no fanatic. He is aware of the changes taking place about him and unconsciously absorbs the spirit of those changes. For Tevye the Dairyman, whose fame as a dealer in milk and butter and cheese has spread like the sound of the *shofar* over the world, can't avoid rubbing elbows with the world. On his rounds with his horse and wagon he has met and had dealings (much to his sorrow) with Menachem-Mendel the *luftmensch*, the entrepreneur, who "deals in things you can't put your hands on," and makes and loses fortunes in less time than it takes Tevye to recite *Shma Yisroel*. He has met and talked with the young students, the sons of shoemakers and tailors, who have turned their backs on the study of the *Torah* and live six in a garret and feast on black bread and herring in order to attend the university. He has had dealings with the pompous *negidim* of Yehupetz who spend their summers in their *datchas* in Boiberik, and whose wives have expensive stomach ailments and travel abroad for cures. He has talked with men who understand a *medresh* and with men who don't know the difference between a *medresh* and a piece of horseflesh.

Tevye has been shaken from his moorings. He is a man in conflict with himself, he is not too sure that his way is always the best; and so we find him aiding and abetting his daughters in spite of his better, that is, more instinctive, judgment.

In "Modern Children," Tevye's oldest daughter Tzeitl defies the convention of "arranged marriages." Her mother wants her to marry the rich widower, Lazer-Wolf the Butcher. Tevye's wife Golde is a realist; she sees only what's in front of her and what she sees she doesn't like. Poverty, illness, and struggle have always been her lot. She wants something better for her daughters. To her "something better" means a pantry full of good food, a fur-lined cloak for weekdays and a cloak with a ruffle for Saturdays, shoes and stockings, linen and bedding—in short, a rich husband like Lazer-Wolf the Butcher. Tevye has no objection to these things either. He doesn't hold with the newfangled notion of romantic love; but when he is confronted with it, he weakens. We find him, against his better judgment, helping Tzeitl marry the poor tailor Motel Kamzoil from Anatevka. "That's modern children for you," says Tevye. "You sacrifice yourself for them, you slave for them day and night—and what do you get out of it?" But in his heart he is proud of his modern children; he is even proud of their defiance of him.

Hodel, the second of Tevye's daughters, has been infected with revolution. She is in love with Pertschik, the revolutionary young student, the son of the cigarette-maker. Again Tevye helps his daughter against his better judgment. He goes so far as to fabricate a story about a rich aunt and an inheritance to explain to Golde why Pertschik has to leave right after the hasty marriage ceremony. Driving Hodel and her brand-new husband to the station in his wagon, Tevye marvels at the young couple's apparent lack of emotion. But he reserves judgment. Tevye is not an old woman, he can wait and see. He waits, and he sees Hodel follow her husband to his prison in exile. Though his heart is broken at parting from her, and though he lays no claim to understanding her motives, in a curious way he is proud of her too.

But with his third daughter, Chava, Tevye comes to real grief. Chava is in love with a gentile, the peasant Fyedka Galagan, who is "another Gorky." Now Tevye might condone modern love, he might even shrug his shoulders at revolution with its crazy nonsense of "what's yours is mine and what's mine is yours," but he will never condone apostasy. When Chava marries her Fyedka and goes over to the gentiles, she severs herself completely from her family. She forfeits all the "mercy" that Tevye might have for the weaknesses of his children. For the essence of Tevye is his religion, it is his chief *raison d'être*, the condition of his survival; and if he condoned his daughter's apostasy, he would become something very much less than Tevye. . . .

The tragedy of Schprintze is of a different sort. Schprintze has fallen in love with a rich young man: she has tried to step out of her class. Or rather she has tried to ignore the division of class. Aarontchik is a good man, she tells her father, and he is surrounded by vulgar people who know nothing but money and money and money. But Tevye is not one to scorn "vulgar money." For the first time since he lost his fortune in the deal with Menachem-Mendel he permits himself to spin a dream of wealth. . . . "Perhaps God has willed it that through this quiet little Schprintze you should be rewarded for all the pain and suffering you have undergone until now and enjoy a pleasant and restful old age? Why not? Won't the honor sit well on you?" But he knows all along that he is deceiving himself, and he tries his best to talk Schprintze out of her infatuation. For in spite of Kishinevs and Constitutions, pogroms and revolutions, in spite of all the edicts of the Tsar's ministers to whom a *Zhyd* is a *Zhyd* whether he resides in a palace in Odessa or is squeezed with a family of ten into a hut in Kasrilev-ka—in spite of all this, the Jews themselves are as rigidly as ever divided into the rich and poor, the haves and have-nots, "those who walk on foot and those who ride on horseback." As Aarontchik's uncle puts it, "You are an intelligent person, how could you permit this, that Tevye the Dairyman, who brings us cheese and butter, should try to marry into *our* family?"

In the story of Beilke, the youngest and most beautiful of Tevye's daughters, the circle swings around again. Here it is Beilke herself, unlike her older sisters, who insists on marrying the rich Padhatzur, who made his pile in the Russo-Japanese war. When Tevye in revulsion against the pretensions and vulgarity of his rich son-in-law tells Beilke that "your sister Hodel would have done differently," she answers him, "I've told you before not to compare me to Hodel. Hodel lived in Hodel's time and Beilke is living in Beilke's time. The distance between the two is as great as from here to Japan." Beilke is the product of disillusionment. She knows very well that Hodel's husband will die in prison unless her Padhatzur, stuffed with money he has made at the expense of the government, will bribe that same government to have Pertschik's sentence lifted. Tevye bows to the inevitable and accepts from his son-in-law a ticket to the Holy Land.

But Tevye never starts out for the Holy Land. More disasters intervene. Even the self-assured Padhatzur who "might have entertained a Rothschild in his home" meets with financial failure, and has to flee to America "where all unhappy souls go." And the wave of pogroms which has engulfed the big cities finally overtakes Tevye who was sure "they would never reach him." Tevye's family from time immemorial had lived in a village, and when the May Laws of 1882 drove the Jews out of the villages, denied them the right to own land, and herded them together in the little towns of the Jewish Pale, Tevye's family was left untouched. But now in the days of Mendel Beiliss, when the whole world "went backwards," in the days just preceding the First World War, Tevye was finally "reached." He was politely told to "Get thee out." He was ordered to leave his "father-land," as he ironically calls it. But even in this extremity, Tevye savored a small triumph, more bitter than sweet, but still a triumph. His daughter Chava, whom he had chosen to count as dead, repents and comes back to her father and to her God. And so at the last Tevye stands vindicated. The religion he clung to so tenaciously through all his reversals of fortune is all that is left to him. "Tell our friends not to worry," he tells Sholom Aleichem at the final parting. "Our ancient God still lives."

To understand Tevye at all we must first understand his peculiar relation to God. To Tevye, God is not a remote Deity to whom one prays on Sabbaths and High Holy Days or in times of great trouble. He is not the Lawgiver to whom Moses spoke amidst thunder and lightning on Mt. Sinai. Tevye is on much more intimate terms with God. He speaks to Him on weekdays, as well as on the Sabbath, indoors and outdoors and in all kinds of weather, just as his forefathers Abraham, Isaac, and Jacob did. "You do not ask questions of God," says Tevye, but he persists in asking questions at all times. He never lets God alone. What are we and what is our life? What is this world and what is the next world? Why do you always pick on Tevye to do Thy will? Why don't you play with someone else for a change, a Brodsky or a Rothschild? What is the meaning of Jew and non-Jew? If Tevye's daughters are at war with society, Tevye himself wages his own war against God and man, and since he believes men's actions to be chiefly inspired by God, God is the chief Adversary.

Tevye gives battle with the only weapon he has at his disposal—the Holy Word. He fights God with God's own weapons and on God's own ground. He would sooner quote Scriptures than eat, and every mouthful he eats is accompanied by a quotation. As Golde says bitterly, "You drum my head full of quotations and you've done your duty by your children." Says Tevye, "I have to answer even this with a quotation." To Tevye talk is not a substitute for action. It is the only wholly satisfying action he knows.

Though Sholom Aleichem was a humorist and Tevye is his most famous character, Tevye is not funny. Nearly everything that happens to him and his daughters is tragic. His humor lies in his evaluation of what happens to him, in what he says and the way he says it. In the fact that he misquotes more often than he quotes, and that usually his interpretation of what he is quoting is completely cockeyed, lies his all-pervading charm to the Yiddish reader. No wonder Sholom Aleichem's audiences used to roll in the aisles with laughter. The juxtaposition of a lofty phrase in Hebrew or Aramaic with a homely Yiddish phrase which is supposed to explain it but has no bearing on it whatever—that is the gist of Tevye's humor. Tevye, of course, has no idea that he is funny. He continues to quote in Hebrew, in Russian, in whatever comes in handy. He likes to use the same quotation over and over, putting it to a different use each time, and, above all, he is never at a loss for a quotation. When nothing apt occurs to him he reaches into his memory and snatches at the first thing that he can lay his hands on.

Tevye is unique among Sholom Aleichem's characters. No other character displays his peculiar blend of innocence and shrewdness, kindliness and irony, weakness and toughness. He is less a type and more a personality than any of the others, but Tevye did not spring full-grown from a desert, he was not "God's only son." Though he lived in the country, and not in one of the little towns where the Jews were packed together "as tightly as herring in a barrel," Tevye was brother and uncle and cousin to the people of Kasrilevka and Anatevka and Mazapevka and even of Yehupetz and Odessa. He was related to Menachem-Mendel by marriage and no doubt to half of Kasrilevka as well. He knew the Benjamin Lastechkys, the Samuel Fingerhuts, the fish peddlers and tinmen, the poultrywomen and traveling salesmen, the Zaidels and the Reb Yozifels. It isn't stretching the point too far to consider them all as minor characters in the drama of Tevye and his daughters, and their stories as a background for the central action. Taken together, all of these stories are a part of the life, forever vanished, which Sholem Aleichem reproduced so faithfully, with tenderness, with humor and sharp penetration, but never with malice or bitterness.

The nearest we come to bitterness in Tevye himself is when he reflects on the ways of the world: "I wasn't worried about God so much. I could come to terms with Him one way or another. What bothered me was people. Why should people be so cruel when they could be so kind? Why should human beings bring suffering to others and to themselves when they could all live together in peace and goodwill?" Tevye contents himself with asking questions. His daughters went a step farther. They challenged the conventions of "cruelty and suffering," they "strained after a new life" and took desperate chances to attain it. Sometimes they won, more often they lost. Their story is as pertinent today as it was when they lived it.

Minneapolis   FRANCES BUTWIN
1983

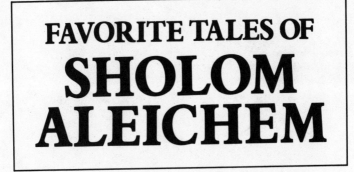

FAVORITE TALES OF
SHOLOM ALEICHEM

The Town of the Little People

THE town of the little people into which I shall now take you, dear reader, is exactly in the middle of that blessed Pale into which Jews have been packed as closely as herring in a barrel and told to increase and multiply. The name of the town is Kasrilevka. How did this name originate? I'll tell you:

Among us Jews poverty has many faces and many aspects. A poor man is an unlucky man, he is a pauper, a beggar, a *schnorrer*, a starveling, a tramp, or a plain failure. A different tone is used in speaking of each one, but all these names express human wretchedness. However, there is still another name—*kasril*, or *kasrilik*. That name is spoken in a different tone altogether, almost a bragging tone. For instance, "Oh, am I ever a *kasrilik*!" A *kasrilik* is not just an ordinary pauper, a failure in life. On the contrary, he is a man who has not allowed poverty to degrade him. He laughs at it. He is poor, but cheerful.

Stuck away in a corner of the world, isolated from the surrounding country, the town stands, orphaned, dreaming, bewitched, immersed in itself and remote from the noise and bustle, the confusion and tumult and greed, which men have created about them and have dignified with high-sounding names like Culture, Progress, Civilization. A proper person may take off his hat with respect to these things, but not these little people! Not only do they know nothing of automobiles, modern travel, airplanes—for a long time they refused to

1

believe in the existence of the old, ordinary railroad train. "Such a thing could not be," they said. "Why," they said, "it's a dream, a fairy tale. You might just as well talk of merry-go-rounds in heaven!"

But it happened once that a householder of Kasrilevka had to go to Moscow. When he came back he swore with many oaths that it was true. He himself had ridden in a train to Moscow, and it had taken him—he shrugged his shoulders—less than an hour. This the little people interpreted to mean that he had ridden less than an hour and then walked the rest of the way. But still the fact of the train remained. If a Jew and a householder of Kasrilevka swore to it, they could not deny that there was such a thing as a train. It had to be true. He could not have invented it out of thin air. He even explained to them the whole miracle of the train, and drew a diagram on paper. He showed them how the wheels turned, the smokestack whistled, the carriages flew, and people rode to Moscow. The little people of Kasrilevka listened and listened, nodded their heads solemnly, and deep in their hearts they laughed at him. "What a story! The wheels turn, the smokestack whistles, the carriages fly and people ride to Moscow—and then come back again!"

That's how they all are, these little people. None of them are gloomy, none of them are worried little men of affairs, but on the contrary they are known everywhere as jesters, story-tellers, a cheerful, light-hearted breed of men. Poor but cheerful. It is hard to say what makes them so happy. Nothing—just sheer joy of living. Living? If you ask them, "How do you live?" they will answer, with a shrug and a laugh. "How do we live? Who knows? We live!" A remarkable thing—whenever you meet them they are scurrying like rabbits, this one here, that one there. They never have time to stop. "What are you hurrying for?" "What am I hurrying for? Well, it's like this. If we hurry we think we might run into something—earn a few pennies—provide for the Sabbath."

To provide for the Sabbath—that is their goal in life. All week they labor and sweat, wear themselves out, live without food or drink, just so there is something for the Sabbath. And when the holy Sabbath arrives, let Yehupetz perish, let Odessa be razed, let Paris itself sink into the earth! Kasrilevka lives! And this is a fact, that since Kasrilevka was founded, no Jew has gone hungry there on the Sabbath. Is it possible that there is a Jew who does not have fish for the Sabbath? If he has no fish, then he has meat. If he has no meat, then he has herring. If he has no herring, then he has white bread. If he has no white bread, then he has black bread and onions. If he has no black bread and onions, then he borrows some from his neighbor. Next week, the neighbor will borrow from him. "The world is a wheel and it keeps turning." The Kasrilevkite repeats this maxim and shows you with his hand how it turns. To him a maxim, a witty remark, is everything. For an apt remark he will forsake his mother and father, as the saying goes. The tales you hear about these little people sound fabulous, but you may be sure they are all true.

For instance, there is the story of the Kasrilevkite who got tired of starving in Kasrilevka and went out into the wide world to seek his fortune. He left the country, wandered far and wide, and finally reached Paris. There, naturally, he wanted to see Rothschild. For how can a Jew come to Paris and not visit Rothschild? But they didn't let him in. "What's the trouble?" he wants to know. "Your coat is torn," they tell him.

"You fool," says the Jew. "If I had a good coat, would I have gone to Paris?"

It looked hopeless. But a Kasrilevkite never gives up. He thought a while and said to the doorman: "Tell your master that it isn't an ordinary beggar who has come to his door, but a Jewish merchant, who has brought him a piece of goods such as you can't find in Paris for any amount of money."

Hearing this, Rothschild became curious and asked that the merchant be brought to him.

"*Sholom aleichem,*" said Rothschild.

"*Aleichem sholom,*" said the merchant.

"Take a seat. And where do you come from?"

"I come from Kasrilevka."

"What good news do you bring?"

"Well, Mr. Rothschild, they say in our town that you are not so badly off. If I had only half of what you own, or only a third, you would still have enough left. And honors, I imagine, you don't lack either, for people always look up to a man of riches. Then what do you lack? One thing only—eternal life. That is what I have to sell you."

When Rothschild heard this he said, "Well, let's get down to business. What will it cost me?"

"It will cost you—" here the man stopped to consider—"it will cost you—three hundred *rubles.*"

"Is that your best price?"

"My very best. I could have said a lot more than three hundred. But I said it, so it's final."

Rothschild said no more, but counted out three hundred *rubles,* one by one.

Our Kasrilevkite slipped the money into his pocket, and said to Rothschild: "If you want to live for ever, my advice to you is to leave this noisy, busy Paris, and move to our town of Kasrilevka. There you can never die, because since Kasrilevka has been a town, no rich man has ever died there."

And then there is the story of the man who got as far as America . . . But if I started to tell all the tales of these little people I'd have to sit with you for three days and three nights and talk and talk and talk. Instead, let us pass on to a description of the little town itself.

Shall I call it a beautiful little town? From a distance it looks —how shall I say it?—like a loaf of bread thickly studded with poppy seed. Some of the houses are built on the slope of a hill, and the rest are huddled together at the base, one on top of the other, like the gravestones in an ancient cemetery. There are no streets to speak of because the houses are not built according to any plan, and besides, where is there room for such a thing? Why should there be vacant space when you can build something on it? It is written that the earth is to be inhabited, not merely to be gazed at.

Yet, don't be upset. There are some streets—big streets, little streets, back streets and alleys. What if they happen to twist and turn uphill and downhill and suddenly end up in a house or a cellar or just a hole in the ground? If you are a stranger, never go out alone at night without a lantern. As for the little people who live there, don't worry about them. A Kasrilevkite in Kasrilevka, among Kasrilevkites, will never get lost. Each one finds the way to his own house, to his wife and children, like a bird to its own nest.

And then in the center of the city there is a wide half-circle, or perhaps it is a square, where you find the stores, shops, market stands, stalls and tables. There every morning the peasants from the surrounding countryside congregate with their produce—fish and onions, horseradish, parsnips and other vegetables. They sell these things and buy from the little people other necessities of life, and from this the Kasrilevkites draw their livelihood. A meager one, but better than nothing. And in the square also lie all the town's goats, warming themselves in the sun.

There also stand the synagogues, the meeting houses, the

chapels and schools of the town where Jewish children study the Holy Writ. The noise they and the rabbis make with their chanting is enough to deafen one. The baths where the women go to bathe are also there, and the poorhouse where the old men die, and other such public institutions. No, the Kasrilev-kites have never heard of canals or water works or electricity or other such luxuries. But what does that matter? Everywhere people die the same death, and they are placed in the same earth, and are beaten down with the same spades. Thus my Rabbi, Reb Israel, used to say—when he was happiest, at a wedding or other celebration, after he had had a few glasses of wine and was ready to lift up the skirts of his long coat and dance a *kazatsky* . . .

But the real pride of Kasrilevka is her cemeteries. This lucky town has two rich cemeteries, the old and the new. The new one is old enough and rich enough in graves. Soon there will be no place to put anyone, especially if a pogrom should break out or any of the other misfortunes which befall us in these times.

But it is of the old cemetery that the people of Kasrilevka are especially proud. This old cemetery, though it is overgrown with grass and with bushes and has practically no upright head-stones, they still value as they might a treasure, a rare gem, a piece of wealth, and guard it like the apple of their eye. For this is not only the place where their ancestors lie, rabbis, men of piety, learned ones, scholars and famous people, including the dead from the ancient massacres of Chmelnitski's time—but also the only piece of land of which they are the masters, the only bit of earth they own where a blade of grass can sprout and a tree can grow and the air is fresh and one can breathe freely.

You should see what goes on in this old cemetery a month before the New Year, during the "days of weeping." Men and women—mainly women—swarm up and down the paths to their ancestors' graves. From all the surrounding country they come to weep and to pour their hearts out at the holy graves. Believe me, there is no place where one can weep so freely and with such abandon as in "the field" of Kasrilevka. In the synagogue a person can weep pretty freely too, but the synagogue doesn't come up to the cemetery. The cemetery is a source of income for the Kasrilevkite stonecutters, innkeepers, cantors and sextons, and the month before the New Year is, for the paupers thereabouts and the old women and the cripples, the real harvest time.

"Have you been in 'our field' yet?" a Kasrilevkite will ask you cheerfully, as though he were asking if you had been in his father's vineyard. If you haven't been there, do him a kindness, and go down into "the field," read the old, half-obliterated inscriptions on the leaning tombstones and you will find in them the story of a whole people. And if you happen to be a man of feeling and imagination then you will look upon this poor little town with its rich cemeteries and repeat the old verses:

"How beautiful are your tents, O Jacob; how good are your resting places, O Israel."

The Inheritors

THE Maiers and the Schnaiers . . .

Actually there was only one Maier and one Schnaier. They were twins and they looked so much alike that there were times when it was impossible to tell which of the two was Maier and which was Schnaier. As babies, the story goes, a queer thing happened to them. They were almost exchanged—and it is possible that they really were exchanged. This is how it happened.

Their mother, you may know, was a tiny woman and quite frail, but very fruitful. Every year without fail she gave birth to a child, but the sickly infant barely lingered through its first twelve months and then died. This went on until she finally stopped having children and thought she would never have another. But in the end a miracle happened. In her old age the Lord blessed her again, and this time with twins. And since it was too hard for her to suckle two babies, she had to hire a wet nurse. What else was there to do? A Kasrilevkite —no matter how poor he may be—will never throw a child of his into the streets or give it to a stranger to raise, unless, God forbid, the child be an orphan.

Having hired the nurse, the mother took Maier for herself (he was older than Schnaier by half an hour) and she gave Schnaier to the nurse. But since the nurse was herself not such a healthy woman, neither Maier nor Schnaier got too much milk. Both babies were equally starved; they screamed all night long; tore the house apart with their noise. It happened one day that the women were bathing the babies, naturally in one basin. They undressed them and put them into the hot water. Then, adding fresh water to the basin, they watched the children, red and bloated, splashing their little hands and feet, rolling about like beetles, enjoying themselves hugely. When they were through bathing them they took the babies out, wrapped them in a sheet (naturally one sheet) and put them to bed (naturally one bed) to dry. But when they started to dress them again, they couldn't tell which was Maier and which was Schnaier. And an argument took place between the two women.

"Look here, I could swear that this is Maier and this is Schnaier."

"How could you say that? This one is Maier and that one is Schnaier. Can't you see?"

"Do you think I'm dreaming? Either you're crazy, or just out of your head!"

"Good Lord! Can't you tell by their eyes that this is Maier and that is Schnaier? Look at those two eyes of his!"

"A fine argument! What do you want him to have—three eyes?"

Well, one of them kept insisting that Maier was Schnaier and Schnaier was Maier, and the other that Schnaier was Maier and Maier was Schnaier. Until at last the men came in and offered a solution. After all, they were men, with superior brains.

"Do you know what?" they suggested. "Try nursing the babies and we shall see. The one who takes his mother's breast must be Maier and the one who takes the nurse's must be Schnaier. That's simple enough."

And so it happened. As soon as the babies snuggled up to the breast, they each began to suck hungrily, smacked their lips, kicked their legs and made sounds like hungry puppies.

"A miracle of God!" said the men, with tears in their eyes. "See how the Almighty has created His world!"

And as a final test they decided to change the babies and see what would happen. The poor infants were torn away from their breasts and changed about, Schnaier taking Maier's place and Maier Schnaier's. And what do you suppose happened? Do you think they stopped sucking? They sucked as hard as ever!

From that time on they gave up trying to tell them apart. Let them be Maier-Schnaier and Schnaier-Maier. And they were given the name of the Maiers and the Schnaiers, as though each one was both a Maier and a Schnaier. More than once it happened in *cheder* that Maier was whipped when Schnaier should have got the whipping, or the other way around, Schnaier was punished for Maier's misdeeds. And in order to avoid hard feelings, the rabbi hit on this scheme (do they not say where there is learning there is wisdom?):

"You know what, children? Both of you stretch out. Then there will be no argument that I beat this one or that one. It will all remain in the family . . ."

But much, much later—after their *Bar Mitzvah,* when the Maiers and Schnaiers had reached manhood—something happened that made it possible to tell them apart a mile away even at night. What wonders God can devise! The brothers began to sprout beards (they must both have begun to smoke cigars too early) and on Maier's cheeks and upper lip there appeared black hairs (black as ink) and on Schnaier's face red hairs (red as fire). These beards grew as if the devil possessed them (they must both have continued to smoke cigars), so that by the time they were married they both had full beards. Did I say beards? Feather dusters was more like it. A black duster and a red one, that looked as if someone had glued them on.

Great are the works of the Lord, and His wonders are without end. For who knows what would have come to pass after their weddings if the beards, too, had been alike? In the confusion, even the wives might not have known which one of the brothers they had married . . . I do not know how it is with you in the big cities, but here in Kasrilevka it has never yet happened that husbands and wives should start exchanging each other. It is possible that there are husbands among us who would not object to this, but they know their wives and they know what they would get from them. However, all this is beside the point. The real story begins now.

Up till now we have concerned ourselves only with the Maiers and Schnaiers, that is with Maier and Schnaier, and we have become slightly acquainted with their mother and nurse, but we have not said a word about their father, as though they had never had a father. God forbid! Such a thing may have happened to others, but never to our kind of people. We have, thank God, no homes for foundlings where children are raised by strangers. It has never happened among us that a child should grow up and not know who his real father was. And if such a thing has happened, it has happened somewhere in Odessa or in Paris or in faraway America . . . As for Kasrilevka, I can swear that such a thing has never happened, and if it did, it happened to some servant girl or some other unfortunate maiden who was led astray by accident, through no fault of her own—an unhappy victim of another's lust . . .

In short, the Maiers and Schnaiers had a father, and a very fine father, too. He was a virtuous and an honest man named Reb Shimshen, and he had a magnificent beard, long and rich and luxurious. In fact, it could be said without exaggeration that Reb Shimshen had more beard than face. And for that reason he was known in Kasrilevka as Reb Shimshen Beard.

And this Reb Shimshen was—I don't even know what he was. But you can be sure that all his life he struggled and sweated for a meager living, waged constant warfare against poverty. Sometimes he overcame poverty; sometimes poverty overcame him, as is usual with Kasrilevkites, who are not afraid of want, but thumb their noses at it . . .

And Reb Shimshen lived out his life and finally he died. And when he died he was given a handsome burial. Almost the whole town followed his remains to the cemetery.

"Who is it that died?"

"Haven't you heard? Reb Shimshen."

"Which Reb Shimshen?"

"Reb Shimshen Beard."

"A great pity. So Reb Shimshen Beard is gone from us too."

That is what they said in Kasrilevka and mourned not so much for Reb Shimshen himself as for the fact that with his death there was one person less in Kasrilevka. Strange people, these Kasrilevkites! In spite of the fact that they are so poor that they almost never have enough for themselves, they would be pleased if no one among them ever died. Their only comfort is that people die everywhere, even in Paris, and that no one can buy his way out. Even Rothschild himself, who is greater than royalty, has to get up and go when the Angel of Death beckons.

Now let us turn back again to the Maiers and Schnaiers.

As long as Reb Shimshen was alive the Maiers and Schnaiers lived as one, brothers in body and soul. But when their father died they became enemies at once, ready to tear each other's beards out. Perhaps you wonder why? Well, why do sons ever

fight after a father's death? Naturally, over the inheritance.
It is true that Reb Shimshen did not leave behind any farms
or woodlands, houses or rental property, and certainly no cash.
Nor did he leave any jewelry, silver or furniture to his children
—not because he was mean or avaricious, but simply because
he had nothing to leave. And yet don't think that Reb Shimshen left his children absolutely nothing. He left them a treasure that could be turned to money at any time, a treasure that
could be pawned, rented or sold outright. This treasure we
speak of was the seat he had had in the old Kasrilevka Synagogue, a seat along the east wall right next to Reb Yozifel, the
Rabbi, who was next to the Holy Ark. It is true that Kasrilevka
wits have a saying that it is better to have an acre outside than
a seat inside, but that is only a saying, and when the Lord is
kind and a person does have his own seat, and along the east
wall at that, it's not so very bad—and certainly better than
nothing . . .

In short, Reb Shimshen left behind a seat in the old Kasrilevka Synagogue. But he forgot one small detail. He didn't
indicate who was to inherit the seat—Maier or Schnaier.

Obviously Reb Shimshen—may he forgive me—did not expect to die. He had forgotten that the Angel of Death lurks
always behind our backs and watches every step we take, else
he would surely have made a will or otherwise indicated in the
presence of witnesses to which of his two sons he wanted to
leave his fortune.

Well, what do you suppose? The very first Saturday after
they arose from mourning, the quarrel began. Maier argued
that according to law the seat belonged to him, since he was the
older (by a good half-hour). And Schnaier had two arguments
in his favor: first, they were not sure which of the two was
older because according to their mother's story they had been
exchanged as infants and he was really Maier and Maier was

really Schnaier. In the second place, Maier had a rich father-in-law who also owned a seat along the east wall of the synagogue, and since the father-in-law had no sons the seat would eventually be Maier's. And when that happened Maier would have two seats by the east wall and Schnaier would have none whatever. And if that was the case, where was justice? Where was humanity?

When he heard of these goings-on, Maier's father-in-law, a man of means, but one who had made his money only recently, entered the battle. "You've got a lot of nerve!" he exclaimed. "I am not forty yet and I have every intention of living a long time, and here you are, dividing up my inheritance already. And besides, how do you know that I won't have a son yet? I may have more than one, see!" he stormed. "There is impudence for you!"

So their neighbors tried to make peace between them, suggested that they determine how much the seat was worth and then have one brother buy his share from the other. That sounds reasonable enough, doesn't it? The only trouble was that neither brother wanted to sell his share. They didn't care a thing about the money. What was money—compared to stubbornness and pride?

"How can one's own brother be so pigheaded as to keep a person away from his rightful seat?" "Why should you have our father's place, and not I?" It became a matter not so much of having things his own way as it was of preventing the other from having his. As the saying is: If I don't, you don't either. And the rivalry between the Maiers and the Schnaiers increased in fury. Stubbornness gave way to cunning as each tried to outwit the other!

The first Sabbath Maier came early and sat down in his father's seat; and Schnaier remained standing throughout the services. The second Sabbath Schnaier came first and occupied his father's place, while Maier remained standing. The third Sabbath Maier got there still earlier, spread himself out in the seat, pulled his *tallis* over his head, and there he was . . .

The next time it was Schnaier who hurried to get there first, sat down in the coveted seat, pulled his *tallis* over his face— and just try to budge him! The following week Maier was the first to get there . . . This went on week after week till one fine Sabbath both of them arrived at the same time—it was still dark outside—took their posts at the door of the synagogue (it was still shut) and glared at each other like roosters ready to tear each other's eyes out. It was like this that long ago the first two brothers stood face to face in an empty field, under God's blue sky, full of anger, ready to annihilate one another, devour each other, spill innocent blood . . .

But let us not forget that the Maiers and Schnaiers were young men of good family, respectable and well behaved—not rowdies who were in the habit of assaulting each other in public. They waited for Ezriel, the *shammes,* to come and open the door of the synagogue. Then they would show the whole world who would get to their father's seat first—Maier or Schnaier . . .

The minutes passed like years till Ezriel arrived with the keys. And when Ezriel, with his tangled beard, arrived he was not able to reach the door because the brothers stood against it—one with the left foot, the other with the right foot, and would not budge an inch.

"Well, what's going to happen?" said Ezriel casually, taking a pinch of snuff. "If the two of you insist on standing there like mean scarecrows I won't be able to open the door and the synagogue will have to remain closed all day. Go ahead and tell me: does that make sense?"

Apparently these words had some effect, because the Maiers

and Schnaiers both moved back, one to the right, the other to the left, and made way for Ezriel and his key. And when the key turned in the lock and the door swung open, the Maiers and Schnaiers tumbled in headlong.

"Be careful, you're killing me!" yelled Ezriel the *shammes,* and before he could finish the words the poor man lay trampled under their feet, screaming in horror: "Watch out! You're trampling all over me—the father of a family!"

But the Maiers and Schnaiers cared nothing for Ezriel and his family. Their only thought was for the seat, their father's seat, and jumping over benches and praying stands they made for the east wall. There they planted themselves firmly against the wall with their shoulders and the floor with their feet and tried to shove each other aside. In the scuffle they caught each other's beards, grimaced horribly, gritted their teeth and growled: "May the plague take you before you get this seat!"

In the meantime Ezriel got up from the floor, felt to see if any of his bones were broken, and approached the brothers. He found them both on the floor clutching each other's beards. At first he tried to reason with them.

"Shame on you! Two brothers—children of the same father and mother—tearing each other's beards out! And in a Holy Place at that! Be ashamed of yourselves!"

But Ezriel gathered that at the moment his lecture was in vain. Actually, his words added fuel to the flame so that the two children of one father became so enraged that one of them clutched in his fist a tuft of black hair (from Maier's beard) and the other a tuft of red (Schnaier's beard); blue marks showed on both faces and from the nose of one streamed blood.

As long as it was merely a matter of pulling beards, slapping and pummeling each other, the *shammes* could content himself with reading a lecture. But when he saw blood streaming, Ezriel could stand it no longer, for blood, even though only from a punched nose, was an ugly thing fit for rowdies and not God-fearing men.

He wasted no time, but ran to the tap, grabbed a dipper of water, and poured it over the two brothers. Cold water has always—since the world was created—been the best means of reviving a person. A man may be in the greatest rage, but as soon as he gets a cold bath he is strangely refreshed and cool; he comes to his senses. This happened to the Maiers and the Schnaiers. At the unexpected shower of cold water to which Ezriel had treated them, they woke up, looked each other in the eyes, and grew ashamed—like Adam and Eve when they had tasted of the forbidden fruit of the Tree of Knowledge and saw their nakedness . . .

And that very Saturday night the Maiers and Schnaiers went together with their friends and neighbors to the home of Reb Yozifel, the Rabbi, to have the dispute settled.

If Kasrilevka had not been such a tiny place, stuck away in a forgotten corner, far from the great world, and if newspapers and periodicals had been printed there, the world would surely have come to know the works of our Rabbi, Reb Yozifel. The papers would have been full of tales about him and his wisdom. The great, the wise and the famous of the world would have traveled far to see him in person and to hear from his own lips the words of wisdom. Photographers and painters would have made portraits of him and spread them to the four corners of the earth. Interviewers would have plagued him, given him no rest. They would have asked him all his views —what his favorite dishes were, how many hours a day he slept, what he thought about this and that, about cigarette smoking and bicycle riding . . . But since Kasrilevka is a tiny place stuck away in a forgotten corner, far from the world, and papers

and periodicals are not printed there, the world knows nothing
of the existence of Reb Yozifel. The papers never mention his
name. The great, the wise and the famous do not come to him,
photographers and painters do not make pictures of him. Interviewers leave him alone. And Reb Yozifel lives his life
quietly, modestly, without noise or fanfare. No one knows
anything about him except the town of Kasrilevka, which
marvels at him, glories in his wisdom, and pays him great
honor (of riches there is little in Kasrilevka, but honor they will
give one as much as he deserves). They say that he is a man
who modestly conceals his wisdom and it is only when you
come to him for judgment that you find out how deep he is,
how profound, how sharp. Another Solomon!

With the Sabbath over and the benedictions completed, the
Maiers and Schnaiers came to Reb Yozifel to have their dispute
settled, and there they found the house already full of people.
The whole town was anxious to hear how he would settle it,
how he would divide one seat between two brothers.

First he gave both sides a chance to unburden themselves.
Reb Yozifel works according to this theory: that before the
verdict is handed down the litigants should have the right to
say anything they want to—because after the verdict all the
talking in the world won't help. After that he let Ezriel, the
shammes, talk. After all, he was the chief witness. And then
other townspeople had their turn—everyone who had the public
welfare at heart. And they talked as long as they wanted. Reb
Yozifel is the kind of person who lets everyone talk. He is
something of a philosopher. He feels this way about it: that
no matter how long a person talks, he will have to stop some
time.

And that is just what happened. They talked and talked and
talked, and finally stopped talking. And when the last person

was through, Reb Yozifel turned to the Maiers and Schnaiers and spoke to them quietly, calmly, as his custom was.

"Hear ye, my friends—this is my opinion. According to what I have heard from you and from all the other citizens it is apparent that both of you are right. You both had one father, and a very noble father, too—may he enjoy the blessings of Paradise. The only trouble is that he left you only one seat in the synagogue. Naturally, this seat is very dear to both of you. After all—it is something to own one's seat along the east wall of the old, old Kasrilevka Synagogue. You can't dismiss that with a wave of the hand. What then? Just as it is impossible for one person to use two seats, so it is impossible for two people to use a single one. On the contrary, it is much easier for one person to use two seats than for two to use one."

And so with example and precept he went on to explain the difficulty of the situation.

"But there is one way," he continued, "in which each of you can sit along the eastern wall in adjoining seats. I have come upon this solution after much reflection. And this is what I have to say. My seat in the synagogue is right next to the one your father left. One of you can have my seat and then both of you brothers can sit next to each other in peace and amity, and you will have no need to quarrel any more. And if you will ask what will I do without a seat? then I will answer you with another question: "Where is it written that a Rabbi or any other man, for that matter, must have his own seat and especially at the east wall, and at the old Kasrilevka Synagogue at that? Let us stop to consider. What is a synagogue? A house of prayer. And why do we go to the synagogue? To pray. To whom? To the Almighty. And where is He found? Everywhere. All the world is filled with His glory. If that is the case, then what difference does it make whether it is east or north or south, whether it is near the Ark or by the door? The important thing is to come to the synagogue and to pray.

"Let me give you an example. Once there was a king . . ."

And there followed another of Reb Yozifel's parables of the two servants who began to tear each other's beards in the presence of the king. And they were sent away with this admonition: "If you want to tear each other's beards, go outside and do it as much as your heart desires, but do not defile my palace . . ."

Thus Reb Yozifel chided them gently, and then he said, "Go home now, my children, in peace and let your father be an advocate in heaven for you, for us, and for all Israel."

Thus the Rabbi handed down his verdict and all the people went home.

The following Sabbath, the Maiers and Schnaiers came to the synagogue and stationed themselves near the door. No matter how much they were entreated by the *shammes* on one side and the Rabbi on the other, they refused to occupy the seats by the east wall.

If there is anyone who would like to have his own seat by the east wall in the old, old Kasrilevka Synagogue, the seat next to Reb Yozifel, the Rabbi, at a reasonable price, let him go to Kasrilevka and see the children of Reb Shimshen Beard, either Maier or Schnaier, it does not matter which. They will sell it to you at any price you say, because neither of them uses that seat any more. It stands there—unoccupied.

What a waste!

Tevye Wins a Fortune

Who raiseth up the poor out of the dust,
And lifteth up the needy out of the dunghill.
—PSALMS, 113:7.

IF YOU are destined to draw the winning ticket in the lottery, Mr. Sholom Aleichem, it will come right into your house without your asking for it. As King David says, "It never rains but it pours." You don't need wisdom or skill. And, on the contrary, if you are not inscribed as a winner in the Books of the Angels, you can talk yourself blue in the face—it won't help you. The *Talmud* is right: "You can lead a horse to water, but you cannot make him drink." A person slaves, wears himself to the bone, and gets nowhere. He might as well lie down and give up his ghost. Suddenly, no one knows how or for what reason, money rolls in from all sides. As the passage has it, "Relief and deliverance will come to the Jews." I don't have to explain that to you. It should be clear to both of us that so long as a Jew can still draw breath and feel the blood beating in his veins, he must never lose hope. I have seen it in my own experience, in the way the Lord dealt with me in providing me with my present livelihood. For how else should I happen to be selling cheese and butter all of a sudden? In my wildest dreams I had never seen myself as a dairyman.

Take my word for it, the story is worth hearing. I'll sit down for a little while here near you on the grass. Let the horse

21

do a little nibbling meanwhile. After all, even a horse is one of God's living creatures.

Well, it was in the late spring, around *Shevuos* time. But I don't want to mislead you; it may have been a week or two before *Shevuos,* or—let's see—maybe a couple of weeks after *Shevuos.* Don't forget, this didn't happen yesterday. Wait! To be exact, it was nine or ten years ago to the day. And maybe a trifle more.

In those days I was not the man I am today. That is, I *was* the same Tevye, and yet not exactly the same. The same old woman, as they say, but in a different bonnet. How so? I was as poor as a man could be, completely penniless. If you want to know the truth I'm not a rich man now either, but compared with what I was then I can now really call myself a man of wealth. I have a horse and wagon of my own, a couple of cows that give milk, and a third that is about to calve. We can't complain. We have cheese and butter and fresh cream all the time. We make it ourselves; that is, our family does. We all work. No one is idle. My wife milks the cows; the children carry pitchers and pails, churn the butter. And I myself, as you see, drive to market every morning, go from *datcha* to *datcha* in Boiberik, visit with people, see this one and that one, all the important businessmen from Yehupetz who come there for the summer. Talking to them makes me feel that I am somebody, too; I amount to something in the world.

And when Saturday comes—then I really live like a king! I look into the Holy Books, read the weekly portion of the Bible, dip into the commentaries, Psalms, *Perek,* this, that, something else . . . Ah, you're surprised, Mr. Sholom Aleichem! No doubt you're thinking to yourself, "Ah, that Tevye —there's a man for you!"

Anyway, what did I start to tell you? That's right. Those days. Oh, was Tevye a pauper then! With God's help I starved to death—I and my wife and children—three times a day, not counting supper. I worked like a horse, pulling wagonloads of logs from the woods to the railroad station for—I am ashamed to admit it—half a *ruble* a day. And that not every day, either. And on such earnings just try to fill all those hungry mouths, not counting that boarder of mine, the poor horse, whom I can't put off with a quotation from the *Talmud*.

So what does the Lord do? He is a great, all-powerful God. He manages His little world wisely and well. Seeing how I was struggling for a hard crust of bread, He said to me: "Do you think, Tevye, that you have nothing more to live for, that the world has come to an end? If that's what you think, you're a big lummox. Soon you will see: if I will it, your luck can change in one turn of the wheel, and what was dark as the grave will be full of brightness." As we say on *Yom Kippur,* the Lord decides who will ride on horseback and who will crawl on foot. The main thing is—hope! A Jew must always hope, must never lose hope. And in the meantime, what if we waste away to a shadow? For that we are Jews—the Chosen People, the envy and admiration of the world.

Anyway, this is how it happened. As the Bible says, "And there came the day . . ." One evening in summer I was driving through the woods on my way home with an empty wagon. My head was bent, my heart was heavy. The little horse, poor thing, was barely dragging its feet. "Ah," I said to it, "crawl along, *shlimazl*! If you are Tevye's horse you too must know the pangs of hunger . . ." All around was silence, every crack of the whip echoed through the woods. As the sun set the shadows of the trees stretched out and lengthened —like our Jewish exile. Darkness was creeping in and a sadness filled my heart. Strange, faraway thoughts filled my mind, and before my eyes passed the images of people a long time dead. And in the midst of it all I thought of my home and my family. And I thought, "Woe unto us all." The wretched dark little hut that was my home, and the children barefoot and in tatters waiting for their father, the *shlimazl*. Maybe he would bring them a loaf of bread or a few stale rolls. And my wife, grumbling as a wife will: "Children I had to bear him—seven of them. I might as well take them all and throw them into the river—may God not punish me for these words!"

You can imagine how I felt. We are only human. The stomach is empty and words won't fill it. If you swallow a piece of herring you want some tea, and for tea you need sugar. And sugar, I am told, is in the grocery store. "My stomach," says my wife, "can get along without a piece of bread, but if I don't take a glass of tea in the morning, I am a dead woman. All night long the baby sucks me dry."

But in spite of everything, we are still Jews. When evening comes we have to say our prayers. You can imagine what the prayers sounded like if I tell you that just as I was about to begin *Shmin-esra* my horse suddenly broke away as if possessed by the devil and ran wildly off through the woods. Have you ever tried standing on one spot facing the east while a horse was pulling you where *it* wanted to go? I had no choice but to run after him, holding on to the reins and chanting, *"God of Abraham, God of Isaac, and God of Jacob."* A fine way to say *Shmin-esra*! And just my luck, at a moment when I was in the mood to pray with feeling, out of the depths of my heart, hoping it would lift my spirits . . .

So there I was, running after the wagon and chanting at the top of my voice, as if I were a cantor in a synagogue: *"Thou sustainest the living with loving kindness* (and sometimes with a little food) *and keepest thy faith with them that sleep in the dust.* (The dead are not the only ones who lie in the dust; Oh, how low we the living are laid, what hells we go through, and I don't mean the rich people of Yehupetz who spend their summers at the *datchas* of Boiberik, eating and drinking and living off the fat of the land . . . Oh, Heavenly Father, why does this happen to me? Am I not as good as others? Help me, dear God!) *Look upon our afflictions.* (Look down, dear God! See how we struggle and come to the aid of the poor, because who will look out for us if you don't?) *Heal us, O Lord, and we shall be healed.* (Send us the cure, we have the ailment already.) *Bless this year for us, O Lord, our God, with every kind of produce* (corn and wheat and every other grain, and if you do, will I get anything out of it, *shlimazl* that I am? For instance, what difference does it make to my poor horse whether oats are dear or cheap?)."

But that's enough. Of God you don't ask questions. If you're one of the Chosen People you must see the good in everything and say, "This too is for the best." God must have willed it so . . .

"*And for slanderers let there be no hope,*" I chant further. The slanderers and rich scoffers who say there is no God—a fine figure they'll cut when they get *there*. They'll pay for their disbelief, and with interest too, for He is one who "breaketh his enemies and humbleth the arrogant." He pays you according to your deserts. You don't trifle with Him; you approach Him humbly, pray to Him and beg His mercy. "*O Merciful Father, hear our voice, pay heed to our lamentations. Spare us and have mercy upon us* (my wife and children too—they are hungry). *Accept, O Lord, thy people Israel and their prayer, even as you did in the days of the Holy Temple, when the priests and the Levites . . .*"

Suddenly the horse stopped. In a hurry I finish *Shmin-esra*, lift up my eyes, and behold two mysterious creatures coming toward me out of the forest, disguised or at least dressed in the strangest fashion. "Thieves," I thought, but corrected myself at once. "What is the matter with you, Tevye? You've been driving through this forest for so many years by day and by night; why should you suddenly begin to worry about thieves?"

And swinging my whip over my head, I yelled at the horse, "Giddap!"

"Mister!" one of the two creatures called out to me. "Stop! Please stop! Don't run away, Mister, we won't do you any harm!"

"An evil spirit!" I said to myself, and a second later, "You ox, Tevye, you ass! Why should evil spirits come to you all of a sudden?" And I stop the horse. I look the creatures over from head to foot: they are ordinary women. One elderly with a silk shawl on her head and the other a younger one with a *sheitel*. Both flushed and out of breath.

"Good evening," I cry out loud, trying to sound cheerful. "Look who's here! What is it you want? If you want to buy something, all I have is a gnawing stomach, a heart full of pain, a head full of worries, and all the misery and wretchedness in the world."

"Listen to him going on," they say. "That's enough. You say one word to a man and you get a lecture in return. There is nothing we want to buy. We only want to ask: do you know where the road to Boiberik is?"

"To Boiberik?" I say, and let out a laugh, still trying to sound cheerful. "You might as well ask me if I know my name is Teyve."

"Oh? So that's what they call you—Tevye? Good evening, then, Mr. Tevye. What is there to laugh at? We are strangers here. We are from Yehupetz, and we are staying at a *datcha* in Boiberik. This morning we went out for a short walk in the woods, and we've been wandering ever since, going round and round in circles. A little while ago we heard someone singing in the forest. At first we thought it was a highwayman, but when we came closer and saw it was only you, we felt relieved. Now do you understand?"

"Ha-ha!" I laughed. "A fine highwayman! Have you ever heard the story about the Jewish highwayman who waylaid a traveler in the forest and demanded—a pinch of snuff? If you'd like, I could tell it to you . . ."

"Leave that for some other time," they said. "Right now, show us how to get back to Boiberik."

"To Boiberik?" I said again. "Why, this is the way to Boiberik. Even if you don't want to, you couldn't help getting there if you followed this path."

"Oh," said they. "Is it far?"

"No, not far. Only a few *versts*. That is, five or six. Maybe seven. But certainly not more than eight."

"Eight *versts*!" they both cried out, wringing their hands and all but bursting into tears. "Do you know what you're saying? Only eight *versts*!"

"What do you want me to do about it?" I asked. "If it were up to me, I'd have made it a little shorter. But people have to have all sorts of experiences. How would you like to be in a carriage crawling up a hill through mud in a heavy rain, late Friday afternoon and almost time to light the candles for the Sabbath? Your hands are numb, you're faint with hunger . . . And crash! The axle breaks!"

"You talk like a half-wit," they said. "You must be out of your head. Why do you tell us these old-wives' tales? We're too tired to take another step. We've had nothing to eat all day except for a glass of coffee and a butter roll in the morning, and you come bothering us with foolish tales."

"Well, that's different," I told them. "You can't expect a person to dance before he's eaten. The taste of hunger is something I understand very well. You don't have to explain it to me. It's quite possible that I haven't even seen a cup of coffee or butter roll for the past year . . ." And as I utter these words a glass of steaming coffee with milk in it appears before my eyes, with rich, fresh butter rolls and other good things besides. "Oh, *shlimazl*," I say to myself, "is that what you've been raised on—coffee and butter rolls? And a plain piece of bread with herring isn't good enough for you?" But there, just to spite me, the image of hot coffee remained; just to tempt me the vision of rolls hovered before my eyes. I smelled the odor of the coffee, I savored the taste of the butter roll on my tongue —fresh and rich and sweet . . .

"Do you know what, Reb Tevye?" the women said to me. "Since we are standing right here, maybe it would be a good idea if we jumped into your wagon and you took us home to Boiberik. What do you say?"

"A fine idea," I said. "Here am I, coming *from* Boiberik, and you're going *to* Boiberik. How can I go both ways at the same time?"

"Well," they said, "don't you know what you can do? A wise and learned man can figure it out for himself. He would turn the wagon around and go back again—that's all. Don't be afraid, Reb Tevye. You can be sure that when you and the Almighty get us back home again, we'll see to it that your kindness won't go unrewarded."

"They're talking Chaldaic," I told myself. "I don't understand them. What do they mean?" And the thought of witches and evil spirits and goblins returned to me. "Dummy, what are you standing there for?" I asked myself. "Jump into the wagon, show the horse your whip, and get away from here!" But again, as if I were under a spell, these words escaped me: "Well, get in."

The women did not wait to be asked again. Into the wagon they climb, with me after them. I turn the wagon around, crack the whip—one, two, three, let's go . . . Who? What? When? The horse doesn't know what I'm talking about. He won't move an inch. "Ah-ha," I think to myself. "Now I can see what these women are. That's all I had to do—stop in the middle of the woods to make conversation with women!" You get the picture: on all sides the woods, silent, melancholy, with night coming on, and here behind me these two creatures in the guise of women. My imagination runs away with me. I recall a story about a teamster who once was riding through the woods by himself when he saw lying on the road a bag of oats. He jumped down, heaved the heavy sack to his back and just managed to tip it into the wagon, and went on. He rode a *verst* or two, looked around at the sack—but there was neither sack nor oats. In the wagon was a goat, a goat with a beard. The teamster tried to touch it with his hand, but the goat stuck out his tongue—a yard long—and let out a wild, piercing laugh and vanished into air . . .

"Well, what's keeping you?" ask the women.

"What's keeping me? Can't you see what's keeping me? The horse doesn't want to play. He is not in the mood."

"Well, you've got a whip, haven't you? Then use it."

"Thanks for the advice," I say. "I'm glad you reminded me. The only trouble with that is that my friend here is not afraid of such things. He is as used to the whip as I am to poverty," I add, trying to be flippant, though all the time I am shaking as if in a fever.

Well, what more can I tell you? I vented all my wrath on the poor animal. I whipped him till with God's help the horse stirred from his place, and we went on our way through the woods. And as we ride along a new thought comes to plague me. "Ah, Tevye, what a dull ox you are! You have always been good for nothing and you'll die good for nothing. Think! Here something happens to you that won't happen again in a hundred years. God Himself must have arranged it. So why didn't you make sure in advance how much it is going to be worth to you—how much you'll get for it? Even if you consider righteousness and virtue, decency and helpfulness, justice and equity and I don't know what else, there is still no harm in earning a little something for yourself out of it. Why not lick a bone for once in your life, since you have the chance? Stop your horse, you ox. Tell them what you want. Either you get so much and so much for the trip, or ask them to be so kind as to jump off the wagon at once! But then, what good would that do? What if they promised you the whole world on a platter? You have to catch a bear before you can skin it . . .

"Why don't you drive a little faster?" the women ask again, prodding me from behind.

"What's your hurry?" I say. "Nothing good can come from rushing too much." And I look around at my passengers. I'll swear they look like women, just plain ordinary women, one with a silk shawl, the other with a *sheitel*. They are looking at each other and whispering. Then one of them asks: "Are we getting closer?"

"Closer, yes. But not any closer than we really are. Pretty soon we'll go uphill and then downhill, then uphill and downhill again, and then after that we go up the steep hill and from then on it's straight ahead, right to Boiberik."

"Sounds like a *shlimazl*," says one to the other.

"A seven-year itch," the other answers.

"As if we haven't had troubles enough already," says the first.

"A little crazy too, I'm afraid," answers the other.

"I must be crazy," I tell myself, "if I let them pull me around by the nose like that."

And to them I say, "Where do you want to be dropped off, ladies?"

"Dropped off? What do you mean—dropped off? What kind of language is that?"

"It's only an expression. You hear it among coarse and impolite drovers," I tell them. "Among genteel people like us we'd say it like this: 'Where would you wish to be transported, dear ladies, when with God's help and the blessings of Providence we arrive at Boiberik?' Excuse me if I sound inquisitive, but as the saying goes, 'It's better to ask twice than to go wrong once.' "

"Oh, so that's what you mean?" said the women. "Go straight ahead through the woods until you come to the green *datcha* by the river. Do you know where that is?"

"How could I help knowing?" I say. "I know Boiberik as well as I know my own home. I wish I had a thousand rubles for every log I've carried there. Last summer I brought a couple of loads of wood to that *datcha* you mention. Somebody from Yehupetz was living there then, a rich man, a millionaire. He must have been worth at least a hundred thousand *rubles*."

"He still lives there," they tell me, looking at each other, whispering together and laughing.

"In that case," I said, "if you have some connections with the man, maybe it would be possible, if you wanted to, that is, if you could say a word or two in my behalf . . . Maybe you could get some sort of job for me, work of some kind. I know a man, a young fellow called Yisroel, who lived not far from our village—a worthless good-for-nothing. Well, he went off to the city, no one knows how it happened, and today, believe it or not, he is an important man somewhere. He makes at least twenty *rubles* a week, or maybe even forty. Who knows for sure? Some people are lucky, like our *shochet's* son-in-law. What would he ever have amounted to if he hadn't gone to Yehupetz? It is true, the first few years he starved to death. But now I wouldn't mind being in his boots. Regularly he sends money home, and he would like to bring his wife and children to Yehupetz to live with him, but he can't do it, because by law he isn't allowed to live there himself. Then how does he do it? Never mind. He has trouble aplenty, only if you live long enough . . . Oh, here we are at the river, and there is the green *datcha*!"

And I drive in smartly right up to the porch. You should

have seen the excitement when they saw us. Such cheering and shouting! "Grandmother! Mother! Auntie! They've come home again! Congratulations! *Mazl-tov!* Heavens, where were you? We went crazy all day! Sent messengers in all directions. . . . We thought—who can tell? Maybe wolves, highwaymen—who knows? Tell us, what happened?"

"What happened? What should happen? We got lost in the woods, wandered far away, till a man happened along. What kind of a man? A *shlimazl* with a horse and wagon. It took a little coaxing, but here we are."

"Of all horrible things! It's a dream, a nightmare! Just the two of you—without a guide! Thank God you're safe!"

To make a long story short, they brought lamps out on the porch, spread the table, and began bringing things out. Hot samovars, tea glasses, sugar, preserves, and fresh pastry that I could smell even from where I was standing; after that all kinds of food: rich fat soup, roast beef, goose, the best of wines and salads. I stood at the edge of the porch looking at them from a distance and thinking, "What a wonderful life these people of Yehupetz must live, praise the Lord! I wouldn't mind being one of them myself. What these people drop on the floor would be enough to feed my starving children all week long. O God, All-powerful and All-merciful, great and good, kind and just, how does it happen that to some people you give everything and to others nothing? To some people butter rolls and to others the plague?" But then I tell myself, "You big fool, Tevye! Are you trying to tell Him how to rule His world? Apparently if He wants it that way, that's the way it ought to be. Can't you see? If it should have been different it would have been? And yet, what would have been wrong to have it different? True! We were slaves in Pharaoh's day, too. That's why we are the Chosen People. That's why we must have faith and hope. Faith, first of all in a God, and hope that maybe in time, with His help, things will become a little better . . ."

But then I hear someone say, "Wait! Where is he, this man you've mentioned? Did he drive away already—the *shlimazl*?"

"God forbid!" I call out from the edge of the porch. "What do you think? That I'd go away like this—without saying anything? Good evening! Good evening to you all, and may the Lord bless you. Eat well, and may your food agree with you!"

"Come here!" they said to me. "What are you standing there for in the dark? Let's take a look at you, see what you are like! Maybe you'd like a little whiskey?"

"A little whiskey?" said I. "Who ever refused a drink of whiskey? How does it say in the *Talmud*? 'God is God, but whiskey is something you can drink!' To your health, ladies and gentlemen."

And I turn up the first glass. "May God provide for you," I say. "May He keep you rich and happy. Jews," I say, "must always be Jews. And may God give them the health and the strength to live through all the troubles they're born to . . ."

The *nogid* himself, a fine looking man with a skullcap, interrupts me. "What's your name?" he asks. "Where do you hail from? Where do you live now? What do you do for a living? Do you have any children? How many?"

"Children?" I say. "Do I have children? Oh . . . if it is true that each child were really worth a million, as my Golde insists, then I should be richer than the richest man in Yehupetz. The only thing wrong with this argument is that we still go to bed hungry. What does the Bible say? 'The world belongs to him who has money.' It's the millionaires who have the money; all I have is daughters. And as my grandmother used to say, 'If you have enough girls, the whole world whirls.' But I'm not complaining. God is our Father. He has His own way. He sits on high, and we struggle down below.

What do I struggle with? I haul logs, lumber. What else should I do? The *Talmud* is right, 'If you can't have chicken, herring will do.' That's the whole trouble. We still have to eat. As my old grandmother—may she rest in peace—used to say, 'If we didn't have to eat, we'd all be rich.' "

I realized that my tongue was going sideways. "Excuse me, please," I said. "Beware of the wisdom of a fool and the proverbs of a drunkard."

At this the *nogid* cries out, "Why doesn't somebody bring something to eat?" And at once the table is filled with every kind of food—fish and fowl and roasts, wings and giblets and livers galore.

"Won't you take something?" they say. "Come on!"

"A sick person you ask; a healthy person you give," I say. "Thanks, anyway. A little whiskey—granted. But don't expect me to sit down and eat a meal like this while there, at home, my wife and children . . ."

Well, they caught on to what I was driving at, and you should have seen them start packing things into my wagon. This one brought rolls, that one fish, another one a roast chicken, tea, a package of sugar, a pot of chicken fat, a jar of preserves.

"This," they say, "take home for your wife and children. And now tell us how much you'd want us to pay you for all you did for us."

"How do I know what it was worth?" I answer. "Whatever you think is right. If it's a penny more or a penny less I'll still be the same Tevye either way."

"No," they say. "We want you to tell us yourself, Reb Tevye. Don't be afraid. We won't chop your head off."

I think to myself, "What shall I do? This is bad. What if I say one *ruble* when they might be willing to give two? On the other hand, if I said two they might think I was crazy. What have I done to earn that much?" But my tongue slipped and before I knew what I was saying, I cried out, "Three *rubles*!"

At this the crowd began to laugh so hard that I wished I was dead and buried.

"Excuse me if I said the wrong thing," I stammered. "A horse, which has four feet, stumbles once in a while too, so why shouldn't a man who has but one tongue?"

The merriment increased. They held their sides laughing.

"Stop laughing, all of you!" cried the man of the house, and from his pocket he took a large purse and from the purse pulled out—how much do you think? For instance, guess! A ten-*ruble* note, red as fire! As I live and breathe . . . And he says, "This is from me. And now, the rest of you, dig into your pockets and give what you think you should."

Well, what shall I tell you? Fives and threes and ones began to fly across the table. My arms and legs trembled. I was afraid I was going to faint.

"*Nu,* what are you standing there for?" said my host. "Gather up the few *rubles* and go home to your wife and children."

"May God give you everything you desire ten times over," I babble, sweeping up the money with both hands and stuffing it into my pockets. "May you have all that is good, may you have nothing but joy. And now," I said, "good night, and good luck, and God be with you. With you and your children and grandchildren and all your relatives."

But when I turn to go back to the wagon, the mistress of the house, the woman with the silk shawl, calls to me, "Wait a minute, Reb Tevye. I want to give you something, too. Come back tomorrow morning, if all is well. I have a cow— a milch cow. It was once a wonderful cow, used to give twenty-four glasses of milk a day. But some jealous person must have cast an evil eye on it: you can't milk it any more. That is, you can milk it all right, but nothing comes."

"Long may you live!" I answer. "Don't worry. If you give us the cow we'll not only milk it—we'll get milk too! My wife, Lord bless her, is so resourceful that she makes noodles out of almost nothing, adds water and we have noodle soup. Every week she performs a miracle: we have food for the Sabbath! She has brought up seven children, though often she has nothing to give them for supper but a box on the ear! ... Excuse me, please, if I've talked too much. Good night and good luck and God be with you," I say, and turn around to leave. I come out in the yard, reach for my horse—and stop dead! I look everywhere. Not a trace of a horse!

"Well, Tevye," I say to myself. "This time they really got you!"

And I recall a story I must have read somewhere, about a gang of thieves that once kidnapped a pious and holy man, lured him into a palace behind the town, dined him and wined him, and then suddenly vanished, leaving him all alone with a beautiful woman. But while he looked the woman changed into a tigress, and the tigress into a cat, the cat into an adder.

"Watch out, Tevye," I say to myself. "No telling what they'll do next!"

"What are you mumbling and grumbling about now?" they ask.

"What am I grumbling about? Woe is me! I'm ruined! My poor little horse!"

"Your horse," they tell me, "is in the stable."

I come into the stable, look around. As true as I'm alive, there's my bony little old nag right next to their aristocratic horses, deeply absorbed in feeding. His jaws work feverishly, as if this is the last meal he'll ever have.

"Look here, my friend," I say to him. "It's time to move

along. It isn't wise to make a hog of yourself. An extra mouthful, and you may be sorry."

I finally persuaded him, coaxed him back to his harness, and
in good spirits we started for home, singing one hymn after
another. As for the old horse—you would never have known
him! I didn't even have to whip him. He raced like the wind.
We came home late, but I woke up my wife with a shout of joy.

"Good evening!" said I. "Congratulations! *Mazl-tov*,
Golde!"

"A black and endless *mazl-tov* to you!" she answers me.
"What are you so happy about, my beloved bread-winner?
Are you coming from a wedding or a *bris*—a circumcision
feast—my goldspinner?"

"A wedding and a *bris* rolled into one," I say. "Just wait,
my wife, and you'll see the treasure I've brought you! But first
wake up the children. Let them have a taste of the Yehupetz
delicacies, too!"

"Are you crazy?" she asks. "Are you insane, or out of your
head, or just delirious? You sound unbalanced—violent!"
And she lets me have it—all the curses she knows—as only a
woman can.

"Once a wife always a wife," I tell her. "No wonder King
Solomon said that among his thousand wives there wasn't one
that amounted to anything. It's lucky that it isn't the custom
to have a lot of wives any more!"

And I go out to the wagon and come back with my arms full
of all the good things that they had given me. I put it all on
the table, and when my crew saw the fresh white rolls and
smelled the meat and fish they fell on it like hungry wolves.
You should have seen them grab and stuff and chew—like the
Children of Israel in the desert. The Bible says, "And they
did eat," and I could say it, too. Tears came to my eyes.

"Well," says my helpmate, "tell me—who has decided to feed

the countryside? What makes you so gay? Who gave you the drinks?"

"Wait, my love," I say to her. "I'll tell you everything. But first heat up the samovar. Then we'll all sit around the table, as people should now and then, and have a little tea. We live but once, my dear. Let's celebrate. We are independent now. We have a cow that used to be good for twenty-four glasses a day. Tomorrow morning, if the Lord permits, I'll bring her home. And look at this, my Golde! Look at this!" And I pull out the green and red and yellow banknotes from my pockets. "Come, my Golde, show us how smart you are! Tell me how much there is here!"

I look across at my wife. She's dumbfounded. She can't say a word.

"God protect you, my darling!" I say to her. "What are you scared of? Do you think I stole it? I am ashamed of you, Golde! You've been Tevye's wife so many years and you think that of me! Silly, this is *kosher* money, earned honestly with my own wit and my own labor. I rescued two women from a great misfortune. If it were not for me, I don't know what would have become of them."

So I told her everything, from *a* to *z*. The whole story of my wanderings. And we counted the money over and over. There were eighteen *rubles*—for good luck, you know—and another eighteen for more good luck, and one besides. In all— thirty-seven *rubles*!

My wife began to cry.

"What are you crying for, you foolish woman?" I ask.

"How can I help crying when my tears won't stop? When your heart is full your eyes run over. May God help me, Tevye, my heart told me that you would come with good news. I can't remember when I last saw my Grandmother Tzeitl—

may she rest in peace—in a dream. But just before you came home I was asleep and suddenly I dreamed I saw a milkpail full to the brim. My Grandmother Tzeitl was carrying it under her apron to shield it from an evil eye, and the children were crying, 'Mama . . .' "

"Don't eat up all the noodles before the Sabbath!" I interrupt. "May your Grandmother Tzeitl be happy in Paradise—I don't know how much she can help us right now. Let's leave that to God. He saw to it that we should have a cow of our own, so no doubt He can also make her give milk. Better give me some advice, Golde. Tell me—what shall we do with the money?"

"That's right, Tevye," says she. "What do you plan to do with so much money?"

"Well, what do you think we can do with it?" I say. "Where shall we invest it?"

And we began to think of this and that, one thing after another. We racked our brains, thought of every kind of enterprise on earth. That night we were engaged in every type of business you could imagine. We bought a pair of horses and sold them at a profit; opened a grocery store in Boiberik, sold the stock and went into the drygoods business. We bought an option on some woodland and made something on that, too, then obtained the tax concession at Anatevka, and with our earnings began to loan out money on mortgages.

"Be careful! Don't be so reckless!" my wife warned me. "You'll throw it all away. Before you know it, you'll have nothing left but your whip!"

"What do you want me to do?" I ask. "Deal in grain and lose it all? Look what's happening right now in the wheat market. Go! See what's going on in Odessa!"

"What do I care about Odessa? My great-grandfather was

never there, and so long as I'm alive and have my senses, my children will never be there, either!"

"Then what *do* you want?"

"What do I want? I want you to have some brains and not act like a fool."

"So you're the brainy one! You get a few *rubles* in your hand and suddenly you're wise. That's what always happens."

Well, we disagreed a few times, fell out, had some arguments, but in the end this is what we decided: to buy another cow—in addition to the one we were getting for nothing. A cow that would really give milk.

Maybe you'll say, "Why a cow?" And I'll answer, "Why not a cow?" Here we are, so close to Boiberik, where all the rich people of Yehupetz come to spend the summer at their *datchas*. They're so refined that they expect everything to be brought to them on a platter—meat and eggs, chickens, onions, pepper, parsnips—everything. Why shouldn't there be someone who would be willing to come right to their kitchen door every morning with cheese and butter and cream? Especially since the Yehupetzers believe in eating well and are ready to pay?

The main thing is that what you bring must be good—the cream must be thick, the butter golden. And where will you find cream and butter that's better than mine?

So we make a living . . . May the two of us be blessed by the Lord as often as I am stopped on the road by important people from Yehupetz—even Russians—who beg me to bring them what I can spare. "We have heard, Tevel, that you are an upright man, even if you are a Jewish dog . . ." Now, how often does a person get a compliment like that? Do our own people ever praise a man? No! All they do is envy him.

When they saw that Tevye had an extra cow, a new wagon, they began to rack their brains. "Where did he get it? How did he get it? Maybe he's a counterfeiter. Maybe he cooks alcohol in secret."

I let them worry. "Scratch your heads and rack your brains, my friends! Break your heads if you begrudge me my small living."

I don't know if you'll believe my story. You're almost the first person I've ever told it to.

But I'm afraid I've said too much already. If so, forgive me! I forgot that we all have work to do. As the Bible says, "Let the shoemaker stick to his last." You to your books, Mr. Sholom Aleichem, and I to my pots and jugs . . .

One thing I beg of you. Don't put me into one of your books, and if you do put me in, at least don't tell them my real name

Be well and happy always.

A Page from the Song of Songs

BUZIE is a name. It is a diminutive of Esther-Libbe. First Esther-Libbe, then Libuzie, then Buzie. She is a year older than I, or maybe two years, and together we are not quite twenty years old. Now, I ask you, how old am I and how old is she? But that is not important. Instead let me give you a short sketch of her life.

My older brother Benny lived in a village, where he owned a mill. He was a wonder at shooting, riding and swimming. One summer day while bathing in the river, he drowned. Thus the old adage that the best swimmers drown was borne out. He left the mill, two horses, a young widow and a child. The mill was abandoned, the horses were sold, the widow remarried and moved to some distant place, and the child was brought to us.

That child was Buzie.

That my father should love Buzie as his own is easy to understand, and that my mother should watch over her like an only daughter is natural. In her they found a comfort for their great sorrow. But that has nothing to do with me. Then why is it that when I come from *cheder* and find Buzie not at home my food is flat and tasteless? And why is it that when Buzie comes in the darkest corners are suddenly lit up? And why is it that when Buzie speaks to me I drop my eyes? And when Buzie laughs at me I weep?

And when Buzie . . .

All through the winter I had been looking forward to the Passover holidays. Then I would be free from *cheder,* free to play with Buzie, free to run outdoors with her. We would run down the hill to the river's edge, where I could show her how the ducklings learn to swim. When I try to tell her about it she only laughs at me. Buzie doesn't believe a thing I tell her. She doesn't believe that I can climb to the top of the highest tree—if I only wanted to. She doesn't believe that I can shoot—if I only had a gun to shoot with. She never says she doesn't believe, she only laughs at me. And I hate nothing more than to be laughed at. But when Passover comes, the beautiful, free days of Passover, when we can run outdoors away from the watchful eyes of my parents, then I will show her such wonders that they will take her breath away.

The wonderful time, the most joyous time of the year, has come.

Buzie and I are dressed in our holiday clothes. Everything we have on twinkles and shines and crackles. I look at Buzie and I am reminded of the *Song of Songs* which I studied before Passover with my rabbi. Verse after verse, it comes back to me:

"Behold, thou art fair, my beloved, thou art fair; thy eyes are as doves, thy hair is a flock of goats that comes down from Mount Gilead.

"Thy teeth are like a flock of white lambs that come up from the river, all are alike; the same mother bore them.

"Thy lips are like a thread of scarlet; thy speech is full of sweetness."

Why is it that when you look at Buzie you are reminded of the *Song of Songs?* Why is it that when you study the *Song of Songs* Buzie comes into your thoughts?

We are ready to go. I can hardly stand still. My pockets are full of nuts. My mother gave us all we wanted. She filled our pockets and told us we could play with them to our hearts'

content. But she made us promise not to crack any before
Passover.

"Are you ready?" says Buzie.

I jump for the door. Away we go. The nuts make a drumming sound, they rattle as we run. At first we are dazzled by
the brilliance outside. The sun is high up already; it is looking
down on the other side of town. The air is free and fresh, soft
and clear. Here and there on the hill beyond the synagogue
there sprouts the first grass of spring, tender, quivering, green
. . . With a scream and a flutter of wings a straight line of
swallows flies over our heads and again I am reminded of the
Song of Songs: "The flowers appear on the earth; the time of
the song of birds has come and the voice of the turtle is heard
in our land."

I feel strangely light. It seems to me that I have wings. Any
minute now I will rise into the air and fly.

From the town strange sounds arise—a roaring, a boiling, a
seething. It is the day before Passover, a rare and wonderful
day. In one instant the world is transformed. Our yard is a
king's court. Our house is a palace. I am a prince and Buzie
is a princess. The logs of wood piled about our door are the
cedars and cypresses that are mentioned in the *Song of Songs.*
The cat that lies near the door warming herself in the sun is
a roe or a young hart that is mentioned in the *Song of Songs.*
The women and the girls who are working outdoors, washing
and cleaning and getting ready for the Passover are the daughters of Jerusalem mentioned in the *Song of Songs.* Everything,
everything is from the *Song of Songs.*

I walk about with my hands in my pockets and the nuts
rattle. Buzie follows me step by step. I cannot walk slowly, I
am treading on air. I want to fly, to swoop, to soar, like an
eagle. I start running and Buzie runs after me. I leap onto the
pile of logs and jump from one log to another. Buzie jumps

after me. I jump up, she jumps up; I jump down, she jumps down. Who will get tired first? I guessed it.

"How-long-will-you-keep-it-up?" asks Buzie all out of breath. And I answer her in the words of the *Song of Songs:*

" 'Till the morning breeze come and the shadows flee away.' There! You are tired and I am not!"

I feel proud that Buzie cannot keep up with me. I gloat over her and at the same time I am sorry for her. My heart aches for her, because I imagine she is unhappy. That is Buzie—full of gaiety one moment, and the next she is hiding in a corner, quietly weeping. At times like these nothing helps. No matter how much my mother tries to comfort her, how much my father caresses her, she continues to cry. For whom does she cry? For her father who died when she was a baby? For her mother who married and went off without as much as a goodbye? Ah, that mother of hers. When you mention her mother her face turns fiery red, as though she were ashamed of her. She never says an unkind word about her, but she looks unhappy. I cannot bear to see Buzie looking so wretched. I sit near her on the logs and try to distract her thoughts.

Rolling a few nuts about, I start:

"Guess what I could do if I wanted to."

"What could you do?"

"If I wanted to, all your nuts would be mine."

"Would you win them away from me?"

"No. We wouldn't even start playing."

"Well then, would you take them away from me?"

"No. They would come to me by themselves."

She raises her eyes to me, her blue eyes, eyes straight out of the *Song of Songs.* I say, "You think I am joking. Well, I know a certain language, I know some magic words . . ."

She opens her eyes wider. I explain, feeling grown and important, all puffed up with pride. "We boys know a lot of things. There is a boy in *cheder,* Shaike, who is blind in one eye—he knows everything. He even knows *Kabala.* Do you know what *Kabala* is?"

"No. How should I know?"

I am suddenly lifted to the seventh heaven because I can give her a lesson in *Kabala.*

"*Kabala,* silly, is a useful thing. By means of *Kabala* I can make myself invisible. With *Kabala* I can draw wine from a stone and gold from a wall. With the help of *Kabala* you and I, just as we are sitting here, could rise to the clouds and above the clouds . . ."

To fly up to the clouds with Buzie and above the clouds, and fly away with her, far, far off over the ocean—that has been one of my fondest dreams. There, beyond the ocean, begins the land of the dwarfs who are descended from King David's time. These dwarfs are kindly little people who live on sweets and almond milk, play all day long on little flutes and dance in a ring, are afraid of nothing and are kind to strangers. When someone arrives from our world they give him food and drink and shower him with costly garments and gold and silver ornaments and before he leaves they fill his pockets with diamonds and jewels which lie about in their streets as trash does in ours.

"Really? Like trash in the streets?" asked Buzie, wonderingly, when I once told her about the dwarfs.

"Don't you believe it?"

"Do you?"

"Why shouldn't I?"

"Where did you hear about it?"

"In *cheder,* of course."

"Oh, in *cheder*!"

Lower and lower sinks the sun, painting the sky a fiery gold

. . . The gold is reflected in Buzie's eyes. They swim in molten gold.

I want very badly to impress Buzie with Shaike's ability and with the wonders I can perform by means of *Kabala*. But Buzie won't be impressed. Instead she laughs at me. She looks at me with her mouth half-open and all her pearly teeth show-ing, and laughs.

Annoyed, I ask, "Don't you believe me?"

Buzie laughs again.

"You think I am boasting. That I am making up lies."

Buzie laughs harder. I have to repay her for this. I know how, too.

"The trouble with you is that you don't know what *Kabala* is. If you knew, you wouldn't laugh. By means of *Kabala*, if I wanted to, I could bring your mother down here. Yes, I can. And if you begged me very hard I could bring her tonight, riding on a broomstick."

At once she stops laughing. A cloud crosses her lovely, bright face and it seems to me that the sun has suddenly disappeared and the day is done. I have gone too far. I have wounded her tenderest feelings. I am sorry I had ever started this. How can I make up to her now? I move closer to her. She turns away from me. I want to take her hand and speak to her with the words of the *Song of Songs:* "Return, return O Shulamite, turn back to me, Buzie . . ."

Suddenly a voice calls out, "Shimek, Shimek!"

Shimek—that's me. My mother is calling me, to go to the synagogue with my father.

To go with Father to the synagogue on the Eve of Passover is one of the pleasures of life. Just to be dressed in perfectly new clothes from head to foot and to show off before one's friends. And the services—the first evening prayer, the first benediction of the holiday season! What delights the Lord has provided for his Jewish children.

"Shimek! Shimek!"

My mother is in a hurry. "I am coming! I am coming right away, I just have to tell Buzie something, just one little thing!"

I tell her just one thing. That what I told her was not true. To make other people fly by means of *Kabala* is impossible. But I myself—I can fly, and I will show her right after the holidays. I will make my first attempt then. I will rise up here from these very logs where we are now sitting, and in one moment I will be above the clouds. From there I will turn to the right—there, see—there where everything ends and the Frozen Sea begins . . .

Buzie listens, absorbed in my story. The sun, about to sink, sends its last rays to kiss the earth.

"What," asks Buzie, "do you mean by the Frozen Sea?"

"Don't you know what the Frozen Sea is? That's far in the north. The water is as thick as jelly and as salty as brine. Ships cannot go there, and people who are caught in it never return."

Buzie looks at me wide-eyed. "Then why are you going there?"

"Am I going to touch the sea, you silly thing? I'll fly high up over it, like an eagle, and in a few minutes I shall be on dry land. That is where the twelve high mountains begin that belch fire and smoke. I shall stop on the tip of the twelfth mountain and walk from there for seven miles till I come to a thick forest. I will cross several forests till I come to a small lake. I shall swim across the lake and count seven times seven. Out of the ground will spring a dwarf with a long white beard. He will say to me, 'What is your wish?'

"And I will say to him: 'Lead me to the Queen's daughter!' "

"Which Queen's daughter?" asks Buzie, startled.

"The Queen's daughter," I explain, "is the beautiful princess

who was snatched away from under the wedding canopy, bewitched, and carried far, far away and locked up in a crystal
palace for seven years . . ."

"What is she to you?"

"What do you mean—what is she to me? I have to set her
free, don't I?"

"You have to set her free?"

"Who, then?"

"You don't have to fly so far, believe me. You don't have to
fly so far," says Buzie, and takes my hand. Her small, white
hand is cold. I look into her eyes and see in them the last
faint reflection of the gold that is draining from the sky.

Slowly the day is going, the first beautiful day of spring is
passing away. Like a spent candle the sun goes down. The
noises that we heard all day are dying too. There is hardly a
person to be seen in the street. From the windows of the houses
there wink the flames of candles lit for Passover Eve. A strange,
a holy stillness surrounds us, and Buzie and I feel ourselves
slowly merging with this stillness.

"Shimek! Shimek!"

This is the third time my mother has called me. As if I didn't
know myself that I had to go to the synagogue! I'll stay only
another minute, not more than a minute. But Buzie hears her
too, pulls her hand out of mine, jumps to her feet and begins to
push me.

"Shimek, your mother is calling you. You'd better go. It's
late. Go."

I am getting ready to go. The day is done, the sun has been
snuffed out. All the gold has turned to blood. A cool breeze
has sprung up. Buzie keeps pushing me toward the house. I
throw a last quick look at her. Her face has changed and it has
a different, an unearthly beauty in the twilight. The thought
of the bewitched princess flits through my head. But Buzie

won't allow those thoughts. She keeps pushing me ahead. I start slowly to go and I look back just once at the bewitched princess who has now completely merged with the weird Passover twilight, and I stand rooted in one spot. But she waves her hand at me, bidding me to go, to go quickly. And it seems to me that I hear her speaking in the words of the *Song of Songs:*

"Make haste, my beloved, be thou like a gazelle or a young hart upon the mountain of spices."

Two Dead Men

(A Tale for *Purim*)

YOU may think this is a strange title for a *Purim* tale; *Purim*—when it is fitting and proper for a Jew to act the drunkard and a storyteller to play the fool! Reader, I know that today is *Purim* and you are supposed to act the drunkard and I the fool; and nevertheless I'll give you a story about two dead men. That's final. All I can do for you is give you this advice: if your nerves are weak, don't read this tale before going to sleep.

I

Chlavne, a short, dark, heavy-set man, had always loved a drink. Fortunately he was brought up in a decent and temperate home, or he would surely have grown up a drunkard. I do not guarantee that it was only his upbringing that saved him from a drunkard's fate. It is possible that in spite of that he might have been able to outdrink a squad of cannoneers, if only he had the means. But his wife Gittel managed all his finances and did not let him have a *groschen* to spend. Wherever money was involved Gittel took care of it. The work itself, the labor that earned their bread, was done by Chlavne (he was, alas, a shoemaker), but when the work was finished it was Gittel who delivered it and collected the money. And

51

naturally Chlavne was not pleased with this state of affairs.

"What do you think I am? A thief—or what?"

That is what Chlavne said to his wife Gittel, and he received a clear, unequivocal answer on the spot.

"Heaven forbid! Who said you were a thief? All you are is a soak. Do you dare tell me you aren't?"

To deny it outright was not easy. And yet to go ahead and confess that he loved to take the bitter drop was not so agreeable either. So he took refuge in a pun, as he frequently did, because Chlavne the shoemaker was fond not only of a glass of brandy, but also of a quip, a pun, a pithy saying, for he was a true Kasrilevkite. So he scratched his beard, looked up at the ceiling, and said:

"Listen to the woman! All she can say is soak. Soak! If I have a bottle in my hand, do I ever soak anybody with it? All I do is drink it."

"Oh, go to the devil!" his wife sputtered.

"Together with you, beloved, I'd go through the fires of hell."

"Here, go with this!" cried Gittel, and from the other side of the room she heaved a boot at him. This, too, Chlavne caught with a laugh, and he replied with a quip, as always.

And what did he do when Gittel came home with some money, and handed him a few *groschen* to go buy thread and wax and brushes? He became soft as butter and sweet as honey. And his respect for women in general and Gittel in particular rose immediately. He stroked his high, white forehead (all shoemakers have high, white foreheads) and mused thoughtfully, philosophically:

"I can't understand what a wise man like King Solomon had against you women. Do you know what King Solomon said about women? Or don't you?"

"Who cares what King Solomon said? You go to the market

for thread and wax and brushes. And see that you don't lose your way in some tavern."

At this far-fetched idea, Chlavne burst out laughing.

"Next you'll be telling me not to wear my heavy mittens in July, or eat *matzo* on *Yom Kippur*! Which way is the market place and which way are the taverns? And besides, who would think, in the middle of the week, on a working day, of going off for a drink?"

But even while he was talking he was counting the money Gittel had given him by transferring it, coin by coin, from one hand to the other, and looking philosophically up at the ceiling with one eye closed, was figuring out exactly how much he would need for thread, how much for wax, and how much for brushes. And with a deep, deep sigh he quietly went out of the house, and straight to the tavern.

II

Who was that wise man, that sage, who after deep thought announced that on *Purim* all drunkards are sober? I doubt if he knew what he was talking about. Why should a drunkard miss his chance on a day when it is fitting and proper for everybody to get drunk as a lord? The first to protest against a notion like that would have been Chlavne the shoemaker. How eagerly he awaited that one day! What agony he suffered before it came! And when it finally arrived he went to the synagogue with everybody else, to settle his account with Haman and hang him up on a gallows fifty ells high together with his ten sons. And afterwards, instead of going home to taste the festive *hamantash* he stopped off for a while at the homes of one or two of his shoemaker friends, old comrades of the bottle, for a holiday toast. "May the good Lord spare

Haman and his ten sons for another year so we can get together next *Purim* and hang them again on a fifty-ell gallows and take another drink in their honor. Amen."

And after this series of toasts our hero became so foggy that no matter how far he went, no matter how many corners he turned, he was unable to find his way home. It began to look as if the street in which he lived had decided to play hide-and-go-seek with him. There it was in front of him, winking to him with all the flickering candles in all the small windows, and when he took another step he found himself bumping his forehead into a wall. Where did the wall come from? As long as he could remember, there had never been a wall here in the middle of the street. Someone must have put up a woodshed here. Imagine the impudence—building woodsheds right in the middle of the street! Who would dare do a thing like that? It must have been Yossi the *nogid's* doings. But he'd never get away with it!

"As sure as my name is Ahasuerus, King of Persia!" cried Chlavne, and he reached up both hands to tear down the wall that Yossi the *nogid* had dared to build right in the middle of the street. But just then the wall moved away, Chlavne lost his balance, and stretched himself out like a baron, full length in the famous Kasrilevka mud.

And there let us leave him for a while, till we have introduced you to the second hero of our tale, a man who was known in our town by the glorious and opulent name of—Rothschild.

III

He was given the name of Rothschild in Kasrilevka obviously because he was the poorest man in town. Though poor people were as numerous in Kasrilevka as the stars in heaven, a pauper as completely wretched and miserable as he could not be duplicated even there. There is a proverb (it must have originated in Kasrilevka) that it takes a special kind of luck to be that unlucky. And as you know, every proverb is founded on truth.

Who this man Rothschild was and where he came from I cannot tell you. He was a pauper—that much you know already. And his occupation was—walking. And I don't mean walking from house to house, asking for alms. His walking was aimless. All day long he walked through the deep mud, with short, quick strides like a very busy man in a great hurry. He paused only when somebody stopped him.

"Greetings. And where are you going, Mr. Rothschild?"

Rothschild stopped, wiped the sweat off his forehead with his sleeve, looked with strangely frightened eyes at the person who spoke to him and his thin, yellow, hungry face wrinkled up into a sort of smile, as he answered so softly that he could barely be heard:

"Nowhere. I keep going . . . Maybe the good Lord will send something my way."

And having explained all this, he resumed his march with short, rapid strides. And the person who had stopped him remained standing a while looking after him, then shrugged his shoulders, spit into the mud, and laughed.

"There is a *shlimazl* for you!"

As long as this poor man had been known as Rothschild no one in Kasrilevka had ever seen him approach anyone with a plea for food, a request for drink or lodging, although every one knew very well that he was always hungry and had no place to lay his head. In Kasrilevka, there are experienced authorities on the subject of hunger, one might even say specialists. On the darkest night, simply by hearing your voice, they can tell if you are simply hungry and would like a bite to eat, or if you are really starving. No doubt they have their symptoms to judge by, like doctors who prod you here and there and can tell if you are slightly indisposed or if you are on the verge of giving up your ghost.

If we are to distinguish between the various degrees of hunger, between those who are simply hungry and those who are dead hungry, we must say without hesitation that our hero Rothschild was in the rank of the dead hungry. He was a man who frequently went along for days on end with nothing at all in his mouth. And more than once he would surely have passed out right on the broad highway if some kind soul had not of his own accord noticed that here was that unfortunate wretch, Rothschild. If you gave him something he did not refuse it, but if you asked him if he was hungry he never answered. And if you asked if he was very hungry he still did not answer, but his yellow, emaciated face wrinkled up into something like a smile and his frightened eyes looked down, apparently ashamed that a person could ever be as hungry as he was, and a weak little sigh stole out unwillingly. And who knows what that sigh meant?

The Kasrilevkites, who loved a jest, gave him something to eat first, but afterwards could not refrain from teasing him.

"Mr. Rothschild, tell us the truth. How many millions do you have and where do you hide them all?"

Rothschild lowered his frightened eyes, wrinkled his starved, waxen features, smiled weakly and said nothing.

And younger wags, who had no respect for anyone, came close to him, pulled at his sleeve.

"Well, well! The great *M'sieu* Rothschild himself! And how are things on the Paris Bourse?"

Again Rothschild lowered his eyes. What was there to say?

Even the youngest of the lot, little school children, not much more than toddlers, did not let him pass. They made up a song about him:

Rothschild is a gentleman
Rolling in riches.
There's nothing he lacks
But a pair of britches.

He was especially afraid of these little children and he ran away from them with his short quick strides. The children ran after him, they would not stop singing. And hearing them, their parents shouted:

"Go away, you scamps, you scoundrels! Go back to *cheder*! Go back to school, you tramps!"

It is possible that there would have been plenty of people in Kasrilevka to look after him and he would not have had to hunger at all. But who is to blame if this penniless wretch would rather die than hold out his hand for help? And besides, is Kasrilevka expected to support every pauper who comes her way? Do not the people have troubles and heartaches and anxieties enough of their own in their struggle for a livelihood? They thank the Lord that they are able to survive the day and live through the week with their wives and children.

And yet—let the truth be known—when the Holy Sabbath came around, Rothschild was provided for. All Kasrilevka was in the synagogue that day, and Rothschild was in front of their eyes. And seeing him there, would the people let him go hungry—on the Sabbath? After all, an extra person at the table means only that you lay another spoon. So one family or another would take him home. And if the feast was not so rich it was no tragedy. His stomach was tolerant. At least he sat at a table with other Jews. In front of them were a few slices of Sabbath bread, some fish bones and the brass candlesticks from the night before. All these things, taken together with the singing and chanting after the meal, had such an attraction for him that he was ready to forget all the fine dishes, the appetizers and the desserts that human fancy has invented in order to lure us and lead us more deeply into Gehenna.

Great is the power of the Holy Sabbath! On that day you would scarcely recognize the householder of Kasrilevka, or his guest, the derelict Rothschild.

IV

Having fasted the whole day according to custom, the good householders of Kasrilevka finally saw the sun sinking and hastened to the synagogue to celebrate the *Purim* services, to chant the *Book of Esther* and take revenge on Haman. And having hurried through the final prayers standing on one foot, the hungry Kasrilevkites rushed out in a body the quicker to come home and the quicker to break the fast, each one under his own grapevine and his own fig tree, with a fresh, warm *hamantash* full of poppyseed. And in their great haste and desire to partake of food they completely forgot about Rothschild, as if there had never been a Rothschild in the whole world. And Rothschild, seeing that everyone was hurrying, hurried off too, with his short strides, over the muddy roads and alleys of the blessed Kasrilevka, without knowing where he was going.

Running past the half-fallen and dimly lighted shacks and cottages, from time to time our hungry hero stole a glance through a window and saw cheeks and jaws and necks, chewing and grinding and swallowing. What the bulging cheeks enclosed, what the jaws were grinding and the necks were swallowing, he could not see, but he felt fairly certain that it must be those sweet and fresh and wonderful triangular *hamantashen,* stuffed with honeyed poppyseed that melted in your mouth and tasted like something in Eden. And something

woke inside of Rothschild and pulled at his heart and said to
him, "Fool, why do you wander around in the darkness? Open
one of those doors, go into the house and say, 'Good evening
and a happy *Purim*. Do you have something that a person can
break his fast with? It is the third day now since I have eaten
anything.' " And Rothschild became frightened by his bold-
ness. Such a thought had never come to him before—to force
his way into a stranger's house like a thief! And lest his Evil
Spirit take hold of him again he turned from the houses directly into the middle of the road where the mud was deepest,
and in the darkness collided with something soft and broad
and alive, and before he could regain his balance fell headlong
over our hero number one—Chlavne the shoemaker.

Let us leave our Rothschild alone for a while and find out
how Chlavne the shoemaker was doing.

V

Chlavne the shoemaker (we beg his pardon a hundred times
for letting him lie in the mud so long) did not feel nearly as
wretched in his new surroundings as the reader would imagine.
It is an old-established trait of man to adapt himself to his
surroundings, no matter how unfavorable they might be. As
soon as he found that before resuming his journey he was
destined to pause a while in this bed of mud, the famous
Kasrilevka mud, he saw to it that he did it like a man, pro-
ductively, and not idly and wastefully. Without rest and
without pause he proceeded to pour his wrath out on the
wealthy of the earth, and especially on Yossi the *nogid*. Did
Yossi think that he, Chlavne, was drunk? He swore on his
honor that he was not. Who could have started that rumor
that he, Chlavne, was a drunkard? It must have been that wife
of his, Vashti.

And having said the name Vashti, Chlavne the shoemaker became silent and thoughtful. This name—Vashti—came back to his mind again and again like nails being hammered into a shoe. He remembered quite clearly that his wife's name used to be Gittel—and now suddenly it was Vashti! How did that happen? Gittel—Vashti? And it was not only her name. Everything else about her was changed, too. She was dressed like a queen with a golden crown, and everything she wore from head to foot was gold. He decided that this was not the time to start a fight with her. With a beauty like that you made your peace. And he pulled himself through the mud, closer and closer to her; but she drew away. She spurned him. Apparently because of his other passion, drink. The devil take her! She was too proud to have people think that her husband was a drunkard!

"May I never live to get up from this spot if I ever let another drop of brandy touch my lips!" he swore. "Do you hear, Vashti? If you don't believe me, here is my hand. I promise . . ."

And Chlavne stretched out his thick, blackened hand with its stubby black fingers in the mud—and he was surprised to find that Vashti's hand was wet and cold and Vashti's fingers were damp and slippery. It was impossible to put one's arms around a woman like that. And once more he held out his arms, and embraced—the bony, shivering body of the unhappy Rothschild.

VI

Philosophers tell you that many things can happen as a result of a shock. A woman can have a miscarriage because of a sudden fright. If the shock is great enough a person can go

out of his mind, and in some cases—Heaven forbid!—it has
even been suggested that it was possible for a drunkard to become suddenly sober. So say the philosophers. And therefore
we should not be too much surprised to learn that as soon as
our hero, Chlavne the shoemaker, had embraced the unfortunate Rothschild, he too became sober. That is, not entirely sober,
not sober enough to pick himself out of the mud and stand
like a man, but enough to make him regain his senses one by
one. First of all, through his sense of touch, he became aware
that Vashti was a man with a beard. Then, with the return
of his sense of hearing, he made out these words distinctly:
"*Shma Yisroel!* Help! Help! Save me!" Through his sense
of sight he became aware that the two of them were lying in
the mud, in the thick, suffocating Kasrilevka mud. But try
as he might, he could not distinguish the person who was in
his arms, for just then the moon had hidden behind a thick
cloud and the dark night had spread its sable wings over all
of Kasrilevka.

Rothschild too began slowly to collect his thoughts. His
deathly fear gradually disappeared, and together our heroes
recovered their speech. And what they said shall now be repeated, word for word:

Chlavne: Who are you?

Rothschild: It's me.

Chlavne: What are you doing here?

Rothschild: Not a thing.

Chlavne: How the devil did you get here?

Rothschild: I don't know.

Chlavne: Don't you know anything at all? What are you?
One of us? A shoemaker?

Rothschild: No.

Chlavne: What then? A businessman?

Rothschild: Oh, no! No!

Chlavne: Then what on earth are you? Do you know! What *are* you?

Rothschild: I'm . . . I'm . . . dead . . . hungry . . .

Chlavne: So that's the story! You're dead hungry, and i'm dead drunk. But wait! If I'm not mistaken, aren't you Mr. Rothschild? Of course. I knew you at once. If that's the case, Brother Rothschild, maybe it would be a good idea if you helped me crawl out of this mud, and then if you are strong enough the two of us can go to my house and have a bite to eat. Something tells me that there is some sort of holiday being celebrated today. *Simchas-Torah? Purim?* I'm not sure which, but I know it's a holiday. If all the kings of the east and west insisted that it wasn't, I'd . . . I'd spit in their faces!

It took a little while before the two of them managed to drag themselves out of the mud, and with great effort they started on their way, each one holding on to the other. That is, Rothschild was doing his best to keep Chlavne upright, because so far only the shoemaker's head had sobered up. His feet still went this way and that. And when they came to . . .

But at this point let us leave both of our heroes, and let us glance for a moment into the home of Chlavne the shoemaker, to see how his wife Gittel was getting along.

VII

No matter how much she may be criticized by cynics, no matter how much the humorists may joke about her, a wife is still a wife. As soon as it was dark, Gittel began to get things ready for her husband who ought to be coming home soon from the synagogue after his long day of fasting. In his behalf she spread a festive tablecloth and brought out those things that Chlavne loved so well—a bottle and a glass. It is possible that the bottle held no more than a single glassful, or perhaps in recognition of the holiday enough for two glasses. On the other hand, the *hamantash* which she placed on the table was a huge one. It was a giant of a *hamantash*, rich and golden, with honeyed poppyseed oozing out of its three corners. It cried aloud to be eaten. You could almost hear it plead: "Chlavne, where are you? Chlavne, come eat me!" But Chlavne did not hear. At that moment he was sitting with the other shoemakers pouring long drinks in honor of the holy *Purim*.

In vain did the shoemaker's wife look out of the window, in vain did she listen for a sound at the door. Every step she heard outside sounded like Chlavne's. But Chlavne was not walking just then. Chlavne was stretched out in the deep mud, whispering to Vashti. Gittel thought all the thoughts that a wife could ever think about her husband, but when it became really late she tore her jacket off its hook, threw it over her shoulders, and went out to search for Chlavne. She did not find him. The shoemakers with whom he had stopped to take a few drinks in honor of the holiday swore that they hoped they would not live till next *Purim* if Chlavne had not hurried straight home from the synagogue. And they swore that not one of them had so much as touched a single drop that evening. That is, unless—so said the shoemakers—he had met up some-where with Shimen-Wolf . . .

At the mention of this name Gittel very noticeably trembled. This man, this Shimen-Wolf, was responsible for so many of her troubles . . .

Shimen-Wolf was also a shoemaker, and his greatest passion was the same as her husband's. But how could you compare Chlavne to him? He was notorious throughout that part of the country—he was known by only one name—Shimen-Wolf the Drunkard. The story is that he inherited this trait from his father, who had died of drink. One holiday long ago he drank so much that he caught fire inside and was burned to death. This had happened to Shimen-Wolf, too, on one occasion, but they had put out the fire in time and he was saved. Gittel could not believe that her husband had gone off with this drunkard. After all, he had given her his hand and sworn on his pair of *tfillin* that as long as he lived he would never have anything to do with Shimen-Wolf. Because she had insisted on this oath a feud had broken out at the time between Chlavne's Gittel and Shimen-Wolf's Hanna-Zissel. The feud had started with plain words which led to taunts and ended with something not at all pleasant to narrate: the two women became tangled up in each other's hair, and it was with the greatest difficulty that they were pulled apart alive. Since then they had not spoken to each other, and when they met somewhere by accident they stepped to the side of the road and spit three times, as one did when one encountered an evil spirit.

Gittel did not know what to do. Should she go to that shrew Hanna-Zissel to find out about her husband, or shouldn't she? She was afraid a new scandal might come of it. But the Lord himself came to her aid. Before she had time to move one way or the other she saw someone draped in black coming her way. She looked closer in the darkness and saw that it was Hanna-Zissel. Both women were ready to spring to the side of the road and spit three times, as always, but some strange power took hold of them and they began to talk. The conversation was short but to the point:

"What are you doing out here so late?"

"And what are you doing?"

"I'm looking for my husband."

"So am I."

"Where can they be?"

"I wish I knew."

"Mine was at the synagogue just a while ago."

"So was mine."

"Maybe they went somewhere together."

"It looks like it."

And both women let out a deep sigh, and continued on their way, one this way, the other that . . .

VIII

Sad and dejected, Gittel came home again, glanced at the *hamantash* on the table, and it seemed to her that the *hamantash* looked back at her and said: "What's the matter with Chlavne?" In her grief she threw herself on the bed and lay there so long that she fell asleep. She dreamt that someone knocked on the window and called her by name. Without moving she asked, "Who is that?" And she received the answer that it was Hanna-Zissel and the *shammes* of the burial society who had come to her for a shroud. Gittel felt so faint that she could not understand where she got the strength to ask as coldly as she might ask the butcher for a chicken-wing: "Were they burned to death?" "Yes, they were burned to death." "Both together?" "Together."

In terror she sat up and heard something stirring on the other side of the door, as if several hands were passing over it. She was barely able to ask:

"Who is that?"

"Us."

"Who is us?"

"Unlock the door and you'll see."

"The door is unlocked."

"But we can't find the handle."

Gittel recognized her husband's voice. She sprang to the door,

opened it, and saw two creatures covered with mud like some
fiends from the depths of the earth. At this sight she leaped
back.

"Happy *Purim,* my Gittel," said one of them, staggering
into the room without letting go of his companion. "I'll swear
that my name isn't Chlavne," he went on, "that you'll never
guess who has come to see you. You have two guests for *Purim,*
Gittel. Two dead men . . . God in heaven, Gittel, why do you
look so scared? . . . Yes, we are dead, but we do not come
from the Other World. One of us is dead drunk, the other
dead hungry. And which is drunk and which is hungry you'll
have to guess for yourself . . .

"What are you staring for, Gittel? Don't you know who this
is? It's Rothschild. May Reb Yossi sink into the earth together
with the Kasrilevka mud! Rothschild is so covered with the
mud that you can't recognize him. You'd think he'd been
rolling around in a pigsty."

Chlavne looked around the room, looked long at the table.

"Do you know, Gittel? You're a wise and thoughtful woman.
Compared to you, Vashti is a silly little hen. You've put a
bottle on the table, I see. Something must have told you what
a holiday the whole world is celebrating today, and how we
ought to celebrate it—with a prayer and a drink and a *hamantash.* To your health, Rothschild! May the Lord save Haman
for another year, so we can hang him again with his ten sons
on one gallows, fifty ells high!

"Gittel—why don't you say amen?"

The Clock that Struck Thirteen

THE clock struck thirteen.

That's the truth. I wasn't joking. I am telling you a true story of what happened in Kasrilevka, in our own house. I was there.

We had a hanging clock. It was an ancient clock that my grandfather had inherited from his father and his father's father straight back to the days of Count Chmelnitzky.

What a pity that a clock is a lifeless thing, mute and without speech. Otherwise what stories it could have told and told. It had a name throughout the town—Reb Nochem's clock—so unfaltering and true in its course that men came from all directions to set their own clocks and watches by it. Only Reb Leibesh Akoron, a man of learning and philosophy, who could tell time by the sun and knew the almanac by heart, said that our clock was—next to his little watch—just so much tin and hardware, not worth a pinch of snuff. But even he had to admit that it was still a clock. And you must remember that Reb Leibesh was the man who, every Wednesday night, climbed to the roof of the synagogue or to the hilltop nearby, before the evening prayers, to catch the exact moment when the sun went down—in one hand his watch, and in the other—his almanac. And just as the sun sank below the housetops he muttered to himself: "On the dot!"

He was always comparing the two timepieces. Walking in without so much as a Good Evening, he would glance up at our hanging clock, then down at his little watch, then over to his almanac, again at our clock, down to his watch, over to the almanac, several times, and away he went.

Only one day when he came in to compare the two timepieces with his almanac, he let out a yell, "Nochem! Quick! Where are you?"

My father, more dead than alive, came running. "What—what's happened, Reb Leibesh?"

"You are asking me?" shouted Reb Leibesh, raising his little watch right up to my father's face, and pointing with his other hand up to our clock: "Nochem, why don't you say something? Can't you see? It's a minute and a half fast! A minute and a half! Cast out the thing!" He hurled the words like an angered prophet with a base image before him.

My father did not like this at all. What did he mean, telling him to cast the clock out? "Where is it written, Reb Leibesh, that my clock is a minute and a half *fast*? Maybe we can read the same sentence backward—that your watch is a minute and a half *slow*. How do you like that?"

Reb Leibesh looked at my father as at a man who has just said that Sabbath comes twice a week or that the Day of Atonement falls on Passover. Reb Leibesh didn't say a word. He sighed deeply, turned around, slammed the door and away he went.

But we didn't care. The whole town knew that Reb Leibesh was a man whom nothing could please. The best cantor you ever heard sounded like a crow; the wisest man was—an ass; the best marriage—a failure; the cleverest epigram—a dull commonplace.

But let us return to our clock. What a clock that was! Its chimes could be heard three doors away. Boom . . . boom . . . boom . . . Almost half of the town ordered its life according to it. And what is Jewish life without a clock? How many things there are that must be timed to the minute—the lighting of the Sabbath candles, the end of the Sabbath, the daily prayers, the salting and the soaking of the meat, the intervals between meals . . .

In short, our clock was the town clock. It was always faithful to us and to itself. In all its existence it never knew a repair man. My father, himself, was its only master. He had "an intuitive understanding of how it worked." Every year before Passover he carefully removed it from the wall, cleaned the insides with a feather duster, took out from within a mass of spiderwebs, mutilated flies which the spiders had lured inside, along with dead cockroaches that had lost their way and had met their sad fate there. Then, cleaned and sparkling, he hung the clock on the wall again, and it glowed. That is, they both glowed, the clock because it had been polished and cleaned, and my father—because the clock did.

But there came a day when a strange thing happened. It was on a beautiful cloudless day when we were sitting at the noon-day meal. Whenever the clock struck I liked to count the strokes, and I did it out loud.

"One, two, three . . . seven . . . eleven, twelve, thirteen . . ."

What . . . thirteen!

"Thirteen!" cried my father, and burst out laughing. "A fine mathematician you are—may the evil eye spare you. Whoever heard of a clock striking thirteen?"

"Thirteen," I said. "On my word of honor. Thirteen."

"I'll give you thirteen smacks," cried my father, aroused. "Don't ever repeat such nonsense. Fool! A clock can't strike thirteen."

"Do you know what," my mother broke in, "I'm afraid that the child is right. It seems to me that I counted thirteen, too."

"Wonderful," said my father. "Another village heard from."

But at the same time he too began to suspect something.

After dinner he went to the clock, climbed on a stool, and prodded around inside until the clock began to strike. All three of us counted, nodding our heads at each stroke: "One, two, three . . . seven . . . nine . . . eleven, twelve, thirteen."

"Thirteen," repeated my father, with a look in his eye of a man who had just beheld the wall itself come to life and start talking. He prodded once more at the wheels. Once more the clock struck thirteen. My father climbed down from the stool pale as a sheet and remained standing in the middle of the room, looking down at the floor, chewing his beard and muttering to himself, "It struck thirteen . . . How is that? What does it mean? If it was out of order it would have stopped. What then?"

"What then?" said my mother. "Take down the clock and fix it. After all, you're the expert."

"Well," agreed my father, "maybe you're right." And taking down the clock he busied himself with it. He sweated over it, he worked all day over it, and at last hung it back in its place. Thank the Lord, the clock ran as it should, and when midnight came we all stood around it and counted each stroke till twelve. My father beamed at us.

"Well," he said, "no more thirteen."

"I've always said you were an expert," my mother said. "But there is one thing I don't understand. Why does it wheeze? It never used to wheeze like this before."

"You're imagining it," my father said. But listening carefully, we heard the clock wheeze when it got ready to ring, like an old man catching his breath before he coughs—"wh-wh-wh"—and then the boom . . . boom . . . boom. But even the boom itself was not the boom of olden days. The old boom had been a happy one, a joyous one, and now something sad had crept in, a sadness like that in the song of an old, worn-out cantor toward the end of the Day of Atonement . . .

As time went on the wheezing became louder and the ringing more subdued and mournful, and my father became melancholy. We could see him suffering as though he watched a live thing in agony and could do nothing to help it. It seemed as though at any moment the clock would stop altogether. The pendulum began to act strangely. Something shivered inside, something got caught and dragged, like an old man dragging a bad leg. We could see the clock getting ready to stop forever. But just in time, my father came to the decision that there was nothing wrong with the clock itself. What was wrong was the weight. Not enough weight. And so he fastened to the weight the pestle of my mother's mortar—a matter of several pounds. The clock began to run like a charm, and my father was happy again, a new man.

But it didn't last long. Again the clock began to fail. Again the pendulum began to act strangely, swinging sometimes fast and sometimes slow. It was heartrending, it tore you apart, to see the clock languish before your eyes. And my father, watching it, drooped also, lost interest in life, suffered anguish.

Like a good doctor devoted to his patient, considering every known treatment or possible remedy, my father tried every way imaginable to save the clock.

"Not enough weight, not enough life," said my father, and attached to the weight more and more objects. First an iron frying pan, and then a copper pitcher, then a flatiron, a bag of sand, a couple of bricks . . . Each time the clock drew fresh life and began to run. Painfully, with convulsions, but it worked. Till one night when a catastrophe took place.

It was a Friday night in winter. We had just eaten the Sabbath meal of delicious spicy fish with horseradish, fat chicken soup with noodles, pot roast with prunes and potatoes, and had said the grace that such a meal deserved. The candles were still flickering. The servant girl had just brought in the freshly roasted sunflower seeds, when in came Muma Yenta, a tooth-less, dark-skinned little woman whose husband had abandoned her years ago and gone off to America.

"Good Sabbath," said Muma Yenta, breathless as usual. "I just knew you'd have sunflower seeds—the only trouble is—what can I crack them with? May my old man have as few years to live as I have teeth in my mouth . . .

"M-m-m," she went on, faster and faster, "I can still smell your fish, Malka . . . What a time *I* had getting fish this morning, with that Sarah-Pearl—the millionairess—standing next to me at the market. I was just saying to Menasha the fishman, 'Why is everything so high today?' when Sarah-Pearl jumps up with, 'Quick, I'm in a hurry. How much does this pickerel weigh?' 'What's your rush?' I say to her. 'The town isn't on fire. Menasha won't throw the fish back into the river. Among the rich,' I let them know, 'there is plenty of money but not much sense.' Then she goes and opens her mouth at me. 'Paupers,' says she, 'shouldn't come around here. If you have no money you shouldn't hanker after things.' What do you think of her nerve? What was she before she married —a peddler herself—standing in her mother's stall at the mar-ket?"

She caught her breath and went on: "These people and their marriages! Just like Abraham's Pessel-Peiseh who is so de-lighted with her daughter just because she married a rich man from Stristch, who took her just as she stood, without dowry. Wonderful luck she has. They say she is getting to look a sight. The life those children lead her . . . What do you think—it's so easy to be a stepmother? God forbid! Look at that Hava for instance. A good, well-meaning soul like that. But you should see the trouble she has with her stepchildren. The screaming you hear day and night, the way they talk back to her. And what's worse—pitch-patch—three smacks for a penny . . ."

The candles begin to gutter. The shadows tremble on the walls, they mount higher and higher. The sunflower seeds crackle. All of us are talking, telling stories to the company at large, with no one really listening. But Muma Yenta talks more than anybody.

"Listen to this," she lets out, "there is something even worse than all the rest. Not far from Yampola, a couple of miles, some robbers attacked a Jewish tavern the other night, killed everyone in the family, even an infant in a cradle. The only one left was a servant girl asleep on top of the oven in the kitchen. She heard the shrieks, jumped down from the oven, and looking through a crack in the door, saw the master and mistress lying murdered on the floor in a pool of blood. She took a chance—this servant girl—and jumped out of the window, running all the way to town yelling, 'Children of Israel, save us! Help! Help! Help!'"

Suddenly, in the midst of Muma Yenta's yelling, "Help! Help!"—we hear a crash—bang—smash—boom—bam! Immersed in the story, all we could think was that robbers were attacking our own home, and were shooting at us from all sides—or that the room had fallen in—or a hurricane had hit us. We couldn't move from our seats. We stared at each other speechless—waiting. Then all of us began to yell, "Help! Help! Help!"

In a frenzy my mother caught me in her arms, pressed me to her heart, and cried, "My child, if it's going to happen, let it happen to me! Oh . . ."

"What is it?" cries my father. "What's happened to him?"

"It's nothing. Nothing," yells Muma Yenta, waving her arms. "Be quiet." And the girl runs in from the kitchen, wild-eyed.

"What's the matter? What's happened? Is there a fire? Where is it?"

"Fire? What fire?" shouts Muma Yenta at the girl. "Go

burn, if you want to. Get scorched, if you like." She keeps scolding the girl as if it's all her fault, then turns to us.

"What are you all making this racket for? What are you frightened of? What do you think it is? Can't you see? It's just the clock. The clock fell down. Now do you know? Everything you could imagine was hung on it—a half a ton at least. So it fell down. What's strange about that? You wouldn't have been any better yourself . . ."

At last we come to our senses. We get up from the table one by one, go up to the clock and inspect it from all sides. There it lies, face down, broken, shattered, smashed, ruined forever.

"It is all over," says my father in a dull voice, his head bent as if standing before the dead. He wrings his hands and tears appear in his eyes. I look at him and I want to cry too.

"Hush, be quiet," says my mother, "why do you grieve? Perhaps it was destined. Maybe it was written in heaven that today, at this minute, the end should come. Let it be an atonement for our sins—though I should not mention it on the Sabbath—for you, for me, for our children, for our loved ones, for all of Israel. Amen. *Selah*."

All that night I dreamed of clocks. I imagined that I saw our old clock lying on the ground, clothed in a white shroud. I imagined that I saw the clock still alive, but instead of a pendulum there swung back and forth a long tongue, a human tongue, and the clock did not ring, but groaned. And each groan tore something out of me. And on its face, where I used to see the twelve, I saw suddenly number thirteen. Yes, thirteen. You may believe me—on my word of honor.

Home for Passover

TWO times a year, as punctually as a clock, in April and again in September, Fishel the *melamed* goes home from Balta to Hashtchavata to his wife and children, for Passover and for the New Year. Almost all his life it has been his destiny to be a guest in his own home, a most welcome guest it is true, but for a very short time, only over the holidays. And as soon as the holidays are over he packs his things and goes back to Balta, back to his teaching, back to the rod, to the *Gamorah* that he studies with the unwilling small boys of Balta, back to his exile among strangers and to his secret yearning for home.

However, when Fishel does come home, he is a king! Bath-Sheba, his wife, comes out to meet him, adjusts her kerchief, becomes red as fire, asks him quickly without looking him in the eye, "How are you, Fishel?" And he answers, "How are you?" And Froike, his boy, now almost thirteen, holds out his hand, and the father asks him, "Where are you now, Ephraim, in your studies?" And Reizel, his daughter, a bright-faced little girl with her hair in braids, runs up and kisses him.

"Papa, what did you bring me for the holidays?"

"Material for a dress, and for your mother a silk shawl. Here, give Mother the shawl."

And Fishel takes a new silk (or maybe half-silk) shawl out of his *tallis*-sack, and Bath-Sheba becomes redder than ever, pulls her kerchief low over her eyes, pretends to get busy around

75

the house, bustles here and there and gets nothing done.

"Come, Ephraim, show me how far you've got in the *Gamorah*. I want to see how you're getting along."

And Froike shows his father what a good boy he has been, how well he has applied himself, the understanding he has of his work and how good his memory is. And Fishel listens to him, corrects him once or twice, and his soul expands with pride. He glows with happiness. What a fine boy Froike is! What a jewel!

"If you want to go to the Baths, here is a shirt ready for you," says Bath-Sheba, without looking him in the eye, and Fishel feels strangely happy, like a man who has escaped from prison into the bright, free world among his own people, his loved and faithful ones. And he pictures himself in the room thick with steam, lying on the top ledge together with a few of his cronies, all of them sweating, rubbing each other and beating each other with birch rods and calling for more, more . . .

"Harder! Rub harder! Can't you make it harder!"

And coming home from the bath, refreshed, invigorated, almost a new man, he dresses for the holiday. He puts on his best gabardine with the new cord, steals a glance at Bath-Sheba in her new dress with the new silk shawl, and finds her still a presentable woman, a good, generous, pious woman . . . And then with Froike he goes to the synagogue. There greetings fly at him from all sides. "Well, well! Reb Fishel! How are you? How's the *melamed*?" "The *melamed* is still teaching." "What's happening in the world?" "What should happen? It's still the same old world." "What's doing in Balta?" "Balta is still Balta." Always, every six months, the same formula, exactly the same, word for word. And Nissel the cantor steps up to the lectern to start the evening services. He lets go with his good, strong voice that grows louder and stronger as he goes along. Fishel is pleased with the performance. He is also pleased with Froike's. The lad stands near him and prays, prays with feeling, and Fishel's soul expands with pride. He glows with happiness. A fine boy, Froike! A good Jewish boy!

"Good *yom-tev!* Good *yom-tev!*"

"Good *yom-tev* to you!"

They are home already and the *seder* is waiting. The wine in the glasses, the horseradish, the eggs, the *haroses,* and all the other ritual foods. His "throne" is ready—two stools with a large pillow spread over them. Any minute now Fishel will become the king, any minute he will seat himself on his royal throne in a white robe, and Bath-Sheba, his queen, with her new silk shawl will sit at his side. Ephraim, the prince, in his new cap and Princess Reizel with her braids will sit facing them.

Make way, fellow Israelites! Show your respect! Fishel the *melamed* has mounted his throne! Long live Fishel!

The wits of Hashtchavata, who are always up to some prank and love to make fun of the whole world (and especially of a humble teacher) once made up a story about Fishel. They said that one year, just before Passover, Fishel sent a telegram to Bath-Sheba reading like this: *Rabiata sobrani. Dengi vezu. Prigotov puli. Yedu tzarstvovat.* In ordinary language this is what it meant: "Classes dismissed. Purse full. Prepare *kneid-lach.* I come to rule." This telegram, the story goes on, was immediately turned over to the authorities in Balta, Bath-Sheba was searched but nothing was found, and Fishel himself was brought home under police escort. But I can tell you on my word of honor that this is a falsehood and a lie. Fishel had never in his life sent a telegram to anyone. Bath-Sheba was never searched. And Fishel was never arrested. That is, he was arrested once, but not for sending a telegram. He was arrested because of a passport. And that not in Balta but in Yehupetz, and it was not before Passover but in the middle of summer. This is what happened.

Fishel had suddenly decided that he would like to teach in Yehupetz that year, and had gone there without a passport to look for work. He thought it was the same as Balta, where he needed no passport, but he was sadly mistaken. And before he was through with that experience he swore that not only he but even his children and grandchildren would never go to Yehupetz again to look for work . . .

And ever since that time he goes directly to Balta every season and in the spring he ends his classes a week or two before Passover and dashes off for home. What do you mean—dashes off? He goes as fast as he can—that is, assuming that the roads are clear and he can find a wagon to take him and he can cross the Bug either over the ice or by ferry. But what happens if the snows have melted and the mud is deep, there is no wagon to be gotten, the Bug has just opened and the ferry hasn't started yet because of the ice, and if you try to cross by boat you risk your very life—and Passover is right in front of your nose? What can you do? Take it the way a man does if he's on his way from Machnivka to Berdichev for the Sabbath, or from Sohatchov to Warsaw—it's late Friday afternoon, the wagon is going up a hill, it's getting dark fast, suddenly they're caught in a cloudburst, he's dead hungry—and just then the axle snaps! It's a real problem, I can assure you . . .

Well, Fishel the *melamed* knows what that problem is. As long as he has been a teacher and has taken the trip from Hashtchavata to Balta and from Balta to Hashtchavata, he has experienced every inconvenience that a journey can offer. He has known what it is to go more than halfway on foot, and to help push the wagon too. He has known what it is to lie together with a priest in a muddy ditch, with himself on bottom and the priest on top. He has known how it feels to run away from a pack of wolves that followed his wagon from Hashtchavata as far as Petschani—although later, it is true, he found out that it was not wolves but dogs. . . . But all these calamities were nothing compared with what he had to go through this year when he was on his way to spend the Passover with his family.

It was all the fault of the Bug. This one year it opened up a little later than usual, and became a torrent just at the time when Fishel was hurrying home—and he had reason to hurry! Because this year Passover started on Friday night—the beginning of Sabbath—and it was doubly important for him to be home on time.

Fishel reached the Bug—traveling in a rickety wagon with a peasant—Thursday night. According to his reckoning he should have come there Tuesday morning, because he had left Balta Sunday noon. If he had only gone with Yankel-Sheigetz, the Balta coachman, on his regular weekly trip—even if he had to sit at the rear with his back to the other passengers and his feet dangling—he would have been home a long time ago and would have forgotten all about the whole journey. But the devil possessed him to go into the marketplace to see if he could find a cheaper conveyance; and it is an old story that the less you pay for something, the more it costs. Jonah the Drunkard had warned him, "Take my advice, Uncle, let it cost you two *rubles* but you'll sit like a lord in Yankel's coach—right in the very back row! Remember, you're playing with fire. There is not much time to lose!" But it was just his luck that the devil had to drag an old peasant from Hashtchavata across his path.

"Hello, Rabbi! Going to Hashtchavata?"

"Good! Can you take me? How much will it cost?"

How much it would cost—that he found it necessary to ask; but whether or not he would get home in time for Passover—that didn't even occur to Fishel. After all, even if he went on foot and took only tiny steps like a shackled person, he should have been able to reach Hashtchavata in less than a week . . .

But they had hardly started out before Fishel was sorry that he had hired this wagon, even though he had all the room in the world to stretch out in. It became apparent very soon that at the rate at which they were creeping they would never be able to get anywhere in time. All day long they rode and they rode, and at the end of the day they had barely got started. And no matter how much he kept bothering the old peasant, no matter how many times he asked how far they still had to go, the man did not answer. He only shrugged his shoulders and said, "Who can tell?"

It was much later, toward evening, that Yankel-Sheigetz overtook them, with a shout and whistle and a crack of the whip—overtook them and passed them with his four prancing horses bedecked with tiny bells, and with his coach packed with passengers inside, on the driver's seat, and some hanging onto the rear. Seeing the teacher sitting alone in the wagon with the peasant, Yankel-Sheigetz cracked his whip in the air again and cursed them both, the driver and the passenger, as only he could curse, laughed at them and at the horse, and after he had passed them he turned back and pointed at one of the wheels:

"Hey, *shlimazl*! Look! One of your wheels is turning!"

"Whoa!" the peasant yelled, and together the driver and passenger climbed down, looked at every wheel, at every spoke, crawled under the wagon, searched everywhere, and found nothing wrong.

Realizing that Yankel had played a trick on them, the peasant began to scratch the back of his neck, and at the same time he cursed Yankel and every other Jew on earth with fresh new curses that Fishel had never heard in all his life. He shouted louder and louder and with every word grew angrier and angrier.

"*Ah, shob tubi dobra ne bulo!*" he cried. "Bad luck to you, Jew! I hope you die! I hope you never arrive! Every one of you die! You and your horse and your wife and your daughter and your aunts and your uncles and your cousins and your second-cousins and—and—and all the rest of your cursed Jews!"

It was a long time before the peasant climbed into his wagon again and was ready to start. But even then he was still angry; he couldn't stop yelling. He continued to heap curses at the head of Yankel-Sheigetz and all the Jews until, with God's help, they came to a village where they could spend the night.

The next morning Fishel got up very early, before dawn, said his morning prayers, read through the greater part of the *Book of Psalms,* had a *beigel* for breakfast, and was ready to go on. But Feodor was not ready. Feodor had found an old crony of his in the village and had spent the night with him, drinking and carousing. Then he slept the greater part of the day and was not ready to start till evening.

"Now, look here, Feodor," Fishel complained to him when they were in the wagon again, "the devil take you and your mother! After all, Feodor, I hired you to get me home for the holidays! I depended on you. I trusted you." And that wasn't all he said. He went on in the same vein, half pleading, half cursing, in a mixture of Russian and Hebrew, and when words failed him he used his hands. Feodor understood well enough what Fishel meant, but he did not answer a word, not a sound, as though he knew that Fishel was right. He was as quiet and coy as a little kitten until, on the fourth day, near Petschani, they met Yankel-Sheigetz on his way back from Hashtchavata with a shout and a crack of the whip and this good piece of news:

"You might just as well turn back to Balta! The Bug has opened up!"

When Fishel heard this his heart sank, but Feodor thought that Yankel was making fun of him again and began to curse once more with even greater vigor and originality than before. He cursed Yankel from head to foot, he cursed every limb and every bone of his body. And his mouth did not shut until Thursday evening, when they came to the Bug. They drove right up to Prokop Baraniuk, the ferryman, to find out when he would start running the ferry again.

And while Feodor and Prokop took a drink and talked things over, Fishel went off into a corner to say his evening prayers.

The sun was beginning to set. It cast its fiery rays over the steep hills on both sides of the river, in spots still covered with snow and in spots already green, cut through with rivulets and torrents that bounded downhill and poured into the river itself with a roar where they met with the running waters from the melting ice. On the other side of the river, as if on a table, lay Hashtchavata, its church steeple gleaming in the sun like a lighted candle.

Standing there and saying his prayers with his face toward Hashtchavata, Fishel covered his eyes with his hand and tried to drive from his mind the tempting thoughts that tormented him: Bath-Sheba with her new silk shawl, Froike with his *Gamorah,* Reizel with her braids, and the steaming bath. And fresh *matzo* with strongly seasoned fish and fresh horseradish that tore your nostrils apart, and Passover borsht that tasted like something in Paradise, and other good things that man's evil spirit can summon . . . And no matter how much Fishel drove these thoughts from his mind they kept coming back like summer flies, like mosquitoes, and they did not let him pray as a man should.

And when he had finished his prayers Fishel went back to Prokop and got into a discussion with him about the ferry and the approaching holiday, explaining to him half in Russian, half in Hebrew, and the rest with his hands, how important a holiday Passover was to the Jews, and what it meant when Passover started on Friday evening! And he made it clear to him that if he did not cross the Bug by that time tomorrow—all was lost: in addition to the fact that at home everybody was waiting for him—his wife and children (and here Fishel gave a heart-rending sigh)—if he did not cross the river before sunset, then for eight whole days he would not be able to eat or drink a thing. He might as well throw himself into the river right now! (At this point Fishel turned his face aside so that no one could see that there were tears in his eyes.)

Prokop Baraniuk understood the plight that poor Fishel was in, and he answered that he knew that the next day was a holiday; he even knew what the holiday was called, and he knew that it was a holiday when people drank wine and brandy. He knew of another Jewish holiday when people drank brandy too, and there was a third when they drank still more, in fact they were supposed to become drunk, but what they called that day he had forgotten . . .

"Good, that's very good!" Fishel interrupted with tears in his voice. "But what are we going to do now? What if tomorrow—God spare the thought . . ." Beyond that poor Fishel could not say another word.

For this Prokop had no answer. All he did was to point to the river with his hand, as though to say, "Well—see for yourself . . ."

And Fishel lifted his eyes and beheld what his eyes had never before seen in all his life, and he heard what his ears had never heard. For it can truthfully be said that never before had Fishel actually seen what the out-of-doors was like. Whatever he had seen before had been seen at a glance while he was on his way somewhere, a glimpse snatched while hurrying from *cheder* to the synagogue or from synagogue to *cheder*. And now the sight of the majestic blue Bug between its two steep banks, the rush of the spring freshets tumbling down the hills, the roar of the river itself, the dazzling splendor of the setting sun, the flaming church steeple, the fresh, exhilarating odor of the spring earth and the air, and above all the simple fact of being so close to home and not being able to get there—all these things together worked on Fishel strangely. They picked him up and lifted him as though on wings and carried him off into a new world, a world of fantasy, and he imagined that to cross the Bug was the simplest thing in the world—like taking a pinch of snuff—if only the Eternal One cared to perform a tiny miracle and rescue him from his plight.

These thoughts and others like them sped through Fishel's head and carried him aloft and bore him so far from the river bank that before he was aware of it, night had fallen, the stars were out, a cool wind had sprung up and had stolen in under his gabardine and ruffled his undershirt. And Fishel went on thinking of things he had never thought of before—of time and eternity, of the unlimited expanse of space, of the vastness of the universe, of the creation of heaven and earth itself . . .

It was a troubled night that Fishel the *melamed* spent in the hut of Prokop the ferryman. But even that night finally came to an end and the new day dawned with a smile of warmth and friendliness. It was a rare and balmy morning. The last

patches of snow became soft, like *kasha,* and the *kasha* turned
to water, and the water poured into the Bug from all directions
. . . Only here and there could be seen huge blocks of ice
that looked like strange animals, like polar bears that hurried
and chased each other, as if they were afraid that they would be
too late in arriving where they were going . . .

And once again Fishel the *melamed* finished his prayers, ate
the last crust of bread that was left in his sack, and went out
to take a look at the river and to see what could be done about
getting across it. But when he heard from Prokop that they
would be lucky if the ferry could start Sunday afternoon, he
became terrified. He clutched his head with both hands and
shook all over. He fumed at Prokop, and scolded him in his
own mixture of Russian and Hebrew. Why had Prokop given
him hope the night before, why had he said that they might
be able to get across today? To this Prokop answered coldly
that he had not said a word about crossing by ferry, he had
only said that they might be able to get across, and this they
could still do. He could take him over any way he wanted to
—in a rowboat or on a raft, and it would cost him another half
~uble—not a *kopek* more.

"Have it your own way!" sobbed Fishel. "Let it be a rowboat. Let it be a raft. Only don't make me spend the holiday
here on the bank!"

That was Fishel's answer. And at the moment he would have
been willing to pay two *rubles,* or even dive in and swim across
—if he could only swim. He was willing to risk his life for
the holy Passover. And he went after Prokop heatedly, urged
him to get out the boat at once and take him across the Bug
to Hashtchavata, where Bath-Sheba, Froike and Reizel were
waiting for him. They might even be standing on the other
side now, there on the hilltop, calling to him, beckoning,
waving to him . . . But he could not see them or hear their

voices, for the river was wide, so fearfully wide, wider than
it had ever been before.

The sun was more than halfway across the clear, deep-blue
sky before Prokop called Fishel and told him to jump into the
boat. And when Fishel heard these words his arms and legs
went limp. He did not know what to do. In all his life he had
never been in a boat like that. Since he was born he had never
been in a boat of any kind. And looking at the boat he thought
that any minute it would tip to one side—and Fishel would
be a martyr!

"Jump in and let's go!" Prokop called to him again, and
reaching up he snatched the pack from Fishel's hand.

Fishel the *melamed* carefully pulled the skirt of his gabardine
high up around him and began to turn this way and that.
Should he jump—or shouldn't he? On the one hand—Sabbath and Passover in one, Bath-Sheba, Froike, Reizel, the scald-
ing bath, the *seder* and all its ceremonial, the royal throne. On
the other hand—the terrible risk, almost certain death. You
might call it suicide. Because after all, if the boat tipped only
once, Fishel was no more. His children were orphans. And he
stood with his coat pulled up so long that Prokop lost his
patience and began to shout at him. He warned him that if
Fishel did not jump in at once he would spit at him and go
across by himself to Hashtchavata. Hearing the beloved word
Hash-tcha-va-ta, Fishel remembered his dear and true ones
again, summoned up all his courage—and fell into the boat.
I say "fell into" because with his first step the boat tipped ever
so slightly, and Fishel, thinking he would fall, drew suddenly
back, and this time he really did fall, right on his face . . .
Several minutes passed before he came to. His face felt clammy,
his arms and legs trembled, and his heart pounded like an
alarm clock: tick-tock, tick-tock, tick-tock!

As though he were sitting on a stool in his own home, Prokop sat perched in the prow of the boat and coolly pulled at his oars. The boat slid through the sparkling waters, and Fishel's head whirled. He could barely sit upright. No, he didn't even try to sit. He was hanging on, clutching the boat with both hands. Any second, he felt, he would make the wrong move, any second now he would lose his grip, fall back or tumble forward into the deep—and that would be the end of Fishel! And at this thought the words of Moses' song in *Exodus* came back to him: "They sank as lead in the mighty waters." His hair stood straight up. He would not even be buried in consecrated ground! And he made a vow . . .

But what could Fishel promise? Charity? He had nothing to give. He was such a poor, poor man. So he vowed that if the Lord brought him back home in safety he would spend the rest of his nights studying the Holy Writ. By the end of the year he would go, page by page, through the entire Six Orders of the *Talmud*. If only he came through alive . . .

Fishel would have liked to know if it was still far to the other shore, but it was just his luck to have sat down with his face to Prokop and his back to Hashtchavata. And to ask Prokop he was afraid. He was afraid even to open his mouth. He was so sure that if he so much as moved his jaws the boat would tip again, and if it did, where would Fishel be then? And to make it worse, Prokop became suddenly talkative. He said that the worst possible time to cross the river was during the spring floods. You couldn't even go in a straight direction. You had to use your head, turn this way and that. Sometimes you even had to go back a little and then go forward again.

"There goes one as big as an iceberg!" Prokop warned. "It's coming straight at us!" And he swung the boat back just in time to let a huge mass of ice go past with a strange roar. And then Fishel began to understand what kind of trip this was going to be!

"Ho! Look at that!" Prokop shouted again, and pointed upstream.

Fishel lifted his eyes slowly, afraid to move too fast, and looked—looked and saw nothing. All he could see anywhere was water—water and more water.

"There comes another! We'll have to get past—it's too late to back up!"

And this time Prokop worked like mad. He hurled the boat forward through the foaming waves, and Fishel became cold with fear. He wanted to say something, but was afraid. And once more Prokop spoke up:

"If we don't make it in time, it's just too bad."

"What do you mean—too bad?"

"What do you think it means? We're lost—that's what."

"Lost?"

"Sure! Lost."

"What do you mean—lost?"

"You know what I mean. Rubbed out."

"Rubbed out?"

"Rubbed out."

Fishel did not understand exactly what these words meant. He did not even like the sound—lost—rubbed out. He had a feeling that it had to do with eternity, with that endless exist-ence on a distant shore. And a cold sweat broke out all over his body, and once again the verse came to him, "They sank as lead in the mighty waters."

To calm him down Prokop started to tell a story that had happened a year before at this same time. The ice of the Bug had torn loose and the ferry could not be used. And just his luck one day an important-looking man drove up and wanted to go across. He turned out to be a tax officer from Ouman, and he was ready to pay no less than a *ruble* for the trip. Half-way across two huge chunks of ice bore down upon them. There

was only one thing for Prokop to do and he did it: he slid in
between the two chunks, cut right through between them.
Only in the excitement he must have rocked the boat a trifle
too much, because they both went overboard into the icy water.
It was lucky that he could swim. The tax collector apparently
couldn't, and they never found him again. Too bad . . . A
ruble lost like that . . . He should have collected in advance . . .

Prokop finished the story and sighed deeply, and Fishel felt
an icy chill go through him and his mouth went dry. He could
not say a word. He could not make a sound, not even a squeak

When they were halfway over, right in the middle of the
current, Prokop paused and looked upstream. Satisfied with
what he saw, he put the oars down, dug a hand deep into his
pocket and pulled out a bottle from which he proceeded to
take a long, long pull. Then he took out a few black cloves
and while he was chewing them he apologized to Fishel for
his drinking. He did not care for the whiskey itself, he said,
but he had to take it, at least a few drops, or he got sick every
time he tried to cross the river. He wiped his mouth, picked
up his oars, glanced again upstream, and exclaimed:

"Now we're in for it!"

In for what? Where? Fishel did not know and he was
afraid to ask, but instinctively he felt that if Prokop had been
more specific he would have added something about death or
drowning. That it was serious was apparent from the way
Prokop was acting. He was bent double and was thrashing
like mad. Without even looking at Fishel he ordered:

"Quick, uncle! Lie down!"

Fishel did not have to be told twice. He saw close by a tower-
ing block of ice bearing down upon them. Shutting his eyes,
he threw himself face down on the bottom of the boat and
trembling all over began, in a hoarse whisper, to recite *Shma*

Yisroel. He saw himself already sinking through the waters. He saw the wide-open mouth of a gigantic fish; he pictured himself being swallowed like the prophet Jonah when he was escaping to Tarshish. And he remembered Jonah's prayer, and quietly, in tears, he repeated the words: "The waters compassed me about, even to the soul; the deep was round about me. The weeds were wrapped about my head."

Thus sang Fishel the *melamed* and he wept, wept bitterly, at the thought of Bath-Sheba, who was as good as a widow already, and the children, who were as good as orphans. And all this time Prokop was working with all his might, and as he worked he sang this song:

> *"Oh, you waterfowl!*
> *You black-winged waterfowl—*
> *You black-winged bird!"*

And Prokop was as cool and cheerful as if he were on dry land, sitting in his own cottage. And Fishel's "encompassed me about" and Prokop's "waterfowl," and Fishel's "the weeds were wrapped" and Prokop's "black-winged bird" merged into one, and on the surface of the Bug was heard a strange singing, a duet such as had never been heard on its broad surface before, not ever since the river had been known as Bug . . .

"Why is he so afraid of death, that little man?" Prokop Baraniuk sat wondering, after he had got away from the icefloe and pulled his bottle out of his pocket again for another drink. "Look at him, a little fellow like that—poor, in tatters . . . I wouldn't trade this old boat for him. And he's afraid to die!"

And Prokop dug his boot into Fishel's side, and Fishel trembled. Prokop began to laugh, but Fishel did not hear. He was still praying, he was saying *Kaddish* for his own soul, as if he were dead . . .

But if he were dead would he be hearing what Prokop was saying now?

"Get up, Uncle. We're there already. In Hashtchavata."

Fishel lifted his head up slowly, cautiously, looked around on all sides with his red, swollen eyes.

"Hash-tcha-va-ta?"

"Hashtchavata! And now you can give me that half-*ruble*!"

And Fishel crawled out of the boat and saw that he was really home at last. He didn't know what to do first. Run home to his wife and children? Dance and sing on the bank? Or should he praise and thank the Lord who had preserved him from such a tragic end? He paid the boatman his half-*ruble*, picked up his pack, and started to run as fast as he could. But after a few steps he stopped, turned back to the ferryman:

"Listen, Prokop, my good friend! Come over tomorrow for a glass of Passover brandy and some holiday fish. Remember the name—Fishel the *melamed!* You hear? Don't forget now!"

"Why should I forget? Do you think I'm a fool?"

And he licked his lips at the thought of the Passover brandy and the strongly seasoned Jewish fish.

"That's wonderful, Uncle! That's wonderful!"

When Fishel the *melamed* came into the house, Bath Sheba, red as fire, with her kerchief low over her eyes, asked shyly, "How are you?" And he answered, "How are *you?*" And she asked, "Why are you so late?" And he answered, "We can thank God. It was a miracle." And not another word, because it was so late.

He did not even have time to ask Froike how he was getting along in the *Talmud,* or give Reizel the gift he had brought her, or Bath-Sheba the new silk shawl. Those things would have to wait. All he could think of now was the bath. And he just barely made it.

And when he came home from the bath he did not say anything either. Again he put it off till later. All he said was, "A miracle from heaven. We can thank the Lord. He takes care of us . . ."

And taking Froike by the hand, he hurried off to the synagogue.

The Enchanted Tailor

ONCE there was a man named Shimmen-Eli who lived in Zolodievka, a little town in the district of Mazapevka, not far from Haplapovitch and Kozodoievka (between Yampoli and Strishtch on the road that runs from Pischi-Yaboda through Petchi-Hvost to Tetrevitz and from there to Yehupetz). And he was known as Shimmen-Eli *Shma-Koleinu,* (the Hebrew for "Hear our voice, O Lord") because in the synagogue he shouted louder, swayed more vigorously, chanted and warbled with greater emotion than anyone else. By trade Shimmen-Eli was a tailor; not, you understand, a master tailor who sewed according to the latest fashion books, but a mender of great skill who excelled at darning holes and making patches that could never be detected, in turning a garment inside out and making the old look like new. He could take a threadbare coat and turn it into a gabardine, the gabardine into a pair of trousers, cut the trousers into a jacket, and the jacket into something else again.

This was by no means such easy work, but Shimmen-Eli *Shma-Koleinu* was an artist at it, and Zolodievka being a poor town where a new garment was a rare thing, Shimmen-Eli was held in high esteem. His only drawback was that he could never get along with the rich men of the town. He was always interfering in public affairs, defending the rights of the poor, speaking out bluntly about the town philanthropists, calling the tax-collector a blood-sucker and

93

cannibal, and the rabbis and *shochtim* who worked together
with the tax-collector a band of thieves, murderers, scoundrels
and highwaymen. Let the devil take them all, together with
their fathers and grandfathers and Uncle Ishmael . . .

Among his fellow workers Shimmen-Eli was considered
a man of great and esoteric learning, for he was always full
of quotations. He quoted passages from the Bible, which some
of them knew, from *Gamorah* and *Midrash* which they had
heard about, and from other commentaries whose existence
they had never even suspected. No matter what the occasion,
he had a Hebrew quotation at the tip of his tongue. If the
quotation was usually garbled, if the beginning did not match
the ending, and if none of it suited the occasion, that is not for
us to judge.

In addition to his learning he had a voice that was not
so bad, though possibly a little too shrill. He knew all the
tunes and traditional renderings of all the prayers by heart,
and he loved to lead the services in the Tailors' Chapel, where
he was president—an office that brought him more grief than
honor. A box in the ear, a slap in the face, was not uncommon
at the Tailors' Chapel, and the president was usually at the
receiving end.

Although Shimmen-Eli had been wretchedly poor all his
life, a pauper actually, nevertheless he did not let his poverty
get the best of him. On the contrary, he always said, "The
poorer I am, the better I feel. The hungrier I am, the louder
I sing. As the *Gamorah* says . . ." And here he let fly one
of his famous quotations, one part Hebrew, one part Chaldaic,
and the rest as often as not a knock-kneed, staggering Russian.

In appearance Shimmen-Eli was short and homely, with pins
and needles sticking out all over him and bits of cotton batting
clinging to his curly black hair. He had a short beard like
a goat's, a flattened nose, a split lower lip and large black eyes

that were always smiling. His walk was a little dance all his own and he was always humming to himself. His favorite saying was, "That's life—but don't worry."

And Shimmen-Eli was blessed with sons and daughters of all ages—mainly daughters. And he had a wife named Tsippa-Baila-Reiza who was his exact opposite; a tall, strong, red-faced, broad-shouldered woman, a regular Cossack in appearance. Ever since the day of their wedding she had taken him in hand and never loosened her hold. She was the head of the house, and her husband had the greatest respect for her. She had only to open her mouth and he trembled. In the Tailors' Chapel it was said openly that Shimmen-Eli may have patched the pants, but his wife wore them. At times, when they were alone, she was not above giving him a good slap in the face. This slap Shimmen-Eli would put into his pocket, and comfort himself with his favorite quotation: "That's life—but don't worry. The Bible says, 'And he shall rule over thee,' but it means nothing. Let all the kings of East and West do what they will, it won't help."

II

And it came to pass that one summer day Shimmen-Eli's wife, Tsippa-Baila-Reiza, came home from the market with her basket of purchases, flung down the bunch of garlic, the few parsnips and potatoes that she had bought, and cried out angrily, "The devil with it! I'm sick and tired of it all. Day after day, day after day, I break my head trying to think what to cook for dinner. You need the brains of a prime minister to think of something new. Every day it's dumplings and beans, beans and dumplings. May God forgive me for complaining, but look at Nechama-Brocha, will you—a pauper like that, without a *kopek* to her name or a whole

dish in her cupboard—and *she* has to have a goat! Why is
it? Because her husband, though only a tailor, is still a man!
So they have a goat, and if there is a goat in the house you
can have a glass of milk for the children, you can cook porridge with milk, you can make a milk soup for dinner,
noodles and milk for supper, and besides you can count on
a pitcher of sour cream, a piece of cheese, a bit of butter.
Think of it. If we only had a goat!"

"You're quite right, I'm afraid," said Shimmen-Eli mildly.
"There is an ancient law that every Jew must own a goat.
Let me quote you . . ."

"What good are your quotations?" cried Tsippa-Baila
Reiza. "I tell you about a goat and you give me quotations.
I'll give *you* a quotation in a minute and you'll see stars!
He feeds me quotations, that breadwinner of mine, the *shli-
mazl*. I wouldn't trade all your quotations and all your learn-
ing for one good borsht with cream! Do you hear?"

With broad hints like this Tsippa-Baila-Reiza plagued her
husband constantly, until Shimmen-Eli promised her on his
word of honor that from then on she could rest easily. With
God's help she would get a goat.

"But how?" asked Tsippa-Baila-Reiza.

"Don't worry," answered Shimmen-Eli.

From that time on Shimmen-Eli began to save his *groschens*.
He denied himself many necessary things, pawned his Sabbath gabardine, and by the greatest economy managed to save
up a few *rubles*. It was decided that he should take the money
and go over to Kozodoievka to buy a goat. Why to Kozodoievka? For two reasons. First of all, because Kozodoievka
was famous for its goats, as the name implies—*koza* meaning
goat in Russian. And secondly, because Tsippa-Baila-Reiza
had heard from a neighbor of hers with whom she had not

been on speaking terms for a number of years, and who in
turn had heard it from her sister who lived in Kozodoievka
and who had visited her not long before, that there was a
melamed, a teacher, in that town, named Chaim-Chana
the Wise (because he was such a fool) who had a wife named
Tema-Gittel the Silent (because she was so talkative), and
this Tema-Gittel owned two goats, both giving milk.

"Now, I ask you," said Tsippa-Baila-Reiza, "why should
she have two goats, both of them giving milk? What harm
would there be if she had only one? There are plenty of
people who don't have even half a goat. And yet they live."

"You are quite right, my wife," said Shimmen-Eli. "That
is an old complaint. As the saying goes . . ."

"There he goes again! Another quotation!" interrupted
his wife. "You talk about a goat and he comes to you with
a quotation. Take my advice. You go to that *melamed* in
Kozodoievka and tell him this: 'It has come to our attention
that you have two goats, both giving milk. What do you
need two goats for? For pets? And since you don't need the
two, why don't you sell one of them to me? Will it hurt
you?' That's the only way to talk to these people, you understand?"

"Of course I understand. Why shouldn't I?" said Shimmen-
Eli. "For my good money do I have to beg them? With
money you can get anything in the world. 'Silver and gold,'
said our wise men, 'make even pigs clean.' The only thing
that's bad is not to have any money at all. As Rashi says,
'A poor man is like a dead man.' Or as it is written elsewhere,
'Without fingers you can't even thumb your nose.' Or, as
another passage so appropriately puts it, *'Abracadabra . . .'*"

"Another passage! Another quotation! My head rings with
his quotations! Oh, why don't you sink into the earth!"

cried Tsippa-Baila-Reiza. "May you be buried nine feet deep!"
And once more she instructed her husband how to approach
the *melamed,* how to feel him out, and how to close the deal.

But suppose he didn't want to sell his goat? . . . Why
shouldn't he want to sell it? Why should he have two goats,
both of them giving milk? There are so many people who
don't have even half a goat. Well, do these people die?
They manage to live.

And so on and so on, in the same vein.

III

And when it was light, our tailor arose from bed, said his
prayers, took his staff and a rope, and started off on foot.

It was Sunday, a bright, warm, summer day. Shimmen-Eli
could not remember when he had seen a beautiful day like
this before. He could not remember the last time that he had
been out in the open country. It had been a long time since
his eyes had beheld such a fresh green forest, such a rich
green carpet sprinkled with many-colored flowers. It had
been a long time since his ears had heard the twitter of
birds and the fluttering of small wings, such a long time
since he had smelled the odors of the fresh countryside.

Shimmen-Eli *Shma-Koleinu* had spent his life in a different
world from that. His eyes had beheld entirely different scenes:
A dark cellar with an oven near the door, with pokers and
shovels leaning against it, and nearby a slop-basin full to
the brim. Near the oven and the basin, a bed made of three
boards, with a litter of small children on it, half-naked, barefoot, unwashed, always hungry.

His ears had heard entirely different sounds: "Mother, I
want some bread! Mother, I'm hungry!" And above these

sounds the voice of Tsippa-Baila-Reiza herself: "You want
to eat? May you eat worms! Together with that father of
yours, the *shlimazl*! Oh, dear God in heaven!"

And his nose was accustomed to entirely different odors:
the odor of damp walls that dripped in winter and molded
in summer; the odor of sour dough and bran, of onions and
cabbage, of wet plaster, of fish and entrails; the odor of old
clothes steaming under the hot iron . . .

And now, having for the moment escaped from that poor,
dark, unhappy world into the fragrant, unaccustomed brightness, Shimmen-Eli felt like a man who on a hot summer day
dives into the ocean. The water lifts him up, the waves lap
around him, he floats blissfully, deeply inhaling the fresh,
salty air. He had never known anything like this before.

Shimmen-Eli walked slowly along thinking to himself,
"What harm would it do if every workingman could come
out here at least once a week, here in the open country, and
enjoy the freedom of God's great world? Ah, what a world,
what a world!" And Shimmen-Eli began to hum and then
to sing under his breath. "Oh, Lord, Thou hast created Thine
own world out beyond the town. Thou hast decreed that we,
Thy people, should live in Zolodievka, huddled together in
stifling quarters. And Thou didst give us woe and troubles,
illness and poverty. These things Thou gavest us, O Lord,
in Thy boundless mercy . . ."

Thus sang Shimmen-Eli under his breath, and he wanted to
throw himself down on the grass, look up at the blue sky
and taste just for a moment the sweetness of God's great
world. But he remembered that he had work to do and he
said to himself, "Enough, Shimmen-Eli, you have loitered
enough. On your way, brother! It is time to go! You will
rest, God willing, when you come to the Oak Tavern, where

your kinsman, Dodi Rendar, will give you a drink. As the passage goes: 'A drop of whisky gladdens man's life' . . .''

And Shimmen-Eli *Shma-Koleinu* hurried on.

IV

On the road from Zolodievka, half way to Kozodoievka, there stands a guest house called the Oak Tavern. This tavern has a power, the power of a magnet, which draws to itself all travelers who pass by. Whether they are going from Zolodievka to Kozodoievka or from Kozodoievka to Zolodievka, they all stop at the Oak Tavern, if only for a few minutes. No one has ever discovered the secret of this. Some say it is because the host, Dodi Rendar, is such a likable fellow and so hospitable. That is, for money he will give you a good glass of whisky and the best of food. Others say that it is because Dodi, although not a thief himself, has dealings with all the thieves in the vicinity, and at the same time protects all his customers from thieves. But since this is only a rumor, perhaps we had better say no more about it.

This Dodi we speak of was a coarse fellow, fat and hairy, with a large belly, a bulbous nose, and the voice of a wild boar. He had nothing to worry about. He made a good living, owned several cows, was a widower without any ties. He had no learning whatsoever; he scarcely knew the difference between a Bible and a prayer book. And for this reason Shimmen-Eli was ashamed of him. He considered it a disgrace that he, a learned man and president of his synagogue, should have such a coarse and ignorant lout for a relative. And Dodi, for his part, was ashamed to have a worthless tailor for a kinsman. Thus each one was ashamed of the other. And yet, when Dodi caught sight of Shimmen-Eli, he greeted him handsomely, not because he respected his kinsman, but because he feared his loud mouth.

"Oh," he said cheerfully, "look who's here! How are you, Shimmen-Eli? How is your Tsippa-Baila-Reiza? And how are the children?"

" 'What are we and what have we been?' " answered Shimmen-Eli, with a quotation. "How should we be? 'Who shall perish in an earthquake and who in a plague?' Sometimes better, sometimes worse . . . The important thing is, we're still alive. As it is written, '*Abracadabra . . .*'

"But how are *you,* my dear kinsman? What is new here in the country? How are your *vareniki* this year? I remember the ones you served a year ago with your drinks. *Vareniki,* that's what's important to you. The Holy Books mean nothing; you never look into them. Ah, Reb Dodi, Reb Dodi, if your father, my Uncle Gedalia-Wolf—may his soul rest in peace— were to arise now and see his son living in the country among peasants, he would die all over again. Ah, what a father you had, Reb Dodi! He was a good and pious man . . . Ah, yes, no matter what we begin with, we always arrive at death. Come, Reb Dodi, give me a drink. As Reb Pimpon says in his sixth book of commentaries, '*Kapota bimashken,*' 'Pawn your shirt, and buy yourself a drink.' "

"So!" said Dodi, bringing him a glass of whisky. "So you're throwing the Bible at me already! Leave that for later, kinsman. First tell me, Shimmen-Eli, where are you traveling to?"

"I am not traveling," said Shimmen-Eli with a shrug. "I am just taking a walk. As we say in our prayers, 'If you have legs you can walk.' "

"If that's the case," said Dodi, "then tell me, my dear friend, where are you walking to?"

"To Kozodoievka," said Shimmen-Eli, making a face. "To Kozodoievka to buy goats. As it is written, 'Thou shalt buy thyself goats.'"

"Goats?" asked Dodi in surprise. "How does a tailor come to be dealing in goats?"

"That's just a way of talking," said Shimmen-Eli. "What I meant actually was just one goat, that is, if the Lord has mercy and sends me the right kind of goat, one that won't cost too much. As far as I'm concerned, I don't want a goat, but my dear wife, Tsippa-Baila-Reiza—you know what she's like when she makes up her mind—has decided once for all that she must have a goat. And a wife, you have always maintained, must be obeyed. That's an old law. It's in the *Talmud*. You remember what the *Talmud* says . . ."

"About these things," said Dodi, "you are better informed than I am. You know well enough that I'm not even on speaking terms with the *Talmud*. But there is one thing I'd like to know, dear kinsman. How do you happen to be such an authority on goats?"

"The same way you're an authority on prayers!" said Shimmen-Eli angrily. "What does an innkeeper know about holiness? And yet when Passover comes, you recite the *Yom Kippur* prayers as well as you can, and get by with it!"

Dodi the innkeeper understood the jibe. He bit his lip and thought to himself, "Wait, wait, you worthless tailor, you. You're a little too smart for your own good today. You're showing off your knowledge too much. You'll get a goat from me yet, and you'll be sorry!"

And Shimmen-Eli brought the conversation to an end by asking for another drink of that strong brew that is a cure for all troubles.

The truth can no longer be held back. Shimmen-Eli loved an occasional drink. But a drunkard he was not. God forbid!

When was he able to buy enough whisky to become a drunkard? And yet he had this weakness: when he took one drink he had to have a second. And with the second he became quite jolly. His cheeks grew red, his eyes shone, his tongue loosened and wagged without stopping.

"Speaking of guilds," said Shimmen-Eli, "the one I belong to is the Tailors' Guild. Our emblem: Shears and Iron! Our people," he said, "have this one trait: we all like honors. At our synagogue, for instance, the least little shoemaker would like to be a chairman of something. If nothing else, then at least of the water basin. Says I, 'My friends, have it your own way. I can live without being president. Elect any shoemaker you want. I don't care for the honor and I don't want the headaches.' But they say, 'Nonsense! Once you've been elected you can't get out of it!' So I say, 'It is written in our Holy *Torah:* "Thou shalt take thy beatings and be a leader amongst men . . ."'

"But there! I've talked too much already. It's getting late. I forgot all about my goat. So goodbye, Reb Dodi, be well. Say your prayers, and look after your *vareniki*."

"Don't forget," replied Dodi. "On your way back, if God permits, you must come in again."

"If God permits and allows and wills it," said Shimmen-Eli. "After all, I am human, nothing but flesh and blood. Where else should I stop? And as for you, be sure there is whisky on hand, and a bite to eat. In the meantime, goodbye. And remember our motto: Shears and Iron!"

V

And Shimmen-Eli *Shma-Koleinu* departed from the Oak Tavern in an exalted mood, cheerful as he could be. And he arrived in Kozodoievka without mishap. And as soon as he

came there he began to inquire where he could find the
melamed, Chaim-Chana the Wise, who had a wife Tema-
Gittel the Silent and two goats. He did not have to search
very long, since Kozodoievka is not such a large town that
a person can get lost in it. The whole town lies spread out
before your view. Here are the butchers' stalls with the cleavers
and the dogs. Here is the marketplace where women go
from one poultry-stand to another, picking up the chickens,
and pinching and feeling them.

"What do you want for this hen?"

"Which hen? Oh, this one! That isn't a hen, it's a rooster."

"So let it be a rooster. But what do you want for it?"

And two steps farther along is the yard of the synagogue
where old women sit over small baskets of pears, sunflower-
seeds and beans; where the teachers conduct their classes and
children recite their lessons out loud; and where goats—big
goats, little goats, goats of all descriptions—jump about,
pull straw off the roofs, or else sit on the ground warming
themselves in the sun and chewing the cud. And only a few
steps beyond that is the bath house, with its dark, smoke-
stained walls. And beyond that, the pond covered with a
green scum full of leeches and croaking frogs. The pond
shines in the sun, sparkles like diamonds—and smells to high
heaven. And on the other side of the pond is nothing but
earth and sky. That is all there is to Kozodoievka.

When the tailor arrived at Chaim's house, he found him
sitting over the *Gamorah* in his *tallis-ḳot'n* and skullcap, leading his pupils in a loud recitation:

"And—when—the—goat—saw—the—food—that—had—been
—left—on—the—barrel—she—went—after—it—greedily . . ."

"'*Abracadabra d' barbanta,*'" said Shimmen-Eli *Shma-
Ḳoleinu* in his own Chaldaic, and quickly translated it into
plain Yiddish. "Good morning to you, Rabbi, and to all your

pupils. You are in the midst of the very subject about which I have come here to see your wife, Tema-Gittel, namely, a goat. True, if it depended on me, I would not be buying one, but my dear wife Tsippa-Baila-Reiza has set her heart on one once for all: she must have a goat. And a wife, you will tell me, should be obeyed. The *Gamorah* says so . . . But why are you staring at me like that? Because I am a plain work-ingman? 'Happy are ye who toil with your hands!'

"No doubt you have heard of me. I am Shimmen-Eli of Zolodievka, member of the Tailors' Guild and president of our synagogue, though I never asked to be chosen. 'I can get along without the honor,' I told them, 'and you keep the beatings for yourselves.' But they shouted, 'It's too late! Once we've picked you, you can't get out of it! A king and a leader you shall be to us. You'll *be* our leader, and you'll *get* the beatings!'

"But here I've been talking, and I almost forgot to greet you properly. How do you do, my Rabbi! How do you do, my boys! A fine crew of imps and mischief-makers, I see. Anxious to get on with your studies. Am I right?"

Hearing these words, the children began to pinch each other under the table and to giggle surreptitiously. They were, indeed, pleased with the interruption. They would have liked such visitors every day. But Chaim-Chana the Wise was not so pleased. He disliked to be interrupted when he was teaching. So he called in his wife Tema-Gittel and he himself returned with his pupils to the goat which had gotten hold of the food on the barrel. And again they began to chant at the tops of their voices:

"And—the—Rabbi—decreed—that—the—goat—must—pay—for—the—food—and—for—the—damage—to—the—barrel."

Shimmen-Eli, seeing that there was no use talking to the *melamed*, turned to his wife, Tema-Gittel the Silent.

"Here I am," said Shimmen-Eli. "As you see, a plain work-ingman. You may have heard of me, Shimmen-Eli of Zolo-dievka, member of the Tailors' Guild and president of our synagogue (though I didn't ask for the honor). I have come to see you about one of your goats. For my part I wouldn't be buying a goat now, but since my dear wife Tsippa-Baila-Reiza has made up her mind that she has to have a goat . . ."

Tema-Gittel, a tiny woman with a nose like a bean that she was always wiping with her two fingers, listened as long as she could, and then interrupted:

"So you want one of my goats, do you? Well, let me tell you this, my dear man. I'm not interested in selling the goat. For let's not fool ourselves: why should I sell it? For the money you offer? Money is round. It rolls away. But a goat is always a goat. Especially a goat like mine. Did I call it a goat? A sweetheart, that's what it is! How easy it is to milk her! And the amount of milk she gives! And how cheap it is to feed her! What does she eat? A measure of bran once a day, and for the rest she nibbles the straw from the roof of the synagogue. Still, if you're ready to pay what it's worth, I might think it over. Money is—how do you say it?—a temp-tation. If I get enough money I can buy another goat. Although a goat like mine would be hard to find. Did I call it a goat? A sweetheart, I tell you! But wait, why waste words? I'll bring the goat in and you'll see for yourself."

And Tema-Gittel ran out and came back leading a goat and carrying a pitcher full of milk that the goat had given that same day.

At the sight of the milk the tailor could not keep from lick-ing his lips.

"Tell me, my dear woman, how much do you ask for this goat of yours? Remember, if it's too much, I'm not interested. You see, I don't even want the animal, but since my wife, Tsippa-Baila-Reiza, has set her heart . . ."

"What do you mean—how much?" burst out Tema-Gittel, wiping her tiny nose. "Let's hear first what you're willing to pay. But let me tell you, no matter how much you pay, you'll be getting a bargain. Because if you buy my goat . . ."

"Listen to that!" interrupted the tailor. "Why do you suppose I'm buying it? Because it's a goat! Naturally! I'm not looking for a snake, am I? Though to tell you the truth, I'd never have thought of buying a goat if my wife hadn't . . ."

"That's what I'm telling you," Tema-Gittel interrupted in her turn and began to recount the virtues of her goat again. But the tailor did not let her finish. They kept interrupting each other until anyone listening to them would have heard something like this:

"A goat? A sweetheart, not a goat . . . I would never be buying a goat . . . A measure of bran . . . Set her heart on it . . . Money is round . . . So easy to milk . . . Tsippa-Baila-Reiza . . . What does she eat? . . . Once for all . . . Straw from the roof of the synagogue . . . A wife must be obeyed . . . A goat? A sweetheart, not a goat!"

At this point Chaim-Chana broke in. "Maybe you've said enough about goats already? Who ever heard of such a thing? Here I am, right in the midst of a point of law, and all I hear is goat, goat, goat, goat! Heavens above! Either sell the goat, or don't sell the goat, but stop talking about it. Goats, goats, goats, goats, goats. My head is ringing with goats!"

"The Rabbi is right," said Shimmen-Eli. "Where there is learning there is wisdom. Why do we have to talk so much? I have the money and you have the goat. That should be enough. Three words can settle it. As it is written . . ."

"What do I care what's written?" said Tema-Gittel softly, arching herself like a cat and brushing her hand back and forth over her lips. "Just tell me what you want to pay."

"What should I say?" Shimmen-Eli answered as softly. "Who am I to say? Ah, well, it looks as if I've wasted a trip.

Apparently I'm not buying a goat today. Forgive me for bothering you . . ."

And Shimmen-Eli turned to go.

"Now, look here, my good man," said Tema-Gittel, catching him by the sleeve. "What's your hurry? Is there a fire somewhere? It seems to me we were talking about a goat . . ."

At last the *melamed's* wife named her price, the tailor named his; they haggled back and forth, and finally agreed. Shimmen-Eli counted out the money and tied the rope around the goat's neck. Tema-Gittel took the money, spit on it to ward off the Evil Eye, wished the tailor luck, and muttering softly looked from the money to the goat, from the goat to the money. And she led the tailor out with many blessings.

"Go in good health, arrive in good health, use the goat in good health, and may God grant that she continue to be as she has been up to now. No worse. May you have her a long time, may she give milk and more milk, and never stop giving milk."

"Amen," said the tailor and started to leave. But the goat would not budge. She twisted her head, reared up her hind legs, and bleated shrilly, like a young cantor trying to impress his congregation.

But Chaim-Chana came to the rescue with the rod he used on the boys, and helped to drive the goat out of the house. And the children helped along by shouting: *"Koza! Koza! Get out, koza!"*

And the tailor proceeded on his way.

VI

But the goat had no desire to go to Zolodievka. She thrust herself against the wall. She twisted and turned and reared her hind legs. And Shimmen-Eli pulled at the rope and gave her to understand that all her kicking and bucking was useless. He said to her:

"It is written that out of necessity must thou bear thy exile. Whether thou wilt or not; nobody asks thee. I, too, was once a free Soul, a fine young man with a starched shirt and shiny boots that creaked and clattered as I walked. What more did I need? A headache? But the Lord said unto me, 'Get thee out of thy country. Crawl, Shimmen-Eli, into thy sack. Marry Tsippa-Baila-Reiza. Beget children. Suffer all thy days and thy years. For what art thou but a tailor?' "

Thus Shimmen-Eli addressed the goat, and pulling her by the rope, he went on his way, quickly, almost at a run. A warm breeze ruffled the skirts of his patched gabardine, stole under his earlocks and stroked his little beard. It brought to his nostrils the fragrance of mint, of rosemary, and other herbs and flowers whose heavenly odors he had never smelled before. And in a spirit of ecstasy and wonder he began the afternoon prayers, very handsomely, with a noble chant like a cantor performing in the presence of an admiring congregation. Suddenly—who knows how?—an Evil Spirit came to tempt him, and whispered these words into his ear:

"Listen to me, Shimmen-Eli, you fool, you! Of all things, why burst into song? It is almost evening, you haven't had a thing in your mouth all day (except two small glasses of whisky), and you gave your kinsman your word of honor that on your way home with the goat, if all was well, you would stop to have a bite with him. It was a promise, so you'll have to keep it."

And Shimmen-Eli finished his prayers as fast as he could. Then he made his way to Dodi Rendar's tavern, entering with a joyful greeting on his lips.

"Good evening to you, dear kinsman, Reb Dodi. I have news for you. Congratulate me. 'I have dwelt with Laban . . .'

I have a goat. And such a goat! Straight from goatland! A goat such as our fathers and forefathers had never known. Look her over, Reb Dodi, and give us your opinion. After all, you're a man of experience. Well, make a guess. How much should I have paid for it?"

Dodi put up his hand to shield his eyes from the setting sun, and like a true expert appraised the goat—at exactly double the figure that Shimmen-Eli had paid. At which Shimmen-Eli was so flattered that he slapped the innkeeper soundly on the back.

"Reb Dodi, dear kinsman, long life to you! This one time you didn't guess right! You were all wrong!"

Reb Dodi pursed his lips and shook his head in speechless admiration, as if to say, "What a bargain! You certainly put one over that time!"

Shimmen-Eli in his turn bent his head sideways, and with a quick gesture as if he were pulling a needle out of his vest and threading it hastily, said, "Well, Reb Dodi, what do you say now? Do I know how to look after my own affairs, or don't I? Why, if you saw how much milk she gave, you would die on the spot!"

"I'd rather see you die," said Dodi in a friendly tone.

"Amen," said Shimmen-Eli. "The same to you. And now, if I'm such a welcome guest, take my goat, Reb Dodi, and put her in the barn where no one can steal her. In the meantime I'll say my evening prayers, and then the two of us will make a toast and take a bite to eat. As the *Megila* says, 'Before eating, one is not disposed to dance.' Is that in the *Megila,* Reb Dodi, or is it somewhere else?"

"Who knows? If you say so, it must be so. After all, you're the scholar around here."

When he had finished his prayers, the tailor said to Dodi, " 'Let me swallow, I pray thee, some of this red, red pottage;

for I am faint . . .' Come, my kinsman, pour out something
out of that green bottle, and let us drink of it, for our health's
sake. Good health, that is our first concern. As we say in our
prayers every day: 'Cause us to lie down in peace and
health . . .' "

Having taken a couple of drinks and a little to eat, our tailor
became very talkative. He talked about his home town of
Zolodievka, the community in general and his synagogue and
Tailors' Guild ("Shears and Iron our emblem!") in particular. And in the process of his discourse he denounced all
the leading citizens of the town, the well-to-do and influential
men, and swore that as sure as his name was Shimmen-Eli,
every one of them deserved to be sent to Siberia.

"You understand, Reb Dodi?" he rounded out his disser-
tation. "May the devil take them, these givers of charity! Is
it their own money they give? All they do is suck the blood of
us poor people. Out of my three *rubles* a week they make me
pay twenty-five *kopeks*! But their time will come, never
fear. God shall hold them to account! Although to tell you
the truth, my cherished wife, Tsippa-Baila-Reiza, has long
told me that I am worse than a *shlimazl,* a fool and a coward,
because if I only wanted to use it, I could hold a strong whip
over them! But who listens to one's wife? After all, I have
something to say, too. Does not our Holy *Torah* tell us:
'V'hu yimshol b' cho?' Shall I translate that for you, kinsman?
'V'hu—and he, that is, the husband'—'yimshol—shall rule!'
But instead, what happens? What should happen? Since you
have started pouring, so pour a little more. Remember what
the Bible says: 'Abracadabra d' barbanta!' "

The more Shimmen-Eli talked, the more he wandered. His
eyelids drooped and soon he was leaning against the wall
and nodding. His head was bent sideways, his arms were
crossed over his chest, and in his fingers he held his thin little

beard like a man deep in thought. Had it not been for the fact that he was snoring out loud, a snore that was at once a whistling, a wheezing and a blowing, no one in the world would have dreamt that he was asleep.

But though he dozed, his brain worked busily, and he dreamed that he was home at his workbench with a strange garment spread out in front of him. Was it a pair of trousers? Then where was the crotch? There was no crotch. Was it an undershirt? Then why did it have such long sleeves? Then what could it be? It had to be something. Shimmen-Eli turned it inside out—it was a gabardine. And what a gabardine! Brand new, soft and silky to the touch, too new to be made into something else. But out of habit he took a knife out of his vest pocket and began to look for a seam. Just then Tsippa-Baila-Reiza rushed in and began to curse him:

"What are you ripping it for? May your entrails be ripped out! You green cucumber, you fine kidney bean! Can't you see it's your Sabbath gabardine that I got for you with the money I earned from the goat?"

And Shimmen-Eli remembered that he had a goat, and he rejoiced. Never in his life had he seen so many pitchers of milk, so many cheeses, and so much butter—crocks and crocks of butter! And the buttermilk, the cream, the clabber! And rolls and biscuits baked with butter, sprinkled with sugar and cinnamon! What appetizing odors! Never in his life had he smelled such odors. And then another odor crept in—a familiar one—pugh! He felt something crawl over his neck, under his collar, around his ears and over his face. It crawled right up to his nose. He reached out his fingers and caught a bedbug. He opened first one eye, then the other, stole a look toward the window . . . Good heavens, day was breaking!

"What do you think of that! I must have dozed off!" Shimmen-Eli said to himself and shrugged his shoulders. He woke up the innkeeper, ran out into the yard, opened the barn, took the goat by the rope, and started for home as quickly as he could, like a man who is afraid that he will miss—the Lord alone knows what.

VII

When Tsippa-Baila-Reiza saw that it was late and that her husband was not yet home, she began to wonder if some evil had not befallen him. Perhaps robbers had attacked him on the way, murdered him, taken his few *rubles* away and thrown him into a ditch; and here she was, a widow for the rest of her days, a widow with so many children. She might as well drown herself. All that night she did not shut her eyes, and when the first cock crowed at dawn she pulled on her dress and went outside and sat down on the door-step to wait for her husband. Maybe God would have mercy and send him home. But what could you expect from a *shlimazl* when he goes off by himself, she thought; and she planned the welcome that he so richly deserved.

But when finally he appeared with the goat following on the rope behind him—both of them tied to the rope, the goat around the neck and Shimmen-Eli around the waist— she was so relieved that she greeted him affectionately:

"Why so late, my little canary, my almond cake? I thought you had been robbed and killed on the way, my treasure."

Shimmen-Eli loosened the rope around his waist, took the goat into the house, and breathlessly began to tell Tsippa-Baila-Reiza all that had happened to him.

"Behold, my wife, the goat which I have brought to you. A goat straight from goatland. The kind of goat that our forefathers dreamt about but never saw. She eats only once a day, a measure of bran, and otherwise she nibbles the straw from the roof of the synagogue. Milk she gives like a cow, twice a day. I saw a full pail with my eyes, I swear. Did I call it a goat? A sweetheart, not a goat. At least that's what Tema-Gittel said. And such a bargain! I practically stole it from her. Six and a half *rubles* was all I paid. But how long do you think I had to bargain with the woman? Actually she didn't want to sell the goat. All night long I had to fight with her."

And while he spoke, Tsippa-Baila-Reiza thought to herself: "So Nechama-Brocha thinks she's the only person in town who amounts to something! She can have a goat and the rest of us can't? Now watch her eyes pop out when she sees Tsippa-Baila-Reiza with a goat too! And Bluma-Zlata? And Haya-Mata? Friends they call themselves, well-wishers. May they have only half the misfortune they wish me!"

And meanwhile she made a fire in the stove and began to prepare some buckwheat noodles for breakfast. And Shimmen-Eli put on his *tallis* and *tfillin* and started the morning prayers.

It was a long time since he had prayed with such feeling. He sang like a cantor on a holiday and made so much noise that he woke the children. When they found out from their mother that their father had brought home a goat and that she was cooking noodles with milk, they screamed with joy, sprang out of their bed still in their nightgowns, and taking each other's hands, started to dance in a circle. And while they danced, they sang this song they had just made up:

> "*A goat, a goat, a little goat!*
> *Papa brought a little goat!*
> *The goat will give us mi-i-lk*
> *And Mama will make noodles!*"

Watching his children dancing and singing, Shimmen-Eli expanded with pleasure. "Poor children," he thought, "so eager for a little milk. That's all right, my children. Today you'll have as much milk as you want. And from now on you'll have a glass of milk every day, *kasha* with milk, and milk with your tea. A goat is really a blessing. Now let Fishel charge as much for his meat as he wants to. He always gave us bones instead of meat, so let him choke on his bones. What do I need his meat for if we have milk? For the Sabbath? For Sabbath we can buy fish. Where is it written that a Jew must eat meat? I have not seen a law on that anywhere. If all good Jews only listened to me, they would all buy themselves goats."

With these thoughts Shimmen-Eli *Shma-Koleinu* put away his *tallis* and *tfillin,* washed himself, made a benediction over a slice of bread, and sat down to wait for the noodles. Instead, the door flew open and in rushed Tsippa-Baila-Reiza with an empty pail, sputtering with anger, her face aflame. And a shower of curses began to descend on the head of poor Shimmen-Eli—not curses but burning stones. Fire and brimstone poured from Tsippa-Baila-Reiza's mouth.

"May your father, that drunkard, move over in his grave and make room for you!" she cried. "May you turn into a stone, a bone! May you end in hell! I could shoot you, hang you, drown you, roast you alive! I could cut you, slice you, chop you to pieces! Go, you robber, murderer, apostate! Take a look at the goat you brought me! May a scourge descend upon your head and arms and legs! God in heaven! Dear, true, loving Father!"

That was all that Shimmen-Eli heard. Pulling his cap down over his eyes, he went out of the house to see the misfortune that had befallen him.

Coming outside and seeing the goat tethered to the gatepost calmly chewing her cud, he stood fixed in his tracks, not knowing what to do or where to turn. He stood there thinking and thinking, and at last said to himself, " 'Let me die with the Philistines!' I'll get even with them yet, that *melamed* and his wife! They found the right person to play tricks on! I'll show them a few tricks they won't forget. He looked so innocent, too, that *melamed:* he didn't want anything to do with the whole transaction. And this is what he did to me . . . No wonder the children laughed when the rabbi led me out with the goat and his wife wished all that milk onto us . . . Milk I'll give them! I'll milk the blood out of those holy Kozodoievkites, those cheats, those swindlers!"

And once more he set out for Kozodoievka, with the intention of giving the teacher and his wife what they had coming . . .

A little later, passing by the Oak Tavern and seeing the innkeeper in the doorway, with his pipe between his teeth, our tailor burst out laughing.

"What are you so happy about?" asked the innkeeper. "What are you laughing for?"

"Listen to this," said the tailor, "and maybe you'll laugh, too." And he roared as though ten devils were tickling him. "Well, what do you think of my luck? Everything has to happen to me! You should have heard what I got from my wife this morning—what Pharaoh's chariots and horsemen got from the Lord. She served it up in every kind of dish, and I had to take it on an empty stomach. If I could only pass it on to the *melamed* and his wife! Believe me, I'll never let them get away with it. It will be an eye for an eye and a tooth for a tooth. I don't like to have people play tricks like this on me. But come, Dodi, put this cursed goat into the barn for a few minutes, and then pour me a drink. I'm a troubled man. I need a little strength before I face those people again.

"Ah, Reb Dodi, here's to your health. We're still men,

that's the main thing. And remember what we are enjoined in the Bible: 'Do not worry . . .' You can be sure that I'll give them something to think about before this morning is over. I'll show them how to play tricks on a member of the Tailors' Guild ('Shears and Iron' our emblem!)."

"Who told you it was a trick?" asked the innkeeper innocently, puffing away at his pipe. "Maybe you made a mistake in picking the goat?"

Shimmen-Eli nearly sprang at the innkeeper's throat. "Do you know what you're saying? I came and asked for a goat that would give milk, even as Jacob asked for Rachel. And I was tricked just as he was!"

Dodi puffed at his pipe, shrugged his shoulders, and threw up his hands as if to say, "Is it my fault? What can I do about it?"

And once more Shimmen-Eli took his goat and went on his way to Kozodoievka. And his anger burned within him.

VIII

And the teacher labored with his pupils, still on the same section in the *Gamorah* dealing with damages and injuries. Their voices resounded over the whole synagogue yard:

"The—cow—swung—her—tail—and—she—broke—the—pitcher!"

"Good morning to you, my Rabbi, and to you boys, and to all Israel," said Shimmen-Eli. "Give me a minute of your time, I pray you. The cow won't run away, and the broken pitcher surely will not mend itself!

"That was a fine trick you played on me, Rabbi. No doubt it was a joke, but I don't like such jokes. It's too much like that story about the two men who were taking their bath one Friday afternoon, stretched out on the top ledge

at the bath house. Said one of the men to the other, 'Here
is my besom. Whip me with it.' And the other, taking the
besom, beat him till he was bleeding. Said the first, 'Listen,
my friend! If I have wronged you and you want to pay
me back now while I am naked and helpless, that is very well.
But if you are doing it as a joke, I want to tell you: I don't
care for such jokes!' "

"What is the point of that?" asked the *melamed,* taking
off his glasses and scratching his ear with them.

"This is the point. Why did you trick me that way—giving
me a goat like this? For that kind of trick," he said, showing him an open hand, "you may get something in return!
You needn't think you're dealing with just anybody! I'm
Shimmen-Eli of Zolodievka, member of the Tailors' Guild
and president of our synagogue ('Shears and Iron' our
emblem!)."

The tailor was so excited that he shook all over, and the
melamed, putting on his glasses, stared at him in amazement.
The whole room rocked with laughter.

"Why do you look at me like a crazy fool?" demanded
the tailor angrily. "I come here and buy a goat from you,
and you send me home with—the devil alone knows what!"

"You don't like my goat?" the teacher asked, slowly.

"The goat? If that's a goat, then you're the governor of
this province."

The boys burst into laughter anew. And at this point
Tema-Gittel the Silent came in and the real battle started.
Shimmen-Eli yelled at Tema-Gittel and Tema-Gittel yelled
back. The *melamed* looked from one to the other, and the
boys laughed louder and louder. Tema-Gittel shrieked, Shimmen-Eli roared, with neither yielding, till Tema-Gittel caught
the tailor by the hand and pulled him out through the door.

"Come!" she cried. "Come to the rabbi. Let the whole world see how a Zolodievka tailor can persecute innocent people—slander them!"

"Yes, let's go," said Shimmen-Eli. "Certainly let the world see how people who are considered honest, even holy, can rob a stranger and ruin him. As we say in our prayers, 'We have become a mockery and a derision . . .' And you come too, *melamed*."

Whereupon the *melamed* put on his plush hat over his skull-cap, and the four of them went to the rabbi together—the tailor, the *melamed*, his wife, and the goat.

When the delegation arrived, they found the rabbi saying his prayers. When he was through, he gathered up the skirts of his long coat and seated himself on his chair, an ancient relic that was little more than feet and armrests, shaky as the last teeth of an old man.

When he had finished hearing both parties, who had hardly let each other talk, the rabbi sent for the elders and the *shochet* and the other leading citizens of the town, and when they arrived he said to the tailor:

"Now be so kind as to repeat your story from beginning to end, and then we'll let her tell hers."

And Shimmen-Eli willingly told his story all over again. He told them who he was—Shimmen-Eli of Zolodievka, member of the Tailors' Guild and president of the synagogue (though he needed that honor like a headache). Harassed by his wife, Tsippa-Baila-Reiza, who was suddenly determined to have a goat, he had come to Kozodoievka, and there had bought from the *melamed* an animal that was supposed to be a goat. But it turned out that these people had taken away his money and passed off on him the devil alone knew what—possibly as a joke, but he, Shimmen-Eli, hated such jokes. "No doubt you have heard," he said, "the story of the two men who were taking their bath on a Friday afternoon . . ."

And the tailor, Shimmen-Eli, repeated the story of the bath, and the rabbi and the elders and the other leading citizens nodded their heads and smiled.

"Now that we have heard one side," said the rabbi, "let us hear the other."

At this Chaim-Chana the Wise arose from his seat, pulled his plush hat down over his skullcap, and began:

"Hear me, O Rabbi, this is my story, just like this. I was sitting with my pupils, sitting and studying, I was studying the Order of Injuries, that's what we were studying. *Bubi-Kama?* Yes, *Bubi-Kama.* And there walks in this man from Zolodievka, and he says he's from Zolodievka, from Zolodievka, you understand, and he greets me and tells me a long story. He tells me that he's from Zolodievka, a Zolodievkite, that is, and he has a wife whose name is Tsippa-Baila-Reiza. Yes, I'm sure it's Tsippa-Baila-Reiza. At least so it seems to me. Isn't that it?"

And he leaned over to the tailor questioningly, and the tailor, who had been standing all this time with his eyes shut, fingering his little beard, his head a little to one side, swaying back and forth, answered, "That is true. She has all three names, Tsippa and Baila and Reiza. She has been called by these names as long as I have known her, which is now—let's see—about thirty years. And now, my dear friend, let's hear what else you have to say. Don't go wandering. Get down to business. Tell them what I said and what you said. In the words of King Solomon, 'Beat not around the bush.'"

"But I don't know anything about it. I don't," said the *melamed,* frightened, and pointed to his wife. "She talked to him. She did the talking. She made the deal with him. I don't know anything."

"Then," said the rabbi, "let's hear what you have to say." And he pointed to the *melamed's* wife.

Tema-Gittel wiped her lips, leaned her chin on one hand and with the other began to tell her side of the story. She talked quickly, without stopping for breath, and her face grew redder and redder as she spoke.

"Listen to me," she said. "Here is the real story of what happened. This tailor from Zolodievka is either crazy or drunk or just doesn't know what he's talking about. Have you ever heard of such a thing? A man comes to me all the way from Zolodievka and fastens himself to us like a grease spot. He won't leave us alone. He insists: I must sell him a goat. (As you know, I had two of them.)

"The tailor makes a speech. He himself would not be buying a goat, but since his wife Tsippa-Baila-Reiza has set her heart on a goat, and a wife, he says, must be obeyed . . . Do you follow me, Rabbi? So I told him, 'What difference does that make to me? You want to buy a goat? I'll sell you a goat. That is, I wouldn't sell it for any amount, for what is money? Money is round. It rolls away, but a goat remains a goat, and especially a goat like this. It's a sweetheart, not a goat. So easy to milk! And the milk she gives! And what does she eat? Once a day a measure of oats, and for the rest some straw from the roof of the synagogue.'

"But thinking it over, I decided: after all, I have two goats, and money is a temptation. Anyway, at this point my husband told me to make up my mind, and we agreed on the price. How much do you think it was? May my enemies never have any more than we asked for that goat. And I gave him the goat, a treasure of a goat. And now he comes back, this tailor does, and tries to tell me that it's not a goat. It doesn't give milk. Do you know what? Here is the goat. Give me a milk pail, and I'll milk her right here in front of your eyes."

And she borrowed a pail from the rabbi's wife and milked
the goat right there in front of their eyes, and she brought
the milk to each one separately to see. First, naturally, to
the rabbi, then to the elders, then to the other leading citizens,
and finally to the assembled populace. And such a clamor
arose! Such a tumult! This one said, "We must punish this
Zolodievka tailor. Let him buy drinks for us all." Another
said, "Punishing him like this is not enough. We ought to
take away the goat." Still another said, "The goat is a goat.
Let him keep it. Let him enjoy it to a ripe old age. What we
ought to do is give him a few good kicks and send him and
the goat both to the devil!"

When he saw this turn of events, Shimmen-Eli quietly
slipped out of the rabbi's house, and disappeared.

IX

The tailor hastened away from the angry multitude like
a man running from a fire. From time to time he looked back
to see if anyone was following him, and he thanked the
Lord for having escaped without a beating.

When he approached the Oak Tavern, Shimmen-Eli said
to himself: "He'll never get the truth out of me."

"Well, what happened?" asked Dodi with feigned interest.

"What should happen?" said Shimmen-Eli. "People have
respect for a man like me. They can't play tricks on me. After
all, I'm not a schoolboy. I showed them a few things. I had
a little discussion with the *melamed* too, about a few points
in the *Gamorah,* and we found out that I knew more than
he did. Anyway, to make a long story short, they begged my
pardon and gave me the goat I had bought. Here she is. Take
her for a little while, my kinsman, and then give me a drink."

"He is not only a braggart," thought Dodi to himself, "but

a liar as well. I'll have to play the same game once more and see what he'll say next time."

And to the tailor he said: "I have just the thing for you—a glass of old cherry wine."

"Cherry wine!" said Shimmen-Eli and licked his lips in anticipation. "Bring it out and I'll tell you what I think of it. Not everyone knows what good wine is."

When he had drained the first glass, the tailor's tongue began wagging again. He said, "Tell me, dear kinsman, you're no fool and you have dealings with many people. Tell me, do you believe in magic, in illusions?"

"For instance?" asked Dodi, innocently.

"Why," said Shimmen-Eli, "*dybbuks,* elves, evil spirits of all sorts, wandering souls . . ."

"What makes you ask?" said Dodi, puffing at his pipe.

"Just like that," said Shimmen-Eli, and went on talking about sorcerers, witches, devils, gnomes, werewolves.

Dodi pretended to listen attentively, smoked his pipe, and then he spat and said to the tailor, "Do you know what, Shimmen-Eli? I'll be afraid to sleep tonight. I'll tell you the truth: I have always been afraid of ghosts, but from now on I'll believe in *dybbuks* and gnomes as well."

"Can you help yourself?" said the tailor. "Try not believing! Just let one good gnome come along and start playing tricks on you—upset your borsht, pour out your water, empty all your pitchers, break your pots, tie knots in the fringes of your *tallis kot'n,* throw a cat into your bed and let it lie on your chest like a ten-pound weight . . ."

"Enough! Enough!" begged the innkeeper, spitting to ward off spirits. "Don't ever tell me stories like that so late at night!"

"Goodbye, Reb Dodi. Forgive me for teasing you. You know I'm not to blame. As the saying is, 'The old woman had no troubles . . .' You know that saying, don't you? Well, good night . . ."

X

When the tailor returned to Zolodievka he walked into the house boldly, determined to give his wife a piece of his mind; but he controlled himself. After all, what can you expect from a woman? And for the sake of harmony he told her this story:

"Believe me, Tsippa-Baila-Reiza, in spite of what you think, people have to look up to me. I wish you could have seen what I gave that *melamed* and his wife! It was as much as they could take. And then I dragged them off to the rabbi and he ruled that they must pay a fine, because when a man like Shimmen-Eli comes to buy a goat from them, he deserves the greatest consideration, for this Shimmen-Eli, says the rabbi, is a man who . . ."

But Tsippa-Baila-Reiza did not want to hear any more about the praise that had been showered on her husband. What she wanted was to see the real goat he had now brought with him, so she took her pail again and ran out of the house. But it was not long before she came running back, speechless with anger. Catching Shimmen-Eli by the collar, she gave him three good shoves, pushed him out of the house, and told him to go to the devil together with his goat.

Outside, a crowd of men, women and children quickly gathered around the tailor and his goat, and he told them the story of the goat which in Kozodoievka had given milk, but every time he brought her home was no longer a she-goat. With many oaths he swore that he himself had seen the full pail of milk that she had given in the rabbi's house. More and more people came by, examined the goat with deep in-

terest, listened to the story, asked to have it repeated, and
wondered greatly at it. Others laughed and teased him, still
others shook their heads, spat on the ground, and said, "A
fine goat that is. If that's a goat, then I'm the rabbi's wife!"

"What, then is it?" asked the tailor.

"A demon, can't you see? It's possessed. It's a *gilgul*."

The crowd caught the word *gilgul*, and soon they all began
to tell each other stories about spirits and ghosts, incidents
that had occurred right here in Zolodievka, in Kozodoievka, in
Yampoli, in Pischi-Yaboda, in Haplapovitch, in Petchi-Hvost,
and other places. Who had not heard the story of Lazer-Wolf's
horse that had to be taken out beyond the town, killed, and
buried in a shroud? Or about the fowl which had been served
up for a Sabbath dinner, and when it was placed on the table
began to flap its wings? Or many other such true and well-
known happenings?

After several more minutes of this, Shimmen-Eli pulled once
more at his rope and proceeded again on his way to Kozodoievka, followed by a band of schoolboys shouting, "Hurrah
for Shimmen-Eli! Hurrah for the milking tailor!"

And everybody roared with laughter.

At this the tailor was deeply hurt. As if it were not enough
to have this misfortune happen to him, they made a laugh-
ing-stock of him too. So, taking the goat, he went through
the town and sounded an alarm among the members of his
Guild. How could they stand by and be silent at such an
outrage? And he told them the whole story of what had
happened to him in Kozodoievka, showed them the goat, and
at once they sent for liquor, held a meeting, and decided
to go to the rabbi, the elders, and the leading citizens of
the community and ask them to come to their aid. Why, who
had ever heard of such an outrage? To cheat a poor tailor,
take away his last few *rubles*, supposedly sell him a goat and

actually palm off the devil alone knew what! And then to
play the same trick on him a second time! Such an outrage
had never been heard of even in Sodom!

And the delegation came to the rabbi, the elders and the
leading men of the town and raised a hue and cry. Why, who
had ever heard of such an outrage? To cheat a poor tailor,
rob him of his last few *rubles*? And they recounted the story
of the tailor and his goat in all its details.

The rabbi, the elders, and the leading men of the town
listened to the complaints, and that evening held a meeting
at the rabbi's house, where it was decided to write a letter
then and there to the rabbi, elders and leading men of Kozodoievka. And this they did, producing a letter in classical
Hebrew, written in a style as lofty as the occasion demanded.

And here is the letter, word for word, as it was written:

"To the honorable Rabbi, Elders, Sages, renowned scholars,
pillars who uphold and support the entire house of Israel!
Joy unto you and joy unto everyone within the sacred community of Kozodoievka! May all that is good come unto
you and remain with you. Amen.

"It has come to our attention, worthy Rabbi and Elders,
that a great wrong has been committed unto one of our townspeople, the tailor Shimmen-Eli, son of Bendit-Leib, known
also as Shimmen-Eli *Shma-Koleinu*, as follows:

"Two of your inhabitants, the *melamed* Chaim-Chana and
his spouse Tema-Gittel, did with cunning extort the following sum, six and one-half *rubles* in silver, which they took
unto themselves, and wiping their lips said, 'We have done
no wrong.' Now, mark you, honorable sirs, such things are not
done by Jews! All of us here undersigned are witnesses that
this tailor is a poor workingman and has many children
whom he supports by the honest toil of his hands. As King
David says in the Book of Psalms: 'When thou eatest the

labor of thy hands, happy shalt thou be, and it shall be well with thee.' And our sages have interpreted it thus: happy in this world, and well in the next world. Therefore do we beg you to search out and inquire as to what has been done, so that your judgment may shine forth like the sun and you may pass this proper decision: that either the tailor receive his money back entirely or that he be given the goat that he had bought, for that one which he brought home with him is not truly a goat! To this last fact our whole town can swear.

"Then let there be peace among us. As our sages have said, 'There is nothing so blessed as peace.' Peace unto you, peace unto the farthest and the nearest, peace unto all Israel. Amen.

"From us, your servants . . ."

And then they all signed their names. First the rabbi himself, then the elders, then the leading citizens, and then, one after the other, proudly if not always legibly, the entire membership of the Tailors' Guild.

XI

And it came to pass that night that the moon shone down on Zolodievka and on all its bleak tumbledown little houses huddled together without yards, without trees, without fences, like gravestones in an old cemetery. And though the air was by no means fresh and the odors of the square and the marketplace were hardly pleasant and the dust was thick everywhere, nevertheless the people all came out, like roaches from their cracks, men and women, old people and little children, for "a breath of fresh air" after the stifling hot day. They sat on their stoops, talking, gossiping, or simply looking up at the sky, watching the face of the moon and the myriads of stars that, if you had eighteen heads, you could not count.

All that night Shimmen-Eli the tailor wandered by himself through the side streets and alleys of the little town with his goat, hiding from the small mischief-makers who had followed him all through the day. He thought that when it was light enough he would start back again toward Kozodoievka. And meanwhile he slipped into Hodel's tavern to take a drink for his sorrow's sake; unburden his heart, and seek the sympathetic tavern-keeper's advice in his grievous plight.

Hodel the tavern-keeper was a widow, a woman with brains, who knew all the public officials and was a good friend in need to all the workingmen in town. As a girl she had been known as a great beauty and had almost married a wealthy man, an excise collector. The story went that once when he was passing through Zolodievka the collector had seen her leading some geese to the *shochet,* and wanted to marry her at once. But the town gossiped so much that the match fell through. Later, against her will, she married some poor fellow, an epileptic, and again the tongues of the gossips began to wag. They said she was still in love with the exciseman, and they made up this song about her, a song which the women and maidens still sing to this day in Zolodievka.

It starts like this:

> *The moon was shining.*
> *It was the middle of the night.*
> *Hodel sat at her door.*

And it ends with these words:
> *I love you, my soul,*
> *Without end.*
> *I cannot live without you.*

And it was to this same Hodel that our tailor now poured

out his heart. It was to her that he came for advice. "What shall I do?" he asked. "Tell me. After all, you are not only beautiful but wise. As King David—or who was it?—said in the *Song of Songs:* 'I am black but comely, O ye daughters of Jerusalem.' So tell me what to do."

"What can you do?" answered Hodel, and spat vigorously. "Can't you see it's an evil spirit? What are you keeping it for? Get rid of her. Throw her out. Or the same thing may happen to you that once happened to my Aunt Pearl, may she rest in peace."

"And what happened to her?" asked Shimmen-Eli, frightened.

"This," said Hodel, with a sigh. "My Aunt Pearl was a good honest woman (all of us have been good and honest in our family, though here in this forsaken town—may it burn to the ground—everybody always has the worst to say about everyone). Well, one day my Aunt Pearl was going to market and on the ground in front of her she saw a spool of thread. 'A spool of thread,' she thought, 'comes in handy,' so she bent down and picked it up. The spool jumped in her face and then fell to the ground. She bent down and picked it up again. Again it jumped in her face and again fell down. This happened again and again till at last she spit on it, said, 'Let the devil take it,' and started back home. Once or twice she looked back, and there was the spool of thread rolling after her. Well, she came home frightened to death, fell in a faint, and was sick for almost a whole year afterward. Now, what do you think that was? Tell me. Guess."

"Ah, they're all alike, these women!" said Shimmen-Eli. "Old wives' tales, nonsense, poppycock! If you wanted to listen to what women babbled about, you'd soon be afraid of your own shadow. It is truly written: 'And a voice was given unto them.' Geese, that's what they are! But never mind. That is life; don't worry. Good night. Good night to you."

And Shimmen-Eli went on his way.

The night was sprinkled with stars. The moon floated past clouds that were like tall dark mountains inlaid with silver. With half a face the moon looked down on the town of Zolodievka sunk in deep slumber. Some of the people of the town who were afraid of bedbugs had gone to sleep out-doors, had covered their faces with homespun sheets and were snoring lustily, dreaming sweet dreams, dreams of profitable transactions, of considerate landlords, of baskets of food brought home, dreams of wealth and honor, or of honor alone: all sorts of dreams. There was not a living creature on the streets. Not a sound was to be heard. Even the butchers' dogs who had barked and fought all day, now burrowed them-selves between the logs in the back yard, hid their muzzles in their paws, and slept. From time to time a short bark escaped one of them when he dreamed of a bone that another dog was gnawing or of a fly that was buzzing in his ear. Now and then a beetle flew by, humming like the string of a bass violin, zh-zh-zh-zh, then fell to the ground and was silent. Even the town watchman who went around every night, keeping an eye on the stores and rattling his sticks over the windows, had this night become drunk, and leaning against a wall, fell fast asleep. In this silence Shimmen-Eli was the only one awake, not knowing whether to move or to stand still or to sit down.

He walked and muttered to himself, "The old woman had no troubles, so she bought herself a horse . . . Oh, this goat, this goat! May it break a leg and die! A goat? Yes, a goat. A little goat. *Chad gadyo, chad gadyo.* One little goat . . ."

He burst out laughing and was frightened by his own laughter. Passing by the old synagogue renowned for the spirits of dead men who prayed there every Saturday night in their shrouds and prayer shawls, he thought he heard a weird singing as of the wind blowing down a chimney on a winter night. And quickly turning away he found himself near the Russian church, from whose steeple a strange bird whistled shrilly. A terrible fear seized him. He tried to take heart, to steel himself with a prayer, but the words would not come.

Then looming before his eyes he saw the forms of friends long dead. And he remembered the terrifying stories he had heard in bygone days of devils, spirits, vampires, ghouls, goblins, of strange creatures that moved on tiny wheels, of some that walked on their hands, others that looked at you through a single eye, and spirits that wandered through eternity in long white shrouds. Shimmen-Eli began to think that the goat he was leading was really not a goat at all, but a sprite of some sort that at any moment would stick out its long, pointed tongue, or flap a pair of wings and utter a loud cock-a-doodle-doo. He felt his head whirling. He stopped, loosened the rope that had been tied around his waist, and urged the goat to leave him. But the goat would not budge. Shimmen-Eli took a few steps; the goat followed. He turned to the right; so did the goat. He turned left; the goat did too.

"Shma Yisroel!" screamed Shimmen-Eli, and started to run as fast as he could. And as he ran he imagined that some-one was chasing him and mocking him in a thin, goatlike voice, but the words were the words of a human: "Blessed art thou . . . O Lord . . . who quickenest the dead . . ."

XII

When the next day dawned and the men arose to go to the synagogue, the women to market, and the young girls to lead the animals to pasture, they found Shimmen-Eli sitting on the ground and near him the goat, wagging his beard and chewing the cud. When they spoke to the tailor he did not answer. He sat like a graven image staring in front of him. Quickly a crowd gathered; people came running from all over town, and a hubbub arose: "Shimmen-Eli . . . goat . . . *Shma-Koleinu* . . . *gilgul* . . . demons . . . spirits . . . werewolves . . ." Rumors flew about, with everybody telling a different story. Someone said he had seen him riding through the night.

"Who rode whom?" asked a man, sticking his head into the circle. "Did Shimmen-Eli ride the goat or did the goat ride Shimmen-Eli?"

The crowd burst out laughing.

"What are you laughing at?" a workingman burst out. "You ought to be ashamed of yourselves! Grown men with beards. Married men with families. Shame on you! Making fun of a poor tailor. Can't you see the man is not himself? He is a sick man. Instead of standing around sharpening your teeth, it would be better if you took him home and called the doctor!"

These words brought the people to their senses, and they stopped laughing at once. Someone ran off for water, others to get Yudel the healer. They took Shimmen-Eli under the arms, led him home and put him to bed. Soon Yudel came running with all his paraphernalia and began to work on him. He rubbed him, blew into his face, applied leeches, tapped his vein and drew a panful of blood.

"The more blood we draw," explained Yudel, "the better it will be, for all illnesses come from within, from the blood itself." And after presenting this bit of medical theory Yudel promised to come again in the evening.

And when Tsippa-Baila-Reiza saw her husband stretched

out on the broken old couch, covered with rags, his eyes rolled upward, his lips parched, raving in fever, she began to wring her hands, beat her head against the wall, wailed and wept as one weeps for the dead.

"Woe is me, wind is me! What will become of me now? What will become of me and all my children?"

And the children, naked and barefoot, gathered about their mother and joined her in her lamentations. The older ones wept silently, hiding their faces; the smaller ones who did not understand what had happened wailed out loud. And the youngest of all, a little boy of three, with a pinched yellow face, stood close to his mother with his tiny crooked legs and protruding belly and screamed loudest of all. "Ma-ma! I'm hun-gry!"

All the neighbors came to find out how Shimmen-Eli was, but the sight of the poor tailor and his family was so heart-rending that nobody could stay long. Only a few women remained, and stood with tear-stained faces near Tsippa-Baila-Reiza, their noses red from blowing, their mouths working, shaking their heads as though to say, "Poor Tsippa-Baila-Reiza. Nothing can help her now."

Wonder of wonders! For fifty years Shimmen-Eli *Shma-Koleinu* had lived in Zolodievka in poverty and oppression. For fifty years he had lain in obscurity. No one spoke of him, no one knew what sort of man he was. But now that he was so close to death, the town suddenly became aware of all his virtues. It suddenly became known that he had been a good and kind man, generous and charitable; that is to say, he had forced money out of the rich and divided it among the poor. He had fought everybody for those poor people, fought staunchly, and had shared his last bite with others. These and many other things they told about the poor tailor, as people tell about a dead man at his funeral. And they all came

to see him from all directions. They did everything they could
to save him, to keep him from dying before his time.

XIII

And when the sun had set and night had fallen, the members of the Tailors' Guild came together at Hodel's tavern,
ordered whisky, and called a meeting. They argued, shouted,
ranted, pounded on the table.

"Why isn't something done? A fine town like Zolodievka—
may it burn to the ground! —with so many rich people in it,
and not one of them willing to lift a finger! They all live
off the sweat of us, and none of them will help us. Who puts
all the money into the community fund? We do. Who is
skinned alive to support the *shochet*, the bath house, the synagogue? We are! Do we have to stand for everything? Come
on, let's go to the rabbi and the elders. Now it's their turn
to be useful. They'll have to keep his family alive! Come, let
us deal with them!"

And they went to the rabbi with their complaint. In reply,
the rabbi read to them the letter that had just been brought
by a teamster from Kozodoievka. And this is what it said:

"To the honorable Rabbis, elders, sages and scholars of
Zolodievka! May peace reign eternally in your holy community!

"No sooner had we received your letter, which, let us assure you, was as honey in our mouths, than we congregated
and carefully studied the matter you referred to. In answer
we can say only this, that you have wrongfully accused a
townsman of ours. This tailor of yours is a wicked man who
with base slander has created a scandal between our two com-
munities and deserves to be punished accordingly. We, the
undersigned, are ready under oath to bear witness that with

our own eyes we saw the goat give milk. May the goats of all our friends be as bountiful.

"Pay no heed to the accusations of the tailor. Pay no heed to the words of ignorant people who speak falsely.

"Peace be unto you and peace unto all Jews everywhere, now and forever, Amen.

"From your younger brothers who bow in the dust at your feet . . ."

When the rabbi had finished reading this letter, the delegation cried out in anger, "Aha, those Kozodoievka hooligans! They're making fun of us! Let's show them who we are and what our emblem is! Shears and Iron! Let them remember that!"

And at once they called another meeting, sent for more whisky, and it was decided to take this imitation of a goat straight to Kozodoievka, take vengeance on the teacher, wreck his *cheder* and overturn the whole town.

No sooner said than done. They mustered about sixty men for the trip, tailors, shoemakers, carpenters, blacksmiths, butchers, strong young men who enjoyed a fight, each one armed with the tools of his trade: this one with a wooden yardstick, that one with a flatiron, one with a last, another with an axe, some with hammers and cleavers, and others with ordinary household utensils, rolling pins, graters, carving knives . . . And it was decided without further delay that they should march off to Kozodoievka and make war on the town, kill and destroy and lay waste.

"Once for all!" they cried. " 'Let us die with the Philistines!' Let's kill them off and be done with it!"

"But wait," one of them called out. "You are ready for the slaughter, fully armed. But where is the goat?"

"That's right! Where did the demon go?"

"He's been swallowed up."

"Then he's not such a fool. But where could he have gone to?"

"Home to the *melamed*. Can't you understand?"

"He'd be crazy to do that!"

"Where else could he go?"

"What difference does it make? Guess what you want to. The point is, the goat has disappeared!"

XIV

Now let us leave the possessed tailor struggling with the Angel of Death and the workingmen of the town preparing for battle, and let us pass on to the demon himself, that is— the goat.

When the goat became aware of the uproar that had arisen in the town, he thought to himself: what was he going to get out of all this? What was the use of being tied to the tailor's waist and following him wherever he went and starving to death? It was better to run off into the wide world and see what freedom meant. So he made his escape, running off madly across the marketplace, his feet scarcely touching the earth, knocking over men and women, jumping over everything that stood in his way—tables of bread and rolls, baskets of grapes and currants. He leaped over crockery and glassware, scattered and shattered everything in his path. The women screamed, "Who is it? What is it? What happened? A goat, a possessed creature, a demon! Woe is me! Where is he? There, there he is! Catch him! Catch him!"

The men picked themselves up and ran after the goat as fast as they could, and the women, naturally, ran after the men. But in vain. Our goat had tasted the joys of freedom and was gone, never to be seen again.

And the unfortunate tailor? What became of him? And

how did the story end? Reader, don't compel me to tell you. The end was not a happy one. The story began cheerfully enough, but it ended like most cheerful stories, very tragically. And since you know that I am not a gloomy soul who prefers tears to laughter and likes to point a moral and teach a lesson, let us part as cheerfully as we can. And I wish that all of you readers and everybody else in the world may have more opportunities to laugh than to cry.

Laughter is healthful. The doctors bid us laugh.

A Yom Kippur Scandal

"THAT'S nothing!" called out the man with round eyes, like an ox, who had been sitting all this time in a corner by the window, smoking and listening to our stories of thefts, robberies and expropriations. "I'll tell you a story of a theft that took place in our town, in the synagogue itself, and on *Yom Kippur* at that! It is worth listening to.

"Our town, Kasrilevka—that's where I'm from, you know—is a small town, and a poor one. There is no thievery there. No one steals anything for the simple reason that there is nobody to steal from and nothing worth stealing. And besides, a Jew is not a thief by nature. That is, he may be a thief, but not the sort who will climb through a window or attack you with a knife. He will divert, pervert, subvert and contravert as a matter of course; but he won't pull anything out of your pocket. He won't be caught like a common thief and led through the streets with a yellow placard on his back. Imagine, then, a theft taking place in Kasrilevka, and such a theft at that. Eighteen hundred *rubles* at one crack.

"Here is how it happened. One *Yom Yippur* eve, just before the evening services, a stranger arrived in our town, a salesman of some sort from Lithuania. He left his bag at an inn, and went forth immediately to look for a place of worship, and he came upon the old synagogue. Coming in just before the service began, he found the trustees around the collection plates. '*Sholom aleichem*,' said he. '*Aleichem sholom*,' they answered.

138

'Where does our guest hail from?' 'From Lithuania.' 'And your name?' 'Even your grandmother wouldn't know if I told her.' 'But you have come to our synagogue!' 'Where else should I go?' 'Then you want to pray here?' 'Can I help myself? What else can I do?' 'Then put something into the plate.' 'What did you think? That I was not going to pay?'

"To make a long story short, our guest took out three silver *rubles* and put them in the plate. Then he put a *ruble* into the cantor's plate, one into the rabbi's, gave one for the *cheder,* threw a half into the charity box, and then began to divide money among the poor who flocked to the door. And in our town we have so many poor people that if you really wanted to start giving, you could divide Rothschild's fortune among them.

"Impressed by his generosity, the men quickly found a place for him along the east wall. Where did they find room for him when all the places along the wall are occupied? Don't ask. Have you ever been at a celebration—a wedding or circumcision—when all the guests are already seated at the table, and suddenly there is a commotion outside—the rich uncle has arrived? What do you do? You push and shove and squeeze until a place is made for the rich relative. Squeezing is a Jewish custom. If no one squeezes us, we squeeze each other."

The man with the eyes that bulged like an ox's paused, looked at the crowd to see what effect his wit had on us, and went on.

"So our guest went up to his place of honor and called to the *shammes* to bring him a praying stand. He put on his *tallis* and started to pray. He prayed and he prayed, standing on his feet all the time. He never sat down or left his place all evening long or all the next day. To fast all day standing on one's feet, without ever sitting down—that only a Litvak can do!

"But when it was all over, when the final blast of the *shofar* had died down, the Day of Atonement had ended, and Chaim the *melamed,* who had led the evening prayers after *Yom Kippur* from time immemorial, had cleared his throat, and in his tremulous voice had already begun—'*Ma-a-riv a-ro-vim* ...' suddenly screams were heard. 'Help! Help! Help!' We looked around: the stranger was stretched out on the floor in a dead faint. We poured water on him, revived him, but he fainted again. What was the trouble? Plenty! This Litvak tells us that he had brought with him to Kasrilevka eighteen hundred *rubles.* To leave that much at the inn—think of it, eighteen hundred *rubles*—he had been afraid. Whom could he trust with such a sum of money in a strange town? And yet, to keep it in his pocket on *Yom Kippur* was not exactly proper either. So at last this plan had occurred to him: he had taken the money to the synagogue and slipped it into the praying stand. Only a Litvak could do a thing like that! . . . Now do you see why he had not stepped away from the praying stand for a single minute? And yet during one of the many prayers when we all turn our face to the wall, someone must have stolen the money . . .

"Well, the poor man wept, tore his hair, wrung his hands. What would he do with the money gone? It was not his own money, he said. He was only a clerk. The money was his employer's. He himself was a poor man, with a houseful of children. There was nothing for him to do now but go out and drown himself, or hang himself right here in front of everybody.

"Hearing these words, the crowd stood petrified, forgetting that they had all been fasting since the night before and it was time to go home and eat. It was a disgrace before a stranger, a shame and a scandal in our own eyes. A theft like that— eighteen hundred *rubles*! And where? In the Holy of Holies, in the old synagogue of Kasrilevka. And on what day? On the holiest day of the year, on *Yom Kippur*! Such a thing had never been heard of before.

"'*Shammes,* lock the door!' ordered our Rabbi. We have our own Rabbi in Kasrilevka, Reb Yozifel, a true man of God, a holy man. Not too sharp witted, perhaps, but a good man, a man with no bitterness in him. Sometimes he gets ideas that you would not hit upon if you had eighteen heads on your shoulders . . . When the door was locked, Reb Yozifel turned to the congregation, his face pale as death and his hands trembling, his eyes burning with a strange fire.

"He said, 'Listen to me, my friends, this is an ugly thing, a thing unheard of since the world was created—that here in Kasrilevka there should be a sinner, a renegade to his people, who would have the audacity to take from a stranger, a poor man with a family, a fortune like this. And on what day? On the holiest day of the year, on *Yom Kippur,* and perhaps at the last, most solemn moment—just before the *shofar* was blown! Such a thing has never happened anywhere. I cannot believe it is possible. It simply cannot be. But perhaps—who knows? Man is greedy, and the temptation—especially with a sum like this, eighteen hundred *rubles,* God forbid—is great enough. So if one of us was tempted, if he were fated to commit this evil on a day like this, we must probe the matter thoroughly, strike at the root of this whole affair. Heaven and earth have sworn that the truth must always rise as oil upon the waters. Therefore, my friends, let us search each other now, go through each other's garments, shake out our pockets—all of us from the oldest householder to the *shammes,* not leaving anyone out. Start with me. Search my pockets first.'

"Thus spoke Reb Yozifel, and he was the first to unbind his gabardine and turn his pockets inside out. And following his example all the men loosened their girdles and showed the linings of their pockets, too. They searched each other, they

felt and shook one another, until they came to Lazer Yossel,
who turned all colors and began to argue that, in the first place,
the stranger was a swindler; that his story was the pure fabri-
cation of a Litvak. No one had stolen any money from him.
Couldn't they see that it was all a falsehood and a lie?

"The congregation began to clamor and shout. What did he
mean by this? All the important men had allowed themselves
to be searched, so why should Lazer Yossel escape? There are
no privileged characters here. 'Search him! Search him!' the
crowd roared.

"Lazer Yossel saw that it was hopeless, and began to plead
for mercy with tears in his eyes. He begged them not to search
him. He swore by all that was holy that he was as innocent in
this as he would want to be of any wrongdoing as long as he
lived. Then why didn't he want to be searched? It was a disgrace to him, he said. He begged them to have pity on his
youth, not to bring this disgrace down on him. 'Do anything
you wish with me,' he said, 'but don't touch my pockets.' How
do you like that? Do you suppose we listened to him?

"But wait . . . I forgot to tell you who this Lazer Yossel was.
He was not a Kasrilevkite himself. He came from the Devil
knows where, at the time of his marriage, to live with his wife's
parents. The rich man of our town had dug him up somewhere
for his daughter, boasted that he had found a rare nugget, a
fitting match for a daughter like his. He knew a thousand
pages of *Talmud* by heart, and all of the Bible. He was a
master of Hebrew, arithmetic, bookkeeping, algebra, penmanship—in short, everything you could think of. When he arrived
in Kasrilevka—this jewel of a young man—everyone came out
to gaze at him. What sort of bargain had the rich man picked
out? Well, to look at him you could tell nothing. He was a
young man, something in trousers. Not bad looking, but with
a nose a trifle too long, eyes that burned like two coals, and a

sharp tongue. Our leading citizens began to work on him:
tried him out on a page of *Gamorah,* a chapter from the Scriptures. a bit of *Rambam,* this, that and the other. He was perfect
in everything, the dog! Whenever you went after him, he was
at home. Reb Yozifel himself said that he could have been a
rabbi in any Jewish congregation. As for world affairs, there
is nothing to talk about. We have an authority on such things
in our town, Zaidel Reb Shaye's, but he could not hold a candle
to Lazer Yossel. And when it came to chess—there was no one
like him in all the world! Talk about versatile people . . .
Naturally the whole town envied the rich man his find, but
some of them felt he was a little too good to be true. He was
too clever (and too much of anything is bad!). For a man of
his station he was too free and easy, a hail-fellow-well-met, too
familiar with all the young folk—boys, girls, and maybe even
loose women. There were rumors . . . At the same time he
went around alone too much, deep in thought. At the synagogue he came in last, put on his *tallis,* and with his skullcap
on askew, thumbed aimlessly through his prayerbook without
ever following the services. No one ever saw him doing anything exactly wrong, and yet people murmured that he was
not a God-fearing man. Apparently a man cannot be perfect . . .

"And so, when his turn came to be searched and he refused
to let them do it, that was all the proof most of the men needed
that he was the one who had taken the money. He begged
them to let him swear any oath they wished, begged them to
chop him, roast him, cut him up—do anything but shake his
pockets out. At this point even our Rabbi, Reb Yozifel, although he was a man we had never seen angry, lost his temper
and started to shout.

" 'You!' he cried. 'You thus and thus! Do you know what
you deserve? You see what all these men have endured. They

were able to forget the disgrace and allowed themselves to be
searched; but you want to be the only exception! God in
heaven! Either confess and hand over the money, or let us see
for ourselves what is in your pockets. You are trifling now
with the entire Jewish community. Do you know what they
can do to you?'

"To make a long story short, the men took hold of this young
upstart, threw him down on the floor with force, and began to
search him all over, shake out every one of his pockets. And
finally they shook out . . . Well, guess what! A couple of
well-gnawed chicken bones and a few dozen plum pits still
moist from chewing. You can imagine what an impression
this made—to discover food in the pockets of our prodigy on
this holiest of fast days. Can you imagine the look on the young
man's face, and on his father-in-law's? And on that of our poor
Rabbi?

"Poor Reb Yozifel! He turned away in shame. He could
look no one in the face. On *Yom Kippur,* and in his synagogue
. . . As for the rest of us, hungry as we were, we could not stop
talking about it all the way home. We rolled with laughter in
the streets. Only Reb Yozifel walked home alone, his head
bowed, full of grief, unable to look anyone in the eyes, as though
the bones had been shaken out of his own pockets."

The story was apparently over. Unconcerned, the man with
the round eyes of an ox turned back to the window and resumed
smoking.

"Well," we all asked in one voice, "and what about the
money?"

"What money?" asked the man innocently, watching the
smoke he had exhaled.

"What do you mean—what money? The eighteen hundred
rubles!"

"Oh," he drawled. "The eighteen hundred. They were gone."

"Gone?"

"Gone forever."

In Haste

For in haste didst thou come forth out of the Land of Egypt
— DEUTERONOMY, 16:3.

TO MY honored, beloved and respected friend, Sholom Aleichem:

I want to begin by informing you that I am still—Bless the Lord—among the living, and that I hope to hear the same from you, Amen. Next I want to tell you that, with God's help, I am now a king; that is, I have come home to Kasrilevka to spend the Passover with my wife and children, my father-in-law and mother-in-law, and with all my loved ones. And at Passover, as we all know, a Jew surrounded by his family is always a king. If only briefly, I hasten to inform you of all this, my dear, true friend. For a detailed account there is no time. It is Passover Eve, and on this day we must all do everything in great haste, standing on one foot. As it is written, "For *in haste* didst thou come forth out of the Land of Egypt."

But what to write of first, I hardly know myself. It seems to me that before anything else I ought to thank you and praise you for the good advice you gave me, to try my hand at matchmaking. Believe me, I shall never, never forget what you have done for me. You led me forth from the Land of Bondage, from the Gehenna of Yehupetz; you freed me from the desolate occupation of a commission salesman, and lifted me to a noble, respected profession. And for this I am obligated to praise and exalt you, to bless and adorn your name, as you well deserve.

It is true that thus far I have not succeeded in negotiating a single match, but I have made a beginning. Things are stirring, and once things begin to stir there is always the possibility and the hope that with God's help something may come of it. Especially in view of the fact that I do not work alone. I operate in partnership with other matchmakers, the best matchmakers in the world. As a result of these connections I now have a reputation of my own. Wherever I come and introduce myself, Menachem-Mendel from Yehupetz, I am invited to sit down, I am given tea with preserves, I am treated like an honored guest. They introduce me to the daughter of the house, and the daughter shows me what she can do. She turns to her governess and begins to speak French with her. Words come pouring like peas out of a sack, and the mother sits gazing at her daughter proudly, as though to say, "What do you think of her? She speaks well, doesn't she?"

And listening to these girls, I have picked up some French myself and I can understand quite a bit of the language. For instance, if someone says to me, *"Parlez-vous Français?"* ("How are you feeling these days?") I say, *"Merci, bonjour."* ("Not bad, praise the Lord.")

Then, after she has given a demonstration of her French, they have her sit down at the pianola to play something— overtures and adagios and finales—so beautiful that it penetrates to the very depth of one's soul! In the meantime the parents ask me to stay for supper and I let them talk me into it. Why not? . . . At the table they serve me the best portions of meat and feed me *tzimmes* even on weekdays. Afterwards, I strike up a conversation with the daughter. "What," I ask, "is your heart's desire—a lawyer, an engineer, a doctor?"

"Naturally," she says, "a doctor." And once more she starts jabbering in French with the governess, and at this point the mother has an opportunity to display her daughter's handiwork. "Her embroidery and her knitting are a feast to the eye," she says, "and her kindness, her goodness, her consideration for others—there is no one like her! And quiet—like a dove. And bright—as the day . . ."

And the father, in his turn, traces his pedigree for me. He tells me what a fine family he comes from, and his wife as well. He tells me who his grandfather was, and his great-grandfather, and all his wife's connections. Every one of them of the finest. Rich people, millionaires, famous and celebrated all over the world. "There is not a single common person in our whole family," he assures me. "And not one pauper," his wife adds. "Not a single workingman," he says. "No tailors and no cobblers," she adds. "You'll find no fakes or frauds among us," he tells me. "Or apostates either, I can assure you," she puts in.

In the doorway, when I'm ready to leave and they wish me a good journey, I sigh and let them know how expensive it is to travel these days. Every step costs money. And if he is not obtuse he knows what I mean, and gives me at least enough for expenses . . .

I tell you, my dear friend, that matchmaking is not at all such a bad profession—especially if God ever intercedes and you actually conclude a match! So far, as I have told you, I have not succeeded in marrying anyone off. I have had no luck. At the start everything looks auspicious. It could hardly be better. It was a match predestined since the Six Days of Creation. But at the last moment everything goes wrong. In this case the youth does not care for the maiden; in the other, the girl thinks the groom is too old. This one has too fine a pedigree; that one does not have enough money. This one wants the moon on a platter; that one doesn't know what he wants. There is plenty of trouble connected with it, and heartaches, and indigestion, I can assure you.

Right now I am on the verge of arranging a couple of matches—naturally with a few partners—which, if the Lord has mercy and they go through, will be something for the whole world to talk about. Both parties come from the wealthiest and finest and oldest families—there is none like them. And the girls are both the greatest beauties. You can't find their equal anywhere. Both are well-educated, gifted, kind, bright, quiet, modest—all the virtues you can think of. And what do I have to offer them? Real merchandise! One—a doctor from Odessa. But he wants no less than thirty thousand *rubles* dowry, and he has a right to it, because according to the practice that he says he has, he should be worth much more. I have another from Byelotzerkiev—a rare find! A bargain at twenty thousand! And another in Yehupetz—only he doesn't want to get married. And a whole flock of young little doctors who are only too anxious to get married.

Besides these I have a pack of lawyers and attorneys and justices at fifteen thousand and ten thousand, and smaller lawyers—young ones just hatched—that you can have for six thousand or five thousand, or even less. On top of that I have a couple of engineers who are already earning a living, and a few engineers still looking for work. And that is not all. I have an assortment of miscellaneous clients, elderly men, relics of past campaigns from Tetrevitz, from Makarevka, from Yampola and from Strishtch, without diplomas, but fine enough specimens, distinguished, skilled, intelligent. In short, there are plenty to pick from. The only trouble is that if the gentleman wants the lady, the lady does not want the gentleman. If the girl is willing, the man is not. Perhaps then you will ask why the man who does not want girl number one will not take num-

ber two, and vice versa? I thought of that myself, but it
doesn't seem to work. Do you know why? Because strangers
are always mixing in. They may be good people. They mean
no harm. But they spoil everything. And meanwhile letters
are flying back and forth. I send telegrams and receive telegrams every day. The whole world rocks and rolls!

And in the midst of it all, Passover gets in the way, like a
bone in the throat, blocking everything. I think it over. My
fortune won't run away from me. The merchandise I deal in
is not so perishable. Why shouldn't I take a few days off and
go to see my family in Kasrilevka? It's been so long since I've
been there. It is not fair to my wife and children to be away
from them so long. It does not look good to others, and it
is even embarrassing to myself. So, to make it short, I have
come home for Passover, and that is where I am writing you
this letter from.

Maybe you will ask, why have I not written to you before
this? Here is the answer. People like us are always worn out,
we never have time. We are always rushing about. We never
rest. I always keep thinking: if not today, then tomorrow.
Soon, soon, with God's help, I'll arrange a worthwhile match,
and then I'll write you all about it in celebration. But as it
happened that all my prospects dragged on and remained
hanging in the air, I kept putting off writing to you till God
should bring me safely home . . .

And now I shall tell you what my homecoming was like.
I'll describe everything just the way you like it. But if my account does not seem rounded out as yours always are, please
excuse me. Each one of us has to tell his story the way he can.

I arrived—that is, the train came into the station—yesterday.
But around here the mud is so deep that it took the wagon
all night to pull through to town. For a time it even looked
as if I might have to spend the Passover on the way some-

where, axle-deep in mud, together with the driver and the horses. You must be familiar with our Kasrilevka mud from the olden times. But ever since they began to talk about paving the roads around here, it seems as if the mud has become thicker and deeper than ever. In fact, people have begun going around without their galoshes, because they were always losing them in the mud. And some women have started a fashion even better than that. They go around without shoes, either. I wonder what they'll think of next!

Well, this morning, when we reached Kasrilevka itself, all the passengers had to get out of the wagon and go the rest of the way by foot. A fine homecoming! I felt my face burning. Acquaintance after acquaintance stopped me on the way, greeted me broadly, shook hands with me knee-deep in the mud—each with his own questions, his own comments. "How goes it with you, Menachem-Mendel?" "What is the latest news on the Yehupetz market?" "Look at the man, will you! In a derby hat and rubber overshoes!"

"Laugh, laugh," I answered, barely able to pull one foot after another out of the mud. "You have the right to laugh! Everywhere else in the world people really need galoshes, but here you can get along without them! Here it's as dry and sandy as in Palestine!"

I barely managed to drag myself home, and here I found a Gehenna. Like the fumes over Gehenna was the thick smoke that rose from the yard and the kitchen, where silverware for the holidays was being boiled, and everything else was being cleaned and scrubbed and scoured. And food, the rich and wonderful Passover food, was being cooked and baked and broiled. The shouting and clamoring of everyone, of mistresses and servants, the commands, the exhortations, the complaints and the threats, were enough to make a person deaf. A small thing—Passover Eve!

The first one to greet me was my mother-in-law, bless her. She is the same as ever, she has not changed in the least. She was in the front yard, standing over a wooden cot, her kerchief tied around her head with two pointed wings sticking out. In one hand she held a can of kerosene, in the other a brush. She was pickling bedbugs. When she saw me, she managed to control her joy. She kept right on with her work, muttering to herself:

"Well, well! You mention the Messiah—and look who comes! Here he is, my bird of Paradise . . . If he doesn't spoil, he'll find his way home. Goats run away, chickens get lost, but men always come back . . . The only place they don't return from is the Other World. Now I know why the cat was washing herself yesterday, and the dog was eating entrails . . . Oh, Sheine-Sheindel, daughter, come here! Welcome your ornament, your jewel, your crown of gold and diamonds! Your holy of holies . . . Quick, take the garbage away!"

At this point my wife runs out, frightened, and sees me. Her welcome is more direct.

"Tfui!" she spat out. "You picked just the right time to come. All year long you roam around that dirty city, lying around in all the attics, engage in every idolatry—and here you come fluttering in on Passover Eve, when we're busy cleaning up and there is no time to say a word to each other. I don't even have the time to put on a clean dress. I look like a fright. And you— fresh from the fine ladies of Yehupetz—may they roast in hell!—who held you in their clutches all year—may they not live through the Passover! Look at him! A plague on him! He doesn't even ask how a person is getting along, how the children are! Soreleh, Feigeleh, Yoseleh, Nechamenu, Moishe-Hershe-leh! Your father has come back! Suddenly remembered you!

May my worst enemies look as beautiful as you look in that derby hat!"

I must tell you the truth, dear friend. I barely recognized the children. And as for them—they didn't know me at all. But though my wife's welcome was not as ardent as I had hoped for, I could see that she was happy, for when I had finished greeting and kissing each of the children, I saw that she had withdrawn to one side and was crying.

But best and friendliest of all was the welcome I received from my father-in-law. He was as happy as if it were his own child he was seeing, or happy like a man who had been locked up in prison all these years and suddenly he sees another prisoner . . . My father-in-law, a distinguished-looking man with fine, dark eyes and a rich beard, had aged noticeably in these past few years, become white as a dove. Quietly he shook hands with me, asked how I was, and with a wink called me into his little alcove, and only when we were there alone did he embrace me.

"Do you know what, Mendel," he said to me with a deep sigh, "I'm growing old. Every year I'm a year older . . . But come, Mendel, sit down. Tell me what's new. You have been all over the world. How are things going on among our people? What is the true story about Dreyfus? What is it people are saying about a new war? What is happening in Palestine? Here we know nothing, we live like cattle . . ."

My father-in-law was getting wound up for a good long talk, but suddenly from outside we heard my mother-in-law's melodious voice:

"Boruch! Boruch!?" (The first Boruch was a shout, the second had a questioning overtone of astonishment in it, as if to say, "Aren't you here yet?")

"Just a minute! Here I come! I'm coming! I'm coming!"

answered my father-in-law, and he bounded from the room.

A few times this happened. No sooner had he got started talking, when her voice rang out, "Boruch! Boruch!?" And each time he jumped. "I'm coming! I'm coming!" A little later, after breakfast, after the last few bread crusts found on the premises had been burned and the house itself had been purified for the holidays, and he was given a clean shirt and told that now he could go to the Baths, he became a different man, as though a new soul had been installed in his body. There at least, in the bath house, he thought he would have a chance for a few words. But again he was mistaken, woefully mistaken. As soon as we came in the crowd swarmed about us like bees, like the locusts in a year of famine. They almost ate me up alive. Every one of them wanted me to tell him what was going on in Yehupetz. Was it true, what they had heard about the bad times everywhere, the failures and bankruptcies? Did millionaire Brodsky still have some money? How was the Dreyfus case going to come out? Why didn't they hear about it any more? And how did it happen that England was still messing around with the Boers? These questions and many more they put to me from all sides. They almost pulled me apart. They didn't let me rest. And my father-in-law could not get a word in anywhere.

The same thing happened when we went to buy wine for the *seder*. As soon as we walked down into Yudel Veinshenker's cellar, I was greeted from all sides and had to shake hands with everybody. In the midst of it someone asked for Palestinian wine, and Yudel Veinshenker (much older now, with all his teeth gone) kept shouting that there was no such thing. There never had been and never would be. But one young man who pretended to be more worldly than the others, kept arguing that he had seen it himself in the papers.

"Papers! What papers?." shouted Yudel Veinshenker. "Lies and falsehoods! Some troublemakers must have thought it up! Those Zionists you hear about!"

The young man was stubborn. "As sure as I see you in front of me," he said, "I saw the Palestinian wines mentioned. And what's more, I'll tell you the exact name. Mount Carmel wine. And they sell it in all the shops in Yehupetz."

"In Yehupetz, you say?" several bystanders broke in. "Here is a man straight from Yehupetz. Menachem-Mendel Boruch-Hersh Leah-Dvoshe's! Let's ask Menachem-Mendel. He'll know!"

I tried to speak, but they wouldn't let me. For every word I say they ask me ten questions, and before I'm through with one answer another of them asks me ten more questions. "Why do they call it Mount Carmel wine? Is it from Mount Carmel itself or just from Palestine? How do they bring it from Mount Carmel? How much does it cost? Who makes it? Jewish colonists? Our own colonists? How many colonies do we have now in Palestine? What are their names, and what connection do they have with Baron Rothschild? Oh, Rothschild! How much is he really worth? Who is worth more—Rothschild or the Yehupetzer Brodsky? Why is Rothschild a Zionist and Brodsky not? Is it true, what they say, that Doctor Herzel is buying up Palestine from the Turks for the Zionists?"

"Come," my father-in-law says to me, "they don't let us get in a word anywhere."

And it was only later in the day, while he was grating horseradish outside, that my father-in-law was able to say a few words to me. But only a few words, because every little while we were interrupted by my mother-in-law.

"Boruch! *Boruch!?*"

"Right away! Here I come! Here I come!"

In the meantime the women had finished their work and had dressed themselves in their finest clothes and all their jewelry, like queens. My mother-in-law wore a dark green poplin dress with a flowered silk kerchief on her head. And Sheine-Sheindel had a flowered yellow silk dress with a dark green poplin kerchief on her head. And even I slipped into the alcove and put on my best clothes. Are we not all kings on Passover? And in the meanwhile I took a few sheets of paper and I'm writing you this letter. And once more, dear friend, I beg you to pardon me if I appear to be in a hurry. It's Passover Eve! If all is well and the Lord grants me strength, I shall write to you again in a few days. Then I shall have more time and I shall be able to write at greater length.

From your truest friend,
Menachem-Mendel

P.S. It is not my fate to enjoy anything in this world. There everything was ready, all was serene. The holiday spirit was in the air, and suddenly a misfortune overtook us. A dog stole into the kitchen, no one knows how, and ate up the greens and the chicken neck and the rest of the symbolic trimmings for tonight's *seder*. Suddenly there was an uproar and a tumult. Heavens were splitting open. I was sure murder was being done, or a fire had broken out, or at least someone had been scalded with boiling water. Everybody was yelling at everybody else, and all the cries melted into one uproar. Sheine-Sheindel was yelling at the servant girl; the servant girl was yelling at my father-in-law. "It's all his fault!" she cried. "The master has no brains! He's always leaving the door open! Always!"

But above them all could be heard my mother-in-law.

"Woe is me! Thunder and lightning! When the world calls a man crazy, you may believe it! A fool is worse than a sinner!

How should a person be a prophet and know that he would leave the door open, and suddenly, on Passover Eve, a dog would steal into the kitchen? And of all things to find the chicken bones? It never rains but it pours. I have always said: the dog always gets the best bite of food, and the pudding comes out according to the company (that must mean me!) . . . What can we do now? Boruch! *Boruch?*"

"Here I am! Right away! Here I am!"

I look at my father-in-law and think: "What a woeful lot is yours, poor unfortunate king, and what a woeful thing is thy kingdom."

Once more, be well, And enjoy a *kosher Pesach*.

Yours

M. M.

Eternal Life

IF YOU are willing to listen, I shall tell you the story of how I once took a burden upon myself, a burden which almost, almost ruined my life for me. And why do you think I did it? Simply because I was an inexperienced young man and none too shrewd. So far as that goes, I may be far from clever now, too, because if I were clever, I might have had a little money by now. How does the saying go? If you have money, you are not only clever, but handsome too, and can sing like a nightingale!

Well, there I was, a young man living with my father- and mother-in-law, as was the custom with young married couples in those days. And, as was also the custom in those days, I sat in the synagogue all day studying the *Torah*. Now and then I glanced into secular books too, but that had to be done on the sly so my father- and mother-in-law should not find out; not so much my father-in-law as my mother-in-law, a woman who was the real head of the family. You can really say she wore the pants. She managed all their affairs herself, picked out the husbands for her daughters herself, and herself arranged the entire match. It was she who had picked me out too, she who examined me in the *Torah,* she who brought me to Zvohil from Rademishli. I am from Rademishli, you know—that's where I was born. You must have heard of the town; it was recently in the papers.

So I lived in Zvohil with my mother-in-law, struggled over

the Rambam's *Guide to the Perplexed,* never stepping out of the house, you might say, till the time came when I had to register for military service. Then, as the custom was, I had to bestir myself, go back to Rademishli, straighten out my papers, see what exemption I could claim, and arrange for a passport which I would need if I ever left the district. That, you could say, was my first venture into the outside world. All by myself, to prove that I was now a responsible person, I went forth into the marketplace and hired a sleigh. God sent me a bargain. I found a peasant who was going back to Rademishli with a freshly-painted, broad-backed sleigh with wings at the sides like an eagle. But I had failed to pay attention to the fact that the horse was a white one, and a white horse, my mother-in-law said, was bad luck. "I hope I'm lying," she said, "but this trip will be an unlucky one." "Bite your tongue," burst out my father-in-law, and at once was sorry, because he had to take his punishment right on the spot. But to me he whispered, "Women's nonsense," and I began to pack up for the trip: my *tallis* and *tfillin,* some freshly baked rolls, a few *rubles* for expenses, and three pillows—a pillow to sit on, a pillow to lean against, and a pillow to keep my feet warm. And I was ready to go.

So I said goodbye to everybody, and started on my way to Rademishli. It was late in winter; the hard-packed snow made a perfect road for the sleigh. The horse, though a white one, went as smoothly as a breeze, and my driver turned out to be one of those silent fellows who answers everything either "Uh-huh," meaning "yes," or "Uh-uh" for "no." That's all. You couldn't get another word out of him.

I had left home right after dinner and made myself as comfortable as I could, with a pillow under me, a pillow at my back, and one at my feet. The horse pranced, the driver cluck-clucked, the sleigh slid along, the wind blew, and snowflakes drifted through the air like feathers and covered the wide expanse around us. My heart felt light, my spirits free. After all, it was my first trip alone into God's world. I was all alone, a free man, my own master! I leaned back and spread myself out in the sleigh like a lord. But in winter, no matter how warmly you are dressed, when the frost goes through you, you feel like stopping somewhere to warm yourself and catch your breath before going on again. And I began to dream of a warm inn, a boiling *samovar,* and a fresh pot roast with hot gravy. These dreams made me crave for food. I actually became hungry. I began to ask the driver about an inn, asked if the next one was far away. He answered, "Uh-uh," meaning "no." I asked if it was close, and he answered, "Uh-huh," meaning "yes." "How close?" I asked. But that he would not answer, no matter how hard I tried to make him.

I imagined what it would have been like if this were a Jew driving the sleigh. He would have told me not only where the inn was, but who ran it, what his name was, how many children he had, how much rent he paid, what he got out of it, how long he had been there, who had been there before him—in short, everything. We are a strange people, we Jews.

But there I was, dreaming of a warm inn, seeing a hot *samovar* in front of me, and other good things like that; till God took pity on me, the driver clucked to the horse, turned the sleigh a little aside, and there appeared before us a small gray hut covered with snow, a country inn standing alone in the wide, snow-covered field, like a forsaken, forgotten tombstone.

Driving up to the inn with a flourish, the driver took the horse and sleigh into the barn and I went straight toward the inn itself, opened the door, and stopped dead. Here is what I saw. On the floor in the middle of the room lay a corpse covered with black, with two copper candlesticks holding small candles at its head. All around the body sat small children in ragged clothes beating their heads with their fists and screaming and wailing, "Mo-ther! Mother!" And a tall, thin man with long, thin legs, dressed in a torn summer coat entirely out of season, marched up and down the room with long strides, wringing his hands and saying to himself, "What shall I do? What shall I do? I don't know what to do!"

I understood right away what a happy scene I had come upon. My first thought was to run away. I turned to leave, but the door was slammed shut behind me and my feet felt rooted to the ground. I could not move from the spot. Seeing a stranger, the tall man with the long legs ran up to me, stretched out both arms like a man seeking help.

"What do you think of my misfortune?" he asked, pointing to the weeping children. "Poor little things . . . their mother just died. What shall I do? What shall I do? I don't know what to do!"

"Blessed is He who gives, and He who takes," I said, and started to comfort him with the words one uses on such occasions. But he interrupted me.

"She was as good as dead for the past year, poor thing. It was consumption. She begged for death to come. And now she's dead and here we are, stuck in this forsaken spot. What can I do? Go to the village to find a wagon to take her to town? How can I leave the children here alone in the middle of this field, with night coming on? God in heaven, what shall I do? What shall I do? I don't know what to begin to do!"

With these words the man began to weep, strangely, without tears, as though he were laughing, and a queer sound came from his lips, like a cough. All my strength left me. Who could think of hunger now? Who remembered the cold?

I forgot everything and said to him, "I am driving from Zvohil to Rademishli with a very fine sleigh. If the town you

speak of is not very far from here I can let you take the sleigh
and I'll wait here. If it won't take too long, that is."

"Long may you live!" he cried. "For this good deed you'll
earn eternal life! As I am a Jew, eternal life!" he exclaimed,
and threw his arms around me. "The town is not far away,
only four or five *versts*. It will take no more than an hour and
I'll send the sleigh right back. You are earning eternal life,
I tell you! Eternal life! Children, get up from the ground
and thank this young man. Kiss his hands and his feet! He
is letting me use his sleigh to take your mother to the burial
ground. Eternal life! As sure as I'm a Jew, eternal life!"

This news did not exactly cheer them. When they heard their
father talk about taking their mother away they threw themselves around her again and began to weep louder than ever.
And yet it was good news that a man had been found to do
them this kindness. God himself had sent him there. They
looked at me as at a redeemer, something like Elijah, and I
must tell you the plain truth: I began to see myself as an
extraordinary being. Suddenly in my own eyes I grew in
stature and became what the world calls a hero. I was ready
to lift mountains, turn worlds upside down. There was nothing
that seemed too difficult for me, and these words tore themselves out of my lips:

"I'll tell you what. I'll take her there myself, that is, my
driver and I. I'll save you the trouble of going and leaving
the children behind."

The more I talked the more the little children wept, wept and
looked up at me as at an angel from heaven, and I grew in
my own eyes taller and taller, till I almost reached the sky.
For the moment I forgot I had always been afraid to touch
a dead body, and with my own hands helped to carry the
woman out and lift her into the sleigh. I had to promise the
driver another half-*ruble,* and a drink of whisky on the spot.

At first he scratched the back of his neck and mumbled something in his nose. But after the third drink he softened up and we started on our way, all three of us, the driver and I and the innkeeper's wife, Chava Nechama. That was her name, Chava Nechama, daughter of Raphael Michel. I remember it as if it had been this morning, because all along the way I kept repeating to myself the name that her husband had repeated to me several times. For when the time came to bury her with the proper ceremony, her full name would have to be given. So all the way I repeated to myself, "Chava Nechama, daughter of Raphael Michel. Chava Nechama, daughter of Raphael Michel. Chava Nechama, daughter of Raphael Michel." But while I kept repeating the woman's name, the husband's name escaped me completely. He had told me his name too and assured me that when I came to the town and mentioned the name, the corpse would be taken from me at once and I would be able to go on my way. He was well known there, he said. Year after year he came there for the holidays, contributed money for the synagogue, for the bath house, and everywhere he paid well. He told me more, filled my head with instructions, where I should go, what I should say and do, and every bit of it flew out of my head. You'd think that at least a word of it would have remained. But it didn't. Not a word.

All my thoughts revolved about one thing only, here I was, carrying a dead woman. That alone was enough to make me forget everything, even my own name; for from early childhood I had been mortally afraid of dead bodies. You'd have to pay me a fortune to make me stay alone with a corpse. And now it seemed to me that the glazed, half-open eyes stared at me and the dead, sealed lips would open any minute and a strange voice would be heard as though from a sepulchre, a voice so terrible that merely thinking of it almost threw me into a faint. It is not for nothing that such stories are told of the dead, of people who have fainted out of mere fright, and lost their minds or their powers of speech.

So we rode along, the three of us. I had given the dead woman one of my pillows and had placed her crossways in the sleigh, right at my feet. In order to keep myself from thinking melancholy thoughts I turned away from the body, began to watch the sky and softly to repeat to myself, "Chava Nechama, daughter of Raphael Michel. Chava Nechama, daughter of Raphael Michel," until the name became jumbled in my mind and I found myself saying, "Chava Raphael, daughter of Nechama Michel," and, "Raphael Michel, daughter of Chava Nechama."

I had not been aware that it was getting darker and darker. The wind was blowing stronger all the time and the snow continued to fall until it was so deep that we could not find the road. The sleigh went hither and yon, without direction, and the driver began to grumble at first softly, then louder and more insistently, and I could swear that he was blessing me with a threefold blessing. I asked him, "What is the matter with you?" He spat into the snow and turned upon me with such murderous anger that I shrank back. "Look what you've done!" he cried. "You've been the ruination of me and my horse!" Because of this, because we had taken a dead woman into the sleigh, the horse had strayed from the road, and here we were wandering, and God alone knew how long we would keep on wandering. For night was almost here, and then we would really be lost.

At this good news I was ready to go back to the inn, unload our baggage, forget eternal life. But it was too late, said the driver. We could neither go ahead nor turn back. We were wandering in the middle of the field, the devil alone knew where. The road was snowed under, the sky was black. It was late. The horse was dead tired. May a bad end come to that innkeeper and all the innkeepers of the world! Why hadn't he broken a leg before he had stopped at the inn? Why hadn't he choked on the first glass of whiskey before he had let himself be talked into this folly, and for a miserable half-*ruble* perish here in the wilderness, together with his poor little horse. As for himself, it didn't matter so much. Maybe it was fated that he should come to a bad end, and at this spot. But the poor little horse, what had he done? An innocent animal, to be sacrificed like that?

I could swear that there were tears in his voice. And to make him feel better I told him that I would give him another half-*ruble* and two more glasses of whiskey. At this he became furious and told me plainly that if I didn't keep my mouth shut he would throw our cargo out of the sleigh altogether. And I thought to myself: what would I do if he threw the corpse and me out into the snow? Who knew what a man like that could do when he lost his temper? I had better be quiet, sit in the sleigh buried in pillows and try to keep from falling asleep, because in the first place, how could a person fall asleep with a dead body in front of him? And in the second place, I had heard that in wintertime you mustn't fall asleep outside, because if you did you might fall asleep forever.

But in spite of myself my eyes kept shutting. I would have given anything at that moment for a short nap. And I kept rubbing at my eyes but my eyes would not obey. They kept shutting slowly and opening and shutting again. And the sleigh slid over the soft deep white snow and a strange sweet numbness poured through my limbs and I felt an extraordinary calm descend on me. And I wished that this sweet numbness and calm would last and last. I wished it would last forever. But an unknown force, I don't know where it came from, stood by and prodded me. "Do not sleep. Do not fall asleep." With a

great effort I tore my eyes open and the numbness resolved
itself into a chill that went through my bones and the calm
turned to fear and shrinking and melancholy—may the Lord
have mercy on me. I imagined that my corpse was stirring,
that it uncovered itself and looked at me with half-shut eyes
as though to say, "What did you have against me, young man?
Why did you drag me off, a dead woman, the mother of
young children, and then fail to bring me to consecrated
ground?"

The wind blew. It shrieked with a human voice, whistled
right into my ears, confided a horrible secret to me. Terrible
thoughts, frightful images followed one another in my mind
and it seemed to me that we were all buried under the snow,
all of us, the driver, the horse, the dead woman and I. We were
all dead, all of us. Only the corpse—isn't it remarkable?—
only the dead woman, the innkeeper's wife, was alive!

Suddenly I heard my driver clucking to his horse cheerfully,
thanking God, and sighing and crossing himself in the dark.
I sat up and looked around. In the distance I saw a gleam of
light. The light glimmered, went out, and glimmered again.
A house, I thought, and thanked God with all my heart. I
turned to the driver. "We must have found the road," I said.
"Are we close to town?"

"Uh-huh," said the driver in his usual brief manner, without
anger, and I could have thrown my arms around his wide
shoulders and kissed him, I was so happy to hear that pleasant
brief "Uh-huh" which was more wonderful to me at that
moment than the wisest discourse.

"What's your name?" I asked, surprised at myself for not
having asked it before.

"Mikita," he answered, in one short word, as was his custom.

"Mikita," I repeated, and the name Mikita took on a strange
charm.

He answered, "Uh-huh."

I wished that he would tell me more. I wanted to hear him say something more, at least a few words. Mikita had suddenly become something dear to me, and his horse too, a charming animal! I began a conversation with him about his horse, told him what a fine horse he had. A very fine horse!

To which Mikita answered, "Uh-huh."

"And your sleigh, Mikita, is a fine sleigh too!"

Again he answered, "Uh-huh."

Beyond that he would not say a word.

"Don't you like to talk, Mikita, old fellow?" I asked.

"Uh-huh," he said. And I burst out laughing. I was as happy as though I had found a treasure, or made a wonderful discovery. In a word, I was lucky. I was more than lucky. Do you know what I wanted to do? I wanted to raise my voice and sing. That's a fact. I have always had that habit. When I am feeling good I burst out singing. My wife, bless her, knows this trait of mine, and asks, "What happened now, Noah? How much have you earned today to make you so happy?" To a woman, with her woman's brains, it is possible for a man to be happy only when he has made some money. Why does it happen that women are so much more greedy than men? Who earns the money, we or they? But there! I'm afraid I've gone off on the road to Boiberik again.

Well, with God's help we came to town. It was still very early, long before daybreak. The town was sound asleep. Not a glimmer of light showed anywhere. We barely distinguished a house with a large gate and a besom over the gate, the sign of a guest house or inn. We stopped, climbed down, Mikita and I, and began to pound at the gate with our fists. We pounded and pounded till at last we saw a light in the window. Then we heard someone shuffle up to the gate, and a voice called out, "Who's there?"

"Open, Uncle," I cried, "and you'll earn eternal life."

"Eternal life? Who are you?" came the voice from behind the gate, and the lock began to turn.

"Open the door," I said. "We've brought a corpse with us."

"A what?"

"A corpse."

"What do you mean, a corpse?"

"By a corpse I mean a dead person. A dead woman that we've brought from out in the country."

Inside the gate a silence fell. We heard only the lock being turned again and then the feet shuffling off. The lights went out and we were left standing in the snow. I was so angry that I told the driver to help me, and together we pounded at the window with our fists. And we pounded so heartily that the light went on again and the voice was heard once more, "What do you want? Will you stop bothering me!"

"In God's name," I begged as if pleading with a highwayman for my life, "have pity on me. We have a corpse with us, I tell you."

"What corpse?"

"The innkeeper's wife."

"What innkeeper are you talking about?"

"I've forgotten his name, but hers is Chava Michel, daughter of Chana Raphael, I mean Chana Raphael, daughter of Chava Michel, Chana Chava Chana, I mean . . ."

"Go away, you *shlimazl,* or I'll pour a bucket of water over you!"

And with this, the innkeeper shuffled off again and once more the light went out. There was nothing we could do. It was only an hour or so later, when day was beginning to break that the gate opened a crack and a dark head streaked with white popped out and said to me, "Was it you that banged at the window?"

"Of course! Who do you think?"

"What did you want?"

"I've brought a corpse."

"A corpse? Then take it to the *shammes* of the Burial Society."

"Where does your *shammes* live? What's his name?"

"Yechiel's his name, and he lives at the foot of the hill right near the Baths."

"And where are your Baths?"

"You don't know where the Baths are? You must be a stranger here! Where are you from, young man?"

"Where am I from? From Rademishli. That's where I was born. But right now I'm coming from Zvohil. And I'm bringing a corpse from a village close by. The innkeeper's wife. She died of consumption."

"That's too bad. But what's that got to do with you?"

"Nothing at all. I was driving by and he begged me, the innkeeper, that is. He lives all alone out there in the country with all those small children. There was nowhere to bury her, so when he asked me to earn eternal life, I thought to myself: why not?"

"That doesn't make sense," he said to me. "You'd better see the officers of the Burial Society first."

"And who are your officers? Where do they live?"

"You don't know the officers of our Burial Society? Well, first there's Reb Shepsel, who lives over there beyond the marketplace. Then there is Reb Eleazer-Moishe, who lives right in the middle of the marketplace. And then there is Reb Yossi, he's an officer too, who lives near the old synagogue. But the one you'd better see first is Reb Shepsel. He's the one who runs everything. A hard man, I'm warning you. You won't persuade him so easily."

"Thank you very much," I said. "May you live to tell people

better news than you've told me. And when can I see these
men?"

"When do you suppose? In the morning after services."

"Thanks again. But what shall I do until then? At least let
me in so I can warm myself. What is this town anyway, another
Sodom?"

At this the innkeeper locked the doors again, and once more
it was as silent as a tomb. What could we do now? Here we
were in the middle of the road with our sleigh, and Mikita
fuming, grumbling, scratching his neck, spitting and roaring
out his three-dimensional curses. "May that foul innkeeper
roast in hell through all eternity, and every other innkeeper
with him!" For himself he didn't care. Let the evil spirits take
him. But his horse, what did they have against his poor little
horse, to torture it, let it starve and freeze like that? An innocent animal being sacrificed. What had it ever done?

I felt disgraced before my driver. What could he be thinking
of us? A Jew treating another Jew like this. We who were
supposed to be the wise and merciful ones and they, the common, unlearned peasants. Thus I blamed the whole tribe for
the discourtesy of one man, as is always our custom.

Well, we waited for daylight to come and the town to begin
to show signs of life. And finally it did. Somewhere we heard
the grating of a door, the sigh of a bucket. From a few chimneys
smoke curled up, and in the distance roosters crowed louder
and stronger. Soon the doors all opened and God's creatures
appeared, in the image of cows, calves, goats, and also men,
women and young girls, wrapped up in shawls, bundled from
head to foot like mummies. In short the whole town had come
to life as if it were a human being. It awoke, washed, pulled
on its clothes, and set out to work: the men to the synagogue
to pray and study and say *T'hilim;* the women to the ovens,
the calves and the goats; and I to inquire about the officers of

the Burial Society, Reb Shepsel, Reb Eleazer-Moishe, Reb Yossi.

Wherever I asked they put me through a cross-examination. Which Shepsel? Which Eleazer-Moishe, which Yossi? There were, they said, several Shepsels, Eleazers and Yossis in town. And when I told them that I wanted the officers of the Burial Society, they looked frightened and tried to find out why a young man should want the officers of the Burial Society so early in the morning. I didn't let them feel me out long, but opened my heart to them and told them the whole secret of the burden I had taken upon myself. You should have seen what happened then. Do you suppose they rushed to relieve me of my misfortune? God forbid! They ran out, all right, every one of them, but it was only to see if there really was a corpse or if I had invented the whole story. They formed a ring about us, a ring that kept shifting because of the cold, some people leaving and others taking their place, looking into the sleigh, shaking their heads, shrugging their shoulders, and asking over and over who the corpse was, and where it came from, who I was, where I had got it, and gave me no help whatever.

With the greatest of difficulty I managed to find out where Reb Shepsel lived. I found him with his face turned to the wall, wrapped in his *tallis* and *tfillin*, praying so ardently, with such a melodious voice and so much feeling that the walls actually sang. He cracked his knuckles, rocked back and forth, made strange movements with his body. I enjoyed it tremendously, because in the first place I love to listen to such spirited praying, and besides, it gave me a chance to warm my frozen bones. When Reb Shepsel finally turned his face to me his eyes were still full of tears and he looked like a man of God, his soul as far removed from earth as his big fat body was from heaven. But since he was still in the midst of his prayers and did not want to interrupt them with secular discourse, he spoke to me in the holy tongue, that is, in a language that consisted of gestures of the hands, winks of the eye, shrugs and motions of the head and even the nose, with a few Hebrew words thrown in. If you wish, I can relate the conversation to you word by word, and no doubt you will understand which words were his and which were mine.

"*Sholom aleichem,* Reb Shepsel."

"*Aleichem sholom. I-yo. Nu-o.*"

"Thank you. I have been sitting all night."

"*Nu-o? Ma?*"

"I have a request to make of you, Reb Shepsel. You will earn eternal life."

"Eternal life? Good! In what way?"

"I have brought you a corpse."

"Corpse! What corpse?"

"Not far from here there is a country inn. The owner is a poor man whose wife just died of consumption, and she left him with several small children, may God have compassion on them. If I had not taken pity on them, I don't know what the poor innkeeper would have done, alone out there in the middle of the field with the corpse."

"God have mercy on them. Well . . . and did he give you anything for the Burial Society?"

"Where is he going to get the money for that? He's a poor man. Poor as can be, and with a houseful of children. You will earn eternal life, Reb Shepsel."

"Eternal life. Good. Very good! Jews. Poor people . . . ah, yes."

And here he broke in with a series of strange sounds accompanied by so many gestures, winks, blinks, shrugs and motions of the head that I could not begin to understand what he was driving at.

And seeing that I could not follow him, he turned his face

to the wall in disgust and once more began to pray, but not with the same ardor as before. His voice was lower, but he rocked back and forth faster than ever, till he came to the end, threw off his *tallis* and *tfillin* and fell on me with such fury that you would have thought I had outwitted him in some transaction and ruined him completely.

"Look," he said to me, "our town is such a poor one, with so many paupers of our own for whom shrouds must be provided when they die, and here you come from some strange place with a corpse. They come here from everywhere. Everybody comes here!"

I defended myself as well as I could. I said I was an innocent man trying to do only what was proper with respect to the dead. Suppose a dead body had been found in the street and had to be buried, laid to his eternal rest. "You are," I said, "an honest man, a pious one. You can earn eternal life with this deed."

At this he became even angrier and began to lash out at me, not with blows, but with words.

"Is that so?" he cried. "You are a man who craves eternal life? Then take a walk around our town and see to it that our own people stop dying of hunger and freezing of cold. Then you will earn eternal life. Ah-hah! A young man who deals in eternal life! Go take your merchandise to the ne'er-do-wells. Maybe they will be interested. We have our own duties to perform, our own poor to bury. And if we suddenly began to yearn for this eternal life you talk about we could find our own way to earn it!"

With these words Reb Shepsel showed me out and slammed the door behind me. And I swear to you on my word of honor that from that morning on I have despised all those overly pious people who pray out loud and beat their breasts and bow low and make crazy motions. I have hated those holy ones who talk with God all the time, who pretend to serve Him, and do whatever they want, all in His name! True, you might say that these modern irreligious people nowadays are no better and may even be worse than the old-timers with their false piety. But they're not so revolting. At least they don't pretend to be on speaking terms with God. But there! I'm on the way to Boiberik again.

Well, the president, Reb Shepsel, had driven me off. So what should I do next? Go to the other trustees, of course. But at this point a miracle occurred. I saved myself the trouble of going to them, because they came to me instead. They met me face to face at the door and said:

"Are you the young man we're looking for?"

"And what young man are you looking for?"

"The one who brought a body here. Is that you?"

"Yes, I'm the one. What do you want me for?"

"Come back with us to Reb Shepsel and we'll talk it over."

"Talk it over?" I asked. "What is there to talk over? You take the body from me, let me go on my way—and you'll earn eternal life."

"You don't like the way we do things? Is anyone keeping you here?" they asked. "Go take your body anywhere you want, even to Rademishli, and we'll be grateful to you."

"Thanks for the advice," I told them.

"You're welcome," said they.

So we went back into Reb Shepsel's house and the three trustees began to talk. They argued and quarrelled, called each other names. The other two said Reb Shepsel was stubborn, a hard man to deal with; and Reb Shepsel yelled back at them, shouted, ranted, quoted the law: the town's own poor came first. At this the other two fell on him.

"Is that so? Then you want the young man to take the body back with him?"

"God forbid," I said. "What do you want, I should take the

body back? I barely came here alive, almost got lost on the way. My driver wanted to throw me out of the sleigh in the open field somewhere. I beg you. Have pity on me. Take the corpse off my hands. You'll earn eternal life."

"Eternal life is a fine enough thing," answered one of them, a tall thin man with bony fingers, the one called Eleazer-Moishe. "We'll take the body away from you and bury it, but it will cost you something."

"What do you mean?" I asked. "Here I undertook a responsibility like this, at the risk of my life, almost got lost on the way, and you want money!"

"But you're getting eternal life, aren't you?" said Reb Shepsel with such an ugly leer that I wanted to go after him as he deserved. But I managed to control myself. After all, I was still at their mercy.

"Let's get to work," said the one called Reb Yossi, a small man with a short scraggly beard. "I suppose you know, young man, that you have another problem on your hands. You have no papers, no papers at all."

"What papers?" I asked.

"How do we know whose body it is? Maybe it's not what you said it was," said the tall man with the bony fingers, the one called Eleazer-Moishe.

I stood looking from one to the other, and the tall one with the bony fingers, the one called Eleazer-Moishe, shook his head and pointed at me with his long fingers and said:

"Yes, yes. Maybe you murdered some woman yourself. Maybe it's your own wife that you brought here and made up this story about a country inn, the innkeeper's wife, consumption, small children, eternal life."

I must have looked frightened to death at these words, for the one they called Reb Yossi began to comfort me, telling me that they themselves had nothing against me. They understood

very well that I was not a robber or a murderer, but still 1 was
a stranger, and a dead body was not a sack of potatoes. We
were dealing with a dead person, a corpse. They had, he explained, a rabbi and a police inspector in their town. A report
had to be made out.

"Yes, of course. A report. A report," added the tall one,
the one called Eleazer-Moishe, pointing with his finger and
looking down at me accusingly as though I had committed
some crime. I couldn't say another word. I felt a sweat break
out on my forehead and I was ready to faint. I was well aware
of the miserable plight I had fallen into. It was a disgrace, a
sorrow and a heartache in one. But, I thought to myself, what
was the use of starting the whole discussion over again with
them? So I took out my purse and said to the three trustees of
the Burial Society:

"Listen, my friends, here is the whole story. I see what I have
fallen into. It was an evil spirit that made me stop at that
country inn to warm myself just when the innkeeper's wife
had to go ahead and die, and I had to listen to the poor wretch
left with all the children begging me, promising eternal life.
And now I have to pay for it. Here is my purse. You'll find
about seventy-odd *rubles* in it. Take it and do what you think
best. Just leave me enough to get me to Rademishli, and take
the body away from me and let me go on my way."

I must have spoken with great feeling for the three trustees
looked at each other and would not touch my purse. They
told me that their town was not Sodom; they were not robbers.
True, the town was a poor one, with more paupers than rich
people, but to fall on a strange man and order him to hand
over his money, that they would not think of. Whatever I
wanted to give of my own free will was all right. To do it
without charging at all was impossible. It was a poor town, and
there were all the expenses, pallbearers, a shroud, drinks, the

cost of the burial lot. But it was not necessary for me to throw my money away. If I started to do that, there would be no end to it.

Well, what more can I tell you? If the innkeeper had had two hundred thousand *rubles,* his wife could not have had a finer funeral. The whole town came to look at the young man who had brought the corpse. They told each other that it was the body of his mother-in-law, a rich woman. (I don't know where they got the mother-in-law story.) At any rate they came to welcome the young man who had brought the rich mother-in-law and was throwing out money right and left. They actually pointed their fingers at me. And as for beggars, they were like the sands of the ocean. In all my life I have never seen so many beggars in one place, not even in front of the synagogue on *Yom Kippur* eve. They pulled at the skirts of my coat, they almost tore me to pieces. How often do they see a young man who throws away money like that? I was lucky that the trustees came to my rescue and kept me from giving away all I had. Especially the tall one with the bony fingers, Eleazer-Moishe, did not step away from me for a moment. He kept pointing at me with his finger and saying, "Young man, do not hand out all your money." But the more he spoke the closer the beggars gathered around me, tearing at my flesh. "It's nothing," yelled the beggars. "It's nothing. When you bury such a rich mother-in-law you can afford to spend a few extra *groschen.* She must have left him enough money. May we have as much!"

"Young man!" yelled one beggar, pulling at my coat, "young man, give the two of us half a *ruble!* At least forty *kopeks.* We were born like this, one lame, the other blind. Give us at least a *gulden,* a *gulden* for two maimed ones. Surely we deserve a *gulden!*"

"Don't pay attention to him!" shouted another, pushing the

first one aside. "Do you call them cripples? My wife is a real cripple. She can't use her arms or legs, she can't move a limb, and our children are sick too! Give me anything at all and I'll say *kaddish* for your mother-in-law all year—may she rest in paradise!"

Now I can laugh about it. Then it was far from a laughing matter, for the crowd of beggars grew and multiplied about me. In half an hour they flooded the marketplace and it was impossible to proceed with the coffin. The attendants had to use sticks to disperse the mob, and a fight broke out. By that time some peasants began to gather about us too, with their wives and countless children, and at last the news reached the town authorities. The police inspector appeared on horseback with a whip in his hand and with one harsh look about him and a few sharp lashes of the whip sent the mob flying in all directions. He himself dismounted and came up to the coffin to investigate. He started by questioning me, asked who I was, where I had come from, and where I was going. I was paralyzed with fear. I don't know why, but whenever I see an officer of the law I go numb with fear, though I have no real reason to worry. In all my life I have never as much as touched a fly on the wall and I know quite well that a policeman is an ordinary human being, flesh and blood like the rest of us. In fact, I know a Jew who is so friendly with a police officer that they visit each other frequently and when there is a holiday the officer eats fish at my friend's house, and when my friend visits the officer he's treated to hard-boiled eggs. He can't praise the officer highly enough. And yet every time I see a policeman I want to run. It must be something I inherited, because, as you know, I come from a region where pogroms came one after another in the days of Vassilchikov, and I'm descended from the victims of those pogroms. If I wanted to, I could tell you stories enough about those days—but there, I must be well past Boiberik this time.

As I said, the officer began to cross-examine me. He wanted to know who I was, and what I was, and where I was going. How could I tell him the whole story—that I live with my father-in-law in Zvohil and I'm going to Rademishli to get a passport? But the trustees, long may they live, saved me the trouble. Before I could even begin, one of them, the one with the thin beard, called the officer aside and began to talk with him, while the tall one with the bony fingers quickly and in guarded language taught me how to answer the officer.

"Be careful what you say," he whispered. "Tell him the whole truth. You live not far from town and this is your mother-in-law and you brought her here to be buried. Tell him your name and your mother-in-law's too. Your real names, you understand, straight out of the *Hagadah*. And give him the burial fee—don't forget."

And saying this he winked at me and continued, "In the meantime, your driver looks tired and thirsty. We'll take him across the street and give him a chance to rest."

Then the inspector took me into a large building and began to make out some papers. I have no idea at all what nonsense I told him. I said anything and everything that came to my mind and he wrote it all down.

"Your name?"

"Moishe."

"Your father's."

"Itzko."

"Your age?"

"Nineteen."

"Married?"

"Married."

"Children?"

"Of course."

"Your trade?"

"Merchant."

"Who is the dead person?"

"My mother-in-law."

"Her name?"

"Yenta."

"Her father's?"

"Gershon."

"Her age?"

"Forty."

"Cause of death?"

"Fright."

"Fright?"

"Yes, fright."

"What do you mean—fright?" he asked, laying down his pen and lighting a cigarette, looking me over from head to foot. Suddenly my tongue stuck to the roof of my mouth. I thought to myself, if I am inventing a story, I might as well do a good job. So I told him how my mother-in-law had been sitting all alone knitting some socks. She had forgotten that her young son, a boy named Ephraim, was in the room with her. A thirteen-year-old boy, very stupid, something of a clown. He was making shadow figures on the wall and he put his hands up high behind his mother's back, and making a goat's shadow on the wall, opened his mouth and bleated, "Ba-a-a-a." Struck with fright, she fell from her chair and died on the spot.

While I was telling him this story he kept looking at me strangely, not taking his eyes off me. He heard me out till the end, spat on the floor, wiped his red mustaches, and led me out again to the coffin. He removed the black cover, looked at the dead woman's face and shook his head. He looked from the corpse to me, and from me to the corpse, and then said to the trustees, "Well, you can go ahead and bury the woman. As for this young man, I'll have to keep him here until I satisfy myself that she was really his mother-in-law and that she died of fright."

You can imagine how I felt when I heard this. I turned aside —I couldn't help it—and burst out crying like a small child.

"Look here, what are you crying for?" asked the little man they called Reb Yossi, and comforted me, cheered me up as best he could. I was innocent, wasn't I? Then what did I have to be afraid of?

"If you don't eat garlic, they'll never smell it on your breath," put in Reb Shepsel with such a smirk that I wanted to give his fat cheeks a couple of good hard slaps.

God in heaven, what good did it ever do me to make up this big lie and drag my mother-in-law into it? All I needed now was to have her find out that I had buried her alive and spread the news that she had died of fright.

"Don't be afraid," Reb Eleazer broke in, prodding me with his bony fingers. "God will take care of you. The officer is not such a bad fellow. Just give him the burial fee I told you about. He'll understand. He knows that everything you told him is true."

I cannot tell you any more. I don't even want to remember what happened to me after that. You understand, of course, that they took the few *gulden* I had left, put me in jail and I had to stand trial. But that was child's play compared to what happened when the news reached my father- and mother-in-law that their son-in-law was in prison for having brought a dead woman from somewhere.

Naturally they came at once, identified themselves as my parents-in-law, and then the excitement really began! On one side the police went after me. "A fine fellow you are! Now, if your mother-in-law Yenta, daughter of Gershon, is alive, then who was the dead woman you brought?" On the other side, my mother-in-law, may she live long! "There is only one thing I want to ask you," she kept saying to me. "What did you have against me, to take me and bury me alive?"

Naturally at the trial it turned out that I was innocent, free from all guilt. Of course that cost some money too. Witnesses had to be brought in, the innkeeper and his children, and finally I was set free. But what I went through afterwards, especially from my mother-in-law, that I don't wish my worst enemy to have to go through!

And from that time on, when anybody mentions eternal life, I run away as fast as I can.

Hannukah Money

CAN you guess, children, which is the best of all holidays? *Hannukah*, of course.

You don't go to *cheder* for eight days in a row, you eat pancakes every day, spin your *dreidel* to your heart's content, and from all sides *Hannukah* money comes pouring in. What holiday could be better than that?

Winter. Outside it's cold, a bitter frost. The windows are frozen over, decorated with beautiful designs, the sills piled high with snow. Inside the house it's warm and cheerful. The silver *Hannukah* lamp stands ready on the table and my father is walking back and forth, his hands behind his back, saying the evening prayers. When he is almost through, but while still praying, he takes out of the chest a waxen candle (the *shammes,* to light the others with) and starting *Oleinu,* the last prayer in the regular services, signals to us:

" '*Shehu noteh shomayim . . .*' *Nu! Nu-o!*"

My brother and I don't know what he means. We ask, "What do you want? A match?"

My father points with his hand toward the kitchen door, " '*Al-kein n'kaveh l'cho . . .*' *E-o-nu!*"

"What then? A bread knife? Scissors? The mortar and pestle?"

My father shakes his head. He makes a face at us, comes to the end of the prayer, and then, able to speak again, says, "Your mother! Call your mother! I'm ready to light the candle!"

The two of us, my brother and I, leap for the kitchen, almost falling over each other in our haste.

"Mother! Quick! The *Hannukah* candles!"

"Oh, my goodness! Here I am! *Hannukah* lights!" cries my mother, leaving her work in the kitchen (rendering goose fat, mixing batter for pancakes) and hurries into the parlor with us. And after her comes Braina the cook, a swarthy woman with a round plump face and mustache, her hands always smeared with grease. My mother stands at one side of the room with a pious look on her face, and Braina the cook remains at the door, wipes her hand on her dirty apron, draws her greasy hand over her nose, and leaves a black smear across her face.

My father goes up to the lamp with his lighted candle, bends down and sings in the familiar tune, "Blessed art thou, O Lord . . ." and ends ". . . to kindle the lights of *Hannukah*."

My mother, in her most pious voice, chimes in, "Blessed be He and blessed be His name." And later, "Amen." Braina nods her approval and makes such queer faces that Motel and I are afraid to look at each other.

"These lights we kindle," my father continues, marching up and down the room with an eye on the *Hannukah* lamp. He keeps up this chant till we grow impatient and wish that he would reach his hand into his pocket and take out his purse. We wink at each other, nudge and push each other.

"Motel," I say, "go ask him for *Hannukah* money."

"Why should I ask?"

"Because you're younger. That's why."

"That's why I shouldn't. You go. You're older."

My father is well aware of what we are talking about, but he pretends not to hear. Quietly, without haste, he walks over to the cupboard and begins to count out some money. A cold shiver runs down our backs, our hands shake, our hearts pound. We look up at the ceiling, scratch our earlocks, try to act as if this meant nothing at all to us.

My father coughs.

"H'm . . . Children, come here."

"Huh? What is it?"

"Here is *Hannukah* money for you."

The money in our pockets, we move off, Motel and I, at first slowly, stiffly, like toy soldiers, then faster and faster with a skip and a hop. And before we have reached our room we lose all restraint and turn three somersaults one after the other. Then hopping on one foot we sing:

> *"Einga beinga*
> *Stupa tzeinga*
> *Artze bartze*
> *Gola shwartze*
> *Eimelu reimelu*
> *Beigeli feigeli*
> *Hop!"*

And in our great joy and exuberance we slap our own cheeks twice, so hard that they tingle.

The door opens and in walks Uncle Benny.

"Come here, you rascals. I owe you some *Hannukah* money."

Uncle Benny puts his hand into his vest pocket, takes out two silver *gulden,* and gives us each one.

II

Nobody in the world would ever guess that our father and Uncle Benny are brothers. My father is tall and thin; my uncle is short and fat. My father is dark, my uncle is fair. My father is gloomy and silent, my uncle jolly and talkative.

As different as day and night, summer and winter. And yet they are blood brothers.

My father takes a large sheet of paper ruled off into squares, black and white, and asks us to bring him a handful of dry beans from the kitchen, dark ones and white ones. They are going to play checkers.

(Once a miracle happened, and this is our celebration.)

Mother is in the kitchen rendering goose fat and frying pancakes. My brother and I are spinning our *dreidel*. My father and Uncle Benny sit down and play checkers.

"One thing I'll have to ask you," my father says. "Once you've made a move it's a move. You can't keep changing your mind."

"A move is a move," my uncle agrees, and makes a move.

"A move is a move," repeats my father and jumps my uncle's bean.

"That's right," says Uncle Benny, "a move is a move," and jumps twice.

The longer they play the more absorbed they become. They chew their beards, beat time under the table with their feet, and together they hum one song:

"Oh, what shall I do? What shall I do? What shall I do?" sings my father, chewing an end of his beard. "If I move here," he chants, as one does over the *Gamorah*, "then he'll move there. Maybe I'd better move . . . over here."

"Over here . . . over here," echoes Uncle Benny in the same tone.

"Why should I worry?" my father hums again. "If he should take this *one* then I'll take those *two*. On the other hand, maybe he thinks he can take three . . ."

"Take three . . . take three . . . take three   ." Uncle Benny helps him out.

"Ah, you're no good, Benny. You're no good at all," sings
my father and makes a move.

"You're worse than no good, my brother," sings Uncle
Benny and pushes a bean forward, then snatches it back.

"You can't do that, Benny!" my father cries. "You said a
move was a move!" And he catches Uncle Benny's hand.

"No!" Uncle Benny insists. "If I haven't finished I can still
move."

"No!" my father declares just as emphatically. "We decided
on that before we started. Remember. You can't change your
mind."

"I can't?" asks Uncle Benny. "How many times did you
change yours?"

"I?" says my father indignantly. "See! That's why I hate
to play with you, Benny!"

"Who is forcing you to play with me?"

At this point my mother comes in from the kitchen, her face
flaming from the heat.

"Already? Fighting already?" she asks. "Over a few beans?"

Behind her comes Braina with a large platter of steaming
pancakes. We all move toward the table. My brother Motel
and I, who only a moment ago had been fighting like cat
and dog, make up quickly, become friends again, and go
after the pancakes with the greatest gusto.

III

In bed that night I lie awake and think: how much would
I be worth if all my uncles and aunts and other relatives gave
me *Hannukah* money? First of all there is Uncle Moishe-
Aaron, my mother's brother, stingy but rich. Then Uncle
Itzy and Aunt Dveira, with whom my father and mother

have not been on speaking terms for years and years. Then
Uncle Beinish and Aunt Yenta. And how about our sister Ida
and her husband Sholom-Zeidel? And all the other relatives?

"Motel, are you asleep?"

"Yes. What do you want?"

"How much *Hannukah* money do you think Uncle Moishe-
Aaron will give us?"

"How should I know? I'm not a prophet."

A minute later: "Motel, are you sleeping?"

"Yes. What now?"

"Do you think anyone else in the whole world has as many
uncles and aunts as we have?"

"Maybe yes . . . and maybe no."

Two minutes later: "Motel, are you asleep?"

"Of course."

"If you're asleep, how can you talk to me?"

"You keep bothering me so I have to answer."

Three minutes later: "Motel, are you awake?"

This time he answers with a snore. I sit up in bed, take
out my father's present, smooth it out, examine it. A whole
ruble.

"Think of it," I say to myself. "A piece of paper, and what
can't you buy with it! Toys, knives, canes, purses, nuts and
candy, raisins, figs. Everything."

I hide the *ruble* under my pillow and say my prayers. A little
later Braina comes in from the kitchen with a platter full
of *rubles* . . . She isn't walking, she's floating in the air,
chanting, "These lights we kindle . . ." And Motel begins
to swallow *rubles* as if they were pancakes.

"Motel!" I scream with all my might. "God help you,
Motel! What are you doing? Eating money?"

I sit up with a start . . . spit three times. It was a dream.
And I fall asleep again.

IV

The next morning after we have said our prayers and eaten breakfast, our mother puts on our fur-lined jackets and bundles us up in warm shawls and we start off for our *Hannukah* money. First of all, naturally, we stop off at Uncle Moishe-Aaron's.

Our Uncle Moishe-Aaron is a sickly man. He has trouble with his bowels. Whenever we come we find him at the wash bowl after having come in from the back yard, washing and drying his hands with the appropriate prayer.

"Good morning, Uncle Moishe-Aaron!" we cry out together, my brother and I. Our Aunt Pessil, a tiny woman with one black eyebrow and one white one, comes forward to meet us. She takes off our coats, unwinds our shawls, and proceeds to blow our noses into her apron.

"Blow!" says Aunt Pessil. "Blow hard. Don't be afraid. Again! Again! That's the way!"

And Uncle Moishe-Aaron, a little man with a moth-eaten mustache and ears stuffed with cotton, dressed in his old ragged fur-lined jacket and with his quilted skullcap on his head, stands at the water bowl, wiping his hands, wrinkling his face, blinking at us with his eyes, while he groans out his prayer.

My brother and I sit down uneasily. We are always miserable and frightened in this house. Aunt Pessil sits opposite us, her arms folded across her chest, and puts us through her usual examination.

"How is your father?"

"All right."

"And your mother?"

"All right."

"Have they killed any geese yet?"

"Oh, yes."

"Did they have much fat?"

"Quite a lot."

"Did your mother make pancakes yet?"

"Yes."

"Has Uncle Benny come yet?"

"Yes."

"Did they play checkers?"

"Yes."

And so on and so on . . .

Aunt Pessil blows our noses again and turns to Uncle Moishe-Aaron.

"Moishe-Aaron, we ought to give the children some *Hannukah* money."

Uncle Moishe-Aaron doesn't hear. He keeps on drying his hands, and comes to the end of his prayer with a drawn-out groan.

Aunt Pessil repeats: "Moishe-Aaron! The children! *Hannukah* money."

"Huh? What?" says Uncle Moishe-Aaron, and shifts the cotton from one ear to the other.

"The children. *Hannukah* money!" Aunt Pessil shouts right into his ear.

"Oh, my bowels, my bowels," groans Uncle Moishe-Aaron (that's the way he always talks), holding his belly with both hands. "Did you say *Hannukah* money? What do children need money for? What will you do with it, huh? Spend it? Squander it? How much did your father give you? Huh?"

"He gave me a *ruble,*" I say, "and him a half."

"A *ruble!* Hm . . . Some people spoil their children, ruin them. What will you do with the *ruble,* huh? Change it? Huh? No! Don't change it. Do you hear what I say? Don't change it. Or do you want to change it? Huh?"

"What does it matter to you whether they change it or don't change it?" breaks in Aunt Pessil. "Give them what they have coming and let them go on their way."

Uncle Moishe-Aaron shuffles off to his room and begins to search through all the chests and drawers, finds a coin here, a coin there, and mutters to himself:

"Hm . . . How they spoil their children. Ruin them. Simply ruin them."

And coming back, he pushes a few hard coins into our hands. Once more (for the last time) Aunt Pessil blows our noses, puts on our coats, wraps the shawls around us, and we go on our way. We run over the white frozen crunchy snow, counting the money that Uncle Moishe-Aaron has given us. Our hands are frozen, red and stiff. The coins are copper, large and heavy, very old six-*kopek* pieces, strange, old-fashioned three-*kopek* pieces rubbed smooth and thin, *groschens* that we've never seen before, thick and green with age. It's hard for us, in fact impossible, to figure out how much *Hannukah* money Uncle Moishe-Aaron has given us.

V

Our second stop for *Hannukah* money is at Uncle Itzy's and Aunt Dveira's, with whom my parents have not been on speaking terms for many years. Why they don't speak to each other I don't know, but I do know that they never speak, although they go to the same synagogue and sit next to each other on the same bench. And at the holidays when it comes to auctioning off the various honors, they always try to outbid each other. A fierce battle takes place each time. The whole congregation takes sides, helps them to bid, eggs them on.

The *shammes,* who acts as auctioneer, stands on the platform, working hard. His skullcap is off to one side, his prayer-shawl keeps slipping off his shoulders.

"Eighteen *gulden* for *Shi-shi!*

"Twenty *gulden* for *Shi-shi!*"

The bidding gets hotter and hotter. My father and Uncle Itzy are bent over their Bibles, from all appearances unaware of what is going on. But every time one of them bids the other one raises it.

The congregation enjoys the spectacle and helps along. "Thirty . . . thirty-five . . . thirty-seven and a half . . ." But the battle is between my father and Uncle Itzy, and they continue the bidding until one or the other has to give up.

And yet whenever there is a celebration in the family, a birth, a circumcision, a *Bar Mitzvah,* an engagement party, a wedding or a divorce, the feud is forgotten. We all attend, exchange gifts, make merry, drink together and dance together like the best of friends.

"Good morning, Uncle Itzy! Good morning, Aunt Dveira!" we cry out together, my brother Motel and I, and they receive us like honored guests.

"Did you come all this way just to see us, or was there something else on your mind?" Uncle Itzy asks and pinches our cheeks. He opens his purse and gives us our *Hannukah* money, a new silver twenty-*kopek* piece to me and another one to my brother. And from there we go straight to Uncle Beinish's.

VI

If you want a picture of complete chaos, go to our Uncle Beinish's house. No matter when you come you find a perfect bedlam. They have a house full of children, half-naked, dirty, unkempt, unwashed, always bruised, usually scratched, often

bloodied and with black eyes. One of the children may be
laughing, another crying; one singing, another shrieking;
one humming, another whistling; this one has put on his
father's coat with the sleeves rolled up, and that one is riding
a broomstick; this one is drinking milk from a pitcher, that
one is cracking nuts, another is walking about with a herring's
head in his hand, and still another is sucking on a stick of
candy while from his nose two runnels flow down toward
his mouth. Aunt Yenta must be strong as an ox to put up
with this crew. She curses them, pinches them, shakes them
all day long. She isn't particular. Whichever one comes within
reach gets a slap or a shove or a prod in the side.

An ordinary slap by itself is not worth mentioning. "I hope
you choke; I hope you die; why doesn't someone kidnap you!"
These are the lesser curses. And words like "the plague" and
"cholera" and "violent death" are uttered casually, without
anger, as one might say "Good evening" or "Good Sabbath."
The house becomes quiet only when Uncle Beinish comes
home. But since Uncle Beinish is a busy man who spends all
his time at the store, coming home only for meals, their house
is a perpetual Gehenna.

When we come in we find little Ezriel riding on his older
brother Getzi's back, with Froike and Mendel whipping Getzi
on, one with the sleeve of an old jacket, the other with the
cover of a prayer book. Chaim'l, who has found the windpipe
of a slaughtered goose somewhere, is blowing at it until he
is blue in the face, and succeeds in producing an eerie sound
like the squeal of a stuck pig. Zeinvilleh is playing a tune on
a comb and David, a small boy of about four, has put his
shoes on his hands and beats time with them. Sender'l rushes
by carrying a kitten by the scruff of the neck. The kitten's
tongue hangs out, its eyes are shut, its feet hang limply. You
can almost hear it say, "See how I suffer here; they torture

me, they make life unbearable." In another corner Esther, the oldest girl, is trying to comb and braid her little sister Haska's hair, but since the hair is curly and has not been combed for a long time, the child stands shrieking at the top of her voice and Esther keeps slapping her to make her stop. The only quiet one is Pinny, a tiny boy with crooked legs, his shirt tail pinned up behind him. The only trouble with him is that wherever he goes he leaves a trail behind him.

But none of this disturbs Aunt Yenta in the least. It does not prevent her from sitting calmly at the table drinking chicory, with an infant at her breast and an older child on her knee. Between sips of chicory she cuddles the baby at her breast and digs her elbow into the child on her knee. "Look at you eat, you pig! May the worms eat you! Esther, Rochel, Haska, where the devil are you? Quick, wipe his nose! Bring me a saucer, quick! Here I am, drinking without a saucer! Mendel, don't make so much noise! I'll give you such a crack that you'll turn over three times! Oh, my heart, my soul, my comfort. What, murderers, you want more food? All you do all day is eat, eat, eat! Why don't you choke!"

When they catch sight of the two of us the children fall on us like locusts, grabbing us by our hands, our feet, some leaping at our heads. Chaim'l blows the windpipe right into my ear. David, still wearing his shoes on his hands, throws his arms around us. Pinny, with the shirt tail pinned behind him, gets hold of one of my legs and wraps himself about it like a little snake. A confusion of sounds and voices surrounds us, deafens our ears.

"May you scream with a toothache!" shouts Aunt Yenta from the other room. "A person can get deaf here! They're devils, not children! May your souls burn forever and ever!"

And in the midst of all this noise and confusion Uncle Beinish comes in with his *tallis* and *tfillin,* apparently on his

way from the synagogue, and at once everything becomes
quiet. The children vanish.

"Good morning, Uncle Beinish!" we cry out together, my
brother Motel and I.

"What are you doing here, you *shkotzim?*" asks Uncle
Beinish. "Ah, *Hannukah* money!" And he gives us each a ten-
kopek piece.

The children peek at us from their corners with bright
little eyes like mice, wink and signal with their hands, make
strange faces at us, try hard to make us laugh. But with great
effort we control ourselves, take the money, and run off as
fast as we can from this living Gehenna.

VII

The next place we go to for *Hannukah* money is our sister
Ida's. Since she was a child Ida has always been a lugubrious
creature. No matter what silly little thing happened, she could
always be counted on to burst out crying. She was always
shedding tears over her own or other people's troubles. But
when she became engaged to Sholom-Zeidel, that was when
she really cried! Perhaps you think it was because the young
man didn't please her? God forbid! She had never even seen
the man! No, she wept because a bride is supposed to weep
before her wedding. When the tailors brought her trousseau
she wept all night long. Later, when her girl friends came
for their last party together she ran off to her room every few
minutes to weep into her pillows. But she was really at her
best on her wedding day! That day she didn't stop crying for
a minute.

But the climax came at the veiling, when Menashe Fiddele,
the fiddler, led her to the dais and Reb Boruch B'dachun
climbed up on the table, folded his arms over his ample

stomach, lowered his head as though he were bemoaning the
dead, and began, in a mournful tone that could move a stone
to tears, the following song:

> *Dearest Bride, dearest bride!*
> *Weep all you please;*
> *Your tears are becoming,*
> *They need not cease.*
>
> *Weeping is ordained*
> *For brides to be.*
> *And soon you will stand*
> *Under the canopy.*
>
> *For you must learn*
> *That now your life*
> *Is full of sadness,*
> *Woe and strife;*
>
> *That man is not made*
> *Of iron or stone.*
> *He is only a being*
> *Of flesh and bone;*
>
> *That sinners are lashed*
> *In the depths of hell,*
> *And they scream and howl*
> *And lament as well.*
>
> *Then learn to practice virtue*
> *And humility.*
> *Weep, maiden, weep,*
> *Let your tears run free."*

And so on and so on without end.

The women who stood around her, helping to undo her

beautiful long braids, could not control themselves. They
gave themselves up to their lamentations wholeheartedly,
made the oddest faces, wiped their eyes and blew their
noses. And poor Ida wept loudest of all. She wailed and
moaned and blubbered so hard that she fainted three times
and they barely revived her in time for the ceremony.

But our brother-in-law, on the other hand, was as merry
as our sister Ida was sad. If anything, Sholom-Zeidel was
too merry, a practical joker, a clown, a zany, who fastened
himself to you like a leech and got under your skin. He was
always teasing us, my brother and me, pinching our ears and
filliping our noses. That gave him his greatest pleasure. The
first year they were married there were times when for days
Motel and I went around with swollen noses, stinging ears. So
when we heard that the young couple was leaving our home
to set up their own establishment we were really overjoyed.
But for the rest of the family the day they moved was a day
of mourning. Ida wept, poured buckets of tears, and my
mother, watching her, wept also. Sholom-Zeidel, who was
supposed to be doing the packing, skipped back and forth,
stole up behind us cunningly, and pinched our ears or filliped
our noses. And when he bade us farewell he had the impudence to tell us not to wait to be invited but to come as often
as we liked. We swore to each other on our honor, my brother
and I, never to set foot in his house as long as we lived.

But a person forgets all things, even a pinched ear. How
can you keep from going to your own married sister for
Hannukah money?

When we come into the house, Sholom-Zeidel greets us
heartily.

"Well, well! Look who's here! I'm glad you came. I've been
waiting. I have some *Hannukah* money for you!"

And Sholom-Zeidel takes out his purse and hands each

one of us several shiny silver coins. And before we can even count how many he has given us, his hand flies out, pinch, fillip go his fingers, and once more our ears and noses feel the sharp sting.

"Leave them alone! Haven't you tortured them enough?" our sister Ida begs him with tears in her eyes, and calling us aside, fills our pockets with cake, nuts and figs, and gives us *Hinnukah* money besides.

We make our escape as quickly as we can and hurry home.

VIII

"Well, Motel," I say, "let's get down to business. Let's figure out how much money we've collected. But I'll tell you what. You wait. First let me count mine and then you'll count yours."

And I begin to count. A *ruble* and three twenty-*kopek* pieces, four *gulden*, five *grivnye*, six *piatekas* . . . how much is that altogether? It must be a *ruble* and three twenties and four *gulden* and five *grivnye* and six *piatekas* . . .

My brother Motel won't wait until I am through, and he gets busy with his own finances. He moves each coin from one hand to the other and counts.

"A twenty and a twenty are two twenties, and one more is three. And two *gulden* is three twenties and two *gulden* and a *grivnye* and another *grivnye* and one more—that makes two twenties and three *gulden,* I mean three *gulden* and two twenties . . . What am I talking about? I'll have to start all over again from the beginning."

And he starts all over from the beginning. We count and we count and we can't get the total. We figure and we figure and we can't get it straight. When we get to Uncle Moishe-

Aaron's old *piatekas*, huge sixes, smoothly rubbed threes and swollen *groschens* we get so mixed up that we don't know where in the world we are. We try to exchange these coins with our mother, our father, with Braina the cook, but it doesn't work. Nobody wants to have anything to do with them.

"What sort of *piatekas* are those? Who palmed them off on you?"

We are ashamed to tell, and we keep quiet.

"Do you know what," says my brother Motel, "let's throw them into the oven, or outside in the snow, when no one is looking."

"What a smart boy you are!" I tell him. "It would be better to give them to a beggar."

But just to spite us no one comes to our door. We wait and we wait and not a single one appears. We can't get rid of Uncle Moishe-Aaron's present.

Tit for Tat

ONCE I was a rabbiner. A rabbiner, not a rabbi. That is,
I was called rabbi—but a rabbi of the crown.

To old-country Jews I don't have to explain what a rabbi
of the crown is. They know the breed. What are his great
responsibilities? He fills out birth certificates, officiates at circumcisions, performs marriages, grants divorces. He gets his
share from the living and the dead. In the synagogue he has
a place of honor, and when the congregation rises, he is the
first to stand. On legal holidays he appears in a stovepipe hat
and holds forth in his best Russian: "*Gospoda Prihozhane!*"
To take it for granted that among our people a rabbiner is
well loved—let's not say any more. Say rather that we put
up with him, as we do a government inspector or a deputy
sheriff. And yet he is chosen from among the people, that is,
every three years a proclamation is sent us: "*Na Osnavania
Predpisania . . .*" Or, as we would say: "Your Lord, the
Governor, orders you to come together in the synagogue, poor
little Jews, and pick out a rabbiner for yourselves . . ."

Then the campaign begins. Candidates, hot discussions,
brandy, and maybe even a bribe or two. After which come
charges and countercharges, the elections are annulled, and we
are ordered to hold new elections. Again the proclamations:
"*Na Osnavania Predpisania . . .*" Again candidates, discussions, party organizations, brandy, a bribe or two . . . That
was the life!

Well, there I was—a rabbiner in a small town in the province
of Poltava. But I was anxious to be a modern one. I wanted
to serve the public. So I dropped the formalities of my position
and began to mingle with the people—as we say: to stick
my head into the community pot. I got busy with the *Talmud
Torah,* the charity fund, interpreted a law, settled disputes or
just gave plain advice.

The love of settling disputes, helping people out, or advising
them, I inherited from my father and my uncles. They—
may they rest in peace—also enjoyed being bothered all the
time with other people's business. There are two kinds of
people in the world: those that you can't bother at all, and
others whom you can bother all the time. You can climb right
on their heads—naturally not in one jump, but gradually.
First you climb into their laps, then on to their shoulders, then
their heads—and after that you can jump up and down on
their heads and stamp on their hearts with your heavy boots—
as long as you want to.

I was that kind, and without boasting I can tell you that I had
plenty of ardent followers and plain hangers on who weren't
ashamed to come every day and fill my head with their clamoring and sit around till late at night. They never refused a glass
of tea, or cigarettes. Newspapers and books they took without
asking. In short, I was a regular fellow.

Well, there came a day . . . The door opened, and in walked
the very foremost men of the town, the sparkling best, the
very cream of the city. Four householders—men of affairs—
you could almost say: real men of substance. And who were
these men? Three of them were the *Troika*—that was what we
called them in our town because they were together all the
time—partners in whatever business any one of them was in.
They always fought, they were always suspicious of each other
and watched everything the others did, and still they never

separated—working always on this principle: if the business is a good one and there is profit to be made, why shouldn't I have a lick at the bone too? And on the other hand, if it should end in disaster—you'll be buried along with me, and lie with me deep in the earth. And what does God do? He brings together the three partners with a fourth one. They operate together a little less than a year and end up in a brawl. That is why they're here.

What had happened? "Since God created thieves, swindlers and crooks, you never saw a thief, swindler or crook like this one." That is the way the three old partners described the fourth one to me. And he, the fourth, said the same about them. Exactly the same, word for word. And who was this fourth one? He was a quiet little man, a little innocent-looking fellow, with thick, dark eyebrows under which a pair of shrewd, ironic, little eyes watched everything you did. Everyone called him Nachman Lekach.

His real name was Nachman Noss'n, but everybody called him Nachman Lekach, because as you know, *Noss'n* is the Hebrew for "he gave," and *Lekach* means "he took," and in all the time we knew him, no one had ever seen him give anything to anyone—while at taking no one was better.

Where were we? Oh, yes . . . So they came to the rabbiner with the complaints, to see if he could find a way of straightening out their tangled accounts. "Whatever you decide, Rabbi, and whatever you decree, and whatever you say, will be final."

That is how the three old partners said it, and the fourth, Reb Nachman, nodded with that innocent look on his face to indicate that he too left it all up to me: "For the reason," his eyes said, "that I know that I have done no wrong." And he sat down in a corner, folded his arms across his chest like an old woman, fixed his shrewd, ironic, little eyes on me, and waited to see what his partners would have to say. And when they had all laid out their complaints and charges, presented all their evidence, said all they had to say, he got up, patted down his thick eyebrows, and not looking at the others at all, only at me, with those deep, deep, shrewd little eyes of his, he proceeded to demolish their claims and charges—so completely, that it looked as if they were the thieves, swindlers and crooks—the three partners of his—and he, Nachman Lekach, was a man of virtue and piety, the little chicken that is slaughtered before *Yom Kippur* to atone for our sins—a sacrificial lamb. "And every word that you heard them say is a complete lie, it never was and never could be. It's simply out of the question." And he proved with evidence, arguments and supporting data that everything he said was true and holy, as if Moses himself had said it.

All the time he was talking, the others, the *Troika,* could hardly sit in their chairs. Every moment one or another of them jumped up, clutched his head—or his heart: "Of all things! How can a man talk like that! Such lies and falsehoods!" It was almost impossible to calm them down, to keep them from tearing at the fourth one's beard. As for me—the rabbiner—it was hard, very hard to crawl out from this horrible tangle, because by now it was clear that I had a fine band to deal with, all four of them swindlers, thieves and crooks, and informers to boot, and all four of them deserving a severe punishment. But what? At last this idea occurred to me, and I said to them:

"Are you ready, my friends? I am prepared to hand down my decision. My mind is made up. But I won't disclose what I have to say until each of you has deposited twenty-five *rubles*—to prove that you will act upon the decision I am about to hand down."

"With the greatest of pleasure," the three spoke out at once, and Nachman Lekach nodded his head, and all four reached into their pockets, and each one counted out his twenty-five on the table. I gathered up the money, locked it up in a drawer, and then I gave them my decision in these words:

"Having heard the complaints and the arguments of both parties, and having examined your accounts and studied your evidence, I find according to my understanding and deep conviction, that all four of you are in the wrong, and not only in the wrong, but that it is a shame and a scandal for Jewish people to conduct themselves in such a manner—to falsify accounts, perjure yourselves and even act as informers. Therefore I have decided that since we have a *Talmud Torah* in our town with many children who have neither clothes nor shoes, and whose parents have nothing with which to pay their tuition, and since there has been no help at all from you gentlemen (to get a few pennies from you one has to reach down into your very gizzards) therefore it is my decision that this hundred *rubles* of yours shall go to the *Talmud Torah,* and as for you, gentlemen, you can go home, in good health, and thanks for your contribution. The poor children will now have some shoes and socks and shirts and pants, and I'm sure they'll pray to God for you and your children. Amen."

Having heard the sentence, the three old partners—the *Troika*—looked from one to the other—flushed, unable to speak. A decision like this they had not anticipated. The only one who could say a word was Reb Nachman Lekach. He got up, patted down his thick eyebrows, held out a hand, and looking at me with his ironic little eyes, said this:

"I thank you, Rabbi Rabbiner, in behalf of all four of us, for the wise decision which you have just made known. Such a judgment could have been made by no one since King Solomon himself. There is only one thing that you forgot to say, Rabbi Rabbiner, and that is: what is your fee for this wise and just decision?"

"I beg your pardon," I tell him. "You've come to the wrong address. I am not one of those rabbiners who tax the living and the dead." That is the way I answered him, like a real gentleman. And this was his reply:

"If that's the case, then you are not only a sage and a Rabbi among men, you're an honest man besides. So, if you would care to listen, I'd like to tell you a story. Say that we will pay you for your pains at least with a story."

"Good enough. Even with two stories."

"In that case, sit down, Rabbi Rabbiner, and let us have your cigarette case. I'll tell you an interesting story, a true one, too, something that happened to me. What happened to others I don't like to talk about."

And we lit our cigarettes, sat down around the table, and Reb Nachman spread out his thick eyebrows, and looking at me with his shrewd, smiling, little eyes, he slowly began to tell his true story of what had once happened to him himself.

All this happened to me a long time ago. I was still a young man and I was living not far from here, in a village near the railroad. I traded in this and that, I had a small tavern, made a living. A Rothschild I didn't become, but bread we had, and in time there were about ten Jewish families living close by—because, as you know, if one of us makes a living, others come around. They think you're shoveling up gold . . . But that isn't the point. What I was getting at was that right in the midst of the busy season one year, when things were moving and traffic was heavy, my wife had to go and have a baby—our boy—our first son. What do you say to that? "Congratulations! Congratulations everybody!" But that isn't all. You have to have a *bris,* the circumcision. I dropped everything, went into town, bought all the good things I could find, and came back with the *Mohel* with all his instruments, and for good measure I also brought the *shammes* of the synagogue. I thought that with these two holy men and myself and the neighbors we'd have the ten men that we needed, with one to spare. But what does God do? He has one of my neighbors get sick—he is sick in bed and can't come to the *bris*, you can't carry him. And another has to pack up and go off to the city. He can't wait another day! And here I am without the ten men. Go do something. Here it is—Friday! Of all days, my wife has to pick Friday to have the *bris*—the day before the Sabbath. The *Mohel* is frantic—he has to go back right away. The *shammes* is actually in tears. "What did you ever drag us off here for?" they both want to know. And what can I do?

All I can think of is to run off to the railroad station. Who knows—so many people come through every day—maybe God will send some one. And that's just what happened. I came running up to the station—the agent has just called out that a train is about to leave. I look around—a little roly-poly man carrying a huge traveling bag comes flying by, all sweating and out of breath, straight toward the lunch counter. He looks over the dishes—what is there a good Jew can take in a country railroad station? A piece of herring—an egg. Poor fellow—you could see his mouth was watering. I grab him by the sleeve. "Uncle, are you looking for something to eat?" I ask him, and the look he gives me says: "How did you know that?" I keep on talking: "May you live to be a hundred— God himself must have sent you." He still doesn't understand, so I proceed: "Do you want to earn the blessings of eternity— and at the same time eat a beef roast that will melt in your mouth, with a fresh, white loaf right out of the oven?" He still looks at me as if I'm crazy. "Who are you? What do you want?"

So I tell him the whole story—what a misfortune had over-

taken us: here we are, all ready for the *bris,* the *Mohel* is waiting, the food is ready—and such food!—and we need a tenth
man! "What's that got to do with me?" he asks, and I tell
him: "What's that got to do with you? Why—everything
depends on you—you're the tenth man! I beg you—come
with me. You will earn all the rewards of heaven—and have
a delicious dinner in the bargain!" "Are you crazy," he asks
me, "or are you just out of your head? My train is leaving in
a few minutes, and it's Friday afternoon—almost sundown.
Do you know what that means? In a few more hours the
Sabbath will catch up with me, and I'll be stranded." "So
what!" I tell him. "So you'll take the next train. And in the
meantime you'll earn eternal life—and taste a soup, with fresh
dumplings, that only my wife can make . . ."

Well, why make the story long? I had my way. The roast
and the hot soup with fresh dumplings did their work. You
could see my customer licking his lips. So I grab the traveling
bag and I lead him home, and we go through with the *bris.*
It was a real pleasure! You could smell the roast all over the
house, it had so much garlic in it. A roast like that, with fresh
warm twist, is a delicacy from heaven. And when you consider
that we had some fresh dill pickles, and a bottle of beer, and
some cognac before the meal and cherry cider after the meal—
you can imagine the state our guest was in! His cheeks shone
and his forehead glistened. But what then? Before we knew
it the afternoon was gone. My guest jumps up, he looks around,
sees what time it is, and almost has a stroke! He reaches for
his traveling bag: "Where is it?" I say to him, "What's your
hurry? In the first place, do you think we'll let you run off
like that—before the Sabbath? And in the second place—who
are you to leave on a journey an hour or two before the Sabbath? And if you're going to get caught out in the country
somewhere, you might just as well stay here with us."

He groans and he sighs. How could I do a thing like that to him—keep him so late? What did I have against him? Why hadn't I reminded him earlier? He doesn't stop bothering me. So I say to him: "In the first place, did I have to tell you that it was Friday afternoon? Didn't you know it yourself? And in the second place, how do you know—maybe it's the way God wanted it? Maybe He wanted you to stay here for the Sabbath so you could taste some of my wife's fish? I can guarantee you, that as long as you've eaten fish, you haven't eaten fish like my wife's fish—not even in a dream!" Well, that ended the argument. We said our evening prayers, had a glass of wine, and my wife brings the fish to the table. My guest's nostrils swell out, a new light shines in his eyes and he goes after that fish as if he hadn't eaten a thing all day. He can't get over it. He praises it to the skies. He fills a glass with brandy and drinks a toast to the fish. And then comes the soup, a specially rich Sabbath soup with noodles. And he likes that, too, and the *tzimmes* also, and the meat that goes with the *tzimmes,* a nice, fat piece of brisket. I'm telling you, he just sat there licking his fingers! When we're finishing the last course he turns to me: "Do you know what I'll tell you? Now that it's all over, I'm really glad that I stayed over for *Shabbes*. It's been a long time since I've enjoyed a Sabbath as I've enjoyed this one." "If that's how you feel, I'm happy," I tell him. "But wait. This is only a sample. Wait till tomorrow. Then you'll see what my wife can do."

And so it was. The next day, after services, we sit down at the table. Well, you should have seen the spread. First the appetizers: crisp wafers and chopped herring, and onions and chicken fat, with radishes and chopped liver and eggs and *gribbenes*. And after that the cold fish and the meat from yesterday's *tzimmes,* and then the jellied neat's foot, or *fisnoga* as you call it, with thin slices of garlic, and after that the potato *choient* with the *kugel* that had been in the oven all night—and you know what that smells like when you take it out of the oven and take the cover off the pot. And what it tastes like. Our visitor could not find words to praise it. So I tell him: "This is still nothing. Wait until you have tasted our borsht tonight, then you'll know what good food is." At that he laughs out loud—a friendly laugh, it is true—and says to me: "Yes, but how far do you think I'll be from here by the time your borsht is ready?" So I laugh even louder than he does, and say: "You can forget that right now! Do you think you'll be going off tonight?"

And so it was. As soon as the lights were lit and we had a glass of wine to start off the new week, my friend begins to pack his things again. So I call out to him: "Are you crazy? Do you think we'll let you go off, the Lord knows where, at night? And besides, where's your train?" "What?" he yells at me. "No train? Why, you're murdering me! You know I have to leave!" But I say, "May this be the greatest misfortune in your life. Your train will come, if all is well, around dawn tomorrow. In the meantime I hope your appetite and digestion are good, because I can smell the borsht already! All I ask," I say, "is just tell me the truth. Tell me if you've ever touched a borsht like this before. But I want the absolute truth!" What's the use of talking—he had to admit it: never before in all his life had he tasted a borsht like this. Never. He even started to ask how you made the borsht, what you put into it, and how long you cooked it. Everything. And I say: "Don't worry about that! Here, taste this wine and tell me what you think of *it*. After all, you're an expert. But the truth! Remember—nothing but the truth! Because if there is anything I hate, it's flattery . . ."

So we took a glass, and then another glass, and we went to bed. And what do you think happened? My traveler overslept,

and missed the early morning train. When he wakes up he boil
over! He jumps on me like a murderer. Wasn't it up to me, out
of fairness and decency, to wake him up in time? Because
of me he's going to have to take a loss, a heavy loss—he doesn't
even know himself how heavy. It was all my fault. I ruined
him. I! . . . So I let him talk. I listen, quietly, and when he's all
through, I say: "Tell me yourself, aren't you a queer sort of
person? In the first place, what's your hurry? What are you
rushing for? How long is a person's life altogether? Does he
have to spoil that little with rushing and hurrying? And in
the second place, have you forgotten that today is the third
day since the *bris*? Doesn't that mean a thing to you? Where
we come from, on the third day we're in the habit of putting on
a feast better than the one at the *bris* itself. The third day—
it's something to celebrate! You're not going to spoil the
celebration, are you?"

What can he do? He can't control himself any more, and he
starts laughing—a hysterical laugh. "What good does it do
to talk?" he says. "You're a real leech!" "Just as you say," I
tell him, "but after all, you're a visitor, aren't you?"

At the dinner table, after we've had a drink or two, I call
out to him: "Look," I say, "it may not be proper—after all,
we're Jews—to talk about milk and such things while we're
eating meat, but I'd like to know your honest opinion: what
do you think of *kreplach* with cheese?" He looks at me with
distrust. "How did we get around to that?" he asks. "Just
like this," I explain to him. "I'd like to have you try the cheese
kreplach that my wife makes—because tonight, you see, we're
going to have a dairy supper . . ." This is too much for him,
and he comes right back at me with, "Not this time! You're trying to keep me here another day, I can see that. But you can't
do it. It isn't right! It isn't right!" And from the way he
fusses and fumes it's easy to see that I won't have to coax him

too long, or fight with him either, because what is he but a man with an appetite, who has only one philosophy, which he practices at the table? So I say this to him: "I give you my word of honor, and if that isn't enough, I'll give you my hand as well—here, shake—that tomorrow I'll wake you up in time for the earliest train. I promise it, even if the world turns upside down. If I don't, may I—you know what!" At this he softens and says to me: "Remember, we're shaking hands on that!" And I: "A promise is a promise." And my wife makes a dairy supper—how can I describe it to you? With such *kreplach* that my traveler has to admit that it was all true: he has a wife too, and she makes *kreplach* too, but how can you compare hers with these? It's like night to day!

And I kept my word, because a promise is a promise. I woke him when it was still dark, and started the samovar. He finished packing and began to say goodbye to me and the rest of the household in a very handsome, friendly style. You could see he was a gentleman. But I interrupt him: "We'll say goodbye a little later. First, we have to settle up." "What do you mean—settle up?" "Settle up," I say, "means to add up the figures. That's what I'm going to do now. I'll add them up, let you know what it comes to, and you will be so kind as to pay me."

His face flames red. "Pay you?" he shouts. "Pay you for what?" "For what?" I repeat. "You want to know for what? For everything. The food, the drink, the lodging." This time he becomes white—not red—and he says to me: "I don't understand you at all. You came and invited me to the *bris.* You stopped me at the train. You took my bag away from me. You promised me eternal life." "That's right," I interrupt him. "That's right. But what's one thing got to do with the other? When you came to the *bris* you earned your reward in heaven. But food and drink and lodging—do I have to give you these things for nothing? After all, you're a businessman, aren't you? You should understand that fish costs money, and that the wine you drank was the very best, and the beer, too, and the cherry cider. And you remember how you praised the *tzimmes* and the puddings and the borsht. You remember how you licked your fingers. And the cheese *kreplach* smelled pretty good to you, too. Now, I'm glad you enjoyed these things; I don't begrudge you that in the least. But certainly you wouldn't expect that just because you earned a reward in heaven, and enjoyed yourself in the bargain, that *I* should pay for it?" My traveling friend was really sweating; he looked as if he'd have a stroke. He began to throw himself around, yell, scream, call for help. "This is Sodom!" he cried. "Worse than Sodom! It's the worst outrage the world has ever heard of! How much do you want?" Calmly I took a piece of paper and a pencil and began to add it up. I itemized everything, I gave him an inventory of everything he ate, of every hour he spent in my place. All in all it added up to something like thirty-odd *rubles* and some *kopeks*—I don't remember it exactly.

When he saw the total, my good man went green and yellow, his hands shook, and his eyes almost popped out, and again he let out a yell, louder than before. "What did I fall into—a nest of thieves? Isn't there a single human being here? Is there a God anywhere?" So I say to him, "Look, sir, do you know what? Do you know what you're yelling about? Do you have to eat your heart out? Here is my suggestion: let's ride into town together—it's not far from here—and we'll find some people—there's a rabbiner there—let's ask the rabbi. And we'll abide by what he says." When he heard me talk like that, he quieted down a little. And—don't worry—we hired a horse and wagon, climbed in, and rode off to town, the two of us, and went straight to the rabbi.

When we got to the rabbi's house, we found him just finishing his morning prayers. He folded up his prayer shawl and put his philacteries away. "Good morning," we said to him, and he: "What's the news today?" The news? My friend tears loose and lets him have the whole story—everything from A to Z. He doesn't leave a word out. He tells how he stopped at the station, and so on and so on, and when he's through he whips out the bill I had given him and hands it to the rabbi. And when the rabbi had heard everything, he says: "Having heard one side I should now like to hear the other." And turning to me, he asks, "What do you have to say to all that?" I answer: "Everything he says is true. There's not a word I can add. Only one thing I'd like to have him tell you—on his word of honor: did he eat the fish, and did he drink the beer and cognac and the cider, and did he smack his lips over the borsht that my wife made?" At this the man becomes almost frantic, he jumps and he thrashes about like an apoplectic. The rabbi begs him not to boil like that, not to be so angry, because anger is a grave sin. And he asks him again about the fish and the borsht and the *kreplach*, and if it was true that he had drunk not only the wine, but beer and cognac and cider as well. Then the rabbi puts on his spectacles, looks the bill over from top to bottom, checks every line, and finds it correct! Thirty-odd *rubles* and some *kopeks,* and he makes his judgment brief: he tells the man to pay the whole thing, and for the wagon back and forth, and a judgment fee for the rabbi himself . . .

The man stumbles out of the rabbi's house looking as if he'd been in a steam bath too long, takes out his purse, pulls out two twenty-fives and snaps at me: "Give me the change." "What change?" I ask, and he says: "For the thirty you charged me—for that bill you gave me." "Bill? What bill? What thirty are you talking about? What do you think I am,

a highwayman? Do you expect me to take money from you?
I see a man at the railroad station, a total stranger; I take his
bag away from him, and drag him off almost by force to our
own *bris,* and spend a wonderful *Shabbes* with him. So am
I going to charge him for the favor he did me, and for the
pleasure I had?" Now he looks at me as if I really am crazy,
and says: "Then why did you carry on like this? Why did you
drag me to the rabbi?" "Why this? Why that?" I say to him.
"You're a queer sort of person, you are! I wanted to show
you what kind of man our rabbi was, that's all . . ."

When he finished the story, my litigant, Reb Nachman
Lekach, got up with a flourish, and the other three partners
followed him. They buttoned their coats and prepared to
leave. But I held them off. I passed the cigarettes around again,
and said to the story-teller:

"So you told me a story about a rabbi. Now maybe you'll
be so kind as to let me tell you a story—also about a rabbi,
but a much shorter story than the one you told."

And without waiting for a yes or no, I started right in, and
made it brief:

This happened, I began, not so long ago, and in a large city,
on *Yom Kippur* eve. A stranger falls into the town—a businessman, a traveler, who goes here and there, everywhere,
sells merchandise, collects money . . . On this day he comes
into the city, walks up and down in front of the synagogue,
holding his sides with both hands, asks everybody he sees
where he can find the rabbi. "What do you want the rabbi
for?" people ask. "What business is that of yours?" he wants to
know. So they don't tell him. And he asks one man, he asks
another: "Can you tell where the rabbi lives?" "What do you
want the rabbi for?" "What do you care?" This one and

that one, till finally he gets the answer, finds the rabbi's house, goes in, still holding his sides with both hands. He calls the rabbi aside, shuts the door, and says, "Rabbi, this is my story. I am a traveling man, and I have money with me, quite a pile. It's not my money. It belongs to my clients—first to God and then to my clients. It's *Yom Kippur* eve. I can't carry money with me on *Yom Kippur,* and I'm afraid to leave it at my lodgings. A sum like that! So do me a favor—take it, put it away in your strong box till tomorrow night, after *Yom Kippur.*"

And without waiting, the man unbuttons his vest and draws out one pack after another, crisp and clean, the real red, crackling, hundred *ruble* notes!

Seeing how much there was, the rabbi said to him: "I beg your pardon. You don't know me, you don't know who I am." "What do you mean, I don't know who you are? You're a rabbi, aren't you?" "Yes, I'm a rabbi. But I don't know *you* —who you are or what you are." They bargain back and forth. The traveler: "You're a rabbi." The rabbi: "I don't know who you are." And time does not stand still. It's almost *Yom Kippur*! Finally the rabbi agrees to take the money. The only thing is, who should be the witnesses? You can't trust just anyone in a matter like that.

So the rabbi sends for the leading townspeople, the very cream, rich and respectable citizens, and says to them: "This is what I called you for. This man has money with him, a tidy sum, not his own, but first God's and then his clients'. He wants me to keep it for him till after *Yom Kippur*. Therefore I want you to be witnesses, to see how much he leaves with me, so that later—you understand?" And the rabbi took the trouble to count it all over three times before the eyes of the townspeople, wrapped the notes in a kerchief, sealed the kerchief with wax, and stamped his initials on the seal. He passed this from one man to the other, saying, "Now look. Here is my signature, and remember, you're the witnesses." The kerchief with the money in it he handed over to his wife, had her lock it in a chest, and hide the keys where no one could find them. And he himself, the rabbi, went to *shul,* and prayed and fasted as it was ordained, lived through *Yom Kippur,* came home, had a bite to eat, looked up, and there was the traveler. "Good evening, Rabbi." "Good evening. Sit down. What can I do for you?" "Nothing. I came for my package." "What package?" "The money." "What money?" "The money I left with you to keep for me." "You gave *me* money to keep for you? When was that?"

The traveler laughs out loud. He thinks the rabbi is joking with him. The rabbi asks: "What are you laughing at?" And the man says: "It's the first time I met a rabbi who liked to play tricks." At this the rabbi is insulted. No one, he pointed out, had ever called him a trickster before. "Tell me, my good man, what do you want here?"

When he heard these words, the stranger felt his heart stop. "Why, Rabbi, in the name of all that's holy, do you want to kill me? Didn't I give you all my money? That is, not mine, but first God's and then my clients'? I'll remind you, you wrapped it in a kerchief, sealed it with wax, locked it in your wife's chest, hid the key where no one could find it. And here is better proof: there were witnesses, the leading citizens of the city!" And he goes ahead and calls them all off by name. In the midst of it a cold sweat breaks out on his forehead, he feels faint, and asks for a glass of water.

The rabbi sends the *shammes* off to the men the traveler had named—the leading citizens, the flower of the community. They come running from all directions. "What's the matter? What's happened?" "A misfortune. A plot! A millstone around our necks! He insists that he brought a pile of money to me yesterday, to keep over *Yom Kippur,* and that you were witnesses to the act."

The householders look at each other, as if to say: "Here is where we get a nice bone to lick!" And they fall on the traveler: how could he do a thing like that? He ought to be ashamed of himself! Thinking up an ugly plot like that against their rabbi!

When he saw what was happening, his arms and legs went limp, he just about fainted. But the rabbi got up, went to the chest, took out the kerchief and handed it to him.

"What's the matter with you! Here! Here is your money! Take it and count it, see if it's right, here in front of your witnesses. The seal, as you see, is untouched. The wax is whole, just as it ought to be."

The traveler felt as if a new soul had been installed in his body. His hands trembled and tears stood in his eyes.

"Why did you have to do it, Rabbi? Why did you have to play this trick on me? A trick like this."

"I just wanted to show you—the kind—of—leading citizens—we have in our town."

A Daughter's Grave

YOU'RE on your way to the Fair, and we're coming home from the Fair. I have done my weeping already, and you're still going to weep . . . So let me make room for you. Here, move a little closer. You'll be more comfortable."

"There, that's good!"

Thus spoke two passengers sitting behind me in the train. That is, one of them spoke, and the other threw in a word like an echo, from time to time.

"We were both there together, my old woman and I," said the first. "There she is over there, sleeping on the floor. Poor thing, she's all worn out. She's done enough weeping for all of us, there at the cemetery. She fell face down on the grave— and you couldn't drag her away! I begged her, 'Isn't that enough? Your tears won't bring her back to life again!' Did she listen to me? But what do you expect? Such a tragedy! An only daughter. A treasure. Gifted and beautiful and clever. A high school graduate . . . It's two years now since she died. Maybe you think it was consumption? Not at all! She was strong and healthy. She did it herself—took her own life . . ."

"Is that a fact!"

From their conversation I understood the kind of Fair they were talking about. I recalled that it was September, the season of mourning, dear to the hearts of Jews. All over the Pale, during those weeks before *Rosh Hashono*, Jews travel from one town to another, paying their respects to the remains

218

of mothers and fathers, sisters and brothers, children and other relatives. Bereaved mothers, orphaned daughters, lonely sisters and just unfortunate women throw themselves on the dear hallowed graves, shed a few tears, pour out their grief, ease their tortured souls . . .

I can tell you: this isn't the first year I've been a traveling man, but I can't remember when we've had such a good crop of mourners as this September. The railroads, bless the Lord, will make money. The carriages are packed. They are full of long-faced men and women with swollen red eyes and shiny noses. Some are on the way *to* the Fair, and others are coming home *from* the Fair . . . Outside you can smell early autumn. In your heart you feel autumn. And you're longing, you're longing for home . . .

I can't help but overhear the rest of the conversation.

"Maybe you think it was one of today's tragedies? Black smocks, red flags, Siberia? Heaven forbid! That much, at least, God has spared me. I saw to that! After all, I had a reason to. An only daughter. Such a gifted girl. So beautiful and clever. And a high school graduate!

"I did everything I could. I watched where she went and whom she talked with, and what she said and what books she read. 'Daughter, darling,' I said. 'If you want to read books, go right ahead! But I have to know,' I said, 'what you're reading.' It's true I don't know too much about such things, but I have a certain intuition, an inner feeling. Me—all I have to do is look into a book—even if it's in French—and I can tell you right away what it smacks of!"

"Imagine that!"

"I didn't want my child to play with fire. I was afraid . . . But don't think I resorted to trickery or force. On the contrary, I was gentle. All I did was remind her of a proverb. 'Daughter, darling,' I said. 'Let the wheel turn as it will. Neither you nor I can stop it . . .' That's the way I talked to her. And what did she say? Not a thing! An angel. Quiet as a dove! . . . And what does God do? The bad times pass. We live through all the troubles . . . Revolutions! Constitutions! Black smocks, red flags, shorn hair, bombs and the devil knows what else! All these things are gone. Although before those times passed, you can understand, I almost lost my wits. After all, didn't I have a right to? There was plenty to be afraid of. An only child. Gifted and beautiful. A high school graduate!"

"So! What happened?"

"To make a long story short . . . Praise the Lord! We lived through those terrible times. Now, with God's help, we could start thinking about marrying her off. A dowry? That's the least of my worries. Let the Lord only send the right man along! And the merry-go-round began. Matches, matchmakers, prospects, suitors! And my daughter shows no interest. You think maybe she doesn't want to get married? Who knows? . . . What then? I'll tell you. I began to look, to check up, and I find something. She's been reading a book—in secret! And not alone. Three of them were reading it together. She, and a friend of hers, our cantor's daughter—a smart girl, too, a high school graduate—and a third. Who is that? A nobody. A good-for-nothing, with a round face full of pimples and weak eyes without lashes, and gold-rimmed glasses to make him look still handsomer. A repulsive creature. And on top of it all, persistent. You couldn't get rid of him. He crawled after them—like a worm! Why do I call him a worm? I'll explain it to you. There are all kinds of people in the world. Some are oxen. Some are horses. Some are dogs. There are some who are pigs. And this one was a worm. Now do you understand?"

"Of course!"

"How did this worm ever find his way into my house?

Through the cantor's daughter. He's a cousin of hers. He was studying to become a druggist—or a lawyer—or a dentist—the devil alone knows what! All I know is that to me he was the Angel of Death. I didn't like him from the very beginning. I even said so to my wife. But she said to me, 'What foolish notions you have!' Still, I keep an eye on them. I keep my ears open, and I'm not at all pleased with the way the three of them are always reading together, and the way they talk together, getting all wrought up and feverish . . .

"So I say to her one time, 'Daughter, darling, what's this book the three of you are so worked up about?'

" 'Nothing,' she says. 'It's just a book.'

" 'I see it's a book,' I tell her, 'but what kind of a book?'

" 'And if I told you,' says she, 'would you know?'

" 'Why shouldn't I know?' says I. And she laughs and tells me, 'It isn't what you're afraid of. It's just an ordinary book. It's name is *Sanni*. A novel by Archie Bashe's.'

" 'Archie Bashe's?' I say to her. 'Why, that was a blind teacher we had in this town. He died a long time ago.'

"Again she laughs, and I say to myself, 'Ah-ha, my daughter! You laugh, and your poor father is bleeding inwardly!' Here is what I thought: the old troubles were beginning again . . . And do you think I didn't get hold of that book and read it myself?"

"My goodness! Really!"

"Not exactly myself . . . But I got somebody to read it for me. A young man who works for me, a clerk in my shop. A very smart young fellow. Reads Russian like a professor . . . So one evening I sneaked the book away from my daughter's room, gave it to this clerk of mine, and said, 'Here, Berel, take it and read it through. And tomorrow you'll tell me what it's all about.' I barely lived through that night. The next morning, as soon as he came to work, I grabbed hold of him. '*Nu*,

Berel,' I said. 'What about the book?' And he says, 'What a book!' And his eyes are about ready to pop out of his head. 'All night long,' he tells me, 'I couldn't sleep. I couldn't tear myself away!'

" 'Is that so?' I ask. 'Well, then, tell me more! Let me in on it too!' And my Berel tells me a story . . . How can I describe it to you? It just made no sense. Listen to this:

"It's about a big, strong Russian named Sanni who was always drinking whiskey and eating sour pickles! And he had a sister whose name was Lida, and she was madly in love with a doctor, but she had an affair with an army officer and became pregnant. And there was a student named Yura who was head-over-heels in love with a girl, a school teacher, named Krasavitza. And this girl went out for a boat ride one evening—do you think she went with her boy friend? Not at all! She went out with that drunkard, Sanni!

" 'Is that all?' I asked.

" 'Wait a minute,' he tells me. 'That isn't all. There's another teacher too, a man named Ivan, and one day he goes with this drunkard to watch some naked girls bathing . . .'

" 'Come, come,' I say. 'What does it all lead up to? What's the point of it?'

" 'The point of it is this,' he tells me. 'This drunkard, Sanni, has a habit—he brays like a stallion and one time he comes home to his own sister Lida and he . . .'

" 'Go to the devil!' I tell him. 'That's enough about that drunkard. Tell me what happens! What is it all about? How does it end?'

" 'Oh,' he says, 'it ends like this. The army officer shoots himself, and the student shoots himself too, and Krasavitza takes poison, and a Jew—there's a Jew in the book too, Soloveitchik, hangs himself.'

"I lose my patience. 'Go!' I say. 'Go hang yourself together with him!' And he says, 'Why do you talk to me like that? Is it my fault?' And I say, 'No, not yours. I mean this Archie Bashe's.' That's what I tell Berel, but in my mind I'm thinking of that repulsive young fellow, the devil take him! And do you suppose one day I didn't catch him alone and take him to one side . . .''

"You did!"

"Of course! And I said to him, 'Look here! Where on earth did you ever pick up that trash?'

" 'What trash?' says he, flashing his gold-rimmed glasses at me.

" 'This story of Archie Bashie's,' I say, 'with that drunkard in it—Sanni.'

" 'Sanni,' he tells me seriously, 'is not a drunkard.'

" 'What else is he?' I want to know.

" 'Sanni,' he tells me, 'is a Hero!'

" 'And what makes him a Hero?' I ask. 'The fact that he drinks brandy out of a tea glass, eats sour pickles, and brays like a stallion?'

"The young fellow becomes furious. He takes off his glasses and looks at me with his red-rimmed eyes. 'You've heard the tune, Uncle,' he says to me, 'but you don't know the words. Sanni,' he says, pointing his finger up in the air, 'Sanni is a Man of Nature—a Free Man! He says what he means and does what he wants!' And he goes on and on, he doesn't stop. Freedom, and love, and again freedom, and once more love . . . And he puffs out his small pigeon's chest, makes gestures with his hands, and rants like a visiting preacher.

"I stand there looking at him, and think to myself, 'Heavenly Father, what is this repulsive thing talking about? How would it be if I took him by the collar and threw him out of doors so hard he would have to stop and pick up all his teeth?' But then I think it over: still, would it be better if he talked about bombs? Well, go be smart and foresee that there are things worse than bombs, and on account of trash like that I would lose my child, my only one, the apple of my eye, and that my wife would very nearly go out of her head, and that I myself out of shame and agony would have to give up my business and sell my home and go to live in another town! But I am getting ahead of myself. Let me tell you exactly how it came about and what started it.

"It started during the agrarian riots. When these riots started we naturally feared that it would end in another pogrom, as such things always do, and we lived in a state of terror. But if the Lord wishes, miracles happen, and from evil good comes out. How so? From the provincial capital authorities sent down a platoon of soldiers, and it became quiet and peaceful again. And besides, because of the soldiers, the whole town came to life, business flourished. For what can be better for any small town than a company of soldiers with doctors and officers and corporals and commanders and I don't know what else they call them?"

"Why, naturally!"

"But go be smart and foresee that the cantor's daughter would fall in love with an officer and declare that she was willing to be converted in order to marry him? You can imagine what went on in our town! But don't worry. The cantor's daughter was *not* converted and she did *not* marry the officer; because as soon as the agrarian riots ended the troops were sent back where they came from, and in his great hurry the officer even forgot to say goodbye to his beloved . . . But the girl did not forget. And woe to her parents! You can imagine what they went through. The whole town seethed. Everywhere, from every mouth: 'The cantor's daughter, the cantor's daughter.' Evil tongues were busy. Someone sent a midwife to the girl. Someone else asked the cantor what they were going to name the child. Though actually it was very possible that the whole story was a lie. You know what damage a few long tongues can do in a small town!"

"How well I know!"

"Oh, what a pitiful sight they were! I mean the cantor and his wife . . . We could hardly stand it. Because after all—were they to blame? But at the same time I warned my daughter, once for all, no matter how friendly they had been before, from that day on she must have nothing to do with the cantor's daughter. And with me—when I say something, there is nothing more to be said. She may be an only daughter, but a father has to be respected! How was I to know that my daughter would keep on seeing her in secret? But when did I find that out? When it was too late. When it was all over . . ."

Suddenly behind my back I heard someone cough and sigh in her sleep, and the man who was telling the story became silent. He waited a few minutes and then continued in a lower tone than before.

"It was the midnight services a week before *Rosh Hashono*. I remember it as if it happened yesterday. You should have seen our poor cantor as he led the services. It was pitiful to hear him. His sobbing was real, his groans were genuine. It was enough to melt a stone. And nobody knew what he was living through the way I did. These modern children! You can pity their parents . . . Well, the very next morning, I came home early from the synagogue, had a bite to eat, took my keys and went to the marketplace. I opened my shop and waited for Berel to come. I waited a half-hour. I waited an hour. No clerk, no Berel. At last I look up and there he is. 'Berel, why so late?' And he tells me, 'I was at the cantor's.' 'Why all of a sudden at the cantor's?' And he tells me, 'Why, haven't you heard what happened to Haika?' 'What happened to Haika?' I ask. 'Why, she poisoned herself . . .'"

"Think of that!"

"As soon as I heard that I ran straight home. My first thought was: what would Etka say? (That was my daughter, you know.) I come into the house and ask my wife, 'Where is Etka?' 'Etka is still in bed. Why, what's the matter?' 'What's the matter?' I say, 'Why, Haika just took poison.' When she heard this my wife threw her hands over her head and began to weep and wail. 'What's the matter?' I ask. 'Why,' she says, 'only last night Etka was with her. They went walking together —for about two hours!' 'Etka—with Haika?' I say. 'What are you talking about? How could that happen?' 'Oh,' she moaned. 'Don't ask me. I had to let her do it. She begged me not to tell you that she saw her every day. Something terrible has happened! I know it! I hope it's not true!' And with these words my wife runs into Etka's room and falls down on the floor in a faint. I come after her, run to the bed, screaming, 'Etka!' Etka? Did I say Etka? There is no Etka . . ."

"No Etka?"

"She was dead. Face down across the bed—dead. On her table was a bottle, and near it a note, in Yiddish, in her own hand. She used to write the most beautiful Yiddish; it was a pleasure to read it. 'My dear, faithful parents,' she had written. 'Forgive me for having caused you this grief and shame. Forgive me. Forgive me. We promised each other that we'd do it—Haika and I. On the same day, at the same hour, by the same means; because without each other we could not live. I know,' she wrote, 'dear parents, that I am committing a great wrong. I fought with myself for a long time, but it had to be. There is only one thing I ask of you, my dear ones, and that is that you bury me together with Haika, in a grave next to hers. Be well, and forget—forget that you ever had a daughter Etka . . .'

"Can you imagine that! To expect us to forget that we ever had a daugter Etka!"

Behind my back I heard a shuffle, the sound of steps, a sigh, and then a woman's voice, stifled and still sleepy:

"Avrom! Avrom!"

"Yes, Gitka—what is it? Did you sleep? Maybe you want some tea . . . Just a minute, we're coming to a station. I'll get some hot water. Where is the teakettle? Where is the tea and sugar?"

The Miracle of Hashono Rabo

THE miracle of *Hashono Rabo*—that was what we called the train wreck that almost took place on *Hashono Rabo,* the day when our judgment is sealed in Heaven, and our fate decided. And it happened right in my home town of Heissin. That is, not in the town itself, but a few stations away, at a place called Sobolivka.

You who have ridden on the train in our region know what the service on the Straggler Special is like. When it reaches a station and stops, it forgets when to start again. According to the timetable, it has a definite schedule. For instance, at Zatkovitz it says that the train is supposed to stop exactly an hour and fifty-eight minutes; and at Sobolivka, the place I am now telling you about, not a second more than an hour and thirty-two minutes. But take my word for it, no matter where it stops—whether at Zatkovitz or at Sobolivka, it stands at least two, and sometimes more than three hours. It depends on how long the switching and fueling take, and what switching and fueling mean to a train like the Straggler Special, I don't have to tell you.

First of all the locomotive has to be uncoupled, and then the train crew—the conductor, the engineer and the fireman— sit down together with the stationmaster, the guard and the telegraph operator, and drink beer—one bottle after another.

And while these important operations, or maneuvers, are going on, what do the passengers do? You have seen what they do. They go crazy with boredom. Some yawn; some find themselves a corner and take a nap; and some walk back and forth on the platform, their hands clasped behind their backs, idly humming a tune.

On the day that I am telling you about, while the Straggler was waiting in the station of Sobolivka, a man was seen standing nearby, his hands clasped behind his back, watching. He was not a passenger, simply an inquisitive onlooker, a resident of Sobolivka. And what was a Sobolivka householder doing there? Nothing! It was *Hashono Rabo*—a half holiday; the man had been at the synagogue already, had eaten already, and as it was a half holiday and there was nothing for him to do at home, he took his walking stick and went out for a walk to the station, to meet the train.

Meeting the train, as you know, is an old custom in our part of the country. When the train is due, everyone who is not otherwise occupied, rushes off to the station. Maybe they'll see somebody there. See whom? See what? A man from Teplik? An old woman from Obodivka? A priest from Golovonievska? In Sobolivka that's great excitement—and you go. And especially since in those days the train was still a novelty, there was always something new to see, something strange to hear. Anyway, on that special *Hashono Rabo,* when the fate of all of us had been sealed already, as I told you before, there stood the train at the station, uncoupled and waiting; and watching it with a mild curiosity, in a half-holiday mood, stood a householder of Sobolivka with a stick under his arm.

Well, you may say, what of that? What if a resident of Sobolivka stands and looks at an uncoupled locomotive? Let him stand and look! But no. It had to happen that on this day, among the waiting passengers, was a priest from Golovonievska, a village not far from Heissin. Having nothing to do, the priest walked back and forth on the same platform,

his hands also clasped behind his back, and he also stopped
to look at the locomotive. Seeing nothing unusual, he turned
to the Sobolivker and said, "Tell me, Yudko, what is there to
stare at?"

The man answered crossly, "What do you mean—Yudko?
My name is not Yudko. My name is Berko."

So the priest said, "Let it be Berko. Well, tell me then,
Berko, what are you looking at so seriously?"

Without taking his eyes from the locomotive, the man answered, "I am standing here beholding the wonders of God.
Think—a simple thing like that. You turn one screw this
way, another screw that way, and this strange and terrifying
machine moves off."

"How do you know that?" the priest asks him. "How
do you know that if you turn one screw this way, another
the other way, the machine will start?"

Answers the man from Sobolivka, "If I didn't know, would
I have said so?"

Says the priest, "What do you know? How to eat potato
pudding? But this is not a pudding."

At this the man becomes angry (the people of Sobolivka
are famous for their tempers), and he says, "Well then, my
Father, maybe you'd care to climb up into the locomotive
with me and have me show you what makes these things
move and what makes them stop?"

This did not sound so good to the priest. What was this
little man trying to say? Was he going to tell *him* the principle whereby a locomotive moved or stood still? So he answered him sharply, "Go, Hershko. Climb up then."

As sharply the other corrected him, "My name is not
Hershko. My name is Berko."

"All right," said the priest. "Let it be Berko. So climb up,
Berko."

"What do you mean—climb up? Why should I climb up? You can go first, Father."

"You're the teacher this time—not I," says the priest, with some bitterness. "So lead the way."

They argued, they bickered; the debate became heated, but in the end they both climbed up, and the Sobolivka householder began to instruct the priest in the workings of modern machinery. Slowly he turned one handle, slowly, he turned another, and before they could say a single word, they were horrified to find that the locomotive had begun to move. And away it went!

Now this is the best time, I think, to leave the two good men to themselves in the roaring locomotive, while we pause and consider who is this man of Sobolivka who was so bold and so brave that he dared to climb together with the priest into the locomotive . . .

Berel Essigmacher—that was the name of the man I'm telling you about. And why did they call him Essigmacher? Because his business was that of making vinegar—*essig* in Yiddish—the very best vinegar in our corner of the world. The business he had inherited from his father, but he himself had invented a machine—so he says—that gave the vinegar its distinctive and superior quality. If he only had the time, he could make enough vinegar to provide for the needs of three whole provinces. But why should he? He didn't have to. He wasn't that greedy. That's the kind of man this Essigmacher was.

He had studied nowhere, and yet he could do the most delicate work you could imagine, and he understood the workings of all kinds of engines. How did this happen? Well, all you had to remember, he explained, was that the manufacture of vinegar had much in common with that of whiskey. Both were made in a distillery; and a still had almost the same machinery as a locomotive. A still whistled, and so did a locomotive. What difference was there? The important thing—so said Berel himself and showed you what he meant with his hands—the important thing was the power that came from the heat. You started, he explained, by heating the boiler, and the boiler heated the water. The water turned to steam, the steam pushed a rod, and the rod turned the wheels. If you wanted to turn it right, you twisted the lever right, if you wanted to turn it left, you twisted it left. It was as plain as the nose on your face.

And now, having introduced you to this man of Sobolivka, I have at the same time no doubt answered many of the questions you had in mind. So we might as well go back to the wreck of the Straggler Special.

You can imagine the horror and dismay of the passengers when they saw the locomotive go off by itself, no one knew by what strange power. And besides that, the confusion that overwhelmed the crew itself. The first thing they did was to jump up and chase after the engine as if they thought they could catch up with it. But it did not take them long to realize that they were wasting their strength; and as if to tease them, the locomotive suddenly proved that it could develop speed. In fact it flew like mad. It was the first time that anyone had ever seen it move so fast. There was nothing to do but turn back, and this they did. And then, together with the guard and station master, they sat down and drew up a complete and detailed report; after which they sent off telegrams to every station along the line: BEWARE RUNAWAY LOCOMOTIVE. TAKE ACTION. WIRE REPLY.

What a panic this telegram created you can well imagine. What does this mean: Beware runaway locomotive? How does a locomotive run away? And what was this: Take action? What action could they take—besides sending telegrams?

And so once more telegrams began to fly back and forth, forth and back, from one end of the line to the other. The instruments clicked and clattered as if they were possessed. Every station wired every other station, and the frightful news spread fast, till every town and every hamlet knew all the tragic details. In our town, for instance, in Heissin, we knew the exact number of people killed and injured. So violent a death! Such innocent victims! And when did it happen? On what day? Exactly on *Hashono Rabo,* when the tickets of our fate are made out, inscribed and sealed high up in Heaven! Apparently Heaven wanted it thus . . .

That is what people said in Heissin and all the nearby towns, and it is impossible to describe the agony and the suffering that we all endured. But how did that compare with the suffering of the poor passengers themselves, who were stranded in the station at Sobolivka without a locomotive, like sheep without a shepherd? What could they do? It was *Hashono Rabo.* Where could they go? Celebrate the holiday in a strange town? And they all huddled together in a corner and began to discuss their plight and to speculate about what had happened to the Fugitive, as they had now named the vanished locomotive. Who knew what might happen to a *shlimazl* like that? Just think of it—a monster like that careening down the track! How could it keep from colliding somewhere along the way with its sister train creeping from Heissin through Zatkovitz on its way to Sobolivka? What would happen to the passengers in the other train? In their imagination they saw the collision—a frightful catastrophe with all its gory details. They saw it before their eyes—overturned carriages, shattered wheels, severed heads, broken legs and arms, battered satchels and suitcases spattered with blood! And suddenly—another telegram! A telegram from Zatkovitz. And what did it say? Here it is:

THIS INSTANT LOCOMOTIVE FLEW PAST ZATKOVITZ WITH BLINDING SPEED CARRYING TWO PASSENGERS ONE A PRIEST. BOTH WAVED THEIR HANDS POINTED. CAN'T SAY WHAT THEY MEANT. NOW ON WAY TO HEISSIN.

What do you think of that? Two men in a runaway locomotive—and one of them a priest? Where were they going—and why—and who could the other man be? Asking here and there they finally found out that it was a resident of Sobolivka. But who? Did anyone know? What a question! Of course they knew! Berel Essigmacher of Sobolivka! How did they know? How does anyone ever know? They knew! Some neighbors of his swore they had seen him and the priest from a distance standing together near the unhitched locomotive, gesturing with their hands. What did that mean? Why should a vinegar maker be standing with a priest near a locomotive, gesturing with his hands?

The talking and the shouting went on so long that soon the story reached Sobolivka, and though the town is only a short distance from the tracks, still by the time the story was relayed from one person to another it had been altered so much, assumed so many different forms, that by the time it reached Berel's home the story was so fantastic that Berel's wife fainted at least ten times and they had to bring a doctor. And all Sobolivka came pouring into the station. The place became so crowded, the noise so deafening, that the stationmaster instructed the guard to clear the platform.

If so, what are we doing there? Let's be off and see what happened to our friend the vinegar maker and the priest on the Fugitive, the runaway locomotive.

It is very easy to talk about seeing what happened in the runaway locomotive, but we'll have to take Mr. Essigmacher's word for it. The stories he tells about his adventure are so remarkable that if only half of them were true, it would be enough! And from what I know of him he doesn't seem to be the sort of person who makes up stories.

At first—this is Essigmacher's version—when the locomotive began to move, he scarcely knew what was happening. Not that he was alarmed; he was simply upset by the fact that the locomotive would not behave as it should. According to logic, he said, it should have stopped dead at the second turn of the lever. Instead, it went faster than ever, as if ten thousand evil spirits were pushing it down the tracks. It flew with such speed that the telegraph poles shimmered and flickered in front of his eyes like the spots you see when you're dizzy. A little later, when he came back to his senses, he remembered that a locomotive had brakes that could slow it down or stop it altogether. There should be brakes somewhere—hand brakes —air brakes—a wheel that you gave a good turn and it came pressing down on the rims of the wheels and they stopped turning . . . How could he ever have forgotten a simple thing like that! And he made a leap for the wheel, was going to give it a turn, when suddenly someone grabbed him by the arm and yelled, "Stop!"

Who was it? The priest, pale as a sheet. "What are you trying to do?" he asked. "Nothing," said Berel, "I'm just trying to stop the engine." "May God help you," cries the priest, "if you ever touch anything on that machine again! If you do, I'll pick you up by the collar and throw you out of here so fast that you'll forget your name was ever Moshko!" "Not Moshko," Berel corrects him. "My name is Berko." And he tries to explain what is meant by a wheel that's called a brake. But the priest won't let him. He was a stubborn man!

"You've turned enough things here already, and look where your turning got us! If you touch that wheel, I'll touch *you*! You'll wish you'd broken your neck before you ever saw me!"

"But, Father!" pleaded Berel. "Don't you think that my life means as much to me as yours does to you?"

"Your life!" snorted the priest bitterly. "What good is your life? A dog like you . . ."

At this Berel became angry and he turned upon the priest with a fury that will not soon be forgotten. "In the first place," he pointed out, "even if I were a dog you ought to feel sorry for me. According to our law even a dog mustn't be harmed. It's a living thing. And in the second place, in the eyes of the Almighty, in what way is my life any less important than any other life? Are we not alike? Do we not all have the same pedigree? Are we not all descended from the same man— Adam? And are all of us not going to the same identical place —the rich, black earth? And thirdly, Father, look at the difference between you and me. I am doing everything I can to make the locomotive stop, that is, I have the welfare of both of us in mind; while you are ready to throw me out of here, that is, to murder a human being!"

That and many other fine things he told him. There in the flying locomotive he delivered a sermon complete with quotations and examples, until the poor, helpless priest was ready to collapse. And in the midst of the lofty discourse the station of Zatkovitz suddenly came into view, with the stationmaster and the guard straining themselves at the edge of the platform. Berel and the priest tried to signal to them; they yelled and waved their arms, but nobody knew what they were trying to say. The station flew past, and the locomotive was on its way to the next town—Heissin. As they went farther on, the priest became more friendly, but on one thing he still insisted. Berel must not touch the machine. But he did say this much:

"Tell me, Leibko . . ."

"My name," corrected Berel, "is not Leibko. It's Berko."

"All right," said the priest, "let it be Berko. Tell me, Berko, would you be willing to jump off this locomotíve together with me?"

"What for?" asked Berel. "Just to get ourselves killed?"

To this the priest answered, "We're going to get killed anyway."

Said Berel, "Where was that decided? What proof do you have? If God wants to—Oh, Father, what He can do!"

Says the priest, "What do you think He'll do?"

Says Berel, "That depends on Him. Listen, Father, I'll tell you something. Today we Jews have a sort of holiday—*Hashono Rabo*. Today up in Heaven, every human being, every living thing, gets a certificate that's signed and sealed, a certificate of life or death. So, Father, if God marked me down for death, there's nothing I can do. What difference does it make to me if I'm killed jumping off the locomotive or standing *in* the locomotive? As a matter of fact, I can be walking along the street, and can't I slip and get killed? But on the other hand, if it was inscribed that I should go on living, then why should I jump?"

This is the way the vinegar maker of Sobolivka tells the story, and he swears that every word is true. He does not remember how it happened or when he first became aware that something had happened. It was somewhere close to Heissin; they could see the chimney on the station. Berel looked at the priest and the priest looked at Berel. What was this? The locomotive was slowing down. Little by little its speed decreased. Soon it was barely crawling. Now it paused, then moved a few feet farther, then thought it over and stopped completely.

What had happened? He suddenly remembered: the fire must have gone out. And when the fire in a locomotive goes out, the water stops boiling, and when the water stops boiling —well, you don't have to be a vinegar maker in Sobolivka to know that the wheels stop turning. And that's all there is to it.

And naturally, being Berel, he turned to the priest right then and there. "Well, Father, what did I tell you?" he said. "If God Almighty had not decided this morning in Heaven that I should go on living here on earth, who knows how much longer the fire might have continued to burn, and how much farther we might have gone by now?"

The priest said nothing. He stood where he was, with his head down, silent. What was there to say? But later, when it came time to part, he came up to Berel and held out his hand. "Goodbye, Itzko," he said. And Berel answered, "My name is not Itzko. It's Berko."

"Let it be Berko," said the priest. "I never knew you were such a . . ." And that was the last he heard. For rolling up the skirts of his cassock, the priest had started off with long strides back to his home in Golovonievska.

Berel himself went on to Heissin and there he had a real holiday. Like the good Jew that he was, he offered up thanks for his deliverance, and then he told his story from start to finish to everyone he saw, each time with new incidents and new miracles.

And everybody wanted the vinegar maker of Sobolivka to come home with him, spend the night with him, and tell him in person the story of the Miracle of *Hashono Rabo*.

And what a celebration we had that night! What a *Simchas Torah* that was! What a *Simchas Torah*!

You Mustn't Weep — It's Yom-Tev

I AM willing to bet any amount you want that no one in the world was as happy at the coming of Spring as were the two of us—I, the cantor Peisi's son, Motel, and the neighbor's calf, Meni. (It was I who had given him that name.) Both of us together had crept out of our narrow winter quarters to greet the first day of spring, both of us together had felt the warm rays of the sun and together we had smelled the fresh odors of the newly sprouted grass. I, Motel, the cantor's son, came out of a cold, damp cellar that smelled of sour dough and medicine and Meni, the neighbor's calf, was let out of even the worse stench of a small, filthy shed with flimsy walls through whose chinks the snow sifted in winter and the rain beat in summer.

Having escaped into God's free world, the two of us, Meni and I, began to show our unbounded joy, each in his own way. I, Motel, the cantor's son, lifted up both my arms above my head, opened my mouth, and drew in as much of the fresh warm air as my lungs could contain. And I felt as though I were growing in height, as though I were drawn up there into the blue sky where the fleecy clouds drifted, up there where the birds dipped and rose and were lost to view. And from my overfilled breast there escaped a song that was even lovelier than the songs my father used to lead in the synagogue during holidays, a song without words, without notes, without motif— more like the song of a waterfall or the waves of the ocean—a sort of *Song of Songs,* a hymn of praise: "O Father," I sang, "O Heavenly Father . . ."

Meni, the neighbor's calf, showed his joy quite differently. First of all, he buried his black, wet muzzle in the dirt, poked at the earth three or four times with his forepaws, lifted up his tail, reared himself up and let out a loud ma-a-a-a. This sounded so funny to me that I had to burst out laughing and to mimic the ma-a-a-a. The calf apparently was pleased by this for it was not long before he repeated it all once more with the same intonation and the same leap. Naturally I did it over again, in every detail. This was repeated, several times—I leaped, the calf leaped; the calf let out his ma-a-a-a. I let out a ma-a-a-a. Who knows how long this might have gone on if it hadn't been for my brother Elihu who came up from behind and slapped me sharply across the neck.

"What's the matter with you! A boy like you, almost nine years old, dancing with a calf! Into the house, you good-for-nothing. You'll get it from father."

Nonsense! My father won't do anything to me. My father is sick. He hasn't led the prayers in the synagogue since the Autumn Festivals. All night long I hear him coughing, and every day the doctor comes to the house. The doctor is a large, heavy-set man with a black mustache and laughing eyes—a cheerful man. He has only one name for me—*Pupik.* Whenever he sees me he pokes me in the belly. He keeps telling my mother not to stuff me with potatoes, and for the patient he prescribes bouillon and milk, milk and bouillon. My mother listens to him quietly and when he is gone she hides her face in her apron and her shoulders shake. Then she wipes her eyes, calls my brother Elihu aside and they whisper in low voices. What they are talking about I do not know, but they seem to be quarreling. My mother wants to send Elihu somewhere and he won't go. He says to her, "Rather than go to them for help I'd kill myself. I'd sooner die."

"Bite your tongue," says my mother in a low voice, gritting her teeth and looking as if she wanted to slap him. But soon she calms down and pleads with him: "What can I do, my son? You see how ill he is. We must do something for him."

"Then sell something," says my brother, looking out of the corners of his eyes at the glass cabinet. My mother follows his glance, wipes her eyes again and sighs, "What can I sell? My soul? There is nothing left. Or shall I sell the empty cabinet?"

"Well, why not?" says my brother.

"Murderer!" cries out my mother. "How did I ever get such murderers for children?"

My mother fumes and rages, cries her heart out, then wipes her eyes and forgives him. The same thing also happened with the books, with the silver collar on my father's *tallis,* with the two gilded goblets, with my mother's silk dress, and all the other things which were sold one by one, each to a different buyer . . .

The books were sold to Michal, the baggage-man, a man with a thin beard which he was constantly scratching. My poor brother had to go to him three times before he brought him to the house. My mother, relieved and happy to see him at last, put her finger across her lips to show him that he must speak softly so my father shouldn't hear. Michal understood, raised his eyes to the shelf, scratched his beard and said to her, "Well, show us, what have you got up there."

My mother beckoned to me to climb up on the table and take down the books. I didn't have to be told twice. I jumped up so eagerly that I sprawled over the table and my brother, snapping at me to stop jumping like a crazy fool, pushed me aside. He climbed up on the table himself and handed the books down to Michal who scratched his beard with one hand, while with the other he leafed through the books and found fault with each one. This one had a poor binding, that one had a worn back, another was simply worthless. And after he had looked through half of them, examined all the bindings, felt all the backs, he scratched his beard again:

"If it was a complete set of *Mishnayos,* I might consider buy-ing it . . ."

My mother turned pale, and my brother on the contrary became red as fire. He leaped angrily at the baggage-man, "Why didn't you tell us in the beginning that all you wanted to buy were *Mishnayos?* What did you have to come here and take up our time for?"

"Be quiet!" my mother begged him, and a hoarse voice was heard from the next room where my father lay.

"Who is there?"

"Nobody," my mother said and pushing my brother Elihv into my father's room, began to bargain with Michal herself and finally sold him the books, apparently for very little, be-cause when my brother came back again and asked her how much, she pushed him aside, saying, "It's none of your busi-ness." And Michal snatched up the books quickly, shoved them into his bag and disappeared.

Of all the things in the house that we sold none gave me as much pleasure as the glass cabinet.

It is true that when they ripped the silver collar off my fa-ther's *tallis,* it was a treat, too. First of all there was the bargain-ing with Yosel the goldsmith, a pale man with a red birthmark on his face. Three times he went away, but in the end he won out, and he sat down crosslegged near the window with my father's *tallis,* took out a small knife with a yellow, bone handle, bent his middle finger and began to rip the collar with such skill that I envied him! And yet you should have seen how my mother carried on. She cried and cried and cried. Even my brother Elihu, who has been confirmed already and is practically a man, ready to be married, turned toward the door and pretended to be blowing his nose.

"What's going on there?" called my father from the sick-room.

"Nothing," my mother answered, wiping her eyes, and her lower lip and the whole lower part of her face trembled so that it was all I could do to keep from laughing.

But how does that compare with the taking away of the glass cabinet?

First of all, how could anybody take it away? I had always taken it for granted that the cabinet was built into the wall, so how could it be moved? And if it was, where would my mother keep the bread and the dishes and the pewter spoons and forks (our two silver spoons and one silver fork, had been sold long ago). And where would we keep the *matzos* at Passover? These thoughts went through my head while Nachman the carpenter was measuring the cabinet with the big red thumbnail of his dirty right hand. He kept insisting that the cabinet wouldn't go through the door. "Here," he said, "is the width of the cabinet, and here is the width of the door— it will never go through here."

"Then how did it ever get in?" asked my brother Elihu.

"Don't ask me," answered Nachman angrily. "Go ask the cabinet. How should I know how it got in?"

For one moment I was really afraid for the cabinet. That is, I was afraid it would remain at our house. But it wasn't long before Nachman returned with his two tall sons, both of them also carpenters, and they took hold of the cabinet as easily as the devil took hold of the *melamed*. First came Nachman, then the two sons, and behind them came I. The father directed them; "Kopel, this way. Mendel, to the right. Kopel, don't rush. Mendel, wait . . ." I imitated the gestures of all three, but my mother and brother refused to have anything to do with it. They stood looking at the empty wall, now covered with cobwebs, and wept . . . A regular circus. Always crying. Suddenly we heard a loud crash. Right in the doorway the glass had shattered. The carpenter and his sons began to roar at each other, and curse, each blaming the other for the broken glass. "Graceful as a lead bird!" "Bears' feet." "The devil take you." "Go break your head in hell."

"What's going on there?" a weak voice called from the sickroom.

"Nothing," my mother answered, wiping her eyes.

But these experiences were as nothing compared with the selling of my brother's couch and my cot. My brother's couch was once the sofa we all sat on, but after Elihu became engaged he began to sleep on it, and I inherited his old cot. Long ago when times were good and my father was still well and conducted services in the butchers' synagogue with his choir of four, the sofa still had springs. Now the springs belonged to me. I did all sorts of tricks with them; cut my hands and almost poked my eyes out. One day I put them around my neck and nearly choked to death. Finally, my brother spanked me and threw the springs up into the attic.

It was old Hannah who bought the couch and the cot from us. Before she paid her deposit my mother wouldn't let her look under the covers.

"You can buy what you see in front of you. There is nothing more to look at." But after she had finished bargaining and had given my mother a deposit she went up to the couch and the cot, lifted up the bedclothes, looked slowly into every corner, and spat violently. My mother resented her spitting and was ready to return the money, but my brother Elihu interfered:

"Once you've bought it, it's final."

That night we put the bedclothes on the floor and my brother and I spread ourselves out like lords, covered ourselves with one blanket (his blanket had already been sold) and I was pleased to hear my brother say that sleeping on the floor wasn't so bad. I waited till he had said his prayers and gone to sleep and then I began to roll around on the floor, over and over again. There was plenty of room, praise the Lord. It was like a field, a field in paradise . . .

"What can we do now?" said my mother one morning, as she looked around with a deep frown at the four empty walls. My brother and I followed her glance. Then looking at me with pity in his eyes my brother said sternly:

"Go outside, Motel. We have something to talk about."

I ran out, skipping on one foot. Naturally I went straight to the neighbor's calf. In the last few months Meni had grown into a handsome calf, with a lovely black muzzle, and brown eyes full of understanding. It was always looking for something to eat and liked to have its throat scratched.

"Again. So you're playing with that calf again? You can't stay away from your dear friend?"

It was my brother Elihu speaking, this time without anger, without curses. And taking my hand he led me to Hirsch-Ber the cantor. There, at Hirsch-Ber's, he told me I would be well off. First of all I would have enough to eat. At home things were bad, he said. Our father was very ill; we had to do everything we could for him. And we were doing everything we could. And he unbuttoned his coat and showed me his vest underneath.

"This is where I used to wear my watch," he said. "A gift

from my father-in-law and I sold it. If he ever found out—I don't know what he'd do. The world would turn upside down.

"Well, here we are," my brother said, in a friendly tone. Hirsch-Ber the cantor was a good musician. That is, he couldn't sing himself, he had no voice at all, poor fellow (so said my father) but he understood music. He had fifteen boys in his choir and he was a terribly mean master. That much I knew. He listened to me sing one or two pieces with all the frills and flourishes, then patted my head and told my brother that my soprano wasn't bad. Not only wasn't it bad, my brother insisted, but it was excellent. Elihu bargained with him, took a payment, and told me I was going to stay here for a while. He told me to obey Hirsch-Ber and not to get homesick.

It was easy for him to say, "Don't get homesick." But how could I keep from being homesick in the summer time when the sun shone, the sky was clear as crystal, and even the mud had already dried up? In front of our house there was a pile of logs, not ours, but Yossi, the *nogid's*. He was planning to build a dwelling and since he had nowhere to keep the logs he kept them in front of our house. God bless Yossi, the *nogid*, for that. Out of his logs I made myself a fortress. In this fortress I was happy, Meni the calf was happy, we ruled alone here. So how could I keep from being homesick?

I have been at Hirsch-Ber's for three weeks already and I have hardly done any singing at all. I have another job—I take care of his Dobtzie. Dobtzie is a deformed child, a hunchback. She is not quite two, but I have to hold her all the time and she is heavy. It's all I can do to lift her. Dobtzie is fond of me. She puts her thin arms about me and clutches me with her thin fingers. She calls me Kiko—I do not know why. But she loves me. She won't let me sleep at night. "Kiko ki." That means that she wants me to rock her. Dobtzie adores me. When I am eating she tears the food out of my hands. "Kiko pi." That means, "Give it to me." How I long for home. The food is not so wonderful here, either. It's a holiday—*Shevuos* eve. I wish I could go outside and see the heavens split open, as they do on *Shevuos,* but Dobtzie won't let me. Dobtzie loves me too much to let me out of her sight. "Kiko ki." She wants me to stay and rock her. I rock and I rock until I fall asleep. In my sleep a visitor comes to me—Meni, the neighbor's calf. He looks at me with his big eyes, like a human being's and says, "Come." And we both run, downhill to the river. I roll up my pants. Hop! I am in the river. I swim and Meni swims after me. It's lovely on the other side. There is no cantor, no Dobtzie, no sick father. I wake. It was all a dream. Oh, if I could only run away, run away. But how can I run away? Where could I run? Home, of course.

Hirsch-Ber is up already. He tells me to dress quickly and go with him to the synagogue. There is a big morning ahead of us. There are some special pieces to sing today. When we get there I see my brother Elihu. What is he doing here? He usually goes to the butchers' synagogue, where our father is cantor. What does this mean? My brother goes up and talks something over with Hirsch-Ber, who does not seem to be well-pleased. Finally he says, "But remember, bring him back right after dinner."

"Come along," my brother says to me, "you're going home to see father." And we start to go off together, Elihu walking sedately, and I skipping along.

"What's your hurry?" says my brother, holding me back. He apparently wants to talk to me.

"You know father is sick. He's very, very sick. God knows what will become of him. We have to save him, but have nothing left and no one wants to help. Mother absolutely won't let him go to the hospital. She will sooner die than let him go there. Here she comes. Be quiet."

With outstretched arms my mother comes to meet me. She falls on my neck and I feel a tear not my own fall on my cheek. My brother Elihu goes inside to my father, and my mother and I remain standing outside. A group of women gather about us—our neighbor's wife, Fat Pessie, and her daughter Mindel and her daughter-in-law Pearl and several others.

"Oh! A guest for *Shevuos*," they say. "May you enjoy his company!"

My mother lowers her tear-swollen eyes. "A guest?" she says. "The child has only come to see his sick father." And then turning to Pessie she adds in a whisper, "A town full of people, but does anyone care? Twenty-three years in one synagogue; he ruined his health. I might still be able to save him, but I have nothing to do it with. We've sold everything, even the pillows. Sent the child out to a cantor. Everything for him. Everything to help him . . ."

While my mother talks I keep turning my head this way and that.

"What are you looking for?" my mother asks.

"What do you suppose?" says Pessie. "He must be looking for the calf." And she turns to me with a strangely pleasant tone in her voice.

"Ah, little one, the calf is gone. We had to sell it to the butcher. What else could we do? It's enough to feed one animal without having two to worry about."

So the calf had become just a mouth to feed!

A strange woman, Pessie. She sticks her nose into everything. She wants to know what we're going to have for dinner.

"Why do you ask?" my mother wants to know.

"Just like that," says Pessie, carelessly, and lifting up her shawl pushes into my mother's hands a bowl of thick cream. My mother shoves it back with both hands.

"For heaven's sake, Pessie, what are you doing? What do you think we are? Beggars? Don't you know us better than that?"

"It's because I do know you," Pessie defends herself. "I'm not giving you anything, just lending it to you. Our cow has been good to us lately. We've had more than we can use. You'll return it some day."

The women talk and I keep thinking of the pile of logs, and my playmate the calf whom I won't see any more. If I weren't ashamed I'd burst out crying.

"If your father asks how you're getting along," my mother tells me, "say, 'God be thanked.' "

My brother explains this further:

"Don't complain about anything to him. Don't tell him any of your childish stories. Just say, 'God be thanked.' Understand?" And with these words my brother Elihu took me into the sick room to see my father. The table was crowded with jars and bottles and boxes of pills. The air smelled like a druggist's shop. The window was tightly closed. In honor of *Shevuos* the room had been decorated with greens. The floor was covered with sweet-smelling grass. My brother had done it all.

When my father saw me come in he beckoned to me with a long, thin finger. My brother pushed me forward. I could hardly recognize my father. His face was like chalk. His gray hairs shone on his head, each hair singly as if pasted on. His dark eyes were sunken deep into his head. His teeth looked artificial. His neck was so thin that it could barely support his head. He made strange movements with his lips, like a tired swimmer trying to breathe. As I approached the bed he placed his hot, bony fingers on my face, and twisted his mouth into a wan smile that was like the smile of death.

Just then my mother came into the room, followed by the jolly doctor with the big, black mustache. He greeted me like an old friend, poked me in the belly and said cheerfully to my father.

"So you have a guest for *Shevuos!* May you enjoy his company!"

"Thank you," said my mother and beckoned to the doctor to examine the patient and prescribe something for him. The doctor threw the window open and began to scold my brother for keeping it shut. "I've told you a thousand times that a window likes to be kept open."

My brother Elihu pointed at my mother. It was her fault. She wouldn't let him open the window because she was afraid my father would catch cold. My mother motioned to the doctor to hurry and examine the patient, give him something. The doctor calmly took out his big gold watch. I could see my brother staring at it. The doctor saw it, too.

"Do you want to know what time it is? I have four minutes to half past eleven. What do you have?"

"My watch has stopped," said my brother, turning red from the tip of his nose to the backs of his ears.

My mother was becoming restless. She wanted the doctor to hurry up and give something for the patient. But the doctor was in no hurry. He asked my mother all sorts of trivial questions. When was my brother getting married? What did Hirsch-Ber think of my singing? I ought to have a good voice, because a voice is inherited. My mother answered him patiently. Suddenly the doctor turned his chair around and faced my father and took the dry, feverish hand in his.

"Well, cantor," he said, "how were the Services this *Shevuos?*"

"God be praised," answered my father, with the smile of a ghost.

"That's good. And the coughing? Are you coughing less? Are you sleeping better?" asked the doctor, bending closer.

"No," said my father, barely catching his breath. "On the contrary, I cough as much as ever. I sleep very little. But God be praised. It's *Shevuos*—a holy day. We received the Commandments this day. And we have a guest—a guest for *Shevuos* . . ."

Everyone's eyes were turned on the "guest," and the guest looked down on the floor. His thoughts were elsewhere. They were outdoors with the logs where reeds and stickers grew, with the neighbor's calf that had been like a dear human friend, and now had been sold to the butcher. They were down by the river that tumbled downhill—far from the sick room that smelled like a drugstore.

The bowl of cream that our neighbor Pessie had lent to us was very useful. My brother and I made a feast out of it, both of us dipping chunks of fresh white bread into the chilled sour cream, and finding it very good.

"The only trouble with it is that there isn't enough . . ." said my brother. He was being unusually friendly that day. He didn't even make me go back to Hirsch-Ber right away. He let me play at home a while instead.

"After all, you're a guest here today," he said, and told me I could go outside and play on the logs for a while. But he warned me not to climb too much and tear my best pair of pants. My best pair of pants! That was a good joke. You should have seen those pants. But let's not talk about them . . . Let's talk about Yossi the *nogid's* logs instead. Yossi the *nogid* thought the logs belonged to him. That's what he thought! Really they were my logs. I made a palace out of them and a vineyard. I was a prince. The prince walked proudly in his vineyard, tore up a reed and marched back and forth with it. Everyone envied me. Even the *nogid's* son, Hennich with the squinting eye, begrudged me my good fortune. He went by in his shiny new clothes, pointed at my pants and laughed and squinted his eye and shouted:

"Watch out, you'll be losing something."

"Better run along," I said, "before I call my brother Elihu."

All the little boys were afraid of my brother Elihu. Hennich with his squinting eyes moved off and I was again alone, once more a prince in his vineyard. What a pity that Meni couldn't be here with me. He had been sold to the butcher, said Pessie. Why? To be slaughtered? Was he born for this—to be slaughtered? For what end is a calf ever born, and for what end a human being?

Suddenly I hear a terrible screaming and wailing from our house. I recognize my mother's voice. I look up. People are running in and out of the house. I continue to lie stretched out on a log. I feel good. But what's this? Here comes Yossi the *nogid*. Yossi is the president of the butchers' synagogue where my father has been cantor for twenty-three years. Yossi was once a butcher himself, but he now deals in cattle and furs, and is a rich man, a very, very rich man.

Yossi is waving his arms, shouting angrily at my mother:

"Why wasn't I told that Peisi the cantor was so sick? Why was everybody so quiet about it?"

"Did you want me to shout?" says my mother, weeping. "The whole town saw how I struggled, how I tried to save him. And he wanted to be saved, too . . ."

My mother was unable to say any more. She wrung her hands and threw her head back. My brother caught her in his arms.

"Mother, why do you have to explain to him? Mother, don't forget this is *yom-tev*—it's *Shevuos*! You mustn't weep! Mother!"

But Yossi continues to shout. "The whole town? Who is the

town? You should have come to me! I'll take care of everything. The funeral, the attendants, the shroud, everything! I'll
pay for it all. And if something has to be done for the children,
come to me, too, don't be ashamed to come."

But that comforted my mother not at all. She kept on weeping and wailing and fainting in my brother's arms. And my
brother, who was almost in tears himself, kept reminding her,
"Today is *yom-tev,* mother! It's *Shevuos,* you mustn't cry,
mother."

And then at once it all became clear to me. My heart shrank.
I felt lost. I wanted to burst out crying, and I didn't know
for whom. I was so sorry for my mother, I couldn't bear to
see her cry like that.

And I left my palace and my vineyard and I came up to her
from behind and cried in the same tone as my brother.

"Mother! Today is *yom-tev.* It's *Shevuos,* mother! You
mustn't weep!"

I'm Lucky—I'm an Orphan

NEVER before in my life have I been the privileged character I am now. What is the reason for this?

As you know, my father, Peisi the cantor, died the first day of *Shevuos,* and I was left an orphan.

The first day after *Shevuos* my brother and I began to say *kaddish,* the prayer for the dead. It was my brother Elihu who taught me how to say it. My brother Elihu is a devoted brother, but a poor teacher. He is quick tempered and he beats me. Taking the prayer book in his hand, that first day after *Shevuos,* he sat down with me and began to teach me the words: *"Yisgadal v'yiskadash shmei rabo."* He expected me to know it by heart right away. He repeated it with me one time after another from beginning to end and then told me to say it by myself. I tried, but it didn't work.

The first few lines weren't bad, but after that I always got stuck. Every time this happened he prodded me with his elbow, and said my mind must be elsewhere (how did he guess?), that I must be thinking about the calf (how could he know?). But he didn't give up. He repeated it with me once more. I started out like a flash, but again, after a few lines, I got stuck. The words wouldn't come. So he grabbed me by the ear and shouted, "If father could only get up from his grave now and see what a stupid child he had . . . !"

"Then I wouldn't have to be saying *kaddish* for him!" I said, promptly.

254

For this I caught a juicy slap on the cheek. Hearing the noise my mother cried out, "God be with you! What are you doing? Whom are you slapping? Have you forgotten that the child is an orphan?"

I sleep with my mother now in the bed my father had slept in—the only piece of furniture left in the house. She lets me have most of the blanket.

"Cover yourself," she says to me, "and go to sleep, my poor little child. You might as well try to sleep; I have no food to give you."

I cover myself with the blanket, but I can't fall asleep. I keep repeating the words of *kaddish* to myself.

I don't go to *cheder* these days. I am not learning anything these days. I don't even pray, I don't sing in the choir.

I'm lucky. I'm an orphan.

Congratulate me. I know the whole *kaddish* by heart now—every bit of it. In the synagogue I stand on a bench and rattle it off without a pause. I have a good singing voice—inherited from my father—a real soprano. All the boys stand around me and envy me. The women weep. Some of the men even give me a *kopek*. Yossi the *nogid's* son, Hennich with the squinting eye (who is by nature very jealous), stands in front of me and sticks out his tongue. He is eager—he is anxious—he is dying —to make me laugh. But just to spite him I won't laugh. One time Aaron the *shammes* caught him at it, and grabbing him by the ear, led him to the door. Served him right!

Since I have to say *kaddish* in the morning and at night, I don't stay with Hirsch-Ber any more, and I don't have to carry Dobtzie around all the time. I am a free man. I spend all day at the river, either fishing or bathing. I have figured out for myself a good way to catch fish. If you like, I'll teach it to you.

You take off your shirt, tie your sleeves into knots, and walk
slowly through the water up to your neck. You have to keep
going a long, long time. When you feel the shirt growing heavy
it's a sign that it is full. Then you come out as quickly as you
can, and shake out the weeds and mud, and look carefully inside. Tangled in the weeds you will sometimes find a few little
tadpoles. These you can throw back; it's a pity to let them die.
In the thick mud you may find a leech. These are worth money:
for ten you can get three *groschen,* a *kopek* and a half. But it
isn't easy work . . . For fish there is no use even looking. At
one time there may have been fish in the river, but now there
are none. I don't care. I'd be glad enough just to find leeches,
but you don't even always find those. This summer I didn't
catch a single one.

How my brother Elihu found out that I have been going
fishing I don't know. When he did find out he almost pulled
my ear off. It was lucky that Fat Pessie, our neighbor, saw
him do it. One's own mother couldn't take up for her child
any better.

"Is that the way to treat an orphan?" she cried.

My brother Elihu is ashamed and lets go my ear. Everybody
takes up for me these days.

I'm lucky. I'm an orphan.

Our neighbor, Fat Pessie, must have fallen in love with me.
She goes after my mother and won't stop bothering her. She
wants me to go and live at her house.

"Why should it bother you?" she asks. "I have twelve at the
table already, so he'll be one more." She almost got my mother
to consent that time, but my brother Elihu spoke up.

"Who will keep an eye on him and see that he goes to say
kaddish?"

"I'll see that he goes," said Pessie. "There, does that satisfy you?"

Pessie is not a rich woman. Her husband is a bookbinder; his name is Moishe. He is known as a very skilled workman, but being skilled is not enough. You need luck besides. That is what Pessie tells my mother. My mother goes her one better. She says that even to be unlucky, to be a *shlimazl*, you have to have luck. As an example she points at me. Here I am, an orphan—and everybody wants me! There are some people who are willing to keep me for good, but my mother says that as long as she is alive she won't give me up. And she bursts out crying. Later she asks my brother's advice.

"What do you think? Should we let him stay at Pessie's?"

My brother is almost a grown man now. If he weren't, would my mother be asking his advice? With his hand he strokes his chin, as though he had a beard already. He likes to talk like a grown man.

"Let him go. So long as he doesn't become a *sheigetz*."

And it is agreed that I should live at Pessie's for the time being, provided that I don't become a *sheigetz*. What do they call being a *sheigetz*? To tie a piece of paper to the cat's tail so she'll chase it around and around—that is being a *sheigetz*. Rattling a stick along the fence around the priest's house and making a lot of noise—that is being a *sheigetz*. Pulling the cork out of the water carrier's tank so that half the water runs out—that is being a *sheigetz*.

"It's your luck that you're an orphan!" cries Leibke the water carrier. "If you weren't, I'd break every bone in your body! You can believe me, too!"

I believe him all right, but I also know that he won't touch me. For I am an orphan.

I'm lucky. I'm an orphan.

Our neighbor Pessie told a big lie. She said she feeds twelve at her table, but according to my reckoning I am the fourteenth. She must have forgotten their blind Uncle Boruch. Maybe she didn't count him because he is so old and has no teeth to chew with. I won't argue about that. It is true that he can't chew, but he still knows how to swallow. He swallows like a goose, and grabs all the food he can reach. Everybody grabs there. I grab too, and for that they jump on me. Under the table each one kicks me. The one who kicks the hardest is Vashti. Vashti is a terror. His name is really Hershel, but they call him Vashti. Everyone in this house has a nickname.

You can be sure that there is a reason for each name. Pinny is called "Barrel" because he is round and fat. Haym is rough and shaggy so they call him "Buffalo." Mendel has a pointed nose so they call him "Sharpnose." Feitel is called "Petelili" because he stammers. Berel is never satisfied with one slice of bread smeared with chickenfat; he always says, "Give me more!" In short, everyone in this house has a nickname. Even the cat—poor innocent creature. What harm did she ever do anyone? And yet she has a nickname too. They call her "Feiga-Leah the *shammeste*." Do you want to know why? Because she is fat and Feiga-Leah, the wife of the *shammes,* is also fat. You can't imagine how many times every one of them has been beaten for calling the cat by a human name. But beatings have no effect. Once they have given someone a nickname, the name sticks.

I have a nickname too. Guess what it is . . . "Motel with the Lips." They don't like my lips. They say that when I eat I always smack my lips. I would like to see a person who can eat without smacking his lips! I am not one of those proud people whose feelings are easily hurt, but this nickname I simply can't stand. And just because I can't stand it they keep on teasing me and calling me by it all the time. Nothing can make them stop. First I was "Motel with the Lips," then "The Lips," and finally just "Lippy."

"Lippy, where have you been?"

"Lippy, wipe your nose."

It annoys me and then it hurts me so that I start crying. Seeing me, their father, Pessie's husband, Moishe the bookbinder, asks, "Why are you crying?"

I answer, "Why shouldn't I cry? My name is Motel and they call me Lippy."

He asks who called me that, and I say Vashti.

He was going to beat Vashti and Vashti said it wasn't he, it was Barrel. And Barrel said it was Buffalo.

And so it went. One blamed another and the other blamed a third. It was like a circle without an end. At last their father made up his mind. He laid them down one by one and gave each one a good whipping with the cover of a prayerbook.

"You rascals!" he cried. "I'll show you how to make fun of an orphan! The devil take every one of you!"

And so it goes. Everybody comes to my defense. Everybody takes up for me.

I'm lucky. I'm an orphan.

Dreyfus in Kasrilevka

I DOUBT if the Dreyfus case made such a stir anywhere as it did in Kasrilevka.

Paris, they say, seethed like a boiling vat. The papers carried streamers, generals shot themselves, and small boys ran like mad in the streets, threw their caps in the air, and shouted wildly, "Long live Dreyfus!" or "Long live Esterhazy!" Meanwhile the Jews were insulted and beaten, as always. But the anguish and pain that Kasrilevka underwent, Paris will not experience till Judgment Day.

How did Kasrilevka get wind of the Dreyfus case? Well, how did it find out about the war between the English and the Boers, or what went on in China? What do they have to do with China? Tea they got from Wisotzky in Moscow. In Kasrilevka they do not wear the light summer material that comes from China and is called pongee. That is not for their purses. They are lucky if they have a pair of trousers and an undershirt, and they sweat just as well, especially if the summer is a hot one.

So how did Kasrilevka learn about the Dreyfus case? From Zeidel.

Zeidel, Reb Shaye's son, was the only person in town who subscribed to a newspaper, and all the news of the world they learned from him, or rather through him. He read and they interpreted. He spoke and they supplied the commentary. He told what he read in the paper, but they turned it around to suit themselves, because they understood better than he did.

One day Zeidel came to the synagogue and told how in Paris a certain Jewish captain named Dreyfus had been imprisoned for turning over certain government papers to the enemy. This went into one ear and out of the other. Someone remarked in passing, "What won't a Jew do to make a living?"

And another added spitefully, "A Jew has no business climbing so high, interfering with kings and their affairs."

Later when Zeidel came to them and told them a fresh tale, that the whole thing was a plot, that the Jewish Captain Dreyfus was innocent and that it was an intrigue of certain officers who were themselves involved, then the town became interested in the case. At once Dreyfus became a Kasrilevkite. When two people came together, he was the third.

"Have you heard?"

"I've heard."

"Sent away for good."

"A life sentence."

"For nothing at all."

"A false accusation."

Later when Zeidel came to them and told them that there was a possibility that the case might be tried again, that there were some good people who undertook to show the world that the whole thing had been a plot, Kasrilevka began to rock indeed. First of all, Dreyfus was one of *ours*. Secondly, how could such an ugly thing happen in Paris? It didn't do any credit to the French. Arguments broke out everywhere; bets were made. Some said the case would be tried again, others said it would not. Once the decision had been made, it was final. All was lost.

As the case went on, they got tired of waiting for Zeidel to appear in the synagogue with the news; they began to go to his house. Then they could not wait that long, and they began to go along with him to the postoffice for his paper. There they read, digested the news, discussed, shouted, gesticulated, all together and in their loudest voices. More than once the postmaster had to let them know in gentle terms that the postoffice was not the synagogue. "This is not your synagogue, you Jews. This is not *kahal shermaki*."

They heard him the way Haman hears the *grager* on *Purim*. He shouted, and they continued to read the paper and discuss Dreyfus.

They talked not only of Dreyfus. New people were always coming into the case. First Esterhazy, then Picquart, then General Mercies, Pellieux Gonse . . .

There were two people whom Kasrilevka came to love and revere. These were Emile Zola and Labori. For Zola each one would gladly have died. If Zola had come to Kasrilevka the whole town would have come out to greet him, they would have borne him aloft on their shoulders.

"What do you think of his letters?"

"Pearls. Diamonds. Rubies."

They also thought highly of Labori. The crowd delighted in him, praised him to the skies, and, as we say, licked their fingers over his speeches. Although no one in Kasrilevka had ever heard him, they were sure he must know how to make a fine speech.

I doubt if Dreyfus' relatives in Paris awaited his return from the Island as anxiously as the Jews of Kasrilevka. They traveled with him over the sea, felt themselves rocking on the waves. A gale arose and tossed the ship up and down, up and down, like a stick of wood. "Lord of Eternity," they prayed in their hearts, "be merciful and bring him safely to the place of the trial. Open the eyes of the judges, clear their brains, so they may find the guilty one and the whole world may know of our innocence. Amen. *Selah.*"

The day when the good news came that Dreyfus had arrived was celebrated like a holiday in Kasrilevka. If they had not been ashamed to do so, they would have closed their shops.

"Have you heard?"

"Thank the Lord."

"Ah, I would have liked to have been there when he met his wife."

"And I would have liked to see the children when they were told, 'Your father has arrived.' "

And the women, when they heard the news, hid their faces in their aprons and pretended to blow their noses so no one could see they were crying. Poor as Kasrilevka was, there was not a person there who would not have given his very last penny to take one look at the arrival.

As the trial began, a great excitement took hold of the town. They tore not only the paper to pieces, but Zeidel himself. They choked on their food, they did not sleep nights. They waited for the next day, the next and the next.

Suddenly there arose a hubbub, a tumult. That was when the lawyer, Labori, was shot. All Kasrilevka was beside itself.

"Why? For what? Such an outrage! Without cause! Worse than in Sodom!"

That shot was fired at their heads. The bullet was lodged in their breasts, just as if the assassin had shot at Kasrilevka itself.

"God in Heaven," they prayed, "reveal thy wonders. Thou knowest how if thou wishest. Perform a miracle, that Labori might live."

And God performed the miracle. Labori lived.

When the last day of the trial came, the Kasrilevkites shook as with a fever. They wished they could fall asleep for twenty-four hours and not wake up till Dreyfus was declared a free man.

But as if in spite, not a single one of them slept a wink that night. They rolled all night from side to side, waged war with the bedbugs, and waited for day to come.

At the first sign of dawn they rushed to the postoffice. The outer gates were still closed. Little by little a crowd gathered outside and the street was filled with people. Men walked up and down, yawning, stretching, pulling their earlocks and praying under their breath.

When Yadama the janitor opened the gates they poured in after him. Yadama grew furious. He would show them who was master here, and pushed and shoved till they were all out in the street again. There they waited for Zeidel to come. And at last he came.

When Zeidel opened the paper and read the news aloud, there arose such an outcry, such a clamor, such a roar that the heavens could have split open. Their outcry was not against the judges who gave the wrong verdict, not at the generals who swore falsely, not at the French who showed themselves up so badly. The outcry was against Zeidel.

"It cannot be!" Kasrilevka shouted with one voice. "Such a verdict is impossible! Heaven and earth swore that the truth must prevail. What kind of lies are you telling us?"

"Fools!" shouted Zeidel, and thrust the paper into their faces. "Look! See what the paper says!"

"Paper! Paper!" shouted Kasrilevka. "And if you stood with one foot in heaven and the other on earth, would we believe you?"

"Such a thing must not be. It must never be! Never! Never!"

And—who was right?

The Convoy

I. HAMAN IVANOVITCH PLISETSKY

THAT was what they called the new Government Inspector who had recently come to Teplik. To be accurate, his real name was Agamemnon Afonagenovitch, but the Jews of Teplik, who love to tamper with names, changed his for two reasons: first, because Haman Ivanovitch was shorter and easier to say. Just try, for instance, to roll your tongue around in your mouth and say, A-ga-mem-non A-fo-na-ge-no-vitch! That is the first reason. And the second is that since Teplik was founded, no one remembers ever having heard of an Inspector so much like the Haman of Scriptures as this Haman Ivanovitch Plisetsky of whom we speak.

In Teplik they have had all kinds of Inspectors—good ones, bad ones, those who take bribes eagerly and those who would not touch a *kopek*—except possibly as a New Year gift, which doesn't count, or a birthday present, which you could hardly refuse. All of us have birthdays, and everywhere a birthday is celebrated as a holiday. It has been that way since the dawn of history, since Pharaoh was king of Egypt, as we read in *Genesis*. Pharaoh, when his birthday came, ordered a feast for all his slaves, set his cupbearer free from prison, and hanged his baker on a tree, as Joseph had foretold in in terpreting the dreams three days before.

But let us go back to this other tyrant, this Haman we have been talking about. When he arrived in Teplik, the first thing he did was to start cleaning up the town. And when I say

cleaning, I mean just that. The horse thieves of Teplik, renowned throughout the world, were smoked out in a month
or two. Even if you needed one for an exhibit you couldn't
find one. If there was any person he had any reason to suspect, he did not wait or hesitate, but packed him off by convoy
to the prison at Heissin. Let them reckon with him there.

After the thieves and petty pilferers, he turned his attention
to the streets of the town and to the Jews. He issued the order
that from that day on, the streets must all be kept clean. No
one must empty rubbish into the streets, pour slops out of
the front door, or do anything else unseemly. And the Jews,
he declared, must not open their shops before noon on Sunday,
teachers must not hold classes without a special permit, and
to make it complete, he forbade the *eirev,* the zone of exemption. As you recall, on the Sabbath we must not carry anything
on our persons, not even a handkerchief. In our own house
we could, and in our yard also, but in the city at large not a
thing. So every Friday afternoon we used to make a fence
around the entire Jewish settlement. A fence? You could
call it that, though it consisted of no more than a strong piece
of cord that ran from tree to tree around the entire village.
This we called an *eirev,* and it made all the village one's own
yard, and people could carry whatever they needed without fear
of committing a sin.

But now Haman said that the *eirev* had to go. The Jews
could get along without their telegraph, without these wires
strung all around the town. Even in the synagogue itself,
when some of the men had a fight over this or that honor and
slapped each other in the face, he liked to interfere. That's the
kind of tyrant he was!

Well, he had his way. The stores were closed Sunday till
noon. And if not right on the dot—if some of them opened

a minute or two earlier—he pretended not to notice. For what choice did he have? He did as much as he could. But to be a watchman at every Jewish shop, to catch anyone who opened the door just an inch—that was not humanly possible.

But the *eirev,* the zone of exemption, gave him trouble at first. Every Friday afternoon the cord was strung up all around the town, and Saturday morning he had it torn down. But the next week a new *eirev* appeared, and the week after that another one. This happened several weeks in succession. No matter how much his spies watched, they could not find the culprit, until he condescended to go himself, hide behind a hedge and spend the whole night watching. Finally toward daybreak he caught Peisi, the *shammes'* son, in the very act of stretching the cord. Without ceremony he grabbed Peisi by the left ear and dragged him off to jail and locked him up for the whole day. From that day on Teplik had to get along without an *eirev.* And still people carried their handkerchiefs and watches around on the Sabbath—with no apparent consequences.

Not so simple was the war he waged against the teachers. They made life wretched for him. Here he arrested a teacher with twenty pupils and closed his *cheder,* and there he discovered him with the same pupils in another street. He closed up this *cheder* too, swore out a warrant; looked around—and there was the same man, high up in the women's balcony of the synagogue with the same twenty pupils shouting at the tops of their voices. A curse on these Jewish children, you couldn't drive them away from their studies! "For heaven's sake, if you have to go up there with those pupils of yours, stay there and be damned! But don't make so much noise! Don't force me to listen to you!"

That is how Plisetsky appealed to the teacher, and he swore that if he ever caught him again he would banish him from

Teplik within twenty-four hours. The teacher heard him out with the greatest respect and discontinued his classes in the women's balcony. But the next day he started again in a cellar not far away, and went on teaching with the very same ear-splitting chant as before—that familiar, deafening chant without which the study of Hebrew apparently has no more flavor than the cold puddings that wealthy people in the big cities eat these days.

Haman Ivanovitch battled with these teachers so long, till with a final curse he shut his eyes and pretended not to know that they were there.

II. THE *NOGID* OF TEPLIK, SHOLOM-BER TEPLIKER OF TEPLIK

Since most of the inhabitants of Teplik were Jews, the new Inspector had to spend the greater part of his time dealing with Jews, and in a short time he became acquainted with most of them, knew them by name, learned all their secrets, spoke to them in a half-Yiddish, half-Russian language of his own, and became quite intimate with many of them—almost like one of the family.

The richer townspeople, the leading citizens—the soup ladles, as we call them, because they are always stirring the community pot—in their turn, when they saw how friendly he was, began to win their way into his good favor—first, with a piece of Sabbath fish ("Jew fish," he called it), a glass of Passover brandy ("Jew brandy"), and a few pieces of *matzo* ("Jew *matzo*"). And afterward, with a fawning smile, they moved on to the next stage—of slipping something into his hand. But his response to this gesture was so unexpected and sharp that they learned something that they remembered forever after, and they passed it on to their children and grandchildren: "Never bribe a man—until you know who he is and what he is."

"If you're trying to bribe me," cried Haman, "it must mean that you've committed some crime. Here, take him and put him away!"

The words, "Take him and put him away!" were always at the tip of his tongue. They meant several different things: to throw a person in jail for a day or two; to put him away for several weeks; or even to send him off to Heissin, where the prison was, by convoy. And once he had given this order, nothing more could be done about it. Not all the kings of east or west could help. That's the kind of a man he was! And yet so inconsistent was he that if some penniless wretch fell into his hands, this tyrant reached into his own pocket and gave the fellow a *ruble* or two, and said to him in his mixture of Russian and Yiddish:

"Here is a loan to help you on your way."

But considerate as he was of poor people, so intolerant was he of the rich. And especially if the rich man was from Teplik. And most especially the *nogid* of Teplik, Sholom-Ber Tepliker of Teplik. Him he could not tolerate at all, and for a long, long time he tried to catch the man at some misdemeanor, without success, till God came to his aid and he had him in his hands. This is how it happened.

This Sholom-Ber Tepliker of Teplik, in addition to being a man of wealth, was as stubborn and proud a creature as you would ever find. If he ever decided to do something, nothing could stop him. It would be easier to pick up all of Teplik and move it somewhere else than to make him change his mind. Thus when Haman Ivanovitch decreed that no one was to throw rubbish or slops out into the street, Sholom-Ber Tepliker of Teplik asked this question, "Whose business is that? It's my rubbish and my slops, and I can do with it as I wish!"

"But, Reb Sholom-Ber," people tried to tell him, "if this Haman ever catches you, there'll be trouble!"

"Don't worry," said Sholom-Ber. He was a man who did not like to waste his words.

"But, Reb Sholom-Ber, he'll serve a warrant."

"Let him serve seventy-seven warrants!"

"But, Reb Sholom-Ber, what if someone should slip in front of your house and break a leg?"

"Let that Haman break a leg!" cried Sholom-Ber, and ordered his servant girl to throw as much rubbish in front of the house as she wanted to.

So Plisetsky came to him with the police and served papers on him, and Sholom-Ber protested vociferously, and told them all what he thought of them, as only a *nogid* can. Plisetsky told him to shut his mouth, and in the course of giving this advice threw in a few words like, "the nerve of the Jew," and "dirty Jewish mouth," and a few other pleasant remarks of the same general type. At this Sholom-Ber became angry and let it be known before all those present that the Inspector was a second Haman, in fact he was Haman himself, the very same one they told about in the Bible. All this was added as an extra clause to the complaint, and between one thing and another, the leading citizen of Teplik, Sholom-Ber himself, was sentenced to two weeks in the district jail. And all the prayers and all the vows and all the pledges to the Almighty could not help him!

It is to be understood that all of Teplik rocked at the news. Imagine it! Two weeks behind bars for Teplik's Sholom-Ber! And the whole town came to see him being led off to jail. They say that not even a babe was left in its cradle. Everybody who could see was there to watch him. And as they led him through the marketplace to the town jail, Sholom-Ber Tepliker of Teplik lowered his eyes for the first time in his life. And his wife, Stissi-Pearl, for very shame, hid herself in her house. And everybody else in town stood along the road watching the spectacle and saying nothing, although deep in their hearts many of them were glad.

In the first place, he had it coming. Just because he was rich was no reason for a man to be so insolent. And in the second place he was disliked by everyone because in spite of his haughty manner he was a low and petty creature and his wife, Stissi-Pearl, begrudged a person a dry crust of bread, though, as everybody in Teplik knew well enough, their very gizzards were stuffed with gold and they had no one to spend it on—not even a child.

"If I had their money," every Tepliker was in the habit of saying, "if I only had half as much, or a third as much, the town would get more pleasure out of it than it does now . . ." And that might very well have been so, but since in all of Teplik there was no one else who had any money at all, there was no one who got any pleasure out of it—neither the town itself, nor Sholom-Ber, nor his wife Stissi-Pearl. Though it may be that the latter two did get some joy out of it. It all depends what you call joy. If you measured it by the position one held in the community, then Sholom-Ber had it. Wherever he was, whether in the synagogue or at a public gathering or a celebration, he had the place of honor. It was always the others who came up to him to wish him a good Sabbath, a good morning, or greet him at the holidays. When Sholom-Ber spoke, the others listened in silence, and whatever he said was a thing of wisdom. And more than that—every year, at *Simchas-Torah,* it was at his home that the whole town gathered. Sholom-Ber sat like a king and asked everyone who came to take some brandy, and Stissi-Pearl his wife watched every glass. There were other occasions also during the year, which, if you were a Tepliker, would have some meaning, but if you were not, would have none at all. And besides all this, there was the simple fact that Sholom-Ber was convinced that he was the only one who was anything at all. Only he, and no one else.

In Teplik there was only one Sholom-Ber Tepliker. In Teplik there was only one like that. There was no other . . .

III. A CHEERFUL PAUPER

In Teplik, if there had been no meddlers and informers, that is, if there had been no people who paid attention to what everybody else was doing, ninety-nine out of every hundred transgressions would have gone unpunished, and Teplik would have had as many sinners as Sodom itself. But since the people of Teplik have a way of keeping very well informed of the activities of their neighbors, every time they see anything that looks wrong, or hear anything, or smell anything, or even imagine anything that might not be just right, they make a note of it and see to it that the information reaches the proper authorities in the proper manner. And Plisetsky could boast that he did not ever have to hire any spies. The householders of Teplik were competent enough spies themselves.

After an introduction like this, you will not be surprised to hear that one bright morning the police surrounded the hut of Berel the Redhead with the crooked leg, just as he was sitting on the ground, the skirts of his gabardine rolled up around his waist, pouring from a large jug into small bottles the raisin wine that he sold to his neighbors for sacramental purposes. With great absorption he pressed each cork in and pounded it down. Plisetsky opened the door quietly, observed the red-haired Berel at his work, remaining standing a few minutes on the threshold, and beckoned to his assistants. When Berel raised his eyes and saw Haman Ivanovitch standing over him, he got up from the ground, came up to the Inspector with his strange limp, and looked him right in the eye as though to say, "Are you going to punish me for this? Go ahead, punish me! What can you take away from me? The hole in my pocket?"

How did it happen that Berel was so bold? Because he had nothing to be afraid of. True, he had made wine out of raisins, poured it into small bottles and sold it to his acquaintances for the Sabbath, and in that way earned his livelihood. But what a wine it was, and what a livelihood! The wine was no wine; the livelihood no livelihood. And yet both served their purpose. Every Friday night a benediction had to be made over wine, so this was wine. And it kept him occupied, gave him something to live on—not much, but enough, as he said, for a thin gruel to dip his hard crust into. And that was better than nothing. Think of how many people there are in Teplik who have no work at all and earn nothing at all and have nothing at all! Really nothing! Absolutely nothing at all!

And it was these very men, who did nothing and earned nothing and had nothing, who were most envious of Berel the Redhead, who had the reputation among them of living like a mogul. Was there not a rumor current that he had fish and meat every Sabbath, and certainly white bread? And did he not send his children to *cheder*? And didn't he clothe them, and have a goat of his own? And all from these raisins that he shook up and made into wine! So they sat down and wrote a letter to Plisetsky with all the necessary information. And this is how it read:

"Whereas we have always been concerned with the public welfare, and whereas the public welfare is threatened by all illegal transactions, and whereas Berel the Redhead, hereafter referred to by his legal name of Berko Krivak, has for so many years dealt in wine without a permit, and whereas the aforementioned Berko Krivak manufactures this wine with his own hands, also without a permit, therefore . . ." And so on and so on and so on . . .

The pride of a pauper is nothing to sneer at. The poorer a man is, the prouder he is—prouder than some of the richest people in the world. I once knew a pauper who met another on the street.

"How can you compare yourself to me, you idiot!" said the first. "You still have a pair of boots and a torn old overcoat, and I don't have these things even in my dreams!"

This was said in such a tone of boastfulness that if Rothschild himself had been standing there, he would have lost confidence in himself.

In the meantime, returning to our story, Haman Ivanovitch stood contemplating Berel's apartments, which consisted of three rooms, or to be more accurate, of two small alcoves and a kitchen, and each of these rooms was filled with beds and the beds were full of children. The children were half-dressed and half-naked, that is, they were dressed from the neck to the navel, and from there down they were naked. To this half-naked audience the Inspector was a rare sight, the like of which they had never seen. Without hesitation the children jumped out of bed, quietly stole up to the dazzling figure and stared up at him, examined his gold buttons and felt the scabbard at his side. And while they drank in all the details of his attire, this conversation took place above their heads:

Plisetsky: According to what they wrote about you, you must be making a lot of money.

Berel: It could have been a little worse. It could have been a lot better.

Plisetsky: Then why are your children naked and barefoot?

Berel: They grow better that way.

Plisetsky: And what do you do with your money?

Berel: I do as the *Talmud* advises us.

Plisetsky: The *Talmud*? And what does that say?

Berel: It tells us to divide our money three ways. One third is to be put away; one third is to be kept in cash, and the rest in merchandise.

Plisetsky: I see you're in good spirits.

Berel: What do I have to worry about? What do I need and what do I have? But tell me, my Lord and Master, what is it that my good neighbors said about me, and what is it that I can expect as a result of this visit of yours?

Plisetsky: If you want to know so much you'll be old and gray in a hurry. But first show me all your chests and drawers. I have to search your home. Maybe in addition to the wine I'll find other good things too.

Berel: With the greatest pleasure. Only this: if you discover any gold or silver or government bonds, let's divide it, half for me and half for you.

Plisetsky: You're a little too cheerful—like some people before their death.

Berel: It may be so. No one knows what tomorrow will bring. As the *Talmud* says, "Repent for your sins a day before you die." And as we never know when the Angel of Death might grab us by the neck, so . . .

At this point Plisetsky interrupted him, called in the police and told them to take him to jail. When he heard the word "jail," Berel felt a chill pass through him, and a wailing arose among the children as if a corpse were being carried out.

Naturally in Teplik it did not take long for the news to get around, and from all sides people came crowding to see another Jew being led off to prison—no one knew why. That is, why he was being led was no secret. How could a thing like that be kept a secret in Teplik? Especially when they saw Haman Ivanovitch carrying a small bottle of wine, the kind they

knew Berel made without a license. The only thing they did
not know was what would come of it. A fine—or prison?
They tried to figure out which. And yet they had much more
sympathy for this pauper than for Sholom-Ber the *nogid*.
But they could do nothing to help him, except sigh as he walked
past.

IV. ANOTHER TRANSGRESSOR

That same day Haman Ivanovitch went after the Jews of
Teplik in one more way. He arrested another Jew, one who,
quite obviously, had not committed any crime. This is how
it happened:

There was a young man in town, a boy you might call him,
named Hennich. This Hennich had an older brother, David-
Leib, who was to be called up for military service that year,
and David-Leib claimed exemption because Hennich was
not yet eighteen years old and thus was technically dependent
on him. That was as the law provided. The papers were all
made out and filed with the authorities in Heissin. But filing
papers was not enough. They also had to produce the brother
in person so that the authorities could see for themselves how
old he was. The order came to Plisetsky, and when Plisetsky
was ordered to produce, he produced. He sent the constable
and had Hennich brought to him at the station.

Hennich, you could see at a glance, was not a very gifted
youth. His complexion was pasty, almost lifeless; he had a
cataract in one eye, and his head shook with some nervous dis-
order. In addition to this, his fright at being picked up by the
constable was such that it gave a touch of madness to his appearance, and the impression he made on the Inspector was not
a very good one.

"Are you Hennich Tellerlecker?" Plisetsky asked, grabbing hold of him and looking him over from head to foot.

"I am Hennich Tellerlecker," answered the boy, and then realizing that he was there on account of his brother, he blurted out, "And I'm not eighteen yet! I swear I'm not!"

"So I see," said Plisetsky. "Only seventeen and a half—not counting Sundays and Holidays." And he looked at Hennich so fiercely that the poor lad went hot and cold all over, his heart sank, and he said to himself, "It's all up. David-Leib is gone from us . . ." But he still wanted to do something for his brother, and suddenly he became bold and cried out, "I swear that I am not more than seventeen and a month. Not a day more. If I am lying I hope I may never come home again. Maybe I look older, but I am not! We are all like that in our family. By fifteen our beards start growing . . ."

Plisetsky looked at him, shook his head and smiled, as though to say, "That's all you need besides the cataract and that complexion of yours—a handsome beard." And then he told his deputy to put him away until he could examine the papers more carefully. And Hennich was put away.

So a third citizen of Teplik took up his residence that day in the town jail.

He was greeted at once by Berel. "Look who's here! And what was it you did now, my little bird, and who was it that told them you had done it?"

Sholom-Ber was more reserved. From his corner he looked the lad over coldly, as if he were a thief who had just been caught stealing. And Hennich looked back like a half-wit, with his mouth open, at the sight of the town's *nogid* in the same cell with him, and he began to babble, without knowing what he was saying.

"I don't know what I did. I don't know anything. It's

on account of David-Leib. If I'm more than eighteen . . ."

Berel interrupted him. "What are you flapping your mouth for? Say something! Make sense!"

"I am telling you about my brother . . ." And suddenly he turned upon Berel with these words: "Tell me! How do I look to you?"

"How do you look? You look like a wild man!" Berel answered with a laugh and looked at Sholom-Ber to see if he was laughing too. But the *nogid* was not laughing at all. He was looking at the wretched Hennich shaking in his rags and tatters, wondering why things like that had to go on living in this world.

"No," said Hennich, looking at the rich man with his good eye and at Berel with the other. "That isn't what I meant. What I mean is, how old do I look?"

"Oh, how old? Well, I'd say about twenty-two or so—or a trifle more . . ."

In his great sorrow and anger Hennich let out a shriek and turned on Berel:

"Are you crazy? What are you talking about? David-Leib was just twenty and he is almost three years older than me. So what are you talking about?"

And he looked so mournful and woebegone that Sholom-Ber himself became interested and asked him:

"There are two of you then—two brothers—is that it?"

"Two brothers and our old mother. And a sister of thirteen who is out doing housework. And a younger brother apprenticed to a shopkeeper. And two smaller girls and a little boy in *Talmud Torah*. And all of us depend on him, on David-Leib—all of us. If they send him away we'll have to get sacks and go begging. House to house. What else can we do?"

And he told the whole story as well as he could—not too clearly, not too consecutively, but always insisting that he was not yet eighteen in spite of the beard and in spite of what everybody said. And he turned aside with a cough, wiping his nose and his eyes.

"It's a pity, the poor fellow," said the *nogid* in spite of himself.

"A *shlimazl*," added Berel with a half-smile. "And his brother, in some ways, is not much better. He'd make as good a soldier as I would." And he stuck out his lame leg and looked at it from all sides.

V. THE CONVOY STARTS

Until the day that we now come to, and until the last minute, Sholom-Ber Tepliker of Teplik did not believe that he would be compelled to go with the convoy to Heissin. All the time that he waited he busied himself, writing letters to the proper people, using what influence he had to free himself. But Plisetsky was busy too and his influence was greater, and he saw to it that our fine citizen of Teplik took that trip to Heissin with the convoy—and on foot!

"I'll see to it that you go," Haman Ivanovitch said to him in half-Russian, half-Yiddish, "with your own feet." And to make it worse, the day was bright and hot, a midsummer day. No one could escape the heat, it was like a furnace, a lime-kiln. Shopkeepers closed their shops, workers left their tools, teachers their schools, and they all went to see the *nogid* being led away. And the people of Teplik, seeing him standing with lowered head, said to each other, "Let that be a lesson to us." But in their hearts they rejoiced. They were having their revenge. Pity they had only for Berel the Redhead and for Hennich.

For Sholom-Ber's journey his wife had sent a large basket with fresh white loaves, roast duck and other good things.

Berel's wife and all their children came to bid Berel farewell, bringing a small loaf of bread, boiled fish and potatoes and a bunch of fresh garlic. Only Hennich had no food at all to take along, but some strangers in the crowd collected enough to buy him a dark loaf, a couple of small salted fish, and onions. And all these delicacies were handed over to the guard, who took them willingly, promising that every bit of it would be safe in his hands. And then Haman Ivanovitch appeared on his porch and told the guard to start moving. The guard moved, and the prisoners with him, and after them all of Teplik.

The convoy consisted of one Lavre, the guard, a hairy creature with a fur jacket that he wore winter and summer, a tall fur hat, and a long knotty staff with a large wooden knob at one end and a sharp iron point at the other. The roast duck and the salt fish under one arm, the bread and garlic under the other, his report for the district officials stuck in his bosom, he started off quickly with his wards, much more quickly than you would have imagined. That was because our prisoners wanted to get rid of their followers, and when the older people had dropped away, they begged the guard to chase the little children back. They had kept them company out beyond the town, beyond the mill, and showed no signs of weariness. Lavre raised his staff with the iron point and the youngsters disappeared like frightened birds, and the prisoners remained alone in the open fields. They did not have to hurry any more, they began to take shorter steps and slower ones, and one of them suggested to the guard that it might be well to sit down for a while on the fresh green grass and take a little rest.

The guard was not such an evil man, and it did not take long to convince him. In fact, it is hard to say who was more eager to stop. He too was willing to rest and to sample the baskets he had been carrying, and to see what those odors were

that had been tickling his nostrils all the way. He had already
broken off a few twists of one of the large white loaves and
found them to his liking. He had tasted one of the fishes too
and found that with garlic it was not at all bad. Walking behind the prisoners, he was able to taste this and that without
their knowledge, until Sholom-Ber happened to look around
and caught him pinching his large white loaf and nibbling at
what he had pinched off.

"Our protector," he said to the others guardedly, "has good
active jaws."

"Pray that he doesn't choke," said Berel, cheerfully. "Now
that you mention it, my own appetite is not so bad either.
What do you say, Hennich, are you beginning to feel a little
weak inside too?"

Hennich moistened his lips and said in his own strange
manner:

"Very hungry, no. But a little something to chew, maybe.
If I had something."

"I have everything," said Sholom-Ber with a quick glance
back at their guard.

"Everything?" wondered Berel. "Without a glass of brandy
you can never say everything." And to make sure that the
guard caught the full meaning, he said it over, in Russian:
"Isn't it true, Lavre, that a meal without brandy is like eating
without teeth?"

"True . . . very true . . ." the guard answered earnestly.

And they juggled their words so long, till they all understood and agreed that as it was not very far from where they
were to Granov, at most a couple of *versts,* one of the prisoners
—naturally Hennich, the youngest—should dash off for a
bottle of brandy; and the other two prisoners, Sholom-Ber
Tepliker of Teplik and Berel the Redhead, guaranteed that he
would not try to escape. And when they had sent him off, the

others sat down on the grass in the middle of the field, under a tree on a hillock, the prisoners talking with each other in low tones, and the guard sitting near them but looking with both eyes up the road to Granov.

VI. HE REMINDS HIM OF OLD WRONGS

If I were a painter or a photographer I would have taken a picture of this group, the three figures sitting there in the middle of the field on the hillock under a wild pear tree with small green leaves and those small, hard pears that no one can eat and that no one ever knows what to do with.

Between Lavre, the guard, with the tall fur cap, on one side, and Berel the Redhead with the crooked leg and the red, freckled face on the other, our Sholom-Ber Tepliker of Teplik, with the small eyes and the thin beard, with his black, satin gabardine and with his black, silk hat, looked like a man of state among two common fellows. A man like that usually knows how to conduct himself. He may act like anybody else, like a plain and modest man, and yet he is not just like anybody else. Other people talk about the things that *he* wants to talk about, and when *he* talks, others listen, and when others talk, he has the right to interrupt.

"What do you think of this heat?" he said to Berel with a sigh and a glance in all directions. And he rolled his sleeves up to the elbows and fanned himself with his silk hat.

"It's not at all cold," answered Berel, following the rich man's glance.

"I hope it doesn't rain," the other went on, with a look up at the sky.

Berel looked up too. "It would be a pity," he agreed, "with all of us dressed up like this."

"Not a bad fellow, this guard of ours," continued Sholom-

Ber, with his eyes on a long, empty wagon that a pair of large oxen were pulling up the road, with a little boy on the driver's seat dangling a whip above their ears.

"Our guard?" echoed Berel. "He's a gentleman compared with those good neighbors of mine who ran to the police with the news that a poor hardworking man was selling a few bottles of raisin wine. It wasn't even anything new. It's been going on for years . . ."

"What do you think," interrupted the *nogid* again, with his eyes on the road that led to Granov. "What do you think? He couldn't have lost his way, could he? I mean, made tracks? That boy—what's his name?"

"Him?" said Berel. "Why should he do a thing like that? What did he ever do that was wrong? He's no more a criminal than I am."

"Speaking of that," said Sholom-Ber, "what do you think they'll do to you?" He was sitting now with his eyes closed, meditatively chewing at a blade of grass.

"For what? For that raisin wine? They won't hang me, that much I know. But beyond that—" he shrugged his shoulders, "let them do what they want. What can they take away from me? The holes in my pockets? And if they want me to sit a while, I'll sit. But what I want to know is what will they do with *you*? You're somebody! You have money, position, property . . .

"I'll tell you the truth, Reb Sholom-Ber. Don't be offended. But if I were you I'd never have given them a chance to throw me into jail like this; for a little thing like that, a bit of rubbish, a pan of dirty water! In the first place, I would not have been so stubborn, especially with the police. In the second, if I were you, I wouldn't have let them march me off this way. Teplik itself should never have allowed it, letting its *nogid* be sent to jail by convoy, like a common nobody, a penniless lout."

At another time Berel would have paid dearly for talking like this to Sholom-Ber. He would certainly have been sent flying head first. But now on his way by convoy to Heissin, Sholom-Ber was not a privileged character. Now a person could say anything he wanted to him. And Berel the Redhead got even with him as well as he could, smoothly, without ever losing his temper. He edged up close to Sholom-Ber with his crooked leg, so close that the rich man had to move away a little, and he spoke to him like this:

"Do you know, Reb Sholom-Ber, how long we have known each other? It's been a long, long time. I remember when you were a brat no taller than that" (Berel held his hand down close to the ground). "You must be about my age, at the most a year older, or two, and you ought to remember me from those days because my grandfather and your father were—don't be afraid, I was not going to say relatives, although they were that too, forty-second cousins once removed on my mother's side. What I was going to say was that we sat close to each other in the synagogue, your father along the east wall and my grandfather in the opposite row so that when we all stood facing east I had your back right in my face. I still remember your father's shiny silk coat and his broad shoulders and the silver stripes on his *tallis;* and my grandfather, Reb Naftali the vintner—you must remember him—used to pull his own yellow *tallis* over his head and pinch me every time I looked up from my prayerbook. Because apparently I was just as anxious to be praying as you were . . . When we were supposed to be standing motionless you were always looking down at your new boots that squeaked. And how I used to envy you, always with new boots while mine were always old, always patched. I could never get good boots on account of my foot. And that was not the only trouble I had on account of that foot. It was hard for me to walk, but that too was nothing.

What was worse was being called Limpy and being mimicked.
And worst of all was the way you did it, Reb Sholom-Ber—
don't be offended! You and others like you, from the richer
families, spoiled little brats . . ."

"I?" cried the *nogid* with a start, and then he remembered
that it was true, they used to mimic Berel, make fun of the
way he jumped on one foot.

"And making fun of me would not have been so bad either,
but what was even worse than that was that you never let
me play with the rest of you. You chased me away with sticks
and stepped with your heels on my ailing foot, right on my
toes, and pretended it had been an accident. Stepped on them
to make me scream, so I screamed, and you laughed and held
your sides . . ."

"Now, *that* you simply made up!" the *nogid* called out, his
face red with shame and he remembered how spoiled he had
been as a child. He had been able to do anything that he wanted
to.

"No, I'm not making it up. It was true and I'll prove it to
you. I told my grandfather and he went and told your father,
and your father would not believe it. He scolded my grandfather, swore that his child was a well-behaved boy who
wouldn't have a thing to do with paupers' children. How do
you like that? Paupers' children! From that time on I knew
what I was—a pauper's child. But I did not know what it
meant and I asked my grandfather, and he told me. He taught
me what it meant to be a poor man's child, and what it was
to be a rich man's. But I still could not understand why a rich
man's child could step on the toes of a poor man's child, and
the poor man's child could do nothing about it. So I asked
my grandfather that too, and he explained it to me this way:
that a rich man is not a poor man and a poor man is not a rich
man. In short, the rich were rich and the poor were poor. And

still that did not make sense, so I looked into his eyes, maybe there 1 could find an explanation that his words could not give me. But all I saw was something like a dark cloud pass over his face, and the wrinkles on his forehead. And that was all . . . And I must admit there is nothing I can do about it. Ever since that time I have had nothing but scorn for the rich and the children of the rich, and most of all I have scorned and hated you . . ."

"Me?"

"You. Yes, you! You were just a child then, no larger than a grasshopper. We were both children. But even later, when we were older, when we were *Bar-Mitzvah,* young men already, you always turned away from me, as if you didn't know me. You were afraid that I might greet you, and you might have to answer me. You begrudged me even that, apparently. It was not worth your time . . ."

The *nogid* of Teplik, Sholom-Ber Tepliker, squirmed and made a weak gesture with his hands. "That couldn't have been," he said without conviction, and at the same time he admitted to himself that it was possible. He remembered that his father was always reminding him that he was not like other children, that the others were not his equal.

"Don't be offended, Reb Sholom-Ber. Foolish little things are never forgotten. When I was married the first time (you were married a short time earlier) I sent you an invitation, but you did not even acknowledge it."

"I swear I don't remember that."

"How should you remember? I bet you don't remember this either, that when my wife died, I sent my Uncle Yossi (my grandfather was dead already by that time) to tell you that I was alone with two small children, forlorn and helpless. Your answer was that you were a man who did not meddle in public affairs."

"Did *I* say that? Oh, no! Your uncle must have told you a lie."

"That may be so. Maybe *you're* right. All I know is that you did nothing to help me that time, or later either, when my house burned down and I was left as naked as when I was born. Or later yet, that time we met at Heissin at the inn, if you remember, during the Fair. You had come, if I remember correctly, to buy some horses or a cow, or maybe to sell some grain."

The rich man rubbed his forehead, like a man trying to remember something, something that eluded him. And he wondered why he should have forgotten and the other had not. And he did not like it that Berel the Redhead, who in Teplik would not have dared say two superfluous words to him, should point out all his shortcomings and remind him of all his past misdeeds. He did not like it at all, and he was on the point of saying so when Hennich arrived from Granov with the bottle of brandy, all out of breath from running, afraid that someone might catch him with the bottle and have him arrested . . .

And the three transgressors sat down to their feast, beginning with a drop of brandy. They offered the guard a glass too, and he did not refuse. But they could see that the drink did not appeal to him. He made a face, wiped his thick mustache with his sleeve, and cursed forsaken Granov and its fiery brandy.

"May seven devils take it! It's too bitter!" he swore, and he lifted up his hand as if he were taking an oath that as long as he lived he would never take another drop. And yet, when they had finished the fish and were about to attack the roast duck, they prevailed upon him to try another sip. It was hard work, but they succeeded, and he agreed to try it again, and when they urged him to finish the glass because they wanted him to take another, he agreed to that too.

When they had finished eating, the four of them lay down

under the pear tree for a little while, not to take a nap—that they did not even have in mind—but simply to look up at the deep blue heavens and watch the tiny white clouds that passed by overhead and disintegrated and then disappeared like smoke, and the ravens that swept and turned and at the same time appeared motionless.

Lying on the ground after eating, and looking up at the sky, is an excellent way of overcoming sleeplessness. The first to prove this was the guard himself, who almost at once let out a snore like a frightened horse. And shortly afterward was heard the only slightly more modest accompaniment that issued from the capable though less consistent nostrils of the boy Hennich. He did well while he tried, but he awoke too often, sat up too frequently to babble something that was on his mind:

"So tired . . . ran four versts . . . afraid, afraid he'd catch me . . . the Inspector . . ."

The only ones who did not sleep were the rich man, Sholom-Ber Tepliker of Teplik, and Berel the winemaker. Sholom-Ber was worrying. He wanted to know what it was that had happened that time in Heissin at the Fair, what it was he had refused to do. And Berel did him a favor and told him the whole story in these words.

VII. A TRIVIAL INCIDENT IS NOT FORGOTTEN

"Don't be offended," Berel began. "A trivial incident is never forgotten. I came to Heissin not for the Fair. My oxen were still in pasture and my ships were still at sea. Then why did I have to come to Heissin at that very time? I came to look over a boy whom the *shadchan* had found for my older daughter, by my first wife. I had finally decided to marry her off. She was still young, poor child, but her stepmother kept nagging me. She wanted her out of the house. And what could

I do? I asked what good it would do her. Who would help her cook and bake and scrub the smaller children's heads, and whom would she be able to curse and pull around by the hair? But try to convince a woman! So we decided to marry her off.

"That's easy to say. But how? What with? With your five fingers? There isn't much that people in our class can do, but clothes at least we have to get. Do I mean fine clothes? No. But even a cotton dress and some shoes and stockings cost money. And you have to get a few nightgowns, a couple of pillows, a bedspread, maybe a blanket. That's not counting the dowry, and how can a person give less than a hundred *rubles*? And here I was, with less than a hundred *kopeks*.

"And as if to tease me, Moishe-Aaron, the matchmaker, keeps swamping me with letters, one letter after another, saying that he had found a young man in Heissin, just the right boy for my daughter, one boy in a hundred, one in a million. I'd never find another one like him. And whose boy is it? Yankel the carpenter's, a poor man's child, but a very gifted one, advanced in his studies, a good penman—everything! And he played the fiddle like the devil himself!

"So I wrote to Moishe-Aaron and told him that first of all I was in no hurry to consider a match, and in the second place I had to know how much dowry he expected, because maybe it was not for my purse at all. And in the third place, why didn't Yankel come here first, at least to take a look at the girl. So he answers me at once—Moishe-Aaron, that is—and tells me that my first point, that I was not interested in a match, was nonsense, because he knew and everybody else knew that a daughter is not a son, and it's never too soon to marry her off. And as for what I had said about a dowry, that was foolish of me. Were we talking about an ox or a cow that we should start bargaining? These were his very words. And as for coming to look at my daughter, that was not necessary, either.

Yankel knew all about her already. A neighbor of his from Heissin had been in my house and had seen the girl and he could not begin to praise her highly enough.

"At any rate—a letter here, a letter there—I took my feet in my hands, as the saying is, and went off to Heissin. And when I saw the boy I felt as if I had never seen anyone like him in my life before. His face was like that of a prince, his brain a prime minister's. When he spoke, every word was a jewel. And when he played the fiddle you could forget every musician who ever lived! I was in love with him myself and I swore that no matter what happened I would have him for my daughter. But go do something when your pocket's empty! If I only had a hundred *rubles!* Or even part of it to give as a deposit! The boy himself did not care about a dowry. Give it to him or don't give it to him, it was all the same. But the carpenter, the devil take him, was stubborn and you couldn't budge him. If a grand duchess herself wanted to marry his son she'd have to pay a dowry before she could lead him to the canopy.

"I turned to the *shadchan.* 'Reb Moishe-Aaron,' I said, 'do something. Say something.' 'What can I say?' he asked. 'Do something quick. It looks bad. You'll never get anywhere with this stubborn ox. Only yesterday I almost hit him over the head with his plane.' Did you ever hear anything like that? Yet there was the boy before my eyes. I couldn't drive him out. I simply had to have him for my daughter. I'd die if I didn't have him!

"In the meantime, I looked around at the inn, and whom did I see? Reb Sholom-Ber Tepliker! God alone, I told myself, could have brought him there. And I wasn't shy. I went right up and greeted you, like an old friend. I was so happy to see you! Why? Because, I thought to myself, you would surely ask me what I was doing here in Heissin, and I would tell you that I was here for a match. And you would say, 'With whom?' And I would say, 'With Yankel the carpenter.' And you would say, 'How much dowry are you giving?' And I would say, 'Ah, that's the whole problem! The carpenter says that I'll have to lay down a hundred, and all I have is a fig.' And then you would say . . .

"But what happened really? You didn't ask me a thing. So without your asking, I told you that I had come not for the Fair, but to arrange a match for my daughter. Why did I do that? Because I thought that then you would have to ask with whom, and then I could say, 'With Yankel the carpenter.' And then you would say, 'What dowry are you giving?' And I'd say . . . But you know already what I was going to say, and yet what happened? Not the trace of a question!

"So I decided to tell you without being asked. I told you whom the match was with, and I praised the boy to the skies, as I could do in all truthfulness. Well . . . I did all the talking. You didn't say a word. My story made no impression, as if it went through one ear and out through the other. So I said to myself, why should I be a diplomat? The time had come to say it directly—tear the tooth out by the root! And what did you do then? You refused me outright. And scolded me besides."

"I scolded you? What did I say?"

"Do you want me to tell you? Ah, trivial things are never forgotten. And so I remember. You asked me what right did I have to bother you, what right did I have to expect you to go throwing out a hundred *rubles* at a time . . ."

"But did you tell me what you needed the money for?"

"Did I tell you? Don't you remember? And this was your answer: 'What makes you so anxious to marry off your daughter to a millionaire?' And when I told you how well the boy played the fiddle, you said to me, 'It's lucky he plays the fiddle. What if it was the trumpet?' Here I was, suffering anguish, desperate for help, and you made fun of me, practiced your jokes on me . . . Apparently you were feeling good that day."

Reb Sholom-Ber Tepliker of Teplik listened to the whole story, sweated, said nothing. What had really happened that day he did not remember, but there had been something to do with a hundred *rubles*. That much he remembered. And he was ashamed of himself, ashamed to think that he had once refused a small thing like that which would have meant so much to this man and his family. The story itself now interested him too, and he asked: "Well, how did the match turn out?"

"There wasn't any."

"What do you mean—there wasn't any?"

"The carpenter wouldn't have anything more to do with me. The devil take him!"

"And your daughter? The girl?"

"My daughter? I buried her long ago. I killed her and buried her myself. You don't believe me? Well, what could I do? Could I make a dowry with my own hands? . . . A year went by, two years went by. There is no such thing, you know, as a Jewish convent. And the stepmother continued to nag. So I married the child off to a bookbinder as penniless as myself. A good man, an honest one, but sickly, tubercular. He struggled along a few years and then he died, leaving me this inheritance —three little children. Yes, I was the one to inherit them, because my daughter had caught his disease and she died too, a year later. Do you see? So now I have not only children from my own two marriages, but three little orphans besides. But such children! You won't find their equal in the richest families. 'Grandpa, where are you going?' they asked when Haman had me taken away. 'To Heissin,' I told them. 'When I come back I'll bring you all some chocolate.' And do you think they didn't know that I was telling them a lie? You should have seen them stand around me, like little lambs, without a sound, but with tears in their eyes. You can imagine what they looked like—if I tell you that Haman Ivanovitch himself reached into his pocket and gave them a *gulden* to buy sweets with."

VIII. WHICH PERTAINS TO HENNICH AND HIS FAMILY

Berel the Redhead had nothing more to say. After a pause he stood up, straightened his ailing leg, and limping over to Hennich snapped his finger across the lad's nose.

"Look here!" he said. "Haven't you slept long enough already?"

Hennich awoke with a start, wiped his eyes, and seeing the *nogid* looking at him, picked himself up quickly and began to babble:

"I didn't begin to sleep! I was thinking about poor David-Leib. They say more than eighteen. And what will happen to the poor children?"

"Listen to him talk!" said Berel to Sholom-Ber. "A real *schlimazl*! I was telling you just now about my bad luck, but compared to him I'm a rich man, a millionaire! And a man of influence, too . . . I'm the man who got David-Leib the job that he supports the family with. Eight mouths!"

"Nine you can say," Hennich corrected him. "Two brothers and an old mother. A sister of thirteen who does house work. And a younger brother in a shop. And two smaller girls. And a boy in *cheder,* a younger one. And where am I?"

"You? You are as good as buried!" Berel told him. "What are you now, and what will you ever be?" And turning to Sholom-Ber he said, "Now his brother David-Leib compared to him is a prime minister. A genius he's not; but he's not a fool, either. He's honest. The whole family is honest; they wouldn't steal a *beigel* from anyone. But David-Leib is both honest *and* capable.

"Well, one day he came to me with this story. In Heissin a sugar refinery had just been built that was owned by Reb Zalmen Rademishler, and Reb Zalmen Rademishler belonged to the Sadagora *chassidim*. Now I belong to the Sadagora *chassidim* too, and David-Leib's father—may he rest in peace—was also one of them. So he wanted me to go to see Reb Zalmen and ask him if he would find work somewhere in his refinery for him. 'What kind of work would you want?' I asked, and he told me, 'Anything at all, so long as it's work.' 'Idiot,' I said, 'tell me what you can do.' And he said, 'I can do anything. I know arithmetic and bookkeeping. I can write and I can copy.' 'Where did you learn all that?' I asked him. 'By myself,' he said, and took a piece of paper out of his pocket for me to show Reb Zalmen what his handwriting was like.

"Well, he bothered me so much that in order to get rid of him I put on my shoes and again went to Heissin, on foot. And when I came to Reb Zalmen's refinery they wouldn't let me in. What's the matter? And they tell me this. If I came just to visit Reb Zalmen, he did not have time to see me. And if I had some business to do, I should go into the office. I said to myself, 'Bah! I don't like this at all!' What kind of talk was this—no time—business—office? We Sadagora *chassidim* don't believe in such tricks. 'Go,' I said, 'tell Reb Zalmen that I, Berel the Redhead from Teplik, am here to see him about something important, and *not* on business, and I *can't* wait, because I have no time either!' So they tell me that Reb Zalmen is at his prayers, he just started a little while ago. 'If so,' I said, 'that's different.' But at the same time, was that an excuse? Couldn't he see me anyway? But the answer to that

is that he was a rich man and people had to show respect for
him. If I were rich, the whole world would respect me too.

"So I sat down and waited. I waited an hour and two and
three, right by the door. All around me was rush and bustle.
People came and went, this one in, that one out. It was getting
late. Someone came past me with a tray and a *samovar* and
food that I'd never even seen before. So I said to myself, 'This
I don't like either!' And I decided: why be formal? So I
opened the door and in I went. 'How do you do, Reb Zalmen,' I said. 'How do you do,' said he, 'and where are you
from?' 'From Teplik,' I answer him. 'Didn't you recognize
me? I'm Berel. I was in Sadagora together with you once,
to see our Rabbi.' 'Maybe so,' he said, 'but I didn't remember
you and I still don't know you. My eyesight is not so good
any more, not good at all. I went to all the doctors around
here and then I went to Mendelstam, and he gave me black
glasses to wear and told me not to read or write and keep
away from sunlight.' 'Oh-ho,' I said to myself, 'you're telling
me a story I heard from my grandmother!' And then to him,
'Listen to me, Reb Zalmen. This is what I came for. You
remember Benny from Teplik, don't you?' And he said, 'Which
Benny?' 'Benny Tellerlecker,' I tell him. 'No,' he says, 'this
is the first time I've heard the name—Tellerlecker.' 'That,'
I said, 'won't help you. You knew him well enough. We all
drank wine together in Sadagora and danced together on the
Rabbi's table, and more than once embraced each other, you
and he and I, and now he's in Eternity—may he intercede
for us there.'

"When he heard his, Reb Zalmen became another man
altogether. These rich men must be very much afraid of
death. 'What do you want?' he asks, 'what do you want of me?'
'What should I want?' I say, 'I want to fulfill my promise to
the dead. A few hours before he died, this same Benny Teller-

lecker called me and a few other friends together and told us that he had gone to see you a couple of times here in Heissin, wanted to talk with you about something, but had not been allowed to come in. He was a quiet little man, you remember, and he never liked intrigue or politics; so when he saw that he was not wanted he turned around and went back home again. But now, that he was about to begin another journey, and a longer one, from which no one ever returns, he wanted to bid farewell to each of us separately, and through each of us he sent his regards first to the Rabbi of our order, and then to you. And he asked me to give this message to you: he leaves everything he has to you—that is, he leaves his whole family to you, and he knows that you will never abandon them.'

" 'What can I do for them?' said he, reaching into his pocket. 'Ah-ha,' thought I, 'a donation. Never!' And I said, 'What I want you to do is to take his eldest son, David-Leib, and give him work, a job.' When a rich man hears the word *job* he has a stroke. 'Where can I get him a job? Where can I find work for him? Every job is taken.' 'That story,' I said, 'you can tell someone else, not me! I don't want to hear any excuses from you. You have to find a job for Benny's son. He knows arithmetic and bookkeeping, he can copy and write. So please be so kind now and call for a glass of brandy and a bite to eat, because I'm starved. I've had nothing in my mouth all day.'

"Well, why should I drag out the story? We Sadagora *chassidim* are simple people. Reb Zalmen promised me that he would take the boy, so when I came home I sent David-Leib back to Heissin. For a while he lay around, waiting. Reb Zalmen told him that he would have to talk it over with his son first, his son Reb Yossil, and Reb Yossil was not in town. Later, when Reb Yossil returned, Reb Zalmen was out of town. But at last they had to take him in, and today he is their chief executioner."

"Cashier," corrected Hennich, and explained to them what a cashier was. "He has to do with money. He takes it and he gives it out."

"Thanks for making it clear," said Berel. "Otherwise we would never have known."

And he went over to the guard, pulled him by the sleeve, and woke him up.

"Hey, Lavre, what's the matter with you? It's time to sober up."

And Lavre obeyed him. Slowly he got up from the ground, slowly he looked up at the sky to see where the sun was, then he picked up his staff, lined up and counted his three wards, and together they continued their journey.

IX. THE *NOGID* REPENTS

The sun was close to setting, the heat had begun to abate, and the convoy was near the outskirts of Granov, the first scheduled stop on their journey, when the three prisoners stopped near a windmill, turned their faces toward the east, and began their evening prayers. Lavre stood a little to one side leaning against his staff, his cap pushed back, and looked with curiosity at the Jews nodding and swaying and once or twice beating their breasts.

Of the three, it was Reb Sholom-Ber Tepliker of Teplik who prayed with the greatest feeling. That evening he was not satisfied with merely touching his breast twice, he really beat it. "Forgive us, Our Father, for we have sinned; pardon us, Our King, for we have transgressed." With all his heart he regretted his past behavior, the things he had done and the things he had neglected to do. And he compared himself to this tattered creature, Berel the Redhead, and he was ashamed of himself. Berel, who had hardly enough to keep himself alive, had not hesitated to go a long distance on foot in someone else's behalf, to force his way into a rich man's presence, humble himself in order to do someone else a favor. And he, Sholom-Ber Tepliker of Teplik, had been unwilling even to hear about someone else's troubles; he had been cold, cold as ice. And he was sorry that he had acted that way, and most of all he was sorry for the way he had treated Berel in connection with the match he had tried to arrange for his young daughter, in Heissin, at the time of the Fair.

He felt now that he owed something to Berel the Redhead for the share he might have had in the killing of his daughter. For if he had listened to Berel's request, if he had shown a trace of pity, a trace of love for a poor man, his daughter might still be alive and happy. And Sholom-Ber felt that if he could still right at least a small part of the wrong, he would feel much better. But he did not know how to do it. And as he went on with his prayers his whole life passed in review before his eyes, almost for the first time. And he could not understand how he had ever been so satisfied with himself, and had thought that he had done his duty if only he said his prayers every day and dropped an occasional three-*kopek* piece in the charity box.

The Tepliker *nogid*, Sholom-Ber Tepliker of Teplik, remembered how he had bargained for every *groschen* that had to be torn from him by force. He had given the Holy Scrolls to the synagogue for his own glory, but he had refused a small loan to the scribe who had made the scrolls. And he burned with shame. He felt that until that day his soul had been asleep, that his heart had lain under a weight somewhere, with ice around it. And he wanted to do something for Berel, and he did not know how.

He had lived fifty-six years, more than three-quarters of the seventy he hoped to live, and all his life had been one long war to add one *groschen* to another. To whom would he leave it all? He had no children, and his kinsmen all hated him. And he remembered things he had long forgotten, and a cold chill gripped his heart. He promised that from now on, at least, in his old age, he would be more considerate of his fellow men.

Having finished their prayers, our convoy resumed its journey. Berel limped along, joking with Hennich, and the *nogid* walked alone, deep in thought. He walked faster and faster, without looking to left or right, without knowing that he was getting ahead of the others.

"What's your hurry, Reb Sholom-Ber?" the redhead called to him. "I can't keep up with you."

"Is it hard for you to walk, Reb Berel?" the *nogid* asked. "Here, give me your hand and we'll go together. And when we come home again, with the Lord's help, I want you to come to me, both of you. There is something I have to tell you."

Berel could not understand. What did he have to tell them? And why at his home? Why not now, where they were? And why had he suddenly become so humble?

Hennich did not even try to understand. All he said was, "If only the Lord has mercy. If only David-Leib is saved."

"Don't worry," said Sholom-Ber. "Even if he goes, I'll take care of all of you. I'll take care of everybody."

When the convoy entered Granov the sun had already set, all but a bright golden strip along the horizon. They were greeted with music, a chorus of the croaking of frogs mingled with the bleating of sheep and goats being led home for the night in a cloud of dust. And that was their good fortune.

In the cloud of dust the people did not see *who* was being led through their town! Otherwise the good people of Granov might have welcomed them with the same respect and escorted them beyond the town with the same parade with which they were greeted and escorted at Michaelovka and Mitchulka and Krasnopilka and Zdakovitz and all the other points along the way between Teplik and Heissin.

The Fiddle

TODAY I'll play you something on the fiddle.

I don't know how you feel, but as for me, there is nothing more wonderful than to be able to play a fiddle. As far back as I can remember my heart has gone out to the fiddle. In fact, I loved everything about music. Whenever there was a wedding in our town I was the first one on hand to greet the musicians. I would steal up behind the bass violin, pluck a string—boom!—and run off. Boom—and run off again. For doing this I once caught the devil from Berel Bass. Berel Bass, a fierce-looking man with a flat nose and a sharp eye, pretended not to see me as I stole up behind his bass violin. But just as I was stretching my hand out to pull at the string he caught me by the ear and led me to the door with a great show of courtesy.

"Don't forget to kiss the *mazuza* on your way out," he said.

But that experience taught me nothing. I couldn't stay away from musicians. I was in love with every one of them, from Shaike Fiddele, with his fine black beard and slim white fingers to round-shouldered Getzie Peikler with the big bald spot that reached down to his ears. Many a time when they chased me away, I hid myself under a bench and listened to them playing. From under the bench I watched Shaike's nimble fingers dancing over the strings and listened to the sweet tones that he so skillfully drew out of his little fiddle.

After that I would go around for days in a trance with Shaike and his fiddle constantly before my eyes and moving through my dreams at night. Pretending that I was Shaike, I would crook my left arm, move my fingers, and draw the right arm across as though I held a bow. All this while I threw my head to one side and dreamily shut my eyes. Just like Shaike. Exactly like him.

When the rabbi caught me—this was in *cheder*—drumming my fingers in the air, throwing my head back and rolling my eyes, he gave me a loud smack. "You rascal, you are supposed to be learning something, and here you are—fooling around— catching flies!"

I vowed to myself, "Let the world come to an end, I must have a fiddle. No matter what it cost, I must have one." But how do you make a fiddle? Naturally, of cedarwood. It is easy to say—cedarwood. But where do you get this wood that is supposed to grow only in the Holy Land? So what does God do? He gives me this idea: we had an old sofa at our house, an inheritance from my grandfather, Reb Anshel, over which my two uncles and my father had quarreled for a long time. My uncle Ben argued that he was the oldest son, therefore the sofa was his. Uncle Sender argued that he was the youngest, therefore the sofa belonged to him. My father admitted that he, being only a son-in-law, had no claim to the sofa, but since his wife, my mother, was my grandfather's only daughter, the sofa rightfully belonged to her. All this time the sofa remained at our house. But my two aunts, Aunt Itke and Aunt Zlatke, entered the feud. They carried their bickerings back and forth between them. The sofa this, the sofa that. Your sofa, my sofa. The whole town rocked with it. Meanwhile, the sofa remained our sofa.

This sofa of which I speak had a wooden frame with a thin veneer which was loose and puffed out in several places. Now this veneer, which was loose in spots, was the real cedarwood that fiddles are made of. That was what I had heard in *cheder*. The sofa had one drawback which was really a virtue. When you sat down on it you couldn't get up, because it sloped—there was a bulge on one end and a depression in the middle. This meant that no one wanted to sit on it. So it was put away in a corner and was pensioned off.

But now I began to cast an eye at this sofa. I had already arranged for a bow a long time ago. I had a friend, Yudel the teamster's Shimeleh, and he promised me as many hairs as I would need from the tail of his father's horse. And a piece of resin, to rub the bow with, I had all my own. I hated to rely on miracles. I got it in a trade with another friend of mine— Maier, Lippe-Sarah's boy—for a small piece of steel from my mother's old crinoline that had been lying up in the attic. Later, out of this piece of steel, Maier made himself a knife sharpened at both ends, and I was even ready to trade back with him, but he wouldn't think of it. He shouted at me:

"You think you're smart! You and your father, too! Here I go and work for three nights, sharpening and sharpening, and cut all my fingers, and you come around and want it back again!"

Well, I had everything. There was only one thing to do—to pick off enough of the cedar veneer from the sofa. And for that I chose a very good time—when my mother was out shopping and my father lay down for his afternoon nap. I crept into the corner with a big nail and began clawing away with real energy. In his sleep my father heard someone burrowing, and apparently thought it was a mouse. He began to hiss: "Shhh, shhhhh." I didn't move, I didn't breathe.

My father turned over on his other side and when I heard that he was snoring again I went back to my work. Suddenly I looked up—there stood my father, watching me with a puzzled look. At first he didn't seem to know what was going on,

but when he saw the gouged-out sofa he dragged me out by the
ear and shook me till I rattled. I thought I was going to faint.

"God help you—what are you doing to the child?" my
mother screamed from the threshold.

"Your pride and joy! He's driving me into my grave!"
gasped my father, pale as the white-washed wall, as he clasped
at his heart and went into a coughing spell.

"Why do you eat yourself up like that?" asked my mother.
"You're sick enough without that. Just take a look at yourself,
just look!"

The desire to play the fiddle grew as I grew. The older I
grew, the more anxious I was to be able to play, and as if in
spite I had to listen to music every day. Just about halfway between home and *cheder* there was a small sod-covered shack,
and whenever you passed that shack you heard all sorts of
sounds, the strains of all kinds of instruments, and especially
the sound of a fiddle. It was the home of a musician, Naftaltzi
Bezborodka, a Jew with a shortened coat, with clipped earlocks
and with a starched collar. His nose was large and looked almost as if it were pasted on, his lips were thick, his teeth black,
his face was pockmarked and without the trace of a beard.
And that was why they called him Bezborodka, the beardless
one. His wife was a crone who was known as Mother Eve, and
they had at least a dozen and a half children—tattered, half-
naked, barefoot, and every one of them, from the oldest to the
youngest, played on some instrument—this one the fiddle, that
one the cello, the other the bass, one the trumpet, another the
flute, the bassoon, the harp, the cymbal, the balalaika, the drum.
Some of them could whistle the most complicated melody with
their lips, or through their teeth, on glass tumblers or pots, or
on pieces of wood. They were magicians—or devils of some
sort!

With this family I became acquainted in a most unexpected way. I was standing under their window one day, drinking in the music, when one of the boys caught sight of me and came out. He was Pinny, the flutist, a boy about fifteen, but barefoot like the rest.

"What do you think of the music?" he asked.

"I wish I could play that well in ten years," I told him.

"You can," he said, and explained that for two *rubles* a month his father would teach me to play. Or, if I wanted, he himself would teach me.

"What instrument would you like to play?" he asked. "The fiddle?"

"The fiddle," I said.

"The fiddle," he repeated. "Could you pay a *ruble* and a half a month—or are you as penniless as I am?"

"I can pay," I told him. "But there is one thing. Neither my father nor my mother nor my rabbi must know a thing about it."

"God forbid!" he exclaimed. "Why should anyone find out?" He moved up closer to me and whispered, "Have you got a cigar butt—or a cigarette?" I shook my head. "No? You don't smoke? Well, then, lend me a few *groschen* so I can buy some cigarettes. But don't tell anybody. My father doesn't know that I smoke, and if my mother found out she'd take the money away and buy some bread."

He took the money and said in a friendly voice, "Come on in. You'll get nothing done standing out here."

With great fear, my heart pounding and my legs trembling, I crossed the threshold of this small paradise.

My new friend Pinny introduced me to his father. "This is Sholom—Nochem-Vevik's. A rich man's son . . . He wants to learn to play the fiddle."

Naftaltzi Bezborodka pulled at his earlock, straightened his

collar, and buttoned up his coat. Then he began a long and
detailed lecture on the subject of music in general and fiddle-
playing in particular. He gave me to understand that the
fiddle was the best and finest of all instruments—there was no
instrument that ranked higher. Else why is the fiddle the chief
instrument in an orchestra, and not the trombone or the flute?
Because the fiddle is the mother of all instruments . . .

Thus Naftaltzi spoke, accompanying his words with motions
of his hands and large nose. I stood gaping at him, swallowing
every word that came out.

"The fiddle," Naftaltzi continued, apparently pleased with
his lecture, "the fiddle, you understand, is an instrument that
is older than all other instruments. The first fiddler in the world
was Tubal Cain or Methuselah, I am not sure which. You
may know, you study such things in *cheder*. The second fiddler
was King David. The third, a man named Paganini, also a
Jew. The best fiddlers have always been Jews. I can name you
a dozen. Not to mention myself . . . They say I don't play
badly, but how can I compare myself to Paganini? Paganini,
we are told, sold his soul to the devil for a fiddle. He never
would play for the great of the world—the kings and the princes
—no matter how much they gave him. He preferred to play
for the common people in the taverns and the villages, or even
in the woods for the beasts and birds. Ah, what a fiddler
Paganini was!"

Suddenly he turned around: "Fellow artists—to your instruments!"

Thus Naftaltzi called out to his band of children, who gathered about him immediately, each with his own instrument.
Naftaltzi himself struck the table with his bow, threw a sharp
look at each child separately and at all of them at once, and
the concert began. They went at it with such fury that I was

almost knocked off my feet. Each one tried to outdo the other, but loudest of all played a little boy named Chemeleh, a thin child with a running nose and bare spindly legs. Chemeleh played a strange instrument—some sort of a sack—and when he blew, it gave out an unearthly shriek, like a cat when its tail is stepped on. With his bare foot Chemeleh marked time and all the while watched me out of his small impish eyes and winked at me as if to say, "I am doing well, ain't I?" . . . But hardest of all worked Naftaltzi himself. He both played and conducted, working with his hands, his feet, his nose, his eyes, his whole body; and if anyone made a mistake, he gritted his teeth and yelled out:

"*Forte,* you fool! *Forte, fortissimo!* Count, stupid—count! One, two, three! One, two, three!"

I arranged with Naftaltzi Bezborodka to take three lessons a week, an hour and a half each time, for two *rubles* a month. I begged him over and over to keep this a secret, or I would get into trouble. He gave me his word of honor that he would breathe it to no one.

"We are people," he said gravely, adjusting his collar, "of small means, but when it comes to honor and integrity, we have more than the richest of the rich. By the way—can you spare me a few *groschen?*"

I pulled a *ruble* out of my pocket. Naftaltzi took it from me like a professor—very refined—with the tips of his fingers. Then he called Mother Eve, and hardly looking at her, said, "Here, get something for dinner."

Mother Eve took the money from him with both hands and every one of her fingers, inspected it carefully, and said, "What shall I buy?"

"Anything you want," he said with a show of indifference.

"Get a few rolls—two or three herring—a sausage. And don't forget—an onion, some vinegar and oil—and, maybe, a bottle of brandy . . ."

When the food was laid out on the table the crowd fell on it with such gusto as after a fast. Watching them made me so ravenous that when they asked me to join them I couldn't refuse. And I don't know when I enjoyed any food as much as I did that meal.

When we were through, Bezborodka winked at the crowd, signaled for them to reach for their instruments, and I was treated to another concert, this time an "original composition." This they played with such verve and spirit that my ears rang and my head swam and I left the house drunk with Naftaltzi Bezborodka's "composition."

All that day in *cheder* the rabbi, the boys and the books all danced before my eyes and the music rang incessantly in my ears. At night I dreamed of Paganini riding the devil. He hit me over the head with his fiddle. I woke screaming, my head splitting, and I began to babble—I don't know what. Later my older sister Pessel told me that I was out of my head. What I said made no sense—crazy words like "composition," "Paganini," "the devil" . . . Another thing my sister told me was that while I was sick someone came to ask about me— somebody from Naftaltzi the musician—a barefoot boy. He was chased away and told never to come back.

"What did that fiddler's boy want from you?" my sister nagged, but I held my tongue.

"I don't know. I don't know a thing. What are you talking about?"

"How does it look?" my mother said. "You are a grown boy already—we are trying to arrange a match for you—and you pick yourself friends like these. Barefoot fiddlers! What have you got to do with musicians anyway? What did Naftaltzi's boy want of you?"

"Which Naftaltzi?" I asked innocently. "What musicians?"

"Look at him!" my father broke in. "He doesn't know a thing. Poor little fellow! At your age I was engaged a long time already, and you are still playing games with children. Get dressed and go to *cheder*. And if you meet Hershel Beltax on the way and he asks what was the matter with you, tell him you had a fever. Do you hear what I said? A fever."

I didn't begin to understand. What did I have to do with Hershel Beltax? And why did I have to tell him about a fever? In a few weeks my question was answered.

Hershel Beltax (he was called that because he and his father and his grandfather had all worked for the tax collector) was a man with a round little belly, a short red beard, small moist eyes and a broad white forehead—the mark of a wise man. He had the reputation in town of being an intelligent man, accomplished and learned—up to a certain point—in the *Torah*. He was a fine writer—that is, he had a clear handwriting. It was said that at one time his writings were known all over the countryside. And besides that he had money and a daughter, an only daughter, with red hair and moist eyes—the exact image of him. Her name was Esther, she was called by a nickname—Flesterl. She was timid and delicate, and terribly afraid of us schoolboys because we teased her all the time. When we met her we sang this song:

Esther, Flester,
Where is your sister?

What was so terrible about that? Nothing, it seemed to

me, and yet when Esther heard it she covered her ears and ran off crying. She would hide in her room and not go out on the street for days.

But that was a long time ago when she was a child. Now she was a grown girl with long red braids and went about dressed in the latest fashion. My mother was very fond of her. "Gentle as a dove," she used to say. Sometimes on Saturday Esther used to come to visit my sister and when she saw me she would turn even redder than she was and drop her eyes. And my sister would call me over and start asking me questions—and watch us both to see how we acted.

One day—into the *cheder* walked my father with Hershel Beltax, and behind them trailed Reb Sholom-Shachne, the matchmaker, a man with a curly black beard, a man with six fingers, as people used to say. Seeing such guests, the rabbi, Reb Zorach, grabbed his coat and put on his hat in such a hurry that one of his earlocks was caught behind his ear, and his skullcap stuck out from under his hat, and his cheeks began to flame. We could see that something unusual was about to happen. Lately Reb Sholom-Shachne the matchmaker had been coming to the *cheder* frequently and each time he came he called the rabbi out of the room and there through the doorway we could see them whispering together, shrugging their shoulders, gesturing with their hands—ending up with a sigh.

"Well, it's the same old story. If it's to be, it will be. Regardless."

Now when these guests came in, the rabbi, Reb Zorach, was so confused he didn't know what to do or where to seat them. He grabbed hold of a low bench on which his wife used to salt the meat, and carried it around the room with him, till he finally put it down and sat on it himself. But he quickly jumped up and said to his guests, "Here is a bench. Won't you sit down?"

"That's all right, Reb Zorach," said my father. "We just came in for a minute. We'd like to hear my son recite something—out of the Bible." And he inclined his head toward Hershel Beltax.

"Surely, why not?" said the rabbi, and picking up the Bible he handed it to Hershel Beltax, with a look that said, "Here—do what you can with it."

Hershel Beltax took the Bible like a man who knew what he was doing, bent his head sideways, shut one eye, shuffled the pages and handed it to me open at the first paragraph of the *Song of Songs.*

"The *Song of Songs?*" said Reb Zorach with a smile, as though to say, "You couldn't find something harder?" "The *Song of Songs,*" says Hershel Beltax, "is not as easy as you think. One has to understand it."

"That's not a lie," said Reb Sholom-Shachne, the matchmaker, with a laugh.

The rabbi beckons to me. I walk up to the table, and begin to chant in a loud voice, with a fine rhythm:

"The *Song of Songs!* A song above all other songs. Other songs have been sung by a prophet, but this song was sung by a prophet who was the son of a prophet. Other songs have been sung by a sage, but this was sung by a sage who was the son of a sage. Other songs have been sung by a king. This was sung by a king who was the son of a king."

While I sang I watched my examiners and saw on the face of each of them a different expression. On my father's face I saw great pride and joy. On the rabbi's face was fear lest I make a mistake. His lips silently repeated each word. Hershel Beltax sat with his head bent sideways, his beard between his lips, one eye shut, and the other raised aloft, listening with a very knowing look. Reb Sholom-Shachne the matchmaker did not take his eyes off Hershel Beltax the whole time. He sat with his body bent forward, swaying back and forth along with me, interrupting me with a sound that was part exclamation, part laugh, part a cough, pointing his fingers at me:

"When I said he knew it I really meant he knew it."

A few weeks later plates were broken, and I became engaged to Hershel Beltax's daughter, Flesterl.

Sometimes it happens that a person ages more in one day than in ten years. When I became engaged I suddenly felt grown up—seemingly the same boy and yet not the same. From the smallest boy to the rabbi himself they all treated me with respect. After all, I was a young man engaged to be married—and I had a watch! No longer did my father scold me—and as for whippings—that was out of the question. How could you whip a young man who wore a gold watch? It would be a shame and a disgrace. Once a boy named Eli who, like me, was engaged to be married, received a whipping in *cheder* because he was caught skating on the ice with some peasant boys. The whole town talked about it, and when his fiancée learned of the scandal she cried so long that her parents broke the engagement. And the young man, Eli, was so heartbroken and so ashamed that he wanted to throw himself into the river. Fortunately, the water was frozen over . . .

Such a calamity befell me, too, but not over a whipping, and not over skating on ice, but over a fiddle. And here is the story:

In our tavern we had a frequent guest, Tchetchek, the bandleader, whom we called Colonel. He was a strapping fellow, tall, with a large, round beard and sinister eyebrows. His speech was a mixture of several languages, and when he spoke he moved his eyebrows up and down. When he lowered his eyebrows his face became black as night, and when he raised them, his face glowed like the sun, because under those thick eyebrows were a pair of eyes that were bright blue and full of laughter. He wore a uniform with gold buttons and that was why we called him Colonel. He came to our tavern frequently—not because he was a heavy drinker, but because my father used to make a raisin wine—"the best—and rarest— Hungarian wine" that Tchetchek could hardly praise enough. He would put his enormous hand on my father's thin shoulder and roar in his queer mixed language:

"Herr Kellermeister, you have the best Hungarian wine in the world. There is no such wine even in Budapest, *pred- bozhe.*"

Tchetchek was very friendly with me. He praised me for my stories and liked to ask questions like: "Who was Adam? Who was Isaac? Who was Joseph?"

"You mean—*Yosef?*" I would say.

"I mean Joseph."

"*Yosef,*" I corrected him again.

"To us he is Joseph, to you he is *Yosef,*" he would say and pinch my cheek. "Joseph or *Yosef, Yosef* or Joseph, it's all the same, all equal—*wszystko yedno.*"

But when I became engaged Tchetchek's attitude also changed. Instead of treating me like a child he began to talk to me as to an equal, to tell me stories of the army and of musicians. (The Colonel had wonderful stories to tell but no one had time to listen except me.) Once, when he was talking about music, I questioned him, "What instrument does the Colonel play?"

"All instruments," he said, and raised his eyebrows.

"The fiddle too?" I asked, and his face became in my eyes the face of an angel.

"Come to my house some day," he said, "and I will play for you."

"I can only come on the Sabbath. But please, Colonel, no one must know." *"Przed bohem,"* he said fervently and raised his eyebrows.

Tchetchek lived far off beyond the town in a small white cottage with small windows and brightly painted shutters, surrounded by a garden full of bright, yellow sunflowers that carried themselves as proudly as lilies or roses. They bent their heads a little, swayed in the breeze and beckoned to me, "Come to us, young man, come to us. Here is space, here is freedom, here it is bright and fresh, warm and cheerful." And after the stench and heat and dust of the town, the noise and turmoil of the crowded *cheder,* I was glad to come, for here was space and freedom, here it was bright and fresh, warm and cheerful. I felt like running, leaping, yelling, singing, or like throwing myself on the ground with my face deep in the fragrant grass. But that is not for you, Jewish children. Yellow sunflowers, green grass, fresh air, the clean earth, the clear sky, these are not for you . . .

When I came to the gate the first time, I was met by a shaggy, black dog with fiery, red eyes, who jumped at me with such force that I was almost knocked over. Luckily he was tied to a rope. When Tchetchek heard me yell he came running out of the house, without his uniform on, and told the dog to be quiet. Then he took me by the hand and led me up to the black dog. He told me not to be afraid. "Here, pat him—he won't hurt you." And taking my hand he passed it over the dog's fur, calling him odd names in a kindly voice. The dog dropped his tail, licked himself all over and gave me a look that said, "Lucky for you my master is standing here, or you would be leaving without a hand."

Having recovered from my fright, I entered the house with the Colonel and there I was struck dumb: all the walls were covered with guns, and on the floor lay a skin with the head of a lion—or maybe a leopard—with fierce teeth. The lion didn't bother me so much—he was dead. But those guns—all those guns! I didn't enjoy the fresh plums and juicy apples with which my host treated me. I couldn't keep my eyes away from the walls. But later, when Tchetchek took out of its red case a small round fiddle with an odd belly, spread over it his large round beard and placed on it his huge powerful hand and passed the bow over it a few times, and the first melody poured out, I forgot in one instant the black dog, the fierce lion and the loaded guns. I saw only Tchetchek's spreading beard, his overhanging eyebrows, I saw only a round fiddle with an odd belly, and fingers which danced over the strings with such speed that it was hard to imagine where so many fingers came from.

Then Tchetchek himself disappeared—with his spreading beard, his thick eyebrows, and his wonderful fingers—and I saw nothing in front of me. I only heard a singing, a sighing, a weeping, a sobbing, a talking, a roaring—all sorts of strange sounds that I had never heard in my life before. Sounds sweet as honey, smooth as oil, kept pouring without end straight into my heart, and my soul soared far far away into another world, into a paradise of pure sound.

"Would you like some tea?" calls out Tchetchek, putting down the fiddle and slapping me on the back.

I felt as though I had fallen from the seventh heaven down to earth again.

After that I visited Tchetchek every Saturday to listen to his playing. I went straight to the house, not afraid of anyone, and I even became so familiar with the black dog that he would wag his tail when he saw me, and try to lick my hand. But I wouldn't allow that. "Let's be friends at a distance," I said.

At home no one knew where I spent my Saturdays. No one stopped me. After all, I was not a child any more.

And they wouldn't have known until now if a fresh calamity had not occurred—a great calamity which I shall now describe.

Who should care if a young fellow takes a Sabbath walk by himself a short distance out of town? Whose business is it? Apparently there are people who care, and one such person was Ephraim Klotz, a busybody who knew what was cooking in every pot. He made it his business to know. This man watched me closely, followed me, found out where I was going, and later swore with many pious oaths that he had seen me at the Colonel's house eating pork and smoking cigarettes on the Sabbath.

Every Saturday when I was on my way to Tchetchek's I would meet him on the bridge, walking along in a sleeveless, patched, summer coat that reached to his ankles. He walked with his arms folded behind him, his overcoat flapping, humming to himself in a thin voice.

"A good Sabbath," I would say to him.

"Good Sabbath," he would reply. "Where is the young man going?"

"Just for a walk," I said.

"For a walk? Alone?" he repeated, with a meaningful smile . . .

One afternoon when I was sitting with Tchetchek and drinking tea, we heard the dog barking and tearing at his rope. Looking out of the window, I thought I saw someone small and dark with short legs running out of sight. From his way of running I could swear it was Ephraim Klotz.

That night, when I got home, I saw Ephraim Klotz sitting at the table. He was talking with great animation and laughing his odd little laugh that sounded like dried peas pouring out of a dish. Seeing me, he fell silent and began to drum with his short fingers on the table. Opposite him sat my father, his face pale, twisting his beard and tearing hairs out one by one —a sign that he was angry.

"Where are you coming from?" asked my father, with a glance at Ephraim Klotz.

"Where should I be coming from?" I said.

"Where have you been all day?" said my father.

"Where should I be all day? In *shul*."

"What did you do there all day?"

"What should I be doing there? Studying . . ."

"What were you studying?" said my father.

"What should I be studying? The *Gamorah* . . ."

"Which *Gamorah*?" said my father.

At this point Ephraim Klotz laughed his shrill laugh and my father could stand it no more. He rose from his seat and leaning over, gave me two resounding, fiery slaps in the face. My mother heard the commotion from the next room and came running in . . .

"Nochem," she cried, "God be with you! What are you doing? The boy is engaged to be married. Suppose his father-in-law hears of this?"

My mother was right. My future father-in-law heard the whole story. Ephraim repeated it to him himself. It was too good to keep.

The next day the engagement was broken and I was a privileged person no more. My father was so upset that he became ill and stayed in bed for days. He would not let me come near him, no matter how much my mother pleaded for me.

"The shame of it," he said. "The disgrace. That is worst of all."

"Forget about it," my mother begged. "God will send us

another match. Our lives won't be ruined by this. Perhaps it was not his lot."

Among those who came to visit my father while he was ill was the bandmaster. When my father saw him, he took off his skullcap, sat up in bed, and extending an emaciated hand, said to him:

"Ah, Colonel, Colonel . . ."

More he could not say because his voice became choked with tears and he was seized with a fit of coughing. This was the first time in my life that I had seen my father cry. My heart ached and my soul went out to him. I stood staring out of the window, swallowing tears. How I regretted the trouble I had caused!

Silently I swore to myself never, never to disobey my father again, never to cause him such grief, never in this world.

No more fiddles.

The Day before Yom Kippur

(Sketches of Disappearing Types)

I. NOAH-WOLF THE BUTCHER

IF THE day before *Yom Kippur* were three times as long as
it is, it would not be long enough for Noah-Wolf the butcher
to finish his work in time for the evening services.

And this is his work: he has to apologize to a townful of
people for his year's misdeeds. He has to go to all the customers
who buy meat from him, all the neighbors who live in the
same street with him or have their shops near his, or sit close
to him in the butchers' synagogue.

There is not a person in our town with whom Noah-Wolf
has not had an argument at one time or another. Not that
Noah-Wolf is such an evil person, but he undoubtedly has,
as he himself says, an ugly temper. He simply has to fight
with people.

If you come into his shop for some meat, you are met with
a pailful of cold water. And he cannot even tell you why.

A housewife comes in: "Reb Noah-Wolf, do you have any
fresh meat today?"

And he answers: "How should I have fresh meat? If you
want rotten meat, you can get it."

Or: "Noah-Wolf, give me a good portion."

"I'll give you just the kind of portion you deserve."

Or this: "What kind of carcass are you giving me, Noah-Wolf! Look at it!"

"What does a carcass like you know about carcasses?"

That is how Noah-Wolf treats his customers, the housewives themselves. So how would you expect him to treat the servant girls? When one of them has to go to his shop, she curses her fate. She knows what a greeting she can expect. Either he will slap her across the face with a beef tongue, or he'll fit her marketbasket over her head, or he'll simply chase her out.

"Get out of here! Go to some other shop! There are enough butchers without me!"

Nevertheless one thing has nothing to do with another. Noah-Wolf the butcher may be stubborn and eccentric, and yet his customers won't go anywhere else, because they know that he is the most honorable butcher in town. They know that his scale is true and that he keeps his word. If he tells you that the meat was slaughtered yesterday, you know that it is so. And if he promises you some sweetbreads, or a piece of lung, or a neat's foot for Saturday, you can sleep in peace. The lung or the foot is as good as yours. Furthermore, he will never connive with your servant girl to rob you behind your back. And he won't combine with other butchers to raise their prices. That is why the servant girls slander him, and the other butchers would like to drown him in a spoonful of water. He sticks in their throats like a bone. He is a stubborn man. If he makes up his mind on anything, he's like an ox being dragged to slaughter. You can't make him budge.

And he even looks like an ox. He is tall and broad and red-faced, and his hands are enormous. When he raises his cleaver to split a side of meat he does it as ferociously as if the ox or cow had committed some crime and had been condemned to be chopped to pieces by him in person.

"That man is a murderer!" they say in our town, and there are grown people who are actually afraid of him.

But if all year long he gets under your skin, he changes with the coming of the New Year. Then you would hardly recognize him. He becomes someone else, pious, God-fearing, virtuous, and sees omens in everything. He stops fighting with the other butchers, becomes soft as butter toward his customers, is considerate to the servant girls, becomes so unctuous you could almost spread him over a boil. Even when he chops his meat now he does it differently, not murderously as before, but gently, mercifully. A different Noah-Wolf altogether.

The day before *Yom Kippur* he locks up very early (he had said his morning prayers when most of us were still asleep), puts on his holiday gabardine, and goes from house to house, to all his customers and neighbors, friends and acquaintances, to offer his apologies, to ask for pardon for the year's misdeeds.

"Good *yom-tev*," he says. "If anything I have said offended you, I want to apologize, and wish you a happy New Year."

And they say to him: "The same to you, Noah-Wolf. May God pardon us all."

And they invite him to sit down and they treat him to a piece of holiday torte.

II. EZRIEL THE FISHERMAN

Since the world was created, you have never seen as ill-tempered a creature as Ezriel the fisherman.

An ill-tempered man with angry eyes, thick eyebrows, bristling mustache, and a beard that looks as if it has been pasted on. And he wears a quilted jacket summer and winter, with the fringes of his *tallis-kot'n* sticking out underneath. And he smells of raw fish a mile away.

All week long you don't see him at all. But before every Sabbath and every holiday he appears in the marketplace with his wagon piled high with fish. On top of the wagon sits a girl with pockmarked face, watching the fish. And his wife, Maita, a heavy, swollen woman, stands alongside the wagon with a stick and watches the fish.

"Fish—fish—fresh and quivering! Women! Fish for Sabbath!"

That is the way Ezriel the fisherman announces his wares across the marketplace, in his loud, familiar chant, and he never takes an eye off the women who have already crowded around his wagon and laid siege to it from all sides, clutching the fish by the heads, peering under the gills, poking at the eyes or prodding at the bellies to see if the fish is fresh. These liberties Ezriel hates and despises like something un-*kosher,* and he chases the women away.

"Away from here! You've pawed over them long enough already!"

This he hurls at them in a quick undertone, and then, once more to the world at large, in his loud, clear chant:

"Fish—fish—fresh and quivering! Women! Fish for Sabbath!"

Every woman, whether a housewife or a servant girl, is treated alike by Ezriel the fisherman. He watches her like a hawk. He does not suspect anyone of being a thief, but he knows that when it comes to fish, you can never tell. The richest, most honorable, most charitable woman is frequently torn by the desire to make off with a good, fresh fish if no one is looking. "Fish," he says, "is a temptation that is hard for a woman to resist."

Every year at least one scandal takes place around Ezriel's

wagon. He slaps some woman across the face with a wet
and shiny pickerel. From all directions men and women come
running up; there is noise and confusion. The crowd puts in
a word for the woman, gives her advice, tells her to file a
complaint with the Justice of the Peace, or have Ezriel dragged
off to the rabbi. But since the pain is moral rather than physical,
it soon wears off, and the whole affair comes to nothing.

Most of the women know him already. They would think
no more of edging too close to his fish than to the gold and
precious stones under a king's guard.

"How much are your rubies and emeralds today?" a woman
may ask, standing with her basket at some distance and
pointing with her little finger at the wagon.

"I deal in fish, not rubies!" Ezriel answers proudly, without even condescending to give the woman a glance with his
angry eyes. And once more he lets out his call to the world
at large:

"Fish—fish—fresh and quivering! Women! Fish!"

"An apoplectic man!" the women say of him. They would
much rather not have anything to do with him, but that is
impossible. There is not another fisherman in town, so what
can one do? Lie down on the ground and die? Or live through
the Sabbath without fish? But that is even worse than dying,
for if a woman dies she knows she is dead: it's all over. But
if she comes home without fish for Saturday, then she has he
husband's wrath to contend with. And that is worse than
dying.

"I wish something terrible would happen to him!"

That is what the women say when *Yom Kippur* eve comes
around and they rush off to the marketplace with their
baskets, afraid that they might be too late, because the day
before *Yom Kippur* Ezriel is in the habit of getting up so early
that God himself is still in bed. And when other people are

just getting ready for their morning prayers, Ezriel is through
with everything and is all dressed up for the holiday. His
heavy, quilted jacket has been put away and he wears the
coarse, shiny, black gabardine that is seen only on the Sabbath and high holidays, but which nevertheless is saturated
through and through with the odor of raw fish.

Ezriel begins his fast earlier than anyone. Earlier than anyone he comes to the synagogue that afternoon, takes his
place close to the back wall, covers his head with his prayer
shawl, and stands without rest for twenty-four hours. He
won't sit down even for a minute. He prays quietly, so that no
one can hear a word. He weeps a great deal, but no one can
ever see a tear.

But that is in the evening. Before that, all day long, he goes
around the town to his customers, bringing his apologies, asking their pardon.

"If anything I have said to you during the year offended
you, I want to apologize, and wish you a happy New Year."

And they say to him:

"The same to you, Reb Ezriel. May God pardon us all."

And they invite him to sit down and they treat him to a
piece of holiday torte.

III. GETZI THE GOVERNOR

Getzi the Governor—that is what we always called the
shammes, the sexton, of the old synagogue.

Everywhere, in all the synagogues of the world, a *shammes*
may be a *shammes.* But Getzi, the *shammes* of our old synagogue, is more like a member of the board of governors than
a *shammes.* Did I say a member of the board? He acts like
the president of the board!

Getzi does not permit any secular business in the synagogue. He says that a synagogue is a place of worship. If you want to talk business you can go to the marketplace. If you want to discuss politics there is a bath house. Under no conditions will he let you talk during an intermission or a recess. Getzi is a man who shows no respect for anyone. You can be the holder of a pew by the eastern wall, you can have seventeen silver stripes on your *tallis,* he won't debase himself before you. You can be the richest person in town, Reb Joshua Hershel himself, if you say a single word out loud, you hear his hand come pounding down on the table, and a cry of "Qui-et!" so loud that you are almost deafened.

Or try to take one of the sacred tomes from the synagogue bookshelf, and forget to bring it back in time! You'll be put in your place soon enough.

Or if on the Sabbath you pledge a half pound of candles for the synagogue, or eighteen *kopeks* for the poor fund, and then forget to give it! You might as well go bankrupt, or leave everything behind and rush off to America!

Or try to send Getzi on an errand that has nothing to do with the synagogue. This is what you'll hear: "Do *you* have feet? Then go yourself!"

That's the kind of man Getzi is.

The only ones who dare to be impudent with Getzi are the small fry. Inquisitive youngsters, small boys barely learning their alphabet, mischief makers, pranksters of all kinds, these make life miserable for him. The things they do to him would make anyone shudder. They turn over the prayer stands when no one is looking, they let water out of the washbowl, tie knots in the towels, let tallow drip on all the holy books, and tear *Yekum Purkon* out of all the prayer books, so that no matter which one you open the prayer is missing.

These little troublemakers shortened Getzi's life, they taught him the terrors of Gehenna. He kept constant watch; maybe he would catch one of them in the act. And when he caught one, he evened accounts for everything the whole band had ever done. To emerge from his grasp with only a light bruise, a black eye, or an ear that was only partly pulled off, that was luck indeed. Getzi hated drawn-out affairs, worthless investigations and formal trials. No matter whom he caught, a rich man's child or an orphan in rags, it made no difference.

Getzi knows all about slapping. When you feel his hand you behold your grandfather in Paradise. A powerful man, from a family known for its strength, although to look at him you would have hesitated to give two broken *kopeks* for him. Lean, dried up, skin and bones. But his sidelocks were thick and black, and he himself was dark as a Tartar, with fierce, black eyes, hollow cheeks, a crooked nose, and black drooping mustache. All these things taken together made him look either as if he was about to sneeze but was trying not to, or as if he had something to tell you but was keeping it to himself, or simply as if he were an ill-tempered, evil man.

The most evil man in town, was what a lot of people called him. A worm-eaten, spiteful creature who knew no master and did whatever he pleased. If he wanted to open the synagogue, he opened it. If he wanted to shut it, he shut it. When winter came, you had to get down and beg him to start the fire. But when he did make up his mind to start it, you thought you were in a steam bath.

Let some wandering pauper beg with his last breath to be allowed to spend the night in the synagogue. "A synagogue is not a poorhouse," says Getzi, and drives the poor man out without a trace of pity.

And when the High Holidays come around, Getzi rules in the synagogue with a strong and ruthless hand. If he has conceived a dislike for you, you will never get his permission

to let your son or son-in-law sit where you would like to
have him. You can resign yourself to this: he will sit where
Getzi wants him to. And if you go up to the trustees with your
complaint, you'll get this answer: "Go to the governor."

And you know that what they mean is Getzi the *shammes.*
To his face you will call him Getzi, but behind his back he is
the Governor.

It's like that all the time. During *Succos,* if Getzi does not
bring the *esrog* to you on time and you complain, he says:
"You can wait a minute, can't you? I waited longer for you!"

So once more you bring your charges to the trustees. But
this is the only answer you get:

"What can a person do with a governor?"

All year long it's the same. Getzi provides the materials
for all the holidays, candles for *Hannukah,* noisemakers for
Purim, matzo for Passover, and greens for *Shevuos.* Getzi
runs the whole town, rules over it like a king. Like a king?
Like a conqueror! All of us have to endure it. The only time
when people dare to talk is on the Sabbath or a holiday, at
dusk, when we sit and wait in the gathering darkness for
the evening services. Then we can say something. For a few
minutes we do not have to be afraid of the *shammes,* we can
talk freely and openly. And no matter what we talk about,
we come finally to the Getzi captivity, which seems worse
to us than the Babylonian captivity we have heard about. We
ask each other, "How long? Till when? How long will this
captivity last?" And that is as far as we go. What else can
we do? We Jews have suffered under so many evil kings
and governors!

But there is one day of the year when Governor Getzi sus-
pends his tyranny. Not a whole day, but a half day, really
only a few hours. That is the day before *Yom Kippur,* right
after the morning prayers, and before people start coming

for the high services, when Getzi once more becomes king. But during those few hours he forgets that he is *shammes,* forgets he is governor. He is dressed in his holiday best, and he runs from house to house, stops everywhere, with these words:

"If anything I have said to you at any time offended you, forgive me. And may you have a happy New Year."

And he gets this reluctant answer: "You too, you too."

And they invite him to sit down and they give him a piece of holiday torte.

Three Little Heads

I OFFER you a present for *Shevuos,* a picture of three little heads, three wonderfully fine heads of three poor, tattered, barefoot Jewish children. All three little heads are dark, with curly hair and eyes big and luminous that stare at you with wonder and always seem to ask the question: "Why?" You look back at them with wonder and a feeling of guilt as if somehow you are to blame for their having been created, three more superfluous creatures on the face of the earth.

The three little heads—Avremchik, Moisechik and Dvorka —are two brothers and their little sister. Avremchik and Moisechik—that was what their father, Peiseh the boxmaker, called them, in the Russian manner. If he hadn't been afraid of what his wife would say, and if he weren't such a bitterly poor man, he'd have changed his own name too, from Peiseh the boxmaker to Piotr Pereplotchik. But since he was afraid of his wife, and since he was as poor as he could be, he remained, for the time being, Peiseh the boxmaker, till the time should some day come, the happy time when everything would be different, as Bebel said and as Karl Marx said, and as all good and wise men say. But until that lucky time arrived, he would have to stand from morning till dark, cutting cardboard and pasting boxes and containers.

So Peiseh the boxmaker stands on his feet all day and cuts cardboard and puts together boxes, and sings songs, some of the old ones and some new ones, some Jewish songs and some not a bit Jewish—many of them not a bit Jewish—happy sad songs with a sad happy tune.

"Will you ever stop singing those outlandish songs? You must have fallen in love with them! Since you have come to the big city you are not a Jew any more."

The three—Avremchik, Moisechik and Dvorka—were born and grew up in the same place, between the wall and the oven in a single crowded room. Every day the three saw the same things before them: their jolly father who cut the cardboard, pasted boxes and sang songs; and their worried, exhausted mother, who cooked and baked, swept and scrubbed and was never finished. Both were always at work, the mother at the oven, the father at his boxes. Who would ever need so many boxes? What would they do with all these boxes? The whole world must be full of boxes. That's how it seemed to the three little heads, and they waited for their father to get so many boxes ready that he would have to pile them on his head, and fill both arms with them—maybe a hundred thousand boxes—and then go out with them. Later he came back without any boxes—with no boxes at all, but with a little money for their mother, and with oddly shaped buns, *beigel* and candy for the children.

How good their father was to them, how wonderfully good! Their mother was good too, but she was the one to scold them. Rushing between washtub and oven, she pushed them out of her way, gave their hands a slap, boxed an ear. She did not want them to upset things playing house. She did not want Avremchik to cut up the scraps of cardboard that fell from his father's work table, or Moisechik to steal paste from the pot, or Dvorka to make mud cakes. Their mother always wanted them to sit quietly and sedately. Their mother forgot that young heads worked all the time, that young spirits tore themselves, pulled with all their might, strained toward—toward what?

Toward the outdoors, toward the light, toward the window—
the window . . .

One window—that's all there was. One small window. The
three little heads try to reach the one small window—and
what can they see there? A wall, a high, broad, gray damp
wall, always damp, always dripping, even in summer. Does the
sun ever come in here at all? Of course the sun comes in—
sometimes. That is, not the sun itself, but a glimmering reflection of the sun. And when that happens it is a time for rejoicing. The three little heads crowd against the small window,
look up, way up, and glimpse a long, narrow, blue strip, like
a long blue ribbon.

"There, do you see that, children? That's the sky!"

That is Avremchik speaking. Avremchik knows. Avremchik
goes to *cheder*. He is already studying the alphabet. The *cheder*
is not so far—two houses away, or rather, two doors away. Oh,
what stories Avremchik tells about *cheder*! Avremchik says
that he himself saw, on his word of honor, a huge brick
building covered with small windowpanes from top to bottom.
He swears that he saw with his own eyes, on his word of honor,
a chimney, a tall chimney reaching to the sky, with smoke pouring out of it, and machines that run by themselves without
anybody operating them, and carts that move without horses.
And other such fabulous tales Avremchik brings back from his
trips to *cheder*, and swears, as his mother swears, on his word
of honor. And Moisechik and Dvorka listen to him and sigh
with envy, because Avremchik knows everything—everything.

For instance, Avremchik knows that a tree grows. Of course
he himself has never seen a tree grow any more than they have
—there are no trees on their street—but he knows (he heard it
in *cheder*) that trees bear fruit. And that is why when you
eat fruit you say, "Blessed art thou, O Lord our God, King of
the universe, who createst the fruit of the tree." Avremchik

knows (what doesn't he know?) that potatoes, for instance, or cucumbers, or onions or garlic grow on the ground. And that is why for these things you say, "Blessed art thou, O Lord our God, King of the universe, who createst the fruit of the earth." Avremchik knows everything! But he doesn't know how or in what manner these things grow either. For on their street there is no field, no garden, there are no trees, there's not a blade of grass—not one! On their street there are only tall buildings, gray walls, high chimneys pouring smoke, and every building is covered with windowpanes, thousands of little windowpanes, and inside the buildings are machines that run by themselves, and carts that move without horses. And aside from that there is nothing, nothing.

Even a bird is rarely seen. Sometimes a sparrow blunders into the neighborhood and the sparrow is as gray as the walls themselves. It pecks once or twice at the cobblestones, rises and flies away. And chickens, ducks, geese? Once in a great while they have a quarter of a chicken for Saturday, chicken with a pale scrawny leg. How many legs does a chicken have? Obviously four. Just like a horse. That is Avremchick's opinion, and Avremchik knows everything.

Sometimes their mother comes from market bringing a chicken's head with glazed filmy eyes. "It's dead," says the older Avremchik, and the three little heads look at each other with large dark eyes and sigh. Born and brought up in the great city, in the large buildings, in crowded quarters, the three children never had a chance to see anything alive—a hen, a cow, or any other creature except a cat. They have their own cat, a live one, a large cat, gray as the tall gray damp walls. The cat is their one joy. They play with it whenever they can. They tie a kerchief around its head and call it Auntie, and laugh uproariously.

But then their mother catches them at it and goes after them.

slaps one's hands, boxes another's ears, sends them back to their place behind the oven. The oldest, Avremchik, begins to talk and the younger ones listen, look up wide-eyed at their older brother, and listen. Avremchik says that their mother is right. He says that you're not supposed to play with a cat, because a cat is an unclean thing, an evil spirit. Avremchik knows everything, everything. Is there anything in the world that he doesn't know?

Avremchik knows everything. He knows that there is a land, a land far away, far, far away, that is called America. There in America they have many friends and relatives. There in America Jews have a better life and a happier one. Next year, or the year after, if all is well and someone sends them tickets from over there, they plan to go to America too. Without tickets you can't go, because there is an ocean you have to cross, and storms come up and toss the ship about. Avremchik knows everything.

Everything . . . Even what goes on in the next world. For instance, he knows that in the next world there is a Paradise —for Jews, of course. In that Paradise you'll find the most brilliant trees with all kinds of fruit, rivers flowing with all good things. Diamonds and precious stones are scattered over the streets; all you have to do is bend down and fill your pockets with them. And pious Jews sit day and night studying the holy books and enjoying the divine presence.

Avremchik tells them all these things, and the children's eyes sparkle and they envy their brother, who knows everything—even what happens in heaven. Avremchik swears that twice a year—one night of *Succos* and one night of *Shevuos*—the skies split open. Of course he has never seen the skies split open, because where they live you can't see the sky. But some of his schoolmates saw it happen. They swore that they saw it. And they wouldn't swear to a lie, would they? That would be a sin. And to prove that the skies really split open, Avremchik runs to his mother and pulls her skirts.

"Mama, isn't it true that this *Shevuos* at midnight the heavens will split open? Isn't it true?"

"Split open? My head is splitting open!" cries their mother, pulling herself away from his grasp.

And getting only this answer from their mother, Avremchik waits for their father to come home. Their father has gone to market with a stack of boxes.

"Children, what do you think he's going to bring us today?"

And the children begin to guess. They count on their fingers—everything that could possibly be at the market, everything that the eye could see and the heart could long for—all those oddly shaped buns and the *beigel* and the candy. But none of them guessed right, and I am afraid that none of you will guess it either. This time Peiseh the boxmaker brought neither buns nor *beigel* nor candy. He brought grasses, a bagful of grasses, strange, long, green, sweetsmelling grasses.

And the three little heads, Avremchik, Moisechik and Dvorka, surrounded their father.

"Oh, what is it? What did you bring? What is it?"

"Greens. Can't you see?"

"What do you mean—greens?"

"Greens for the holidays. It's *Shevuos* tonight. All Jews need greens for *Shevuos*."

"Where do you get them?"

"Where do you get them? M-m-m . . . You buy them at the market."

And saying this, he scatters the green, fragrant grasses over the freshly swept floor. He keeps some of it in his hands and fingers it and sniffs at it joyfully.

"Isn't it wonderful?"

"Wonderful for you!" says their mother. "A wonderful litter. Something new for the children to mess with."

That's how their mother takes it, as she goes on with her work, always worried, always burdened, just the opposite of their father.

And the three little heads look at their mother, look at their father, look at each other. And when their parents' backs are turned for a moment, they throw themselves on the floor, bury their heads in the fragrant grasses, fondle and kiss the rough blades that are called greens, and that Jews must have for their holidays, and that you buy at the market.

Everything can be found at the market, even greens. Their father brings them everything. There are so many things that Jews must have, and they get them. Even greens . . . Even greens . . .

A Country Passover

LET the winds blow. Let the storms rage. Let the world turn upside down. An old oak that has been standing since the beginning of time, whose roots have sunk deep into the earth, cares nothing about winds. He pays no heed to storms . . .

This old oak is not a symbol. It is a living person named Nachman Verebivker of Verebivka. He is tall and broad shouldered, a giant of a man. The whole town envies him his strength, and at the same time pokes fun at him. "How do you do?" they greet him. "How is your health today?" Nachman knows they are making fun of his height, so he bends his shoulders to make himself look smaller, a little less like a peasant. But it doesn't help. God has made him big.

Nachman is an old settler in Verebivka. The peasants who call him "Our Lachman" consider him a pretty good fellow, a man of intelligence, with whom they like to talk things over once in a while. They come to ask him what to do about their grain. "Lachman" has an almanac, so he ought to know if grain will be high or low this year. Sometimes they discuss affairs of the world. "Lachman" goes to town occasionally, he sees people, he knows what goes on outside of their village.

It is impossible to imagine Verebivka without Nachman Verebivker. Not only did his father Feitel Verebivker live and die there, but also his grandfather, Aryah, may he rest in peace. Aryah, a wise man and one who liked to play with words.

used to boast that the town was named Verebivka because
Aryah Verebivker lived there. Actually he had lived there long
before the town was ever known by that name. And do you
think he said this only to be talking? He was not that kind
of a man. What he was referring to was the decrees against
the Jews. Even in those days they spoke of driving the Jews out
of the villages; and not only talked but actually drove them.
All of them were driven out, that is, all but old Aryah Verebivker. It is said that the governor himself could do nothing
about it, for Aryah proved that according to law he could not be
forced out of Verebivka. He had lived there too long for that
. . . Oh, those men of old!

Naturally if one is such an exception as to be permitted to
live in Verebivka, one has a right to feel secure, and can
laugh at the whole world. Why does a man have to worry about
decrees, proclamations or statutes? Why does he have to pay
attention to the stories that the peasant Kurachka, his neighbor,
is always bringing from the district office? Kurachka was a
short, heavy-set man who wore a short, heavy jacket and tall
boots and a large watch on a silver chain, like a landed pro-
prietor. He was clerk in the district office and knew everyone's
troubles. In addition he read all the choice newspapers that
printed inflammatory stories against the Jews.

By nature Kurachka was not such a bad fellow. He was a
neighbor of Nachman's and supposedly a good friend. When
Kurachka had a toothache, "Lachman" gave him a remedy for
it. When Kurachka's wife was having a baby, "Lachman's"
wife acted as midwife. But for some time now, since he had
started reading those choice newspapers, Kurachka had become a changed man. The spirit of Esau had entered into
him. He was always coming with another piece of news:
a new governor had been appointed, a new proclamation had

been issued, a new decree had been announced about the Jews. And hearing this, the Jew Nachman felt heavy-hearted. A chill went through him, but he never let on that he was disturbed. He heard him out with a smile and showed him the palm of his hand, as though to say, "When hair grows on this hand, then I'll begin to worry."

Let governors change, let ministers issue proclamations. What did Nachman Verebivker of Verebivka care about that?

The living that Nachman Verebivker made was a fairly good one, though it did not compare to that of former years. When his grandfather Aryah was alive, times had been different. Ah, those times! Then all Verebivka, you might say, belonged to them. They owned a tavern, a store, a mill, a granary. They had everything they wanted. But that was long ago. Now they had lost all these things. No tavern, no store, no granary. Nothing, simply nothing. But if that was so, you ask, then why did he remain in Verebivka? Well, then, where else could he go? Should he go dig a hole for himself? If he sold his home he would not be a Verebivker any more. He would become an outcast, a stranger. This way, at least, he had a place he could call his own, a roof over his head, a home of his own. And behind his house he had a garden. His wife and daughters worked the garden themselves and all summer they had greens to eat and then potatoes for the whole winter and into spring. But you can't live on potatoes alone. You have to have bread, too, and bread there was none. So Nachman would take his stick and go through the countryside looking for something to buy. He never came back empty-handed. Whatever God sent his way he bought—some scrap metal, a basket of millet, an old sack, a hide. The hide he would stretch, air out, and take to Avrom-Eli the tanner in town. And from all these great transactions he either made a *ruble* or lost a *ruble*. That's what happens in business. *"Kupetz kak streletz,"* Nachman would say in Russian: "A businessman is like a hunter," and Avrom-Eli the tanner, a man with a bluish nose, and fingers that looked as though they had been dipped in ink, laughed at him for being so coarsened by country living that even his jokes were now of peasant origin.

Nachman agreed. He had become coarse. It was lucky that his grandfather could not see him now. What a man he had been! Also a giant of a man, but learned as well. He knew his prayers and all the Psalms by heart. Those men of old! And he, Nachman—what did he know? He could barely read his prayers; but that at least was something. His children would not know that much . . .

When he looked at his children, growing up big and burly like himself, and unable to read or write, also like himself, he grew sick at heart. And most of all was he saddened by the sight of his youngest child, his baby, a boy named Feitel, after his father, Feitel Verebivker. A fine, promising little boy, different from the others, smaller in build, more gentle and refined in appearance. A true child of Israel. And what a brain! Just one time, for the fun of it, they had shown him the letter *aleph* and the letter *beis* in a prayer book, and he never forgot which was which. And a child like that had to grow up in a village among calves and pigs, with Kurachka's son Pedka as his playmate. Feitel and Pedka rode a broomstick together, pretending it was a horse. Together they chased cats, dug caves, amused themselves as small children will. When Nachman saw his favorite child playing with the peasant boy, his heart was heavy within him.

Pedka was an alert child, too, the same age as Feitel, with a bright winning face and flaxen hair. They liked to be together and would do anything in the world for each other. All winter

long they remained indoors, close to the oven, but they longed
for each other and often stood by the window each hoping to see
the other. But now the winter, the long dark winter, was past.
The snow was gone. The sun shone. The wind had dried the
earth. The grass sprouted. And down below the hill the brook
gurgled once more. The little calf spread its nostrils and took
a deep breath. The rooster shut an eye and stood lost in thought.
Everything was coming to life again everywhere. Everything
was growing, rejoicing. It was Passover Eve. Neither Pedka
nor Feitel could be kept at home any longer. They burst out
into God's green world, took each other by the hand, and
raced toward the hill which beckoned to them both, "Come,
children, come." They leaped up toward the sunlight, which
greeted them both, "Come children, come." And when they
grew tired of running and leaping they sat down on God's
earth which knew neither Jew nor Gentile, but invited them
both, equally : "Come to me, children, come . . ."

There was so much to talk about after not having seen
each other all winter. Feitel boasted to his friend that he knew
almost the whole alphabet by heart. And Pedka boasted about
his new whip. Then Feitel said that they were having their
Passover Feast that very night. They had baked *matzos* for
the whole eight days and they had wine too. "Do you remember, Pedka, that *matzo* I brought you last year?" "*Matza?*"
said Pedka, and over his fair face there spread a broad smile,
as he remembered. "Would you like to taste some *matzo* now,
Pedka, fresh *matzo*?" What a question to ask. Would he like
some *matzo!* "Then let's go there," said Feitel, pointing to
the green hill that beckoned to them. They climbed up the
hill and stood enchanted, looking between their outspread
fingers at the rays of the sun, and then threw themselves on
the earth, still damp but already fragrant with the coming

growth. Feitel reached inside his shirt and pulled out a fresh round white *matzo* punctured with rows of tiny holes. He broke the *matzo* in half and divided it with his friend, "Well, what do you think about it?" he asked. But what could Pedka say with his mouth full of matzo that crackled between his teeth and melted on his tongue like snow? One more minute and the *matzo* was gone.

"Do you have any more?" asked Pedka, looking with his gray eyes into Feitel's shirt, and licking his lips like a cat that had swallowed the butter. "Would you like some more?" said Feitel, laughing and chewing his last crumbs, and looking at his friend out of mischievous black eyes. What a question! Would Pedka like more? "Then wait a while," said Feitel, "next year you'll get some more!" At this promise they both burst out laughing, and then without any signal, as if they had arranged it before, they threw themselves on the ground and rolled down hill faster and faster like two balls . . .

On the other side of the hill they stood up and watched the foaming brook, which ran off to the left, and they themselves ran to the right farther and farther across the fields which were not yet green but gave promise of becoming green soon. They could not smell the grass itself yet, but there was an odor in the air of coming grass. They walked on and on without words, as though in a dream, over the soft, sweet-smelling earth under the kindly sun. They seemed to be flying rather than walking, flying together with the birds that soared overhead, dipping and rising in the open sky which God had created for all living creatures.

Now they had come to the mill—the mill that belonged to the village mayor. Once it had belonged to Nachman Verebivker, but now it belonged to the mayor, a shrewd and rich man. He had tricked Nachman out of the mill and also a store

he had once owned in the village. Usually at this time of the
year the mill was turning, but now it stood still. There was
no wind. Strange to have no wind in the early spring. For
the boys this was a piece of good luck. Now they could examine the mill. There was plenty to see. They looked closely at
the stones, the wheels, and finally sat down and began to talk,
one of those conversations that has no beginning and no end.
Feitel told Pedka all the wonders of the city, where his father
had taken him once. He had gone to market, had seen stores,
not one store as in Verebivka, but many stores. Then in the
evening they had gone to the synagogue, because it was the
anniversary of his grandfather's death. "Do you understand,
Pedka, or don't you?"

Perhaps Pedka understood, but he wasn't listening. Suddenly
he dove in with a story of his own. He told Feitel how last
year he had seen a bird's nest high up in a tree, how he had
tried to climb the tree but couldn't, how he tried to reach
it with a stick, but it was too high and finally how he had
started to throw stones at the nest, and kept on throwing
them until he knocked down two small bleeding birds.

"Were they dead?" asked Feitel, incredulous, frightened.

"But they were so small," Pedka defended himself.

"But you killed them?"

"They had no feathers yet, they were nothing but tiny birds
with yellow bills and round little bellies."

"But you killed them. You killed them."

It was quite late when the two young comrades saw by the
sun that it was time to go home. Feitel had forgotten all about
the holiday that night and he suddenly remembered that his
mother still had to wash his head and put new clothes on
him. He jumped up, with Pedka after him, and together they
started for home, running and leaping with the same joy and

eagerness with which they had started out hours ago. And so that neither one should be left behind they took each other by the hand like true comrades and began to run toward the village as fast as they could. And when they arrived this is what they saw.

Nachman Verebivker's house was surrounded by all the people of the village. Kurachka, the clerk; Aponas, the mayor; the constable; the inspector; the sheriff—all the officials were there. Everybody was talking at once. Nachman and his wife stood in the middle of the crowd explaining, defending themselves, making all sorts of motions with their hands. Nachman stood with his shoulders bent, trying to make himself less conspicuous, wiping the sweat from his brow. Near by stood the older children with frightened faces. Suddenly the whole picture changed. Someone pointed at the two boys and the whole crowd—the clerk, the mayor, the police officers, all stood open-mouthed. Only Nachman looked over the crowd, straightened his broad shoulders, cried out, "Well?" and burst out laughing. His wife clapped her hands together and burst out crying.

The mayor, the constable, the inspector, the sheriff all stepped out of the crowd and turned to the boys.

"Where were you all this time, you . . . you . . ."

"Where were we? We were at the mill, that's where we were."

Both boys, Feitel and Pedka, got what they had coming and neither understood why. Feitel's father gave him a good beating so that he'd know better next time. But what should he know next time? And apparently out of pity his mother took him away from his father, gave him a few cuffs of her own and quickly began to wash his head for the holiday. Then she put on his new pants, his only new clothes for Passover, and as she did so she sighed. Why did she sigh? Feitel could not understand. But a little later he heard her say to his father. "Ah, if *Pesach* were only over already. I hope it goes by without trouble. For my part it could have gone by before it started." Feitel racked his brain but he could not understand why she wanted the holiday to be over before it had started. He couldn't understand his father's whipping or his mother's cuffs. What kind of Passover Eve was this?

Pedka understood as little as Feitel did. First of all his father Kurachka had grabbed him by the hair, swung him around savagely and given him a resounding slap for good measure. Pedka accepted the slaps like a philosopher. He was accustomed to them. A little later he heard his mother talking with the other peasant women. Such queer stories they told! There was one about a child who had been lured into a cellar by some Jews on the eve of Passover. They kept him there a day and a night and were just about to begin torturing him when people heard the screams of the child, came running from all directions, and rescued him. His body had already been pierced on four sides in the sign of the cross. The woman who told the story was a heavy, red-faced, blustering creature in a wide headdress. The other women in their brightly colored kerchiefs, stood around her in a circle, listening to the story, shaking their heads and crossing themselves. "Poor child, they said, "Poor little thing." And some of the women looked at him—at Pedka. And Pedka couldn't understand why they looked at him so strangely and what the story had to do with him and with Feitel. He could not understand why his father Kurachka had pulled him by the hair and slapped him in the bargain. He didn't enjoy hair pullings and slaps, but they didn't bother him too much. What did bother him was the reason for these things. Why—on this day of all days? Why?

"Well?" Feitel heard his father say joyfully to his mother the morning after Passover, as though some great good fortune had come to him. "You were afraid, just like a woman. Our Passover is gone, their Passover is gone, and nothing has happened."

"God be thanked," his mother answered, and still Feitel did not understand what his mother had been afraid of. And why they were so happy that Passover was gone. Wouldn't it have been much better if it had lasted and lasted? That afternoon when Feitel met Pedka outdoors he blurted everything out. He told how they had celebrated Passover and what good things they had to eat, and he described what all the good Passover dishes tasted like, and how sweet the wine was that they had drunk. Pedka listened solemnly, then looked inside Feitel's blouse. He was still dreaming about the *matzo* he had tasted the other day. Suddenly a shrill voice was heard calling, "Hvedka—H-vedka!"

That was Pedka's mother calling him for dinner. But he was in no hurry. This time he wouldn't have his hair pulled. In the first place they were not at the mill. And in the second place it was "after Passover." After Passover they did not have to be afraid of the Jews. And he lay on the grass on his stomach with his flaxen head between his hands and opposite him lay Feitel also on his stomach with his dark head between his hands. The sky was blue, the sun was warm and a soft breeze played about their heads. The calf stood nearby and so did the rooster with all his wives. And the two young heads, the fair one and the dark one, were propped up facing each other and the boys talked and talked and talked . . .

Nachman was not at home. Early in the morning with his stick in his hand he had gone out over the countryside looking for something to buy. He stopped at every house. He

greeted each peasant with a friendly good morning, calling
each one by name, and talked about everything under the
sun except what had happened the day before Passover and
the terror that had lasted all through Passover. And before
leaving he touched the peasant's wagon. "Do you have something you don't need, neighbor?"

"Nothing, Lachman."

"Some metal, millet, anything at all? A skin maybe?"

"Believe me, Lachman, I don't have a thing. Times are
hard."

"Hard? You must have drunk everything up. A holiday
like that."

"I—drink—on a holiday? These are hard times, I tell you."

The peasant sighed and Nachman sighed with him. Then
they talked about other things so that it wouldn't look as if
he had come to buy anything.

From this peasant's house he went to that of another and
then to a third, till at last he found something, so that he
shouldn't have to come home empty-handed.

Nachman Verebivker, loaded down and sweating, hurried
home with his long strides and thought of only one thing:
how much could he earn, how much could he lose . . .

He had completely forgotten the Passover incident. He had
completely forgotten the Passover terror. And Kurachka and
his governors and his decrees had fled his mind. He had forgotten about them completely.

Let the winds blow. Let the storms rage. Let the world
turn upside down. An old oak that has been standing since
the beginning of time whose roots are sunk deep in the earth
cares nothing about winds. He pays no heed to storms . . .

The Lottery Ticket

BENYOMCHIK—that boy of mine—is a regular lottery ticket."

That is the way Yisroel, the *shammes* at the old synagogue, described his young son, Benjamin, who was known in our town as a promising lad when he was still a pupil in Yarachmiel-Moishe's *cheder*. Yarachmiel-Moishe could not praise him highly enough.

"Your youngster," he said to Yisroel the *shammes* one morning in the synagogue, "is one of the best boys I have. He is a hard worker—a very hard worker. And the understanding he has! The memory! Oh-ho!"

The "Oh-ho" Yarachmiel-Moishe sang out with such enthusiasm that Yisroel the *shammes* glowed with pride.

"May God grant you health and fortune for these words," Yisroel said to the teacher and helped him put away his *tallis* and *tfillin*. This he did out of gratitude for the teacher's praise of his son. For the lessons the boy received Yisroel paid the same amount that all the other parents did—two *rubles* a quarter besides the usual presents at *Hannukah* and *Purim*, although Yisroel supported his own family on little more than the *Hannukah* and *Purim* gifts that others gave him.

Afterwards, when Benyomchik had gone through all of Yarachmiel-Moishe's classes, Yisroel the *shammes* wanted very much to send him to Eli-Maier, the *Gamorah* teacher, but Eli-Maier would not take him. In the first place, his school wa already full. In the second place, Yisroel could not begin to pay what the well-to-do householders did. So Benyomchik did what many other boys do. If they have nothing to pay with, they study by themselves. That's what we have a large synagogue for, with a lot of bookstands, and candle-ends salvaged from memorials for the dead, and books—all the books one needs: Bibles, the tracts and commentaries, and whatnot. If a person only wants to, he can study anywhere, even in an attic. Do you know how many great people, scholars of renown, grew up among us that way, bent over tiny candle-ends in the synagogue? And how many more we might have had by now—holy men of genius, *Talmudists* and *Kabalists*—we cannot even guess.

But something happened: in the last forty or fifty years a ray of wordly light has stolen into our corner of the earth and has reached even into our very synagogues, even there where the impoverished lads sat with their tomes. There you found them secretly snatching their first taste of secular food, some rhetoric as an appetizer, then swallowing—or choking over—a Russian grammar, with maybe a few chapters of a novel for dessert. From studies like these, naturally, no *Talmudic* scholars or famous rabbis emerged. Instead, Jewish youths wandered off into the world and were ruined, became doctors, lawyers, writers of prose and verse, teachers—and plain non-believers. Not a single rabbi who was worth anything. That is, there were a number of rabbis. But what kind? Crown rabbis wished onto us by the czar, whether we wanted them or not. As if he had said, "Here is a loaded bomb; hold on to it." But let us proceed . . .

Benyomchik did not study in the synagogue all alone. He had two companions, penniless boys like himself, and that was how the trouble started. One man by himself cannot do wrong as easily as he can with others. It was always that way.

Look at Adam. So long as he walked in the Garden alone, all was still and heavenly. But as soon as Mother Eve appeared, all was changed. She talked him into eating of the fruit of the Tree of Knowledge, and who knows what more she would not have done if they had not been driven out in time?

It was the same with Benjamin. If Benjamin had sat alone in the synagogue, all would have been well. But he studied together with these comrades, boys as naked and barefoot, as hungry and thirsty as himself; and together they longed for the large, bright world, the world of wisdom and knowledge. They sat at the table, bent over the yellowed pages, but their thoughts were far away, among the great of the earth, among the learned ones, the fortunate ones. It pulled and dragged at them like a magnet—this outside world. So was it strange that one Saturday night three boys left their study table in the synagogue—Itzik, Yossil and Benyomchik—and disappeared? They were hunted everywhere, all over town, in every corner and hole, but they were gone without a trace. Well, the other two lads, Itzik and Yossil, were waifs, orphans without father or mother. Whom did they run away from? But Benyomchik! Yisroel the *shammes* turned the town upside down, searched everywhere, and calmed down only on the following day, when a letter came from the three boys, asking everybody not to worry; they were, bless the Lord, safe and sound. They had become aware (that is how they wrote) that here in the synagogue there was no future for them, and therefore they had gone off to attend a seminary, a *yeshiva*, in Vilna or Volozhin or Mir. They had cleverly listed all three seminaries so that no one should know where to go and look for them.

But all that was unnecessary. No one ran after them. The town itself was in fact happy about it. In the first place, it meant that there would be two or three fewer people to keep alive—you could not let them starve to death. And in the second place, it was such a fine thing to see poor boys who wanted to become educated. If all the others in the town could only have done it, they would have gone off somewhere too, rather than stay here and struggle for a living.

Whatever happened to the two other lads—Itzik and Yossil—no one knows, but after about six months Yisroel the *shammes* got a letter from Benyomchik—not from Volozhin, not from Vilna and not from Mir, but from another large city. He told them not to worry because at last he was on the right path, some day he would amount to something—if only, with the help of God, he succeeded in passing his examinations to enter the *gymnasium*. He wanted to prepare himself for the study of medicine and when he became a doctor he would be able to make a good living and could then support his father and mother in their old age. His father would not have to work so hard any more, being a *shammes,* and his mother a *shammeste*.

"And there is one thing, my dear and loyal parents," he wrote, "that you must never worry about. A person can have all the education there is and still remember his debt to God. I want you to know that I pray every day, that I use the *tfillin,* and wash before meals and say grace before and after I eat—that is, when there is something to eat. Usually we eat every other day, sometimes a piece of dry bread alone and sometimes dry bread with salt water. And when there is nothing at all, we suck a piece of sugar. Sugar is a remedy for hunger, it drives away the appetite. But there is something besides food, and that we have in plenty! Don't forget: we have four grammar texts to go through, and geography and history, and how many other things! Mathematics we won't even talk about. That is too simple. When we were still home we used to study algebra in the synagogue, and the rhetoric books we devoured in those days help us now when we have compositions to write. There is only one thing wrong: we have so far not been able to correct our accent altogether. But that will be done in time. So don't worry; everything will turn out all right. The important thing is not to become discouraged. We must have faith in the Eternal."

When Yisroel the *shammes* received this letter he went at once to Yarachmiel-Moishe the *melamed,* an old colleague, an honest man and a confidant.

"Do me a favor," he said. "Read this letter through and answer it. I could have written to him myself, but I am sure you can do it better."

Yarachmiel-Moishe the *melamed* knew very well that the *shammes* was telling a big lie, but you can't make it appear that you know. So he took out his glasses and put them on his nose—a strange pair of glasses, held together by a piece of wire and two pieces of string; lenses there were none—one frame was covered with a circular piece of tin and the other was empty, just a hole.

Yisroel could not resist asking, "What good are these glasses, Rabbi? Can you see anything with them?"

"They're better than nothing, and besides, I'm used to them," Yarachmiel-Moishe answered, and held the letter off at a distance, one eye (the one behind the tin) closed; and with the other he read like water going over a dam, in a loud clear voice, stopping every so often to look at Yisroel as if to say, "How is that for reading?" And Yisroel stood by, his head a little to one side, beaming with joy, as if to say. "And the letter itself—how is that for writing?"

And when Yarachmiel-Moishe took off his glasses and gave him the letter back again, Yisroel asked, "Well, Rabbi, what do you think of it?"

"What can I tell you? It's good. It's very good. He says

that he prays every day, with his *tfillin* too. May it be no
worse in the future."

"What I meant was that he is growing up. My Benyomchik
is becoming something," said Yisroel. At the tip of his tongue
were other words but he was afraid to use them—words like
"gymnasium," "examinations," and finally "doctor" itself.
So he said, "I'm wondering what to think about it. You said
that he was studying to be a—doctor? What do you think
of that? What is your opinion, Rabbi? You're a man of
experience."

Yarachmiel-Moishe knows that he is a man of experience,
but what can he say? Naturally, if it were up to him, he
would not have let him study in the *gymnasium*. What does
a man like Yisroel want to have a son in the *gymnasium* for?
And studying to be a doctor! But he wants advice . . .

Yarachmiel-Moishe looks with glazed eyes at the wall and
sighs. The *shammes* understands what the sigh means; he
feels a little like that himself, he is not too well pleased with
the *gymnasium*. If it were only a *yeshiva* . . . And yet, there
was the other side too: his son, Benyomchik—a doctor!

"But, Rabbi, he says he is not forgetting. He prays every
day. He is still one of us."

And then, after another pause: "Rabbi, I asked you to do
me a favor. Won't you answer the letter? And another thing,
Rabbi. You know our town. People love to talk. So I want
to ask you: keep it to yourself. You understand?"

"I understand. Of course I understand," said Yarachmiel-
Moishe, and once more saddling his nose with the strange
glasses, he took a piece of paper, pen and ink, dipped the pen
into the ink, and waited for the *shammes* to tell him what to
write.

"Tell him this," says the *shammes*, and dictates:

"To my beloved son, Benjamin. To begin with I want to

tell you that we are all, bless the Lord, in the best of health, and may we hear no worse from you now or in the future, Amen. And secondly, tell him that Simma, my wife, and I send our friendliest greetings and ask him to write to us frequently, let us know how he is getting along, and tell him that we wish him all the luck in the world and that he should succeed in his work, and tell him not to worry. God is our father. The main thing is that he should take care of himself, in his health and in his habits and in his prayers: he should remember that he is a Jew. That is the main thing, and tell him that I am sending him a *ruble,* a *ruble* I'm sending him" (here the *shammes* feels through all his pockets) "and tell him that I would have sent more if I had it, but right now conditions are very bad. I am not earning a thing; no one is dying and no one is getting married and no one is having children. And what else do I make a penny from? I don't remember when there has been a wedding, not one since Reb Hersh married off his youngest daughter. That is, a few weddings there have been, but I am speaking of *real* weddings, weddings worth mentioning . . ."

"Sh-h . . . don't rush like that," says the teacher. "You're pounding away like a post horse. I can't catch up to you . . . Mmmmmm. Well. What next?"

"And tell him further . . . that there is nothing to say. And tell him that I send him my friendliest regards, and Simma, his mother, sends her friendliest regards, and all his sisters too, Pessil and Sossil and Brochele. And remind him to be sure to remember that he is a Jew, not to forget the synagogue. That is the main thing. And when you're through, I'll sign my name to it."

When the teacher had written all this down, Yisroel the *shammes* rolled up his sleeve, took the pen carefully with two fingers and prepared himself for the delicate operation. He spelled out his own name carefully—Y-i-s-r-o-e-l—and the name of his father—N-a-f-t-o-l-i—and the family name—R-i-t-e-l-m-a-n. And while he wrote, his tongue moved from side to side, following his fingers from right to left and from left to right.

It is to be understood that it did not take long for people all over town to learn the secret, that Yisroel the *shammes'* young son was studying, or getting ready to study, to be a doctor. And this did not hurt Yisroel in the least, though there were some people who teased him:

"So you're going to have a doctor in the family—going around bareheaded? With brass buttons, maybe, like a state official? How will that look, Yisroel? I mean for you—like a hen that hatches ducklings . . ."

Yisroel the *shammes* let them talk, and himself said nothing. But deep in his heart he thought: "Laugh, laugh at my Benyomchik! He's still my lottery ticket!"

One day—it was Passover eve—Simma the *shammeste* and her three daughters, Pessil, Sossil and Brochele, were cleaning up for the holiday, when the door opened, and in came a striking young man in a coat with white buttons and an odd-looking cap on his head. He fell on Simma's neck and then on the three girls, hugging and kissing and squeezing them.

The young man was Benjamin.

Simma was so happy she burst out crying. And Yisroel hurried in, frightened and out of breath. He shouted at his wife, "Stop crying, will you! Look how upset she is! Do you know what you're crying about?"

But when he himself had looked the boy over and seen how much he had grown and changed, he almost began to cry too. But a man does not do such things.

"When did you get here?" he asked his son. "Turn around,

let me see what you look like from the back. What kind of suit is that? Take off your coat—why don't you take off your coat?"

And when Benjamin took off his coat and stood there in his blue uniform with silver buttons—his cheeks rosy and his eyes shining—he charmed not only the rest of the family, but everyone who saw him. "What do you think of Yisroel-the-*shammes'* son?" they said. "How he has grown! What a fine looking boy he is!" And Mintzi, the neighbor's daughter, a girl of nineteen with black eyes and a heavy black braid tied with a red ribbon that suited her so well, came in to see if Simma had an extra pot that she could borrow, although she knew very well that in all her life Simma had never had an extra pot. But it gave her a chance to see Benjamin close up, to glance at him with her lively black eyes and to toss her head with the thick black braid and the bright red ribbon—it gave her a chance to turn around and run off, and a little later to come back again under another pretext, until Benjamin's three sisters looked at each other as if to say: "How do you like the way she runs in and out?"

In the meantime Benjamin called his mother aside. "Here is something for *Pesach*," he said, and pushed some money into her hand. Poor Simma! She had never held so much money before in all her life! And for the girls he had presents and presents—ribbons and combs and mirrors and trinkets without number! And for his mother a silk shawl, a yellow one with red and blue flowers. And once more Simma the *shammeste* burst out crying.

And Yisroel asked with a laugh, "What's all this? How did you ever get so much money, my boy?"

"Why shouldn't I have money?" asks Benjamin, proudly. "I'm earning money now, bless the Lord. Eight *rubles* a month. I'm a tutor. I have a few children to teach and I get paid for it. I'm in the fifth class at the *gymnasium*. There are eight classes altogether, so in three more years I'll be through. And then—the university, to study medicine."

Benjamin talks and talks, and they all stand around him. They can't take their eyes off him, and they think, "Can that really be Benjamin? That barefoot Benyomchik who used to spend all his time in the synagogue, studying? Eight *rubles* a month . . . eight classes . . . a silk shawl . . . the university . . . doctor . . .

The Lord alone knows if anyone else had such a happy Passover, such a cheerful *seder,* that year. And I am not talking about the wine, or the brandy, or the fish, or the dumplings, or the pudding. I am speaking now of the *Hagadah,* the Passover ceremonial, that Yisroel and Benjamin both chanted, one louder than the other. It was wonderful to listen to! When they came to *"Rabbi Eleazer omer, minayin shekol mako umako,"* and the men both began to sway with a new vigor and struck up a louder tone, Simma, who had been sitting all the time with her eyes on Benjamin, suddenly began to pucker up her lips as if to cry, and the three sisters, Pessil and Sossil and Brochele, seeing her, could control themselves no longer and began to laugh; and seeing them, the others began to laugh too, even Simma herself . . . Ah, what a Passover that was! You can well imagine!

The next morning, the first day of Passover, when Benjamin came to the synagogue, everybody gaped at the boy in the student's uniform with the silver buttons as if he were a strange animal from the jungle. The smallest boys, full of mischief, crowded around him and pointed at him with their fingers and laughed right in his face. But Benjamin stood all the time with his small prayerbook in his hand and prayed. And when he was called up to the *Torah* (Reb Monish, the *gabai,* arranged it in order to please Yisroel) and

Benjamin recited the benediction in a loud clear tone with an accent and an emphasis that one saved for the holidays, the whole synagogue was agog with wonder: "What do you think about Yisroel's young scholar?"

And when they were all ready to leave the synagogue, the rich man of the village, Reb Hersh, turned to the *shammes.* "Yisroel," Reb Hersh said broadly, as a rich man does when he speaks to one of the lesser creatures, looking a little to one side and clearing his throat and nose in a double cough, "Yisroel, ah-h, come here, hm-m, with that young man of yours. Let me—hm-m—take a look at him."

Hearing that Reb Hersh wanted to talk to Yisroel-the-*shammes'* "young scholar" the crowd gathered around to hear what the rich man would say and what the other would answer. Benjamin approached Reb Hersh as if he were an equal, not at all self-consciously, greeted him like an acquaintance of old, and Reb Hersh looked him over from head to foot, not quite knowing how to start. Should he address him in the respectful plural—a child like that? That would be showing too much respect for the son of the *shammes.* And yet, to use the singular, to say *du,* as you might say, "Hey, there . . ."—maybe that would not be right either. After all, he was a *gymnasium* student with silver buttons, he looked almost like a young prince . . . So at last he spoke to him neither one way nor the other, but vaguely and impersonally: "How are things? When did the visitor come? When is he going back?"

Benjamin put his right foot forward. With one hand he toyed with a button at his chest, with the other he stroked his upper lip. And he answered every question—confidently, without any shame or hesitation. Reb Hersh liked it—and yet he did not like it. "Not a foolish lad at all, but he doesn't know his place." And he became involved in a broad discussion about his school: "How many classes are there? What is the significance of eight classes? Why not nine? And what is the difference between one class and another?"

And Benjamin thought: "He looks so important, and yet he is such an ox!" And he gave him to understand what the difference was between one class and another. Reb Hersh did not like this at all, having a child explaining things to him, and making it sound so simple that it needed no explanation. He said, "Why, everybody knows that. But what is the sense of having eight classes instead of nine?"

"Simply because if there were nine classes, you would say: Why should there be nine and not ten?"

At this the crowd begins to laugh, that is, everybody laughs except Reb Hersh. He thinks: "A tramp—that's all he is." And with his double cough he says, "Hm-m. It's time to go home. Hm-m . . ."

If you did not see Yisroel the *shammes* then, standing a little to one side, looking from one to the other and swallowing each word of Benjamin's, you have never seen a happy and fortunate man. He was waiting for Reb Hersh to stop questioning his son so he could take him home, where the women were waiting anxiously. On the table, the fresh crisp *matzos* were also waiting, and in the oven a delicious Passover borsht was simmering, and hot *kneidlach* with chicken fat, and maybe even a potato pudding! And at last when Reb Hersh had coughed his double cough again and gone off with a few of his close friends, Yisroel the *shammes* invited his one and only good friend and confidant, Yarachmiel-Moishe the teacher, to come along with them, as the others had gone with Reb Hersh, for a glass of wine. And when they arrived he poured out for the old teacher a glass of genuine raisin wine, and Simma brought in such wonderful *chremzlach* that it would have been hard even for an epicure to tell if there was more honey in them or more chicken fat, because they were so sugary and so rich that they stuck to the gums and ran down his beard. Yarachmiel-Moishe, a quiet man, who rarely said a word, now at the first glass of genuine raisin wine found his head whirling round and his tongue running loose and wild. He called Benjamin over to him, and put him through a quick but thorough examination of the Scriptures and commentaries that he had once studied in his *cheder*.

Benjamin remembered not only the Scriptures, but the commentaries as well, so thoroughly that Yisroel the *shammes'* heart almost burst with pleasure. He followed the teacher out through the door. "What do you think of him?" he asked.

"A perfect vessel—a saint!" answered Yarachmiel-Moishe, puckering his lips and shaking his head.

"But a Jew all the same? He hasn't forgotten that?" said the *shammes,* and watched the teacher's eyes for the answer.

"With God's help," said the teacher.

"A lottery ticket! A lottery ticket! Do you agree with me?"

At this Yarachmiel-Moishe tossed his head—it was hard to tell if it was a nod or a shake—blinked his eyes and made a gesture with his hands that meant that he thought the boy either was, or was not, a lottery ticket.

"A good day!" he cried, and once more kissed the *mazuza.* "May God keep us alive and well another year, and may we come to each other in joy—for your daughters' weddings and then your son's—and may the Jews have some relief from all their troubles, may there be good news for all of us, it's time that God had mercy on us, improved our lot, lightened our load . . . And may all things be good everywhere, and cheer in every heart. And—ah . . ."

Yarachmiel-Moishe himself did not know what more he wanted. It seemed as if he had already poured out everything that was on his mind. He stood with his tongue out, unable

to say one thing or another . . . Yet how can a man go
away like this, without a word of farewell of any kind?
Fortunately he remembered one more thing:

"And may—may the Messiah come soon!"

"Amen!" answers Yisroel the *shammes,* and in his heart
he thinks: First let my Benjamin graduate as a doctor. And
then let the Messiah come.

As cheerful and bright as everything was at Yisroel the
shammes' when Benjamin arrived, so was it dark and gloomy
when he went away again.

And the three years passed, the three years before Benjamin
could enter the university. It was not an easy time. Yisroel
the *shammes* experienced one trouble after another at home,
and his son Benjamin over there in the city. Many a night
Yisroel could not fall asleep here, and Benjamin his son
there. Yisroel could not sleep because he kept thinking of the
difficult time Benjamin had, of all the hard work he had to
do. And Benjamin could not sleep because he was getting
ready for his examinations.

"If God helps me and I pass my examinations," Benjamin
wrote home, "I'll come to see you again, my dear and faithful ones, and be with you all summer to rest my bones."

And Yisroel the *shammes* waited for the good news of the
examination as a pious Jew waits for the Messiah.

At last summer came, but Benjamin did not. His letters
began to come less and less often, and as time went on they
became shorter and more gloomy. All he ever said was that
on such and such a day he would have to take this or that
examination.

"The next examination," wrote Benjamin in his last letter, "is my Day of Judgment, because if I get less than a ninety-

four I shall not be able to get in, and if I can't get in now I shall have to stay over another year. And who knows what will happen next year? Maybe next year it will be even worse. What will I do then? What will happen to me? Why did I ever have to work so hard, wear myself out like this? Study so hard, starve day after day, freeze in unheated rooms and spend so many sleepless nights? I am not the only one to ask these questions. There are many others like me—Jewish boys—who stayed over from last year and can't get in because their average is not quite high enough. I don't know what I shall do . . ."

Yisroel the *shammes* went around in a daze. He could not understand why Benjamin's letters suddenly should have become so melancholy. He asked Yarachmiel-Moishe to write to Benjamin and ask him what he meant by "average" and "ninety-four." In short, he asked Benjamin to write and explain everything, and not to worry, but rely on the Eternal One who could do everything. And the main thing still was that he should remember he was a Jew, and if the Lord willed, all would be well . . .

But this letter was never answered, and neither were all the others that Yisroel sent later. But he kept writing and writing, until at last, ashamed to come again to Yarachmiel-Moishe, he gave up writing.

"What can be the matter?" Simma asked her husband. "There has been no letter for such a long time."

And she got an answer: "What do you expect? Is that all he has to do? Write letters? Wait a little. Let him finish his examinations, whatever they are, and then he'll write!"

But Yisroel himself went around with a heavy heart and low spirits. He could not find a place to turn. What went through his head during those days, may no other father ever know. And his dreams every night were frightful and horrible, with black canopies, black candles, everything black . . .

Have you ever heard of Lemel the *starosta*? Or is this the first time you have heard his name? In addition to being the *starosta,* the mayor, a man of substance and influence, what in plain Yiddish we refer to as a soup-ladle, right here in town, he was also a power of some sort in the provincial capital, knew all the important people, dealt with them, was intimate with them. Whenever he comes to the capital, he says, he never knows where to go first. Everybody wants to drag him off to himself. "*Pan* Lemel!" shout the Poles. "*Gospodin* Lemel!" plead the Russians. "*Reb* Lemel, you're ours!" say the Jews. He simply does not know what to do! And every time that he comes back from the capital he has news to bring, something startling to talk about for the next three months. A sensational bankruptcy, a terrible fire, a murder to make your hair stand on end. And although Lemel's bankruptcies took place too often, his fires and murders almost every week, it never occurred to anyone to contradict him. They knew he could not help it—he liked to talk, to tell stories, and if necessary, to make them up himself.

So you can imagine what a time our *starosta* had when an envelope came to his office from the provincial capital with a document instructing him to remove from the rolls of the Jewish community the name of Benjamin, son of Yisroel Ritelman, because of the fact that he had assumed another faith.

As soon as Lemel the *starosta* finished reading the message he forgot all his work and ran out into the street with the paper, stopped everyone he saw, whispered the secret into each one's ear, and soon had the story spread all over town.

No doubt you have heard of the halcyon days. The skies are clear, there is no breeze, not a drop of rain, everything is quiet, serene. The people are asleep, the town itself looks dead. Suddenly, no one knows how or where, something explodes, like a bomb from the sky, like an earthquake. The people awaken, start to run. They run this way and that. "What is it? Where? What happened?"

The story of Yisroel-the-*shammes'* son was like that bomb. It tore the town to pieces and woke up everybody. They were all as upset and excited as if this had to do with their own health or livelihood, as if this were the only thing they had to worry about. Some dropped their work, others left the table with their food untouched and went off to the marketplace to see what was going on. Around Reb Hersh's house there stood a whole ring of people, and Reb Hersh himself stood by the porch in a gabardine and skullcap, surrounded by his kinsmen, intimate friends, acquaintances, total strangers—men who catered to him, scraped and bowed and showed their respect for the man who might be able to do them a favor some time. Reb Hersh held forth and his followers echoed:

"Of course! Naturally! That's right, Reb Hersh!"

And Reb Hersh went on:

"A *shammes*, a ne'er-do-well, a pauper—and he wants to be better than anyone else! He has a son, so what does he have to become? A doctor. Nothing less. And if he became a *shammes* like his father, or, heaven spare us, a teacher, what would happen then? I'd like to hear what our *shammes* has to say now. Or maybe he doesn't know yet. I don't see him anywhere around? Where can he be?"

Where was he? There were some in the crowd who did not hesitate to hurry off to the synagogue to look for him. And some even went to his home, but they could not find him anywhere.

And the truth is that Yisroel knew nothing about it. At that moment, when all the town was in an uproar, Yisroel was sitting with his one and only good friend and confidant, Yarachmiel-Moishe the teacher. In the same mail that brought the document to the town hall there was a large envelope for Yisroel himself, and it was from his son. It was the longest letter that had ever come from Benjamin. With great difficulty he had read through a couple of pages, but had understood little more than a word here and there. So he took it to Yarachmiel-Moishe.

"It's here!" he shouted from the doorway, with joy.

"A letter from your son?"

"And what a letter! It's like a cushion!"

When he heard these words, Yarachmiel-Moishe told his pupils to take a rest, and he himself put on the glasses we had seen before, and began to read the letter in a loud, clear voice, almost a chant. At the start all was well, but soon he began to halt and stutter, as if he were walking over pointed rocks. He came upon hard, strange words he had never seen before. He had to set his glasses straight, he held the letter up to the window, shrugged his shoulders, chewed his words, muttered, "Hm-m . . . What language is this? Nation . . . emancipation . . . quota . . . he's beginning to use strange words, that son of yours . . ."

Yisroel sat at the end of the table, holding his head in his hands, and looked only at Yarachmiel-Moishe, listened to every word, tried to catch the meaning—and made nothing of it. He could not begin to understand why suddenly Benjamin should have to defend himself, try to justify himself, insist with so many oaths that he was the same person as before, that what he had done was out of greater love and greater loyalty . . . Yisroel could not understand why he should be any different now, and why he should ask his forgiveness.

What was there to forgive? "But it could not have been otherwise," he wrote. "I have struggled so long with myself. I know the pain I am giving you, but the fight I have carried on since childhood for an education, my need, my desire for learning has become so great, so strong, that I *finally yielded*."

"What? What was that? Read it again, read it once more. What did he say?"

Yarachmiel-Moishe adjusted his glasses to read it again, but just then the door was pushed open and in came Bassya-Hinda, the teacher's wife, a tall gaunt woman with a sallow face, carrying a large market basket. In the basket were all sorts of good things—potatoes and onions, two black radishes, a small piece of beef-lung that she had barely managed to coax from the butcher, because there are always customers by the hundred who want beef-lung. Women fight over it as men do over the greatest honors at the synagogue, and the reason is this: it costs so little and there are no bones in it, and if you cook it with potatoes and onions and a lot of pepper and it simmers long enough, it tastes quite well . . .

Coming in and seeing the *shammes* sitting with her husband and reading something, Bassya-Hinda took a quick glance to see if the poor *shammes* knew already. But she could not tell from their faces, so she put the basket down, and while she wiped her face with her hand, winked at her husband.

" 'Chmiel-Moishe, come here," she said, and he, seeing that she wanted to say something to him, took off his glasses and excused himself for a minute. And there on the other side of the doorway, this conversation took place between husband and wife:

She: Does he know?
He: Who?
She: The *shlimazl*.
He: Which *shlimazl*?

She: The *shammes.*
He: Know what?
She: About his son.
He: Which son?
She: Benjamin.
He: What about him?
She: The whole town is full of it.
He: Full of what?
She: His son.
He: But what about?
She: Oh, you make me tired!

The Lord knows how long this conversation would have dragged on, if at this point the *shammes* himself had not forced his way into the room and in a frightened voice, asked, "What—what are you saying? What did you say Benjamin did? What?"

Bassya-Hinda did not know what to do now. Why should she be the one to tell him? Better send him straight to Lemel the *starosta,* let him take care of it himself.

"Nothing," she said, wiping her face again. "What do I know? They say a paper came in. I don't know—something about your son."

"What kind of paper?"

"Something. In the town hall."

"Who has it—the paper?"

"The *starosta.*"

"What is it about?"

"Your Benjamin. Something."

"What's the matter with Benjamin?" he asked, this time angrily. "What happened to him?"

"I should know? Ask me! Go over there, go to Lemel. He's somewhere in the marketplace. He has the paper."

Paper . . . Lemel . . . the town hall . . . Benjamin . . .

what did all this mean? Yisroel felt his cheeks grow hot and
he heard a whistling in his ears. He pulled down his cap, bent
over double, and stumbled out . . .

There are people who love to watch a person in agony, who
stare at him when he weeps, look after him when he follows
a corpse at a funeral, stand by when he wrings his hands.
I do not care for such scenes. Say what you will, I don't like
mournful pictures. My muse does not wear a black veil on her
face. My muse is a poor—but cheerful one . . .

Where did Yisroel run? Whom did he see? What did he
hear? What did he say? Do not ask, it will give you no joy
to know. What will you have gained, for instance, when you
have learned that there were people who finally lived to
have revenge on Yisroel the *shammes,* who had gone around
so long showing off his lottery ticket?

"He had it coming," said Reb Hersh, with his peculiar
double-cough, and stroked his paunch comfortably. "It should
be a lesson for people. A pauper should be careful how he
jumps in your face. A doctor he had to have . . ."

Others, it is true, had pity on the *shammes,* "poor fellow"—
and you know what that means. My grandfather Minda had
a saying, "Look out for people who pity you, and God protect
you from those who call you 'poor fellow.'"

So I won't tell you what Yisroel did or whom he saw, but
it was dusk when he turned in at his cottage, looking like
a ghost. Entering without a word, he sat down on the ground,
took off his boots, tore his shirt at the heart as one does for
the dead, and prepared to sit in mourning for an hour, as one
does at a time like that. Simma did the same, and so did the
three sisters. Together they sat on the ground, moaning and
weeping for the one they had lost.

Later, when Yarachmiel-Moishe the teacher came to offer

condolence, this is what he found: Yisroel sitting with his head thrown forward between his knees, Simma with her hands covering her face and Pessil, Sossil and Brochele sitting with red swollen eyes, each one looking with expressionless face into a separate corner, as if in their shame and pain they could not face each other openly.

He came into the house quietly without a greeting of any kind, as one does in a house of mourning, and slowly lowering himself to the edge of a bench at one side of the room, sighed. That was all. He didn't say a word. A little later, another sigh, and again silence; and later still a sigh again. It was only after a while that he looked around and decided that it was not right to sit there and not say a word, he ought to say something to comfort them. But what was there to say? When a family is in mourning because a person has died, you can come to sit with them for a while, and say, "The Lord giveth and the Lord taketh away." Or, "Man is, after all, like a fly." Or, "Death—that is something none of us can escape." Or, "Vanity of vanities, all of us will die." Or other such sayings that cannot make one especially happy, but are still a comfort. If a person says something, gets it off his chest, he feels a trifle better. But what can one say at a time like this, when it is a living person they are mourning for? Yarachmiel-Moishe turned a little on his bench with a shy cough, wanted to say something, but the words would not come. He tried a few different times, till finally he started again and it worked. And now he was unable to stop, he did not know where or how to end it.

"Ah, well, it's the same story as always. What can you call it—a trial from heaven, from the Lord. For everything is from Him; without Him nothing is done, nothing occurs, not a finger here on earth is lifted. He is a real Master, let us agree on that. Oh, what a Master! And we obey Him—how we obey Him! . . . So it was decreed that this had to happen, exactly as it happened. And here is the proof: that if it did not have to happen this way, it would not have happened. But it did happen, so it must have been ordained. If He had wanted something else to happen, it would have happened the other way. It would have . . ."

Yarachmiel-Moishe began to feel that he did not know what he was saying, so he paused, took a pinch of snuff, lowered his head to one side, and heaved a deep sigh. He told himself that it was time to go, but talking about going is an easy matter. How are you going to do it, though, if you are glued to the bench? There is no visit that is worse than one to a house of mourning. You are supposed to leave without a word of parting, without a sign or a look. But how can you do it? Yarachmiel-Moishe sat waiting for a miracle to happen. If only they would doze off a little so he could leave while they slept. Or if something happened outside, a riot, a fire—anything—so he could escape in the excitement. He sat looking around at the ceiling, at the four walls, and then he said to himself: "It is time to think about going. The children will turn the *cheder* upside down . . ."

When the hour was up, Yisroel and his family rose from the floor, quietly, without talking, put on their shoes and crawled off each to his own corner, to his own work. Yisroel rushed through his late-afternoon prayers and hurried off to the synagogue to be in time for evening services. After all, he was the *shammes,* his time was not his own. He had to be where he was needed. Work—that was the only remedy, the means of chasing all worries away, of forgetting all troubles . . .

In the synagogue a few busybodies came up to him.

"What do you hear from your lottery ticket? How is your son getting along?"

"A son? Have I got a son?" answered Yisroel with a bitter little smile.

And seeing the bitterness and the ache in the smile, the meddlers retreated. All they had to do was look at his face and they did not want to talk to him any more about his son.

What happened afterward? What became of Benjamin? Did he write any more letters? And what did he write? And did his father answer him? And if he answered, what did he say? Don't press me with questions. I shall not say a word. I'll tell you only that as far as Yisroel was concerned, there was no Benjamin any more anywhere. Benjamin was dead. In the lottery, Yisroel had drawn a blank.

Cnards

NOWADAYS a game of cards is an everyday affair. *Where* don't we play cards nowadays? *When* don't we play cards? And *who* doesn't play cards nowadays?

There was a time, if you know what I mean, when we used to play cards only once a year—at *Hannukah.*

That is, if you want the whole truth, people used to get together for a game in those days too—a real game, a hot game! But where? In a secret chamber, behind locked doors.

In winter, in *cheder,* between the late-afternoon and evening prayers, when the rabbi was at the synagogue warming himself by the stove and we were left alone; or in summer, in a dark corner of the stable, near a thin crack in the wall; or at other times of the year when we bribed Getzel, the *shammes,* and locked ourselves up in the synagogue, high up in the women's balcony, turned a lectern face down for a table, and dealt out a hand of *Starshy Kozir* or Thirty-one or Turtle-myrtle.

One day Riva-Leah, the *gabai's* wife, of blessed memory (she has gone to her rest these many years) found a strange object in her lectern and almost fainted dead away. Who could have planted a thing like that—in her lectern?

Aghast, she ran out of the synagogue into the street, shouting at the top of her voice:

"Help, fellow Jews! Help! A misfortune has come to pass! A calamity! A plot! Come with me and I'll show you!"

What was the calamity and what kind of a plot? You

couldn't get any answer from Riva-Leah. Only this: "Come, come with me and I'll show you!"

And before long she had drawn around her a fine assemblage, consisting of the rabbi, the *shochet,* a few of the elders, and the cantor, together with a liberal sprinkling of our secular aristocracy.

Naturally, when the rest of the people saw Riva-Leah proceeding up the street followed by the rabbi, the *shochet,* a few of the elders and the cantor and so many of our leading citizens, they joined the procession too. And then the women and boys, and the little children, torn by curiosity, fell in behind, and together they marched into the synagogue. At the head, came Riva-Leah, and behind her, the townspeople.

You can imagine what a terror gripped the town. People thought—it must be something serious. Either someone had left a foundling, or some poor wretch had been found hanging from the rafters, or, God forbid, someone had been murdered.

Worried and frightened, they clattered up to the women's balcony—Riva-Leah first, followed by the rabbi, the *shochet,* the cantor, with the rest of the town after them.

"Where—where is it?" the crowd asked Riva-Leah, and listened for the cry of the foundling and looked for the hanging body or the trail of blood leading to the corpse that some unknown enemy had left there to bring trouble on our town.

And then imagine how astounded they all were when, instead of a foundling or a bleeding corpse, they found this strange and ominous object in Riva-Leah's lectern: a picture of a bearded man—obviously a Russian Orthodox priest—with an odd black cross at his side. And not just one priest, but two priests and two crosses, one priest upright, and the other one standing on his head . . .

They all bent down and peered into Riva-Leah's lectern: first the rabbi, then the *shammes,* then the *shochet* and the elders and the cantor; then the leading citizens; then the common people. They looked and drew away. For to touch the thing with their hands—for that no one was bold enough. That is, no one except one man, Velvel Ramshevitch, the cantor's son-in-law.

When Velvel Ramshevitch looked and saw what it was his face lit up, and then with a laugh, he cried, "It's nothing! What's there to get excited about? It's just the king of clubs!"

"And what is the king of clubs?"

"A card. A card—that you play with."

"How did it get here?" they wanted to know. "In the lectern of Riva-Leah, the *gabai's* wife, in the women's balcony of the synagogue? That's one thing. And the other is, how does it happen that you, the cantor's son-in-law, know what a card is, and that it's called the king of clubs? And that it's a game that people play?"

At this our Velvel realized that he had fallen into a trap. And he turned every color imaginable and began to babble and to bleat, make sounds like a sheep or a goat, sounds that no one could understand, no human being, at any rate . . .

But that is not the story I started to tell. It is only an introduction to our tale about cnards. I merely wanted to show you what a forbidden thing cards used to be and how carefully we had to hide our knowledge of them.

There was only one lucky week in the year when we could play cards freely and openly.

That was the week of *Hannukah.*

And freely and openly we gathered that week at Velvel Ramshevitch's house. He was a free soul even then: he had shaved his beard and sidelocks, smoked on Saturdays on his front porch where all could see, and ate pork sausage—even on fast days! And he dared anyone to criticize him.

And his wife, Chayela, the cantor's daughter, imitating him, threw away the wig that all respectable married women wore in those days and went about in her own yellow hair; sprinkled powder over her pockmarked face and spent all her time with a gay young crowd, laughing and making merry—showing everybody her large, stained teeth.

The Chapel—that was what we all called Ramshevitch's house—was open to all the young people in town. There we could read a newspaper or a secular book, there we could smoke a cigarette on the Sabbath, nibble at sausage on fast days, and—most important of all—play a game of cards.

They both loved a good game of cards, and if anything she loved it even more than he did. She could hardly keep away from the table. It was even rumored that they made their living that way, for it was obvious that she was always winning. No matter who dealt she always had trumps. She beat everybody. There was nothing we could do about it.

As you remember, in those days many young men were supported by their fathers-in-law while they themselves went on with their holy studies. And in our town, because of this same Chayela with the blond hair and pockmarked face, more than one such son-in-law gambled away his entire dowry and his wife's pearls, and even drove his father-in-law into bankruptcy.

With one such son-in-law, in fact, she once played through a whole winter, and before she was through with him he had divorced his wife, a wonderful girl, a beauty, and come to live with the Ramshevitches. No use telling you what a scandal it made in our town. Everybody was horrified.

But that is still not the story of cnards that I started to tell. It is only the introduction to the scene of the story which took place in the Chapel I have mentioned—the Ramshevitch home —on the first night of *Hannukah.*

As I was saying, it was the first night of *Hannukah*. We were all sitting in the Chapel, playing our favorite Jewish card game, a real *kosher* game of Okeh.

And we played, as usual, in shifts. One group finished a game and the next group sat down to play. It was that way all the time. One group played in the morning, another in the afternoon, and a third at night. And one of the Ramshevitches played with each group. Either he—or she—or both. At night, if he was sleeping, she played; and if she was asleep, then he played. And sometimes it happened that one night passed, and two nights, and three nights, and neither of them slept. They both played. Except for a half-hour or so when one of them dropped out between games and took a nap.

That was something all of us learned to do. Whenever we got too tired to play, we found something to lean against and dozed off.

It was the same with eating. On the table there was always a bottle and a small glass, herring and sausage. And when you were hungry you took a few minutes off and ate.

Naturally, you understand, we paid for all this. At each game part of the winnings were taken out for "the maid," though in the Chapel there never had been a maid. The Ramshevitches did not need a maid. There was no cooking to do, no beds to make—and no house to clean. There was no time for these things. So what did they need a maid for? Nevertheless with every hand the few cents were put aside and all of us knew that this went for rent and heat, for new decks of cards, and for food. Human beings must eat. And this I can say: there was as much to eat and drink as any of us ever wished for.

And it was the same with cigarettes. Whole boxes full of cigarettes. And whoever wanted to reached for one. And the Ramshevitches smoked more than anybody; and she smoked more than he did. I cannot imagine Chayela Ramshevitch without a cigarette in her mouth. Add to this the powdered pockmarked face and the uncombed blond hair, with the tired, puffy eyes. And the rooms thick with smoke, and the noise and the tumult. Think of all these together and you can picture to yourself what the Chapel looked like at *Hannukah,* when we could play cards openly and freely and we did not have to hide ourselves, or worry about being seen by any of the good people of the town.

That day—I am now coming to the story of the cnards—I was on the third shift. That is, I was one of the group that sat down to play in the evening, when the second candle was lit, and didn't get up until it was time for the third candle the next evening.

It was not the host—Velvel Ramshevitch—who lit the *Hannukah* candles that evening, but one of the guests, an elegant specimen—Eli Rafalski, one of those sons-in-law I mentioned earlier, who loved a card game more than almost anything else in the world, but who, nevertheless, had not strayed from the path in matters of Godliness. That was one thing you could say about the Ramshevitches: they didn't ask you what you were. You could be as pious as you wanted to be: so long as you had something in your pocket, and you played Okeh, and there was room at the table for another hand, you were welcome to sit down with us and were an honored guest! May my enemies have as many plagues and I as many lucky years as the number of times we played with people five nights and five days in succession, and then broke up without ever knowing who they were or what they were or where they had come from. A game of cards is not a marriage contract. You can play a very good game without knowing your opponent or his pedigree.

Well, there we were, sitting around the table, so absorbed in our work that we did not notice that two strangers had come

in, men so unusual and odd in appearance that when we heard
their "Good evening," and looked up at them, we were struck
motionless and dumb.

Perhaps you want to know what they looked like to have
frightened us so? I'll describe them to you as well as I can, and
briefly.

One of them was a tall man—long and thin—in a long, black
silken coat; earlocks—long and narrow, curly, reaching almost
to his belt; a fur cap on his head; and a long beard and a pair
of whiskers so thick and black that if you had met this man
on a dark night on a deserted road, you'd want to say your
prayers.

The other was just the opposite: short and round, also with
earlocks and with a strange beard and whiskers, but not quite
as overgrown as the other. In one hand he held a lantern and
in the other a kerchief full of money.

Noticing the effect they had on us, the tall, thin one with
the curly earlocks smiled at us gently through his whiskers,
and repeated, "Good evening, my dear people. We have come
here to greet you in honor of *Hannukah*."

And as he spoke he looked around at the *Hannukah* candles
at the far end of the room, then at the table with the cards, and
heaved a deep sigh. His companion, the short, round one,
sighed also. Both of them sought with their eyes for a place to
sit down.

Luckily the host, Ramshevitch, remembered that it was his
duty to be polite, so he got up from the table and shook hands
with the newcomers and asked them to sit down. And the rest
of us followed suit, each one separately, some of us shaking
hands with them and others just nodding from a distance.

The two sat down, looked at each other again, and gave
another deep sigh. And once more the host remembered his
manners.

"What's your name?" he asked, as one always should. "Where are you from? Have you been here long? Where are you going to?"

It was the tall, thin one who answered, in a tone as sweet as honey. Speaking slowly, one word at a time and with a delicate sweet smile that came out of his thick and frightful whiskers (he did not even seem to be talking to us, but looked rather as if he were deep in prayer, in humble communion with the Lord), he said:

"My dear friends, I am the grandchild of the *Bal-Shem-Tov*, the founder of Chassidism. I have but one duty, to wander about the world and collect money for the *yeshivas*, the holy seminaries, both here and in the Holy Land of our fathers."

And he sighed again. "And this is my companion who goes with me everywhere and who guards the contributions." With his eyes he indicated the fat one, and this time both of them sighed deeply. "We have devoted our whole life to the *yeshivas*, in order that God's Law may not be forgotten.

"And so, my friends," he continued, with another sigh, "give us a contribution—whatever you are able. One," he said, nodding his head as if in prayer, "can give more, and another can give less."

And his companion, rolling his eyes aloft, added, "And all who give more, will receive more from Heaven."

And he laid his kerchief full of money on the table with a clang. A corner came open and we could see the glint of silver and gold.

Money, they say, attracts money. Seeing all the money already in the kerchief, we had no choice but to add more from our own pockets, and as we did it each one of us thought (I am sure of it): "Ah, if I had the money in that kerchief! What couldn't I do with it . . ."

Our hostess, Chayela Ramshevitch, could not conceal her

excitement. Her eyes fairly blazed. We were all aware of it, even the *Bal-Shem-Tov's* grandchild and his companion, who was in no apparent hurry to remove the kerchief from her sight. The two continued to sit there with their eyes on the cards scattered around the table, and we could see that this was the first time in their lives that either one of them had seen such a thing.

At last the *Bal-Shem-Tov's* grandchild raised his eyes. "I hope I am not disturbing you, but I'd like to ask a question," he said in his unctuous voice and with his soft, sweet smile, pointing with an extended little finger at one card after another. "What sort of thing is this—on the table here?"

"Why, cards," answered our host and hostess together, with a glance at us that seemed to say, "So there are still people on earth so uncivilized that they don't even know what cards are!"

The *Bal-Shem-Tov's* grandchild shut an eye, wrinkled up his nose and forehead, turned his face toward his companion, and with an unearthly sigh, repeated: "Cnards?"

And his companion, with a sigh of his own, repeated after him, "Cnards."

"No, that's wrong," Chayela Ramshevitch undertook to correct them, without once taking her eyes off the kerchief full of money. "Not cnards—cards!"

Naturally they did not say a word to her, nor did they turn their soft, smiling, clever eyes upon her. They were holy men, and such men, you understand, never glance at a female.

But turning to their host, Velvel himself, the *Bal-Shem-Tov's* grandchild said, "I don't want to disturb you, but tell me— what are these things—these cnards? What are they good for? That is, what do you do with them?"

"You play with them," answered Ramshevitch. "Don't you know? When *Hannukah* comes, people play cards."

Again the *Bal-Shem-Tov's* grandchild shut an eye, and turning his face slowly toward his companion, said:

"When *Hannukah* comes—they play cnards."

"Imagine that," echoed his companion.

"But what does that mean?" asked the *Bal-Shem-Tov's* grandchild, slowly, unctuously. "How does one play with these—
cnards? And why? What for?"

"For money," answered Ramshevitch, looking from us to
the kerchief on the table.

Apparently this answer sounded wild and meaningless to
both of them, for they turned upon each other with such a
strange, bewildered expression that all of us burst out laughing.

But our hostess come to their defense. "What is there to
laugh at?" she demanded, and lit a cigarette to hide her own
laughter. And Ramshevitch helped her out by explaining to
them briefly and clearly the meaning and the use of cards;
concluding with the observation that cards were both a diversion
and a vocation. In short, you could say that cards were a trade.
A trade like any other.

And saying this, Velvel the cantor's son-in-law picked up
the cards again with a quick glance at all of us to see if we
were ready, and to show the meddlers that we were busy and
that time was short. Let them stop bothering us; it was time for
them to get up and be on their way.

But that was apparently not their intention. On the contrary, they edged still closer to the table and stared at our host
who was now shuffling the cards. Their eyes grew large as
though they were expecting something to pop out at any minute.

"I hope I am not disturbing you," said the *Bal-Shem-Tov's*
grandchild again in his unctuous tone and with his fine sweet
smile . . .

"Do you want to watch us play?" Ramshevitch interrupted. "Then go ahead and watch. You can't do us any harm. Well, children! Let's get to work! Time doesn't stand still! Whose deal is it now?"

And the interrupted work was resumed with a new vigor, a new warmth, with skill and cunning; as they say in society, with *éclat*.

And the visitors looked on, listened to every word we said, and studied our hands. And every time that one of us cautiously looked at our covered card, our two guests bent and turned and twisted until they could see the card too, and made such strange faces that it was all we could do to keep from splitting with laughter. It was lucky we were all so absorbed in the game that nothing less than an earthquake could have disturbed us.

I am afraid that I was the only one who really kept an eye on them. From time to time I looked up and I began to think that to them we must look even stranger than they did to us. We and not they were peculiar, involved in a strange pursuit, speaking a wild language and conducting ourselves in general like savages: sitting bareheaded, inhaling smoke, exchanging little squares of paper, throwing money into a plate, and talking to each other in a language that might have been Turkish or Greek. For who could understand the meaning of *pass, deuce, pair, flush, jack, queen, king, ace,* and other such words that belong to the language of cards?

I can swear to you that we had forgotten all about the two holy men in our midst, when suddenly a pale white hand came slapping down on the deck of cards, and we heard these words:

"There! Now we understand it! We've caught on to it! It's a temptation, I tell you! A terrible temptation! The work of the devil himself and all the evil spirits! Do us a favor, please! Give us some too! Oh, what a diabolic invention! I hope the Lord will pardon us. Man is sinful. I beg you, give us some! We want to feel the taste of these cnards too!"

It was the *Bal-Shem-Tov's* grandchild who said this. He said it in such a trembling voice, with such fire and feeling, almost with tears in his eyes, that it almost tore our hearts out. And to our sympathy was added the sight of the kerchief full of gold and silver . . . Each one of us, I am afraid, would have liked the kerchief and what was in it to become his personal property. You should have seen our Chayela Ramshevitch. Her eyes were aflame and her cheeks were flushed, and she said to her husband and to the rest of us:

"They are asking us a favor. Why shouldn't we let them? After all, it's *Hannukah*." And her eyes were on the kerchief with the money which the *Bal-Shem-Tov's* grandchild had now drawn close to him, and from which with trembling fingers he was taking out coin after coin, one for himself and one for his companion, making two even piles of silver, one for each of them. At the same time he murmured to himself apologetically:

"Never mind! We have a great and powerful God! If we win, the *yeshivas* will have more money. And if we should lose, then the Lord will pardon us. He is long-suffering, as Jeremiah so truthfully said."

Thus he spoke, with a glance aloft, and his companion followed him, also with an upward glance and with these holy words:

"Long-suffering and full of kindness and truth."

All of this happened so suddenly, so unexpectedly, that not one of us had time even to be surprised. It seemed as natural as could be. And in addition I must confess that our minds were playing with the kerchief of money and our eyes were fixed on the two piles of silver.

There was only one thing left to decide: which of us should drop out. With two new players added, the question now was, which of us should make room for them. You understand, of course, that none of us was anxious to retire when the rare opportunity presented itself of playing with the grandchild of so holy a man as the *Bal-Shem-Tov,* especially when he had been so thoughtful as to have brought with him a kerchief full of money. And the argument began.

"You go take a rest." "No, you." "Why should I?" "You look tired."

The first to be sacrificed on the altar of hospitality was the pampered son-in-law I have already told you about, Eli Rafalski, the one who a little earlier in the evening had lit the *Hannukah* candles for us. And it was our hostess, Chayela Ramshevitch, who decided that. She insisted that it was time for him to go home. It was late, his wife's parents would complain; they might even create a scandal, and it would get them all into trouble.

That was her excuse, but all of us knew the truth. Eli had lost all he had and no one wanted to let him have any more. In the midst of a game no one loans out money.

That took care of one. For the second we drew lots. And then we went to work. Little by little the two fresh even stacks of silver disappeared, the kerchief became lighter and lighter, while in front of each of us now appeared the funds once destined for the *yeshivas* of all the world. Soon the kerchief was almost empty and it began to look as if the *Bal-Shem-Tov's* grandchild would be lucky if he still had his gabardine to go away in. We were beginning to wonder what would happen if we took their last *kopek* away. What would the town say? What would the whole world say?

But all of you who play the game know the mysterious

quality that cards possess. One minute you're flat on the ground, ready to be carried out in a blanket, and suddenly your luck changes—you don't know yourself how it happened! That's just what happened to our visitors. They began to win hand after hand, especially when the *Bal-Shem-Tov's* grandchild began to deal.

"They are possessed by the devil. Let me have them," he said, taking the cards and beginning to deal them out, at first clumsily and inaccurately, with trembling, inexperienced hands, and eyes that followed each card until it landed. Looking at him we could not suppress our laughter. But as time went on he began to do it faster and faster until the cards sped from his hands in an endless stream. And everything went his way. No matter what cards you had, he had better ones. If you had three jacks, he had three queens. If you had kings, he had aces. If you had aces, he had a flush. And if you became frightened and dropped out with an unpromising pair, he had nothing at all! Until, with a start, he pushed his chair back, sprang to his feet, and stretched himself.

"*Raboisa!*" he cried, gathering up his winnings and stuffing them not into the kerchief but into his own pockets. And then with a glance aloft he sighed, and his companion followed him with the same upward glance and the same sigh, and finished the quotation from the Passover services which the other had started:

"*Masters, the time has come to say the morning prayers!*"

Stunned and sleepy, hungry and depressed, sulking as losers always do, we remained sitting a while, unable to move. Then gradually one by one we got up and went to the table for a drink and a bite to eat. That is, all except our two guests, who were ready to take their leave, and coming to the doorway did not forget to kiss the *mazuza*.

But suddenly our host, Velvel Ramshevitch, jumped in front of them, and spreading our his arms, blocked their way with these words:

"Oh, no! You can't go away from here without taking a bite to eat!"

Velvel could not have imagined a vengeance more complete. Our poor guests stood as though trapped, looking at each other as if we were forcing them to empty their pockets of all their winnings. The first to recover his speech was the *Bal-Shem-Tov's* grandchild, who addressed us once more with his unctuous tone and his sweet little smile:

"We thank you wholeheartedly for your kindness. Hospitality to wayfarers is, according to our Law, one of the greatest of all acts of virtue. But you must not forget that my companion and I are careful about what meat we allow to touch our lips. No doubt it's *kosher,* but . . ."

That was too much for us. "Oh, so you can't eat our food!" we cried. "You're afraid it isn't *kosher* enough for you, but our cards were *kosher* enough? To take our money away was proper enough? No, we won't let you get away with that! You tasted our hospitality at the card table; now you must taste some sausage too!"

Crestfallen, they looked at each other. Then the *Bal-Shem-Tov's* grandchild let out a deep sigh, almost a groan, and said to us. "Just as you say, my friends. After all, we are in a Jewish home, and we must never be suspicions of our own people. And what if the food, heaven forbid, is not as *kosher* as it might be? Our Lord is a great and mighty One . . ."

And murmuring a prayer that none of us could make out, he turned humbly toward the table were our hostess was preparing sardines, herring and sausages. Picking up a glass he turned to us. "Your health, my friends. I drink your health," he said, and lifted the glass and barely moistened his lips.

Then, with a trembling hand he took a bite of herring, and then a thin slice of sausage. His companion followed him, and together they struggled with their food, almost choking on it. And only when they were through did Velvel take his full revenge. Without a trace of pity, he addressed them in these words:

"Do you know what you have just eaten? It was not Jewish food at all. Do you know what kind of sausage that was? Do you know what it was made of? Gentlemen, you have just been eating real, genuine . . ."

Before he could finish the sentence our two visitors clutched their heads in terror, opened their mouths wide as if to spit everything out, and then with a bitter groan sprang for the door and swept out of the house like a cyclone.

Our vengeance was so complete that we almost forgot how much we had lost that night, forgot the depths to which we had sunk, and looking at each other we laughed and laughed and laughed. We thought we would never stop laughing, but we did—and suddenly too—when from the table where we had been playing we heard a shriek that was barely human.

"Quick! Quick! Come here! Oh, may lightning strike me! I can't bear it!"

It was Chayela Ramshevitch. We had not even noticed that as soon as she had finished eating she had gone back to the table to clean things up. First, as always, she gathered up the cards we had played with; they could still be sold or traded for new decks. And in sorting out the cards she had noticed something strange. There were too many aces—far too many. Six or seven to the deck.

We grabbed up the rest of the cards and discovered not only aces but a wealth of everything else as well: kings and queens and jacks, in fact everything! And many of them! Well, we didn't go home to rest as we had planned. Instead, we made a

pilgrimage. We went to every synagogue in town, visited
every chapel and prayer house. We looked everywhere, searched
everywhere, asked everywhere. But no one had seen the *Bal-
Shem-Tov's* grandchild and his companion. No one had even
heard of them.

Unsuccessful, dejected, we decided to try the railroad station. There we searched everywhere. We went through the
station itself, through every carriage in the waiting train. Not
a sign of the grandchild or his companion. The earth must
have swallowed them both!

It was after the third bell had rung, the last whistle had
blown, that we heard a familiar voice from one of the carriages.

"Cnards!"

We sprang toward the carriage from which the word had
come. From an open window of a second-class carriage, two
strange men were watching us with interest and amusement.
One was tall and thin, the other short and fat. Both were
clean-shaven, both wore short tailored jackets and derby hats.
And yet they were familiar. Not so much the faces as the eyes—
soft, smiling, shrewd little eyes.

The first to recognize them was the pampered son-in-law,
Eli Rafalski. As soon as he saw their smiling faces he pointed
straight at them:

"There they are!" he cried. "There they are! The two cnard
players—as sure as my name is Rafalski!"

But the train was already moving. The wheels had just begun
to turn. And slowly passing us by, the two men looked at us
once more with their soft, smiling shrewd eyes. And for Eli
Rafalski, who had been so acute as to recognize them, they
had a special farewell.

Together they raised their thumbs to their noses, and made
a broad arc with their outstretched fingers.

The Bubble Bursts

"THERE are many thoughts in a man's heart." So I believe it is
written in the Holy *Torah.* I don't have to translate the passage for
you, Mr. Sholom Aleichem. But, speaking in plain Yiddish, there is
a saying: "The most obedient horse needs a whip; the cleverest man
can use advice." In regard to whom do I say this? I say it in regard
to myself, for if I had once had the good sense to go to a friend and
tell him such and such, thus and so, this calamity would never have
taken place. But how is it said? *"Life and death issue from thine own
lips.*—When God sees fit to punish a man he first takes away his good
sense."

How many times have I thought to myself: Look, Tevye, you
dolt, you are not supposed to be a complete fool. How could you have
allowed yourself to be taken in so completely and in such a foolish
way? Wouldn't it have been better for you if you had been content
with your little dairy business whose fame has spread far and wide,
everywhere from Boiberik to Yehupetz? How sweet and pleasant it
would have been if your little hoard still lay in its box, buried deep
where not a soul could see or know. For whose business is it whether
Tevye has money or not? Was anyone concerned with Tevye when
he lay buried nine feet deep, wrapped in his poverty like a dead man
in his shroud? Did the world care when he starved three times a day
together with his wife and children?

But lo and behold! When God turned his countenance on Tevye and
caused him to prosper all at once, so that at last he was beginning to

389

arrive somewhere, beginning to save up a *ruble* now and then, the world suddenly became aware of his presence, and overnight, mind you, plain Tevye became Reb Tevye, nothing less. Suddenly out of nowhere a multitude of friends sprang up. As it is written: *"He is beloved by everyone."* Or, as we put it: "When God gives a dot, the world adds a lot."

Everyone came to me with a different suggestion. This one tells me to open a drygoods store, that one a grocery. Another one says to buy a building—property is a sound investment, it lasts forever. One tells me to invest in wheat, another in timber. Still another suggests auctioneering. "Friends!" I cry. "Brothers! Leave me alone. You've got the wrong man. You must think I'm Brodsky, but I am still very far from being a Brodsky. It is easy to estimate another's wealth. You see something that glitters like gold at a distance. You come close and it's only a brass button."

May no good come to them—I mean those friends of mine, those well-wishers—they cast an evil eye on me. God sent me a relative from somewhere, a distant kinsman of some kind whom I had never seen before. Menachem-Mendel is his name—a gadabout, a wastrel, a faker, a worthless vagabond, may he never stand still in one place. He got hold of me and filled my head with dreams and fantasies, things that had never been on land or sea. You will ask me: *"Wherefore did it come to pass?"* How did I ever get together with Menachem-Mendel? And I will answer in the words of the *Hagadah: "For we were slaves."* It was fated, that's all. Listen to my story.

I arrived in Yehupetz in early winter, with my choicest merchandise —over twenty pounds of butter fresh from Butterland and several pails of cheese. I had salted away everything I had, you understand, didn't leave a smidgen for myself, not as much as a medicine spoon would hold. I didn't even have the time to visit all of my regular customers, the summer people of Boiberik, who await my coming as a good Jew waits for the coming of the Messiah. For say what you will, there isn't a merchant in Yehupetz who can produce a piece of goods that comes up to mine. I don't have to tell you this. As the prophet says: *"Let another praise thee.*—Good merchandise speaks for itself."

Well, I sold out everything to the last crumb, threw a bundle of hay to my horse and went for a walk around the town. *"Man is born of dust and to dust he returneth."* After all, I am only human. I want to see something of the world, breathe some fresh air, take a look at the wonders Yehupetz displays behind glass windows, as though to say: "Use your eyes all you want, but with your hands—away!"

Standing in front of a large window filled with seven and a half *ruble* gold pieces, with piles of silver *rubles,* and stacks of paper money of all kinds, I think to myself: God in Heaven! If I had only a tenth of what all of this is worth! What more could I ask of God and who would be my equal? First of all, I would marry off my oldest daughter, give her a suitable dowry and still have enough left over for wedding expenses, gifts, and clothing for the bride. Then I would sell my horse and wagon and my cows and move into town. I would buy myself a Synagogue seat by the Eastern Wall, hang strings of pearls around my wife's neck, and hand out charity like the richest householders. I would see to it that the Synagogue got a new roof instead of standing as it does now, practically roofless, ready to cave in any minute. I would open a school for the children and build a hospital such as they have in other towns so that the town's poor and sick wouldn't have to lie underfoot in the Synagogue. And I would get rid of Yankel Sheigetz, as president of the Burial Society. There's been enough guzzling of brandy and chicken livers at public expense!

"Sholom aleichem, Reb Tevye," I hear a voice right in back of me. I turn around and take a look. I could swear I have seen this man somewhere before.

"Aleichem sholom," I answer. "And where do you hail from?"

"Where do I hail from? From Kasrilevka," he says. "I am a relative of yours. That is, your wife Golde is my second cousin once removed."

"Hold on!" I say. "Aren't you Boruch-Hersh Leah-Dvoshe's son-in-law?"

"You've hit the nail right on the head," he says. "I am Boruch-Hersh Leah-Dvoshe's son-in-law and my wife is Sheina Sheindel Boruch-Hersh Leah-Dvoshe's daughter. Now do you know who I am?"

"Wait," I say. "Your mother-in-law's grandmother Sarah-Yenta and my wife's aunt, Fruma-Zlata, were, I believe, first cousins, and if I am not mistaken you are the middle son-in-law of Boruch-Hersh Leah-

Dvoshe's. But I forget what they call you. Your name has flown right out of my head. Tell me, what is your name?"

"My name," he says, "is Menachem-Mendel Boruch-Hersh Leah-Dvoshe's. That's what they call me at home, in Kasrilevka."

"If that's the case," I say, "my dear Menachem-Mendel, I really owe you a *sholom aleichem* and a hearty one! Now, tell me, my friend, what are you doing here, and how is your mother-in-law, and your father-in-law? How is your health, and how is business with you?"

"As far as my health," he says, "God be thanked. I am still alive. But business is not so gay."

"It will get better, with God's help," I tell him, stealing a look meanwhile at his shabby coat and the holes in his shoes. "Don't despair, God will come to your aid. Business will get better, no doubt. As the proverb says: '*All is vanity.*—Money is round, it is here today, gone tomorrow.' The main thing is to stay alive and keep hoping. A Jew must never stop hoping. Do we wear ourselves down to a shadow in the meanwhile? That's why we are Jews. How is it said? If you're a soldier you have to smell gunpowder. '*Man is likened to a broken pot.*—The world is nothing but a dream.' Tell me, Menachem-Mendel, how do you happen to be in Yehupetz all of a sudden?"

"What do you mean how do I happen to be in Yehupetz all of a sudden? I've been here no less than a year and a half."

"Oh," said I, "then you belong here. You are living in Yehupetz."

"Sshh" he whispers, looking all about him. "Don't talk so loud, Reb Tevye. I *am* living in Yehupetz, but that's just between you and me."

I stare at him as though he were out of his mind. "You are a fugitive," I ask, "and you hide in the middle of the public square?"

"Don't ask, Reb Tevye. You are apparently not acquainted with the laws and customs of Yehupetz. Listen and I'll explain to you how a man can live here and still not live here." And he began telling me a long tale of woe, of all the trials and tribulations of life in the city of Yehupetz.

When he finished I said to him, "Take my advice, Menachem-Mendel, come along with me to the country for a day and rest your tired bones. You will be a guest at our house, a very welcome guest. My wife will be overjoyed to have you."

Well, I talked him into it. He went with me. We arrive at home. What rejoicing! A guest! And such a guest! A second-cousin-once-removed. After all, blood is thicker than water. My wife starts right in, "What is new in Kasrilevka? How is Uncle Boruch-Hersh? And Aunt Leah-Dvoshe? And Uncle Yossel-Menashe? And Aunt Dobrish? And how are their children? Who has died recently? Who has been married? Who is divorced? Who has given birth? And who is expecting?"

"What do you care about strange weddings and strange circumcisions?" I tell my wife. "Better see to it that we get something to eat. As it is written, *'All who are hungry enter and be fed.—*Nobody likes to dance on an empty stomach.' If you give us a *borsht,* fine. If not, I'll take *knishes* or *kreplach,* pudding or dumplings. *Blintzes* with cheese will suit me too. Make anything you like and the more the better, but do it quickly."

Well, we washed, said grace, and had our meal. *"They ate,"* as Rashi says. "Eat, Menachem-Mendel, eat," I urged him. *"'Forget the world,'* as King David once said. It's a stupid world, and a deceitful one, and health and happiness, as my grandmother Nechama of blessed memory used to say—she was a clever woman and a wise one—health and happiness are only to be found at the table."

Our guest—his hands trembled as he reached for the food, poor fellow—couldn't find enough words in praise of my wife's cooking. He swore by everything holy that he couldn't remember when he had eaten such a dairy supper, such perfect *knishes,* such delicious *vertutin.*

"Stuff and nonsense," I tell him. "You should taste her noodle pudding. Then you would know what heaven on earth can be."

After we had eaten and said our benedictions, we began talking, each one naturally talking of what concerned him most. I talk about my business, he of his. I babble of this, that, and the other, important and unimportant. He tells me stories of Yehupetz and Odessa, of how he had been ten times over, as they say, "on horseback and thrown off the horse." A rich man today, a beggar tomorrow, again a rich man, and once more a pauper. He dealt in something I had never heard of in my life—crazy-sounding things—stocks, bonds, shares-shmares, Maltzev-shmaltzev. The devil alone knew what it was. The sums that he reeled off his tongue were fantastic—ten thousand, twenty thousand, thirty thousand—he threw money around like matches.

"I'll tell you the truth, Menachem-Mendel," I say to him. "Your business sounds very involved, you need brains to understand all of that. But what puzzles me most is this: from what I know of your better half it's a wonder to me that she lets you go traipsing around the world and doesn't come riding after you on a broomstick."

"Don't remind me of that," he says with a deep sigh. "I get enough from her as it is, both hot and cold. If you could see the letters she writes me you would admit that I am a saint to put up with it. But that's a small matter. That's what a wife is for—to bury her husband alive. There are worse things than that. I have also, as you know, a mother-in-law. I don't have to go into detail. You have met her."

"It is with you as it is written: *The flocks were speckled and streaked and spotted.*—You have a boil on top of a boil and a blister on top of that.'"

"Yes," he says. "You put it very well, Reb Tevye. The boil is bad enough in itself, but the blister—ah, that blister is worse than the boil."

Well, we kept up this palaver until late into the night. My head whirled with his tales of fantastic transactions, of thousands that rose and fell, fabulous fortunes that were won and lost and won again. I tossed all night long dreaming in snatches of Yehupetz and Brodsky, of millions of *rubles,* of Menachem-Mendel and his mother-in-law.

Early the next morning he begins hemming and hawing and finally comes out with it. Here is what he says. "Since the stock market has for a long time been in such a state that money is held in high esteem and goods are held very low, you Tevye have a chance to make yourself a pretty penny. And while you are getting rich you will at the same time be saving my life, you will actually raise me from the dead."

"You talk like a child," I say to him. "You must think I have a big sum of money to invest. Fool, may we both earn before next Passover what I lack to make me a Brodsky."

"I know," he says, "without your telling me. But what makes you think we need big money? If you give me a hundred *rubles* now, I can turn it in three or four days into two hundred or three hundred or six hundred or maybe even into a thousand *rubles.*"

"It may be as it is written: '*The profit is great, but it's far from my pocket.*' Who says I have anything to invest at all? And if there is no hundred *rubles,* it's as Rashi says: '*You came in alone and you go out by yourself.*' Or, as I put it, 'If you plant a stone, up comes a boulder.' "

"Come now," he says to me, "you know you can dig up a hundred *rubles.* With all the money you are earning and with your name . . ."

"A good name is an excellent thing," I tell him. "But what comes of it? I keep my name and Brodsky has the money. If you want to know the truth, my savings come all in all close to a hundred *rubles.* And I have two dozen uses for it. First of all, to marry off my daughter . . ."

"Just what I've been trying to tell you," he breaks in. "When will you have the opportunity to put in a hundred *rubles* and to take out, with God's help, enough to marry off your daughter and to do all the other things besides?"

And he went on with this chant for the next three hours, explaining how he could make three *rubles* out of one and ten out of three. First you bring in one hundred *rubles* somewhere, and you tell them to buy ten pieces of I-forget-what-you-call-it, then you wait a few days until they go up. You send a telegram somewhere else to sell the ten pieces and buy twice as many for the money. Then you wait and they rise again. You shoot off another telegram. You keep doing this until the hundred *rubles* become two hundred, then four hundred, then eight hundred, then sixteen hundred. It's no less than a miracle from God. There are people in Yehupetz, he tells me, who until recently went barefoot—they didn't have a pair of shoes to their names. They worked as errand boys and messengers. Now they own palatial homes, their wives have expensive stomach ailments, they go abroad for cures. They themselves fly all over Yehupetz on rubber wheels, they don't recognize old friends any more.

Well, why should I drag out the story? I caught the fever from him. Who knows, I think to myself, maybe he was sent by my good

angel? He tells me that people win fortunes in Yehupetz, ordinary
people with not more than five fingers to each hand. Am I any
worse than they? I don't believe he is a liar, he couldn't make all these
things up out of his own head. Who knows, suppose the wheel turns,
and Tevye becomes a somebody in his old age? How much longer
can I keep on toiling and moiling from dawn until dark? Day in and
day out—the same horse and wagon, night and day the same butter
and cheese? It's time, Tevye, that you took a little rest, became a man
among men, went into the Synagogue once in a while, turned the
pages of a holy book. Why not? And on the other hand, if I lose out,
if it should fall buttered side down? But better not think of that.

"What do you say?" I ask my wife. "What do you think of his
proposition?"

"What do you want me to say?" she asks. "I know that Menachem-
Mendel isn't a nobody who would want to swindle you. He doesn't
come from a family of nobodies. He has a very respectable father, and
as for his grandfather, he was a real jewel. All his life, even after he
became blind, he studied the *Torah*. And Grandmother Tzeitl, may
she rest in peace, was no ordinary woman either."

"A fitting parable," I said. "It's like bringing *Hannukah* candles to
a *Purim* Feast. We talk about investments and she drags in her
Grandmother Tzeitl who used to bake honeycake, and her grandfather who died of drink. That's a woman for you. No wonder King
Solomon traveled the world over and didn't find a female with an
ounce of brains in her head."

To make a long story short, we decided to form a partnership. I
put in my money and Menachem-Mendel, his wits. Whatever God
gives, we will divide in half. "Believe me, Reb Tevye," he says, "you
won't regret doing business with me. With God's help the money will
come pouring in."

"Amen and the same to you," I say. "From your lips into God's
ears. There is just one thing I want to know. How does the mountain
come to the prophet? You are over there in Yehupetz and I am here
in the country; and money, as you know, is a delicate substance. It
isn't that I don't trust you, but as Father Abraham says, '*If you sow
with tears you shall reap with joy.*—It's better to be safe than sorry.'"

"Oh," he says, "would you rather we drew up a paper? Most willingly."

"Listen," I say to him, "if you want to ruin me, what good will a piece of paper do me? *'The mouse is not the thief.*—It isn't the note that pays, but the man.' If I am hung by one foot I might as well be hung by both."

"Believe me, Reb Tevye," he says to me, "I swear to you on my word of honor, may God be my witness, that I have no tricks up my sleeve. I won't swindle you, but I will deal with you honestly. I will divide our earnings equally with you, share and share alike—a hundred to you, a hundred to me, two hundred to you, two hundred to me, four hundred to you, four hundred to me, a thousand to you, a thousand to me."

So I dug out my little hoard, counted the money over three times, my hands shaking the whole time, called over my wife as a witness, and explained to him again that this was blood-money I was giving him, and sewed it carefully inside his shirt so that no one would rob him of it on the way. He promised that he would write me not later than a week from Saturday and tell me everything in detail. Then we said good-bye with much feeling, embraced like close friends, and he went on his way.

When I was left alone there began to pass in front of my eyes all sorts of visions—visions so sweet that I wished they would never end. I saw a large house with a tin roof right in the middle of town, and inside the house were big rooms and little rooms and pantries full of good things, and around it a yard full of chickens and ducks and geese. I saw the mistress of the house walking around jingling her keys. That was my wife Golde, but what a different Golde from the one I knew. This one had the face and manner of a rich man's wife, with a double chin and a neck hung with pearls. She strutted around like a peacock giving herself airs, and yelling at the servant girls. And here were my daughters dressed in their Sabbath best, lolling around, not lifting a finger for themselves. The house was full of brightness and cheer. Supper was cooking in the oven. The samovar boiled merrily on the table. And at the head of the table sat the master of the house, Tevye himself, in a robe and skullcap, and around him sat the foremost householders of the town, fawning on him. "If you please, Reb Tevye. Pardon me, Reb Tevye."—And so on.

"What fiendish power money has!" I exclaimed.

"Whom are you cursing?" asked Golde.

"Nobody. I was just thinking," I told her. "Daydreams and moonshine . . . Tell me Golde, my love, do you know what sort of merchandise he deals in, that cousin of yours, Menachem-Mendel?"

"What's that?" she said. "Bad luck to my enemies! Here he has spent a day and a night talking with the man, and in the end he comes and asks me, 'What does he deal in?' For God's sake, you made up a contract with him. You are partners."

"Yes," I said. "We made up something, but I don't know what we made up. If my life depended on it, I wouldn't know. There is nothing, you see, that I can get hold of. But one thing has nothing to do with the other. Don't worry, my dear wife. My heart tells me that it is all for the best. We are going to make a lot of money. Say amen to that and go cook supper."

Well, a week goes by and two and three. There is no news from my partner. I am beside myself with worry. It can't be that he has just forgotten to write. He knows quite well how anxiously we are waiting to hear from him. A thought flits through my head. What shall I do if he skims off the cream for himself and tells me that there is no profit? But that, I tell myself, can't be. It just isn't possible. I treat the man like one of my own, so how can he turn around and play a trick like that on me? Then something worse occurs to me. Profit be hanged. Who cares about profit? *"Deliverance and protection will come from the Lord."* May God only keep the capital from harm. I feel a chill go up and down my back. "You old fool," I tell myself. "You idiot. You made your bed, now lie on it. For the hundred *rubles* you could have bought yourself a pair of horses such as your forefathers never had, or exchanged your old wagon for a carriage with springs."

"Tevye, why don't you think of something?" my wife pleads with me.

"What do you mean why don't I think of something? My head is splitting into little pieces from thinking and she asks why don't I think."

"Something must have happened to him on the road," says my wife. "He was attacked by robbers, or else he got sick on the way. Or he may even be dead."

"What will you dream up next, my love?" I ask. "All of a sudden she has to start pulling robbers out of thin air." But to myself I think: "No telling what can happen to a man alone on the road."

"You always imagine the worst," I tell my wife.

"He comes of such a good family," she says. "His mother, may she intercede for us in Heaven, died not long ago, she was still a young woman. He had three sisters. One died as a girl; the other one lived to get married but caught cold coming from the bath and died; and the third one lost her mind after her first child was born, ailed for a long time, and died too."

"To live until we die is our lot," I tell her. "We must all die sometime. A man is compared to a carpenter. A carpenter lives and lives until he dies, and a man lives and lives until he dies."

Well, we decided that I should go to Yehupetz. Quite a bit of merchandise had accumulated in the meanwhile—cheese and butter and cream, all of the best. My wife harnessed the horse and wagon, and *"they journeyed from Sukos"*—as Rashi says. On to Yehupetz!

Naturally my heart was heavy and my thoughts gloomy as I rode through the woods. I began to imagine the worst. Suppose, I think to myself, I arrive and begin to inquire about my man and they tell me, "Menachem-Mendel? Oh, that one? He has done well by himself. He has feathered his own nest. He owns a mansion, rides in his own carriage, you wouldn't recognize him." But just the same I gather up courage and go to his house. "Get out!" they tell me at the door, and shove me aside with their elbows. "Don't push your way, Uncle. We don't allow that."

"I am his relative," I tell them. "He is my wife's second cousin once removed."

"Mazl-tov," they tell me. "We are overjoyed to hear it. But just the same it won't hurt you to wait a little at the door."

It occurs to me that I should slip the doorman a bribe. As it is said: *"What goes up must come down";* or, "If you don't grease the axle the wheels won't turn." And so I get in.

"Good morning to you, Reb Menachem-Mendel," I say.

Who? What? *"There is no speech. There are no words."* He looks at me as though he has never seen me before. "What do you want?" he says.

I am ready to faint. "What do you mean?" I say. "Don't you recognize your own cousin? My name is Tevye."

"Tevye . . ." he says slowly. "The name sounds familiar."

"So the name sounds familiar to you. Maybe my wife's *blintzes* sound familiar too? You may even remember the taste of her *knishes* and *kreplach?"*

Then I imagine exactly the opposite. I come in to see Menachem-Mendel and he meets me at the door with outstretched arms. "Welcome, Reb Tevye. Welcome. Be seated. How are you? And how is your wife? I've been waiting for you. I want to settle my account with you." And he takes my cap and pours it full of gold pieces. "This," he tells me, "is what we earned on our investment. The capital we shall leave where it is. Whatever we make we shall divide equally, share and share alike, half to me, half to you, a hundred to me, a hundred to you, two hundred to you, two hundred to me, five hundred to you, five hundred to me. . . ."

While I am lost in this dream, my horse strays from the path, the wagon gets caught against a tree, and I am jolted from behind so suddenly that sparks fly in front of my eyes. "This is all for the best," I comfort myself. "Thank God the axle didn't break."

I arrive in Yehupetz, dispose of my wares quickly and, as usual, without any trouble, and set out to look for my partner. I wander around for an hour, I wander around for two hours. It's no use. It's as Jacob said about Benjamin: *"The lad is gone."* I can't find him anywhere. I stop people in the street and ask them, "Have you seen or have you heard of a man who goes by the elegant name of Menachem-Mendel?"

"Well, well," they tell me, "if his name is Menachem-Mendel, you can look for him with a candle. But that isn't enough. There is more than one Menachem-Mendel in the world."

"I see, you want to know his family name. At home in Kasrilevka he is known by his mother-in-law's name—Menachem-Mendel Leah-Dvoshe's. What more do you want? Even his father-in-law, who is a very old man, is known by his wife's name, Boruch-Hersh Leah-Dvoshe's. Now do you understand?"

"We understand very well," they say. "But that isn't enough. What does this Menachem-Mendel do? What is his business?"

"His business? He deals in seven and a half *ruble* gold pieces, in Putilov shares, in stocks and bonds. He shoots telegrams here, there, and everywhere—to St. Petersburg, Odessa, Warsaw."

They roll with laughter. "Oh you mean Menachem-Mendel-who-deals-in-all-and-sundry? Turn left and follow this street and you will see many hares running around. Yours will be among them."

"Live and learn," I say to myself. "Now I am told to look for hares." I follow the street they pointed out to me. It's as crowded as our town square on market day. I can barely push my way through. People are running around like crazy—shouting, waving their hands, quarreling. It's a regular bedlam. I hear shouts of *Putilov*, "shares," "stocks . . ." "he gave me his word . . ." "here is a down payment . . ." "buy on margin . . ." "he owes me a fee . . ." "you are a sucker . . ." "spit in his face . . ." "look at that speculator." Any minute they will start fighting in earnest, dealing out blows. *"Jacob fled,"* I mutter to myself. "Get out, Tevye, before you get knocked down. God is our Father, Tevye the Dairyman is a sinner, Yehupetz is a city, and Menachem-Mendel is a breadwinner. So this is where people make fortunes? This is how they do their business? May God have mercy on you, Tevye, and on such business."

I stopped in front of a large window with a display of clothing in it and whom should I see reflected in it but my partner Menachem-Mendel. My heart was squeezed with pity at the sight. . . . *I became faint.* . . . May our worst enemies look the way Menachem-Mendel looked. You should have seen his coat. And his shoes. Or what was left of them. And his face! A corpse laid out for burial looks cheerful by comparison. "Well, Tevye," I said to myself as Esther had once said to Mordecai, " 'if I perish, I perish.—I am done for.' You may as well kiss your savings good-bye. 'There is no bear and no woods.—No merchandise and no money.' Nothing but a pack of troubles."

He looked pretty crestfallen on his part. We both stood there, rooted to the ground, unable to speak. There seemed to be nothing left to say, nothing left to do. We might as well pick up our sacks and go over the city begging.

"Reb Tevye," he says to me softly, barely able to utter the words, the tears are choking him so, "Reb Tevye, without luck, it's better never to have been born at all. Rather than live like this, it is better to hang from a tree or rot in the ground."

"For such a deed," I burst out, "for what you've done to me, you deserve to be stretched out right here in the middle of Yehupetz and flogged so hard that you lose consciousness. Consider for yourself what you've done. You've taken a houseful of innocent people who never did you a speck of harm, and without a knife you slit their throats clear through. How can I face my wife and children now? Tell me, you robber, you murderer, you—"

"It is all true, Reb Tevye," he says, leaning against the wall. "All true. May God have mercy on me."

"The fires of hell," I tell him, "the tortures of Gehenna are too good for you."

"All true," he says. "May God have pity on me. All true. Rather than to live like this, Reb Tevye, rather than to live—" And he hangs his head.

I look at him standing there, the poor shlimazl, leaning against the wall, his head bent, his cap awry. He sighs and he groans and my heart turns over with pity.

"And yet," I say, "if you want to look at it another way, you may not be to blame either. When I think it over, I realize that you couldn't have done it out of plain knavery. After all, you were my partner, you had a share in the business. I put in my money and you put in your brains. Woe unto us both. I am sure you meant it for the best. It must have been fate. How is it said? 'Don't rejoice today, because tomorrow—' Or, 'Man proposes and God disposes.'

"If you want proof, just look at my business. It seems to be completely foolproof, a guaranteed thing. And yet when it came to pass last fall that one of my cows lay down and died and right after her a young calf—was there anything I could do about it? When luck turns against you, you are lost.

"I don't even want to ask you where my money is. I understand only too well. My blood money went up in smoke, it sank into the grave. . . . And whose fault is it if not mine? I let myself be talked into it. I went chasing after rainbows. If you want money, my friend, you have to work and slave for it, you have to wear your fingers to the bone. I deserve a good thrashing for it. But crying about it won't help. How is it written? *'If the maiden screamed*—You can shout until you burst a blood vessel.' Hindsight, as they say . . . It wasn't fated that Tevye should be a rich man. As Ivan says, 'Mikita never had anything and never will.' God willed it so. *'The Lord giveth and the Lord taketh away.'* Come, brother, let's go get a drink."

And that, Mr. Sholom Aleichem, is how my beautiful dream burst like a bubble and vanished into thin air. Do you think I took it to heart? Do you think I grieved over the loss of my money? Not at all. We know what the proverb says: *"The silver and the gold are mine.*—Money is worthless." Only man is important, that is, if he is really a man, a human being. For what did I grieve then? I grieved for the dream I had lost, the dream of wealth that was gone forever. For I had longed, how I had longed, to be a rich man, if only for a short while. But what did it avail me? The proverb says, *"Perforce you live and perforce you die.*—You live in spite of yourself and you wear out your shoes in spite of yourself."

"You, Tevye," says God, "stick to your cheese and butter and forget your dreams." But what about hope? Naturally, the harder life is the more you must hope. The poorer you are the more cheerful you must be.

Do you want proof? But I think I have talked too long already, I have to be on my way, I have to tend to business. As it is said: *"Every man is a liar.*—Everyone has his affliction." Farewell, be healthy and happy always. . . .

If I Were Rothschild

IF I WERE ROTHSCHILD, ah, if I were only Rothschild—a Kasrilevka *melamed* let himself go once upon a Thursday while his wife was demanding money for the Sabbath and he had none to give her. If I were only Rothschild, guess what I would do. First of all I would pass a law that a wife must always have a three-*ruble* piece on her so that she wouldn't have to start nagging me when the good Thursday comes and there is nothing in the house for the Sabbath. In the second place I would take my Sabbath gabardine out of pawn—or better still, my wife's squirrel-skin coat. Let her stop whining that she's cold. Then I would buy the whole house outright, from foundation to chimney, all three rooms, with the alcove and the pantry, the cellar and the attic. Let her stop grumbling that she hasn't enough room. "Here," I would say to her, "take two whole rooms for yourself—cook, bake, wash, chop, make, and leave me in peace so that I can teach my pupils with a free mind."

This is the life! No more worries about making a living. No more headaches about where the money for the Sabbath is coming from. My daughters are all married off—a load is gone from my shoulders. What more do I need for myself? Now I can begin to look around the town a little. First of all I am going to provide a new roof for the old Synagogue so the rain won't drip on the heads of the men who come to pray. After that I shall build a new bathhouse, for if not today, then tomorrow—but surely soon—there is bound to be a catastrophe—the roof is going to cave in while the women are inside bathing. And while we are putting up a new bathhouse we might as well throw down the old poorhouse too and put up a hospital in its place, a real hospital such as they have in big towns, with beds and bedding, with a doctor and attendants, with hot broths for the sick every day. . . . And I shall build a home for the aged so that old men, scholars who have fallen upon hard times, shouldn't have to spend their last days on the hearth in the Synagogue. And I shall establish a Society for Clothing the Poor so that poor children won't have to run around in rags with—I beg your pardon for mentioning it—their navels showing. Then I shall institute a Loan Society so that anyone at all—whether he be a teacher or a workman, or even a merchant—could get money without having to pay interest and without pawning the shirt off his back. And a Society for Outfitting Brides so that any girl old enough to marry and without means should be outfitted properly and married off as befits a Jewish girl. I would organize all these and many other such societies in Kasrilevka.

But why only here in Kasrilevka? I would organize such societies everywhere, all over the world, wherever our brethren the Sons of Israel are to be found. And in order that they should all be run properly, with a system, guess what I would do. I would appoint a Society to head them all, a Board of Charity that would watch over all the societies under it. This Board of Charity would keep watch over all of Israel and see to it that Jews everywhere had enough to live on, and that they lived together in unity. It would see to it that all Jews sit in *yeshivas* and study the Bible, the *Talmud,* the *Gamorah,* and the various Commentaries and learn all the seven wisdoms and the seventy-seven languages. And over all these *yeshivas* there would be one great *yeshiva* or Jewish Academy which would naturally be located in Vilno. And from there would come the greatest scholars and wise men in the world. And all of this education would be free to everyone, all paid for out of my pocket. And I would see to it that it was all run in orderly fashion, according to plan, so that there should be none of this grab-and-run, hit-and-miss, catch-as-catch-can business. Instead, everything would be run with a view to the common welfare.

But in order to have everyone think only of the common welfare, you have to provide one thing. And what is that? Naturally, security. For, take it from me, security from want is the most important thing in the world. Without it there can be no harmony anywhere. For alas, one man will impoverish another over a piece of bread, he will kill, poison, hang his fellow-man. Even the enemies of Israel, the Hamans of the world—what do you think they have against us? Nothing at all. They don't persecute us out of plain meanness, but because of their lack of security. It's lack of money, I tell you, that brings envy and envy brings hatred, and out of hatred come all the troubles in the world, all the sorrows, persecutions, killings, all the horrors and all the wars. . . .

Ah, the wars, the wars. The terrible slaughters. If I were Rothschild I would do away with war altogether. I would wipe it off completely from the face of the earth.

You will ask how? With money, of course. Let me explain it to you. For instance, two countries are having a disagreement over some foolishness, a piece of land that's worth a pinch of snuff. "Territory" they call it. One country says this "territory" is hers and the other one says, "No, this territory is mine." You might think that on the First Day, God created this piece of land in her honor. . . . Then a third country enters and says, "You are both asses. This is everybody's 'territory,' in other words, it's a public domain." Meanwhile the argument goes on. "Territory" here, "territory" there. They "territory" each other so long that they begin shooting with guns and cannon and people start dying like sheep and blood runs everywhere like water. . . .

But if I come to them at the very beginning and say, "Listen to me, little brothers. Actually, what is your whole argument about? Do you think that I don't understand? I understand perfectly. At this feast you are concerned less with the ceremonial than with the dumplings. 'Territory' is only a pretext. What you are after is something else—something you can get your hands on—money, levies. And while we are on the subject of money, to whom does one come for a loan if not to me, that is, to Rothschild? I'll tell you what. Here, you Englishmen with the long legs and checkered trousers, take a billion. Here, you stupid Turks with the scarlet caps, take a billion also. And you, Aunt Reisel, that is Russia, take another billion. With God's help you will pay me back with interest, not a large rate of interest, God forbid, four or five percent at the most—I don't want to get rich off you."

Do you understand what I've done? I have not only put over a business deal, but people have stopped killing each other in vain, like oxen. And since there will be no more war, what do we need weapons for? What do we need armies and cannons and military bands for, and all the other trappings of war? The answer is that we don't. And if there are no more weapons and armies and bands and other trappings of war, there will be no more envy, no more hatred, no Turks, no Englishmen, no Frenchmen, no Gypsies and no Jews. The face of the earth will be changed. As it is written: "Deliverance will come—" The Messiah will have arrived.

And perhaps, even—if I were Rothschild—I might do away with money altogether. For let us not deceive ourselves, what is money anyway? It is nothing but a delusion, a made-up thing. Men have taken a piece of paper, decorated it with a pretty picture and written on it, *Three Silver Rubles*. Money, I tell you, is nothing but a temptation, a piece of lust, one of the greatest lusts. It is something that everyone wants and nobody has. But if there were no more money in the world there would be no more temptation, no more lust. Do you understand me or not? But then the problem is, without money how would we Jews be able to provide for the Sabbath? The answer to that is—How will I provide for the Sabbath now?

Modern Children

MODERN children, did you say? Ah, you bring them into the world, sacrifice yourself for them, you slave for them day and night—and what do you get out of it? You think that one way or another it would work out according to your ideas or station. After all, I don't expect to marry them off to millionaires, but then I don't have to be satisfied with just anyone, either. So I figured I'd have at least a little luck with my daughters. Why not? In the first place, didn't the Lord bless me with handsome girls; and a pretty face, as you yourself have said, is half a dowry. And besides, with God's help, I'm not the same Tevye I used to be. Now the best match, even in Yehupetz, is not beyond my reach. Don't you agree with me?

But there is a God in heaven who looks after everything. *"A Lord merciful and compassionate,"* who has His way with me summer and winter, in season and out. And He says to me, "Tevye, don't talk like a fool. Leave the management of the world to Me."

So listen to what can happen in this great world of ours. And to whom does it have to happen? To Tevye, *shlimazl.*

To make a long story short, I had just lost everything I had in a stockmarket investment I had gotten involved in through that relative of mine, Menachem-Mendel (may his name and memory be forever blotted out), and I was very low. It looked as if it was all over with me. No more Tevye, no more dairy business.

"Fool," my wife says to me. "You have worried enough. You'll get nowhere worrying. You'll just eat your heart out. Pretend that robbers had broken in and taken everything away. . . . I'll tell you what," she says to me. "Go out for a while. Go see Lazer-Wolf, the butcher, at Anatevka. He wants to see you about something very important."

"What's the matter?" I asked. "What is he so anxious to see me about? If he is thinking of that milch cow of ours, let him take a stick and knock that idea out of his head."

"What are you so anxious about her for?" she says to me. "The milk that we get out of her, or the cheese or butter?"

"I'm not thinking about that," I answer. "It's just the idea. It would be a sin to give the poor thing away to be slaughtered. You can't do that to a living creature. It is written in the Bible. . . ."

"Oh, enough of that!" she comes back at me. "The whole world knows already that you're a man of learning! You do what I tell you. You go over and see Lazer-Wolf. Every Thursday when our Tzeitl goes there for meat, he won't leave her alone. 'You tell your father,' he keeps saying, 'to come and see me. It's important.' "

Well, once in a while you have to obey your wife. So I let her talk me into it, and I go over to Anatevka, about three miles away. He wasn't home. "Where can he be?" I ask a snub-nosed woman who is bustling around the place.

"They're slaughtering today," says the woman, "and he went down to bring an ox. He'll be coming back pretty soon."

So I wait. And while I'm waiting I look around the house a little. And from what I see, it looks as if Lazer-Wolf has been a good provider. There is a cupboard filled with copperware—at least a hundred and fifty *rubles'* worth; a couple of samovars, some brass trays, silver candlesticks and gilded goblets. And a fancy *Hannukah* lamp and some trinkets made of porcelain and silver and everything.

"Lord Almighty!" I think to myself. "If I can only live to see things like that at my children's homes. . . . What a lucky fellow he is—such wealth, and nobody to support! Both his children are married, and he himself is a widower. . . ."

Well, at last the door opens and in stamps Lazer-Wolf.

"Well, Reb Tevye," he says. "What's the matter? Why is it so hard to get hold of you? How goes it?"

"How should it go?" I say to him. "I go and I go, and I get no-where. '*Neither gold nor health nor life itself,*' as the *Torah* says."

"Don't complain, Reb Tevye," he answers me. "Compared with what you were when I first knew you, you're a rich man today."

"May we both have what I still need to make me a rich man," I say. "But I am satisfied, thank God. '*Abracadabra askakudra,*' as the *Talmud* says."

"You're always there with a line of *Talmud*," he comes back. "What a lucky man you are, Reb Tevye, to know all these things. But what does all that wisdom and knowledge have to do with us? We have other things to talk about. Sit down, Tevye." He lets out a yell, "Let's have some tea!" And as if by magic the snub-nosed woman appears, snatches the samovar, and is off to the kitchen.

"Now that we are alone," he says to me, "we can talk business. Here is the story. I've been wanting to talk to you for a long time. I tried to reach you through your daughter. How many times have I begged you to come? You understand, I've been casting an eye . . ."

"I know," I say, "that you have been casting an eye on her, but it's no use. Your pains are wasted, Reb Lazer-Wolf. There is no use talk-ing about it."

"Why not?" he asks, with a frightened look.

"Why yes?" says I. "I can wait. I'm in no hurry. My house isn't on fire."

"But why should you wait, if you can arrange it now?"

"Oh, that's not important," I say. "Besides, I feel sorry for the poor thing."

"Look at him," says Lazer-Wolf with a laugh. "He feels sorry for her. . . . If somebody heard you, Reb Tevye, he'd have sworn that she was the only one you had. It seems to me that you have a few more without her."

"Does it bother you if I keep them?" I say. "If anyone is jeal-ous . . ."

"Jealous? Who is talking of jealousy?" he cries. "On the contrary, I know they're superior, and that is exactly why—you understand? And don't forget, Reb Tevye, that you can get something out of it too!"

"Of course . . . I know all a person can get from you. . . . A piece of ice—in winter. We've known that from way back."

"Forget it," he says to me, sweet as sugar. "That was a long time ago. But now—after all—you and I—we're practically in one family, aren't we?"

"Family? What kind of family? What are you talking about, Reb Lazer-Wolf?"

"You tell me, Reb Tevye. I'm beginning to wonder. . . ."

"What are you wondering about? We're talking about my milch cow. The one you want to buy from me."

Lazer-Wolf throws back his head and lets out a roar. "That's a good one!" he howls at me. "A cow! And a milch cow at that!"

"If not the cow," I say, "then what *were* we talking about? You tell me so I can laugh too."

"Why, about your daughter. We were talking about your daughter Tzeitl the whole time. You know, Reb Tevye, that I have been a widower for quite a while now. So I thought, why do I have to go looking all over the world—get mixed up with matchmakers, those sons of Satan? Here we both are. I know you, you know me. It's not like running after a stranger. I see her in my shop every Thursday. She's made a good impression on me. I've talked with her a few times. She looks like a nice, quiet girl. And as for me—as you see for yourself—I'm pretty well off. I have my own house. A couple of stores, some hides in the attic, a little money in the chest. I live pretty well. . . . Look, Tevye, why do we have to do a lot of bargaining, try to impress each other, bluff each other? Listen to me. Let's shake hands on it and call it a match."

Well, when I heard that I just sat and stared. I couldn't say a word. All I could think was: Lazer-Wolf . . . Tzeitl. . . . He had children as old as she was. But then I reminded myself: what a lucky thing for her. She'll have everything she wants. And if he is not so good looking? There were other things besides looks. There was only one thing I really had against him: he could barely read his prayers. But then, can everybody be a scholar? There are plenty of wealthy men in Anatevka, in Mazapevka, and even in Yehupetz who don't know one letter from another. Just the same, if it's their luck to have a little money they get all the respect and honor a man could want. As the saying goes, "*There's learning in a strong-box, and wisdom in a purse. . . .*"

"Well, Reb Tevye," he says. "Why don't you say something?"

"What do you want me to do? Yell out loud?" I ask mildly, as if not wanting to look anxious. "You understand, don't you, that this is something a person has to think over. It's no trifle. She's my eldest child."

"All the better," he says. "Just because she is your eldest . . . That will give you a chance to marry off your second daughter, too, and then, in time with God's help, the third. Don't you see?"

"Amen. The same to you," I tell him. "Marrying them off is no trick at all. Just let the Almighty send each one her predestined husband."

"No," he says. "That isn't what I mean. I mean something altogether different. I mean the dowry. That you won't need for her. And her clothes I'll take care of too. And maybe you'll find something in your own purse besides. . . ."

"Shame on you!" I shout at him. "You're talking just as if you were in the butcher shop. What do you mean—my purse? Shame! My Tzeitl is not the sort that I'd have to sell for money!"

"Just as you say," he answers. "I meant it all for the best. If you don't like it, let's forget it. If you're happy without that, I'm happy too. The main thing is, let's get it done with. And I mean right away. A house must have a mistress. You know what I mean. . . ."

"Just as you say," I agree. "I won't stand in your way. But I have to talk it over with my wife. In affairs like this she has her say. It's no trifle. As Rashi says: '*A mother is not a dust rag.*' Besides, there's Tzeitl herself to be asked. How does the saying go? 'All the kinsmen were brought to the wedding—and the bride was left home'. . . ."

"What foolishness!" says Lazer-Wolf. "Is this something to *ask* her about? *Tell* her, Reb Tevye! Go home. Tell her what is what, and get the wedding canopy ready."

"No, Reb Lazer-Wolf," I say. "That's not the way you treat a young girl."

"All right," he says. "Go home and talk it over. But first, Reb Tevye, let's have a little drink. How about it?"

"Just as you say," I agree. "Why not? How does the saying go? *'Man is human*—and a drink is a drink.' There is," I tell him, "a passage in the *Talmud.* . . ." And I give him a passage. I don't know myself what I said. Something from the *Song of Songs* or the *Hagadah.* . . .

Well, we took a drop or two—as it was ordained. In the meantime the woman had brought in the samovar and we made ourselves a glass or two of punch, had a very good time together, exchanged a few toasts—talked—made plans for the wedding—discussed this and that—and then back to the wedding.

"Do you realize, Reb Lazer-Wolf, what a treasure she is?"

"I know. . . . Believe me, I know. . . . If I didn't I would never have suggested anything. . . ."

And we both go on shouting. I: "A jewel! A diamond! I hope you'll know how to treat her! Not like a butcher . . ."

And he: "Don't worry, Reb Tevye. What she'll eat in my house on weekdays she never had in your house on holidays."

"Tut, tut," I said. "Feeding a woman isn't everything. The richest man in the world doesn't eat five-*ruble* gold pieces, and a pauper doesn't eat stones. You're a coarse fellow, Lazer-Wolf. You don't even know how to value her talents—her baking—her cooking! Ah, Lazer-Wolf! The fish she makes! You'll have to learn to appreciate her!"

And he: "Tevye, pardon me for saying it, but you're somewhat befuddled. You don't know your man. You don't know me at all. . . ."

And I: "Put gold on one scale and Tzeitl on the other. . . . Do you hear, Reb Lazer-Wolf, if you had a million *rubles,* you wouldn't be worth her little finger."

And he again: "Believe me, Tevye, you're a big fool, even if you are older than I am."

We yelled away at each other that way for a long time, stopping only for a drink or two, and when I came home, it was late at night and my feet felt as if they had been shackled. And my wife, seeing right away that I was tipsy, gave me a proper welcome.

"Sh . . . Golde, control yourself," I say to her cheerfully, almost ready to start dancing. "Don't screech like that, my soul. We have congratulations coming."

"Congratulations? For what? For having sold that poor cow to Lazer-Wolf?"

"Worse than that," I say.

"Traded her for another one? And outsmarted Lazer-Wolf—poor fellow?"

"Still worse."

"Talk sense," she pleads. "Look, I have to haggle with him for every word."

"Congratulations, Golde," I say once more. "Congratulations to both of us. Our Tzeitl is engaged to be married."

"If you talk like that then I know you're drunk," she says. "And not slightly, either. You're out of your head. You must have found a real glassful somewhere."

"Yes. I had a glass of whiskey with Lazer-Wolf, and I had some punch with Lazer-Wolf, but I'm still in my right senses. Lo and behold, Golde darling, our Tzeitl has really and truly and officially become betrothed to Lazer-Wolf himself."

And I tell her the whole story from start to finish, how and what and when and why. Everything we discussed, word for word.

"Do you hear, Tevye," my wife finally says, "my heart told me all along that when Lazer-Wolf wanted to see you it was for something. Only I was afraid to think about it. Maybe nothing would come of it. Oh, dear God, I thank Thee, I thank Thee, Heavenly Father. . . . May it all be for the best. May she grow old with him in riches and honor—not like that first wife of his, Fruma-Sarah, whose life with him was none too happy. She was, may she forgive me for saying it, an embittered woman. She couldn't get along with anybody. Not at all like our Tzeitl. . . . Oh, dear God, I thank Thee, dear God . . . Well, Tevye, didn't I tell you, you simpleton. . . . Did you have to worry? If a thing has to happen it will happen. . . ."

"I agree with you," said I. "There is a passage in the *Talmud* that covers that very point. . . ."

"Don't bother me with your passages," she said. "We've got to get ready for the wedding. First of all, make out a list for Lazer-Wolf of all the things Tzeitl will need. She doesn't have a stitch of underwear, not even a pair of stockings. And as for clothes, she'll need a silk dress for the wedding, and a cotton one for summer, a woolen one for winter, and petticoats, and cloaks—she should have at least two—one, a fur-lined cloak for weekdays and a good one with a ruffle for Saturdays. And how about a pair of button-shoes and a corset, gloves, handkerchiefs, a parasol, and all the other things that a girl nowadays has to have?"

"Where, Golde, darling, did you get acquainted with all these riggings?" I ask her.

"Why not?" says she. "Haven't I ever lived among civilized people? And didn't I see, back in Kasrilevka, how ladies dressed themselves? You let me do all the talking with him myself. Lazer-Wolf is, after all, a man of substance. He won't want everybody in the family to come bothering him. Let's do it properly. If a person has to eat pork, let him eat a bellyful. . . ."

So we talked and we talked till it was beginning to get light. "My wife," I said, "it's time to get the cheese and butter together so I can start for Boiberik. It is all very wonderful indeed, but you still have to work for a living."

And so, when it was still barely light I harnessed my little old horse and went off to Boiberik. When I got to the Boiberik marketplace— Oho! Can a person ever keep a secret? Everybody knew about it already, and I was congratulated from all sides. "Congratulations, congratulations! Reb Tevye, when does the wedding come off?"

"The same to you, the same to you," I tell them. "It looks as if the saying is right: 'The father isn't born yet and the son is dancing on the rooftops'. . . ."

"Forget about that!" they cry out. "You can't get away with that! What we want is treats. Why, how lucky you are, Reb Tevye! An oil well! A gold mine!"

"The well runs dry," I tell them, "and all that's left is a hole in the ground."

Still, you can't be a hog and leave your friends in the lurch. "As soon as I'm through delivering I'll be back," I tell them. "There'll be drinks and a bite to eat. Let's enjoy ourselves. As the Good Book says, *'Even a beggar can celebrate.'* "

So I got through with my work as fast as I could and joined the crowd in a drink or two. We wished each other good luck as people do, and then I got back into my cart and started for home again, happy as could be. It was a beautiful summer day, the sun was hot, but on both sides of the road there was shade, and the odor of the pines was wonderful. Like a prince I stretched myself out in the wagon and eased up on the reins. "Go along," I said to the little old horse, "go your own way. You ought to know it by now." And myself, I clear my throat and start off on some of the old tunes. I am in a holiday mood, and the songs I sing are those of *Rosh Hashono* and *Yom Kippur*. As I sing I look up at the sky but my thoughts are concerned with things below. The heavens are the Lord's but the earth He gave to the Children of Adam, for them to brawl around in, to live in such luxury that they have time to tear each other apart for this little honor or that. . . . They don't even understand how one ought to praise the Lord for the good things that He gives them. . . . But we, the poor people, who do not live in idleness and luxury, give us but one good day and we thank the Lord and praise Him; we say, "*Ohavti, I love Him*"—the Highest One—"*for He hears my voice and my prayer, He inclines His ear to me . . . For the waves of death compassed me, the floods of Belial assailed me. . . .*" Here a cow falls down and is injured, there an ill wind brings a kinsman of mine, a good-for-nothing, a Menachem-Mendel from Yehupetz who takes away my last penny; and I am sure that the world has come to an end—there is no truth or justice left anywhere on earth. . . . But what does the Lord do? He moves Lazer-Wolf with the idea of taking my daughter Tzeitl without even a dowry. . . . And therefore I give thanks to Thee, dear God, again and again, for having looked upon Tevye and come to his aid. . . . I shall yet have joy. I shall know what it is to visit my child and find her a mistress of a well-stocked home, with chests full of linens, pantries full of chicken fat and preserves, coops full of chickens, geese and ducks. . . .

Suddenly my horse dashes off downhill, and before I can lift my head to look around I find myself on the ground with all my empty pots and crocks and my cart on top of me! With the greatest difficulty I drag myself out from under and pull myself up, bruised and half-dead, and I vent my wrath on the poor little horse. "Sink into the earth!" I shout. "Who asked you to show that you know how to run? You almost ruined me altogether, you devil!" And I gave him as much as he could take. You could see that he realized he had gone a little too far. He stood there with his head down, humble, ready to be milked. . . . Still cursing him, I turn the cart upright, gather up my pots, and off I go. A bad omen, I tell myself, and I wonder what new misfortunes might be awaiting me. . . .

That's just how it was. About a mile farther on, when I'm getting close to home, I see someone coming toward me. I drive up closer, look, and see that it's Tzeitl. At the sight of her my heart sinks, I don't know why. I jump down from the wagon.

"Tzeitl, is that you? What are you doing here?"

She falls on my neck with a sob. "My daughter, what are you crying about?" I ask her.

"Oh," she cries, "father, father!" And she is choked with tears.

"What is it, daughter? What's happened to you?" I say, putting my arm around her, patting and kissing her.

"Father, father, have pity on me. Help me. . . ."

"What are you crying for?" I ask, stroking her head. "Little fool, what do you have to cry for? For heaven's sake," I say, "if you say *no* it's *no*. Nobody is going to force you. We meant it for the best, we did it for your own sake. But if it doesn't appeal to you, what are we going to do? Apparently it was not ordained. . . ."

"Oh, thank you, father, thank you," she cries, and falls on my neck again and dissolves in tears.

"Look," I say, "you've cried enough for one day. . . . Even eating pastry becomes tiresome. . . . Climb into the wagon and let's go home. Lord knows what your mother will be thinking."

So we both get into the cart and I try to calm her down. I tell her that we had not meant any harm to her. God knows the truth: all we wanted was to shield our daughter from poverty. "So it was not meant," I said, "that you should have riches, all the comforts of life; or that we should have a little joy in our old age after all our hard work, harnessed, you might say, day and night to a wheelbarrow—no happiness, only poverty and misery and bad luck over and over. . . ."

"Oh, father," she cries, bursting into tears again. "I'll hire myself out as a servant. I'll carry rocks. I'll dig ditches. . . ."

"What are you crying for, silly child?" I say. "Am I forcing you? Am I complaining? It's just that I feel so wretched that I have to get it off my chest; so I talk it over with Him, with the Almighty, about the way He deals with me. He is, I say, a merciful Father, He has pity on me, but He shows me what He can do, too; and what can I say? Maybe it has to be that way. He is high in heaven, high up, and we are here below, sunk in the earth, deep in the earth. So we must say that He is right and His judgment is right; because if we want to look at it the other way round, who am I? A worm that crawls on the face of the earth, whom the slightest breeze—if God only willed it—could annihilate in the blink of an eye. So who am I to stand up against Him with my little brain and give Him advice on how to run this little world of His? Apparently if He ordains it this way, it has to be this way. What good are complaints? Forty days before you were conceived, the Holy Book tells us, an angel appeared and decreed: 'Let Tevye's daughter Tzeitl take Getzel, the son of Zorach, as her husband; and let Lazer-Wolf the Butcher go elsewhere to seek his mate.' And to you, my child, I say this: May God send you your predestined one, one worthy of you, and may he come soon, Amen. And I hope your mother doesn't yell too much. I'll get enough from her as it is."

Well, we came home at last. I unharnessed the little horse and sat down on the grass near the house to think things over, think up some fantastic tale to tell my wife. It was late, the sun was setting; in the distance frogs were croaking; the old horse, tied to a tree, was nibbling at the grass; the cows, just come from pasture, waited in the stalls to be milked. All around me was the heavenly smell of the fresh grass—like the Garden of Eden. I sat there thinking it all over. . . . How cleverly the Eternal One has created this little world of His, so that every living thing, from man to a simple cow, must earn its food. Nothing is free. If you, little cow, wish to eat—then go, let yourself be milked, be the means of livelihood for a man and his wife and children. If you, little horse, wish to chew—then run back and forth every day with the milk to Boiberik. And you, Man, if you want a piece of bread—go labor, milk the cows, carry the pitchers, churn the butter, make the cheese, harness your horse, drag yourself every dawn to the *datchas* of Boiberik, scrape and bow to the rich ones of Yehupetz, smile at them, cater to them, ingratiate yourself with them, see to it that they are satisfied, don't do anything to hurt their pride. . . . Ah, but there still remains the question: *'Mah nishtano?'* Where is it written that Tevye must labor in their behalf, must get up before daybreak when God Himself is still asleep, just so that they can have a fresh piece of cheese, and butter for their breakfast? Where is it written that I must rupture myself for a pot of thin gruel, a loaf of barley bread, while they—the rich ones of Yehupetz—loll around in their summer homes without so much as lifting a hand, and are served roast ducks and the best of *knishes, blintzes* and *vertutin?* Am I not a man as they are? Would it be a sin, for instance, if Tevye could spend one summer himself in a *datcha* somewhere? But then—where would people get cheese and butter? Who would milk the cows? The Yehupetz aristocrats, maybe? And at the very thought of it I burst out laughing. It's like the old saying: "If God listened to every fool what a different world it would be!"

And then I heard someone call out, "Good evening, Reb Tevye." I looked up and saw a familiar face—Motel Kamzoil, a young tailor from Anatevka.

"Well, well," I say, "you speak of the Messiah and look who's here! Sit down, Motel, on God's green earth. And what brings you here all of a sudden?"

"What brings me here?" he answers. "My two feet."

And he sits down on the grass near me and looks off toward the barn where the girls are moving about with their pots and pitchers. "I have been wanting to come here for a long time, Reb Tevye," he says at last, "only I never seem to have the time. You finish one piece of work and you start the next. I work for myself now, you know, and there is plenty to do, praise the Lord. All of us tailors have as much as we can do right now. It's been a summer of weddings. Every-

body is marrying off his children—everybody, even the widow Tri-
hubecha."

"Everybody," I say. "Everybody except Tevye. Maybe I am not
worthy in the eyes of the Lord."

"No," he answers quickly, still looking off where the girls are.
"You're mistaken, Reb Tevye. If you only wanted to you could marry
off one of your children, too. It all depends on you. . . ."

"So?" I ask. "Maybe you have a match for Tzeitl?"

"A perfect fit!" the tailor answers.

"And," I ask, "is it a good match at least?"

"Like a glove!" he cries in his tailor's language, still looking off
at the girls.

I ask, "In whose behalf is it then that you come? If he smells of a
butcher shop I don't want to hear another word!"

"God forbid!" he says. "He doesn't begin to smell of a butcher
shop!"

"And you really think he's a good match?"

"There never was such a match!" he answers promptly. "There are
matches and matches, but this one, I want you to know, was made
exactly to measure!"

"And who, may I ask, is the man? Tell me!"

"Who is it?" he says, still looking over yonder. "Who is it? Why,
me—myself!"

When he said that I jumped up from the ground as if I had been
scalded, and he jumped too, and there we stood facing each other like
bristling roosters. "Either you're crazy," I say to him, "or you're
simply out of your mind! What are you—everything? The matchmaker, the bridegroom, the ushers all rolled into one? I suppose you'll
play the wedding march too! I've never heard of such a thing—arranging a match for oneself!"

But he doesn't seem to listen. He goes right on talking.

"Anyone who thinks I'm crazy is crazy himself! No, Reb Tevye,
I have all my wits about me. A person doesn't have to be crazy in
order to want to marry your Tzeitl. For example, the richest man in
our town—Lazer-Wolf, the Butcher—wanted her too. Do you think
it's a secret? The whole town knows it. And as for being my own

matchmaker, I'm surprised at you! After all, Reb Tevye, you're a man of the world. If a person sticks his finger in your mouth you know what to do! So what are we arguing about? Here is the whole story: your daughter Tzeitl and I gave each other our pledge more than a year ago now that we would marry. . . ."

If someone had stuck a knife into my heart it would have been easier to endure than these words. In the first place, how does a stitcher like Motel fit into the picture as my son-in-law? And in the second place, what kind of words are these, "We gave each other our pledge that we would marry"? And where do I come in? . . . I ask him bluntly, "Do I still have the right to say something about my daughter, or doesn't anyone have to ask a father any more?"

"On the contrary," says Motel, "that's exactly why I came to talk with you. I heard that Lazer-Wolf has been discussing a match, and I have loved her now for over a year. More than once I have wanted to come and talk it over with you, but every time I put it off a little. First till I had saved up a few *rubles* for a sewing machine, and then till I got some decent clothes. Nowadays almost everybody has to have two suits and a few good shirts. . . ."

"You and your shirts!" I yell at him. "What childish nonsense is this? And what do you intend to do after you're married? Support your wife with shirts?"

"Why," he says, "why, I'm surprised at you, Reb Tevye! From what I hear, when you got married you didn't have your own brick mansion either, and nevertheless here you are. . . . In any case, if the whole world gets along, I'll get along, too. Besides, I have a trade, haven't I?"

To make a long story short, he talked me into it. For after all— why should we fool ourselves?—how do all Jewish children get married? If we began to be too particular, then no one in our class would ever get married at all. . . . There was only one thing still bothering me, and that I still couldn't understand. What did they mean—pledging their troth? What kind of world has this become? A boy meets a girl and says to her, "Let us pledge our troth." Why, it's just too free-and-easy, that's all!

But when I looked at this Motel standing there with his head bent like a sinner, I saw that he was not trying to get the best of anybody, and I thought: "Now, what am I becoming so alarmed about? What am I putting on such airs for? What is my own pedigree? Reb Tzotzel's grandchild! And what huge dowry can I give my daughter —and what fine clothes? So maybe Motel Kamzoil is only a tailor, but at the same time he is a good man, a worker; he'll be able to make a living. And besides, he's honest too. So what have I got against him?

"Tevye," I said to myself, "don't think up any childish arguments. Let them have their way." Yes . . . but what am I going to do about my Golde? I'll have plenty on my hands there. She'll be hard to handle. How can I make her think it's all right? . . .

"You know what, Motel," I said to the young suitor. "You go home. I'll straighten everything out here. I'll talk it over with this one and that one. Everything has to be done right. And tomorrow morning, if you haven't changed your mind by that time, maybe we'll see each other."

"Change my mind!" he yells at me. "You expect me to change my mind? If I do, I hope I never live to go away from here! May I become a stone, a bone, right here in front of you!"

"What's the use of swearing?" I ask him. "I believe you without the oath. Go along, Motel. Good night. And may you have pleasant dreams."

And I myself go to bed, too. But I can't sleep. My head is splitting. I think of one plan and then another, till at last I come upon the right one. And what is that? Listen, I'll tell you. . . .

It's past midnight. All over the house we're sound asleep. This one is snoring, that one is whistling. And suddenly I sit up and let out a horrible yell, as loud as I can: "Help! Help! Help!" It stands to reason that when I let out this yell everybody wakes up, and first of all—Golde.

"May God be with you, Tevye," she gasps, and shakes me. "Wake up! What's the matter with you? What are you howling like this for?"

I open my eyes, look around to see where I am, and call out in terror, "Where is she? Where is she?"

"Where is who?" asks Golde. "What are you talking about?"

I can hardly answer. "Fruma-Sarah. Fruma-Sarah, Lazer-Wolf's first wife . . . She was standing here a minute ago."

"You're out of your head," my wife says to me. "May God save you, Tevye. Do you know how long Fruma-Sarah has been dead?"

"I know that she's dead," I say, "but just the same she was here just a minute ago, right here by the bed, talking to me. Then she grabbed me by the windpipe and started to choke me. . . ."

"What on earth is the matter with you, Tevye?" says my wife. "What are you babbling about? You must have been dreaming. Spit three times and tell me what you dreamt, and I'll tell you what it meant."

"Long may you live, Golde," I tell her. "It's lucky you woke me up or I'd have died of fright right on the spot. Get me a drink of water and I'll tell you my dream. Only I beg you, Golde, don't become frightened: the Holy Books tell us that sometimes only three parts of a dream come true, and the rest means nothing. Absolutely nothing. Well, here is my dream. . . .

"In the beginning I dreamt that we were having a celebration of some kind, I don't know what. Either an engagement or a wedding. The house was crowded. All the men and women we knew were there—the *rov* and the *shochet* and everybody. And musicians, too. . . . In the midst of the celebration the door opens, and in comes your grandmother Tzeitl, may her soul rest in peace. . . ."

"Grandmother Tzeitl!" my wife shouts, turning pale as a sheet. "How did she look? How was she dressed?"

"How did she look?" I say. "May our enemies look the way she looked. Yellow. A waxen yellow. And she was dressed—how do you expect?—in white. A shroud. She came up to me. 'Congratulations,' she said, 'I am so happy that you picked such a fine young man for your Tzeitl who bears my name. He's a fine, upstanding lad —this Motel Kamzoil. . . . He was named after my uncle Mordecai, and even if he is a tailor he's still an honest boy. . . .'"

"A tailor!" gasps Golde. "Where does a tailor come into our family? In our family we have had teachers, cantors, *shamosim,* undertakers' assistants, and other kinds of poor people. But a tailor—never!"

"Don't interrupt me, Golde," I tell her. "Maybe your grandmother Tzeitl knows better. . . . When I heard her congratulate me like that, I said to her, 'What is that you said, Grandmother? About Tzeitl's betrothed being a tailor? Did you say Motel? . . . You mean a butcher, don't you? A butcher named Lazer-Wolf?'

" 'No,' says your grandmother again. 'No, Tevye. Your daughter is engaged to Motel, and he's a tailor, and she'll grow old with him— if the Lord wills—in comfort and honor.'

" 'But Grandmother,' I say again, 'what can we do about Lazer-Wolf? Just yesterday I gave him my word. . . .'

"I had barely finished saying this when I looked up, and your grandmother Tzeitl is gone. In her place is Fruma-Sarah—Lazer-Wolf's first wife—and this is what she says: 'Reb Tevye, I have always considered you an honest man, a man of learning and virtue. But how does it happen that you should do a thing like this—let your daughter take my place, live in my house, carry my keys, wear my clothes, my jewelry, my pearls?'

" 'Is it my fault,' I ask her, 'if Lazer-Wolf wanted it that way?'

" 'Lazer-Wolf!' she cries. 'Lazer-Wolf will have a terrible fate, and your Tzeitl too, if she marries him. It's a pity, Reb Tevye. I feel sorry for your daughter. She'll live with him no more than three weeks, and when the three weeks are up I'll come to her by night and I'll take her by the throat like this. . . .' And with these words Fruma-Sarah grabs me by the windpipe and begins choking me—so hard that if you hadn't waked me up, by now I'd have been—far, far away. . . ."

"Ptu, ptu, ptu," spits my wife three times. "It's an evil spirit! May it fall into the river; may it sink into the earth; may it climb into attics; may it lie in the forest—but may it never harm us or our children! May that butcher have a dream like that! A dark and horrible dream! Motel Kamzoil's smallest finger is worth more than all of him, even if Motel is only a tailor; for if he was named after my uncle Mordecai he couldn't possibly have been a tailor by birth. And if my grandmother—may she rest in peace—took the trouble to come all the way from the other world to congratulate us, why, all we can do is say that this is all for the best, and it couldn't possibly be any better. Amen. Selah. . . ."

Well, why should I go on and on?

The next day they were engaged, and not long after were married. And the two of them, praise the Lord, are happy. He does his own tailoring, goes around in Boiberik from one *datcha* to another picking up work; and she is busy day and night, cooking and baking and washing and tidying and bringing water from the well. . . . They barely make enough for food. If I didn't bring her some of our cheese and butter once in a while—or a few *groschen* sometimes—they would never be able to get by. But if you ask her—my Tzeitl, I mean—she says everything is as good as it could be. Just let Motel stay in good health.

So go complain about modern children. You slave for them, do everything for them! And they tell you that they know better.

And . . . maybe they do. . . .

Competitors

ALWAYS, right in the midst of what some of us call the Reign of Terror—when everyone is pushing and shoving, this one getting in, that one getting out; when people are fighting for a seat in the carriage, as though they were vying for honors in the Synagogue—then you see both of them appear. There they are—the two of them—he and she.

He—swarthy, stout, hairy, with a cataract over one eye. She—red-faced, bony, pock-marked. Both of them in rags and tatters, both in patched shoes, both with identical baggage—he with a basket, and she with a basket; his filled with twisted white rolls, hard-boiled eggs, oranges, bottles of seltzer water; and hers, also with twisted white rolls, hard-boiled eggs, oranges, and bottles of seltzer water.

Sometimes it happens that he has in his basket small bags of purple grapes, black cherries, or green grapes as sour as vinegar. Then she also comes in with the same purple grapes, black cherries, or green grapes as sour as vinegar.

And always the two of them come at the same time, push their way through the same door of the carriage, and cry out their wares together, in the very same words. Only their accents are different. He speaks in a slightly asthmatic voice, slurring the r's, mumbling his words as though he had no tongue. She speaks out clearly, in a loud sharp voice, all tongue.

Maybe you think that they cut prices, try to compete with each other, engage in unfair trade practices? Not at all. Their prices are identical. Their competition consists only of this: which of them can arouse the greatest sympathy. Both of them implore you to take pity on their five orphaned children (he has five orphans and she has five orphans). Both of them peer right into your eyes, push their wares under your nose and argue so persistently that whether you need it or not, you are forced to buy something.

Only they talk so much, cry and beg and plead with you so much, that you become confused. Which one should you buy from—him or her? You decide to solve the problem by buying a little from each, but they won't let you do this.

No, my friend. If you're going to buy something, you'll have to but it from one or the other. You can't dance at two weddings with one pair of shoes.

So, wanting to be fair, you think you'll buy from one of them one time and from the other next time. But if you try it you'll find yourself abused by both sides.

"Look here, mister, anything wrong with the way I look to you today?"

Or, "My good man, it seems to me that last week you bought some food from me and you didn't become poisoned or choke on it."

You decide to make a moral issue of it. You read them a lecture on ethics. After all, you say, the other party has a soul too, he or she has to keep body and soul together. You know what they say in German: *"Leben und leben lassen*—Live and let live." To this you get an answer not in German, but in plain Yiddish, a trifle disguised, but quite easy to understand.

"Uncle! You can't sit on two horses with one behind."

Yes, dear friend, that's the way it is. Never try to please the whole world, you won't succeed. And think twice before you try to become a peacemaker—it doesn't work. I know from sad experience. I could tell you a good story of the time I made a fool of myself trying to make peace between a husband and wife. And what was the upshot? I caught the devil from my own wife. But I don't want to confuse one story with another. Though it sometimes happens in business that you show a person a piece of goods—let's say cowhides—and you start talking about silks from China. However, let's get back to our story.

It happened one time in the fall, on a rainy day when the sky was overcast and down below everything was dark and gloomy and wet. The station was packed with travelers both coming and going. They were all in a hurry, all of them running and pushing and crawling over each other with suitcases, with bundles of different shapes and sizes, pillows, quilts, featherbeds. You should have heard the clatter and rattle, the shouting and scolding. And right in the thick of it, the two of them have to appear—he and she. Both loaded with things to eat, as always. Both pushing through one door, as always. Suddenly—how did it happen? Both baskets are on the ground. The rolls and the eggs, the oranges and the bottles of seltzer water, are scattered in the mud; and our ears are filled with cries and shrieks and sobs and curses that mingle with the laughter of the train crews and the noise and tumult of the passengers. The whistle blows, the bell rings. Another minute and we'll be on our way.

Inside the carriage there is a hubbub too. The passengers are talking it over, airing their views on the subject—and, naturally, all together, like women in the Synagogue, or geese in the marketplace. It is hard to follow their conversation, to get the gist of it, except for a phrase here and there.

"A bumper crop in rolls this year."

"A massacre of eggs."

"What did anybody have against the oranges?"

"What did you expect from him—an Esau, a nonbeliever."

"Just offhand—at how much would you estimate the loss?"

"Serves them right. Do they have to push their way where they are not wanted?"

"But what else can they do? It's their livelihood."

"Ha-ha-ha," booms a deep bass voice. "A fine livelihood. A Jewish livelihood."

"A fine livelihood, you say," pipes up a young, thin, squeaking voice. "Do you know of a better way a poor Jew can make his livelihood? If so, let's hear it."

"Young man!" thunders the bass. "I wasn't talking to you."

"Not talking to me? But *I* am talking to you. Do you know of a better way of making a living? So. You are silent. You have nothing to say."

"How do you like that leech? He won't let me go."

"Quiet, everybody. Be still. Here she comes."

"Who?"

"She herself, the woman with the basket."

"Where is she, the beauty? Where?"

"Here, here she is."

Pock-marked, red-faced, her eyes swollen with weeping, she pushed her way through the crowd with her empty basket, looking for a vacant place, and finally she sat down on the floor on her upturned basket, hid her swollen eyes in her torn shawl and wept quietly.

A strange silence descended on the carriage. Not a word was uttered, not a sound was heard. We were all tongue-tied until a deep bass voice called out, "Why is everybody so quiet?"

"What do you want us to do—shout?"

"Come, let's take up a collection."

Do you know who is talking? Just guess. The same man who only a few minutes ago was laughing at a poor Jew's livelihood. He is a strange-looking creature with an odd cap on his head, a cap with a broad shiny visor in front. Besides this he is wearing smoked glasses so that you can't see his eyes. He has no eyes, only a nose, a broad, fleshy, bulbous nose.

Without any more ado he pulls his cap off his head, throws in a couple of silver coins and begins going from one person to another, all the while thundering in his deep bass voice: "Come, everybody. Give what you can. A little or a lot, whatever you can afford. You know what the *Talmud* says, 'Never look a gift horse in the mouth.'"

We all reached into our pockets, opened our wallets, and the change began to ring out—all kinds of change, silver and copper, large and small. There was a Russian peasant in the crowd, with high boots and a silver chain around his neck. He yawned, crossed himself, and threw in a coin too. Only one passenger refused, he wouldn't give a thing. And who do you suppose he was? The same fellow who a few minutes ago had taken it upon himself to defend a poor Jew's means of livelihood. A young intellectual with well-nourished plump cheeks, a small yellow pointed beard, and golden pince-nez. One of these fellows with rich parents, rich parents-in-law and plenty in his own pocket, who travels third-class to save money.

"Young man, put something into the cap," says the personage with the smoked glasses and the bulbous nose.

"I am not giving anything," says the young intellectual.

"Why not?"

"Just because. It's a matter of principle with me."

"I knew before I came to you that you wouldn't give anything."

"And how did you know?"

"I could tell by your looks. Your secret was divulged by the way your cheeks bulged. As the *Talmud* says, 'You can spot a gentleman by his boots.'"

The young intellectual went into such a rage that his pince-nez almost fell off. He began screaming, "You are an ignorant lout, a low vulgarian, an impudent ass."

"Thank heavens," answered the bulbous nose calmly. "Thank heavens I am not also a robber and a highwayman." He went up to the weeping woman. "Aunty, haven't you cried enough for one time? You'll spoil your pretty eyes. Here, hold out both your hands and I'll pour the money into them."

A strange woman. I thought that when she saw all the money he had collected she would overwhelm us with thanks, melt with gratitude. But instead of thanks, she overwhelmed us with curses. A fountain, a torrent of abuse began pouring from her lips.

"It's all his fault, may he fall by the wayside and break his neck and bones and skull, dear Father in Heaven. He is to blame for everything. It all comes from him, may no good come to him. May he sink into the ground, sweet Father. May he never live to come home again, but meet with violent death instead, from cholera or fire or plague or pestilence. May he dry up and his flesh shrink from his bones."

Dear Lord, where does a person find so many maledictions? Luckily the man with the smoked glasses interrupted her. "Enough, my woman, enough. Enough of your blessings and benedictions. Tell us instead what the conductor and the guards had against you?"

The woman lifted her swollen eyes to him.

"It's all on account of him, curse him. He was afraid I'd grab all the customers away from him, so he tried to push into the carriage ahead of me. So I squeezed past him, so he caught my basket from behind, and then I let out a yell; and the guard winked at the conductor and both of them together heaved our baskets and scattered everything in the mud—may *his* bones be scattered like that. Believe me, I am telling the truth, when I say that as long as I've traveled on this route with my merchandise no one has ever before as much as touched a hair on my head. Why do you think they left me alone? Because of their kind hearts? May *he* have a boil for every egg I've had to give away, for every roll I've handed out at the station. Everyone, from the lowest to the highest, has to have his gullet stuffed with something. From early morning I have to be handing it out—if I could only hand out chills and fever to them. The head conductor takes his share first, anything he wants. Then I have to start dividing it up among the other conductors, this one gets a loaf, that one some eggs, a third gets an orange. What more do you want? Even the fellow who fires the ovens, do you think he doesn't demand his share? A plague on him! He threatens to report me to the guard if I don't give him something. He doesn't know that the guard has been taken care of long ago. Every Sunday I bring him a bag of oranges. He always picks the biggest, the finest, the best oranges. . . ."

"Aunty, from the looks of things," says the man with the smoked glasses, "you must be rolling in wealth."

"What are you saying?" She looks at him quickly, as though offering an apology. "I barely, barely come out even. And I sometimes lose and have to take it out of my own hide. I am getting poorer all the time."

"Then what's the use of doing business at all?"

"What else do you want me to do—become a thief? I have five little children to support—may *he* have five different kinds of pains in his bowels. And I myself am a sick woman—may *he* lie sick in the hospital, dear God, from now until the fall. The way he has ruined my business, run it into the ground. May he rot in the ground. It was such a good business, such a fine thriving business."

"A good business, did you say?"

"A wonderful business. With a steady income. How do you say it —a gilt-edged investment."

"But just a minute ago you were saying that you are getting poorer all the time."

"Of course. How can I make a living if I have to give away more than half of my merchandise to the head conductor and the rest of them? What do you think I have there? A well, a bottomless spring? A stolen fortune?"

Our friend with the bulbous nose and smoked glasses begins to lose patience. "Aunty, you are pulling my leg now."

"Me, pulling your leg?" She is indignant. "May *his* legs fester and drop off. He has wrecked my life, may God wreck his. Actually he is only a tailor, a pants-patcher. He spent most of his life jabbing a needle through cloth, and he was lucky to make enough for water for his *kasha*. Then he got jealous of me. He saw me eating a slice of bread, may the worms eat him. He saw—may his eyes drop out of his head—how with this basket I kept five little orphans alive. So he goes and buys himself a basket too. One of these days I will buy him a shroud, dear Lord. So I ask him, 'What's this?' And he says, 'A basket.' 'And what are you going to do with this basket?' I ask. And he says, 'The same as you are doing.' 'And what's that?' And he says, 'You should know. I have five children too, and they also have to eat once in a while. You won't raise them on dry bread.' And ever since then he's been following me around everywhere with his basket. He drags the customers away from me, may his teeth be dragged out of him one by one. He tears the bread right out of my mouth, may he be torn into bits, sweet Father, dear loving Father."

Our friend with the smoked glasses hits upon an idea, an idea that has already occurred to most of us.

"But why do you both have to pound the same piece of earth? Why do you both follow the same route?"

The woman stares at him with her red swollen eyes. "What else do you want us to do?"

"Find yourself another route. The railway line is a long one."

"And what about him?"

"Who?"

"My husband."

"Which husband?"

"My second husband."

"Which second husband?"

The woman's red pock-marked face gets redder still. "What do you mean, which second husband? That's him over there, the *shlimazl* I've been talking about."

All of us leap out of our seats.

"That man, that competitor of yours, that's your second husband?"

"What did you think he was? My first husband? Oh-ho. If my first husband were only still alive . . ."

There is a lilt in her voice as she draws out the words, a strange light in her eyes as she gets ready to tell us who her first husband was and what sort of man *he* was. But who wants to listen to her? We are all busy talking, laughing, making wisecracks. We laugh and laugh and can't stop laughing.

Perhaps you can guess what we are laughing about.

Another Page from the Song of Songs

"FASTER, Buzie, faster," I tell Buzie and take her hand in mine and together we race up the hill. It is the day before *Shevuos* and we are setting out to pick greens. "We haven't all day," I tell her. "We have a big mountain to climb and after the mountain there is a river. Over the river there is a trestle made of boards, that's the 'bridge.' The water runs under the bridge, the frogs croak, the boards creak and shake—and there, over there on the other side of the bridge, that's where the real Garden of Eden is, Buzie. That's where my Estates begin."

"Your Estates?"

"I mean the big meadow. It's a great field that stretches far and wide without any end. It has a green blanket over it, sprinkled with yellow dots and covered with tiny red shoots. Wait till you smell it. It has the most wonderful smells in the world. And wait till you see my trees. I have many, many trees—tall, spreading trees. And I have a little hill all my own to sit on. I can sit on top of my hill, or I can say the Magic Word and fly off like an eagle straight above the clouds. I can fly over forest and field, over sea and desert, till I come to the other side of the mountain of darkness."

"And from there," Buzie interrupts me, "you walk seven miles on foot until you come to a lake."

"No, to a deep wood. First I walk through this wood, then through another wood, then I come to the lake."

"And you swim across the lake and count seven times seven."

"And there springs up in front of me a tiny gnome with a long beard."

"And he asks you, 'What is your heart's desire?'"

"And I tell him, 'Lead me to the Queen's daughter.'"

Buzie snatches her hand out of mine and starts running downhill. I run after her. "Buzie, why are you running away?"

Buzie does not answer. I've offended her. She doesn't like to have me talk about the Queen's daughter. She likes all my stories except the one about the Queen's daughter.

You probably remember who Buzie is. I have told you about her once before. But in case you've forgotten I shall tell you again.

I had an older brother named Benny who was drowned. He left behind him a mill, a young widow, two horses and a child. The mill was abandoned. The horses were sold. The widow remarried and moved to some distant place and the child was brought to us. That child was Buzie.

Do you want to hear something funny? Everybody thinks that Buzie and I are sister and brother. She calls my father "Father" and my mother "Mother." We live together just like sister and brother and love each other just like a sister and a brother.

Like a sister and a brother? Then why is Buzie so shy with me? Why does she act so strange sometimes?

Let me tell you something that happened once. We had been left alone, she and I, all by ourselves in the house. My father had gone to the Synagogue to say *kaddish* for my brother Benny, and my mother had gone out to buy matches. Buzie and I sat huddled together in a corner and I was telling her stories. Buzie loves to hear me tell stories, stories from *cheder* or else fairy tales I make up for her. She moved quite close to me. Her hand was clasped in mine.

"Go on, Shimek. Go on, tell me more."

Silently, night descends. Slowly the shadows cover the walls, quiver in the half-light, then creep to the ground and melt. We can barely make each other out. I can only feel her little hand trembling in mine. I can hear her heart beating and see her eyes gleaming in the dark.

Suddenly she snatches her hand away. "What is it?" I ask, surprised.

"We mustn't do it," she says.

"Mustn't do what?"

"Hold hands like this."

"Why not? Who told you we mustn't?"

"Nobody. I know it myself."

"But we aren't strangers. Aren't we brother and sister?"

"If we were only brother and sister," says Buzie softly, and it seems to me that she is speaking in the words of the *Song of Songs:* "*O that thou wert as my brother* . . ."

It is always like this. Whenever I speak of Buzie, I think of the *Song of Songs.* . . .

Where were we? It is the day before *Shevuos.* We are running down the hill. Buzie runs ahead and I run after her. Buzie is offended because of the Queen's daughter. She likes all my stories except the one about the Queen's daughter. But Buzie can't hold a grudge very long. She has forgotten about it in less time than it takes me to tell it. She is looking at me once more with her big lovely eyes. She tosses her hair back and calls out to me, "Shimek! Look, Shimek, can you see what I see?"

"Of course I see, silly. Why shouldn't I see? I can see the blue sky, I can feel the warm breeze. I can hear the birds chirping and see them sailing over our heads. It is our sky, our breeze, our birds. Everything is ours, ours, ours. Give me your hand, Buzie."

"No," she says. She won't give me her hand. She is suddenly shy. Why should Buzie be shy with me? Why should she blush?

"Over there," calls Buzie, running ahead. "Over there, on the other side of the bridge." And it seems to me that she speaks in the words of the Shulamite. "*Come, my beloved, let us go forth into the fields. Let us lodge in the villages. Let us get up early to the vineyards. Let us see whether the vine has budded, whether the vine blossom be opened.*"

And here we are, at the bridge.

The river runs under the bridge, the frogs croak, the boards creak and shake, and Buzie trembles. "Oh, Buzie, you are . . . What are you afraid of, silly? Hold on to me or, better still, let me put my arm around you and you put your arm around me. See? Like this."

We have crossed the bridge.

And now we walk ahead, still with our arms tightly around each other, she and I, all by ourselves in the holy stillness of the first morning of Creation. Buzie holds on tightly to me, very tightly. She is silent, but it seems to me that she is speaking in the words of the *Song of Songs: "I am my beloved's and my beloved is mine."*

The meadow stretches far and wide without end. It is like a green blanket sprinkled with yellow dots, covered with red shoots. And the smells that rise from it—they are the most wonderful smells in the world. We walk along, the two of us, arm in arm, over the Garden of Eden, in the morning of the world.

"Shimek," says Buzie, looking into my eyes and moving closer to me, "when are we going to start picking greens for *Shevuos?"*

"The day is long, silly," I tell her. I am burning with excitement. I don't know where to look first, whether up at the blue cup of the sky, or down at the green blanket of the fields. Or over there, toward the end of the world, where the sky melts into the earth. Or should I look into Buzie's lovely face? Into her big thoughtful eyes, as deep as the sky, as pensive as the night? Her eyes are always pensive, always troubled. A deep sorrow lies hidden in them. I am familiar with her sorrow, I know what is troubling her. She grieves for her mother who married a stranger and went off far away, never to return.

At our house, Buzie's mother is never mentioned. It's as though Buzie never had a mother. My parents have become her parents. They love her as though she were their own child; they watch over her anxiously, let her have anything her heart desires. This morning Buzie said she wanted to go with me to pick greens for *Shevuos* (I had put her up to it). At once my father turned to my mother. "What do you think?" As he spoke, he looked at her over the tops of his silver-rimmed spectacles and with his fingers he combed the silver strands of his beard. A conversation took place between my father and mother that went something like this:

Father: What do you say?
Mother: What do *you* say?
Father: Should we let them go?
Mother: Why shouldn't we let them go?
Father: Am I saying no?
Mother: What are you saying then?
Father: I'm only saying, should they go?
Mother: Why shouldn't they go?

And so on. I know on which foot the shoe pinches. My father
has told me twenty times over, and after him my mother has warned
me that over there is a bridge and under the bridge there is water.
A river . . . a river . . . a river . . .

Buzie and I have long ago forgotten the bridge and the river. We
are wandering over the wide, open field, under the wide, open sky.
We run and we fall down and roll over and over in the sweet-smelling grass. Then we get up and run, and fall down again. We haven't
even started to pick greens for *Shevuos.* I lead Buzie over the broad
meadow and boast to her about my possessions.

"Do you see these trees? Do you see the sand? Do you see this
hill?"

"And is all of it yours?"

Buzie looks at me as she says this and her eyes laugh at me. She
is always laughing at me. I can't bear to have her laughing at me.
I sulk and turn away from her. Buzie sees that I am offended. She
runs in front of me, looks into my eyes earnestly, takes my hand and
says, "Shimek." My anger disappears and I feel good again. I take
her hand and lead her to my little hill, the little hill on which I sit
every year. If I want to I can sit on my hill and look over my Estates.
Or else I can utter the Magic Word and be borne aloft like an eagle.
I can fly above the clouds, over forest and field, over sea and
desert. . . .

We sit on my hill (we still haven't picked any greens for *Shevuos*)
and tell stories, that is I tell stories and Buzie listens. I tell her about
how it is going to be some far-off day when we are both grown up

and marry each other. We will rise up by magic and fly above the clouds, and travel over the whole world. First we will travel over the countries that Alexander of Macedonia had traveled over. Then we will take a trip to the Holy Land. There we will visit all the mountains and the vineyards, and we will fill our pockets with figs and dates and olives. Then we will get up and fly further. And everywhere we go we will play different tricks on people, because no one will be able to see us.

"No one will see us?" asks Buzie, and catches me by the hand.

"No one, no one at all. We will be able to see everybody and nobody will be able to see us."

"If so, Shimek, I want to ask a favor of you."

"A favor?"

"A tiny favor."

I know beforehand what this favor is. She wants us to fly over there where her mother is living with her new husband. She wants me to play a trick on her stepfather.

"Why not?" I tell her. "With the greatest pleasure. You can depend on me. I will play them a trick that they will remember me by."

"Not them, just him, just him," Buzie pleads with me. But I don't consent right away. When someone has made me angry, I am terrible in my wrath. How can I forgive her so easily? The insolence of a woman—marrying a perfect stranger and going off somewhere, the devil knows where, and deserting her own child, never even writing her a letter. . . . Whoever heard of such an outrage?

I got all wrought up for nothing and now I am sorry. But it's too late. Buzie has covered her face with her hands. Is she weeping? I would gladly tear myself into little pieces for making her weep. Why did I have to wound her tenderest feelings so? In my own mind I call myself all sorts of harsh names: "You ox, you ass, you idiot, you blabber-mouth." I come close to her, take her hand in mine. "Buzie. Buzie!" I want to speak to her in the words of the *Song of Songs:* "*Let me see thy countenance. Let me hear thy voice.*"

Suddenly I look up. Where did my father and mother come from? My father's silver-rimmed spectacles gleam at a distance. The silver strands of his beard are whipped by the breeze. My mother beckons to us from afar, waving her shawl. Buzie and I sit there as though we were turned to clay. What can our parents be doing here?

They have come to see where we are. They want to make sure that no harm has come to us. Who can tell—a bridge, a river . . . a river . . .

What queer people our parents are.

"And where are the greens?" they ask.

"The greens?"

"Yes, the greens you were going to pick for *Shevuos.*

Buzie and I look at each other. I understand the look in her eyes. It seems to me that she is saying, *"O that thou wert as my brother."*

"Well, as for the greens, I am sure we will find some," says my father, smiling, and the silver strands of his beard shine in the rays of the noonday sun. "God be thanked that the children are well and that no harm has come to them."

"God be thanked," echoes my mother, wiping her red perspiring face with her shawl. They both look at us tenderly, beaming with unconcealed pride. . . .

What queer, queer people our parents are. . . .

Hodel

YOU LOOK, Mr. Sholom Aleichem, as though you were surprised that you hadn't seen me for such a long time. . . . You're thinking that Tevye has aged all at once, his hair has turned gray. . . .

Ah, well, if you only knew the troubles and heartaches he has endured of late! How is it written in our Holy Books? *"Man comes from dust, and to dust he returns.*—Man is weaker than a fly, and stronger than iron." Whatever plague there is, whatever trouble, whatever misfortune—it never misses me. Why does it happen that way? Maybe because I am a simple soul who believes everything that everyone says. Tevye forgets that our wise men have told us a thousand times: "Beware of dogs. . . ."

But I ask you, what can I do if that's my nature? I am, as you know, a trusting person, and I never question God's ways. Whatever He ordains is good. Besides, if you do complain, will it do you any good? That's what I always tell my wife. "Golde," I say, "you're sinning. We have a *medresh.* . . ."

"What do I care about a *medresh?*" she says. "We have a daughter to marry off. And after her are two more almost ready. And after these two—three more—may the Evil Eye spare them!"

"Tut," I say. "What's that? Don't you know, Golde, that our sages have thought of that also? There is a *medresh* for that, too. . . ."

But she doesn't let me finish. "Daughters to be married off," she says, "are a stiff *medresh* in themselves."

So try to explain something to a woman!

441

Where does that leave us? Oh, yes, with a houseful of daughters,
bless the Lord. Each one prettier than the next. It may not be proper
for me to praise my own children, but I can't help hearing what the
whole world calls them, can I? Beauties, every one of them! And
especially Hodel, the one that comes after Tzeitl who, you remember,
fell in love with the tailor. And is this Hodel beautiful. . . . How can
I describe her to you? Like Esther in the Bible, *"of beautiful form
and fair to look upon."* And as if that weren't bad enough, she has
to have brains, too. She can write and she can read—Yiddish and
Russian both. And books—she swallows like dumplings. You may
be wondering how a daughter of Tevye happens to be reading books,
when her father deals in butter and cheese? That's what I'd like
to know myself. . . .

But that's the way it is these days. Look at these lads who haven't
got a pair of pants to their name, and still they want to study! Ask
them, "What are you studying? Why are you studying?" They can't
tell you. It's their nature, just as it's a goat's nature to jump into
gardens. Especially since they aren't even allowed in the schools.
"Keep off the grass!" read all the signs as far as they're concerned.
And yet you ought to see how they go after it! And who are they?
Workers' children. Tailors' and cobblers', so help me God! They go
away to Yehupetz or to Odessa, sleep in garrets, eat what Pharaoh ate
during the plagues—frogs and vermin—and for months on end do
not see a piece of meat before their eyes. Six of them can make a ban-
quet on a loaf of bread and a herring. Eat, drink and be merry! That's
the life!

Well, so one of that band had to lose himself in our corner of the
world. I used to know his father—he was a cigarette-maker, and as
poor as a man could be. But that is nothing against the young fellow.
For if Rabbi Jochanan wasn't too proud to mend boots, what is
wrong with having a father who makes cigarettes? There is only
one thing I can't understand: why should a pauper like that be so
anxious to study? True, to give the devil his due, the boy has a good
head on his shoulders, an excellent head. Pertschik, his name was, but
we called him "Feferel"—"Peppercorn." And he looked like a pepper-

corn, little, dark, dried up and homely, but full of confidence and with a quick, sharp tongue.

Well, one day I was driving home from Boiberik where I had got rid of my load of milk and butter and cheese, and as usual I sat lost in thought, dreaming of many things, of this and that, and of the rich people of Yehupetz who had everything their own way while Tevye, the *shlimazl,* and his wretched little horse slaved and hungered all their days. It was summer, the sun was hot, the flies were biting, on all sides the world stretched endlessly. I felt like spreading out my arms and flying!

I lift up my eyes, and there on the road ahead of me I see a young man trudging along with a package under his arm, sweating and panting. *"'Rise, O Yokel the son of Flekel,'* as we say in the synagogue," I called out to him. "Climb into my wagon and I'll give you a ride. I have plenty of room. How is it written? *'If you see the ass of him that hateth thee lying under its burden, thou shalt forbear to pass it by.'* Then how about a human being?"

At this the *shlimazl* laughs, and climbs into the wagon.

"Where might the young gentleman be coming from?" I ask.

"From Yehupetz."

"And what might a young gentleman like you be doing in Yehupetz?" I ask.

"A young gentleman like me is getting ready for his examinations."

"And what might a young gentleman like you be studying?"

"I only wish I knew!"

"Then why does a young gentleman like you bother his head for nothing?"

"Don't worry, Reb Tevye. A young gentleman like me knows what he's doing."

"So—if you know who *I* am, tell me who *you* are!"

"Who am I? I'm a man."

"I can see that you're not a horse. I mean, as we Jews say, *whose* are you?"

"Whose should I be but God's?"

"I know that you're God's. It is written: *'All living things are*

His.' I mean, whom are you descended from? Are you from around here, or from Lithuania?"

"I am *descended*," he says, "from Adam, our father. I *come* from right around here. You know who we are."

"Well then, who is your father? Come, tell me."

"My father," he says, "was called Pertschik."

I spat with disgust. "Did you have to torture me like this all that time? Then you must be Pertschik the Cigarette-maker's son!"

"Yes, that's who I am. Pertschik the Cigarette-maker's son."

"And you go to the university?"

"Yes—the university."

"Well," I said, "I'm glad to hear it. Man and fish and fowl—you're all trying to better yourselves! But tell me, my lad, what do you live on, for instance?"

"I live on what I eat."

"That's good," I say. "And what do you eat?"

"I eat anything I can get."

"I understand," I say. "You're not particular. If there is something to eat, you eat. If not, you bite your lip and go to bed hungry. But it's all worth while as long as you can attend the university. You're comparing yourself to those rich people of Yehupetz. . . ."

At these words Pertschik bursts out, "Don't you dare compare me to them! They can go to hell as far as I care!"

"You seem to be somewhat prejudiced against the rich," I say. "Did they divide your father's inheritance among themselves?"

"Let me tell you," says he, "it may well be that you and I and all the rest of us have no small share in *their* inheritance."

"Listen to me," I answer. "Let your enemies talk like that. But one thing I can see: you're not a bashful lad. You know what a tongue is for. If you have the time, stop at my house tonight and we'll talk a little more. And if you come early, you can have supper with us, too."

Our young friend didn't have to be asked twice. He arrived at the right moment—when the *borsht* was on the table and the *knishes* were baking in the oven. "Just in time!" I said. "Sit down. You can say grace or not, just as you please. I'm not God's watchman; I won't

be punished for your sins." And as I talk to him I feel myself drawn
to the fellow somehow; I don't know why. Maybe it's because I like a
person one can talk to, a person who can understand a quotation
and follow an argument about philosophy or this or that or something
else. . . . That's the kind of person I am.

And from that evening on our young friend began coming to our
house almost every day. He had a few private students and when he
was through giving his lessons he'd come to our house to rest up
and visit for a while. What the poor fellow got for his lessons you
can imagine for yourself, if I tell you that the very richest people
used to pay their tutors three *rubles* a month; and besides their regular duties they were expected to read telegrams for them, write out
addresses, and even run errands at times. Why not? As the passage
says, *"If you eat bread you have to earn it."* It was lucky for him that
most of the time he used to eat with us. For this he used to give my
daughters lessons, too. One good turn deserves another. And in this
way he became almost a member of the family. The girls saw to it
that he had enough to eat and my wife kept his shirts clean and his
socks mended. And it was at this time that we changed his Russian
name of Pertschik to Feferel. And it can truthfully be said that we
all came to love him as though he were one of us, for by nature he
was a likable young man, simple, straightforward, generous. Whatever he had he shared with us.

There was only one thing I didn't like about him, and that was the
way he had of suddenly disappearing. Without warning he would
get up and go off; we looked around, and there was no Feferel.
When he came back I would ask, "Where were you, my fine-feath-
ered friend?" And he wouldn't say a word. I don't know how you
are, but as for me, I dislike a person with secrets. I like a person to
be willing to tell what he's been up to. But you can say this for him:
when he did start talking, you couldn't stop him. He poured out
everything. What a tongue he had! *"Against the Lord and against
His anointed; let us break their bands asunder."* And the main thing
was to break the bands. . . . He had the wildest notions, the most
peculiar ideas. Everything was upside down, topsy-turvy. For instance, according to his way of thinking, a poor man was far more

important than a rich one, and if he happened to be a worker too, then he was really the brightest jewel in the diadem! He who toiled with his hands stood first in his estimation.

"That's good," I say, "but will that get you any money?"

At this he becomes very angry and tries to tell me that money is the root of all evil. Money, he says, is the source of all falsehood, and as long as money amounts to something, nothing will ever be done in this world in the spirit of justice. And he gives me thousands of examples and illustrations that make no sense whatever.

"According to your crazy notions," I tell him, "there is no justice in the fact that my cow gives milk and my horse draws a load." I didn't let him get away with anything. That's the kind of man Tevye is. . . .

But my Feferel can argue too. And how he can argue! If there is something on his mind, he comes right out with it. One evening we were sitting on my stoop talking things over—discussing philosophic matters—when he suddenly said, "Do you know, Reb Tevye, you have very fine daughters."

"Is that so?" said I. "Thanks for telling me. After all, they have someone to take after."

"The oldest one especially is a very bright girl," said he. "She's all there!"

"I know without your telling me," said I. "The apple never falls very far from the tree."

And I glowed with pride. What father isn't happy when his children are praised? How should I have known that from such an innocent remark would grow such fiery love?

Well, one summer twilight I was driving through Boiberik, going from *datcha* to *datcha* with my goods, when someone stopped me. I looked up and saw that it was Ephraim the Matchmaker. And Ephraim, like all matchmakers, was concerned with only one thing—arranging marriages. So when he sees me here in Boiberik he stops me and says, "Excuse me, Reb Tevye, I'd like to tell you something."

"Go ahead," I say, stopping my horse, "as long as it's good news."

"You have," says he, "a daughter."

"I have," I answer, "seven daughters."

"I know," says he. "I have seven, too."

"Then together," I tell him, "we have fourteen."

"But joking aside," he says, "here is what I have to tell you. As you know, I am a matchmaker; and I have a young man for you to consider, the very best there is, a regular prince. There's not another like him anywhere."

"Well," I say, "that sounds good enough to me. But what do you consider a prince? If he's a tailor or a shoemaker or a teacher, you can keep him. I'll find my equal or I won't have anything. As the *medresh* says . . ."

"Ah, Reb Tevye," says he, "you're beginning with your quotations already! If a person wants to talk to you he has to study up first. . . . But better listen to the sort of match Ephraim has to offer you. Just listen and be quiet."

And then he begins to rattle off all his client's virtues. And it really sounds like something. . . . First of all, he comes from a very fine family. And that is very important to me, for I am not just a nobody either. In our family you will find all sorts of people, spotted, striped and speckled, as the Bible says. There are plain, ordinary people, there are workers, and there are property owners. . . . Secondly, he is a learned man who can read small print as well as large; he knows all the Commentaries by heart. And that is certainly not a small thing, either, for an ignorant man I hate even worse than pork itself. To me an unlettered man is worse—a thousand times worse—than a hoodlum. You can go around bareheaded, you can even walk on your head if you like, but if you know what Rashi and the others have said, you are a man after my own heart. . . . And on top of everything, Ephraim tells me, this man of his is rich as can be. He has his own carriage drawn by two horses so spirited that you can see a vapor rising from them. And that I don't object to, either. Better a rich man than a poor one! God Himself must hate a poor man, for if He did not, would He have made him poor?

"Well," I ask, "what more do you have to say?"

"What more can I say? He wants me to arrange a match with you. He is dying, he's so eager. Not for you, naturally, but for your daughter. He wants a pretty girl."

"He is dying?" I say. "Then let him keep dying. . . . And who is this treasure of yours? What is he? A bachelor? A widower? Is he divorced? What's wrong with him?"

"He is a bachelor," says Ephraim. "Not so young any more, but he's never been married."

"And what is his name, may I ask?"

But this he wouldn't tell me. "Bring the girl to Boiberik," he says, "and then I'll tell you."

"Bring her?" says I. "That's the way one talks about a horse or a cow that's being brought to market. Not a girl!"

Well, you know what these matchmakers are. They can talk a stone wall into moving. So we agreed that early next week I would bring my daughter to Boiberik. And driving home, all sorts of wonderful thoughts came to me, and I imagined my Hodel riding in a carriage drawn by spirited horses. The whole world envied me, not so much for the carriage and horses as for the good deeds I accomplished through my wealthy daughter. I helped the needy with money—let this one have twenty-five *rubles,* that one fifty, another a hundred. How do we say it? "Other people have to live too. . . ." That's what I think to myself as I ride home in the evening, and I whip my horse and talk to him in his own language.

"Hurry, my little horse," I say, "move your legs a little faster and you'll get your oats that much sooner. As the Bible says, *'If you don't work, you don't eat.'* . . ."

Suddenly I see two people coming out of the woods—a man and a woman. Their heads are close together and they are whispering to each other. Who could they be, I wonder, and I look as them through the dazzling rays of the setting sun. I could swear the man was Feferel. But whom was he walking with so late in the day? I put my hand up and shield my eyes and look closely. Who was the damsel? Could it be Hodel? Yes, that's who it was! Hodel! So? So that's how they'd been studying their grammar and reading their books together? Oh, Tevye, what a fool you are. . . .

I stop the horse and call out: "Good evening! And what's the latest news of the war? How do you happen to be out here this time of the day? What are you looking for—the day before yesterday?"

At this the couple stops, not knowing what to do or say. They stand there, awkward and blushing, with their eyes lowered. Then they look up at me, I look at them, and they look at each other. . . .

"Well," I say, "you look as if you hadn't seen me in a long time. I am the same Tevye as ever, I haven't changed by a hair."

I speak to them half angrily, half jokingly. Then my daughter, blushing harder than ever, speaks up: "Father, you can congratulate us."

"Congratulate you?" I say. "What's happened? Did you find a treasure buried in the woods? Or were you just saved from some terrible danger?"

"Congratulate us," says Feferel this time. "We're engaged."

"What do you mean—engaged?"

"Don't you know what engaged means?" says Feferel, looking me straight in the eye. "It means that I'm going to marry her and she's going to marry me."

I look him back in the eye and say, "When was the contract signed? And why didn't you invite me to the ceremony? Don't you think I have a slight interest in the matter?" I joke with them and yet my heart is breaking. But Tevye is not a weakling. He wants to hear everything out. "Getting married," I say, "without matchmakers, without an engagement feast?"

"What do we need matchmakers for?" says Feferel. "We arranged it between ourselves."

"So?" I say. "That's one of God's wonders! But why were you so silent about it?"

"What was there to shout about?" says he. "We wouldn't have told you now, either, but since we have to part soon, we decided to have the wedding first."

This really hurt. How do they say it? It hurt to the quick. Becoming engaged without my knowledge—that was bad enough, but I could stand it. He loves her; she loves him—that I'm glad to hear. But getting married? That was too much for me. . . .

The young man seemed to realize that I wasn't too well pleased with the news. "You see, Reb Tevye," he offered, "this is the reason: I am about to go away."

"When are you going?"

"Very soon."

"And where are you going?"

"That I can't tell you. It's a secret."

What do you think of that? A secret! A young man named Feferel comes into our lives—small, dark, homely, disguises himself as a bridegroom, wants to marry my daughter and then leave her—and he won't even say where he's going! Isn't that enough to drive you crazy?

"All right," I say. "A secret is a secret. Everything you do seems to be a secret. But explain this to me, my friend. You are a man of such —what do you call it?—integrity; you wallow in justice. So tell me, how does it happen that you suddenly marry Tevye's daughter and then leave her? Is that integrity? Is that justice? It's lucky that you didn't decide to rob me or burn my house down!"

"Father," says Hodel, "you don't know how happy we are now that we've told you our secret. It's like a weight off our chests. Come, father, kiss me."

And they both grab hold of me, she on one side, he on the other, and they begin to kiss and embrace me, and I to kiss them in return. And in their great excitement they begin to kiss each other. It was like going to a play. "Well," I say at last, "maybe you've done enough kissing already? It's time to talk about practical things."

"What, for instance?" they ask.

"For instance," I say, "the dowry, clothes, wedding expenses, this, that and the other. . . ."

"We don't need a thing," they tell me. "We don't need anything. No this, no that, no other."

"Well then, what do you need?" I ask.

"Only the wedding ceremony," they tell me.

What do you think of that! . . . Well, to make a long story short, nothing I said did any good. They went ahead and had their wedding, if you want to call it a wedding. Naturally it wasn't the sort that I would have liked. A quiet little wedding—no fun at all. And besides there was a wife I had to do something about. She kept plaguing me: what were they in such a hurry about? Go try to ex-

plain their haste to a woman. But don't worry. I invented a story—
"great, powerful and marvelous," as the Bible says—about a rich aunt
in Yehupetz, an inheritance, all sorts of foolishness.

And a couple of hours after this wonderful wedding I hitched up
my horse and wagon and the three of us got in, that is, my daughter,
my son-in-law and I, and off we went to the station at Boiberik.
Sitting in the wagon, I steal a look at the young couple, and I think to
myself: what a great and powerful Lord we have and how cleverly
He rules the world. What strange and fantastic beings He has
created. Here you have a new young couple, just hatched; he is going
off, the Good Lord alone knows where, and is leaving her behind—
and do you see either one of them shed a tear, even for appearance's
sake? But never mind—Tevye is not a curious old woman. He can
wait. He can watch and see. . . .

At the station I see a couple of young fellows, shabbily dressed,
down-at-the-heels, coming to see my happy bridegroom off. One of
them is dressed like a peasant with his blouse worn like a smock over
his trousers. The two whisper together mysteriously for several
minutes. "Look out, Tevye," I say to myself. "You have fallen among
a band of horse thieves, pickpockets, housebreakers or counterfeiters."

Coming home from Boiberik I can't keep still any longer and tell
Hodel what I suspect. She bursts out laughing and tries to assure me
that they were very honest young men, honorable men, whose whole
life was devoted to the welfare of humanity; their own private welfare
meant nothing to them. For instance, the one with his blouse over his
trousers was a rich man's son. He had left his parents in Yehupetz
and wouldn't take a penny from them.

"Oh," said I, "that's just wonderful. An excellent young man! All
he needs, now that he has his blouse over his trousers and wears his
hair long, is a harmonica, or a dog to follow him, and then he would
really be a beautiful sight!" I thought I was getting even with her for
the pain she and this new husband of hers had caused me; but did
she care? Not at all! She pretended not to understand what I was
saying. I talked to her about Feferel and she answered me with "the
cause of humanity" and "workers" and other such talk.

"What good is your humanity and your workers," I say, "if it's all a secret? There is a proverb: 'Where there are secrets, there is knavery.' But tell me the truth now. Where did he go, and why?"

"I'll tell you anything," she says, "but not that. Better don't ask. Believe me, you'll find out yourself in good time. You'll hear the news—and maybe very soon—and good news at that."

"Amen," I say. "From your mouth into God's ears! But may our enemies understand as little about it as I do."

"That," says she, "is the whole trouble. You'll never understand."

"Why not?" say I. "Is it so complicated? It seems to me that I can understand even more difficult things."

"These things you can't understand with your brain alone," she says. "You have to feel them, you have to feel them in your heart."

And when she said this to me, you should have seen how her face shone and her eyes burned. Ah, those daughters of mine! They don't do anything halfway. When they become involved in anything it's with their hearts and minds, their bodies and souls.

Well, a week passed, then two weeks—five—six—seven . . . and we heard nothing. There was no letter, no news of any kind. "Feferel is gone for good," I said, and glanced over at Hodel. There wasn't a trace of color in her face. And at the same time she didn't rest at all; she found something to do every minute of the day, as though trying to forget her troubles. And she never once mentioned his name, as if there never had been a Feferel in the world!

But one day when I came home from work I found Hodel going about with her eyes swollen from weeping. I made a few inquiries and found out that someone had been to see her, a long-haired young man who had taken her aside and talked to her for some time. Ah! That must have been the young fellow who had disowned his rich parents and pulled his blouse down over his trousers. Without further delay I called Hodel out into the yard and bluntly asked her: "Tell me, daughter, have you heard from him?"

"Yes."

"Where is he—your predestined one?"

"He is far away."

"What is he doing there?"

"He is serving time."

"Serving time?"

"Yes."

"Why? What did he do?"

She doesn't answer me. She looks me straight in the eyes and doesn't say a word.

"Tell me, my dear daughter," I say, "according to what I can understand, he is not serving for a theft. So if he is neither a thief nor a swindler, why is he serving? For what good deeds?"

She doesn't answer. So I think to myself, "If you don't want to, you don't have to. He is your headache, not mine." But my heart aches for her. No matter what you say, I'm still her father. . . .

Well, it was the evening of *Hashono Rabo*. On a holiday I'm in the habit of resting and my horse rests too. As it is written in the Bible: *"Thou shalt rest from thy labors and so shall thy wife and thine ass. . . ."* Besides, by that time of the year there is very little for me to do in Boiberik. As soon as the holidays come and the *shofar* sounds, all the summer *datchas* close down and Boiberik becomes a desert. At that season I like to sit at home on my own stoop. To me it is the finest time of the year. Each day is a gift from heaven. The sun no longer bakes like an oven, but caresses with a heavenly softness. The woods are still green, the pines give out a pungent smell. In my yard stands the *succah*—the booth I have built for the holiday, covered with branches, and around me the forest looks like a huge *succah* designed for God Himself. Here, I think, God celebrates His *Succos,* here and not in town, in the noise and tumult where people run this way and that panting for breath as they chase after a small crust of bread and all you hear is money, money, money. . . .

As I said, it is the evening of *Hashono Rabo*. The sky is a deep blue and myriads of stars twinkle and shine and blink. From time to time a star falls through the sky, leaving behind it a long green band of light. This means that someone's luck has fallen . . . I hope it isn't my star that is falling, and somehow Hodel comes to mind. She has changed in the last few days, has come to life again. Someone, it seems, has brought her a letter from him, from over there. I wish I knew what he had written, but I won't ask. If she won't speak, I won't either. Tevye is not a curious old woman. Tevye can wait.

And as I sit thinking of Hodel, she comes out of the house and sits down near me on the stoop. She looks cautiously around and then whispers, "I have something to tell you, father. I have to say good-bye to you, and I think it's for always."

She spoke so softly that I could barely hear her, and she looked at me in a way that I shall never forget.

"What do you mean—good-bye for always?" I say to her, and turn my face aside.

"I mean I am going away early tomorrow morning, and we shall possibly never see each other again."

"Where are you going, if I may be so bold as to ask?"

"I am going to him."

"To him? And where is he?"

"He is still serving, but soon they'll be sending him away."

"And you're going there to say good-bye to him?" I ask, pretending not to understand.

"No. I am going to follow him," she says. "Over there."

"There? Where is that? What do they call the place?"

"We don't know the exact name of the place, but we know that it's far—terribly, terribly far."

And she speaks, it seems to me, with great joy and pride, as though he had done something for which he deserved a medal. What can I say to her? Most fathers would scold a child for such talk, punish her, even beat her maybe. But Tevye is not a fool. To my way of thinking anger doesn't get you anywhere. So I tell her a story.

"I see, my daughter, as the Bible says, *'Therefore shalt thou leave thy father and mother'*—for a Feferel you are ready to forsake your parents and go off to a strange land, to some desert across the frozen wastes, where Alexander of Macedon, as I once read in a story book, once found himself stranded among savages. . . ."

I speak to her half in fun and half in anger, and all the time my heart weeps. But Tevye is no weakling; I control myself. And Hodel doesn't lose her dignity either; she answers me word for word, speaking quietly and thoughtfully. And Tevye's daughters can talk.

And though my head is lowered and my eyes are shut, still I seem to see her—her face is pale and lifeless like the moon, but her voice trembles. . . . Shall I fall on her neck and plead with her not to go? I know it won't help. Those daughters of mine—when they fall in love with somebody, it is with their heads and hearts, their bodies and souls.

Well, we sat on the doorstep a long time—maybe all night. Most of the time we were silent, and when we did speak it was in snatches, a word here, a word there. I said to her, "I want to ask you only one thing: did you ever hear of a girl marrying a man so that she could follow him to the ends of the earth?" And she answered, "With him I'd go anywhere." I pointed out how foolish that was. And she said, "Father, you will never understand." So I told her a little fable— about a hen that hatched some ducklings. As soon as the ducklings could move they took to the water and swam, and the poor hen stood on shore, clucking and clucking.

"What do you say to that, my daughter?"

"What can I say?" she answered. "I am sorry for the poor hen; but just because she stood there clucking, should the ducklings have stopped swimming?"

There is an answer for you. She's not stupid, that daughter of mine.

But time does not stand still. It was beginning to get light already, and from within the house my old woman was muttering. More than once she had called out that it was time to go to bed, but seeing that it didn't help she stuck her head out of the window and said to me, with her usual benediction, "Tevye, what's keeping you?"

"Be quiet, Golde," I answered. "Remember what the Psalm says, *'Why are the nations in an uproar, and why do the peoples mutter in vain?* Have you forgotten that it's *Hashono Rabo* tonight? Tonight all our fates are decided and the verdict is sealed. We stay up tonight . . . Listen to me, Golde, you light the samovar and make some tea while I go to get the horse and wagon ready. I am taking Hodel to the station in the morning." And once more I make up a story about how she has to go to Yehupetz, and from there farther on, because of that same old inheritance. It is possible, I say, that she may have to stay there through the winter and maybe the summer too, and maybe even another winter; and so we ought to give her something to take along—some linen, a dress, a couple of pillows, some pillow slips, and things like that.

And as I give these orders I tell her not to cry. "It's *Hashono Rabo* and on *Hashono Rabo* one mustn't weep. It's a law." But naturally they don't pay any attention to me, and when the time comes to say good-bye they all start weeping—their mother, the children and even Hodel herself. And when she came to say good-bye to her older sister Tzeitl (Tzeitl and her husband spend their holidays with us) they fell on each other's necks and you could hardly tear them apart.

I was the only one who did not break down. I was firm as steel —though inside I was more like a boiling samovar. All the way to Boiberik we were silent, and when we came near the station I asked her for the last time to tell me what it was that Feferel had really done. If they were sending him away, there must have been a reason. At this she became angry and swore by all that was holy that he was innocent. He was a man, she insisted, who cared nothing about himself. Everything he did was for humanity at large, especially for those who toiled with their hands—that is, the workers. That made no sense to me. "So he worries about the world," I told her. "Why doesn't the world worry a little about him? Nevertheless, give him my regards, that Alexander of Macedon of yours, and tell him I rely on his honor—for he is a man of honor, isn't he?—to treat my daughter well. And write to your old father some times."

When I finish talking she falls on my neck and begins to weep. "Good-bye, father," she cries. "Good-bye! God alone knows when we shall see each other again."

Well, that was too much for me. I remembered this Hodel when she was still a baby and I carried her in my arms, I carried her in my arms. . . . Forgive me, Mr. Sholom Aleichem, for acting like an old woman. If you only knew what a daughter she is. If you could only see the letters she writes. Oh, what a daughter. . . .

And now, let's talk about more cheerful things. Tell me, what news is there about the cholera in Odessa?

The Happiest Man in Kodno

THE BEST TIME of the year to travel is in the autumn, right after the High Holidays. It is neither too hot nor too cold and you are not obliged to look at the dripping sky or at the dark dismal earth. Drops of rain beat against the windows and roll down the sweating windowpanes, like tears. You sit in the third-class carriage like a Lord in his castle, surrounded by other nobles just like yourself. You take a look outside and you see at a distance a wagon creeping along, the wheels sloshing in the mud. On the wagon sits one of God's creatures, bent over double, with a sack on his shoulders, and whips along his poor little horse who is also one of God's creatures. You lean back and thank God that you are sitting under a dry roof in company with others. I don't know about you, but for me autumn is the best time of the year to travel.

The first thing I do is grab a seat. If I am lucky enough to get a seat by a window, then I am really a king. I take out my tobacco pouch and begin smoking cigarette after cigarette. I look around to see who my fellow-passengers are, to see if there is anyone worth talking to. The car is packed tight with people, row upon row of beards, noses, caps, protruding stomachs—all in the image of man. But wait! Off in a corner by himself sits an odd creature, different from the others. My eyes are sharp. I can spot an odd character among a hundred others.

At first glance he seems to be an ordinary fellow—a Jew like the rest, the kind we call an "everyday Jew." But he is dressed strangely.

457

His coat is not quite a coat and yet not a gabardine. He has something on his head that is not quite a hat and yet not a skullcap. In his hands he holds something that might be either an umbrella or a broomstick. An odd-looking character.

But it isn't his clothes that attract me so much as his manner. He can't seem to sit still in one spot. He keeps moving about restlessly from place to place. And his face isn't still either. His eyes shoot sparks, his face is glowing, it has a rapt joyous look on it, as though he had just won a fortune in the lottery, or married off a daughter to a millionaire, or entered his son in a gymnasium. Every few minutes he jumps up, and runs to the window and mutters to himself, "A station? Not yet?" And he sits down again, each time a little closer to where I am sitting. And his face continues to shine. . . .

You must know that by nature I am not the sort of person who likes to worm secrets out of people. I never pry into other people's affairs. I go according to this theory, that if a man has something on his chest he will unburden himself of his own accord.

And I am not wrong this time either. At the very next station the restless passenger moved closer to me, so close this time that his mouth almost touched my nose.

"And where are you going?" he asked me.

I could tell from the way he asked the question, from the eager look in his eyes and the restless motion of his hands, that he was not so eager to know where I was going, as to tell me where *he* was going. And so I humored him, I didn't answer his question, but asked instead, "And where are you going?" This started him off.

"Where am I going? To Kodno. Have you ever heard of Kodno? That's where I'm from. It isn't far, just three stations away. That is, you get off at the third station from here and then you still have to ride an hour and a half by wagon to get to Kodno. I say an hour and half. It's closer to two hours, two solid hours and a little bit over. And that only if the road is clear and you're riding in a carriage. I am going to have a carriage meet me today. I sent a telegram ahead to have a carriage meet me at the station. Do you think it's for myself? Don't worry—for my part I can squeeze into a wagon with six others, and if not, I can take my umbrella in one hand, my bundle in the other and make the trip on foot too. I can't afford to hire carriages every day. Business being what it is, I can sit at home altogether."

Here he paused, sighed, looked all around him first to make sure that no one was listening, then began to speak softly right into my ear:

"I am not traveling alone. I am traveling with a Professor—a famous doctor. How do I happen to be traveling with a Professor? I'll tell you. Have you ever heard of Kashavarevka? That's a town near here. A certain very rich man lives there—maybe you have heard of him—his name is Borodenko, Itzik Borodenko. How do you like his name? An odd name, isn't it? But he's a rich man, rolling in wealth. In Kodno we value him at half a million. For my part, I will allow him a whole million. And seeing how stingy he is, I will even make it two million. For example, you must have traveled widely in these parts—have you ever heard of a man named Borodenko giving great sums to charity? So far we've never heard of it in Kodno either. But let that go. I am not—how do you say it—God's deputy. I am not collecting charity. Everybody is too generous with other people's money.

"It isn't charity I speak of now, but plain ordinary human decency. If God has blessed you with so much money that you can afford to send for a famous specialist for your sick child, will it hurt you if another benefits from your good fortune? Nobody is asking you for money. All we want is a kind word. But wait till you hear this.

"We heard in Kodno that a daughter of this same Borodenko that I am telling you about had suddenly become ill. (In Kodno we hear about everything.) What sort of illness do you think it was? Not an illness, but an unhappy love affair. She fell in love with a gentile and he jilted her, so she took poison. (In Kodno we hear about everything.) This happened only yesterday. Well, they made haste and sent off for a doctor, a famous Professor from the big city. A rich man can afford to get the best. So I got an idea. Since this doctor, this Professor, won't be staying very long, he will be leaving today or tomorrow and on his way back he has to pass our station anyway —why can't he get off and run over to Kodno between trains and see my son?

"I have a son who is sick, at home. You ask what's wrong with him? I don't know myself. It's something they call internal. He has no pains of any kind, and he doesn't cough either, thank God. But he has no strength—he is weak, as weak as a fly. That's because he won't touch any food, he won't eat a thing. Sometimes he will drink a glass of milk, and that only by force. You have to weep and plead with him to take it. Aside from that he won't take a spoonful of soup or a bite of bread. And meat? He won't look at meat. He turns his head away.

"He has been this way since he had a hemorrhage last summer. He hasn't had any since then, thank God. But he is so weak, you can't imagine how weak he is. He can't move a limb. But what can you expect when the boy has been running a fever since before *Shevuos*. There is no remedy for it. We've taken him to the doctor more than once. But what do our doctors know? Give him a lot of food, he says, give him fresh air. But he won't touch any food, and as for fresh air—where would we get that? Fresh air—in Kodno? Kodno is a fine little town, we have a good number of Jews living there. We have a Synagogue, two Synagogues in fact. We have a Rabbi, we have everything. But from two things God has delivered us—from fresh air and a livelihood.

"Still we scrape up a living somehow. We live off each other. But fresh air? If we want fresh air, we have to go outside the town to the Landowners' Estate. There you will find fresh air. When Kodno belonged to the Polish Squire we were not allowed on the estate. The Squire didn't permit it, and not so much the Squire as the Squire's dogs. But now the estate belongs to Jewish landowners and we are allowed to go in. When I say Jewish landowners, I don't mean they are Jews like us. They don't go to our Synagogue and certainly not to our Baths. And they don't mind eating chicken with butter. Naturally they are clean-shaven and go without hats, that's taken for granted. Even in Kodno there are certain young men nowadays who find a hat too weighty for their heads.

"But we have nothing to complain about. The landowners are good to us. In autumn they send down a hundred sacks of potatoes for the poor. In winter they give us straw for fuel. For Passover they provide us with *matzos*. Recently, they donated some bricks for the Synagogue. If it wasn't for that chicken cooked in butter, I wouldn't find fault. Mind you, I don't want to slander them. They think very highly of me. They wouldn't exchange me for a barrel of *borsht*. Whenever something comes up, they call on Reb Alter—my name is Alter. Whether it's a calendar for the new year or *matzos* for Passover —anything to do with Jewish customs—they send for me. And they give my wife a good bit of business too—my wife has a shop—they buy salt and pepper and matches from her. I can't complain about our landowners.

"And their sons—the young students—are wild about my boy. In summer when they all come home from St. Petersburg they gather at my house and read with him. They spend days reading books with him. And books, you must know, are my son's first love. They are dearer to him than his father and his mother. I hate to say it, but I'm afraid that it's these books that have ruined his health, though my wife insists that it's his military service. That's nonsense. He's forgotten his military service long ago. But whatever it is, books or military service, there he is—sick, sick to death, wasting away like a candle. . . ."

For a moment something like a cloud passed over the shining face of my acquaintance. But only for a moment. The sun came out quickly again and drove away the cloud. His face began to glow once more, his eyes lit up, and a smile appeared on his lips. He went on talking:

"Well, where were we? Oh, yes, I decided to run over to Kashavarevka. Naturally I didn't set out just so, how do you say it—empty-handed? I took along a letter from the Rabbi of Kodno. (The Rabbi of Kodno is known all over.) A very handsomely written letter, addressed to Itzik Borodenko: 'Whereas, God has blessed you to such an extent that you are in a position to summon a Professor to your home when you need his services, and since our Alter has a son who is lying on his deathbed, perhaps a spark of pity will awaken in your breast and warm your heart so that you will enter into his need, and prevail upon the Professor to stop off in Kodno between trains and visit the sick boy.' And so on and so on. A very handsome letter."

Suddenly a whistle sounds, the train stops.

"Aha. A station. I'll just run over to the first-class carriage for a second. I want to take a peek at my Professor. When I get back I'll finish my story."

In a few minutes he came back, looking even happier and more exalted than before. If I might express myself thus, he looked as though he had "beheld the divine Presence." Moving up close to me he whispered into my ear as though he was afraid he might wake up someone. "He is asleep. The Professor is sleeping. May he rest well with God's help, so that when he comes to us, it will be with a clear head. Where were we? Oh, yes, in Kashavarevka. I arrived in Kashavarevka and went straight to Itzik Borodenko's house. I rang the bell once, twice, three times. Out came a big fellow with a red face, licking his chops like a cat, and he says to me in Russian, 'Chto nada?'—What do you need? And I say in Yiddish, 'It must be nada. If I didn't need anything I wouldn't have traveled here all the way from Kodno.'

"He listens to me, keeps on chewing and licking his chops, and finally shakes his head and says, 'You can't get in today. The Professor is sitting in consultation.'

" 'That's just why I came here,' I tell him. 'On account of the Professor.'

"And he says in an insulting tone, 'What business can you have with a Professor?'

"Instead of explaining, I handed him the Rabbi's letter. 'It's easy for you to stand there talking,' I said. 'You are snug and dry inside, and I am standing here with the rain pouring on me. Here, take this document and be so kind as to give it to your employer, put it right into his hands.'

"He went in, and I remained standing there, waiting for them to send for me. I wait half an hour. I wait an hour. I wait two hours. The rain keeps coming down on me in a torrent and still nobody sends for me. I was beginning to feel offended, not so much for my sake as for the Rabbi's. Imagine them ignoring a letter from the Rabbi of Kodno! So I rang the bell again, several times. The same red-faced lout jumps out and shouts at me furiously, 'What's the idea of ringing that bell? Who do you think you are?' And I answer, 'And who do you think you are, letting me stand out here in the rain for two hours?' I try to push my way in, but he quickly slams the door in my face. What's to be done? It looks bad. I am ashamed to go home empty-handed. After all, I am a leading citizen of Kodno, not some tramp that can be chased away from the door. And above all, my heart aches for my son.

"But there is a merciful God in heaven. I look up—a carriage pulled by four horses drives up and stops right at the door. I ask the coachman whose carriage and horses these are, and I learn that they are Borodenko's carriage and horses and they have come to take the Professor to the station. If so, I think to myself, very good. In fact, excellent.

"Before I am through asking, the door opens and out comes the Professor himself, a tiny, shrunken little old man with a face—how shall I describe it—the face of an angel. An angel from heaven. Behind him comes Borodenko himself, and behind him the red-faced lout carrying the Professor's suitcase. I wish you could have seen this Borodenko, this millionaire, homely and cross-eyed and dressed in a jacket of ordinary cloth, the kind we wear in Kodno, standing there with his hands in his pockets. I look at him and think to myself, 'Dear God in Heaven, so this is the creature you blessed with millions.' But you can't argue with God. The millionaire looks at me sideways, with his cross-eyes and says, 'What do you want here?'

"I go up to him and tell him why I came. 'I brought you a letter from the Rabbi,' I say.

"And he says, 'Which Rabbi?'

"How do you like that? He wants to know which Rabbi. 'From the Rabbi of Kodno,' I tell him. 'I came from Kodno especially to see the Professor and to ask if he wouldn't be so kind as to do me the favor of stopping at my house for a quarter of an hour between trains to see my sick son.'

"I was thinking to myself, 'The man has just suffered a misfortune, his daughter took poison, maybe he will have some pity in his heart for a poor father's plight.'

"But there wasn't a sign of pity on his face. He didn't even answer me. He turned to the red-faced lout as though to say, 'How about clearing this beggar out of the way?'

"Meanwhile the Professor had stepped into the carriage with his suitcase. A moment more and he would be gone. What should I do? Seeing that the game was as good as lost anyway, I had no choice. I said to myself, 'What will happen will happen! I must save my child.' I took a deep breath and jumped in front of the horses. What would you like to know? Shall I tell you how it felt to be trampled by the horses' hooves? I am not sure whether I was trampled under their hooves or not. I am not sure just what happened or how long I lay there, or if I lay there at all. I only know that in less time than it takes to tell this, the little Professor was standing by me and saying, 'Chto takoie?'—What's the matter? And calling me 'golubtchik,' dear one, and asking me to tell him my request, not to be afraid, to tell him everything.

"So I began talking while the millionaire stood by looking at me with his cross-eyes. You must know that I don't speak Russian fluently, but this time God gave me extra strength and I talked! I poured out everything there was in my heart. 'Herr Professor,' I said, 'God himself must have sent you as His messenger to save my son's life. He is my only son, the only one left to me of six. And if it has to cost money, I have twenty-five rubles. It isn't my own money— where would I get so much money? It's my wife's money that she has been saving up to buy merchandise for her shop. But I will give you the twenty-five rubles and the devil take my wife's shop. I must save my son.'

"I unbuttoned my coat and was about to take out the money. But the Professor put his hand on my shoulder and said, 'Nitchevo.'—It doesn't matter. And he told me to get into the carriage with him. Do you think that I am inventing this? I swear to you by everything holy, by my hope of seeing my son well, that I am telling the truth. So I ask you, isn't the millionaire Borodenko worth less than the least little fingernail of the Professor? He almost ruined me, this Borodenko; he was ready to kill me, without a knife. Luckily my trick worked. But suppose it hadn't? Eh? What do you say?"

Suddenly there was a stir in the carriage. My friend ran up to the conductor.

"Is this Kodno?" he asked.

"This is Kodno."

He turned to me. "Good-bye, and have a good trip and don't tell anyone whom I am traveling with. I don't want them to know in Kodno that I am bringing a Professor. The whole town will come running."

He whispered this hurriedly, pressed my hand, and was gone.

A few minutes later when we were ready to start again I looked out of the window and saw a rickety old carriage with a couple of broken-down nags hitched to it. Inside sat a tiny old man wearing glasses, with youthful pink cheeks, and a short gray beard. Opposite him in the carriage sat my friend, barely hanging on to the edge of his seat. He was looking into the old man's eyes and you could see him quivering all over with emotion—his face was glowing and his eyes almost popped out of his head with excitement.

I was sorry that I didn't have a camera with me. I would have liked to take a picture of him, to let the whole world see what a really happy man looked like, the happiest man in Kodno.

A Wedding without Musicians

THE LAST TIME I told you about our Straggler Special, I described the miracle of *Hashono Rabo*. This time I shall tell you about another miracle in which the Straggler Special figured, how thanks to the Straggler Special the town of Heissin was saved from a terrible fate.

This took place during the days of the Constitution when reprisals against the Jews were going on everywhere. Though I must tell you that we Jews of Heissin have never been afraid of pogroms. Why? Simply because there is no one in our town who can carry out a pogrom. Of course you can imagine that if we looked very hard we could find one or two volunteers who wouldn't deny themselves the pleasure of ventilating us a little, that is, breaking our bones or burning down our houses. For example, when reports of pogroms began drifting in, the few Squires, who are enemies of our people, wrote confidential letters to the proper authorities, saying it might be a good idea if "something were done" in Heissin also; but since there was no one here to do it, would they be so kind as to send help, in other words, would they dispatch some "people" as quickly as possible.

And before another twenty-four hours had passed a reply came, also confidentially, that "people" were being sent. From where? From Zhmerinko, from Kazatin, Razdilno, Popelno and other such places that had distinguished themselves in beating up Jews. Do you want to know how we learned of this deep secret? We found it out through our regular source of news, Noah Tonkonoy. Noah Tonkonoy is a

466

man whom God has endowed with a pair of extra-long legs and he uses them to good purpose. He never rests and he is seldom to be found at home. He is always busy with a thousand things and most of these things have to do with other people's business rather than his own. By trade he is a printer, and because he is the only printer in Heissin he knows all the squires and the police and has dealings with officialdom and is in on all their secrets.

Noah Tonkonoy spread the good news all over town. He told the secret to one person at a time, in strictest confidence, of course, saying, "I am telling this only to you. I wouldn't tell it to anyone else." And that was how the whole town became aware of the fact that a mob of hooligans was on the way, and that a plan for beating up Jews had been worked out. The plan told exactly when they would start, on which day, at which hour, and from which point, and by what means —everything to the last detail.

You can imagine what terror this struck in our hearts. Panic spread quickly. And among whom do you think it spread first? Among the poor, of course. It's a peculiar thing about poor people. When a rich man is afraid of a pogrom, you can understand why. He is afraid, poor fellow, that he will be turned into a pauper. But those of you who are already paupers, what are you afraid of? What have you got to lose? But you should have seen how they bundled up their children and packed up their belongings and began running hither and yon, looking for a place to hide. Where can a person hide? This one hides in a friendly peasant's cellar, another in the Notary's attic, a third in the Director's office at the factory. Everyone finds a spot for himself.

I was the only one in town who wasn't anxious to hide. I am not boasting about my bravery. But this is the way I see it: what's the sense of being afraid of a pogrom? I don't say that I am a hero. I might have been willing to hide too, when the hour of reckoning came. But I asked myself first, "How can I be sure that during the slaughter the friendly peasant in whose cellar I was hiding, or the Notary, or the Director of the factory himself, wouldn't . . ." You understand? And all that aside, how can you leave a town wide open like that? It's no trick to run away. You have to see about doing something. But, alas, what can a Jew do? He appeals to a friendly official. And that is just what we did.

In every town there is at least one friendly official you can appeal to. We had one too, the Inspector of Police, a jewel of a fellow, willing to listen to us and willing to accept a gift on occasion. We went to the Inspector with the proper gifts and asked for his protection. He reassured us at once. He told us to go home and sleep in peace. Nothing would happen. Sounds good, doesn't it? But we still had our walking newspaper, Noah, who was broadcasting another secret through the length and breadth of the town. The secret was that a telegram had just arrived. He swore by everything holy that he had seen it himself. What was in that telegram? Only one word—*Yediem*. An ugly word. It means simply, "We are coming." We ran back to the Inspector. "Your honor," we told him, "it looks bad." "What looks bad?" he asked, and we told him, "A telegram has just arrived." "From where?" We told him. "And what does it say?" We told him, "*Yediem*." At this he burst out laughing. "You are big fools," he said. "Only yesterday I ordered a regiment of Cossacks from Tolchin."

When we heard this we breathed more easily. When a Jew hears that a Cossack is coming, he takes courage, he can face the world again. The question remained: who would arrive first, the Cossacks from Tolchin, or the hooligans from Zhmerinko? Common sense told us that the hooligans would arrive first, because they were coming by train, while the Cossacks were coming on horseback. But we pinned all our hopes on the Straggler Special. God is merciful. He would surely perform a miracle and the Straggler would be at least a few hours late. This wasn't too much to hope for, since it happened nearly every day. But this one time it looked as though the miracle wouldn't take place. The Straggler kept going from station to station as regular as a clock. You can imagine how we felt when we learned, confidentially of course, through Noah Tonkonoy, that a telegram had arrived from the last station, from Krishtopovka. *Yediem* it said, and not just *yediem*—but *yediem* with a *hurrah!* in front of it.

Naturally we took this last bit of news straight to the Inspector. We begged him not to rely on the Cossacks who might or might not arrive from Tolchin sometime, but to send police to the station, at

least for the sake of appearances, so that our enemies wouldn't think
that we were completely at their mercy. The Inspector listened to our
pleas. He did what we asked, and more. He got himself up in full
uniform, with all his orders and medals, and took the whole police
force, that is the gendarme and his assistant, to the station with him
to meet the train.

But our enemies weren't asleep either. They also put on their full-
dress uniforms, complete with ribbons and medals, took a couple of
priests along, and also came to meet the train. The Inspector asked
them sternly, "What are you doing here?" And they asked him the
same question, "What are you doing here?" They bandied words
back and forth, and the Inspector let them know in no uncertain
terms that their trouble was for nothing. As long as he was in charge,
there would be no pogrom in Heissin. They listened, smiled know-
ingly, and answered with insolence, "We shall see."

Just then a train whistle was heard from the distance. The sound
struck terror to our hearts. We waited for another whistle to blow
and after that for the shouts of *"Hurrah!"* What would happen after
the *"Hurrah!"* we knew only too well from hearsay. We waited, but
heard nothing more. What had happened? The sort of thing that
could only happen to our Straggler Special.

When the Straggler Special drew into the station, the engineer
stopped the locomotive, stepped out calmly and made his way toward
the buffet. We met him halfway. "Well, my good fellow, and where
are the cars?" "Which cars?" "Can't you see that you are here with
the locomotive and without cars?"

He stared at us. "What do I care about the cars? They are the
business of the crew." "Where is the crew?" "How should I know
where the crew is? The conductor blows the whistle when he is ready
and I whistle back to let him know that I am starting, and off we
go. I don't have an extra pair of eyes in back of my head to see what's
going on behind me." That was his story and according to that he
was right. But right or wrong, there stood the Straggler Special without cars and without passengers. In other words, it was a wedding
without musicians.

Later we learned that a band of hooligans had been on the way to

Heissin, all of them handpicked youths, armed to the teeth with clubs and knives and other weapons. Their spirits were high and liquor flowed freely. At the last station, Krishtopovka, they invited the crew to join them and treated everybody to drinks—the conductor, the fireman, the gendarme. But in the midst of this revelry they forgot one little detail, to couple the cars back to the locomotive. And so the locomotive went off at the usual time to Heissin and the rest of the Straggler Special remained standing in Krishtopovka.

Neither the hooligans nor the other passengers nor the crew noticed that they were standing still. They continued to empty bottle after bottle and to make merry, until the station master suddenly noticed that the locomotive had gone off and left the cars behind. He spread the alarm, the crew came tumbling out. A hue and cry was raised. The hooligans blamed the crew, the crew blamed the hooligans, but what good did it do? The cars couldn't budge without the locomotive. At last they decided that the only thing to do was to set out for Heissin on foot. They took heart and began marching toward Heissin, singing and shouting as they went.

And so they arrived in their usual good form, singing and yelling and brandishing their clubs. But it was already too late. In the streets of Heissin the Cossacks from Tolchin were riding up and down on horseback with whips in their hands. Within half an hour not one of the hooligans remained in town. They ran off like rats in a famine, they melted like ice in the summer.

Now I ask you, didn't the Straggler Special deserve to be showered with gold, or at least written up?

What Will Become of Me?

SUPPOSE you try to guess where the Garden of Eden is. You will never guess. Do you know why? Because it's different for everybody. For instance, for my mother the Garden of Eden or the true Paradise is where my father, Peissi the Cantor, is now. There, she says, dwell all the pure souls who suffered on this earth. Because they have lost this world they have gained the next. That is as plain as day. The best example is my father. For where else should he be but in the Garden of Eden? Didn't he suffer enough in this world? And my mother wipes her eyes, as she always does when she speaks of my father.

But ask my friends and they will tell you something else. For them Paradise is somewhere on a mountain of pure crystal that reaches up to the sky. There boys run and jump and play all day long as free as birds. They have no lessons to do. They bathe in rivers of milk and eat honey by the fistfuls. Is that good enough for you? Then along comes a bookbinder and tells me that the only true paradise is to be found Friday in the bath. I swear by all that is holy that this is what I heard from our neighbor Pessie's husband, Moses the Bookbinder. Now try to figure out who is right. If you asked me, for instance, I would tell you that the Garden of Eden is in Menashe the Doctor's orchard. In all your life you have never seen such an orchard. Neither on our street, nor in our whole town, nor in the whole wide world has there ever been such an orchard. There never has been and never will be. Everybody knows that.

Now what shall I tell you about first? Shall I tell you about

471

Menashe the Doctor and his wife, or about their paradise, I mean their orchard? I think that first of all I should tell you about Menashe and his wife. They are the owners of the orchard and they should have the honor of being first.

Menashe the Doctor wears a cape both summer and winter, in imitation of the "black doctor." One of his eyes is smaller than the other and his mouth is twisted to one side. It became twisted once when he was sitting in a draft. I don't understand how a mouth can become twisted from a draft. Think of all the winds and hurricanes I've been through in my short life. My head should have been turned around on my shoulders by now. I think it's only a habit with him. For instance, there is my friend Berel who blinks his eyes. Another boy Velvel lisps. Everything in the world is a habit. But in spite of his twisted mouth, Menashe makes out better than any of the other doctors. In the first place, he isn't as proud as the others. When you call him, he drops everything and comes at a run, sweating and out of breath. In the second place, he doesn't bother writing prescriptions. He makes his own medicines.

It happened one time that I suddenly came down with chills and fever and sharp pains in my chest. (I must have been playing in the river too long.) My mother rushed off to get Menashe the Doctor. He looked me over and said to my mother out of his crooked mouth, "You have nothing to worry about. It's a joke. The rascal caught a cold in his lungs."

And he took a blue bottle out of his pocket and poured something white out of the bottle into six pieces of white paper. He called these "powders." He wanted me to take one of those "powders" at once. I twisted and squirmed and tried to get out of taking it, for my heart told me that it would taste as bitter as gall. I had guessed right. There are bitter things and bitter things. Have you ever tasted the bark of a young tree? That was how this "powder" tasted. I took it and saw the Angel of Death face to face. He left the other five powders with my mother and told her to give me a powder every two hours until they were all gone.

But they didn't reckon with me. My mother had barely turned her back on me—she had gone to tell my brother Elihu that I was sick—

when I poured the five powders into the washbasin and filled the five papers with flour. My mother had taken a chore on herself that day. Every two hours she had to run to our neighbor Pessie's to look at the clock. After each powder that I took she noticed that I looked a little better. After the sixth one I got out of bed, completely cured.

"That's what I call a doctor," my mother said joyfully. She kept me home from *cheder* all day and gave me sweet tea and white rolls to eat. "Menashe is the best doctor of them all, may God grant him health and a long life. His powders work miracles, they make the dead come to life again," my mother boasted to the neighbors, wiping her eyes, as usual.

Menashe the Doctor's wife is known as Menashacha. She is a terrible woman, a regular witch. She wears men's boots and she has a deep gruff voice like a man. Whenever she talks, she seems to be scolding. She has a wonderful reputation in town. They say that in all her life she has never given a beggar a crust of bread to eat. And her house and pantry are filled with the best of everything. In her cellar you will find preserves from last year and the year before last and the year before that and from ten years ago. What does she do with all these preserves? She herself won't be able to tell you. She only knows that when summer comes she has to start making jams and preserves. Do you think that she cooks them over a coal fire? Not on your life. A fire made of thistles and pine cones and even of last year's leaves is good enough for her. This fire gives off such an acrid smoke that a person can choke to death. If you happen to stray into our neighborhood during the summer and smell something scorching, don't be frightened. There is no fire. It's only Menashacha cooking preserves. She makes them herself out of the fruits that grow in her own orchard. And now, at last, we have come to the orchard itself.

What fruits won't you find in this orchard? Apples and pears and cherries, plums and gooseberries and currants, peaches, raspberries, rough cherries, blackberries. What more can you ask for? Even grapes for *Rosh Hashono* grow in Menashe the Doctor's orchard. It's true that when you taste these grapes you behold Krakov and Lvov in front of you, they are that sour. But she gets good money for them.

She gets money for everything, even for her sunflowers. God help you if you ask her to let you pick a sunflower. She would sooner pull a tooth out of her head than a sunflower from her garden. So you can imagine what it's like asking for an apple or a pear or a plum. You take your life into your hands if you try.

I know the orchard by heart, inside and out, the way a good Jew knows his Psalms. I know where every tree grows, and what fruit it bears and whether it produced a good crop this year or not. How do I know all that? Don't get excited, I've never been inside the orchard. How could I when it's surrounded by a tall fence which is covered with sharp barbs? And do you think this is all? Inside the orchard there is a dog tied to a rope. Did I say a dog? He is more like a wolf. Just let anyone go by, or let him think he heard someone go by, and he begins tearing at the rope and jumping in the air and barking as though the devil had him by the throat. Then how did I become so familiar with the inside of the orchard? Listen, and I will tell you.

Do you know Mendel the *Shochet?* You don't? Then you certainly don't know Mendel's house. It's right next door to Menashe the Doctor's house and it faces the orchard. When you are on the roof of Mendel's house you can see everything that's going on in Menashe the Doctor's orchard. The problem is how to get up on Mendel's roof. To me that's no problem. Do you know why? Because Mendel's house is right next door to ours and it's much lower than our house. When you climb up into our attic (I do it without a ladder, some day I may tell you how) and put your foot out of the little window, you are on Mendel's roof. Once on the roof you can stretch out on its slope, either with your face down or your face up, but you have to stretch out flat, or someone will see you and ask, "What are you doing on Mendel the *Shochet's* roof?" I always used to pick the early evening to go up on the roof, just before sundown, when I was supposed to be in the Synagogue saying *kaddish* for my father. That's the best time, when it's neither light nor dark. Lying on Mendel the *Shochet's* roof in the twilight I would look down on the orchard and I can swear to you that here was the true paradise. . . .

Early in the summer when the trees start budding and become covered with white fluff, you can start hoping that if not today, then to-morrow—any minute now—in the short prickly bushes, gooseberries will appear. This is the first fruit you wish you could taste. There are people who wait until the gooseberries are ripe. They are fools. May I have as many blessings how much better they are when they are still green. You will say that they are sour? That they set your teeth on edge? What of that? Sour things sharpen the appetite. And there is a remedy against having your teeth set on edge. The remedy is salt. You pour salt on your teeth and keep your mouth open for half an hour. Then you can start eating gooseberries again.

After the gooseberries come the currants. Bright red, tiny, with black muzzles, and yellow kernels, there are dozens of them growing on each sprig. If you pass one sprig between your lips you get a whole mouthful of currants—sweet, winy, delicious.

When currants are in season my mother buys me a small bag for a *groschen,* so that I can make the blessing over the first fruit of the season, and I eat them with bread. In Menashe's orchard there are two rows of currant bushes growing close to the ground, studded with currants. They glisten and twinkle in the sun and you long to pick one twig, or at least take one currant between your fingers and pop it into your mouth. Would you believe it, when I talk about green gooseberries and red currants my teeth are set on edge? Let's better talk about cherries.

Cherries don't stay green long. They ripen very quickly. I can swear to you by anything you wish that I myself saw, from Mendel the *Shochet's* roof, several cherries that were green as grass in the morning. I looked at them and marked in my mind the spot where they grew. During the day their cheeks reddened in the sun. That same evening they were as red as fire. My mother used to buy me cherries too. How many did she buy? Five cherries on a string. What can you do with five cherries? You fondle them and play with them until you don't know where they've disappeared to.

There are as many cherries in Menashe's orchard as there are stars in heaven. I once tried to count the cherries on one branch. I counted and counted and couldn't finish counting. Cherries cling very tightly to the branch. It's very seldom that a cherry will fall to the ground.

Before it falls it has to be over-ripe, and as black as a plum. But peaches are different. Peaches fall to the ground as soon as they turn yellow. Don't let me start talking about peaches. I love them more than any other fruit. In all my life I have eaten only one peach, and the taste still lingers in my mouth. That was several years ago, when I was not quite five years old and my father was still alive, and we still had the glass cabinet, the sofa, the books and all our beds. One day my father came home from the Synagogue and called me and my brother Elihu over to him. "Children," he said, "how would you like to taste a peach? I brought you two peaches, one peach for each of you."

He put his hand into his back pocket and brought out two large, round, yellow, fragrant pieces of fruit. My brother Elihu couldn't wait. He rushed through the words, "Blessed be the fruit of the earth . . ." and stuck the whole peach into his mouth at once. But I wasn't in such a hurry. I wanted to hold it in my hand awhile, to fondle it, smell it, play with it, and then when I was through playing, I began eating it, and that not in one gulp, but in little bites, a bite of peach and a bite of bread. Peaches taste very good with bread. Since that time I have never tasted another peach, but I have never forgotten the taste of that first one. Now a whole peach tree stands in front of me and I lie on Mendel's roof and watch the ripe peaches falling to the ground one by one. One ripe golden peach, streaked with pink, has split open and lies there with its fat kernel showing. What will Menashacha do with so many peaches? She will shake down the tree, gather them up, and make preserves. She will put the preserves on the back of the hearth and in winter she will take them down to the cellar. There they will stand until they become sugared over and are coated with mold.

After the peaches, the plums ripen. Not all the plums at once. I have two kinds of plum trees in Menashe's orchard. One tree bears plums called "chernitza." That's a hard, sweet, dark plum. The plums on the other tree are called "bucket plums" because they are sold by the bucket. They have thin skins and are slippery and sticky to the touch and they have a watery taste. Still, they are not as bad as you might think. I only wish I could have some of them. But Menashacha is not one of your generous givers. She would rather make plum jam for the winter. When in the world does she expect to eat up all this jam?

When I am through with the cherries, peaches and plums, then there begins for me a succession of apples. Apples, as you know, are not like pears. The best pears in the world, if they are not quite ripe, are absolutely no good. They are as dry as dust. Apples, though they are as green as grass and their seeds are still white, already taste like apples. You bury your teeth in a green apple and your whole mouth puckers up. And yet I wouldn't change half a green apple for two ripes ones. If you want your apples ripe you have to wait until late, late in the summer. But you can have green apples as soon as the tree has finished blooming. The difference is only in size. The longer an apple is left to ripen the larger it gets, just like a human being. But that doesn't mean that a large apple is the best. It often happens that a tiny apple tastes better than a big one. Take the little *Eretz-Isroel* apples for instance, they are tart but delicious. Or "kislitzas" or wine-saps. Is there anything wrong with them, I ask you?

This will be a great year for apples. There will be so many apples that they will be carted around in wagonloads. I heard Menashacha herself tell it to Rueben the Appleman when the trees were still in bloom. Rueben the Appleman came to see her orchard, he wanted to buy the apples and pears "on the tree." Rueben knows all about apples and pears. He can glance at a tree out of the corner of his eye and tell you at once how much money the tree will bring. He won't be off by so much—unless the winds are unusually strong and the apples fall before their time, or worms get them or else the blight. All these are things a person can't foresee. A wind is sent by God and so is a blight. Though I can't understand what God wants with worms and blights. Unless it's to take the bread away from Rueben the Appleman. Rueben says that all he wants from a tree is a piece of bread. He has a wife and children and he has to find bread for them. Menashacha promises him not only a piece of bread, but bread with meat. "Are they ordinary trees?" she asks. "They are gold mines, not trees.

"You know yourself," says Menashacha," that I don't wish you any ill luck. May all the good fortune I wish to you come to me also."

"Amen," says Rueben with a smile on his kindly, red face that's peeling from the sun. "If you will sign a contract against winds, worms, and blights, I will give you even more than you asked for."

Menashacha gives him a peculiar look and says in her gruff, man's voice, "How about signing a contract that you will walk out of here and won't slip and break a leg?"

"No one is assured against falling and breaking a leg," says Rueben, looking at her with his kindly, smiling eyes. "That can happen to a rich man even quicker than to a poor man, for a rich man can afford it better."

"You are very smart," says Menashacha angrily. "But a man who wishes that another break his leg deserves to have his tongue shrink up in his mouth."

"Why not?" says Reuben, still with the same gentle smile. "A shrunken tongue isn't so bad either, as long as it doesn't happen to a poor man."

It's a great pity that the orchard doesn't belong to Rueben the Appleman. It would be much pleasanter for me. You've never seen such a witch as Menashacha. Let one little, wormy, dried-up apple, as wrinkled and shrunken as an old woman's face, fall to the ground and she will bend down, pick it up, hide it in her apron and carry it off. Where does she carry it off to? Either up into her attic or down into the cellar. I've heard it told that last year a whole cellarful of apples rotted on her. Now tell me, doesn't she deserve to have her apples picked by others? But how can you get to them? To steal into the orchard at night when everyone is asleep and fill your pockets would be one way. But there is that wild dog guarding it. And to make things worse the trees are loaded with apples this year. They beg you, they plead with you, to pick them. What to do? If only there were some charm, some magic words by which I could make them come to me of their own will. I think and I think and at last think up something.

What I have thought up is neither charms nor magic words, but an ordinary stick, a long stick with a nail at the end of it. If you reach the tree with the stick and catch the stem of the apple with the nail, and pull it gently toward yourself, the apple is yours. You just have to know how to hold the stick so that the apple won't fall to the ground. And if an apple does fall it isn't such a loss either. She will think the wind tore it off. But you must be careful not to touch the apple itself with the nail or you will bruise it. I promise you that I have never bruised an apple yet. And my apples don't fall to the ground either. I know how to operate the stick. The important thing is not to be caught at it. Just don't hurry. Take your time about it. Have you got an apple in your hands? Eat it quietly, rest a little, then start picking again. I give you my word not a soul will know. . . .

How could I have guessed that the witch Menashacha would know the exact number of apples on her trees? She must have counted them one day and counted them again the next day and found that some were missing. Then she hid herself in her attic and began spying to see if she could catch the thief. That's how I figured it out. For how else could she have found out that I lay on Mendel's roof and plied my stick in her orchard? If she had only caught me herself, without any witnesses, I might have begged off. After all, I am an orphan. She might have had pity on me. But she thought of a better way. She went to my mother and to our neighbor Pessie and to Mendel's wife, and took all three women up into our attic with her. (Only a witch could do a thing like that.) Crouching in the attic they could look through the window and see me operating the stick. . . .

"Well, and what have you got to say for your precious son? Do you believe me now?"

I recognized Menashacha's gruff voice and turned my head and saw the four women watching me. I didn't throw my stick away. It fell out of my hands. It was lucky that I didn't fall off the roof too. I couldn't look them in the face. If the dog weren't down there in the orchard I would have leaped to my death for very shame. Worst of all were my mother's tears. She began weeping and wailing and wringing her hands. "Woe is me, woe is me. That I should live to see this day. Here I am thinking that my orphan is at the Synagogue saying *kaddish* for his father, and instead he is lying on a roof—may thunder and lightning strike me—and picking apples from a stranger's orchard."

And Menashacha added in her deep, gruff voice, "He should be beaten, he should be whipped, the young apostate. Whipped till the blood comes. A boy should be taught not to be a th—"

My mother wouldn't let her finish the word "thief." "He is an orphan," she pleaded. "The poor child is an orphan." And she began kissing the witch's hands and begging her to forgive me, promising that it would never happen again. She swore with sacred oaths that this was the last time, the very last time, may she die if it wasn't, or else live to bury me. . . .

"I want him to swear that he will never even look into my orchard," demanded Menashacha ruthlessly, without a trace of pity for a poor orphan.

"Let my hand dry up," I swore. "Let my eyes drop out, before I touch another apple." Then I went home with my mother and had to listen to her scolding and weeping, and I began weeping lustily myself.

"What will become of you?" my mother asked with tears in her eyes. She told the story to my brother Elihu, and when my brother heard of the incident of the apples he went pale with rage. My mother saw this and whispered something into his ears. She whispered to him not to thrash me, I was an orphan.

"Who wants to touch him?" said my brother Elihu. "I would like to know just one thing. What will become of him? *What will become of him?*"

My brother gnashed his teeth and looked at me as though asking me if I knew what would become of me. How should I know? Do you know what will become of me?

Chava

"*GIVE thanks unto the Lord, for He is good.*—Whatever He ordains, His way is the best." It has to be the best, for if you had the wisdom of a Solomon could you improve on it? Look at me—I wanted to be clever, I turned and twisted, this way and that, and tried everything I knew, and then when I saw it was no use, I took my hand off my chest, as the saying is, and said to myself, "Tevye, you're a fool, you won't change the world. The Lord has given us the '*pain of bringing up children*,' which means that in raising children you have to accept the bad with the good and count them as one."

Take, for instance, my oldest daughter, Tzeitl, who went and fell in love with the tailor Motel Kamzoil. Have I got anything against him? True, he is a simple, unlettered fellow, who can't read the learned footnotes at the bottom of the page, but is that anything against him? Everybody in the world can't be a scholar. At least he is an honest man and a hard-working one. She's already borne him a whole brood of young ones; they have a houseful of hungry mouths to feed, and both of them, he and she, are struggling along "*in honor and in riches*," as the saying is. And yet if you ask her, she will tell you that she is the happiest woman in the world, no one could be happier. There is only one tiny flaw—they don't have enough to eat. "*That's the end of the first round with the Torah.*—There's Number One for you."

About my second daughter, about Hodel, I don't have to tell you. You know about her already. With her I played and I lost. I lost her

481

forever. God knows if my eyes will ever behold her again, unless it should be in the next world. To this day I can't bring myself to talk about her calmly. I mention her name and the old pain returns. Forget her, you say? How can you forget a living human being? And especially a child like Hodel! If you could only see the letters she writes me. . . . They are doing very well, she tells me. He sits in prison and she works for a living. She washes clothes all day, reads books in between, and goes to see him once a week. She lives in the hope that very soon the pot will boil over, as they say, the sun will rise and everything become bright. He will be set free along with many others like him, and then, she says, they will all roll up their sleeves and get to work to turn the world upside down. Well, what do you think of that? Sounds promising, doesn't it?

But what does the Lord do next? He is, after all, *"a gracious and merciful Lord,"* and He says to me, "Wait, Tevye, I will bring something to pass that will make you forget all your former troubles."

And so it was. It's a story worth hearing. I would not repeat it to anyone else, for while the pain is great, the disgrace is even greater. But how is it written? *"Shall I conceal it from Abraham?*—Can I keep any secrets from you?" Whatever is on my mind I shall tell you. But one thing I want to ask of you. Let it remain between you and me. For I repeat: the pain is great, but the disgrace—the disgrace is even greater.

How is it written in *Perek?* *"The Holy One, blessed be He, wished to grant merit to Israel—"* The Lord wanted to be good to Tevye, so He blessed him with seven female children, that is, seven daughters, each one of them a beauty, all of them good-looking and charming, clever and healthy and sweet-tempered—like young pine trees! Alas, if only they had been ill-tempered and ugly as scarecrows, it might have been better for them, and certainly healthier for me. For what use is a fine horse, I ask you, if you have to keep it locked up in a stable? What good are beautiful daughters if you are stuck away with them in a forsaken corner of the world, where you never see a live person except for Anton Poperilo, the village mayor, or the clerk Fyedka Galagan, a young fellow with a long mane of hair and tall peasant boots, or the Russian priest, may his name be blotted out?

I can't bear to hear that priest's name mentioned, not because I am a Jew and he is a priest. On the contrary, we've been on friendly terms for a number of years. By that I don't mean that we visit at each other's homes or dance at the same weddings. I only mean that when we happen to meet we greet each other civilly. "Good morning." "Good day. What's new in the world?"

I've never liked to enter into a discussion with him, for right away the talk would turn to this business of *your God* and *my God.* Before he could get started I would recite a proverb or quote him a passage from the Bible. To which he replied that he could quote me a passage from the Bible also, and perhaps better than I, and he began to recite the Scriptures to me, mimicking the sacred language like a Gentile: *"Berezhit bara alokim*—In the beginning the Lord created the Heavens. . . ." Then I told him that we had a folk tale, or a *medresh* to the effect that. . . . "A *medresh*" he interrupted me, "is the same as *Tal-mud,"* and he didn't like *Talmud,* "for *Tal-mud* is nothing but sheer trickery." Then I would get good and angry and give him what he had coming. Do you think that bothered him? Not in the least. He would only look at me, and laugh, and comb his long beard with his fingers. There is nothing in the world, I tell you, so maddening as a person who doesn't answer when you abuse him. You shout and you scold, you are ready to burst a gut, and he stands there and smiles. . . . At that time I didn't understand what that smile of his meant, but now I know what was behind it. . . .

Well, to return to my story. I arrived at home one day—it was toward evening—and whom should I see but the clerk Fyedka standing outside with my Chava, that's my third daughter, the one next to Hodel. When he caught sight of me, the young fellow spun around quickly, tipped his hat to me, and was off. I asked Chava, "What was Fyedka doing here?"

"Nothing," she said.

"What do you mean nothing?"

"We were just talking."

"What business have you got talking with Fyedka?" I asked.

"We've known each other for a long time," she said.

"Congratulations!" I said. "A fine friend you've picked for yourself."

"Do you know him at all?" she asked. "Do you know who he is?"

"No," I said, "I don't know who he is. I've never seen his family tree. But I am sure he must be descended from a long and honorable line. His father," I said, "must have been either a shepherd or a janitor, or else just a plain drunkard."

To this Chava answered, "Who his father was I don't know and I don't care to know. All people are the same to me. But Fyedka himself is not an ordinary person, of that I am sure."

"Tell me," I said, "what kind of person is he? I'd like to hear."

"I would tell you," she said, "but you wouldn't understand. Fyedka is a second Gorky."

"A second Gorky? And who, may I ask, was the first Gorky?"

"Gorky," she said, "is one of the greatest men living in the world today."

"Where does he live," I asked, "this sage of yours, what is his occupation and what words of wisdom has he spoken?"

"Gorky," she said, "is a famous author. He is a writer, that is, a man who writes books. He is fine and honest and true, a person to be honored. He also comes from plain people, he was not educated anywhere, he is self-taught . . . here is his portrait." Saying this, she took a small photograph from her pocket and handed it to me.

"So this is he," I said, "this sage of yours, Reb Gorky? I can swear I have seen him somewhere before, either at the baggage depot, carrying sacks, or in the woods hauling logs."

"Is it a crime then if a man works with his hands? Don't you yourself work with your hands? Don't all of us work?"

"Yes, yes," I said, "you are right. We have a certain proverb which says, *'When thou eatest the labor of thine own hands—*If you do not work, you shall not eat.' But I still don't understand what Fyedka is doing here. I would be much happier if you were friends at a distance. You mustn't forget *'Whence thou camest and whither thou goest—* Who you are and who he is.'"

"God created all men equal," she said.

"Yes, yes," I said, "God created Adam in his own image. But we mustn't forget that each man must seek his own kind, as it is written: *'From each according to his means . . .'"

"Marvelous!" she cried. "Unbelievable! You have a quotation for everything. Maybe you also have a quotation that explains why men have divided themselves up into Jews and Gentiles, into lords and slaves, noblemen and beggars?"

"Now, now, my daughter, it seems to me you've strayed to the *'sixth millennium.'*" And I explained to her that this had been the way of the world since the first day of Creation.

"And why," she wanted to know, "should this be the way of the world?"

"Because that's the way God created the world."

"And why did God create the world this way?"

"If we started to ask why this, and wherefore that, *'there would be no end to it*—a tale without end.'"

"But that is why God gave us intellects," she said, "that we should ask questions."

"We have an old custom," I told her, "that when a hen begins to crow like a rooster, we take her away to be slaughtered. As we say in the morning blessing, *'Who gave the rooster the ability to discern between day and night. . . .'*"

"Maybe you've done enough jabbering out there," my wife Golde called out from inside the house. "The *borsht* has been standing on the table for an hour and he is still out there singing Sabbath hymns."

"Another province heard from! No wonder our sages have said, *'The fool hath seven qualities.*—A woman talks nine times as much as a man.' We are discussing important matters and she comes barging in with her cabbage *borsht*."

"My cabbage *borsht*," said Golde, "may be just as important as those 'important matters' of yours."

"*Mazl-tov!* We have a new philosopher here, straight from behind the oven. It isn't enough that Tevye's daughters have become enlightened, now his wife has to start flying through the chimney right up into the sky."

"Since you mention the sky," said Golde, "I might as well tell you that I hope you rot in the earth."

Tell me, Mr. Sholom Aleichem, what do you think of such crazy goings-on on an empty stomach?

Now let us, as they say in books, leave the prince and follow the fortunes of the princess. I am speaking of the priest, may his name and memory be blotted out. Once toward nightfall I was driving home with my empty milk cans—I was nearing the village—when whom should I see but the priest in his cast-iron *britzka* or carriage, approaching from the other direction. His honor was driving the horses himself, and his long flowing beard was whipped about by the wind.

"What a happy encounter!" I thought to myself. "May the bad luck fall on his head."

"Good evening," he said to me. "Didn't you recognize me, or what?"

"It's a sign that you will get rich soon," I said, lifted my cap and was about to drive on. But he wouldn't let me pass. "Wait a minute, Tevel, what's your hurry? I have a few words to say to you."

"Very well. If it's good news, then go ahead," I said. "But if not, leave it for some other time."

"What do you mean by some other time?" he asked.

"By some other time, I mean when the Messiah comes."

"The Messiah," said he, "has already come."

"That I have heard from you more than once," I said. "Tell me something new, little father."

"That's just what I want to tell you. I want to talk to you about yourself, that is, about your daughter."

At this my heart almost turned over. What concern could he have with my daughter? And I said to him, "My daughters are not the kind, God forbid, that need someone to do the talking for them. They can manage their own affairs."

"But this is the sort of thing she can't speak of herself. Someone else has to speak for her. It's a matter of utmost importance. Her fate is at stake."

"And who, may I ask, concerns himself with the fate of my child? It seems to me that I am still her father, am I not?"

"True," he said, "you are her father, but you are blind to her needs. Your child is reaching out for a different world, and you don't understand her, or else you don't wish to understand her."

"Whether I don't understand her, or don't wish to understand her, is besides the point. We can argue about that sometime if you like. But what has it got to do with you, little father?"

"It has quite a lot to do with me," he said, "for she is now under my protection."

"What do you mean she is under your 'protection'?"

"It means she is now in my care."

He looked me straight in the eye as he said this and stroked his long, flowing beard with his fingers.

"What!" I exclaimed. "My child is in your care? By what right?" I felt myself losing my temper.

He answered me very calmly, with a little smile, "Now don't start getting excited, Tevel. We can discuss this matter peaceably. You know that I am not, God forbid, your enemy, even though you are a Jew. As you know, I am very fond of the Jewish people, even though they are a stiff-necked race. And my heart aches for them because in their pride they refuse to admit that we mean everything for their own good."

"Don't speak to me of our own good, little father," I said, "for every word that comes from your lips is like a drop of poison to me— it's like a bullet fired straight at my heart. If you are really the friend you say you are, I ask only one thing of you—leave my daughter alone."

"You are a foolish person," he said to me. "No harm will come to your daughter. She is about to meet with a piece of great good luck. She is about to take a bridegroom—and such a bridegroom! I couldn't wish a better fate to one of my own."

"Amen," I said, forcing a laugh, though inside me burned all the fires of hell. "And who, may I ask, is this bridegroom, if I may have the honor of knowing?"

"You must be acquainted with him," he said. "He is a gallant young man, an honest fellow and quite well-educated, though he is self-taught. He is very much in love with your daughter and wants to marry her, but cannot, because he is not a Jew."

"Fyedka!" I thought to myself, and the blood rushed to my head, and a cold sweat broke out all over my body, so that I could barely sit upright in my cart. But show him how I felt? Never. Without replying I picked up the reins, whipped my horse, and *"departed like Moses."* I went off without as much as a fare-thee-well.

I arrived at home. What a scene greeted me! The children all lying with their faces buried in pillows, weeping; my Golde weaving around the house like a ghost. I looked for Chava. Where is Chava? She is nowhere to be found. I didn't ask where she was. I knew only too well. Then it was that I began to feel the tortures of a soul that is damned. I was full of rage and I didn't know against whom. I could have turned on myself with a whip. I began yelling at the children, I let out all my bitterness toward my wife. I couldn't rest in the house, so I went outside to the barn to feed my horse. I found him with one leg twisted around the block of wood. I took a stick and began laying it into him, as though I were going to strip off his skin and break his bones in half. "May you burn alive, you *shlimazl.* You can starve to death before I will give you as much as an oat. Tortures I will give you and anguish and all the ten plagues of Egypt. . . ."

But even as I shouted at him I knew that my horse did not deserve it; poor innocent creature, what did I have against him? I poured out some chopped straw for him, went back to the house and lay down. . . . My head was ready to split in two as I lay there thinking, figuring, arguing with myself back and forth. What could it all mean? What was the significance of all this? *"What was my sin and what my transgression?"* How did Tevye sin more than all the others that he should be punished thus above all the others? *"'Oh, Lord Almighty, what are we, and what is our life?'"* What sort of cursed creature am I that you should constantly bear me in mind, never let any plague that comes along, any blight or affliction pass me by?"

As I lay there torturing myself with such thoughts, I heard my wife groaning and moaning beside me. "Golde," I said, "are you sleeping?"

"No," she said. "What is it?"

"Nothing," I said. "Things are bad with us, very bad. Maybe you can think of what's to be done."

"You ask me what's to be done. Woe is me, how should I know?

A child gets up in the morning, sound and fresh, gets dressed, and falls on my neck, kissing and hugging me, and weeping all the time, and she won't tell me why. I thought that, God forbid, she had lost her mind. I asked her, 'What's the matter with you, daughter?' She didn't say a word, but ran out for a while to see to the cows, and disappeared. I waited an hour, two hours, three hours. Where is Chava? There is no Chava. Then I said to the children, 'Run over and take a look at the priest's house. . . .'"

"How did you know, Golde, that she was at the priest's house?"

"How did I know? Woe is me. Don't I have eyes in my head? Am I not her mother?"

"If you do have eyes in your head, and if you are her mother, why did you keep it all to yourself? Why didn't you tell me?"

"Tell you? When are you at home that I can tell you anything? And if I do tell you something, do you listen to me? If a person says anything to you, you answer him with a quotation. You drum my head full of quotations and you've done your duty by your children."

After she finished I could hear her weeping in the dark. "She is partly right," I thought to myself, "for what can a woman understand of such matters?" My heart ached for her, I could not bear to listen to her moaning and groaning. "Look here, Golde," I said, "you are angry because I have a quotation for everything. I have to answer you even that with a quotation. It is written: *'As a father has mercy on his children.'* This means that a father loves his child. Why isn't it written: *'As a mother has mercy on her children'?* For a mother is not the same as a father. A father can speak differently with his child. You will see—tomorrow I will go and speak to her."

"I hope you will get to see her, and him also. He is not a bad man, even if he is a priest. He has compassion in his heart. You will plead with him, get down on your knees to him, maybe he will have pity on us."

"Whom are you talking about?" I said. "That priest? You want me to bow down to the priest? Are you crazy or out of your head? *'Do not give Satan an opening,'* it is said. My enemies will never live to see that day."

"What did I tell you?" she said. "There you go again."

"Did you think," I said, "that I would let a woman tell me what to do? You want me to live by your womanish brains?"

In such talk the whole night passed. At last I heard the first cock crow. I got up, said my morning prayers, took my whip with me, and went straight to the priest's house. A woman is nothing but a woman. But where else could I have gone? Into the grave?

Well, I arrived in the priest's yard and his dogs gave me a royal welcome. They leaped at me and tried to tear off my coat and sink their teeth into my calves to see if they liked the taste of a Jew's flesh. It was lucky that I had taken my whip along. I gave them this quotation to chew on—*"Not a dog shall bark."* Or, as they say in Russian: *"Nehai sobaka daram nie breshe."* Which means, "Don't let a dog bark for nothing."

Aroused by the barking and the commotion in the yard the priest came running out of his house and his wife after him. With some effort they drove off the happy throng that surrounded me, and invited me to come in. They received me like an honored guest and got ready to put on the samovar for me. I told the priest it wasn't necessary to put on the samovar, I had something I wanted to say to him in private. He caught on to what I meant and motioned to his spouse to please be so kind as to shut the door on the outside.

When we were alone I came straight to the point without any preambles, and asked him first of all to tell me if he believed in God. Then I asked him to tell me if he knew what it felt like to be parted from a child he loved. And then I asked him to tell me what, according to his interpretation, was right and what was wrong. And one more thing I wanted him to make clear for me. What did he think of a man who sneaked into another man's house, and began tearing it apart, turning beds, tables, and chairs—everything, upside down.

Naturally he was dumbfounded by all this, and he said to me, "Tevel, you are a clever man, it seems to me, and yet you put so many questions to me and you expect me to answer them all at one blow. Be patient and I shall answer them one at a time, the first question first and the last question last."

"No, dear little father," I said. "You will never answer my questions. Do you know why? Because I know all your answers beforehand. Just tell me this: is there any hope of my getting my child back, or not?"

He leaped up at this. "What do you mean getting her back? No harm will come to your daughter—just the opposite."

"I know," I said. "I know. You want to bring her a piece of great good luck. I am not speaking of that. I only want to know where my child is, and if I can see her."

"Everything, yes," he said, "but that, no."

"That's the way to talk," I said. "Come to the point. No mincing of words. And now good-bye. May God repay you in equal measure for everything you have done."

I came home and found Golde lying in bed all knotted up like a black ball of yarn. She had no more tears left to weep. I said to her, "Get up, my wife, take off your shoes, and let us sit down and mourn our child as God has commanded. *'The Lord hath given and the Lord hath taken away.'* We are neither the first nor the last. Let us imagine that we never had a daughter named Chava, or that like Hodel she went off to the ends of the earth. God is All-Merciful and All-Good. He knows what He does."

As I said this I felt the tears choking me, standing like a bone in my throat. But Tevye is not a woman. Tevye can restrain himself. Of course, you understand, that's only a way of speaking. First of all, think of the disgrace! And second, how can I restrain myself when I've lost my child, and especially a child like Chava. A child so precious to us, so deeply embedded in our hearts, both in her mother's and mine. I don't know why she had always seemed dearer to us than any of the other children. Maybe because as a baby she had been so sickly, and we had gone through so much with her. We used to stay up whole nights nursing her, and many a time we snatched her, literally snatched her, from the jaws of death, breathed life into her as you would into a tiny crushed chick. For if God wills it, He makes the dead come to life again, as we say in Hallel: *"I shall not die, but I will live.*—If you are not fated to die, you will not die." And maybe we loved her so because she had always been such a good child, so thoughtful and devoted, both to her mother and me. Now I ask you, how could she have done this thing to us?

Here is the answer: first of all, it is fate. I don't know about you, but as for me, I believe in Providence. Second, it was witchcraft. You may laugh at me, and I want to tell you that I am not so misguided as to believe in spirits, elves, *domovois* and such nonsense. But I do believe in witchcraft, in the evil eye. For what else could it have been? Wait, listen to the rest of the story, and you will agree with me.

Well, when the Holy Books say, *"Perforce you must live.—*Man does not take his own life—" they know what they are talking about. There is no wound so deep that it does not heal in time, there is no sorrow so great that you do not forget it eventually. That is, you do not forget, but what can you do about it? *"Man is likened to a beast. —*Man must work, man must till the earth in the sweat of his brow." And so we all went to work. My wife and children got busy with the pitchers of milk, and I took to my horse and wagon and *"the world continued in its course—*the world does not stand still." I told everyone at home to consider Chava as dead. There was no more Chava. Her name had been blotted out. Then I gathered up some dairy stuff— cheese and butter and such, all fresh merchandise—and set off for Boiberik to visit my customers in their *datchas.*

I arrived in Boiberik and I was met with great rejoicing. "How are you, Reb Tevye?" "Why don't we see you any more?" "How should I be?" I told them. *" 'We renew our days as of old.—*I am the same *shlimazl* as always.' One of my cows just dropped dead." They appeared surprised. "Why do so many miracles happen to you, Reb Tevye?" And they began questioning me, wanting to know what kind of cow it was that had dropped dead, how much she had cost, and if I had many cows left. They laughed and joked and made merry over me as rich people will make merry over a poor man and his troubles, when they have just eaten their fill and are in a good mood, and the weather is perfect, sunny and warm and balmy, just the weather to drowse in. But Tevye is the sort of person who can take a joke even at his own expense. I would sooner die on the spot than let them know how I felt.

When I got through with my customers, I set out for home with my empty milk cans. As I rode through the woods I slackened the horse's reins, let him nibble at will, and crop a blade of grass now and then. I let my thoughts roam at will also. I thought about life and death, this world and the next, what the world is altogether about, what man has been created for, and other such things. Anything to drive my gloom away, to keep from thinking about Chava. But just as if to spite me she kept creeping in among my thoughts.

First she appeared before me in her own image, tall, lovely, blooming, like a young tree. Then I saw her as a little baby, sick and ailing, a frail little nestling, snuggled in my arms, her head drooping over my shoulder. "What do you want, Chaveleh? Something to suck on? A piece of candy?" And for the moment I forgot what she had done to me and my heart went out to her in longing. Then I remembered and a great anger seized me. I burned with anger against her and against him and against the whole world, but mostly against myself because I wasn't able to forget her, even for a minute. Why couldn't I forget her, why couldn't I tear her out of my heart completely? Didn't she deserve to be forgotten?

For this, I thought, Tevye had to be a Jew among Jews, to suffer all his life long, to keep his nose to the grindstone, bring children into the world—in order to have them torn from him by force, to have them fall like acorns from a tree and be carried away by wind and by smoke. I thought to myself, "It's like this: a tree grows in the forest, a mighty oak with outspread branches, and an ignorant lout comes along with an axe and chops off a branch, then another and another. What is a tree without branches, alas? Go ahead, lout, chop down the whole tree and let there be an end. . . . What good is a naked oak in the forest?"

In the midst of these thoughts I suddenly became aware that my horse had stopped. What's the matter? I lift up my eyes and look. It is she, Chava. The same as before, not changed at all, she is even wearing the same dress. My first impulse was to jump off the wagon

and take her in my arms. But something held me back. "What are
you, Tevye? A woman? A weakling?" I pulled in my horse's reins.
"Giddap, *shlimazl*." I tried to go to the right. I look—she is also going
to the right. She beckons to me with her hand as though to say,
"Stop a while, I have something to tell you."

Something tears at my insides, something tugs at my heart. I feel
myself going weak all over. Any moment I will jump off the wagon.
But I restrain myself, pull the horse's reins in and turn left. She also
turns left. She is looking at me wildly, her face is deathly pale. What
shall I do? Should I stop or go on? And before I know what's happened, she's got the horse by the bridle and is saying to me, "Father,
I will sooner die on the spot before I let you move another step.
I beg you, father, listen to me."

"So," I think to myself, "you want to take me by force. No, my
dear, if that's what you are trying to do, I see that you don't know
your father very well." And I begin whipping my horse with all my
might. The horse obeys me, he leaps forward. But he keeps moving
his ears and turning his head back. "Giddap," I tell him. "*'Judge
not the vessel but its contents.—*Don't look where you aren't supposed to.'" But do you think that I myself wouldn't like to turn my
head and look back at the place where I left her standing? But Tevye
is not a woman. Tevye knows how to deal with Satan the Tempter.

Well, I don't want to drag my story out any longer. Your time is
valuable. If I have been fated to suffer the punishments of the damned
after death, I surely have expiated all my sins already. If you want to
know about the tortures of hell that are described in our Holy Books,
ask me. I can describe them all to you. All the rest of the way, as I
drove, I thought I could hear her running after me, calling, "Listen,
father, listen to me." A thought crossed my mind, "Tevye, you are
taking too much upon yourself. Will it hurt you if you stop and
listen to her? Maybe she has something to say that is worth hearing.
Maybe—who can tell—she is regretting what she has done and wants
to come back to you. Maybe she is being badly treated and wants you
to save her from a living hell." Maybe and maybe and maybe . . .
And I saw her as a little child once more and I was reminded of the
passage: *"As a father has mercy on his children . . ."* To a father

there is no such thing as a bad child. I blamed myself and I told myself, *"I do not deserve to be pitied*—I am not worthy of the earth I walk upon.

"What are you fuming and fretting for?" I asked myself. "Stubborn mule, turn your wagon around and go back and talk to her, she is your own child." And peculiar thoughts came into my mind. What is the meaning of Jew and non-Jew? Why did God create Jews and non-Jews? And since God did create Jews and non-Jews why should they be segregated from each other and hate each other, as though one were created by God and the other were not? I regretted that I wasn't as learned as some men so that I could arrive at an answer to this riddle. . . .

And in order to chase away these painful thoughts I began to chant the words of the evening prayer: *"Blessed are they who dwell in Thy house, and they shall continue to praise Thee. . . ."* But what good was this chanting when inside of me a different tune was playing? *Chava,* it went. *Cha-va.* The louder I recited the prayer, the plainer the word *Cha-va* sounded in my own ears. The harder I tried to forget her, the more vividly she appeared before me, and it seemed to me that I heard her voice calling, "Listen, father, listen to me." I covered my ears to keep from hearing her voice and I shut my eyes to keep from seeing her face, and I started saying *Shmin-esra,* and didn't know what I was saying. I beat my breast and cried out loud, *"For we have sinned,"* and I didn't know for what I was beating my breast.

I didn't know what I was saying or doing. My whole life was in a turmoil, and I myself was confused and unhappy. I didn't tell anyone of my meeting with Chava. I didn't speak about her to anyone and didn't ask anyone about her, though I knew quite well where they lived and what they were doing. But no one could tell from my actions. My enemies will never live to see the day when I complain to anyone. That's the kind of man Tevye is.

I wonder if all men are like me, or if I am the only crazy one. For instance, let us imagine—just suppose it should happen—if I tell you this, you won't laugh at me? I am afraid that you will laugh. But just let us suppose that one fine day I should put on my Sabbath gabardine and stroll over to the railway station as though I were

going away on the train, going to see them. I walk up to the ticket
window and ask for a ticket. The ticket seller asks me where I want
to go. "To Yehupetz," I tell him. And he says, "There is no such
place." And I say, "Well, it's not my fault then." And I turn myself
around and go home again, take off my Sabbath clothes and go back
to work, back to my cows and my horse and wagon. As it is written:
"*Each man to his labor*—The tailor must stick to his shears and the
shoemaker to his last."

I see that you are laughing at me. What did I tell you? I know
what you're thinking. You're thinking that Tevye is a big imbecile.
. . . That's why I say: "*Read to this part on the great Sabbath before
Passover,*" meaning, it's enough for one day. Be well and happy and
write me often. And don't forget what I asked you. Be silent as the
grave concerning this. Don't put what I told you into a book. And if
you should write, write about someone else, not about me. Forget
about me. As it is written: "*And he was forgotten—*" No more Tevye
the Dairyman!

The Joys of Parenthood

A RICH MAN, I am not. Far from it. But I am not complaining. I have a place of my own to live in. Though what do I get out of that? A headache. But there is one thing I can really boast of—more than the richest man in Kasrilevka—and that is my children. For instance, at the holidays, when all my children come together—my sons and daughters, daughters-in-law, and all the grandchildren—who can be compared to me?

For example, consider the *Purim sudah*. What satisfaction is there in a *sudah*, I ask you, if you sit down all alone with your wife and you eat? Well, picture it to yourself. So I've had my fish already, and noodle soup, *tzimmes,* this, that and the other. What satisfaction is there in that? None whatever. A horse can eat too. But a human being is not a horse. Especially a Jew. And on a holiday. And particularly a holiday like *Purim,* when there are so many good traditional dishes to feast on!

First of all—my children, long may they live. . . .

There are eight of them, may God protect them. All married. (There were twelve altogether, but four passed away.) Half are sons and half are daughters; four sons-in-law and four daughters-in-law. That makes a total of sixteen.

And then the grandchildren, Lord bless them!

I don't want to boast, but all my daughters and daughters-in-law are fruitful, they all bear children every year. One has eleven, one nine, another seven. Barren ones, that is, with no children at all, not

497

one! Though with one son, the middle one, I had some difficulty. For a long time my daughter-in-law had no children at all. We wait and wait—not a sign of one. We tried everything. We went to doctors, rabbis. . . . We even tried a gypsy. Nothing helped.

Finally there was only one thing left to do. He had to divorce her. Well and good, he'll divorce her. But when it came down to getting the divorce . . . Who . . . What . . . She didn't want it.

"What do you mean, she doesn't want it?" I ask my son. And he tells me, "She loves me." "Fool!" I say. "Are you going to listen to that?" And he says, "But I love her too." Now what do you think of that smart boy? I tell him *children,* and he answers me *love.* What do you think of such an idiot?

To make a long story short, they didn't get divorced. But God had mercy on them; it's six years now since she started having them—a child every year. She showers me with grandchildren.

And you ought to see my grandchildren, all of them gifted and handsome, one better looking than the other. A joy to behold. I tell you—jewels!

And they're such good students, too. If you ask for a page of *Gamorah* they give you a page of *Gamorah* by heart. As for the Bible and all the commentaries, grammar, and all the modern nonsense they teach now, there's no use talking. They read and they write Yiddish, Russian, German, French, and anything you can think of. When I have a letter to be read or an address to be written, or anything else, a war starts: "Grandpa, I'll do it! Grandpa, let me."

What did you say? How do we all live? Never mind. God is all-powerful. He provides. Sometimes this way, sometimes that, sometimes better, sometimes worse. Naturally more often worse than better. We struggle along. We get through the year. We live. That's the important thing.

My oldest son was getting along pretty well for a long time. He lived in a village, in Zolodoievka, and made a pretty good living. But when the decrees of the Third of May were announced, he was politely asked to move on. Naturally he did everything he could to prove that he was not a newcomer, produced papers to show that he had lived there since the world was created, even appealed to the courts. Well, the Lord himself couldn't help him. He was driven out, and he hasn't recovered from it yet. So he lives with me, he and his wife and children. What else could we do?

My second son, poor fellow, just can't get along. No matter what he tries, he fails to make good. Everything falls, as they say, buttered side down. If he buys grain, the price drops; if he buys oxen, they die. If he tries wood, there is a warm winter. That's his luck. If he looked at the river, all the fish would die. So I thought it over and I said to him, "Do you know what? Pack up your things and move over with us."

My third son was getting along very well. But in the Great Fire, his house had to go and burn down, and he was left as naked as the day he was born. Besides that he had other troubles: a lawsuit, trouble with the record of his military service, various other things. Now he is living with me together with his whole family. Naturally!

But my youngest son is really doing well. What do I mean by that? He has nothing himself, but he has a rich father-in-law. That is, not really rich, but he makes a good living. A businessman, a conniver, a manipulator, may the Lord forgive him. He manipulates so long that he gets both himself and the other party all tangled up. But somehow he always squeezes out himself, the scoundrel. More than once he has gone through not only his own money but his children's as well. I tell him, "Why did you have to fool around with my son's money?" And he says, "Was any of it yours?" So I say, "My son is still my child." Says he, "And my daughter isn't mine?" "Huh," I say. "Bah" he says. "But after all," I say. "What do you want?" says he. And so one word leads to another. I called my boy aside and I said to him, "Go, spit on that father-in-law of yours, that conniver. Come, live with me. Whatever the Lord gives us, at least we'll be together."

But when it comes to sons-in-law, I have no luck at all. None whatever. That is, I have nothing against them either. I am not ashamed of them. For, believe me, I have such sons-in-law that the wealthiest man could envy me. Fine boys, from good families, handsome, brilliant, every one of them.

I have one son-in-law who comes from a very superior family. He is really something to brag about—a young man of refinement, talent, education, a great scholar. Day in and day out he sits and studies. I have been keeping him with us ever since the wedding, for if you knew him you would admit that it would be a sin to let him out into the world. What would ever become of him?

The next one is of not quite such a good family, but he's just as intelligent as the first. Whatever you think of, he can do. He can write, read, figure, sing, dance—everything. And what a chess player he is! And yet he is not a success. What does King Solomon say? "For the wise man there is often no bread." I have started him in every kind of business. He had a concession, he ran a store, he was a teacher, a matchmaker—he just couldn't make good. Now he and his family live with me. I can't throw my daughter out into the street, can I?

Then there is another son-in-law who is not a scholar like the others, but who still is not just a nobody. He has a good head, a fine handwriting, knows the *Gamorah,* can quote you Scriptures. It's a pleasure to listen to him.

He has only one drawback. He is too delicate, too spiritual—that is, he's none too healthy. He doesn't look so bad, but he sweats a great deal and he has a cough. He's had this cough, together with a wheeze, for quite a while now, and he has a hard time breathing. The doctors tell him to drink milk and to go to Boiberik for the summer. That's where all the sick people go. The pine trees, they say, are good for a cough. So I am planning to take him with me to Boiberik next summer, if God grants us life. In the meantime, until he gets well some day, he and his wife and children are naturally saddled on my shoulders. What choice do I have?

I have one more son-in-law. This one is very plain, but a hard-working fellow. Not, God forbid, an ordinary workingman, a tailor or a cobbler, but not a student either.

He is a fish peddler. He deals in fish. His father sells fish and his grandfather before him sold fish too. The whole family knows nothing but fish and fish and more fish. They're honest people, you understand, respectable people, but very common, ordinary people.

Maybe you will ask, how do I happen to have such a son-in-law? There must be a reason. What do they say? "In a river there are all kinds of carp." It must have been my daughter's luck to get a man like that.

Not that I have anything against him. My daughter is very happy with him, for he is a good man, a devoted husband, as kind to all of us as he can be. Whatever he earns he hands over to her and he helps my other sons-in-law and my sons also, as much as possible. I can even say that almost all the work he does is for us. He has great respect for us too. He understands well enough who he is and who we are. He is what he is and after all we are something else. You can't dismiss *that* with a shrug.

For whenever the rest of us get together with other people and my sons and other sons-in-law begin to talk over things—a sacred law or regulation passages from the *Talmud* or a passage in the *Gamorah,* he has to sit by himself, poor fellow, without opening his mouth. To him these things are all a deep mystery.

It's only right that he should be proud to have such brothers-in-law and he should be glad to labor in their behalf. Don't you agree?

And now that you know my family a little better, you can understand my pride in them and my enjoyment of their company, especially when the holidays come around. For instance, the *Purim sudah,* when all my children and grandchildren gather about the table and we make a blessing over the big shiny *Purim* loaf covered with saffron and studded with raisins, and my wife serves the good strong spicy fish with horseradish and the rich soup with the long yellow noodles in it. And we take a drop of something, if the Lord permits—a glass of port or cherry wine, if we have it, and if we don't, a sip of ordinary brandy is welcome too. And we sing in a chorus. I begin the song and the children come in on the refrain and the little ones, the grandchildren, pipe the second refrain in their high shrill voices. And then we get up and join in a dance. Who is equal to me then? What is Rothschild to me then? What is any other millionaire to me? I am a King. Look at me, a King—that's what I am.

A rich man, you understand, I am not. But one thing I can really boast of—my children! In that respect I am wealthier than the wealthiest man in Kasrilevka.

The Littlest of Kings

A LUCKY CHILD, ISAAC. The whole world loves him. He is everyone's darling; everyone fondles him, kisses him, showers him with endearments. If he were an only child, say the neighbors, his parents couldn't dote on him the way his two sisters, Sarah and Rebecca, dote on the boy. From morning till night it's Isaac and Isaac and Isaac. "Isaac, eat." "Isaac, drink." "Go to sleep, Isaac." "Isaac, here is some candy for you." "Isaac, we are making a new pair of pants for you for the holidays." "Isaac, we are going to send you to the baths before Passover." "Isaac, you will conduct the Passover ceremony this year." Isaac. Isaac. Isaac. A person gets sick and tired hearing that name from morning till night. "They have taken a child," say the neighbors, "a wonder child, a beautiful boy like Isaac, and between them they are spoiling him to death."

And yet these same neighbors who do the complaining are always calling Isaac over, slipping him a piece of candy, a slice of *shtrudel,* a baked chicken liver, a spoonful of jam. . . .

And they all do it because of pity. The whole world pities him, everyone feels sorry for the boy. For Isaac, the wonder child, the beautiful boy, is an orphan.

There was once a man named Raphael. He had been a poor man all his life and on top of that he was an asthmatic. Every time he drew a breath or let it out you heard strange music coming from his breast, as though a bow that hadn't been rubbed with rosin were drawn across some violin strings. And he was a most upright and honest man, but may God forgive me for saying this, also a very impractical man, in fact he was pretty much of a *shlimazl*. It was said about him in Kasrilevka that if he hadn't been so impractical, that is if he hadn't been such a *shlimazl*, he might have become a wealthy man.

And Raphael was in such sorry circumstances because all his life he had worked for Reb Simche Weiner as overseer in his wine distillery, and aside from his wages he could honestly say that he had never received a *groschen* from anyone. . . .

Reb Simche Weiner knew that he could depend on his overseer to the utmost. In return he treated him well, paid him regularly his six *rubles* a week, gave him an extra ten *rubles* before a holiday, wine for Passover and a bottle of Passover brandy besides. Why shouldn't he? Reb Simche was the sort of man who knew the value of an honest employee.

It is true that Raphael got rheumatism working in the damp wine cellar and later a heavy cold settled in his lungs and he began to cough and to wheeze. But who was to blame for that? Health—that is something that comes from God. The healthiest man can drop dead walking in the street. Our wise men have long ago said concerning this . . . but then you probably know what our wise men have said.

Well, our Raphael coughed and wheezed and sang like an untuned violin so long until one day—it was between the first and last days of Passover—he took to his bed, began to run a high fever, and never got up again.

Raphael died—and what a splendid funeral he had. Reb Simche outdid himself. He carried the body out of the house himself, put his own shoulder to the coffin, followed the hearse to the cemetery on his own two feet, saw to it personally that Raphael got a choice spot for his burial, himself supervised the digging of the grave, threw in the first shovelful of dirt with his own hands, and when he heard the

boy Isaac repeat the first *kaddish* after the *shammes,* how Reb Simche wept!

"If only you knew . . . If you only knew," he told everyone he met
separately, "what a loss this is to me. What a terrible loss!"

And to the widow he said, "Don't weep. You know that I won't
forsake you and the orphans. Put your trust in God first, and then
in me."

And Reb Simche kept his word as well as he was able. That is, for
the first few weeks he paid the widow the same sum that Raphael used
to receive from him. It is true she had to go after the money every
week, and not once but several times, and she did not enjoy doing
this. But I ask you, what did you expect? That he send the money
to her house? It was enough that he should keep on paying a man's
wages after the man was dead.

"You come to me for money," he said to her one day, "just as though
I owed it to you, as though you had a share in my winery."

That day the widow wept more than she had wept when Raphael
lay dead, and when her two daughters, Sarah and Rebecca, found out
why their mother was weeping they made her swear that she would
never go to him for money again.

"But what shall we do?" she asked.

"We'll do what others have done. We'll go into service, we'll wash
clothes, we'll sew on a machine."

Sewing on machines had become quite an occupaion in Kasrilevka.
You could earn as much as two *guldens* a day if you were willing to sit
over a machine sixteen or seventeen hours a day. As for getting enough
work, that was no problem. You got work. If you didn't get dresses,
you got underwear; if you didn't get underwear, you got shirts; if not
shirts then handkerchiefs to hem. The trouble was that they needed
a machine, or, worse yet, two machines.

You could get a machine and pay for it in installments. But where
to get enough money for the down payment?

"Go over to your *nogid,* your rich benefactor," the neighbor women
advised the widow. "Tell him that you need money for a machine,
that the girls will work and pay him back."

"Go to the *nogid.*" That was easier said than done. But what won't one do to earn a living? The widow went over to Reb Simche Weiner and found him in his most relaxed state, right after he had eaten. If you want to ask someone for a favor always lie in wait for him until he has eaten. After a meal the meanest man is more tender-hearted than before a meal. Before he has eaten, man is—a beast!

"And what good news do you bring today?" asked Reb Simche.

The widow made her request. She told him the whole story; in a word, she needed machines.

Reb Simche listened to her attentively the whole time. He picked his teeth, got red in the face, sweated a little, dozed a little. He didn't fall asleep—God forbid, no—he only dozed, looking at her with one eye shut, thinking meanwhile partly about business, and partly about his digestion. Reb Simche was somewhat lazy, somewhat too plump, and the doctors had told him to eat more meat and less starchy foods. But starchy foods were just what Reb Simche liked best—things such as bread, noodles, puddings, anything made of flour. He knew that they were bad for him, but he couldn't keep from eating when they were in front of him, and after he had eaten he had reason to be sorry.

"Well, and how are you getting along?" he said when the widow became silent. He looked at her now with one eye open and the other only half shut.

"How should I be getting along?" she said. "I've just told you how I am getting along. May my enemies get along as well. But if I had the money for a machine, better yet for two machines, or even for one machine . . ."

"What machines?" he asked, looking at her in astonishment, with both eyes open.

"I've just told you that my daughters want to take in sewing. They want to become seamstresses, to sew on machines. But we have no machines. They need two machines and they can get them on credit, they can pay for them in installments. . . ."

"That's a fine idea. A very proper thing . . . seamstresses. They will sew, they will earn money. Fine. Very good."

But while he was speaking to her he thought to himself, "Why does my stomach feel so loaded? It seems to me I didn't eat so much today." And one eye began to grow smaller. But because the widow became silent again he woke up and began talking to her.

"Well, well. That's fine. Sewing. *So be it*. Why not?"

"I wanted to ask you, Reb Simche, since you've already done so much for us, perhaps it might be possible that you . . ."

It suddenly dawned on Reb Simche that she was making a request of him, that this smelled of a loan, that she wanted money, and he at once became wide awake.

"What?" he said.

"That you lend us money for the first payment on the machines."

"Which machines?"

"Those I told you about. The two machines for my daughters. Or at least one machine."

"Where will I get machines? What kind of dealings do I have with machines?"

"Money," said the widow, "is what we need. They can get the machines themselves—on credit. For instance if I pay fifty *rubles* now and three months later I pay twenty-five *rubles,* and a little later . . ."

"I know, I know, you don't have to explain it to me. I am satisfied that they get along without machines. Machines all of a sudden!"

"How else can they sew? You can't get much sewing done by hand. All seamstresses have machines nowadays."

"So you want to make seamstresses out of your daughters? You've come to this! If your husband were to rise from the dead and hear that you were going to make seamstresses out of your daughters he would lie down and die all over again. Let me tell you, your Raphael was an honest, God-fearing man. There aren't many like him. He would never have stood for this seamstress business. He would have— God alone knows what he would have done."

Reb Simche spoke with feeling. He meant every word he said. And the more he talked the louder his voice grew.

"Seamstresses! Hah! A fine calling for Jewish girls. We know what it means to be a seamstress nowadays. Raphael's daughters, seamstresses. And what about me? Where am I? Do you know that I practically raised Raphael!? I made him the man he was, first God, then I. And who married him off, if not I? And you expect me to permit such a thing. Never in this world. What am I? A stone? A bone? A block of wood?"

The widow left Reb Simche's house exactly as she had come, empty-handed.

She went home and made a vow with herself—she swore by everything holy that she would sooner not live to bring up her children than put a foot into Reb Simche's house again. She would go into service instead.

It is easy to say "go into service." But how could Raphael the Overseer's wife, a housewife like the other Kasrilevka housewives, become a servant? How could she stand at a stranger's oven, sit at a stranger's table? Rather than live like this it was better to die. And the widow wished for death to come.

And this time God, the great merciful God, father of orphans and protector of widows, took pity on the poor woman and did not allow her to linger long on this earth. He sent her an easy death, some sort of swelling inside. She suffered for three and a half months and then she died. And it so happened that aside from little children, no one had died in Kasrilevka during that time, so that the widow was buried next to her husband; their graves were almost side by side. Such a piece of luck must have been ordained from above.

From that time on, Isaac began to say *kaddish* for both his parents, his mother as well as his father. And he became the darling of all the neighbors and all the people who saw him standing on a bench in the Synagogue reciting in his high childish voice the words, "*Yisgadal v'yiskadash . . .*" Everyone who saw the small boy with his big brown eyes, his red cheeks, and the round cap on his head, standing on a bench in the Synagogue chanting the *kaddish,* was dazzled by the sight, and stood bemused, sighing deeply and thinking sad, sad thoughts. For every man may die and every man has young children who, God forbid, may become fatherless orphans. And this one gave the little orphan a *kopek,* that one slipped him an apple, partly out of pity, partly because "charity delivereth from death."

The truth was that Isaac was an unusual child, a child with a face one couldn't help loving. And he had a good head besides. He was the brightest boy in the Kasrilevka *Talmud Torah*. Reb Noah the *melamed* didn't have enough words to laud him. The whole town rang with his praises.

"Raphael's boy is very bright, they say."

"Isaac? They say he is going to be a great scholar some day."

"And where do you find such a treasure? Among the rich? Of course not. You find it among paupers on an ash heap."

"It's always this way. Who goes on living? Old Moishe Aaron, a cripple without hands or feet. And who has to die? Reb Simche's son-in-law, a young, healthy man, the head of a family, a man with money. He has to die."

"You talk about Reb Simche's son-in-law? What about Peisie the *Nogid's* daughter-in-law?"

"How is she getting along?"

"Getting along? They've had a specialist from Yehupetz for her, three times already."

"So? I wish I had at least half of what it will cost them."

"This is certainly a strange world!"

"A world with little worlds revolving around it."

This is how they talk in Kasrilevka, ceaselessly criticizing the works of the Almighty. They don't like the way He prolongs the life of some and cuts it short for others. They don't approve of the way He gives wealth to one, and nothing but bad luck to another. They can't understand why He blesses the poor with gifted children and punishes the wealthy with who-knows-what. No one ever stops to consider: How do these gifted children live? What do they eat? Who clothes them? Do they freeze during the long winter nights in their damp cellars? Will they not grow up crippled, hunchback, paupers from birth, unhappy and unwanted, a burden to humanity and themselves?

Luckily the two sisters, Sarah and Rebecca, scraped up enough for a sewing machine. They had to thank their neighbors for this, the three women who lived in the same house with them—Basha the Healer, Pessie the *Shammes'* Assistant, and Sossie the Second-hand Dealer. The three women each put in some money and raised enough

for the first payment on the machine. The girls would pay the rest
out of their work. What is so strange about that? A person has to
live. And what else can two grown girls, with a small boy on their
hands, do? They say even a snake looks out for its young. Can a
human being do less?

The only drawback is that the machine makes such an infernal
racket day and night. For there is plenty of work, God be thanked,
and both sisters use the machine, which never stands idle. They take
turns running it, "changing hands," so that while Sarah is sewing,
Rebecca is making the fire in the oven or sweeping the floor. Or,
while Sarah is cooking dinner, Rebecca is sewing on the machine.
The machine never stops clattering and the neighbors grab their
heads with both hands, stop up their ears, and mutter softly to themselves, "Rattle, rattle. There is a rattle for you."

But God is merciful. He sends a remedy for every disease. In this
case the remedy was Isaac. There are times in every home when
everything goes wrong, everyone's spirits are low, and life becomes
dreary. Then a little creature is born and everything changes. At first
the little one whines and screams, yells with colic, doesn't let anyone
sleep nights. But soon *it* grows a little older, stops crying at night,
opens its eyes and looks about. "See, he is looking around. He sees
us." Then the creature opens its mouth, sticks out its tiny tongue and
laughs, and everyone's heart grows lighter. "Look, the child is
laughing." The gloom is dissolved, bad times are forgotten. A new
soul has entered the house.

And that was how it was with our Isaac. He was the darling of
the house. He was the creature that brought laughter and cheer with
him. When Passover came they dressed him up like a king in a little
coat and trousers with suspenders. His sisters had a pair of boots made
for him and bought him a new cap. They promised to give him nuts
to play with, and the neighboring women made him pans full of
pancakes out of *matzo* meal. They stuffed him with pancakes and
chicken fat until he got sick and almost died of overeating.

"Who asked you to feed him all this stuff?" the two sisters scolded
the neighbors.

"Just listen to them. We give the child a pancake or two and they pounce on us like this."

Bashe the Healer used all the knowledge at her command and saved the boy's life. The day before Passover they gave Isaac a clean shirt and three *groschen* and sent him to the baths. When he came home they put his new clothes on him and he was a joy to behold.

"A royal child. A young prince," they nodded to each other.

"May no evil eye fall on him."

And Isaac took his small prayer book and went to the Synagogue. He said his *kaddish* and came home and greeted everyone with a cheery good *yom-tev*. The table was laid out for the *seder*, with *matzos*, a bottle of raisin wine, and bitter herbs and *charoses*, potatoes, and salt water. Everything was there except for one thing. There was no one to conduct the service. There was no king!

The three women were all widows; that is, two were widows and the third was divorced. They had no children; that is, they had children, but not at home. Their children were scattered far and wide over the whole world. This one was a workingman, that one had a store, others had emigrated to far-off America. Their various fortunes or perhaps misfortunes had drawn the three women together into one house, a house which belonged to Basha the Healer who was the wealthiest of the three.

The three lived under one roof, cooked at one oven, and set the dough for bread in one trough, but each kept her own table. For it is difficult for three women to live peacefully together at all times.

Out of the three hundred and sixty-five days in the year, the three women quarreled on about three hundred of them. But it depends on what you mean by quarreling. They never took anything from each other, they did not insult one another, never hurt one another's feelings. It was just that three different personalities had to disagree sometimes.

For instance Pessie the *Shammes'* Assistant liked to bank the fire in the stove and cover it with an oven lid. What harm was there in that? But Sossie the Second-hand Dealer had a habit of putting a pot of chicory on the hearth every morning. That wasn't so terrible either. She would never shove her pot of chicory in among the pots in which meat was cooking. But Pessie the *Shammes'* Assistant said it wasn't right that the bread in the oven should be ruined because of a mere pot of chicory. Sossie retorted to this, "May my enemies be ruined like this."

Said Pessie, "You must have quite a few enemies."

"I have enough, God be thanked," countered Sossie. "May they be planted in great numbers and fail to come up."

"Since when have you become such a shrew?" asked Pessie.

"Since I've come to live in this God-forsaken place."

At this Bashe the Healer, the owner of the house, who had been standing near by, rolling pin in hand, rolling out dough for noodles, spoke up.

"So it's a God-forsaken place to you? What makes it so? The high rent you are paying?"

Said Sossie the Second-hand Dealer, "You are the lucky one, you are so rich."

"What difference does it make how rich I am? Did I take it away from you?"

And Sossie replied, "What could you take from me? My bad luck? Go ahead, take it."

Said Bashe, "Keep it for yourself."

Pessie spoke up, "No one is guaranteed against bad luck. I've seen some people with homes of their own who have enough bad luck."

"Enough and to burn," added Sossie.

Bashe got angry and leaped at Sossie. Pessie the *Shammes'* Assistant took up for her. A hubbub arose among the three women; they began screaming and shouting all together: "Look at the defender she has." "How do you like the nerve of the woman?" "If you don't like it you don't have to marry me." "You are looking for scissors and the top of the mortar shows up." "Tavern talk!" "The rich lady—ruling over pokers and shovels." "Be still, loud-mouth, or I will throw a poker at you." "You'll get it first." "Here, take it then." "You take it." "Both of you take this."

Do you think it was blows they gave each other? God forbid. They shouted, gestured and threatened, thumbed noses at each other, and that was the end of it.

In spite of all the controversies and conflicts that took place among them, the three women harbored no enmity toward each other. For actually what did they have against each other? Had any of them taken away the other's livelihood? One moment they quarreled, the next they made up. And invariably when Passover came they declared peace by common consent, and all three became one in spirit, for all three baked their *matzos* on the same day, put up their beet juice in the same crock, dickered for and bought the same bargain, a sack of potatoes, and then sat down together at the same table to celebrate the Passover. They all sat at the table of the landlady, Bashe the Healer, ate together with her, followed the *Hagadah* softly after her word for word as she read it in Yiddish translation from a thick prayer book.

Some time ago, when Bashe the Healer's husband, Israel the Healer, had been alive, he had conducted the Passover service. After Israel's death the son of one of the other women officiated. Now that they were all scattered and gone to the four corners of the world and the only male person who remained in the house was little Isaac, there arose among the women some talk, the gist of which was that it might be a good idea to let Isaac lead the service. Isaac was already studying the Bible and he read Hebrew fluently. Why couldn't he be the man of the house, the king for one night?

"Isaac," they said to him, "would you like to be the king?"

"A king? Why not? Who would refuse a kingdom, even for one night?"

"Woe to the kingdom of which Isaac has to be king."

Nevertheless the three women and the two girls went to work and prepared a royal throne, well padded with pillows, for little Isaac. And when Isaac came home from the Synagogue with his cheery good *yom-tev,* he sat down on the throne and in his handsome new clothes, he looked like a real king.

There are three actions over which we have no control—yawning, laughing and weeping. Let anyone in the room begin to yawn or to laugh or to weep and everyone present will sooner or later be yawning or laughing or weeping.

And so it was during the *seder* we are describing. At the high point of the ceremony—after Isaac, the Littlest of Kings, had said, "Therefore we are bound to thank and praise Thee," and then "Halleluiah," and was lifting the second cup of wine to his lips and beginning to intone: "Behold I am about to observe the commandment of the second cup" —there arose on all sides of him such a weeping and wailing and sobbing you might have thought someone had just died in the house.

How it happened, which of the women started weeping first, is hard to say. When Isaac had finished the *kiddush* and began chanting, "For we were slaves," one of the sisters suddenly remembered that a year ago at this time they had also been sitting at a *seder*. But what a different *seder*. Their father and mother had both been alive, and the two girls had new dresses made for them for the holiday. Who would have dreamed then that this year they would be sitting at a strange table with three strange women and that little Isaac would be performing the Passover ceremony? She began to blink her eyes very fast and her lower lip trembled. Looking at her, the other sister began to blink also and tears fell from her eyes.

Glancing over at the girls, one of the women recalled her own sad plight. When her husband Nossi the *Shammes* was alive she had been as happy as anyone could be, that is, she had never been happy, but she had certainly been happier than she was now as assistant to the new *shammes* who had taken her husband's place. When her husband died his former assistant had been elevated to the rank of *shammes*, and his wife Gnessi put on such airs it was impossible to come near her. Thinking of her sorry lot, Pessie the *Shammes*' Assistant made such wry faces that Sossie the Second-hand Dealer, who sat by her, had to be stronger than iron to keep from tears.

Sossie remembered her own sad lot. The seventy-seven women who were so envious of her second-hand business, who dragged customers away from her, did everything they could to keep her from earning a *groschen,* tried to ruin her, ruin her completely. She thought of her oldest girl who had died long ago as a small child. Her name had been Rosie. If Rosie hadn't died she would be a grown woman by now, probably married and a mother herself. Then she thought of her husband who had been an unfortunate cripple, a good-for-nothing without a trade, and a sickly man besides. And Sossie the Second-hand Dealer, who had been softly repeating the words of the *Hagadah* after Bashe the Healer, swaying backwards and forwards in the same rhythm with her, was suddenly bathed in tears.

And Bashe the Healer did not hear the words of the *Hagadah* which flowed so easily from her lips, for she too was thinking of her troubles. She thought of her children who had gone off, far, far away to America. It is true, they wrote her pretty satisfactory letters, they assured her that they were making a living—that is, they worked hard and were as good as anybody. To demonstrate how well off they were they sent her photographs or as they called them "pictures." They promised her that if their affairs or as they called them "business" improved a little they would send her a few *rubles* or as they called them "dollars" and a ship's ticket so that she could come to this great and happy land where everyone made a living and where all men were free and equal. A person could lie down in the middle of the street and starve to death and no one would tell him he was in the way. But nothing could make Bashe move over there. She had children here too. They might not be so well off, but what of that? Their fate was in God's hands. Everything was in God's hands.

That is how Bashe the Healer thought and the words of the *Hagadah* kept pouring from her lips and she herself didn't notice that the tears were also pouring from her eyes. But when they reached the part in the ceremony when the Littlest of Kings stopped chanting and lifted the second cup of wine to his lips, the women stopped chanting also and looking around became frightened at their own noise. Bashe the Healer was the first to recover. She wiped her eyes on her apron, blew her nose and began scolding the others in a loud voice:

"What's all this yammering and yowling for? What is this? *Yom Kippur?* A fast day? Just look at them."

At this the women began to calm down. Sossie got up and handed the king a pitcher of water and a towel so that he could perform the washing-up ceremony, Pessie went to the oven and brought out the hot fish, Bashe put the horseradish on the table. The Littlest of Kings made the blessing over *matzos,* the women followed with a loud *Amen* and quietly, without any more talk, they began the Passover meal.

The Man from Buenos Aires

TRAVELING by train is not as dull as some people think. Not if you happen to run into congenial company. Sometimes you happen to be traveling with a merchant, a man who understands business. Then you don't know where the time goes. Or if not a merchant, then you run into some other man of experience, a witty fellow, shrewd and well-informed, a man who knows his way around. With such a person, it is a pleasure to travel. You can pick up a few choice tidbits from him. And sometimes the Lord sends you a fellow-passenger who is just good company, a lively, cheerful, talkative person. He talks and he talks and he talks. His mouth doesn't shut for a moment. And all he talks about is himself, nothing but himself.

I once had occasion to travel with such a man for quite a distance.

Our acquaintance began—how does an acquaintance in a railway car begin? With some such trifle, as, "Do you know what station this is?" Or, "Can you tell me the time?" Or, "Do you happen to have a match?" Very quickly we became friends, as though we had known each other for who knows how long. At the first station at which we happened to stop for a few minutes, he grabbed me by the arm, led me straight to the buffet and, without asking me whether I drank or not, he ordered two glasses of brandy. Right after that he motioned to me to pick up a fork and when we were through with the various snacks and appetizers that you find at a railway buffet, he ordered two mugs of beer, gave me a cigar, lit one for himself—and our friendship was as good as sealed.

516

"I want to tell you very frankly, without an ounce of flattery," said my new acquaintance when we were once more seated in the railway car, "that I took a liking to you, will you believe it or not, from the first moment I laid eyes on you. As soon as I saw you I said to myself, 'Here is a man you can talk to.' I don't like to sit by myself like a dummy. I like to talk to someone that's wide-awake. That's the reason I bought a third-class ticket, to have someone to talk to. Otherwise I would be traveling second class. And do you think I can't manage first class? I can swing that too. You may think I am boasting. Look!" And with these words my fellow-passenger reached into his back pants pocket, pulled out a fat wallet and showed it to me, stuffed full of banknotes. He slapped it with the palm of his hand as though it were a sofa cushion, then put it back into his pocket. "Don't worry," he said, "there is more where this came from."

I looked the fellow over curiously, but try as I might I couldn't figure out how old he was. You might say he was forty, and then again you might say he was a little over twenty. His face was smooth and round, and heavily tanned, without a sign of a beard or mustache. He had small, unctuous, laughing eyes. He was short, and round in build, sprightly and full of life and movement, dressed nattily from top to toe the way I like to see a man dress. He had on a snow-white shirt with gold buttons, a rich silk tie pierced by a showy tiepin, an elegant new suit made of real English broadcloth, and a pair of smartly shined shoes. On his finger, he wore a heavy gold ring with a diamond that blinked with a thousand facets in the sun. (The diamond, if it was real, must have been worth not less than four or five thousand *rubles*.)

To be well dressed is in my opinion the most important thing of all. I like to dress well myself and I like to see others well dressed. From the way a man is dressed I will tell you whether he is an upright person or not. True, there are those who maintain that this is no indication. A man can be most elegantly gotten up, they argue, and yet be a scoundrel. Then I will ask you this: Why is it that the whole world wants to dress well? Why does one man wear one kind of suit and another wear a different outfit? Why does one man buy himself a flowing tie of smooth satin, sea-green in color, and another insist on a bow tie, and a red one with white dots at that?

I could give you many more such examples, but there is no point to it. Why waste your time? Let us better return to our friend and listen to what he has to tell us.

"—and so you see, my friend, I can afford to travel second class, too. Do you think that I begrudge the expense? Expense is no object. But will you believe it or not—I like to travel third class. I am a plain person myself and I like plain people. I am, you understand, a democrat. I began my career at the bottom of the ladder, at the very bottom, like this." (My new acquaintance showed me with this hand to the ground how he had begun his career at the very bottom.) "And I came up higher and higher." (Here he reached with his hand to the ceiling to show me how high he had come up.) "Not all at once, mind you. But slowly, little by little, little by little. At the beginning I worked for others. I was just an employee. An 'employee' did I say?" (Here he laughed out loud.) "Believe me, before I attained the dignity of being called an 'employee,' much water flowed under the bridge.

"When I remind myself sometimes of what I was as a child, my hair—will you believe it or not—my hair, stands on end. I can't bear to remind myself of it, and what's more I don't want to. Do you think it's because I am ashamed of my past? Just the opposite. I tell everyone who I am. When people ask me, 'Where are you from?' I don't hesitate for a moment. I tell them right off that I come from that illustrious city, Somashken. Do you know where Somashken is? There is a tiny town in Kurland, not far from Mitau, that's called Somashken. The whole town is so big that I could easily buy it up today complete with all its assets. It is possible, of course, that the town has changed, that it has grown—I can't tell you, I don't know. But in my day the whole town of Somashken, will you believe it or not, owned exactly one orange, which traveled like a worn-out tune from one hostess to the next to be set before the guests every Saturday afternoon.

"In this very town of Somashken I was brought up on resounding slaps, ironclad kicks, and plain beatings. I saw stars in front of my eyes, wore black and blue marks on my body and nursed an empty stomach. There is nothing, I tell you, nothing, that I remember so well as hunger. I came into God's world hungry, I suffered hunger from the moment I became conscious of who I was. Painful, wracking hunger, the kind that knots up your belly and makes you retch with nausea . . . Wait! Have you ever heard of the sap of a pine tree? Musicians use it instead of rosin to rub on their fiddle strings. I lived on this sap, will you believe it or not, for one whole summer. That was the summer my stepfather, a snub-nosed tailor, dislocated my arm and drove me from my mother's house, the summer I ran away from Somashken to Mitau. This is the arm, see—there should still be a mark on it." And my new-found friend rolled up his sleeve and showed me a soft, healthy, plump arm. Then he went on talking.

"Wandering around, half-naked and hungry in Mitau, living in unbelievable filth, I at last with God's help landed a job. My first job. I became a companion to a blind old cantor. He had been a famous cantor at one time, but he had become blind in his old age and had to go begging from house to house. I was hired to lead him around. The job itself wouldn't have been so bad, but you had to be stronger than iron to put up with the old man's whims. He was never satisfied. Never. He was always grumbling at me, pinching me, tearing pieces of flesh out of me. He would complain that I didn't lead him where I was supposed to. To this day I don't know where I was supposed to lead him. He was certainly a cantankerous old man. Besides, he set me a fine example. He boasted in front of everyone, will you believe it or not, that my parents had turned Christian and had wanted to baptize me too, but he had rescued me with nobody knew how much trouble and anguish from the hands of the Christians. I had to listen to those lies and keep a straight face. More than that, he expected me to look woebegone when he told these wild tales. . . .

"I quickly saw that I wasn't going to live to a ripe old age in the service of my cantor, so I made a burnt offering of my 'job' and left Mitau for Libau. After I had wandered around in Libau for a while, homeless and hungry, I attached myself to a group of poor emigrants. These emigrants were getting ready to go by ship somewhere far off, all the way to Buenos Aires. I began to plead with them to take me along. It was impossible, they told me. It didn't depend on them, but on the

Committee. The Committee had the say-so. So I went to the Committee, wept and fell in a faint before them, implored them to have pity on me and finally they consented to take me to Buenos Aires.

"You ask me, why Buenos Aires? What drew me there, of all places? Nothing. Everybody was going to Buenos Aires, so I went too. Later I found out that Buenos Aires was only a point of departure and that actually we were going to be sent further out. And so it came to pass. No sooner had we arrived in Buenos Aires than our papers were taken away and we were reassigned to different places, such places as Adam himself had never seen in his wildest dreams. There they put us to work.

"No doubt you would like to know what kind of work. You'd better not ask. I am sure that our ancestors in Egypt never labored as we did. And the torments they endured as they are described in the *Hagadah* are not even a tenth as bad as what we had to endure. They tell us that our grandfathers kneaded clay with their hands, made bricks without straw and built the pyramids in that way. Do you call that an achievement? They should have tried, as we did, to plow, with their bare hands, the wild steppes overgrown with thistles, or drive tremendous oxen that could kill a man with one touch, or chase wild horses for a hundred miles with a lasso. They should have known for only one night what it felt like to be bitten by ferocious mosquitoes, or eaten dry biscuits that had the flavor of stones, or drunk stagnant worm-infested water. One day, will you believe it or not, I happened to look down into a river and I became frightened at my own image. My skin was all peeled off, my eyes were swollen shut, my arms were like sausages and my feet were bloody. I was covered with hair from top to toe.

" 'Is that you, Motek from Somashken?' I said to myself, and burst out laughing. That same day I spat at the huge oxen and the wild horses and the untamed steppes and the wormy water and went back on foot to Buenos Aires.

"It seems to me that the station we are stopping at now should have a large buffet. Look into your book. Don't you find it's time to get a bite to eat? It will give us strength to go on with the story."

After we had had a substantial "bite," and washed it down with some beer, we again lit cigars, fine aromatic cigars, genuine Havanas from Buenos Aires, and settled ourselves down in the railway car. My new acquaintance from Buenos Aires resumed his story.

"Buenos Aires is the sort of place, believe me, that since God created the world . . . Wait! Have you ever been in America? In the city of New York? Never? Or in London? No? In Madrid? Constantinople? Paris? Not there either? Well, then I can't explain to you what Buenos Aires is like. I can only tell you that it's an inferno. A *Gehenna*. A Hell and a Heaven rolled into one. That is, it's a hell for some and a heaven for others. If you just keep your eyes open and watch out for the main chance, you can make your fortune there. It's a place where, will you believe it or not, you will find gold lying in the streets. Bend down, stretch out your hand, pick up as much as you want. But you have to watch out that no one crushes you underfoot. The thing is—not to stop. Don't stop for anything. Don't stop to think, don't weigh one thing against another. Don't worry about what is proper and what isn't proper. Everything is proper. Is it a job waiting on tables in a restaurant? Good. Clerking in a store? Good. Washing bottles in a tavern? Good. Running through the streets shouting headlines in the papers? Good. Washing dogs? Good. Raising cats? Good. Catching rats? Also good. Skinning the rats? That too. In a word, everything is good. I have tried everything, and everywhere I have seen the same thing. Simply this, that it doesn't pay to work for someone else. It's a thousand times better to have someone else working for you.

"Can we help it if God created the world once and for all so that one man has to sweat brewing the beer and I can sit here and drink it? That another has to work at rolling the cigars and I can smoke them? That the engineer has to drive the locomotive, the stoker to stoke coal, the workman to oil the wheels, and you and I can sit here in the car and tell stories? There are those who don't like it? Then let them go ahead and change the world."

I looked at my companion and thought to myself, "What can the creature be? A man who has just struck it rich? A former tailor in

America who now has a ready-to-wear store? Maybe even a manu-
facturer? Or a landlord? Or just a capitalist living off interest?" But
let him go on with the story. He tells it much better himself.

"This is a great world, I tell you, a sweet world and a lovely world,
and it's a pleasure to be alive in this world. You just have to make
sure that no one spits into your porridge. I have tried every occupation in the world. I have served, as they say, every kind of master. No
work was too difficult for me, no occupation too mean. And if you
want to know something, there is no such thing as an occupation that
is too mean. All work is good, if you only deal honestly and keep your
word. I know it from personal experience. I won't boast to you that I
am as virtuous as the chief rabbi of Lemberg. But you can take my
word of honor for it, that I am no thief either. And certainly not a
robber. Nor am I a swindler. I swear to you by everything good, that
I am an honest merchant. I carry on my business honorably. I don't
cheat anyone. I sell only what I have to sell. I have no pig in the poke
to sell. In short, do you want to know what I am? I am no more than
a middleman, a jobber, or as you call it a 'podradchik.' I supply the
world with merchandise, something that everyone knows and nobody
speaks of. Why? Because it's a cunning world and people are too
shifty. They don't like it if you tell them that black is black and
white is white. They would rather have you tell them that black is
white and white is black. So what can you do with them?"

I looked at my friend from Buenos Aires and thought to myself,
"Dear Lord, what is he anyway? What sort of goods does this jobber
supply the whole world with? And what's all this strange talk about
black and white and white and black?" I didn't like to interrupt and
ask, "Uncle, what do you actually deal in?" So I let him go on.

"In short—where were we? At my present business in Buenos Aires.
The business itself is actually not in Buenos Aires. My business, if
you want to know, is everywhere, over the whole world. In Paris,
in London, Budapest, Boston . . . but the main office is in Buenos
Aires. It's too bad we are not in Buenos Aires right now. I would take
you up to my place of business and show you my office and the people
who work for me. My employees all live, will you believe it or not,
like Rothschilds. Eight hours a day, that's all they work, not a minute

more. The men who work for me are treated like human beings. Do you know why? Because I was an 'employee' once myself; I worked for my present partners. We are three partners now. At one time there were two partners and I worked for them. I was their right-hand man. The entire business, you might say, rested on my shoulders. I did all the buying and selling, the estimating, the sorting, everything. I have an eye for good merchandise, will you believe it or not; all I need is to take one look at a piece of goods and I will tell you right away how much it's worth and where it can go. But that alone is not enough. In our business you have to have a sense of smell too. You have to be able to smell out where something is hidden. And you need still another sense, to tell you where you can make a good transaction and where you can break your neck and sink into mire so deep that you won't talk your way out of it. . . .

"The trouble is that there are too many curious people in the world. Too many prying eyes. And in our business we fear the evil eye. . . . If you make one false step you won't wash yourself clean in a hundred waters. The least little thing and there is a hue and a cry and it's smeared all over the newspapers. That's all the papers need, you know. They are only too happy to publish the least little breath of a scandal, fan it into a huge conflagration and bring the police of the world down on us. Although I must tell you this in strict confidence, that the police of the whole world are in our pockets. If I were to mention the sums of money the police collect from us every year, you would just gape at me. But then to us, will you believe it or not, a sum like ten thousand, fifteen thousand, even twenty thousand, is a mere trifle. . . ."

Saying this, my friend waved his hand carelessly like a man who could afford to throw thousands around. The diamond on his finger flashed in the light and the man from Buenos Aires who threw thousands around so lightly looked at me briefly to see what impression he had made. Then he pushed forward with his story.

"And if it's necessary to put out a little more sometimes, do you think that stops us? On the other hand, we have complete confidence in each other, we three partners. No matter how many thousands we give the police, we trust each other implicitly. All our business is carried on in good faith. One of us wouldn't cheat the other by so much. Just let him try . . . he will live to regret it. We know each other very well, we know the place, and we know all that goes on in the world. Each of us has his own spies and agents. What do you expect? Business that is done on faith can't be carried on any other way. Don't you think it would be a good idea if we jumped off at this station and rinsed our throats a bit?" Saying this he took my hand and looked into my eyes.

Naturally I had nothing against his proposal and we jumped out at the next station and "rinsed our throats." The corks of the lemonade bottles popped one after the other. My friend drank with such evident enjoyment that it was a pleasure to watch him. But one thing still preyed on my mind. What sort of merchandise did he deal in, this man from Buenos Aires? How did he come to throw all those thousands around? And how could the police of the whole world be in his pockets? And what did he need agents and spies for? Did he deal in contraband goods? In false diamonds? Stolen merchandise? Or was he just a bluffer and a windbag, one of those creatures whose tongue wags at both ends and everything that rolls off is a hundred times more wonderful than life? We traveling salesmen have a name of our own for such a creature. We call him a "wholesaler," because everything he deals in is wholesale, on a large scale, blown up. In plain language he is nothing but a liar or a teller of tall tales.

Well, we lit fresh cigars, settled down in our seats again, and the man from Buenos Aires plunged on.

"Where were we? Oh, yes, I was talking about my partners. That is, my present partners. At one time they were my employers and I was, as I have already told you, their employee. I won't try to discredit them or to pretend that they treated me badly. How could they treat me badly when I was as faithful to them as a dog? Every cent of theirs was as precious to me as if it were my own. Over and over I made myself enemies for their sake, deadly enemies. There were times, will you believe me or not, when I came near being poisoned because of my faithfulness. Yes, poisoned. I can pride myself on the fact that I served them loyally, as loyally as a man could. True, I didn't forget about myself either. A person must never forget about himself. You have to remember you are only human, here today and gone to-morrow. And there is no point in slaving for someone else all your life. Why should I? Have I no hands? No feet? No tongue in my head? And especially since I knew that without me they couldn't get along for even one day. They couldn't and they shouldn't. There were too many secrets . . . as is natural in any business.

"One fine day I made up my mind and said to them, *'Adieu, gentlemen.'* They looked at me. 'What do you mean *adieu?*' *'Adieu* means good-bye,' I said. 'What's the matter?' they asked me. 'I've had enough,' I said, 'I am fed up.' They exchanged glances, and asked me how much capital I had. I told them whatever I had would be enough to start with and if it wasn't enough God was our Father and Buenos Aires was a city. They understood me at once. Why shouldn't they? Were their brains dried up? And that was how we became partners. Three partners, three bosses, all sharing equally in the business. There is no such thing among us as one getting more and the other getting less. Whatever God sends, we split three ways. And we don't quarrel among ourselves either. Why should we? We are doing quite well, God be thanked, and the business is growing. The world is getting bigger and our merchandise is getting dearer. Each of us takes out of the partnership as much as he needs for his personal expenses. And our expenses, I can tell you, are pretty large.

"I myself, will you believe it or not, without a wife and children to support, spend three times as much as another who has a wife and children. Some people would be glad to make what I give to charity alone each year. There isn't a thing in the world that doesn't cost me money—synagogues, hospitals, emigrant funds, concerts. Buenos Aires, God be praised, is a big city. And what about other places? Palestine alone, will you believe it or not, costs me a pretty penny. Not so long ago I received a letter from a *yeshiva* in Jerusalem. A handsome letter with a Star of David on top, with seals and signatures of rabbis. The letter was addressed to me personally in very impressive language: 'To our Master, the Renowned and Wealthy Reb Mordecai.'

" 'Oho,' I thought, 'since they address me in such respectful language and call me by my first name, I can't be small either. I have to send them a hundred at least.' These are only incidental donations. What about my native town, Somashken? Somashken costs me, will you believe it or not, a hatful of money as big as this, every year. I keep getting letters from there all the time. There is always a fresh catastrophe, one thing after another. Money for Passover—that goes without saying. Every Passover I send a hundred. That's become a rule. Right now I am on my way to Somashken and I know beforehand that I won't get by with less than a thousand. Why do I say a thousand? I hope I get by with two thousand. If not, I'll have to make it three thousand. Just think, I haven't been back home all these years, since childhood. And after all, Somashken is my *home*. I know beforehand what a commotion my coming will cause, how excited everybody will be to see me. The whole town will come running. 'Have you heard the news? Motek is here. Our Motek from Buenos Aires.' That's an occasion for them. Believe me, those poor souls are waiting for me as though I were the Messiah. From each station I send them a message that I am on the way. I send them a telegram every day. Just these words, 'I am coming. Motek.' And I myself, will you believe it or not, can't wait to get there. To see Somashken again, to kiss the earth of Somashken, the dust of Somashken. . . . Who cares about Buenos Aires? Or New York? Or London and Paris? Let them all perish. Somashken is my home town."

As he spoke his face was transformed. It seemed to grow younger, handsomer. His bright little eyes had a new light in them, a new glow of happiness and of love. Of genuine love. But there was one thing still troubling me. . . . I still didn't know what it was that he dealt in. But he didn't let me ponder long. He forged ahead with his story.

"Do you want to know the real reason for my going to Somashken? I am going there partly because I am lonesome for my home, and partly to visit the graves of my ancestors. My father and mother are buried there, and my brothers and sisters—my whole family. But the main reason is that I want to get married. How much longer can a man remain a bachelor? And when I marry, I want to marry a girl from Somashken, a girl from my own town, my own class, my own kind. I have already written about it to my friends in Somashken. I have asked them to look around, and find me something good . . .

They write me that if I only arrive safely, everything is bound to be for the best. That's the kind of crazy fool I am. . . . In Buenos Aires, will you believe it or not, the greatest beauties in the world have been offered to me in marriage. I could pick up something that the Sultan of Turkey doesn't boast of. But I've told myself once for all. No! I shall find myself a wife in Somashken. I want a girl of good family. A respectable Jewish girl. I don't care how poor she is. I will make her rich. I will shower her parents with gold, make her whole family wealthy.

"And the girl herself I will take to Buenos Aires with me and I will build her a palace fit for a princess. I won't let a speck of dust fall on her. She will be happy with me, believe me. She will be the happiest woman in the world. Nothing will touch her, she won't have to give a thought to a single thing, except her household and her husband and children. I will send my children to the best schools. My sons will all enter the professions. One will become a doctor, another a lawyer, another an engineer. . . . And my daughters I will send to private boarding schools. . . . Do you want to know where? In Frankfurt."

At this point the conductor came up to collect our tickets. The conductor (I have noticed this many times) always appears just when you least want him. A hubbub arose in the carriage, people began running back and forth, collecting their baggage, pushing and shoving. I reached for my luggage too. I had to get out and change to another train. The man from Buenos Aires helped me tie up my luggage, and in the meanwhile we carried on this conversation which I will transmit to you word for word.

Man from Buenos Aires: "Too bad you aren't going further. I won't have anybody to talk to."

I: "What can I do? Business is business."

Man from Buenos Aires: "Well said. Business is business. I am afraid I will have to pay the difference and move over to second class. I can swing first class too, thank God. When I travel . . ."

I: "Forgive me for interrupting you. We have only half a minute left. I wanted to ask you something."

Man from Buenos Aires: "For instance?"

I: "For instance, I wanted to ask you. . . . Oh, there goes the whistle. What, in short, is your business? What do you deal in?"

Man from Buenos Aires: "What do I deal in?" (He burst out laughing.) "Not in prayer books, my friend, not in prayer books . . ."

I was at the far end of the car now with my luggage, but I could still see the man from Buenos Aires with the smug look on his smooth round face and the fine aromatic cigar between his teeth and his laughter still rang in my ears. . . . "Not in prayer books, my friend, not in prayer books."

May God Have Mercy

ZAIDEL REB SHAYE'S was a young man who sat in his father-in-law's house and studied the *Torah*—never lifted a finger, only sat and studied, though he already has several children of his own. Why should he exert himself when he was the only son and his father-in-law, Reb Shaye, was a wealthy man and some day that wealth would pass on to him?

Reb Shaye's business was that of money-lender. His "capital" was scattered all over the town. There wasn't a single Kasrilevkite who didn't owe Reb Shaye money. His house was always full of people—some coming, others going, this one borrowing, that one paying back.

Reb Shaye had what might pass for an office or a bank—a bank, it is true, without highly polished desks and tables, without clerks in white coats, with curled mustaches and long fingernails, without grated windows and iron safes, without massive account books and ledgers heavy enough to knock a man down.

Reb Shaye had only a small table with an inkstand and sand-dispenser, and whenever he had to write something down he had to spit into the inkstand before it would produce any ink. Besides that, the table also had a drawer with two rings and a huge lock on it. In this drawer was locked up the account book with all the transactions which Reb Shaye kept according to his own peculiar bookkeeping system. This is how it went:

The book consisted of fifty-two pages; on each page were written out the days of the week, and each day was divided into two parts.

One side was headed *Received* and the other side, *Paid*. This is how the side labeled *Received* looked:

Rec'd from Gershon Pipik on the note of the weekly portion of *Genesis: 2 rubles.*

Received from Feivel Shmaye's on the note of the last portion of *Exodus: 5 rubles.*

Received from Simcha Lemeshke on the note of the Eleventh reading: 1 *ruble.*

Didn't receive from Gershon Pipik on the note of the second weekly reading of *Genesis: 5 rubles.*

And the *Paid* side:

Paid to Simcha Lemeshke on the note of the last week of *Exodus:* 13 *rubles.*

Paid again to Gershon Pipik: 7 *rubles.*

Didn't pay again to Feivel Shmaye's: 10 *rubles.* Bad debt.

I promised Reb Simcha to give him 11 *rubles.*

How Reb Shaye ever deciphered these jottings, God alone knew. And yet you may rest assured that there were never any protests, no quarrels, and no lawsuits. Everyone simply knew this: that if he stopped paying, he lost his credit, never to regain it.

And so it went, the borrowing and the paying back, smoothly, without a hitch for many years, until. . . .

Until Reb Shaye died.

When Reb Shaye died, Zaidel took over the business.

After the thirty-day period of mourning was over, Zaidel went to work on the accounts. He sat and labored over the account books for three weeks in a row, writing, jotting, figuring, computing. Finally he sent for the citizens of the town and said to them, "Gentlemen, I wish to announce to you that I have gone over your accounts carefully, and I have figured out that you don't owe me anything. You are all clear."

"What do you mean we don't owe you anything? What do you mean we are all clear?"

"Let me explain. According to algebra you have been paying interest and interest on top of interest until you've paid your debts seventeen times over. Here, take your I.O.U. notes."

When they heard this, the Kasrilevkites became furious. They thought he was playing a trick on them, trying to outwit them with clever words. They threw the notes back in his face and began yelling, "He is murdering us. Without a knife or gun he is killing us. Reb Shaye, may he enjoy everlasting glory, did business with us for so many years; his purse was always open to us, and this—this creature comes along and wants to make fools of us."

"Fools!" shouted Zaidel. "What kind of fools and imbeciles are you? I told you, you've paid your debts. I didn't make this up out of my own head. I worked it out according to algebra."

"What nonsense is this? What's this *albegra* he is blabbing about? Let's take our case to someone else. Let's go to the Rabbi."

"To the Rabbi! To the Rabbi!" they shouted in unison, and went straight to the Rabbi, Reb Yozifel.

Almost everybody in town had gathered at the Rabbi's house. There was a tumult and a shouting, loud enough to split the heavens. Zaidel let the others talk first; he allowed each one to say what was on his mind. Then when everyone had made his complaint and yelled to his heart's content, he asked that they all step out for a while, so that he could talk to the Rabbi alone.

What took place between Zaidel and the Rabbi, no one ever found out. They say that Zaidel and the Rabbi had a long discussion. Zaidel demonstrated to the Rabbi that it was wrong to take interest, for, according to the wise men, taking interest was the same as stealing. He who lives off unearned money is the lowest of the low. Everyone, he said, must labor in the sweat of his brow. There is no justice otherwise.

Reb Yozifel the Rabbi tried to discuss the point with him. He tried to prove that according to the Edict of *Mahram* of blessed memory the taking of interest was a necessary thing. He said that otherwise the world could not exist, and so on and so forth. But Zaidel answered him that this sort of "existence" was not to his taste. He didn't like the way the world was run. What sort of world was this? If a hungry man steals a *groschen's* worth of bread, that is considered a crime; but to rob a town full of widows and orphans, to take the last bite out of their mouths, was that righteousness? For cutting off a finger you got sent to hard labor in Siberia; but for killing off eighty-thousand men in South Africa as though they were oxen you got a medal for bravery.

"Is that justice?" he shouted, grabbing Reb Yozifel's lapels. "Is that righteousness? Here old Kruger, the governor of the Boers, is going around knocking on all the doors of the world, begging that we have pity on his poor country. All he wants is a court of justice, he wants impartial mediators to decide the rights of the matter. But this one says he doesn't want to interfere, that one says it won't look proper, this one says this, that one something else. In the meanwhile, blood is running like water.

"Where is justice? Where is humanity? You keep telling me about settlements, about customs, about the ways of the world. . . . A fine way I call it. A wonderful world."

He gave the Rabbi more such arguments, going off the subject into all sorts of speculations, denying the basic laws of what is "mine" and "yours" and "ours," making fun of everything sacred and proper.

Reb Yozifel finally refused to listen any further, stopped up his ears with both hands and shouted, "Enough. Enough. Enough."

When Zaidel had gone home, Reb Yozifel turned to the assembly and said with a deep sigh, "Poor fellow. Such a fine young man, so well-educated, so well-bred, and good-looking . . . but, may God have mercy on him."

Saying this the Rabbi touched his finger to his forehead, and everyone in the assembly understood what he meant.

Schprintze

I OWE you a greeting, a hearty greeting, Mr. Sholom Aleichem. It's a score of years since we've seen each other. My, my, how much water has flown under the bridge! How much agony we have lived through, you and I, and all of Israel, in these last few years! Oh, thou Father of the Universe, our dear God in Heaven! We have lived through a Kishinev and a Constitution, through pogroms and disasters of every kind. I am only surprised, if you will forgive me for saying this, that you haven't changed by a hair. May the evil eye spare you! But look at me: *"Behold, I look like a man of seventy.—*I am not sixty yet, and see how white Tevye has grown." It's the same old thing: *"the pain of bringing up children."* And who has suffered as much pain because of his children as I have? Since the last time I saw you a new misfortune happened to me, this time with my daughter Schprintze, something that put all my former troubles in the shade! And yet, as you see, I am still alive, still here. . . . As it is written: *"Perforce you must live."* Live, though you burst asunder singing this song:

> "The world doesn't please me and life isn't funny
> If I have no luck and I have no money."

In short what does it say in *Perek? "The Holy One, Blessed be He, wished to grant merit to Israel.—*God wanted to favor His chosen people." So a fresh calamity descended upon us, this time a Constitution. And such a panic overtook our rich people that they began

533

leaving Yehupetz in droves, running off abroad, supposedly for their health, for mineral baths, salt water cures, nerves, and other such nonsense. And when Yehupetz is deserted then Boikerik with its fresh air, its pine woods, and its summer homes becomes a desert too. As we say in the morning prayer: *"Blessed be He who bestows mercy upon this earth."*

But that isn't all. We have a great God and a mighty God who watches over His poor and sees to it that they continue to struggle a little longer on this earth. What a summer we had! People began running to Boiberik from all over, from Odessa and Rostov, from Ekaterineslav and Mogilov, and Kishinev. There descended *"thousands upon thousands of rich men."* All the millionaires and plutocrats came to us. Apparently the Constitution was even worse for them than for us in Yehupetz, for they kept on coming, they didn't stop coming. The question is: Why should they run to us? And the answer is: Why do we run to them? It's become a custom with our people, God be praised, that as soon as there is a rumor of a pogrom we begin flying from one town to another, as it is written: *"They journeyed and they encamped, they encamped and they journeyed. . . ."* Which means, "You come to me and I will come to you."

Meanwhile you can imagine how crowded Boiberik became. It overflowed with people, it spilled over with women and children. And since children have to eat three times a day and they like to nibble besides, the demand for milk and butter and cheese kept growing. And from whom does one get milk and butter and cheese if not from Tevye? Overnight, Tevye became all the rage. From all sides you heard nothing but Tevye and Tevye and Tevye. "Reb Tevye, come to me." "Reb Tevye, you promised me." What more need I say? If God wills it, that's enough.

"And it came to pass—" Here is how it all began. Shortly before *Shevuos* I brought my wares to one of my new customers, a young widow and a rich one, from Ekaterineslav, who had just arrived with her son Aarontchik to spend the summer in Boiberik. And naturally the first person she became acquainted with in Boiberik was myself. "You've been recommended to me very highly," she says. "They tell me you have the best butter and cheese in these parts."

"How can it be otherwise?" I asked her. "Not in vain does King Solomon say that a good name can be heard like the sound of the *shofar* all over the world. And if you like," I added, "I can also tell you what a certain *medresh* has to say about that." She cut me short, however, saying that she was only a widow and inexperienced in such matters. She didn't even know what you ate it with. The important thing, she tells me, is that the butter should be fresh and the cheese taste good. There's a female for you.

Well, I began coming to the widow from Ekaterineslav twice a week, every Monday and Thursday, regularly, by the calendar. I brought her butter and cheese each time, without asking whether she needed it or not. I made myself at home in her house, took a friendly interest in the household, stuck my nose into the kitchen, told her a few times, whatever I saw fit to tell her, about the management of the house. The first time, as you might expect, I got a dressing-down from the servant who told me to mind my own business and not to stick my nose into strange pots. The second time, however, they stopped to listen, and the third time they asked my advice, because by then the widow had become aware of who Tevye was.

And so it went, until at last the widow disclosed to me her big problem, her secret sorrow, the thing that was eating away at her, and that was—Aarontchik! There he was, a young man, over twenty years old, and all he could think of was horseback riding, bicycling, fishing, and aside from that nothing! He wouldn't have anything to do with business, with the making of money. His father had left him a nice little fortune, almost a million *rubles,* but did he as much as look into it? All he cared about was spending money; his purse was wide open.

"Where is this young man?" I asked her. "Just turn him over to me. I'll have a good talk with him. I'll read him a lecture, quote him a passage or two, give him a *medresh.* . . ." She laughed at this. "A *medresh* did you say? A horse would be more like it."

Just at this moment *"the lad arrived."* Aarontchik himself walked in. He was a handsome young fellow, tall and husky, and bursting with good health. He wore a wide sash across his middle, with a watch stuck in the side, and his sleeves were rolled up above the elbows.

"Where have you been?" his mother asked him.

"I've been out in a boat," he said, "fishing."

"A fine occupation," I said, "for a young man like you. Over there in the city your inheritance is being frittered away, and you are out on the river catching fish."

I looked at the widow. She had turned as red as a beet. She must have thought her son would pick me up by the collar, *"and smite me as the Lord smote the Egyptians, with signs and symbols,"* that is, give me two slaps in the face, and throw me out of the house like a broken potsherd. Nonsense! Tevye is not afraid of such things. When I have something to say, I say it.

"And so it was." When the young man heard me, he stepped back, folded his arms over his chest, looked me over from head to foot, gave a long, low whistle, and then burst out laughing. We both thought he had lost his mind. And what shall I tell you? From that moment on we became like two comrades. And I must confess that the longer I knew him the better I got to like him, even though he was a rake and a spendthrift, much too free with his money, and something of a fool besides. For instance, who else but a fool would put his hand into his pocket when he met a beggar, and give him all he had without counting it? Or take a perfectly good coat off his back and give it away? Talk about folly.

I was honestly sorry for his mother. She wept and wailed and asked me what she should do. She begged me to have a talk with him. So I did her the favor. Why should I begrudge it to her? Did it cost me anything? I sat down with him, told him stories, cited examples, plied him with quotations and drummed proverbs into his ears, as only Tevye can do. And I must say that he seemed to enjoy listening to me. He kept asking me questions about how I lived and what my home was like. "You know what, Reb Tevye," he said, "I would like to come over and see you at home some day."

"That's easy," I said. "If you want to see me at home, just pick yourself up and drive over to my farm. It seems to me you have enough horses and bicycles. And if necessary, you can even pick up your two feet and walk over. It isn't far. You just have to cut through the woods."

"And when can I find you at home?" he asked me.

"You can find me at home only on Sabbaths and holidays. But hold on!" I said. "Do you know what? A week from Friday is *Shevuos*. If you want to come over to my house for *Shevuos,* my wife will treat you to such *blintzes* as your *'blessed ancestors never ate in Egypt.'*"

"What are you referring to?" he asked me. "You know that I'm weak in Biblical quotations."

"I know you are weak," I said. "If you had studied in *cheder* the way I did, you would have known not only what the rabbi, but also what the rebbitzen, the rabbi's wife, had to say."

He laughed at this. "Good," he said, "you can expect me on the first day of *Shevuos* along with a couple of friends. But see to it that the *blintzes* are good and hot."

"At white heat, inside and out," I said. "From the frying pan right into your mouth."

I came home and said to my wife, "Golde," I said, "we are going to have guests for *Shevuos."*

"Mazl-tov," she said. "And who are they?"

"That," I said, "you will find out later. Just get some eggs ready. We have plenty of butter and cheese, praise the Lord. I want you to make enough *blintzes* for three guests. And remember, they are the kind of people who believe in filling their stomachs; fine words mean nothing to them."

"I suppose you've picked up some starving wretches, some cronies of yours from Hungerland."

"You talk like a fool, Golde," I told her. "In the first place what harm would there be if we did feed some poor hungry wretch on *Shevuos?* In the second place, be thou informed, my dear spouse, my modest and pious wife, Madam Golde, that one of our guests is the widow's son, Aarontchik, the one I told you about."

"Oh," she said, "that's different."

Look at the power money has! Even my Golde, when she gets wind

of money, becomes a different person. That's the way of the world.
How is it written? *"Gold and silver, the work of man's hands—*
Wealth is the undoing of man."

Well, *Shevuos* arrived. And how beautiful *Shevuos* in the country
can be; how warm and sunny and fragrant, I don't have to tell you.
The richest man in the city would envy us such a blue sky, such a
green forest, such aromatic pine trees. Even the cows in the pasture
keep chewing their cuds and look up at you as though to say, "Give
us such grass all year round and we'll give you all the milk you
want." You can tempt me all you like, you can offer me the richest
livelihood in town, I wouldn't change places with you. Where can
you get such a sky in town? How do we say it in Hallel: *"The
heavens are the heavens of the Lord*—God's own sky." In town when
you raise your head, what do you see? A brick wall, a roof, a chimney. Where will you find a tree? And if some scrubby little bush has
crept in somewhere, you smother it with an overcoat.

Anyway, when my guests arrived, they couldn't find enough words
to praise the beauty of the country. They came riding, three abreast,
on horseback. You should have seen those horses, especially the one
Aarontchik rode. An Arab steed. I figured that you couldn't buy him
for three hundred *rubles.*

"Welcome, guests," I said to them. "I see that in honor of *Shevuos*
you have come riding on horseback. Never mind. Tevye is not so pious
either. And if you should be whipped for your sins in the next world,
my back won't be sore. Golde," I called my wife, "get the *blintzes*
ready and let's bring the table outdoors. I have nothing to show off to
my guests inside."

Then I called my daughters, "Schprintze, Teibel, Beilke, where are
you? Get a move on you." Soon the table was brought outside, and
then benches, a tablecloth, plates, forks, salt. And right after that Golde
appeared with the *blintzes* piled high on a platter, plump and juicy,
and as *"sweet as the life-giving manna from heaven."* My guests ate
and ate and couldn't praise them enough.

"What are you standing there for?" I said to Golde. "Repeat the
same verse over again. Today is *Shevuos* and we have to say the same
prayer twice." Golde didn't waste any time, but filled up the platter

again, and Schprintze brought it to the table. I happened to look over at Aarontchik just then and saw him watching Schprintze. He couldn't take his eyes off her. What had he seen in her all of a sudden? "Go on and eat," I said to him. "Why aren't you eating?"

"What else am I doing if not eating?" he said. "You are looking at Schprintze," I told him. Everybody at the table burst out laughing, and Schprintze laughed too. Everybody was happy, everybody felt gay; it was a wonderful, happy *Shevuos*. How was I to know that from all this good cheer would come so much sorrow and misery? That God's punishment would descend on my head and blackest grief on my soul?

Man is a fool. If he was wise he would never let anything touch him too deeply. He would know that if things are a certain way that's the way they were intended to be. For if things were intended to be different, they wouldn't have been as they are. Don't we say in the Psalms: *"Put your trust in God?"*—Have faith in Him and He will see to it that you stagger under a load of trouble and keep on reciting: *"This too is for the best."* Listen to what can happen in this world, but listen carefully, for this is where my story really begins.

"It was evening and it was day." Once toward evening, I came home, worn out from the day's labors, from running all over Boiberik, delivering milk and cheese from *datcha* to *datcha*. When I approached my house I saw a familiar-looking horse hitched to my front door. I could have sworn it was Aarontchik's horse, the one I had valued at three hundred *rubles*. I went up to the horse, slapped him on the rump, scratched his throat and shook him by the mane. "Here, my fine fellow," I said to him, "what are you doing here?" He turned his engaging face toward me and gave me a look, as though to say, "Why ask me? Ask my master."

I went inside and asked my wife, "Tell me, Golde my treasure, what is Aarontchik doing here?"

"How should I know?" she said. "He is a friend of yours, isn't he?"

"Where is he now?" I asked.

"He went strolling in the woods with the children."

"What's all this strolling around for all of a sudden?" I said, and told my wife to give me supper. After I had eaten, I thought to myself,

"What are you getting so rattled about, Tevye? If someone comes to visit you, do you have to get so upset? You should be pleased."

As I tell myself this, I take a look outside and see my girls approaching with the young man, carrying bouquets of freshly picked flowers. The two younger girls, Teibel and Beilke, are walking together in front, and behind them are Schprintze and Aarontchik.

"Good evening."

"Good day."

Aarontchik stands at a side, stroking his horse, chewing at a blade of grass, and there is a strange look on his face. He says to me, "Reb Tevye, I want to do business with you. Let's exchange horses."

"You've found just the person to play a joke on," I said.

"No," he said, "I'm in earnest."

"So you're in earnest. And how much is your horse worth?"

"How much would you value him at?" he asks.

"I would value him at three hundred *rubles,* if not a shade more."

He burst out laughing at this and told me that the horse had cost him over three times as much. "Well, is it a deal then?"

I didn't find this kind of talk to my taste. What did he mean by wanting to change his expensive horse for my broken-down nag? I told him to put the deal off for some other time and I asked him jokingly if he had come all the way to my farm just to exchange horses. If so, I told him, he had wasted the train fare. . . .

He answered me quite seriously, "I came to see you, actually, in regard to something else. Shall we take a little stroll together, Reb Tevye?"

"What's he taken to strolling around for?" I thought to myself as I began walking with him in the direction of the wood. The sun had set some time ago and the little green wood was in darkness, the frogs were croaking in the marsh, and the grass was fragrant. Aarontchik walked and so did I. He was silent and so was I. All at once he stopped, cleared his throat and said to me, "Reb Tevye, what would you say if I told you that I am in love with your daughter Schprintze and that I want to marry her?"

"What would I say? I would say that a crazy man's name should be erased and yours put in his place."

He gave me an odd look and said, "What do you mean?"

"Just what I said."

"I don't understand you," he said.

"That shows that you are not very clever. As it is written: *'A wise man hath his eyes in his head.'* Which means that a smart man can understand a nod, but a fool needs a stick."

He said in a hurt tone of voice, "I ask you a plain question and you put me off with proverbs and quotations."

"Every cantor sings according to his ability and every orator speaks of what concerns him. If you want to know what kind of orator you are, talk it over with your mother. She will put you straight."

"I see that you take me for a child that has to run and ask his mother."

"Of course you have to ask your mother, and of course she will tell you that you are an imbecile, and what's more, she will be right."

"And she will be right?"

"Certainly she will be right. What sort of bridegroom would you make my Schprintze? And what kind of match is she for you? And most important of all, what kind of relative-by-marriage will I be to your mother?"

"If that's what's bothering you, Reb Tevye, you can rest easy. I am not a boy of eighteen and I am not looking for rich connections for my mother. I know who you are, and I know who your daughter is. She suits me and that's the way I want it, and that's the way it's going to be."

"Forgive me for interrupting you," I said to him. "I see that you are all done with one side. But have you settled it with the other side?"

"I don't know what you mean," he said.

"I mean my daughter Schprintze. Have you talked to her about all this? And what did she have to say?"

He pretended to look insulted, and then he said with a smile, "Of course I have talked with her, and more than once. I've talked to her many times. I've been coming here every day."

Did you hear that? He's been coming here every day and I knew nothing about it. "You're a donkey, not a man." I said to myself. "You should be given straw to chew on. Letting yourself be led by the nose like that. Your table and chairs could be sold out from under you and you wouldn't know it."

Thinking thus, I walked back to the house with Aarontchik. He took his leave of my family, jumped on his horse, and *"departed like Moses—"* He was off to Boiberik.

And now, it is time, as they say in books, to leave the hero, and follow the fortunes of the heroine, meaning in this case, Schprintze.

"Listen to me, my daughter," I said. "And listen well. Tell me, what did Aarontchik talk to you about behind my back?"

Does a tree answer when you speak to it? That's how she answered me. She blushed like a bride, lowered her eyes, and wouldn't utter a word.

I thought to myself, "If you won't talk now, you will later on. Tevye is not a woman. Tevye can wait." And I waited, as they say, till *"his day will come."* I watched for the moment when we should be alone. Then I said to her, "Schprintze, answer my question. Do you at least know this Aarontchik?"

She said, "Of course I know him."

"Do you know that he is nothing but a penny-whistle?"

"What is a penny-whistle?" she asked.

"It is an empty walnut-shell that whistles when you blow into it."

"You are mistaken," she said. "Arnold is a fine person."

"So he is Arnold to you, not Aarontchik—the charlatan!"

"Arnold is not a charlatan, father," she said. "Arnold has a kind heart. He is a man with principles. He is surrounded by a house full of vulgar people who think of nothing but money, money, and more money."

"So you've become an enlightened philosopher too, Schprintze?" I said to her. "And you've learned to despise money."

I could tell from this conversation that things had gone pretty far with them and that it was too late to undo them. For I know my daughters. Tevye's daughters, as I've told you before, when they fall in love with someone, it's with their hearts and souls and bodies. And I said to myself, "Fool, why do you try to outsmart the whole world?

Perhaps God has willed it that through this quiet little Schprintze you should be rewarded for all the pain and suffering you have undergone until now, and enjoy a pleasant and restful old age, and learn what life can really be like. Maybe it was fated that you should have one daughter, a millionairess. Why not? Won't the honor sit well on you? Where is it written that Tevye should be a pauper all his life, that he should always drag himself around with his horse and wagon, serving the rich people of Yehupetz who like to gorge themselves on butter and cheese? Who knows, maybe it has been inscribed above that I should become an important person in my old age, that I should dispense charity and entertain guests at my home, and sit together with the learned men and study the *Torah?*"

These and other such golden thoughts crowded through my head; as it is written in the morning prayer: *"Many thoughts are in man's heart."* Or, as they say in Russian, "An idea enriches a fool."

I came into the house, took my wife aside and said to her, "How would you like it if your Schprintze became a millionairess?"

"What is a millionairess?" she asks me.

"A millionairess is a millionaire's wife," I tell her.

"And what is a millionaire?" she wants to know.

"A millionaire is a man who has a million."

"How much is a million?" she asks.

"If you are so simple that you don't know how much a million is, how can I talk to you?"

"Who asked you to talk to me?" she says. And she was right.

A day passed, and I came home and asked, "Has Aarontchik been here?" "No, he hasn't." Another day passed. "Was the young man here today?" "No, he wasn't." To go to the widow and ask for an explanation didn't seem proper. I didn't want her to think that Tevye was running after the match. And besides I had a feeling that this whole affair was to her like *"a rose among thorns,"* or like a fifth wheel to a wagon. Though I couldn't understand why. Because I didn't have a million? So I was getting my daughter a mother-in-law who was a millionairess. And whom would her son get for a father-in-law? A pauper, a man who had nothing, a poor wretch called Tevye the Dairyman. Of the two, who had more to boast of? I'll tell you the honest truth, I began to be a little eager for the match myself. Not so much for the sake of the money as for the honor. The devil take those rich people of Yehupetz. It was time Tevye showed them a thing or two. All you had heard in Yehupetz till now was Brodsky and Brodsky and Brodsky. Just as though the rest of us weren't human beings.

This was how I reflected one day driving home from Boiberik. When I came into the house my wife met me with glad tidings. "A messenger has just been here from Boiberik. The widow wants to see you right away. Even if you come home after dark, she wants you to turn right around and go back to Boiberik. She must see you tonight."

"What's the hurry?" I asked. "Can't she wait?" I looked over at Schprintze. She didn't say a word, but her eyes spoke for her. How they spoke! No one could understand what was in her heart as well as I. I had been afraid all along that, who knows, the whole affair might come to nothing, and I wanted to save her heartache. I had said this and that against Aarontchik, belittled him in every way I knew. I might as well have talked to a stone wall. Schprintze was wasting away like a candle.

I harnessed my horse and wagon again and toward evening I set off for Boiberik. Riding along, I thought to myself, "Why should they want to see me so urgently? To arrange a betrothal? He could have come to me for that. After all, I am the girl's father." Then I laughed at the very thought. Who had ever heard of a rich man coming to a poor man? It would mean that the world was coming to an end, and the times of the Messiah had dawned, as some of those modern young people tried to tell me. The time will come, they said, when the rich will divide up everything with the poor, share and share alike— what's yours is mine and what's mine is yours, and everybody will be equal. It seems to me that it's a clever world we live in, and yet there are such fools in it!

I arrived at Boiberik and went straight to the widow's house. I stopped my horse and got off the wagon. Where is the widow? Nowhere in sight. Where is her son? I don't see him either. Then who sent for me? "I sent for you," said a short, round barrel of a man, with a sparse little beard and a heavy gold chain around his stomach.

"And who are you?" I asked.

"I am the widow's brother, Aarontchik's uncle," he said. "I was summoned from Ekaterineslav by telegram and I have just arrived."

"If so, *sholom aleichem* to you," I said, and sat down.

When he saw me sit down, he said, "Be seated."

"Thanks, I am already sitting," I said. "How are you, and how is the Constitution in your part of the country?"

He didn't even listen to me. Instead, he spread himself out in a rocking chair, with his hands in his pockets; and with his big stomach with the gold chain around it turned toward me and said, "I understand your name is Tevye."

"That's right. When I am summoned to read the *Torah,* that's the name they call me by. 'Arise, Reb Tevye, son of Reb Shneour Zalman.' "

"Listen to me, Reb Tevye," he said. "Why should we enter into a long discussion? Let's get right down to business."

"With pleasure. King Solomon said long ago, *'There is a time for eevrything.'* If you have to talk business, then talk business. I am a businessman myself."

"I can see you're a businessman. That's why I'm going to talk to you like one businessman to another. I want you to tell me, but tell me frankly, how much it will cost us all told. Remember now, speak frankly."

"Since you ask me to speak frankly," I said, "I must tell you that I don't know what you are talking about."

"Reb Tevye," he said once more, without taking his hands out of his pockets, "I am asking you how much this affair will cost us?"

"It depends on what kind of affair you mean. If you want an elaborate wedding, the sort of affair you're accustomed to, I'm not in a position to do it."

He looked at me as though I were out of my mind. "Either you are playing the oaf, or you really are one. Though I don't believe you are an oaf. If you were, you wouldn't have gotten my nephew into your clutches the way you did. Pretending to invite him to your house to eat *blintzes* on *Shevuos,* then putting a pretty girl in front of him—whether she is a daughter or not a daughter I won't go so far as to say. . . . But it's plain that she turned his head, made him take a fancy to her, and she took a fancy to him, that goes without saying. She may be a good girl and mean no harm, I won't go so far as to say. But you mustn't forget who *you* are and who *we* are. It seems to me you are a man with brains, how could you permit such a thing? That Tevye the Dairyman who delivers our cheese and milk should marry into our family! You will tell me that they made promises to each other? They can take them back. It's not a great catastrophe one way or the other. If it has to cost us something, we won't argue about it either. A girl is not a young man, whether a daughter or not a daughter, I won't go so far as to say. . . ."

"God in Heaven," I thought to myself, "what does the man want from me?" But he doesn't stop ranting. I needn't think, he tells me, that it will do any good to create a scandal, to spread the news that his nephew wanted to marry my daughter. And I should get it out of my head that his sister is a person who can be milked dry. If I don't make any trouble, well and good, I can get a few *rubles* from her. She will put it down to charity. After all, they are only human, they have to help another person once in a while.

Do you want to know how I answered him? *"May my tongue cleave to the roof of my mouth."* I didn't answer him at all. I had lost my powers of speech. I got up, turned my back on him, and went. I ran as from a fire, I escaped as from a dungeon. My head was humming, everything was going around in front of my eyes, in my ears buzzed bits of his conversation—"Speak frankly now . . ." "A daughter or not a daughter . . ." ". . . milking the widow dry." "Put it down to charity." I went up to my horse, buried my face in the wagon and—you won't laugh at me?—I burst into tears. When I had cried myself out, I got up on the driver's seat, and gave my horse as much as he could hold with the whip. Then I asked God, as Job had once asked Him, "What hast Thou seen in old Job, dear Lord, that Thou never leavest him be for a moment? Are there no other people in the world but him?"

I came home and found my family sitting around the supper table very cheerful, talking and laughing. Only Schprintze was missing.

"Where is Schprintze?" I asked.

"What happened?" they all wanted to know. "What did they want you for?"

"Where is Schprintze?" I asked again.

And again they asked me, "What happened? Tell us."

"Nothing," I said. "What should happen? Everything is quiet, thank God. There is no news of pogroms."

At these words Schprintze came in, looked into my eyes, then sat down at the table, without a word, as though this had nothing to do with her. There was no expression on her face and her silence was unnatural. I didn't like the way she sat there, sunk in thought, and the way she did everything we told her to do. When we told her to sit down, she sat. When we told her to eat, she ate. When we told her to go, she went. And when we called her name, she jumped. My heart ached at the sight of her and inside me burned a fire, against whom I didn't know. "O thou Heavenly Father, God Almighty, why do you punish me so? For whose sins?"

Well, do you want to hear the end of the story? I wouldn't wish such an end to my worst enemies. It would be wrong to wish it to any human being. For the curse of the children is the worst curse in the chapter of *Admonitions*. How do I know that someone didn't visit that curse on me? You don't believe in such things? What else could it be then? Tell me if you know, but what's the good of arguing about it? Better listen to the end of the story.

One evening I was driving home from Boiberik with a heavy heart. Just imagine the grief and the feeling of shame. And then, too, my heart ached for my child. You ask what happened to the widow and her son? They had gone, vanished without a trace. They left without so much as saying good-bye. I am almost ashamed to mention this, but they left owing me a small debt for butter and cheese. But I don't hold it against them, they must have forgotten. What hurt me most was that they went without saying good-bye. What my poor child went through no living person ever knew, except me. I am her father and a father's heart understands. Do you think she uttered a word to me? Or complained, or wept, even once? Then you don't know Tevye's daughters. She kept her grief to herself, but she wasted away, she flickered like a dying candle. Only once in a while she would let out a sigh, and that sigh was enough to tear out your heart.

Well, I was driving home that evening, sunk in meditation, asking questions of the Almighty and answering them myself. I wasn't worried about God so much, I could come to terms with Him, one way or another. What bothered me was people. Why should people be so cruel to each other, when they could be so kind? Why should human beings bring suffering to one another as well as to themselves, when they could all live together in peace and good will? Could it be that God had created man on this earth just to make him suffer? What satisfaction would He get out of that?

Thinking these thoughts, I drove into my farm and saw at a distance that over by the pond a big crowd had gathered, old people, young people, men, women, children, everybody in the village. What could it be? It was not a fire. Someone must have drowned. Someone had been bathing in the pond and had met his death. No one knows where the Angel of Death lurks for him, as we say on the Day of Atonement.

Suddenly I saw Golde running, her shawl flying, her arms outstretched, and in front of her the children, Teibel and Beilke, and all three of them screaming and weeping and wailing: "Daughter!" "Sister!" "Schprintze!" I jumped off the wagon so fast that I don't know to this day how I reached the ground in one piece. But when I got to the pond it was too late. . . .

There was something I meant to ask you. What was it? Oh, yes. Have you ever seen a drowned person? When someone dies he usually dies with his eyes closed. A drowned person's eyes are wide open. Do you know the reason for this? Forgive me for taking up so much of your time. I am not a free man either. I have to get back to my horse and wagon and start delivering milk and cheese. The world is still with us. You have to think of earning a living, and forget what has

been. For what the earth has covered is better forgotten. There is no
help for it, and we have to return to the old saying that as long as
"my soul abides within me"—you have to keep going, Tevye. Be well,
my friend, and if you think of me sometimes, don't think ill of me.

The Merrymakers

(Sketches of Disappearing Types)

CELEBRATING SIMCHAS TORAH

"THE CREW of Merrymakers," we call them in our town, or simply the "Merry Crew." Ordinarily they are timid, unpretentious folk, most of them quite poor, who have nothing to do with each other all year round. But when *Simchas Torah* comes they become jolly and full of life. They get together in one band, and go about the streets arm in arm, singing and dancing, as though they had planned it all out before. They visit every home in town, and wish one and all a merry good *yom-tev*. They invade the homes of the well-to-do householders and treat them to an elaborate *Simchas Torah kiddush,* the ceremonial blessing over wine. The unwilling hosts have no choice but to bring out the best brandy and wine and set the table with food. If they don't, the revelers will get it themselves. They know where everything is kept. They can find their way to the oven, they can drag the preserves out of the cupboard, they can go down to the cellar and bring up the cherry wines, the pickled melons and the cucumbers that the wealthy housewives have prepared for the winter. You wouldn't believe that God-fearing pious Jews would do such things, would you? But on *Simchas Torah* everything is possible.

But all that is nothing. In bygone days (ah, the bygone days!) they themselves would not only get as drunk as Lot, they would also get the mayor and the constables drunk, and all of them together would go dancing coatless and hatless over the roofs of the rich householders.

But times have changed and the mayor and constables have changed with the times. Now we are thankful if they permit us Jews to get drunk once a year and go freely from house to house singing holiday songs. For in some towns, they tell us, even this is forbidden.

Obviously the "Merry Crew" is getting smaller, is shrinking from year to year. Many of the revelers have died out and those who are left will soon go too. And so I hasten to set down their names and to describe each one separately with all his quirks and oddities. Let there be a memorial no matter how small, let there be a record of how Jews used to celebrate and make merry in their exile when *Simchas Torah* came. . . .

Aleck the Mechanic

He is not a mechanic at all, but a tailor, and a little bit of a tailor at that, a dwarf with short legs, tiny hands and a scrap of a beard. But his voice is that of a much bigger man, it's a deep resonant bass voice. Everyone marvels at how such a tiny man can have such a deep voice. But if you are in a mood to ask questions, you might also ask how such a small man can pour so much liquor into himself on *Simchas Torah*.

But it's only on *Simchas Torah*. All year round he drinks nothing, neither whisky nor wine. Not because he is averse to the bitter drop. Far from it. He doesn't drink for the simple reason that he can't afford to. He is a very poor man, almost a pauper. He has a houseful of children to support, but as for work, every year there is less and less. And it's all because of Lazer Ready-to-Wear, may the plague take him. Ever since he opened his Ready-to-Wear store it has become the fashion to buy ready-made clothes and on credit at that, and Aleck the Mechanic has been losing his customers one by one.

You might think that Lazer Ready-to-Wear might at least shove a little work his way, an alteration, a mending job. Not on your life. It all goes to an outsider from the city. Granted that this city tailor is more up-to-date in his work, does one have to go to him for some plain stitching, for making a lining or turning a garment inside out? Can't an ordinary tailor sew on a button, baste a ribbon, press a collar? It seems that he can't!

If this Lazer Ready-to-Wear were a merchant from the city at least! But no! He is one of our own people, a former tailor, a pious, "holier than thou" sort of fellow. He owns his home, he is on friendly terms with the mayor and the police; he travels abroad every summer and brings back all the latest styles and fashion plates. In the Synagogue, he has the best seat, right up front. He is always being called up to read the juiciest portions of the Law. He finds matches for his children among the best families. He has entirely forgotten that he was once a poor tailor himself, in fact the very word "tailor" is distasteful to him. He won't look at an ordinary workman. Poor people are chased from his door with sticks. And the good Lord sees it all and does nothing about it!

On the contrary. Each year Reb Lazer gets more prosperous. It's getting so that it's an honor to be a visitor in his house. You have to ring a bell to get in!

But there is one day in the year when you can get in without special intermediaries, without bells, and without announcements. That day is *Simchas Torah*.

Early in the morning when everyone else is still in the Synagogue, Aleck the Mechanic and the rest of the "Merry Crew," who have prayed and eaten and had something to drink before dawn, go up and down the streets arm in arm singing and making merry. They make the rounds of the houses to wish everyone a merry good *yom-tev*, and first of all they go to the house of the newly rich Reb Lazer Ready-to-Wear. (In honor of *Simchas Torah* the bell has been removed from the door.) Since early morning the table has been set with whisky and beer and a bottle of wine and all sorts of delicacies. Reb Lazer himself meets them at the door with a set smile on his face and asks Aleck to make the *kiddush*. Aleck obliges him by intoning the blessing in his deepest voice, chanting it in real holiday style, mimicking with his motions a cantor in the Synagogue. And the "Merry Crew" answers him like a choir: "A-a-a-men."

Lazer Ready-to-Wear goes into raptures over the *kiddush,* and his wife pretends to rejoice also, while inwardly she is trembling lest they spill wine on her best tablecloth or break one of her wineglasses.

They both consider themselves more than lucky if they escape without a scene. For when Aleck has had a few drinks and is somewhat tipsy he can tell Reb Lazer a few unpleasant truths.

He can take him by the hand and express himself thus, very delicately and subtly: "Listen to me, Brother Ready-to-Wear! Though you hate a poor Jew worse than a Jew hates pork, still because we are celebrating a holiday over the whole world today, and since you treated us to cake and wine, let us now drink each other's health and pray that we live until next *Simchas Torah* and remain as good Jews as we are now. Now let us kiss each other tenderly, and may the world never learn that you are a tailor and the son of a tailor as well as a scurvy knave and a low-down cur and an enemy of all Israel."

When they are through with Reb Lazer, the "Merry Crew" moves on to the next house. There they repeat the *kiddush* with the same flourishes and the same choral accompaniment. They even add a few choice bits to their performance. Aleck the Mechanic is a past master at this sort of thing. For instance, if you beg him very hard he will give you an imitation of a woman going into labor for the first time. Anything to divert the crowd, anything to make them lively and gay, for it's *Simchas Torah* and on *Simchas Torah* everyone must rejoice and make merry.

KOPEL THE BRAIN

That's what he is called, because he has a high, glistening forehead. "A forehead like a prime minister's," they say. But Kopel is not a prime minister. He is only a poor workman. He is a shoemaker.

Kopel is very gloomy by nature. He is always sad, worried, bedraggled-looking, unhappy and pessimistic.

What's the reason for this? Is it because he looks out at the world from a dark cellar? This cellar is his workshop; here is where he pounds on his last. This cellar is also his home; that's where he and his family live. For a shoemaker is not a tailor. A tailor must have light, while a shoemaker can get by in the dark. That is, if you stop to think about it, a shoemaker also has to see where to put his awl through and where to pound the pegs in. But a little window is enough for that, a quarter of a window with a greenish-yellow pane. A man who has sat for so many years on a round leather stool hammering away in the dark can't have a cheerful outlook on life.

And perhaps his melancholy stems from the fact that God has blessed him with such a terror of a wife who, aside from the fact that she makes life miserable for him, never stops talking; her mouth doesn't shut for a moment.

The neighbors call her "Sarah the Speechmaker" because she talks continually without pause and without rest. One thing leads to another, her voice goes on and on without end, its source never seems to run dry.

But we don't expect our reader to take our word for this. And so we present as proof a sample of the talk that Sarah the Speechmaker runs through of a fine morning, while Kopel is pounding on his last and his two apprentices are working alongside of him, one pulling a thread through with an awl, the other trimming a sole. Don't think that Sarah sits with her arms folded. She is doing three tasks at one time; she is peeling potatoes with her hands, she is rocking the cradle with her foot, and with her mouth she is talking away, talking to herself.

"What a day this has been . . . open the doors and gates and windows wide. . . . It's a madhouse, upstairs, downstairs, this one here, that one there. If this hammering would only stop—there he sits and hammers, may it hammer in his head. And she too, that sister of his, the way she claps her tongue, like a bell going ding-dong-ding. A wonderful piece of good luck has happened to her, she got a letter from her Doli, all the way from America. She is ready to lie down and die with gratitude, because he hasn't gone and married another woman out there, that fine husband of hers, may a plague take him, the way Chaya Kayla's husband did. May it sink into the ocean and never rise again—I mean that golden country, America. When they arrive there they forget they ever had a wife at home, they are as free as birds of passage. Shoo phoo, go away, chickens . . . may she sink into the earth. It's impossible to put up with her, with that poultry-woman, I mean, she and her fowls. She doesn't feed them a thing and expects them to get fat. Do you think they would do you a favor and lay an egg once in a while, just enough to brush the Sabbath loaf with? The way they charge for everything now, you can't touch a thing, neither an egg nor a potato nor an onion, though you run looking through the whole town. . . . May her face break out in a rash, may she get a sore in her insides—I mean that peasant, she is so smart she thinks she can swindle a Jew. 'Will you buy one of my chickens for the Sabbath?' It's a chicken just as you are a rabbi. 'And where is your chicken?' She shoves a pullet as big as a flea into your face. 'Is that a chicken?' She gets furious at that and begins teasing you: 'You have no money anyway.' And hides her fine chicken in her bosom. 'Give it to the cats.' As though it wasn't enough, now a tom-cat has stolen in among the cats, the way Peisi Chaim has stolen into that stylish Riva Leah's graces, every morning and every night like a clock, sticking his nose into all the pots and kettles. 'Get out, scat! There is nothing left. It's all dried out.' May your intestines dry out and your brain and your . . ."

"Whom are your cursing?" Kopel asks her curiously, putting down his hammer and turning his high glistening brow toward his wife.

"You and your bastards, that's who," Sarah answers promptly and continues her three occupations—peeling potatoes, rocking the cradle, and talking as before—delighted to have found new material for her tongue to work over, her tongue that goes blabbing on and on, without pause and without rest. Her speech is as bottomless as the ocean, as long as the Jewish exile, as endless as Kopel's misery. Poor Kopel. How he would long to run away, if he weren't chained to his leather stool. But he has to finish a piece of work, or he wouldn't have money to provide for the Sabbath, and if he doesn't provide for the Sabbath he will get the sharp edge of Sarah's tongue.

Yes, Kopel the shoemaker is gloomy and sad, unhappy and depressed. But he doesn't utter a word of complaint. He bears his lot in silence; he carries his sorrow quietly within himself. A man has to be a philosopher to keep so much within himself. Kopel the Brain is a philosopher. A quiet philosopher and a gloomy one.

But if Kopel is gloomy all year round, there is one day when he is cheerful, and that day is *Simchas Torah*. Did I say cheerful? He is like a new-born soul, beside himself with joy, mad with happiness, literally mad. Just imagine Kopel the Brain among the crew of merry-makers, and the merriest one of them all. He has changed hats with Aleck the Mechanic. Since the one has a hat like a washbasin, and the other's hat is no bigger than a fig, you can split your sides laughing to watch them. But hold on, they wanted to change coats too, only Aleck's tiny coat didn't begin to cover Kopel's broad shoulders. It's comical to watch the two of them cavorting together, with their arms around each other, dancing in the streets. And though Kopel has a high thin voice, almost no voice at all you might say, still he summons all the strength he has in his lungs and sings along with Aleck like a faithful choir boy helping his cantor. And when Aleck starts intoning the holiday *kiddush,* Kopel helps him in that too, ending up with a "Bom." And when Aleck has ended the prayer with a drawn out *"M'kadesh Isroel"* and a beautifully warbled *"V'hasminim"* and starts to carry the glass to his lips, Kopel snatches the glass from his hand and before you know what's happened he has drained it and is ready to start dancing. Then Aleck begins to sing and the "Merry Crew" joins in, some singing, others clapping their hands. Here is the song they sing, half in Hebrew, half in Russian:

> Thou has cho-o-osen us
> Out of all the rest.
> Of all the na-a-a-tions
> Thou hast loved us best.

"Louder, men, louder," shouts Kopel the Brain, and his forehead runs with sweat. "Don't worry, brothers, the main thing is not to worry. Just keep on singing, keep on dancing, rejoice and make merry!"

MENDEL THE TINMAN

"Tinsmith" would be more correct, for Mendel is a tinsmith by trade. But we call him the Tinman because he looks just as though he were made of tin. He is tall and thin and erect, and he wears a stiff narrow coat that looks like a tube made of tin. His face is the color of tin and his beard looks like a sheet of tin. Even his voice is tinny. His work is that of glazing samovars. But since samovars in our town are glazed only for Passover, that is the only time when Mendel is busy. The rest of the year he doesn't look a samovar in the face. With such a thriving business, Mendel the Tinman would starve to death if he didn't have more irons in the fire, other means of making a livelihood.

For instance, he knows how to doctor cows, how to make them give milk. You ask what this has to do with tinsmithing? Nothing whatever. But if a man has a talent for something else, what harm is there in using it? For instance, if a man also happens to know how to build ovens? Or to mend broken pots so that no one can recognize that they had ever been broken? And if you think he has no conception of the art of housepainting, then you are mistaken. When a man is talented there is no limit to what he can do.

But don't jump to conclusions. Out of all these trades and occupations Mendel barely gets enough to provide water for his *kasha*. And even for that his wife Reisel has to help him out.

Reisel is a midwife, but without a practice. It isn't that she is not a competent midwife, but there is a new fashion now of training licensed midwives. There is a name for them—*akusherka*. In recent years we have acquired these midwives, or *akusherkas,* in plenty. There isn't a home without its midwife. If a man has three daughters, two of them are *akusherkas,* and the third is studying to be one.

"A town full of midwives," shouts Mendel the Tinman going into a fine rage. "For every woman who gives birth there are two midwives— no, three, for the woman in labor is a midwife herself."

Mendel disapproves of the system. But then Mendel disapproves of everything. He is sharply critical of everything. There isn't a person in town with whom he doesn't find fault, no one of whom he will say a kind word. That's the sort of nature he has. He is a man whom nothing can satisfy and no one can please. For instance, if it's raining outside, he will never say it's a rain, it's always a downpour, a deluge. And on the other hand, if it isn't raining, that's bad too. Then you have a drought, the earth is parched, it's becoming a desert. The sun is never just warm, it's always blazing. Every snowfall is a blizzard. An ordinary frost is not enough for him. It's a "killing frost."

If anyone dies, then the whole town is dying out, people are dropping like flies. Whenever there is a funeral to attend, a condolence call to make, a sickbed to visit, Mendel is among the first. He offers comfort in these words, "It could have been worse." If you have a toothache, Mendel will say, "Do you call that a toothache? If you want to know what a toothache is, ask me." And he will tell you the agony he went through with a bad tooth, or will recount how a friend of his almost died from a sore tooth, he was barely, barely saved. . . .

Or try complaining of a cough. At once he will ask, "Are you spitting blood?" This is not because he wishes you ill or wants you to spit blood. It is just his temperament. He sees everything in the worst possible light; he likes to heap stones on everyone's head. He can't do otherwise. That is the way he was made.

Now would you ever believe that a misanthrope like Mendel the Tinman would be one of the crew of merrymakers on *Simchas Torah* —the greatest comedian, the biggest clown, the craziest buffoon of them all?

On *Simchas Torah*, Mendel becomes a "German." On that day he dresses up like a German and speaks no other language but German. He rolls up his long tube-like coat to look like a short jacket, he combs his earlocks behind his ears till there isn't a sign of hair on his face. And the hat he puts on his head—friends, where in the world does anyone find such a hat? From what ashheap did he rescue it? It is supposedly a "cylinder," a top-hat, but it's all bent out of shape, full of holes and as high as a chimney pot—it has no lid, only a hole on top, a regular factory chimney. And though this chimney pot is well known in town from last year and the year before and the year before that, he is greeted this year with the same joy and amazement with which he was greeted last year and the year before last and the year before that. The band of small boys gives him the same ovation: "Good *yom-tev*, German. Hurrah! Chimney! Hurrah, 'cylinder.' "

But Mendel the Tinman pays no attention to them. He won't have anything to do with the youngsters. Mendel the German has been created for the edification of grownups. The whole town has to enjoy his antics. Tables and chairs are dragged out of doors and Mendel the Tinman (now Mendel the "German") with the tall

chimney pot on his head, one hand on his hip, and in the other a
bottle, dances a German dance and sings a song in German:

> We are Germans,
> Free from sorrow.
> If we have no money,
> We go out and borrow.

And the rest of the crew joins in on the chorus:

> Bim bom, bim bom
> Bim bim, bim bom.

And Mendel sings further:

> For we are Germans,
> One, two, there and here,
> If we can't get whisky
> We'll drink beer.

And the chorus answers:

> Bim bom, bim bom
> Bim bim, bim bom.

And Mendel goes on:

> For we are Germans
> Known to great and small.
> If you won't give us a little,
> We'll take it all.

And the chorus picks it up from there:

> Bim bom, bim bom
> Bim bim, bim bom.

And so on. Suddenly Mendel stops. "Friends!" he shouts in a trans-
port of joy. "I want to know, is there anything better than to be a
Jew? I ask you one thing: What can be finer than to be a Jew on
Simchas Torah?"

The crowd agrees with him that there is nothing better in the world
than being a Jew on *Simchas Torah*. They become noisier and merrier
all the time. They leap higher and higher, spin faster and faster. They
take hands and make a big circle and go around and around, dancing
and stamping their feet in wilder and wilder revelry.

An Easy Fast

AN EXPERIMENT which the famous Dr. Tanner was not able to perform was carried through successfully by a poor little Jew in poor little Kasrilevka. Dr. Tanner set out to prove that a man could fast for forty days, and he tortured himself for twenty-eight days and almost passed away. All through the experiment he was fed teaspoonfuls of water, given pieces of ice to swallow, attendants sat by him day and night watching his pulse. It was a great event.

While Chaim Chaikin showed that a man could fast much longer than forty days. Naturally, not consecutively, one day after another, but at least a hundred days through the year, if not more.

But real fasting!

Did anyone pour drops of water into his mouth? Was he given pieces of ice to swallow? No such thing. To him, fasting meant neither eating nor drinking for a day and a night, twenty-four hours in a row.

There were no doctors sitting at his side, no attendants counting his pulse. Nobody heard. Nobody knew. . . .

What's the story?

The story is that Chaim Chaikin is a poor man with a large family and it's his family that supports him.

His children are for the most part girls, and these girls work in a factory making cigarettes. This one earns a *gulden,* another half a *gulden* a day. And that, not every day. Sabbaths are not included. Nor holidays. Nor the days on which they are out on strike. For everywhere, God be thanked, and even here in Kasrilevka, we have learned how to strike.

And out of these earnings they have to pay rent for the damp corner of the cellar in which they all live.

And out of these earnings they have to buy dresses and shoes. Each girl has a dress of her own, but one pair of shoes has to serve two. And out of these earnings they have to eat. If you can call it eating. A piece of bread smeared with garlic, sometimes a barley soup, once in a while a piece of dried bloater that burns your gullet so that you have to drink all night long.

When the family sits down to eat, they have to divide up the bread and dole out a piece to each one as though it were cake.

"Eat. Eat. All they do is eat," complains Chaika, Chaim Chaikin's wife, a sickly woman who coughs all night long.

"May no harm come to them," observes Chaim Chaikin, and watches the children swallowing chunks of bread without chewing them. He himself would like to take a bite of bread too, but if he did, then the two little ones, Freidka and Beilka, would have to go without supper.

And so he divides his portion of the bread in half and calls over the two small children.

"Freidka, Beilka, here is another piece of bread for each of you. You'll have it for supper." Freidka and Beilka stretch out their thin, scrawny arms and look into their father's face not knowing whether to believe him or not. Could he be teasing them? They take the bread and play with it, stealing little bites out of it every now and then. Their mother sees them and begins scolding, "Always eating, always eating."

The father can't bear to listen to her scolding the children. He would like to say something, but he keeps his peace. He cannot speak, he must not speak. What is he anyway in this house but a broken reed? He is the meanest of the mean. Superfluous to everyone, superfluous to his family, and even superfluous to himself.

What else, alas, can he be, if he does no work? Absolutely none. Not because he doesn't want to, nor because he is too proud, but simply because there is no work for him. None whatever. The whole town complains that there is no work. The town is overflowing with Jews who have been driven there from other places. So many Jews gathered together in one spot. Something to rejoice about. Well, well.

"This too is for the best," reflects Chaim Chaikin. It's a lucky thing he has children who work, others don't even have that. But who likes to be dependent on his children?

For it isn't a good thing to be dependent on one's children. Not because they begrudge him the food. Not at all. It is just that he can't bear to accept it. He simply can't.

He knows how hard the children work all day long. He knows how they are being sweated. He knows it only too well.

Every bite of bread he takes is like a drop of blood to him. He is drinking his children's blood. Do you hear? He, Chaim Chaikin, is drinking his children's blood. And that is more than he can bear.

"Father, why don't you eat?" the children ask him.

"Today is a fast day," he says.

"Another fast day. How many fast days do you observe?"

"Less than there are days in the week."

Chaim Chaikin is not lying. He observes fast days frequently. But there are also days on which he eats.

But the days on which Chaim Chaikin fasts are for him the best days.

"First of all, fasting is an act of piety. With every fast I get closer to winning Eternal Life, my interest in the Hereafter keeps growing . . . my investment in Heaven gets bigger.

"In the second place, nothing is being spent on me, and I don't have to account to anyone. True, nobody asks for an accounting. But why should I owe anything when I can get by just as easily without it?

"And isn't it worth something to me that I feel a little superior to a dumb beast, a cow? A cow eats every day. I can get by, eating only every other day. A man has to rise above an animal."

If a man could only rise so high above an animal that he could get along without eating altogether! But his gizzard, the devil take it, won't let him. Being hungry, Chaim Chaikin begins to spin theories, to philosophize. It's all on account of this cursed gizzard, he thinks, all because of this wretched habit of eating, that most of the troubles of the world come about. It's all because of this habit of eating that I am a poor man and my children have to work and sweat and risk their very lives for a crust of bread.

"Just think, if a person only didn't have to eat, my children would all be home. There would be no more sweatshops. No more strikes. No factories. No factory owners. No rich. And no poor. No fanaticism and no hatred. We would then have a true paradise on earth."

Thus Chaim Chaikin reflects, and he grieves for this wretched world and it pains him. It pains him deeply that God created man so that he is not much better than a cow.

The days on which Chaim Chaikin fasts are, as I've told you, the happiest days for him. And the day of a real fast, the day of *Tish'abov* for instance is (he is almost ashamed to admit it) a real holiday.

Just figure it out for yourself. By not eating that day, he gains so much. He cannot be counted among the dumb beasts, nor does he profit from his children's sweated labor. He performs an act of piety, and he weeps, as a man is supposed to weep, for the destruction of the Temple.

For how can you weep when you are well fed? How can a man with a full belly feel honest grief? To feel real grief a man has to suffer hunger pangs first.

"Look at them, pampering their gizzards. They are afraid to fast, so they bribe the Lord with a *groschen*." Thus Chaim Chaikin rages against those who in order to avoid fasting buy themselves out by putting a *kopek* in the charity box.

The most difficult of all fast days is *Tish'abov*. So the whole world says. Chaim Chaikin can't understand why. Because the day is longer? And the night shorter? Because it's hot outdoors? Who tells you to stroll around in the sun? Sit in the Synagogue and pray. There are enough prayers, God be thanked.

"And I tell you," insists Chaim Chaikin, "that *Tish'abov* is the easiest of all the fasts. For it's the best, the very best of them all. Take, for instance, *Yom Kippur*.—'Ye shall discipline yourselves,' it is written. Which means, 'You shall chastise your bodies.' For what purpose? To win for yourself a lucky number for the coming year. On *Tish'abov*, you are not required to fast, but you fast anyway. For how can you eat on the anniversary of the day the Temple was destroyed? When all the Jews—men, women and children—were slaughtered?

"It is not written that you must weep on *Tish'abov* and yet you weep. For how can you hold back the tears when you remember what we lost on that day?

"The pity of it is that there is only one *Tish'abov*. Only one *Yom Kippur.*"

"And what about the Fast of the 17th day of *Tamuz?*" asks a bystander.

"Only one 17th day of *Tamuz,*" says Chaim Chaikin with a deep sigh.

"And the Fast of Gedaliah? And the Fast of Queen Esther?" the other continues.

"Only one Fast of Gedaliah, only one Fast of Queen Esther," says Chaim Chaikin with another sigh.

"Why, Reb Chaim, you're a regular glutton for fasts."

"There are not enough fast days," repeats Chaim Chaikin. "Not enough fast days." And he undertakes to fast the day before *Tish'abov* too. He will fast two days in a row.

The only difficulty is with drinking. It's hard to go so long without a drink. Chaim Chaikin then resolves to fast a whole week, except for a glass of water every day.

Do you think this is idle talk? Not at all. Chaim Chaikin is a man who "saith and doeth." He does what he says.

For a whole week before *Tish'abov* he stopped eating, he lived on nothing but water.

Who is there to pay any attention to him? His wife, poor thing, is sick. The older children are at the factory, and the little ones are too young to understand. Freidka and Beilka only know that when they are hungry (and they are always hungry) their insides are all twisted up, and they crave food.

"Today you will get an extra piece of bread," their father tells them, and cuts his share in half, and Freidka and Beilka reach out their scrawny hands and grab the bread with delight.

"Father, why aren't you eating?" the older girls ask him. "Surely there is no fast today."

"Who said I was fasting?" he tells them, and he thinks to himself, "I fooled them and yet I didn't tell a falsehood. For what is a drink of water? It is neither fasting nor eating."

When *Tish'abov* Eve came, Chaim Chaikin felt free and happy. He was happier than he had ever been before. He had no desire for food. On the contrary, he felt that if he put a piece of solid food into his mouth it just wouldn't go down. It would simply stick in his throat.

That is to say, that actually he did feel some hunger pangs. His arms and legs trembled and he felt himself sinking, his strength was ebbing, his head was going around, and he was ready to faint. He thought, shame! To have fasted a whole week and then to give in on the very eve of *Tish'abov*. Unthinkable!

And Chaim Chaikin took his portion of bread and potatoes and called over the little girls, Freidka and Beilka, and told them in a low voice, "Children, take this and eat. But don't let your mother see you." The children took their father's share of bread and potatoes, looked up into his face, and saw that it was deathly pale and that his hands were trembling.

Chaim watched the children snatch the food, he watched them chew and swallow and he swallowed his saliva and shut his eyes. Then he got up, unable to wait any longer for the older girls to come home from the factory. He picked up his prayer book, took off his shoes as a sign of mourning, and went to the Synagogue, barely able to drag his feet.

At the Synagogue he was the first to arrive. He got himself the seat right next to the cantor's stand, on an upturned bench which lay against the wall of the pulpit. He provided himself with a bit of snuff which he stuck to the bench, stretched himself out with his head against the pulpit and began to read, "Mourn O Zion, weep O Zion, and all thy cities." He shut his eyes and saw "Zion" in front of him, in the shape of a tall woman dressed in black with a black veil over her face, weeping and lamenting and wringing her hands, mourning for her sons who fall every day on strange battlefields for strangers' sins.

> "You ask O Zion for thy wretched sons
> Who mourn thy fate upon a foreign shore.
> I bring you news of the surviving ones,
> The last sad remnant . . . the others are no more. . . ."

Opening his eyes he no longer saw "Zion" the beautiful woman in black. He saw instead, through the smoke-stained, dirty windowpane, a brilliant ray of the sun that was setting on the other side of the town. And though he shut his eyes again he still saw the rays of the sun, and not only the rays of the sun but the sun itself, the bright sun which no one else could behold and live. He, Chaim Chaikin, was looking straight at the sun and nothing happened to him. Why? Perhaps because he had shed the world and all its possessions. He was happy at last, he was light of heart, he knew that he could endure anything. He would have an easy fast, a very easy fast. . . .

And Chaim Chaikin kept his eyes closed and saw before him a strange world—many strange worlds—which he had never seen before. Angels floated in front of him and he looked at them and recognized the faces of his children, the older ones as well as the younger ones. He wanted to tell them something, but he couldn't speak. He wanted to ask their forgiveness, to explain that he wasn't to blame. Was it his fault that so many people had been herded together into one small spot, so that they were obliged to squeeze and shove and devour each other alive? Was it his fault that there were people who found it necessary to exploit others and suck their blood? Or that human beings hadn't yet attained such a high degree that they didn't have to drive others to work as they might drive a horse? That even a horse should be treated kindly? For he was one of God's creatures too.

Chaim Chaikin with his eyes shut saw the whole world and the world was clear and bright and he saw something rolling upwards like smoke. He felt something leaving his arms and legs, his bowels and his heart, and, pulling itself upward, separating itself from his body. He felt hollow and strangely light and he let out a deep sigh and a long, long groan. Then he felt nothing, absolutely nothing.

When Berel the *Shammes,* a little man with bushy red hair and puffy lips, came to the Synagogue in his stockinged feet with holes in the heels and saw Chaim Chaikin lying with his head against the pulpit, his eyes half open, he was very much annoyed. Thinking that Chaim was dozing, he began mumbling angrily and shaking his fist at him.

The impudence of the man. Spreading himself out like that. Count Pshagnitzky himself wouldn't dare. Probably had a big meal and came here to sleep it off. "Reb Chaim, get up. Reb Chaim, Say—Reb Cha-im."

The last ray of the setting sun burst through the Synagogue window and fell straight on Chaim Chaikin's peaceful face with its shiny, black, curly hair, its thick black eyebrows and its half-open fine dark eyes and it illumined his pale, waxen, starved features through and through. . . .

The Little Pot

RABBI, I want to ask your opinion. . . .

I don't know if you know me or not. I am Yenta—that's who I am—Yenta the Poultrywoman. I sell eggs and chickens and geese and ducks. I have my regular customers, two or three families that keep me going, may God grant them health and fortune. Because if I had to start paying interest, I wouldn't have enough bread to make a prayer over. But this way I borrow three *rubles* here, or three *rubles* there. I take from one and pay back the other, pay this one, borrow from that one—you twist and turn and keep going! Of course, you understand, if my husband were still alive—oh me, oh my! And yet to tell the truth, I wasn't exactly licking honey when he was alive either. He was never the bread-winner, may he forgive me for saying this, all he did was sit and study; he sat over his holy books all day long, and I did the work. I am used to hard work, I've worked all my life, even as a child I used to help my mother, Bashe her name was, Bashe the Candler. She used to buy tallow from the butchers and make candles, she twisted candles from tallow and sold them. That was long before anybody knew anything about gas or about lamps with chimneys that crack all the time—only last week I cracked a chimney and the week before I cracked another chimney. . . .

How did we get around to that? Oh, yes, you say about dying young . . . When he died, my Moses Ben-Zion, he was only twenty-six years old. What? Why do I say twenty-six? Because he was nineteen when we were married, and it's now eight years since he died, and nineteen and eight taken together make—twenty-three. Then how did I get twenty-six out of that? Because I forgot the seven years that he was sick. Actually, he was sick much longer than seven years, he was ailing all his life. That is, in some ways, he was healthy enough, but he coughed all the time, it was his cough that finished him. I shouldn't say that he coughed all the time, but once he got started he couldn't stop coughing—he coughed and coughed and coughed. The doctors said he had a kind of "spasm," this means that when he had to cough he coughed and when he didn't have to, he didn't cough. Doesn't that sound like nonsense? May goats know as much about jumping into strange gardens as these doctors know about curing the sick.

Take Reb Aaron the *Shochet's* boy, Yokel they call him. He had a very bad toothache, and they tried everything—prayers and potions, poultices, lotions. Nothing helped. Then he, that is Yokel himself, goes and puts a piece of garlic into his ear—they say that garlic is good for the toothache. The boy was in torture, he almost hit the ceiling, but he never said a word about the garlic. They call the doctor, and the doctor comes and feels his pulse. What are you feeling his pulse for, you idiot? If they hadn't taken the boy to Yehupetz right then—do you know where he would be resting now? In the same place where his poor sister Pearl is now, the one who passed away in childbirth.

How did we get around to that? Oh, yes, you said about widows . . . I was left a young widow with a small child and with half a house on Pauper's Row—next door to Lazer the Carpenter's, if you know where that is—it's not far from the bathhouse. You will ask me, why only half a house? It's because the other half isn't mine. It belongs to my brother-in-law Ezriel. You must know him, he is a Vaselikuter, he comes from a town called Vaselikut, and he deals in fish. He makes a good living too, depending on the river and the weather. If the weather is mild, the fish bite, and there's a good catch; and when there's a good catch, fish is cheap. But if it's windy, the catch is poor and fish is high. But it's better for everyone if the catch is good and fish is cheap. That's what he says, Ezriel, that is. "What's the sense of that?" I ask him. And he says it's very simple. "If the weather is mild, there's a good catch, and when there's a good catch, fish is cheap. But if the weather is rough, the catch is poor and fish is high. But it's better for everyone if the catch is good and fish is cheap." So I ask again, "Yes, but what's the sense of that?" And he repeats, "It's very simple. If the weather is mild there's a good catch and when there's a good catch fish is cheap. . . ." "Get out!" I tell him. How can you talk to a dummy like that?

Now how did we get around to that? Oh, yes, you say about owning one's home. . . . Naturally it's better to have a corner of your own than to rent from other people. How do you say it, "What's mine is mine and not another's." So I have my own half of a house, my inheritance or property, if you want to call it that. But I ask you, what does a widow with only one child need a whole half house for? If she has a place to rest her head, that's enough. Especially when the house needs a roof—it's been needing a roof for years. He keeps pestering me, that dear brother-in-law of mine, to have a roof put on. "It's time," he says, "we put on a roof." And I say, "Well, why don't we put on a roof then?" And he repeats, "Let's put on a roof." And I, "Come, let's put on a roof." Roof here, roof there—that's as far as it gets. Because if you're going to put on a roof, you need straw. I am not talking about shingles. Where would I get money for shingles?

So I rent out two rooms. In one lives Chaim-Choneh the Deaf, an old man in his dotage. His children pay me five *gulden* a week rent for his room, and he eats with them every other day, that is, one day he eats, and the next day he fasts, and the day that he eats he gets little enough. At least that's what he tells me, I mean Chaim-Choneh the Deaf. And maybe he is lying! Old folks like to grumble. No matter how much you give them, it isn't enough. No matter where you seat them, the place is no good. No matter where you let them sleep, the bed is too hard.

What were we talking about? Oh, yes, you say tenants and neighbors . . . May no good Jew ever have to put up with them. At least, that one, the deaf one, is deaf and he is a quiet old man. You neither see him nor hear him. But it was just my bad luck to rent the other room to a different sort, to a flour-dealer, Gnessi is her name and she has a small shop where she sells flour. What a harridan! At first she was as soft as honeycake. You should have heard her talk. She was all lovey-dovey. "My dear Yenta." "Yenta, my soul." She was going to do this and that for me. What did she need for herself? Nothing but a corner of the oven, just enough room for a small pot, an end of the wooden bench to salt her meat on once a week, an edge of the table to roll a sheet of dough on for noodles once in a blue moon.

"And the children?" I asked. "Where are you going to put those children of yours, Gnessi? You have a family of small children, may no harm come to them." "What are you talking about, Yenta, my life?" she says to me. "Do you have any idea what kind of children they are? They are jewels, they are diamonds—not children. In the summer they play outside all day, and when winter comes they climb up on the oven, quiet as lambs, you don't hear a peep out of them. The only trouble with them is that they eat so much, they have big appetites, God bless them, always chewing on something."

Well, well, if I had only known what I was getting into. Children are children—may God not punish me for my words. But you should see these children. Day and night, night and day, they deafen you with their noise, screaming, shouting, scrapping, fighting. It's a regular *Gehenna*. Did I say *Gehenna*? *Gehenna* is mild by comparison. But don't think that's the end. The children would be half a headache, because after all you can silence a child. You smack it or pinch it or shake it—it's only a child.

But God gave Gnessi a husband too. Ezer, his name is. You must know him, he is assistant *shammes* at the Basement Synagogue—an honest, pious man, poor fellow, and not such a fool either, it seems to me. But you should see the way she treats him, that Gnessi of his. "Ezer, do this." "Ezer, do that." Ezer here, Ezer there—Ezer—Ezer— Ezer. And Ezer? Either he answers with one of his quips—he is a quipster, he likes to make up jokes on top of everything else—or he pulls his cap down low over his eyes and runs out of the house.

How did we get around to that? Oh, yes, you say bad tenants . . . There are bad tenants and bad tenants. I hope God doesn't put me down as a back-biter—I shouldn't speak evil of Gnessi. What have I got against her? She is a woman who won't refuse a beggar a piece of bread. But when she's in a bad humor—may God have mercy! It's a shame to repeat things like that. I wouldn't say it to anyone else but you, and I know that you will keep it a secret. Sssh. She gives him a slap now and then, her husband I mean, when nobody is looking. "Gnessi, Gnessi," I say to her, "have you no fear of God at all?" But all she says is, "It's none of your business." And I say, "You can go— you know where." And she says, "Let him go there, who looks into other people's pots." And I say, "May his eyes fall out, who can't find a better place to look." And she says, "Let him become deaf who listens." Well, what do you think of such a foul-mouth?

What were we talking about? Oh, yes, you said a clean house . . . Why should I lie about it? I like a clean house, clean in every corner. Is there anything wrong with that? Maybe she can't stand it, I mean Gnessi, that my room is so clean and neat, so bright and sweet. And hers? You should see it—always dark and dingy, unswept, unkempt, with dirt and refuse as high as your neck and the water basin always full of slops—Ugh.

And when morning comes, you'd think the heavens were splitting open. Did I say they were children? They are devils, not children. Just compare them with my David. There is no comparison. My David, may he be strong and healthy, is in *cheder* all day; and when he comes home at night he gets to work again, saying his prayers, studying, or just reading a book. And her children? May God not punish me for these words—either they are eating or crying or pounding their heads against the wall. Is it my fault that God blessed her with such a crowd of hooligans and rewarded me with such a prize, such a jewel, may the Lord watch over him, he has cost me so many tears already.

And don't say it's because I am a woman. A man, if he was in my place, would never have lived through it all. I don't want to embarrass you, but there are men who are a thousand times worse than women. Let anything happen to them and they think the world is coming to an end. For example, how much proof do you need? Take Yossi, Moses Abraham's, as long as his Fruma-Necha was alive he was as good as anybody, but as soon as she died, he went to pieces completely. "Reb Yossi," I say to him, "God be with you. It's true that your wife died, but what can you do about it? It's God's work. 'He gives

and He takes away.'" How is it written in the Holy Books? I don't
have to tell you. You must know it better than I do.

Well, how did we get to talking about that? Oh, you were saying
an only child . . . He is my only one, my Dovidl, how do we say
it? The apple of my eye. Don't you know him? He is named after
my father-in-law, David Hersch. If you could only see him, he is just
like his father, just likes Moses Ben-Zion, the same build, the same
face, just like my husband's, yellow, lean, drawn—skin and bones—
and weak, so weak, all worn out from *cheder,* tired out from his
studies. I say to him, "That's enough, Dovidl. Enough, my son, rest
up a little. Just look at yourself. See how pale you look. Take something to eat," I say. "Eat something, drink something. Here, take a
glass of chicory, take it." "Chicory?" he says. "You'd better drink it
yourself, mother. You are working beyond your strength. I wish I
could help you. Let me carry your basket from the marketplace."

"What an idea!" I say. "What are you saying? Do you know what
you are talking about? What do you mean—you will carry baskets?
My enemies will never live to see the day. And I have enough enemies.
I want you to study, just sit there and study." And I look at him, at
my David, sitting there, just like his father. Exactly like him, even to
his cough. Every time he coughs, part of my heart is torn loose. Oh, if
you knew what I went through before I lived to see him grow up.
When he was a baby, you understand, nobody believed he would
survive at all. Every sickness, every ailment, every malady you ever
heard of—he had it. Was it measles? He had the measles. Smallpox?
He had smallpox. Diphtheria also, and scarlet fever and stomachaches
and toothaches. All the nights that I sat up with him—may God
Himself not count them. But with all my prayers and tears, and a
little grace from Heaven, I lived to see him *Bar Mitzvah* at last.

But do you think that was the end of my troubles? Then just listen
to this. He is on his way from *cheder* one night, it's the middle of
winter, and he sees someone coming his way draped in pure white
and slapping his hands together at every step. The poor child is scared
out of his wits, he falls in a faint right into the snow, and they bring
him home half-dead. We barely revive him, and when he comes to, he
runs up a fever and he lies there on fire for six whole weeks.

How I ever lived through those six weeks, I don't know. It must have been a miracle from heaven. What didn't I do to save him? I made vows, I sold him and bought him back again, I gave him an extra name—Chaim-David-Hersch—I did all the customary things. And then my tears, who could count the tears I poured out over him? "Dear God," I pleaded with the Eternal One, "do you want to punish me? Punish me then in any way you like, but don't take my child from me." And God heard me, He granted my wish, the boy became well again, and when he sat up he said to me, "Do you know what, mother? I have a message to you from father. He came to see me." When I heard that my soul almost leaped out of my body and my heart began pounding. "That's a good omen," I told him. "It's a sign that you will get well and live to a ripe old age." But my heart kept on pounding inside of me.

It was much later that I found out what this thing in white had been that scared him so. Can you guess, Rabbi? Well, it was Reb Lippa, that's who it was, Lippa the Water-Carrier. Just that day he had bought himself a coat of white fur, and because it was so bitterly cold outside, he was trying to get warm by slapping his hands together. Have you ever heard anything like it? A man has to go dress himself up in a white fur coat all of a sudden!

How did we get around to that? Oh, yes, you were saying, good health . . . Good health, that's the main thing in life. That's what the doctor says, and he warns me to take good care of my David. "Give him soup," he says. "Make him a soup every day out of at least a quarter of a chicken, if you can manage it." He says to feed him on milk and butter and chocolate, provided I can manage it. Did you ever hear anything like it? *Provided,* he says, that I can manage it. As if there was anything in the world I couldn't manage for my David's sake. For instance, if I were told, "Go, Yenta, dig in the earth, chop wood, carry water, knead clay, rob a church!" If it were for my David's sake, I would do it all, even in the middle of the night and in a bitter frost.

For instance—this was last summer—he decides that he needs certain books. I don't know anything about books and I have no such books. But he says that when I go to the homes of my rich customers I can borrow these books, and he writes the names down on a piece of paper. So I go to them and show them the paper and ask for the books—I ask once, twice, thrce times. They laugh at me. "What do you nced these books for, Yenta? Do you feed them to your chickens and ducks and geese?" "Laugh, laugh, if you like," I think to myself, "just so my Dovidl gets his books." Night after night, all night long, he reads these books, and then asks me to bring him others. Am I going to begrudge him a few books? So I take these back, and bring him others. And now along comes this clever doctor and asks me if I can manage to make soup out of a quarter of a chicken. And if he told me to make it out of three-quarters of a chicken, would that stop me? Tell me, where do they get such smart doctors? Where do they grow them? On what kind of yeast do they raise them and in what oven do they bake them?

How did we get to that? Oh, yes, you were saying, chicken soup . . . So every day I make him a chicken soup out of a quarter of a chicken, and every night when he comes home from *cheder* he eats it. And I sit across the table from him with some work in my hands and rejoice at the sight. I pray to God that He should help me so that tomorrow I should be able to make him another soup out of another quarter of a chicken. "Mother," he asks me, "why don't you eat with me?" "Eat," I say, "eat all you want. I ate already." "What did you eat?" "What did I eat? What difference does it make what I ate, as long as I ate?" And when he is through reading or studying, I take a couple of baked potatoes out of the oven, or rub a slice of bread with onion and make myself a feast. And I swear to you by all that is holy, that I get more enjoyment and satisfaction out of that onion than I would out of the finest roast or the richest soup, because I remember that my Dovidl, may the evil eye spare him, had some chicken soup and that tomorrow he will have chicken soup again.

But still he doesn't stop coughing, he coughs all the time—cough—cough—cough. I beg the doctor to give him some medicine for that cough and he says to me, "How old was your husband when he died, and what did he die of?" "What should he die of?" I say. "Death came to him. His time ran out and he died. What's that got to do with my Dovidl?" "I have to know," he says. "I have examined your boy, he's a good boy and a gifted boy. . . ." "Thank you," I tell him. "That's very kind of you, but I know that myself. What I want is medicine for his cough, something to make him stop coughing." "That I can't give you," he tells me. "But you have to watch him, don't let him study too much." "What then should he do?" "He should eat a lot and go for a walk every day, and the most important thing of all—don't let him sit up nights over those books. If he is fated to be a doctor, tell him he'll become a doctor a few years later." "What kind of nightmare is that? What foolish dream?" I ask myself. "The man is talking out of his head. What does he mean that my Dovidl should become a doctor? Why not a governor? What's wrong with being a governor?"

So I go home and tell David what the doctor said. He becomes red as fire and says to me, "Do you know what, mother? Don't go to the doctor any more—don't even talk to him." "I don't want to see his face," I tell him. "I can see that he's a fool, with that ridiculous habit he has of asking questions of sick people, wanting to know how they live, and where they live and what they live off. What difference does it make to him? Do we begrudge him the half-*ruble* fee? Let him write a prescription, that's what we came for!"

How did we get around to that? Oh, yes, you say I am always hustling and bustling. But who wouldn't hustle and run her legs off with a basketful of eggs and chickens and geese and ducks, and the customers always on my neck, each one wanting to be the first, each one afraid that the others will pick out the largest eggs and the best fowl? Tell me yourself, when do I have the time to cook a chicken soup if I am never home? But how do you say it—a clever person finds a way.

So early in the morning, before it's time to go to market, I light the oven and salt a piece of chicken. Then I run to the marketplace, and later in the morning I run back home, rinse off the chicken, and put the pot on the stove. I ask my tenant Gnessi to watch the pot for me; when the soup comes to a boil, I ask her to put the cover on and bank the pot with ashes and let the soup simmer. Is that too much to expect of a neighbor? Many is the time I have cooked a whole supper for her. After all, we are human beings, we live among people, not off in the woods somewhere. Then at night when I come from work I blow the ashes away, and get the blaze started again, and heat the pot and he has a fresh bowl of soup to eat.

Sounds simple, doesn't it? But then that tenant of mine is a great big—— I won't say the word. Just this morning of all mornings she decides to cook a meal for her children, buckwheat dumplings with milk. With milk, mind you. Now what kind of delicacy are buckwheat dumplings with milk? And why of all times does she have to make them on Friday—the day before the Sabbath? She is a peculiar woman, that Gnessi. With her it's either everything or nothing. For a whole week she won't even light the oven, and then suddenly something gets into her and she has to stir up a whole panful of millet or barley soup, though you'd have to put on a pair of glasses to see a grain of barley in the soup—or else she puts on a pot of fish-and-potatoes with so much onion in it that you can smell it a mile away, and so strongly seasoned with pepper that they go around for a day after with their mouths open and their tongues hanging out trying to cool off. . . .

What were we talking about? Oh, yes, you say a *shlimazl* . . . So my tenant decides to stir up some buckwheat batter, and she puts a pitcher of milk in the oven to boil, and her children start dancing with joy, you'd think they had never seen milk before. . . . And actually, how much milk do you think there was in the pitcher? Not more than two spoonfuls, and the rest water. But to paupers like them, even that's something.

In the meantime some ill wind brings her husband the *shammes* along. It seems that over there in the Synagogue he smelled a feast cooking at home. And he comes flying in with one of his quips, "Good *yom-tev*." "A miserable good *yom-tev* to you," she snarls at him. "What brings you home so early?" "I was afraid I might miss a few blessings," he says. "What are you cooking over there?" "A little pot full of misery, and all for you," she says. "Why not a bigger pot, so there'd be enough for both of us?" he says. "To the devil with you and your jokes," she says and reaches for the milk and upsets the pitcher. The pitcher turns over and splash!—the milk gushes all over the oven.

Then hell breaks loose. Gnessi curses her husband with the deadliest curses. Lucky for him that he took himself off just in time. The children climb off the top of the oven and begin crying and wailing just as though both of their parents had been murdered. "Your dumplings are a small loss," I say, "but my Dovidl's soup is ruined, and I am afraid that my pot has become *treif* in the bargain." "The devil take your pot and your soup," she cries. "My dumplings are just as important to me as all your pots and all the soups that you cook for your pride and joy are to you." "Do you want to know something?" I tell her. "The whole lot of you aren't worth my Dovidl's tiniest fingernail." "You can't say that," she screams. "What's so great about him? He is only one." What do you think of the slut? Doesn't she deserve to be smacked across the face with a wet towel?

How did we get around to that? Oh, yes, you say no good can come of cooking milk and meat at the same time. Well, her pitcher of milk had turned over and the milk splashed over the whole oven. And if a drop of the milk touched my soup pot, then I am lost! Even though you might ask, how could a drop of milk touch it if my pot is banked with ashes and stands far in back of the oven? Still, how can I be sure? Who can tell? It's just my miserable luck. To tell you the truth, I am not worrying so much about the soup. Of course it's something of a heartache, for what will my Dovidl eat tonight? But I will probably think of something. Just yesterday I had some geese killed, and cut up the portions to sell for the Sabbath, and I left a few odds and ends for myself, heads, entrails, this, that—you can make a meal out of those things. But the trouble is I have no pot to cook it in. If you decide that my pot is *treif*, then I am left without a pot, and being without a pot is like being without a hand, because all I have is this one pot to cook meat in.

I had three pots to begin with, but Gnessi borrowed one from me, a brand-new pot, and brought back one that was all scratched and chipped. "What kind of pot is that?" I asked her. And she says, "It's your pot." And I say, "What do you mean by bringing me this broken old pot when I gave you a clean new pot?" "Don't yell like that," she says. "You are not doing me any favors. In the first place, I brought back a fine, clean pot. In the second place, when I got the pot from you it was all scratched and chipped, and, in the third place, I never borrowed a pot from you at all, I have my own pot. So go away and leave me alone." A slut like that!

How did we get to talking about that? Oh yes, you say a housewife can't have too many pots. So I was left with two pots, the chipped one and two good ones, that is, only two pots. But how can a pauper have two good pots? So it has to happen that I come home from the market one day with some chickens, and one chicken gets loose and is frightened by the cat. Maybe you will ask, how did the cat get to be there? It's those children of hers again. They have to go and find a kitten somewhere and bring it home and torture it. "Poor little thing," says my David. "A living creature . . ." But how can you talk to such hoodlums, such loafers? They keep torturing the cat. They tie something to its tail and the cat starts jumping and clawing; the chicken gets frightened and flies to the top shelf and crash!—goes a pot to the ground. And maybe you think it was the chipped one? Of course not. If it had to break, it had to be a good one. That's the way it's always been since the world was created. I want to know, why does it have to be this way? For instance, two men are walking down the street—one walking this way, the other walking the other way—one of them an only child, his mother's darling, and the other one . . .

Rabbi! What's the matter? What's happened to you? Rebbitzen! Rebbitzen! Where are you? Come here, quick. The Rabbi looks sick, he's fainting. Help! Water! Water!

Two Shalachmones

or

A *Purim* SCANDAL

KASRILEVKA had not seen such a warm, mild *Purim* for a long time. The ice had melted early this year, and the snow had turned into mud that stood as high as a man's waist. The sun was shining. A lazy breeze was blowing. A foolish calf sniffing spring in the air lifted up his tail, lowered his head and let out a short me-e. In the streets, snakelike rivulets wound downhill carrying with them anything they came across—splinters, bits of straw, scraps of paper. A lucky thing that almost nobody in town had money for *matzos* yet, or you might have thought it was Passover and not *Purim*.

Right in the middle of town where the mud was deepest, two girls met. Both of them were named Nechama. One was dark-haired and stocky, with thick, dark eyebrows and a pug nose; the other was pale and scrawny with red hair and a pointed nose. The dark-haired girl's short, stocky legs were bare and she wore no shoes. The other girl had on shoes whose mouths gaped open as though begging for something to eat. As she sloshed along in the mud, one of the soles dragged behind making now a slapping, now a squeaking, sound. When she took them off they weighed a ton. Each of the girls was holding aloft in both hands a plate of *Shalachmones* covered with a white napkin. When they saw each other they stopped.

"Hello, Nechama."

"Hi, Nechama."

"Where are you going, Nechama?"

"What do you mean where am I going? I am carrying *Shalachmones.*"

"Where are you carrying it?"

"To your house. And where are you going?"

"What do you mean where am I going? Can't you see that I am carrying *Shalachmones?*"

"Where are you carrying the *Shalachmones?*"

"What do you think? Right to your house."

"That's a good joke."

"A regular farce."

"Come on, Nechama, let's see your *Shalachmones.*"

"You show me yours first."

Both girls looked around for a dry spot where they could sit down. The Lord sent them such a spot. They saw a block of wood in front of a doorway, lifted their feet out of the clayey mud, and sat down on the block. They put their plates on their laps, lifted up their napkins and examined the *Shalachmones.*

First Red Nechama uncovered her *Shalachmones.* She worked for Zelda, the wife of Reb Yossie. She was paid four and a half *rubles* for the winter season and was provided with shoes and clothes besides. But such shoes and such clothes! The dress she wore was covered with patches, still, it was a dress. But her shoes! She wore men's shoes that had belonged to Zelda's son Menashe who had tremendous feet and the habit of turning his heels in. Elegant shoes.

The *Shalachmones* which Red Nechama carried consisted of a large *hamantash* filled with poppyseed, two cushion cakes—one open-faced and filled with *farfel,* the other round and handsomely decorated on both sides—a sugar cooky with a plump raisin stuck right in the middle of it, a large square of *torte,* a big slice of nut-bread, two small cherub cakes, and a large piece of spice cake which had turned out better than any that Zelda had ever made. Whether the flour was exceptionally good this year or the honey purer, or whether the cake had baked just long enough, or she had beaten it more than usual, it doesn't matter. It was light and puffy as a feather cushion.

After she had examined Red Nechama's *Shalachmones,* Black Nechama lifted the napkin off her plate. She worked for Zlata, the wife of Reb Isaac, and got six *rubles* a season, without shoes or clothing. That was why she went barefoot; and Zlata scolded her continually, "How the devil can a big wench like you go around barefoot all winter? You'll catch your death."

But Nechama paid no attention to her. She was saving up her money for Passover. Then she would get herself button shoes with high heels and a new dress. Let Kopel the Shoemaker who was courting her drop dead in his tracks when he saw her.

The *Shalachmones* that Black Nechama carried consisted of a fine slice of *shtrudel,* two big sugar cookies, a large honey *teigl,* two cushion cakes stamped with a fish on both sides and filled with tiny sweet *farfel,* and two large slabs of a poppyseed confection, black and glistening, mixed with ground nuts and glazed with honey. Besides all this, there lay on the plate, smiling up at them, a round, golden sweet-smelling orange that wafted its delicious odor right into their nostrils.

"Listen, Nechama, do you know what? I think that your *Shalachmones* is better than mine," said Red Nechama to Black Nechama, graciously, giving her a compliment.

"Your *Shalachmones* isn't bad either," Black Nechama answered her, returning the compliment. As she spoke she touched her *hamantash* with the tip of her finger.

"What a *hamantash!*" said Black Nechama, licking her lips. "That's what I call a real *hamantash.* I'll tell you the truth, I begrudge my mistress such a delicious *hamantash.* The Lord knows she deserves to get a boil on her face instead. I haven't had a thing to eat all day. I ought to get at least a bite of this *hamantash.*"

"What about me? Do you think I had anything to eat today? If only they got as little to eat the rest of their lives!" Red Nechama looked about her cautiously. "Go on, Nechama, listen to me, take the *hamantash* and break it in half, we'll both have a bite. There is no rule that says that there must be a *hamantash.* See, you haven't any."

"God knows you are right," said Black Nechama, breaking the *hamantash* in half and sharing it with Red Nechama.

"M-m-m. It's perfectly delicious. Too bad there isn't any more. Now that you have given me some *hamantash* I owe you a piece of cake. The way they've been tipping me, they can have a piece of cake less. Just think, I've been running around since early this morning, and guess how much I've made so far. Barely one *gulden* and two *groschen*. And the two *groschen* has a hole in it. How much did you make, my dear?"

"I didn't even make that much, a plague on them," said Red Nechama, taking big bites of cake and swallowing them whole like a goose. "I'll be lucky if I get a *gulden* for the day's work."

"Generous, aren't they, those rich women? I hope they die and get buried," said Black Nechama, licking the crumbs from her fingers. "I came to Chiena the Haberdasher's wife with my *Shalachmones*. She takes it and begins scratching around in her pocket, then tells me to come back later. May the Angel of Death come to her instead."

"That's what I got from Keilah Reb Aaron's," said Red Nechama. "I came to her with my *Shalachmones* and she offers me a cooky. May God offer her a new soul."

"And throw the old one to the dogs," Black Nechama finished for her, and took one of Zlata's big sugar cookies and broke it in half. "Here, eat this, my dear. May the worms eat them. If your mistress has one cooky less, it won't hurt me any."

"Oh, my goodness!" Red Nechama jumped up suddenly and began wringing her hands. "Look at what's left of my *Shalachmones*."

"They will never find out," Black Nechama comforted her. "Don't be frightened, foolish girl. They are so busy with their *Shalachmones* today, they won't notice anything."

And the two girls covered up their *Shalachmones* with their napkins and went off through the mud, one this way, and one that way, as though nothing had happened.

Zelda, Reb Yossie's wife, a round-faced, rather good-looking woman in a red silk apron with white dots, stood at her table arranging and distributing the *Shalachmones* she had received and that which she had to send out. Reb Yossie Milksop (that was the nickname he was known by in Kasrilevka) lay on the sofa snoring, and Menashe, her eighteen-year-old son, a large boy with red cheeks and a shiny long coat, hung around his mother snatching now a piece of honeycake, now two poppyseed bars, now a cooky. He had stuffed himself so full of these good things that his teeth and lips were black and his stomach was beginning to rumble.

"Menashe, when will you stop eating? Menashe, haven't you had enough?" Zelda kept saying to him.

"Enough, enough," he mimicked her, and stuffed another chunk of cake into his mouth, "the very last one" this time, and licked his lips with his tongue.

"Good *yom-tev*, my mistress sent you *Shalachmones*," said Black Nechama, walking in and handing her the covered plate.

"Whom do you work for?" said Zelda, smiling graciously and taking the plate from her.

"I work for Zlata, Reb Isaac's-May-his-tribe-increase," said Black Nechama, and waited for Zelda to take the *Shalachmones* and return the plate to her.

Zelda put one hand into her pocket to give the girl a *kopek* for the trip and with the other she uncovered the plate. She took one look and stood there as if turned to stone.

"What is this? Menashe, just take a look."

Menashe took one look at the *Shalachmones,* grabbed himself around the middle and doubled over with laughter. He laughed so hard that Reb Yossie Milksop almost rolled off his couch in fright.

"Ha?" he cried. "What is it? What's happened? Who's there?"

"Look at this *Shalachmones,*" said Zelda, folding her arms over her stomach. Menashe kept on laughing, and Reb Yossie spat in disgust, turned himself around to the wall and went back to sleep.

Zelda threw the plate with the napkin back at Nechama and said to her, "Tell your mistress that I hope she lives until next year and isn't able to afford a better *Shalachmones* than this."

"Amen, the same to you," said Black Nechama, taking the plate.

"To the devil with you," said Zelda angrily. "The insolence of the wench! Did you ever see the like of it, Menashe?"

Zlata, Reb Isaac's wife, a woman who gives birth to a child every year and is always doctoring in between, was so worn out from receiving and sending *Shalachmones* that she had to sit down on a chair and order her husband Isaac around. (He was known as Isaac-May-his-tribe-increase because of the fact that his wife presented him with a child every year.)

"Isaac, take this piece of *torte* there and put it right here. And take that piece of nut-bread and those two poppyseed bars from over there and put them here. Isaac, hand me that cushion cake—not that one, this one. Get a move on you, Isaac. Look at the way I have to show him how to do the least little thing, like a baby. And take that cake there, the bigger one, and put it here, like this. And cut that piece of *torte* in half, this piece is too large. Isaac! Get out of here, you brats. Get!"

These last words were addressed to a swarm of half-naked youngsters who stood around her watching the sweets with greedy eyes and drooling mouths. Though she chased them away, the children kept stealing back to the table, trying to lift a cooky or a sweet from the pile. The mother would catch them at it, and give them now a slap, now a shove, now a cuff on the nape of the neck.

"Good *yom-tev,* my mistress sends you *Shalachmones,*" said Red Nechama, bringing in the covered plate of *Shalachmones.*

"Whom do you work for?" asked Zlata, smiling sweetly and taking the plate out of her hands.

"I work for Zelda, Reb Yossie Milksop's," said Red Rechama, and waited for her plate to be returned to her.

Zlata reached one hand into her pocket to tip the girl and with the other she uncovered the plate, and almost fainted on the spot.

"Of all the black, miserable, ugly nightmares that anybody ever had. Of all the bad luck that I wish to my enemies. Look at this *Shalachmones.* She's insulting me, the slut.

"Here, give this back to your mistress," and Zlata flung the plate with the napkin with the *Shalachmones* straight into Red Nechama's face.

Reb Yossie Milksop and Reb Isaac-May-his-tribe-increase are both shopkeepers in Kasrilevka. Their stores are right next door to each other. Though they are competitors and don't hesitate to drag customers away from each other, still they are good friends and neighbors. They borrow money from each other, go to each other's homes for *kiddush* during the holidays, help each other celebrate family events such as weddings and circumcisions. In summer they sit together all day playing dominoes, and in winter they run in to warm themselves at each other's stoves. Their wives are close friends also. They gossip together about the whole world, borrow flour and sugar from each other, entrust each other with their deepest secrets. They seldom quarrel, and if they do fall out over some trifle, they make up very quickly. In short, they live together as peacefully as doves in a dovecote.

The day after *Purim* when Reb Isaac-May-his-tribe-increase went to open his shop, Reb Yossie Milksop already stood in front of his shop all puffed up like a turkey cock waiting for Reb Isaac to come up and tell him good morning so that he could snub him. Reb Isaac, who had been well-primed by his wife also, unlocked the door and stood waiting for Reb Yossie to come up to him first so that he could snub him. And so they stood there, opposite each other, like two angry cocks, and they would have stood there all day if their wives hadn't appeared just then from the marketplace with angry faces and eyes flashing fire.

"Isaac, why don't you thank him for the wonderful *Shalachmones* that his wife sent me?" said Zlata to her husband.

"Yossie, why don't you say something about the *Shalachmones* we got?" Zelda demanded of her husband.

"Isaac, did you hear that? Isaac, she is picking on us. Why don't you speak to him, Isaac?"

"How can I talk to a milksop like him?" said Reb Isaac, speaking loudly enough for Reb Yossie to hear.

"I am afraid to start anything with a fellow with such a fine name as Isaac-May-his-tribe-increase."

What's so terrible in the words "May his tribe increase?" It seems to me it's a harmless enough blessing, but Reb Isaac could put up with anything in the world better than with being called Isaac-May-his-tribe-increase. He would rather be cursed with the blackest curses, and he would gladly tear the person apart who called him by that nickname.

It was the same with Reb Yossie. He would rather get a slap in the face than be called a milksop.

People came running from all over the marketplace, and tried to separate the two men. They couldn't understand how two such close friends and neighbors had suddenly become tangled in each other's beards. But Reb Isaac and Reb Yossie, Zelda and Zlata were all talking together, one trying to outshout the other, and making such a racket that all that anyone could make out was the word *Shalachmones* repeated over and over. Which *Shalachmones?* What about the *Shalachmones?* It was impossible to get to the bottom of it.

"If you don't report the Milksop to the Magistrate, you might as well put an end to your life," Zlata screamed at her husband.

And Reb Yossie appealed to the gathering.

"Good people, you are witnesses here that the slut called me 'Milksop.' I am going to report her to the Magistrate, and her husband, Isaac-May-his-tribe-increase."

"Friends," called out Reb Isaac, "I ask you to be witnesses before the Magistrate that this—this—this—I don't want to call him by his elegant name—just called me Isaac-May-his-tribe-increase."

Within the hour both parties went to Zaidel the Clerk, each of them bringing his own witnesses, and drew up a complaint to the Magistrate.

The Kasrilevka Magistrate, Pan Milinewsky, a portly squire with a long beard and a high forehead, had been magistrate for so long that he was acquainted with the whole town, was on good terms with everyone, and especially with the Jews of Kasrilevka. He knew each one's weaknesses and peculiarities thoroughly and spoke Yiddish as well as any of them. "He has a real Jewish head on his shoulders," they used to say about him in Kasrilevka.

In autumn, around the time of the high holidays, he was deluged with written complaints, all of them from Jews. They were not, God forbid, reports of thefts or robberies or serious crimes. No! They were all concerned with petty quarrels, and fights over precedence in the Synagogue and interpretations of the Law over the privilege of closing and reopening the reading of the *Torah*. Pan Milinewsky didn't stand on ceremony with the Jews of Kasrilevka. He didn't like to enter into long disputes with them and never let them talk much, because he knew that once started they would never stop. If they were willing to make peace, good. He was all for making peace. If not, he put on his chain and laid down the judgment, *"Po ukazu na osnowanie, takoio-to i takoio.* I hereby pronounce that Hershko may read for three days and Yankel may read the next three." As you see, he made no exceptions and he had no favorites.

Exactly two weeks before Passover the case of the *Shalachmones* came up. The Magistrate's office was crowded with people, most of whom were witnesses for either one or the other party. They were wedged in so tightly there wasn't room for a pin to squeeze through among them.

"Izak, Yosek, Zlata, Zelda," Pan Milinewsky called out, and from the front row stepped out Reb Yossie Milksop, Reb Isaac-May-his-tribe-increase and their wives. Before the Magistrate could say a word, all four began talking at once, and of course the women outtalked the men.

"Gospodin Mirovoi," said Zelda, pushing her husband aside and pointing at Zlata. "This here slut sent me this *Purim* a *Shalachmones* that made me a laughing stock before the town. A wretched little piece of *shtrudel* and one cooky. It's an insult, a disgrace." And she spat.

"Oh, oh, I can't stand it, I can't," shouted Zlata, beating her breast. "May God give me such a piece of gold . . ."

"Amen," said Zelda.

"Shut up, you loud-mouth. Two cushion cakes, *Gospodin Mirovoi,* as I live, and one nut-bread, and a cake, may God punish her, and macaroons. May the plagues descend on her. And a *hamantash*. Woe is me."

"What *hamantash?* There was no *hamantash*. She is lying."

The Magistrate tried to calm down the women, first gently and then with force, ringing his bell for them to be quiet. When he saw that he was getting nowhere and that it was impossible to shut them up, he chased them out of the room so that he could hear himself talk and he advised the men to go to the Rabbi.

"*Do rabina,*" he told them. "Go to the Rabbi with your *hamantash.*"

And the crowd all went off to the Rabbi.

Reb Yozifel, the Rabbi, as our readers know, is a man who can bear up under anything. He is willing to hear everyone out to the end. Reb Yozifel goes according to the theory that every person, no matter how long he talks, must finally stop; for a man, he says, is not a machine. The only trouble was that this time all four of the litigants talked at once and even the bystanders each tried to get a word in.

But what did it matter? Everything in the world must come to an end; and when everyone had talked himself out, and it grew quiet again, Reb Yozifel addressed himself to both sides, speaking calmly and pleasantly as was his custom. He gave a sigh, and began:

"Ah, my children, we are now approaching a holiday, a blessed holiday, Passover. Does it mean anything to you? Reflect, my children. Our ancestors escaped from Egypt, they came to a sea and the sea divided itself and they crossed upon dry ground. They wandered in the desert for forty years. Think of it, forty years. They received the Holy *Torah* on Mt. Sinai. The *Torah* in which it is written '*V'ahavta* —and thou shalt love—*l'reachta*—thy neighbor—*kamocha*—as thyself.' And now it has come to this, that we quarrel and bicker among ourselves 'because of our many sins'; we tear each other's beards out, and over what? Over foolishness, mere childishness. It's a disgrace, I tell you, a disgrace and a reproach. At a time like this we should be thinking instead of providing the poor with *matzos* for Passover. There are many people in our town who will be without *matzos.* Of eggs and chicken fat and other things, I do not even speak. But *matzos,* God in Heaven, we must provide them with *matzos.* Reflect, my children. Our ancestors escaped from Egypt, they came to the sea and the waters divided themselves and they crossed upon dry ground. They wandered in the desert for forty years. They received the blessed *Torah* on Mt. Sinai. Take my advice, my children, you are all children of Israel, ask each other's forgiveness, make peace with each other and go home and bear in mind the blessed holiday that is approaching. . . ."

Slowly, one by one, one by one, the people began slipping out of the Rabbi's house. They made a jest about Reb Yozifel's verdict, in typical Kasrilevka fashion—"It's not a sentence, but a discourse." But each one felt deep in his own heart that Reb Yozifel was right and they were ashamed to talk further about the *Shalachmones*.

On the first day of Passover, after the services at the Synagogue, Reb Yossie Milksop (he was the younger of the two) went to the home of Reb Isaac-May-his-tribe-increase, for *kiddush*. He praised the Passover wine which had turned out exceptionally well this year and licked his fingers after Zlata's *falirchiks*. On the second day of Passover, after the services, Reb Isaac (he was the older of the two) went to Reb Yossie's house, praised the raisin wine to the skies and smacked his lips over Zelda's *falirchiks*.

And that afternoon, after dinner, when the two women got together and talked over the *Shalachmones*, the truth rose like oil on the waters and both girls, Red Nechama and Black Nechama, got their just deserts. Right after Passover they were both sent packing.

Tevye Goes to Palestine

WELL, well, look who's here! Reb Sholom Aleichem, how are you? You're almost a stranger. I never dreamed of this pleasure. Greetings! Here I've been wondering over and over, why we haven't seen him all this time, either in Boiberik, or in Yehupetz. Who can tell? Maybe he had packed up and left us altogether—gone off yonder where people don't even know the taste of radishes and chicken fat. But then I thought: Why should *he* do such a foolish thing? A man of wisdom and learning like *him*? Well, thank God, we meet again in good health. How does the passage go? *"A wall cannot meet a wall*—Man meets man. . . ."

You are looking at me, sir, as though you didn't recognize me. It's me, your faithful old friend, Tevye. *"Look not at the pitcher but at its contents."* Don't let my new coat fool you; it's still the same *shlimazl* who's wearing it, the same as always. It's just that when a man puts on his Sabbath clothes, right away he begins to look like somebody—as though he were trying to pass for a rich man. But when you go forth among strangers you can't do otherwise, especially if you are setting out on a long journey like this, all the way to Palestine. . . .

You look at me as if you're thinking: How does it happen that a plain little man like Tevye, who spent all his life delivering milk and butter, should suddenly get a notion like this into his head— something that only a millionaire like Brodsky could allow himself in his old age? Believe me, Mr. Sholom Aleichem, *"it is altogether questionable. . . .*" The Bible is right every time. Just move your suit-case over this way, if you will be so good, and I will sit down across from you and tell you the whole story. And then you'll know what the Lord can do. . . .

But first of all, before I go on, I must tell you that I have been a widower for some time. My Golde, may she rest in peace, is dead. She was a plain woman, without learning, without pretensions, but extremely pious. May she intercede for her children in the other world; they caused her enough suffering in this one, perhaps even brought on her untimely death. She couldn't bear it any longer, seeing them scatter and disappear the way they did, some one way, some ·another. "Heavens above!" she used to say. "What have I left to live for, all alone without kith or kin? Why, even a cow," she would say, "is lonesome when you wean her calf away from her."

That's the way she spoke, and she wept bitterly. I could see the poor woman wasting away, day by day, going out like a candle, right before my eyes. And I said to her with my heart full of pity, "Ah, Golde, my dear, there is a text in the Holy Book: *'Im ḳ'vonim im ḳ'vodim—Whether we're like children or like slaves,'* which means that you can live just as well with children as without them. We have," I told her, "a great Lord and a good Lord and a mighty Lord, but just the same I'd like to be blessed for every time He puts one of His tricks over on us."

But she was, may she forgive me for saying this, only a female. So she says to me, "It's a sin to speak this way, you mustn't sin, Tevye." "There you go," said I. "Did I speak any evil? Did I do anything contrary to the Lord's will? All I meant was that if He went ahead and did such a fine job of creating this world of His so that children are not children, and parents are no better than mud under one's feet, no doubt He knew what He was doing."

But she didn't understand me. Her mind was wandering. "I am dying, Tevye," she said. "And who will cook your supper?" She barely whispered the words and the look in her eyes was enough to melt a stone. But Tevye is not a weakling; so I answered her with a quip and a quotation and a homily. "Golde," I said to her, "you have been faithful to me these many years, you won't make a fool of me in my old age." I looked at her and became frightened. "What's the matter with you, Golde?" "Nothing," she whispered, barely able to speak. Then I saw that the game was lost. I jumped into my wagon and went off to town and came back with a doctor, the best doctor I could find. When I come home, what do I see? My Golde is laid out on the ground with a candle at her head, looking just like a little mound of earth that had been raked together and covered with a black cloth. I stand there and think to myself: " '*Is that all that man is? —Is this the end of man?*' Oh, Lord, the things you have done to your Tevye. What will I do now in my old age, forsaken and alone?" And I threw myself on the ground.

But what good is shouting and weeping? Listen to me and I will tell you something. When a person sees death in front of him he becomes a cynic. He can't help thinking, "*What are we and what is our life?*—What is this world altogether with its wheels that turn, its trains that run wildly in all directions, with all its tumult and confusion, noise and bustle?" And even the rich men with all their possessions and their wealth—in the end they come to nothing too.

Well, I hired a *kaddish* for her, for my wife Golde, and paid him for the whole year in advance. What else could I do if God had denied us sons to pray for us when we were dead, and given us only daughters, nothing but daughters one after another? I don't know if everybody else has as much trouble with his daughters, or if I'm the only *shlimazl,* but I've had no luck with any of my daughters. As far as the girls themselves are concerned, I have nothing to complain about. And as for luck—that's in God's hands. I wish I had half the happiness my girls wish me to have. If anything, they are too loyal, too faithful—and too much of even the best is superfluous. Take my youngest, for instance—Beilke we call her. Do you have any idea of the kind of girl she is? You have known me long enough to know that I am not the kind of father who will praise his children just for the sake of talking. But since I've mentioned Beilke I'll have to tell you this much: Since God first began making Beilkes, He never created another like this Beilke of mine. I won't even talk about her looks. Tevye's daughters are all famous for their great beauty, but this one, this Beilke, puts all the others in the shade. But beauty alone is nothing. When you speak of Beilke, you really have to use the words of the Proverbs regarding *"a woman of valor."* Charms are deceitful. I am speaking of character now. She is pure goodness all the way through. She had always been devoted to me, but since Golde died I became the apple of her eye. She wouldn't let a speck of dust fall on me. I said to myself, as we say on the High Holy Days: *"The Lord precedes anger with mercy.*—God always sends a remedy for the disease." Only sometimes it's hard to tell which is worse, the remedy or the disease.

For instance, how could I have foreseen that on my account Beilke would go and sell herself for money and send her old father in his declining years to Palestine? Of course that's only a way of speaking. She is as much to blame for this as you are. It was all his fault, her chosen one. I don't want to wish him ill, may an armory collapse on him. And yet if we look at this more closely, if we dig beneath the surface, we might find out that I am to blame as much as any-one, as it says in the *Gamorah: "Man is obligated* . . ." But imagine my telling *you* what the *Gamorah* says.

But I don't want to bore you with too long a tale. One year passed, then another. My Beilke grew up and became a presentable young woman. Tevye kept on with his horse and wagon, delivering his milk and butter as usual, to Boiberik in the summer, to Yehupetz in the winter—may a deluge overtake that town, as it did Sodom. I can't bear to look at that place any more, and not so much the place as the people in it, and not so much the people as one man, Ephraim the *Shadchan,* the matchmaker, may the devil take him and his father both. Let me tell you what a man, a *shadchan,* can do.

"And it came to pass," that one time, in the middle of September, I arrived in Yehupetz with my little load. I looked up—and behold! *"Haman approacheth.* . . ." There goes Ephraim the *Shadchan.* I think I've told you about him before. He is like a burr; once he at-taches himself to you, you can't get rid of him. But when you see him you have to stop—that's the power he has in him.

"Whoa, there, my sage!" I called out to my little horse. "Hold on a minute and I'll give you something to chew on." And I stop to greet the *shadchan* and start a conversation with him. "How are things going in your profession?" With a deep sigh he answers, "It's tough, very tough." "In what way?" I ask.

"There's nothing doing."

"Nothing at all?"

"Not a thing."

"What's the matter?"

"The matter is," says he, "that people don't marry off their children at home any more."

"Where do they marry them off?"

"Out of town, out of the country in fact."

"Then what can a man like me do," I say, "who has never been away from home and whose grandmother's grandmother has never been away either?"

He offers me a pinch of snuff. "For you, Reb Tevye," he says, "I have a piece of merchandise right here on the spot."

"For instance?"

"A widow without children, and with a hundred and fifty *rubles* besides. She used to be a cook in the very best families."

I give him a look. "Reb Ephraim, for whom is this match intended?"

"For whom do you suppose? For you."

"Of all the crazy fantastic ideas anybody ever had, you've dreamed up the worst." And I whipped my horse and was ready to start off. But Ephraim stopped me. "Don't be offended, Reb Tevye, I didn't want to hurt your feelings. Tell me, whom did *you* have in mind?"

"Whom should I have in mind? My youngest daughter, of course."

At this he sprang back and slapped his forehead. "Wait!" he cried. "It's a good thing you mentioned it! God bless you and preserve you, Reb Tevye."

"The same to you," I said. "Amen. May you live until the Messiah comes. But what makes you so joyful all of a sudden?"

"It's wonderful! It's excellent! In fact, it's so good, it couldn't possibly be any better."

"What's so wonderful?" I ask him.

"I have just the thing for your daughter. A plum, a prize, the pick of the lot. He's a winner, a goldspinner, a rich man, a millionaire. He is a contractor and his name is Padhatzur."

"Hmm. Padhatzur? It sounds familiar, like a name in the Bible."

"What Bible? What's the Bible got to do with it? He is a contractor, this Padhatzur, he builds houses and factories and bridges. He was in Japan during the war and made a fortune. He rides in a carriage drawn by fiery steeds, he has a lackey at the door, a bathtub right in his own house, furniture from Paris, and a diamond ring on his finger. He's not such an old man either and he's never been married. He is a bachelor, a first-class article. And he's looking for a pretty girl; it makes no difference who she is or whether she has a stitch to her back, as long as she is good-looking."

"Whoa, there! You are going too fast. If you don't stop to graze your horses we'll land in Hotzenplotz. Besides, if I'm not mistaken you once tried to arrange a match for this same man with my older daughter, Hodel."

When he heard this, the *shadchan* began laughing so hard I was afraid the man would get a stroke. "Oh-ho, now you're talking about something that happened when my grandmother was delivered of her firstborn. That one went bankrupt before the war and ran off to America."

"*'When you speak of a holy man, bless him. . . .'* Maybe this one will run off too."

He was outraged at this. "How can you say such a thing, Reb Tevye? The other fellow was a fraud, a charlatan, a spendthrift. This one is a contractor, with business connections, with an office, with clerks, everything."

Well, what shall I tell you—the matchmaker became so excited that he pulled me off the wagon and grabbed me by the lapels, and shook me so hard that a policeman came up and wanted to send us both to the police station. It was lucky that I remembered what the passage says: *"You may take interest from a stranger.*—You have to know how to deal with policemen."

Well, why should I drag this out? Padhatzur became engaged to my daughter Beilke. *"The days were not long."* It was quite a while before they were married. Why do I say it was quite a while? Because Beilke was no more eager to marry him than she was to lie down and die. The more he showered her with gifts, with gold watches and rings and diamonds, the more distasteful he became to her. I am not a child when it comes to such matters. I could tell from the look on her face and from her eyes red with weeping how she felt. So one day I decided to speak to her about it. I said to her as if I had just this minute thought of it, "I am afraid, Beilke, that this groom of yours is as dear and sweet to you as he is to me."

She flared up at this. "Who told you?"

"If not," I said, "why do you cry nights?"

"Have I been crying?"

"No, you haven't been crying, you've just been bawling. Do you think if you hide your head in your pillow you can keep your tears from me? Do you think that your father is a little child, or that he is in his dotage and doesn't understand that you are doing it on his account? That you want to provide for him in his old age, so he will have a place to lay his head and won't have to go begging from house to house? If that's what you have in mind, then you are a big fool. We have an all-powerful God, and Tevye is not one of those loafers who will fold his hands and live on the bread of charity. *'Money is worthless,'* as the Bible says. If you want proof, look at your sister Hodel, who is practically a pauper; but look at what she writes from the ends of the earth, how happy she is with her Feferl." Well, do you know what she said to this? Try and make a guess.

"Don't compare me to Hodel," she said. "Hodel grew up in a time when the whole world rocked on its foundations, when it was ready at any moment to turn upside down. In those days people were concerned about the world and forgot about themselves. Now that the world is back to where it was, people think about themselves and forget about the world." That's how she answered, and how was I to know what she meant?

Well. You know what Tevye's daughters are like. But you should have seen my Beilke at her wedding. A princess, no less. All I could do was stand and gaze at her, and I thought to myself, "Is this Beilke, a daughter of Tevye? Where did she learn to stand like this, to walk

like this, to hold her head like this, and to wear her clothes so that
she looked as though she'd been poured into them?"

But I wasn't allowed to gaze at her very long, for that same day at
about half past six in the evening the young couple arose and departed.
—They went off, the Lord knows where, to Nitaly somewhere, as is
the custom with the rich nowadays, and they didn't come back until
around *Hannukah*. And when they came back I got a message from
them *to be sure* to come to see them in Yehupetz at once, *without fail*.

What could it mean? If they just wanted me to come, they would
simply have asked me to come. But why *be sure to come* and *without
fail?* Something must be up. But the question was, what? All sorts
of thoughts, both good and bad, crowded through my head. Could
the couple have had a fight already and be ready for a divorce? I
called myself a fool at once. Why did I always expect the worst?
"Maybe they are lonesome for you and want to see you? Or maybe
Beilke wants her father close to her? Or perhaps Padhatzur wants
to give you a job, take you into the business with him, make you the
manager of his enterprises?" Whatever it is, I had to go. And I got
into my wagon, and *"went forth to Heron."* On to Yehupetz!

As I rode along, my imagination carried me away. I dreamed that
I had given up the farm, sold my cows, my horse and wagon and
everything else, and had moved into town. I had become first a fore-
man for my son-in-law, then a paymaster, then a factotum, the general manager of all his enterprises, and finally a partner in his business, share and share alike, and rode along with him behind the
prancing steeds, one dun-colored and the other chestnut. And I
couldn't help marveling, *"What is this and what is it all for?"* How
does it happen that a quiet, unassuming man like me should have
suddenly become so great? And what do I need all this excitement
and confusion for, all the hurry and flurry, day and night, night and
day? How do you say it? *"To seat them with the mighty*—hobnob-
bing with all the millionaires?" Leave me be, I beg of you. All I want
is peace and quiet in my old age, enough leisure so that I can look
into a learned tome now and then, read a chapter of the Psalms. A
person has to think once in a while of the next world too. How does

King Solomon put it? Man is a fool—he forgets that no matter how
long he lives he has to die sometime.

It was with thoughts like these running through my head that I
arrived in Yehupetz and came to the house of Padhatzur. What's the
good of boasting? Shall I describe to you his *"abundance of wealth"*?
His house and grounds? I have never had the honor of visiting Brodsky's house, but I can hardly believe that it could be more splendid
than my son-in-law's. You might gather what sort of place it was
from the fact that the man who stood guard at the door, a fellow
resplendent in a uniform with huge silver buttons, wouldn't let me
in under any consideration. What kind of business was this? The
door was of glass and I could see the lackey standing there brushing
clothes, may his name and memory be blotted out. I wink at him, I
signal to him in sign language, show him with my hands that he
should let me in because the master's wife is my own flesh and blood,
my daughter. But he doesn't seem to understand me at all, the pigheaded lout, and motions to me also in sign language to go to the
devil, to get out of there.

What do you think of that? I have to have special influence to get
to my own daughter. "Woe unto your gray hairs," I told myself.
"So this is what you have come to." I looked through the glass door
again and saw a girl moving about. A chambermaid, I decided,
noticing her shifty eyes. All chambermaids have shifty eyes. I am at
home in rich houses and I know what the maids who work there are
like.

I wink at her. "Open up, little kitty." She obeys me, opens the door
and says to me in Yiddish, "Whom do you want?" And I say, "Does
Padhatzur live here?" And she says, louder this time, "Whom do you
want?" And I say still louder, "Answer my question first. 'Does
Padhatzur live here?'" "Yes," she says. "If so," I tell her, "we can talk
the same language. Tell Madame Padhatzur that she has a visitor.
Her father Tevye has come to see her and has been standing outside
for quite some time like a beggar at the door, for he did not have
the good fortune to find favor in the eyes of this barbarian with the
silver buttons whom I wouldn't exchange for your littlest finger."

After she heard me out, the girl laughed impudently, slammed the door in my face, ran into the house and up the stairs, then ran down again, opened the door and led me into a palace the like of which my father and grandfather had never seen, even in a dream. Silk and velvet and gold and crystal, and as you walked across the room you couldn't hear your own step, for your sinner's feet were sinking into the softest carpets, as soft as newly fallen snow. And clocks. Clocks everywhere. Clocks on the walls, clocks on the tables. Clocks all over the place. Dear Lord, what more can you have in store? What does a person need that many clocks for? And I keep going, with my hands clasped behind my back. I look up—several Tevyes at once are cutting across toward me from all directions. One Tevye comes this way, another Tevye that way; one is coming toward me, another away from me. How do you like that? On all sides—mirrors. Only a bird like him, that contractor of mine, could afford to surround himself with all those mirrors and clocks.

And he appeared in my mind's eyes the way he had looked the first day he came to my house—a round, fat little man with a loud voice and a sniggering laugh. He arrived in a carriage drawn by fiery steeds and proceeded to make himself at home as though he were in his own father's vineyard. He saw my Beilke, talked to her, and then called me off to one side and whispered a secret into my ear—so loud you could have heard it on the other side of Yehupetz. What was the secret? Only this—that my daughter had found favor in his eyes, and one-two-three he wanted to get married. As for my daughter's finding favor in his eyes, that was easy enough to understand, but when it came to the other part, the one-two-three—that was *"like a double edged sword to me"*—it sank like a dull knife into my heart.

What did he mean—one-two-three and get married? Where did I come into the picture? And what about Beilke? Oh, how I longed to drum some texts into his ears, and to give him a proverb or two to remember me by. But thinking it over, I decided: "Why should I come between these young people? A lot you accomplished, Tevye, when you tried to arrange the marriages of your older daughters. You talked and you talked. You poured out all your wisdom and learning. And who was made a fool of in the end? Tevye, of course."

Now let us forsake the hero, as they say in books, and follow the fortunes of the heroine. I had done what they asked me to do, I had come to Yehupetz. They greeted me effusively: *"Sholom Aleichem." "Aleichem sholom."* "How are *you?"* "And how are things with you?" "Please be seated." "Thank you, I am quite comfortable." And so on, with the usual courtesies. I was wondering whether I should speak up and ask why they had sent for me—*"Today of all days"*—but it didn't seem proper. Tevye is not a woman, he can wait.

Meanwhile, a man-servant with huge white gloves appeared and announced that supper was on the table, and the three of us got up and went into a room that was entirely furnished in oak. The table was of oak, the chairs of oak, the walls panelled in oak and the ceiling of oak, and all of it was elaborately carved and painted and curlicued and bedizened. A kingly feast was set on the table. There was coffee and tea and hot chocolate, all sorts of pastries and the best of cognacs, appetizers and other good things, as well as every kind of fruit. I am ashamed to admit it, but I am afraid that in her father's house, Beilke had never seen such delicacies.

Well, they poured me a glass, and then another glass and I drank their health. I looked over at my Beilke and thought to myself, "You have really done well by yourself, my daughter. As they say in Hallel: *'Who raiseth up the poor out of the dust . . .'* When God has been kind to a poor man, *'and lifteth up the needy out of the dunghill,'* you can't recognize him any longer." She is the same Beilke as before and yet not the same. And I thought of the Beilke that used to be and compared her to this one and my heart ached. It was as though I had made a bad bargain—let us say I had exchanged my hard-working little horse for a strange colt that might turn out to be a real horse or nothing but a dummy.

"Ah Beilke," I thought, "look at what's become of you. Remember how once you used to sit at night by a smoking lamp, sewing and singing to yourself? Or how you could milk two cows in the blink of an eye. Or roll up your sleeves and cook a good old-fashioned *borsht,* or a dish of beans or dumplings with cheese, or bake a batch of poppyseed cakes. 'Father,' you would call, 'wash up, supper is ready.' And that was the finest song of all to my ears."

And now she sits there with her Padhatzur, like a queen, and two men run back and forth waiting on the table with a great clatter of dishes. And she? Does she utter a single word? But let me tell you, her Padhatzur isn't silent. He talks enough for two. His mouth doesn't shut for a moment. In all my life I had never seen a man who could jabber so endlessly and say so little, interspersing all his talk with that sniggering laugh of his. We have a saying for this: "He makes up his own jokes and laughs at them himself."

Besides us three, there was another guest at the table—a fellow with bulging red cheeks. I don't know who or what he was, but he seemed to be a glutton of no mean proportions. All the time Padhatzur was talking and laughing, he went on stuffing himself. As it is written: *"Three who have eaten*—he ate enough for three." This one guzzled and the other one talked, such foolish empty talk—I couldn't understand a word of it. It was all about contracts, government pronouncements, banks, money, Japan.

The only thing that interested me was his mention of Japan, for I too had had dealings with that country. During the war, as you know, horses *"commanded the highest prices*—they went looking for them with a candle." Well, they finally found me too, and took my horse with them. My little horse was measured with a yardstick, put through his paces, driven back and forth, and in the end he was given a white card—an honorable discharge. I could have told them all along that their trouble was for nothing. *"The righteous man knoweth the soul of his animal."* No horse of Tevye's will ever go to war. But forgive me, Mr. Sholom Aleichem, for straying away from my subject. Let's get back to the story.

Well, we had eaten and drunk our fill, as the Lord had bade us do, and when we got up from the table, Padhatzur took my arm and led me into an office that was ornately furnished, with guns and swords hanging on the walls, and miniature cannon on the table. He sat me down on a sort of divan that was as soft as butter, and took out of a gold box two long, fat, aromatic cigars, lit one for himself and one for me. He then sat down opposite me, stretched out his legs and said, "Do you know why I have sent for you?"

"Aha," I thought, "Now he is getting down to business." But I played dumb and said, "'*Am I my brother's keeper?*'—How should I know?"

So he said, "I wanted to talk to you, and it's you yourself I want to talk about."

"If it's good news," I replied, 'go ahead, let's hear it."

He took the cigar out from between his teeth, and began a long lecture. "You are a man of sense, I believe, not a fool, and you will forgive me for speaking frankly with you. You must know already that I am doing business on a very big scale, and when a man does business on such a tremendous scale . . ."

"Now he is getting there," I thought to myself, and interrupted him in the middle of his speech. "As the *Gamorah* says in the Sabbath portion: '*The more business the more worries . . .*' Do you happen to be familiar with that passage in the *Gamorah?*"

He answered me quite frankly. "I will tell you the honest truth, I have never studied the *Gamorah* and I wouldn't recognize it if I saw it." And he laughed that irritating laugh of his. What do you think of a man like that? It seems to me that if God has chastised you by making you illiterate, at least keep it under your hat instead of boasting about it. But all I said was, "I gathered that you had no knowledge of these things, but let me hear what you have to say further."

"Further I want to tell you, that it isn't fitting, considering the scale of my enterprises, and the repute in which my name is held, as well as my station in life, that you should be known as Tevye the Dairyman. I'll have you know that I am personally acquainted with the Governor, and that it is very likely that one of these days Brodsky might come to my house or Poliakov or maybe even Rothschild, whomever the devil sends."

He finished speaking, and I sat there and looked at his shiny bald spot and thought to myself, "It may be true that you are personally acquainted with the Governor, and that Rothschild might even come to your house some day, but just the same you talk like a common cur."

And I said, not without a touch of resentment in my voice, "Well, and what shall we do about it, if Rothschild does happen to drop in on you?"

Do you suppose that he understood the dig? Not a bit of it. As we say: *"There was neither bear nor woods."*

"I would like you to give up the dairy business," he said, "and go into something else."

"And what," said I, "would you suggest that I go into?"

"Anything you like. Aren't there enough different kinds of business in the world? I'll help you with money, you can have whatever you need, as long as you quit being Tevye the Dairyman. Or, look here, do you know what? Maybe you'd like to pick yourself up one-two-three and go to America?"

Having delivered himself of this, he put the cigar back between his teeth, looked me straight in the eye, and his bald head glistened.

Well, what would you say to such a vulgar person?

At first impulse I thought, "What are you sitting there for like a graven image? Get up, kiss the *mazuza,* slam the door in his face, and —'*he went to his eternal rest'*—get out without as much as a good-bye." I was as stirred up as all that. The colossal nerve of this contractor. Telling me to give up an honest, respectable livelihood and go off to America. Just because it might come to pass that on some far-off day Rothschild might condescend to enter his house, Tevye the Dairyman had to run off to the ends of the earth.

I was boiling inside and some of my anger was directed at her, at Beilke herself. How could she sit there like a queen among a hundred clocks and a thousand mirrors while her father Tevye was being tortured, was running the gauntlet? "May I have as many blessings," I thought to myself, "how much better your sister Hodel has made out than you. I grant you this, she doesn't have a house with so many fancy gew-gaws in it, but she has a husband who is a human being who can call his soul his own, even if his body is in prison. And besides that he has a head on his shoulders, has Feferl, and not a pot with a shiny cover on it. And when he talks there is something to listen to. When you quote him a passage from the Bible he comes back at you with three more in exchange. Wait, my contractor, I will drum a quotation into your ears that will make your head swim."

And I addressed myself to him thus: "That the *Gamorah* is a closed book to you, I can easily understand. When a man lives in Yehupetz and his name is Padhatzur and his business is that of contractor, the *Gamorah* can very well hide itself in the attic as far as he is concerned. But even a peasant in wooden sandals can understand a simple text. You know what the *Targum* says about Laban the Arameian?" And I gave him a quotation in mixed Hebrew and Russian. When I finished he threw an angry look at me and said, "What does *that* mean?"

"It means this—that out of a pig's tail you cannot fashion a fur hat."

"And what, may I ask, are you referring to?"

"I am referring to the way you are packing me off to America."

At this he laughed that snickering laugh of his and said, "Well, if not America, then how would you like to go to Palestine? Old Jews are always eager to go to Palestine."

Something about his last words struck a chord in my heart. "Hold on, Tevye," I thought. "Maybe this isn't such a bad idea after all. Maybe this is the way out for you. Rather than to stay here and suffer such treatment at the hands of your children, Palestine would be better. What have you got to lose? Your Golde is dead anyway, and you are in such misery you might as well be buried six feet underground yourself. How much longer do you expect to pound this earth?" And I might as well confess, Mr. Sholom Aleichem, that I've been drawn for a long time toward the Holy Land. I would like to stand by the Wailing Wall, to see the tombs of the Patriarchs, Mother Rachel's grave, and I would like to look with my own eyes at the River Jordan, at Mt. Sinai and the Red Sea, at the great cities Pithom and Raamses. In my thoughts I am already in the Land of Canaan—*"the land flowing with milk and honey"*—when Padhatzur breaks in on me impatiently: "Why waste all this time thinking about it? Make it one-two-three and decide."

"With you, thank the Lord, a trip to Palestine is one-two-three like a simple text in the Bible. But for me it's a difficult passage to interpret. To pack up and go off to Palestine one has to have the means."

He laughs scornfully at this, gets up and goes over to a desk, opens a drawer, takes out a purse, and counts out some money—not a trifling sum, you understand—and hands it to me. I take the wad of paper he has handed to me—the power of money!—and lower it into my pocket. I would like to treat him to a few learned quotations, a *medresh* or two, that would explain everything to him, but he won't listen to me.

"This will be enough for your trip," says he, "and more than enough. And when you arrive and find that you need more money, write me a letter, and I will send it to you—one-two-three. I hope I won't have to remind you again about going, for, after all, you are a man of honor, a man with a conscience."

And he laughed again that sniggering laugh of his that penetrated to my very soul. I was tempted to fling the money into his face and to let him know that you couldn't buy Tevye for money and that you didn't speak to Tevye of "honor" and "conscience." But before I had time to open my mouth, he rang the bell, called Beilke in, and said to her, "Do you know what, my love! Your father is leaving us, he is selling everything he owns and going one-two-three to Palestine."

" 'I dreamed a dream but I do not understand it,' as Pharaoh said to Joseph. What sort of nightmare is this?" I think to myself, and I look over at Beilke. Do you think she as much as frowned? She stood there rooted to the ground, pale and without expression on her face, looking from one to the other of us, not uttering a word. I couldn't speak either, and so we both stood there looking at each other, as the Psalm says: "May my tongue cleave to the roof of my mouth." We had both lost our powers of speech.

My head was whirling and my pulse beating as though I had been breathing in charcoal fumes. I wondered why I felt so dizzy. Could it be that expensive cigar he had given me? But he was still smoking his and talking away. His mouth didn't shut for a moment, though his eyelids were drooping as though he were ready to fall asleep.

"You have to go to Odessa by train first," he said. "And from Odessa by sea all the way to Jaffa, and the best time for a sea voyage is right now, for later on the winds and the snows and the hurricanes begin and then and then. . . ." His words were getting jumbled, he was asleep on his feet, but he didn't stop jabbering. "And when you are ready to start let us know and we'll both come to see you off at the station, for when can we hope to see you again?" He finished at last, with a huge yawn, and said to Beilke, "Why don't you stay here awhile, my soul? I am going to lie down for a little bit."

"That's the best thing you have said so far," I thought to myself. "Now I will have a chance to pour my heart out to her." I was ready to spill out all the wrath that had been accumulating in my breast all morning. But instead Beilke fell on my neck and started weeping. You should have heard her weep! My daughters are all alike in this respect. They can be very brave and manly up to a point—then all of a sudden, when it comes to something, they break down and weep like willow trees. Take my older girl Hodel. How she carried on at the last moment when she was telling me good-bye and went to join her Feferl in his exile. But how can I compare the two? This one isn't worthy of lighting the oven for the other. . . .

I will tell you the honest truth. I myself, as you well know, am not a man who is given to tears. I wept once in my life when my Golde lay stretched out on the ground with the candles at her head, and once when Hodel went off to join her husband and I was left standing alone at the station with my horse and wagon. There may have been one or two other occasions on which I weakened, I don't remember. I am not given to weeping. But Beilke's tears wrung my heart so that I couldn't hold myself in. I didn't have the heart to scold her. You don't have to explain things to me. I am Tevye. I understood her tears. She was weeping for *"the sin I have sinned before thee"*—because she hadn't listened to her father. Instead of scolding her and voicing my anger against Padhatzur, I began to comfort her with this story and that proverb as only Tevye can do.

But she interrupted me, "No, father, that isn't why I am crying. It's only because you are leaving on my account and there is nothing I can do to stop it, that's what hurts me."

"You talk like a child," I told her. "Remember we have a merciful God and your father is still in possession of all his faculties. It's a small matter for him to take a trip to Palestine and back again. As it is written: *'They journeyed and they encamped—Tuda i nazad—*I will go and I will return.'"

As though she had guessed my thoughts, she said, "No, father, that's the way you comfort a little child, you give it a toy or a doll and tell it a story about a little white goat. If you want a story, let me tell you one instead. But the story I will tell you is more sad than beautiful."

And she began telling me a long and curious tale, a story out of the thousand and one nights, all about Padhatzur, how he came up from obscure beginnings, worked himself up by his own wits to his present station in life, rose from the lowest to the highest rank. Now that he was rich he wanted the honor of entertaining important people in his home, and to that end he was pouring out thousands of *rubles,* handing out charity in all directions. But money, it seems, isn't everything. You have to have family and background, as well. He was willing to go to any length to prove that he wasn't a nobody, he boasted that he was descended from the great Padhatzurs, that his father was a celebrated contractor too. "Though he knows," she said, "quite well, and he knows that I know, that his father was only a poor fiddler. And on top of that he keeps telling everyone that his wife's father is a millionaire."

"Whom does he mean? Me? Who knows, maybe I *was* destined at one time to be a millionaire. But I'll have to let this suffice me."

"If you only knew how I suffer when he introduces me to his friends and tells them what an important man my father is, and who my uncles were and the rest of my family. How I blush at the lies he makes up. But I have to bear it all in silence for he is very eccentric in those matters."

"You call it being an 'eccentric.' To me he sounds like a plain liar or else a rascal."

"No, father, you don't understand him. He is not as evil as you think. He is a man whose moods change very frequently. He is really very kind-hearted and generous. If you happen to come to him when he is in one of his good moods he will give you anything you ask for. And nothing is too good for me. He would reach down and hand me the moon and the stars on a platter if I expressed a wish for them. Do you suppose I have no influence over him at all? Just recently I persuaded him to get Hodel and her husband out of exile. He promised to spend as much money as necessary on only one condition —that they go from there straight to Japan."

"Why to Japan?" I asked. "Why not to India, or to Persia to visit the Queen of Sheba?"

"Because he has business in Japan. He has business all over the world. What he spends on telegrams alone in one day would keep us all alive for a half year." Then her voice dropped. "But what good is all this to me? I am not myself any more."

"It is said," I quoted, " *'If I am not for myself who will be for me?— I am not I and you are not you!'* "

I tried to distract her with jokes and quotations and all the time my heart was torn into pieces to see my child pining away—how do we say it—*"in riches and in honor."*

"Your sister Hodel," I told her, "would have done differently."

"I've told you before not to compare me to Hodel. Hodel lived in Hodel's time and Beilke is living in Beilke's time. The distance between the two is as great as from here to Japan." Can you figure out the meaning of such crazy talk?

I see that you are in a hurry, but be patient for just a minute and there will be an end to all my stories. Well, after having supped well on the grief of my youngest child, I left the house *"in mourning and with bowed head,"* completely crushed and beaten. I threw the vile cigar he had given me into the street and shouted, "To the devil with you."

"Whom are you cursing, Reb Tevye?" I heard a voice behind my back. I turned around and looked. It was he, Ephraim the *Shadchan,* may no good come to him.

"God bless you, And what are you doing here?" I asked.

"What are *you* doing here?"

"I've been visiting my children."

"And how are they getting along?"

"How should they be getting along? May you and I be as lucky."

"Then I see you are satisfied with my merchandise."

"Satisfied, did you say? May God bless you doubly and trebly for what you have done."

"Thank you for the blessings. Now if you could only add to them something more substantial."

"Didn't you get your matchmaker's fee?"

"May your Padhatzur have no more than I got."

"What's the matter? Was the fee too small?"

"It isn't the size of the fee so much as the manner of giving it."

"What's the trouble then?"

"The trouble is," said he, "that there isn't a *groschen* of it left."

"Where did it disappear to?"

"I married off my daughter."

"Congratulations. Good luck to the couple and may you live to rejoice in their happiness."

"I am rejoicing in it right now. My son-in-law turned out to be a crook. He beat up my daughter, took the few *guldens* away and ran off to America."

"Why did you let him run off so far?"

"How could I stop him?"

"You could have sprinkled salt on his tail."

"I see you are feeling pretty chipper today, Reb Tevye."

"May you feel half as good as I feel."

"Is that so? And I thought you were fixed for life. If that's the case, here is a pinch of snuff."

I got rid of the matchmaker with a pinch of snuff, and went on home. I began selling out my household goods. It wasn't easy, I can tell you, to get rid of all the things that had accumulated through the years. Every old pot, every broken kettle wrenched my heart. One thing reminded me of Golde, another of the children. But nothing hurt me so much as parting with my old horse. I felt as though I owed him something. Hadn't we labored together all these years, suffered and hungered together, known good luck and bad luck together? And here I was up and selling him to a stranger. I had to dispose of him to a water-carrier, for what do you get from a teamster? Nothing but insults. Here is how the teamsters greeted me when I brought my horse to them.

"God be with you, Reb Tevye. Do you call this a horse?"

"What is it, then, a chandelier?"

"If it isn't a chandelier then it's one of the thirty-six saints who hold up the world."

"What do you mean by that?"

"We mean an old creature thirty-six years old without any teeth, with a gray lip, that shivers and shakes like an old woman saying her prayers on a frosty night."

That's teamsters' talk for you. I could swear that my little horse understood every word, as it is written: *"An ox knows his master.—* An animal knows when you are offering him for sale." I was sure he understood, for when I closed the deal with the water-carrier and wished him luck, my horse turned his patient face to me and gave me a look as though to say: *"This is my portion for all my efforts.—* Is this how you reward me for my years of faithful service?"

I looked back at him for the last time as the water-carrier led him away and I was left standing all alone. I thought, "Almighty, how cleverly You have fashioned Your world. You have created Tevye and You have created his horse and to both You have given the same fate. A man can at least talk, he can complain out loud, he can unburden his soul to another, but a horse? He is nothing but a dumb beast, as it is said: *'The advantage of man over animal.'*"

You wonder at the tears in my eyes, Mr. Sholom Aleichem. You are probably thinking that I am weeping for my horse. Why only for my horse? I am weeping for everybody and everything. For I shall miss everybody and everything. I shall miss my horse and the farm, and I shall miss the mayor and the police sergeant, the summer people of Boiberik, the rich people of Yehupetz, and I shall miss Ephraim the Matchmaker, may a plague take him, for when all is said and done, if you think the whole matter over, what is he but a poor man trying to make a living?

When God brings me safely to the place where I am going, I do not know what will finally become of me, but one thing is clear in my mind—that first of all I shall visit the grave of Mother Rachel. There I will offer a prayer for my children whom I shall probably never see again and at the same time I will keep in mind Ephraim the Matchmaker, as well as yourself and all of Israel. Let us shake hands on that, and go your way in good health and give my blessings to everyone and bid everyone a kind farewell for me. And may all go well with you.

Gy-Ma-Na-Si-A

LISTEN to me, your worst enemy can't do to you what you can do to yourself, especially if a woman—I mean a wife—interferes.

Why do I say this? I'm thinking of my own experience. Look at me, for instance. Well, what do you see? A man, you'd say—just an average man. You can't tell from my face whether I have money or not. It is possible that once I may have had some money, and not only money—for what is money?—but a decent livelihood, an honorable position, without rush and bustle and noise. No, the way I look at it, the quiet, unassuming way is best. I've always operated in a quiet, unspectacular way. In a quiet unspectacular way, I've gone broke twice. Quietly, and without fuss, I settled with my creditors and started all over again. . . .

But there is a God who rules over all of us, and through my own wife, He chastened me. She isn't here, so we can talk freely. To look at her you might say she is a wife like all wives. A pretty decent woman as women go. A big woman, God be praised, twice as big as I am, and not bad-looking. Really handsome, you might say, and not a fool either. She is smart—very smart, you might say—in fact, a woman with a masculine brain. And that's just the trouble. It's not so good when a woman has brains like a man. It doesn't matter how smart she is—after all, the good Lord created Adam first, and Eve after him! But try to point that out to her, and she answers, "If the Highest One wanted to create you first and then us—that's His affair.

613

But if He saw fit to put more brains into my little toe than into your whole head, I'm not to blame for that either."

"How did we come around to that?" I ask.

"Very simply," says she. "Whenever there is a decision to be made around here, I am the one who has to rack her brains. Even when our boy has to be sent to the *Gymnasia,* I have to do the planning."

"Where is it written?" I ask, "that he has to go to the *Gymnasia?* I'll be just as happy if he studies the *Torah* right here at home."

And she says, "I've told you a thousand times already that you won't succeed in setting me against the whole world. Nowadays the whole world sends its children to the *Gymnasia.*"

"To my way of thinking," I say to her, "the whole world is crazy."

"And I suppose you are the only sane one," says she. "The world would come to a pretty pass if everybody did what you wanted."

And I tell her, "Everybody acts according to his way of thinking."

"May all my enemies and my friends' enemies," says my wife, "have in their pockets, in their chests, and in their cupboards as much as you have in your head! They'd starve to death."

"Pity the poor man," says I, "who has to listen to a woman's advice."

And she says, "Pity the poor woman who has a husband who needs her advice."

Well, try to argue with a woman. If you say this, she says that. If you say one word she gives you back twelve. And if you stop talking altogether she bursts into tears or better still falls in a faint. To make a long story short, she had her way. For let's not fool ourselves: if a woman makes up her mind, is there anything we can do?

Well, what shall I tell you? *Gy-ma-na-si-a!*

First of all we had to start getting him ready to enter the *Mladshi Prigotovitelnie,* the junior preparatory school. "What's there to worry about?" I said with a shrug. "A trifle like that—*Mladshi Prigotovitelnie.* It seems to me that any little schoolboy among us can put them all in the shade. Especially a child like ours!" If you travel the length and breadth of the Empire, you won't find another like him. I'm his own father and I may be prejudiced, but you can't get away from it—the child has a head on him. He's the talk of the province. . . .

Well, why should I make a long story out of it? He made his application, went for his examination, took his examination, and—he didn't pass! What happened? He failed in arithmetic. He's a little weak, they tell me, in figuring. In math-e-ma-tics, they call it. How do you like that? Here's a boy with such a head—he's the talk of a province—you can travel the length and breadth of the Empire . . . And they tell me: math-e-ma-tics. At any rate, he failed. That made me good and mad. If he took that examination, he should have passed it. But after all, I'm a man, not a woman. So I thought it over: the devil take it! We Jews are used to such treatment. Let's forget the whole thing.

But try to convince *her* once she'd got that crazy idea into her head! She's made up her mind once for all—*Gy-ma-na-si-a!* So I plead with her. "Tell me," I say, "my dear wife, what does he need it for? Will it keep him out of the army? For that, the Lord has already provided. He's an only son. What then? To help him make a living? I can get along without it. What do I care if he becomes a store-keeper like me, or some other kind of businessman? And if it's his luck to become a millionaire or a banker, I'll bear up under that too." Thus I plead with her. But does it do any good?

"It's just as well," she tells me, "that he didn't get into the *Mladshi Prigotovitelnie* after all."

"Why?" I ask.

She says, "He might just as well go right into the *Starshi Prigo-tovitelnie,* the advanced preparatory school." "Well," I think, "why not? After all, with a head like that . . . you can travel the length and breadth . . ."

But what happened? When it came to the final test, he failed again! Not in math-e-ma-tics this time. Something new. His spelling is not what it might be. That is, he spells the words all right, but there is one letter on which he is a little weak. The letter *yati.* He puts it in all right, but the trouble is that he doesn't put it where it belongs. So I'm heart-broken! I don't know how I'll ever be able to go to Poltava or

to Lodz for the fairs, if he doesn't learn to put the letter *yati* where
they want him to. . . .

Anyway, when they told us the glad tidings, *she* almost had a fit.
She rushed right off to the director and insisted that the boy could
do it; he knew how to spell. Just let them try him out again right
from the beginning. Naturally, they paid no attention to her. They
gave him a *two*—the failing grade—and what kind of a *two*? *A two
minus!* And go do something about it. Help! Murder! He failed
again. So I say to her, "What do you want us to do? Commit suicide?
We're Jews. We're used to such treatment."

At this, she flares up at me and starts to yell and to curse as only a
woman can do. That doesn't bother me. The only one I feel sorry for
is my boy, poor child. Think of it. All the other boys will be wearing
uniforms with silver buttons and he won't. So I plead with him. "You
dummy!" I say. "You fool! Is it a law that everybody has to go to
Gymnasia? Silly child, somebody has to stay home, doesn't he? And
besides . . ."

But she doesn't let me finish. "Such comfort he offers! Who asked
for your sympathy? What you can do instead is to go and find a good
teacher for him, a tutor, a Russian tutor to teach him *gra-ma-ti-ka,*
grammar."

Listen to her. She wants two tutors. One tutor and one *melamed*
for Hebrew isn't enough for her. Well, we argued back and forth, but
in the end she won the point. Because when she makes up her mind,
is there anything I can do?

Well, what shall I say? We hired another tutor, a real Russian
this time, because the examination in Grammar for First Class is a
tough proposition. It's strong medicine to take, as strong as horseradish. You can't trifle with *gra-ma-ti-ka* with the *bukva yati,* the
letter *yati*. And what kind of tutor does the good Lord send us? I am
ashamed to talk about it. He made life unbearable for us. He belittled
us and made fun of us right to our faces. May he burn in hell! For
instance, he couldn't find another word to practice on than garlic—
Tchasnok! Tchasnok, tchasnoka, tchasnoku, tchasnokoi . . . If it
hadn't been for *her,* I'd have taken him by the collar and thrown him
out together with his grammar. But to her it was worth going

through. Why? Because the boy was going to know where to put a *yati* and where not to put it. Think of it! All winter we tortured him and it was not until late spring that he had to go to the slaughter. And when the time came, he made his application, took his examination, and this time he didn't fail. He got the best marks, a four and a five. Hurrah! Let's celebrate! *Mazl-tov!* Congratulations! But wait! Don't be in such a hurry. We don't know yet if he'll be admitted. We won't know till August. Why not? Go ask them. What can we do about it? It's *their* world. A Jew is used to such treatment. . . .

Comes August, my wife can't rest. She rushes around, from the director to the inspector, from the inspector to the director. "Why do you keep running, like a poisoned rat, from one hole to the next?" I ask her.

"What do you mean—why do I keep running?" she says to me. "Are you a stranger around here? Don't you know what goes on these days? Haven't you heard about quotas?"

And what finally happened? He *didn't* get in. Why not? Because he didn't get two *fives*. If he had gotten two fives, they told us, then *maybe* he would have got in. How do you like that? *Maybe*. Well, I'd just as soon forget what I got from her that day. But the one I felt sorry for was *him*. The poor boy. He lay there with his head in the pillow and wouldn't stop crying. So there was nothing else to do; we had to get another tutor, a student at the *Gymnasia,* and we started grooming him all over again, this time for second class. And that was a real task, because to get into the second class you had to know not only math-e-ma-tics and grammar, but geography and penmanship and I don't know what else besides. Though, if you ask me, for three *groschen,* you can have it all. Any Bible text our boys have to learn in *cheder* is harder than all their studies and much more to the point. But what can we do about it? A Jew is used to such treatment. . . .

There followed a round of lessons. We lived on lessons. When we got up in the morning—lessons. After we had finished the morning prayer and eaten—lessons. All day long—lessons and more lessons. Until late at night we could hear him reciting: "Nominative, genitive, dative, accusative . . ." It rang in my ears, it pounded in my head. I couldn't eat. I couldn't sleep. "Look," I said, "you take an innocent creature and you torture him. It's a crime. The poor child will get sick."

And she exclaims, "Bite your tongue for these words!"

And once more he went to the slaughter, and this time he brought home nothing but *fives!* But, then, did you expect anything different? A head like his—you can travel the length and breadth of the Empire and you won't find another like it! It sounds good, doesn't it? Well, listen to this then. When they posted the names of the boys who were accepted, and we looked—ours wasn't there. Help! Murder! It's a disgrace, a crime! He had perfect marks. Watch her go! Watch her run! She'll show them. Well, she went, she showed them—and all they told her was to stop annoying them. In plain language, they showed her the door. And she came rushing into the house with a roar that could be heard in heaven.

"You!" she yelled. "A fine father you are! If you were a real father like other fathers, if you had an ounce of love for your child, you'd find some way. You'd see people. You'd do something. You'd use your influence, with the director, the inspector, somebody. . . ."

What do you think of that? There's a woman for you! "Is that all I have to do? Isn't it enough that I have to carry on my mind all the seasons, the markets, the fairs, and notes and receipts and checks and drafts, and I don't know how many more things? Maybe you want me to go bankrupt on account of your *Gy-ma-na-si-a* and your classes? You know what I think of them! You know where you can put them!"

After all, I'm only human and there is a limit to what a person can stand. So I let her have it. But it was she who had her way, not I. Because when she makes up her mind . . .

And what did I do then? I began trying to use influence. I humbled myself, I underwent all sorts of humiliations; because everyone I came to asked me the same questions and everyone of them was correct. "Here you are, Reb Aaron," they said, " a person of some consequence, with an only son. What possesses you to go sticking your head where you're not wanted?"

Go tell them the whole story—that I have a wife—may she live to be a hundred and twenty years old—who has one obsession: *Gy-ma-*

na-si-a and *Gy-ma-na-si-a* and *Gy-ma-na-si-a!* But I'm not such a half-wit either. With God's help I worked my way in where I wanted to be, right into the office of the director himself, and I sat down to talk it over with him. After all, thank the Lord, I know how to talk too. No one has to show me how.

"*Tchto was ugodno?*" he says to me. "What is your wish?" And he asks me to sit down.

I come close and whisper into his ear, "*Gospodin* Director," I say, "*mi ludi ne bogati,* we are not rich people, but we have a boy, an only child who," I say, "wants to study, and I want him to study too, and my wife," I say, "wants very much . . ."

So he says to me again, "*Tchto was ugodno?*—What is your wish?"

So I come a little closer and say to him, "Your honor, we are not rich people, but we have a boy, an only child, who" I say, "wants to study, and my wife," I say, "wants *very much* . . ." And I stretch out the *ve-ry* so he'll understand. But he's thick-headed and slow. He doesn't seem to know what I'm talking about. He repeats angrily, "*Tak tchtozhe was ugodno*—once and for all, what is your wish?"

So slowly, cautiously I put my hand into my pocket. Slowly, cautiously I pull it out again, and slowly and cautiously I say, "I beg your pardon, *Gospodin* Director, *mi ludi ne bogati*—we are not rich people, but we have a boy"—and I pause—"an only child"—and I pause again—"who wants to study." And I look meaningfully at the director. "And my wife," I almost whisper, "wants *very, very* much to have him study." And this time I stretch out the *ve-e-ry* even longer than before, and I put my hand into his. . . .

All at once he knew what I meant. He took a little book out of his drawer, and asked me what my name was, and what my boy's name was, and which class I wanted him to enter. I thought to myself, "That's the way to talk!" And I told him that my name was Katz, Aaron Katz, and my boy was named Moishe or Moshka, and I wanted him to enter third class. So he told me that seeing that my name was Katz, and my boy's name was Moishe or Moshka, and he wanted to enter the third class, I should bring him back in January and then he'd surely get in. You understand. An entirely different language. Apparently if you grease the axle the wheels will turn. The only trouble was that we still had to wait. But what could we do about it? They told us to wait, so we waited. A Jew is used to such treatment. . . .

Came January, and again a tumult, a clamor, a rushing around. Any day now a meeting would be held, a *soviet,* they called it. The director and the inspector and all the teachers of the *Gymnasia* were going to come together, and when the meeting was over we'd know if they were going to take him in. The day came; my wife wasn't home. There was no dinner, no samovar, not a thing in the house to eat. Where was she? She was at the *Gymnasia.* That is, not at the *Gymnasia* itself, but in front of it. All day long she trudged back and forth in the deep snow, back and forth, waiting for them to come out of the meeting. It's a bitter frost, the wind is sharp, it cuts your breath off. And she walks back and forth outside, waiting. What for? She must know that a promise is sacred . . . and specially since . . . you understand? But try to tell that to a woman!

Well, she waited an hour, she waited two, three, four hours. All the boys have gone home already, and still she waits. At last the door opens and one of the teachers comes out. She jumps at him and grabs him by the arm. Does he know how the meeting—the *soviet*—came out? So he says, why shouldn't he know? They decided to admit, all in all, eighty-five boys. Eighty-three Christians and two Jews. So she asks, who were the Jews? And he tells her a Shepselson and a Katz. When she hears the name Katz, she turns around and comes running home all out of breath, falls into the house in ecstasy. *"Mazl-tov,"* she cries. "Oh, I thank Thee, Heavenly Father, I thank Thee! They've accepted him! They've accepted him!" And tears stand in her eyes. Naturally, I am pleased too, but do I have to start dancing to show my joy? After all, I'm a man, not a woman.

"It looks to me," my wife says, "as if you're not too excited about all this."

"What makes you think so?" I ask her.

"Oh," she says, "you're a cold, heartless person. If you only saw how eager the child is, you wouldn't be sitting there so calmly. You would have been on your way long ago to buy him a uniform, a cap, and a satchel for his books. And you'd be doing something about a celebration for our friends."

"Why a celebration all of a sudden?" I ask her. "Is the boy being confirmed, or getting married?" So she gets angry and stops talking to me altogether. And when a woman stops talking it's a thousand times worse than when she's cursing, because if she is cursing you, at least you hear a human voice. But this way it's like talking to a brick wall. Well, who do you think won out? She or I? Naturally, she did, because if she makes up her mind, is there anything I can do?

And so we had a celebration. We invited all our friends and relatives and we dressed the boy up from head to foot in a handsome uniform with shiny buttons and a cadet's cap with a metal gadget in front— just like a general. You should have seen him. He was a different lad altogether, with a new soul, a new life. He shone, like the sun in July! The guests drank toasts to him, wished that he might study in the best of health and go on and on to higher studies.

"That," I said "is not so important. We can get along without that. Just let him go through the first few years of the *Gymnasia*," I said, "and with God's help I'll get him married off."

My wife smiles at the guests and gives me a funny look. "You can tell him that he's very much mistaken," she says. "He has old-fashioned ideas."

"And you can tell her," I say, "that I wish I had a hundred blessings for every way in which the old-fashioned ideas are better than the new-fangled ones."

And she says, "You can tell *him* that he is a . . ."

At this everybody starts laughing. "Oh, Reb Aaron, Reb Aaron," they cry, "have you got a wife, God bless her! A Cossack, not a wife!"

On the strength of that everybody took another drink, somebody struck up a tune, the crowd made a ring with the two of us and our boy in the middle, and we lifted our feet and danced. We danced until dawn. As soon as it was light outside we took the boy and went straight to the *Gymnasia*. When we got there it was still early, the door was locked, there wasn't even a cur in sight. . . . We stood there until we were frozen stiff, and when the door was finally opened we went in and began to thaw out. Before long the youngsters began coming, with knapsacks full of books on their shoulders. Soon the place was full of them, talking, laughing, joking, shouting—like a circus. In the midst of all this a man comes up to us, obviously one of the teachers, with a sheet of paper in his hands.

"What are you here for?" he asks me.

So I point to the boy and tell him that I had just brought him to start *cheder* here, that is, the *Gymnasia*. So he asks me what class he's in and I say the third. He's just been admitted.

So he asks, "What's his name?"

And I tell him, "Katz. Moishe Katz. That is, Moshka Katz."

So he says, "Moshka Katz? There is no Moshka Katz in the third class. There *is* a Katz in the class" he says, "but not Moshka. Morduch. That's the only one. Morduch Katz."

So I say, "What do you mean—Morduch? Not Morduch—Moshka." He says, "Morduch!" And he waves the paper in front of my face. I say "Moshka!" He says "Morduch!" Well, what shall I tell you? Moshka—Morduch, Morduch—Moshka. We Moshka'd and Morduch'ed until at last we found out what had happened. Would you believe it? They did take in a boy named Katz. But they made a mistake and took in a different Katz. There were two Katzes in our town.

Well, what shall I tell you? You should have seen the boy's face when we told him to take that gadget off his cap. A bride doesn't shed as many tears when she is led to the canopy as my boy did that day. I begged him to stop, I threatened him. It didn't help. "Look!" I said to my wife. "See, what you've done to him! Didn't I tell you that this *Gy-ma-na-si-a* of yours would be the death of him yet? May God help us," I said. "I only hope we don't have more trouble on account of this. I hope he doesn't get sick."

"Let my enemies get sick, if they like," says she, "but my child *must* get into the *Gymnasia!* If he didn't get in now, he'll get in a year from now. If he didn't get in here, he'll get in somewhere else. But," she says, "he must get in—unless I die first and you bury me."

Did you ever hear the like of that? And who do you think won out? Let's not fool ourselves. If she makes up her mind, can I do anything?"

Well, I won't take up much more of your time. We traveled from one end of the country to the other. Wherever there is a city, wherever there is a *Gymnasia,* there we went. We registered him, he took his

examinations, he passed his examinations, he passed with top grades—
and he *didn't* get in. Why not? Because of the quota. Always the
quota.

I began to think that I had really gone crazy. "Fool!" I said to
myself. "What is this? What are you flying around for, from one
city to the next? What good will it ever do you? What do you need
it for? And if he does get in, so what?" Well, you can say what you
want, ambition is a great thing. It finally got me too. I became stubborn. I wouldn't give up. At last the Almighty had pity on me and
sent across my path, in Poland somewhere, a certain *Gymnasia,* a
komertcheska, they called it, a business school, where for every
Christian they were willing to take in one Jew—a quota of fifty percent, that is. But here was the catch. Every Jew who wanted to have
his son admitted had to bring along with him a Christian boy, and
if he passed the examination, this Christian, that is, and if all his fees
and expenses were paid, then there was a chance! In other words, you
had not one headache, but two. It was bad enough to have my own
son to worry about, but now I had to eat my heart out over somebody
else's son too. For—woe is me!—if Esau fails to make the grade, then
Jacob lies in the dust together with him.

So I set out to find a Christian youth, and what I went through
before I found one! He was a shoemaker's boy, a shoemaker named
Holiava. And then what do you think happened? The shoemaker's
boy failed in his examinations. And in what? In religion. And my boy
had to sit down and drill him in religion! You ask, how does my boy
come to know religion? You don't have to ask. After all, with a
head like his! As I told you, you can travel the length and breadth
of the Empire. . . .

Well, in spite of that, at last God came to our aid. The lucky day
arrived. They both got in. But do you think we're through? No.
When it came to paying the fees, I look around; my man has vanished.
What's the matter? He doesn't want his son to go to school with so
many Jews. You can't budge him. He says, "What good is it to me?
Aren't all schools open to me anyway? Can't my boy go to any school
he wants to?" And can I contradict him?

"What do you want, *Panie* Holiava?" I say. And he says,

"Nothing." I try this, I try that. I went to see some friends of his, drinking companions, we went into a tavern together, had a glass or two, maybe three. Well, before I lived to see him enrolled, my hair almost turned gray. But anyway, praise the Lord, my work was done.

When I came home I found a new headache. What now? My wife has made up her mind. After all, he is an only child, the apple of her eye. . . . Was it right to leave him out there all by himself?

"What," I ask, "are you driving at now?"

"What am I driving at?" she asks. "Don't you know what I'm driving at? I want to be with him."

"Oh," says I. "And the house?"

"The house," says she, "is nothing but a house."

And what do you think she did? She packed up and went over there to be with him, and I remained all alone at home. You can imagine what it must have been like. May my enemies live like that! My life was no life any more, my business was no business. Everything went wrong. And we kept writing letters to each other. I write to her. She answers. Letters go back and forth. "To my beloved and cherished wife—peace!" "Peace to my dear husband."

"In the name of God," I write to her, "what will be the outcome of all this? I am only human. And what's a house without a mistress? Listen to reason, my wife."

Well, she paid as much heed to my pleas as she might to the snows of last year. She won her point, not I. For if she makes up her mind— is there anything I can do?

Well, I'm coming to the end of my story. I was ruined. I went broke. I lost everything. My business disappeared, my last few remnants were sold. I was left penniless. I had no choice. I had to swallow my pride and move over there with them. There, I had to start all over again. I looked around, sniffed here and there and tried to figure out where I was in the world. At last I found something. I went into partnership with a merchant from Warsaw, a man of some means, a householder, a president of a synagogue, but at bottom a manipulator, a swindler, a pickpocket! He just about ruined me all over again. I couldn't hold up my head any more.

In the meanwhile, I come home one day and my boy opens the door for me. He has a strange look on his face. He is blushing and I see that the fancy gadget, the insignia, is gone from his cap. I say to him, "Look, Moishe, my boy, what happened to the gadget?"

He says to me, "What gadget?"

I say, "The insignia, the thing-a-ma-jig."

The boy turns redder still and says, "I tore it off."

"What do you mean, you tore it off?"

And he says, "I am free."

"What do you mean—you are free?"

And he tells me, "We're through. We are not going back to school any more."

So I say, "What do you mean *you're* not going any more?"

And he says, "We're all free. We didn't like the way they treated us. So we went out on strike. We all agreed not to go back."

"What do you mean—strike?" I shout. "What do you mean—agreed? Was it for this that I gave up my home and my business? Was it for this that I sacrificed myself? So that you could go out on strike? Woe is me. And woe is you. May God protect us. Who will suffer for it? We Jews."

That's the way I talk to him, warn him, lecture him, the way a father naturally does to a child. But I also have a wife, God bless her. She comes running in and lays down the law to me. I'm slightly backward, she tells me. I don't know what's going on in the world. We're living in a new era, she tells me. A better life, a newer life has come into existence, she tells me, where all are equal. There are no rich, no poor; no master, no slave; no lamb, no shears; no cats, no mice. . . .

"Tut-tut, my dear," I say to her. "Where did you learn all this funny talk? It sounds like a new language to me. By the same token, maybe you want to open up the chicken coops and let out all the chickens? Here, chickie-chickie! Shoo, chickie! You're free."

At this, she flares up at me. It's just as if I had poured a bucket full of boiling water at her. She went after me. . . . I had to listen to a whole sermon, from beginning to end. The only trouble is, there was no end. "Just a second," I beg. "Listen to me. Just a minute." And I beat my breast with my fist, as we do on *Yom Kippur:* "I have sinned I have subverted, I have transgressed. Now let's call a halt."

But she pays no attention to me. "No," she says. And she wants to know "why" and "how" and "besides" and "for Heaven's sake," and "what do I mean," and "how does it happen" and "who says so"? And then a second time and a third time, and once again for good measure. I was lucky to escape alive. . . .

Tell me, I beg you. Who ever invented wives?

The Purim Feast

"I DON'T know what's to become of the child, what he's going to grow up into. He's like a dripping dishrag, a soggy handkerchief, like a professional mourner. . . . A child that can't stop crying."

This was my mother talking to herself as she dressed me in my holiday clothes. As she spoke she gave me now a shove, now a push, now a cuff over the head; she grabbed me by the hair or pulled my ear, pinched me, and slapped me—and with all that she expected me to be laughing instead of crying! She buttoned me up from top to toe in my best coat which was much too tight for me. I could barely breathe and my eyes almost popped out of my head. The sleeves were so short that my bluish red wrists stuck out of my cuffs as though they were swollen. This was more than my mother could bear.

"Look at that pair of hands!" And she slapped me smartly across my wrists to make me drop them. "When you sit at Uncle Hertz's table remember to keep your hands down, do you hear me? And don't let your face get as red as Yadwocha the peasant girl's. And don't roll your eyes like a tomcat. Do you hear what I'm telling you? And sit up like a human being. And the main thing—is your nose. Oh, that nose of yours. Come here, let me put your nose in order."

Alas for my poor nose when my mother decides to "put it in order." I don't know what my nose has done to deserve such a fate. It seems to me that it's a nose like all noses, short and blunt, slightly turned up at the end, pinkish in color, and usually dripping. But is that a reason for such cruel treatment? Believe me, there have been

627

times when I have begged the Almighty to take my nose away altogether, to cause it to fall off and end my misery once for all. I used
to imagine that I would wake up one fine morning without a nose.
I would come up to my mother after breakfast and she would grab
hold of me and cry out in a terrible voice, "Woe is me, where is
your nose?"

"Which nose?" I would say innocently, passing my hand over my
face. I would look at my mother's horror-stricken face and taste the
joys of revenge. "Serves her right. Now she can see what her son
looks like without a nose."

Childish dreams! Foolish imaginings! God didn't hear my prayer.
My nose kept on growing, my mother kept on "putting it in order"
and I went on suffering. My nose had to take the worst punishment
when a holiday approached, for instance before *Purim* when we were
getting ready to go to Uncle Hertz's for the *Purim* Feast.

Uncle Hertz was not only the rich uncle in the family, he was also
the foremost citizen in our town, and in all the surrounding towns
you heard nothing but Hertz and Hertz and Hertz. Of course he had
a pair of high-spirited horses and a carriage of his own, and when he
rode out in his carriage the wheels made such a clatter that the whole
town ran outside to see Uncle Hertz riding by. There he sat, high
up in his carriage, with his handsome, round, copper-colored beard
and his fierce gray eyes, rocking himself back and forth and looking
down at everyone through his silver-rimmed spectacles, as though to
say, "How can you worms compare yourselves to me? I am Hertz
the *Nogid* and I ride in a carriage, while you poor Kasriliks, you
paupers, you crawl in the mud."

I don't know how the rest of the world felt about him, but I
detested Uncle Hertz so that I couldn't bear to look at his fat, red
face, his copper-colored beard and his silver-rimmed spectacles. I
hated his big paunch and the massive gold chain that rode around his
paunch, the round silk skullcap that he wore on his head, and above
all I hated his little cough. He had a peculiar little cough which went
along with a shrug of the shoulders, a toss of the head, and pout of
the lips, as though he were saying, "Show respect. It was I, Hertz,

who coughed, not because, God forbid, I have caught cold, but just because I wanted to cough."

I can't understand my family at all. What's the matter with them that they are so excited over going to Uncle Hertz's for *Purim?* It seems to me that they all love him as they love a toothache, and even my mother who is his own sister is not too crazy about him either, for when the older children are not at home (she apparently isn't embarrassed by my presence) she showers strange blessings on his head. She hopes that next year, "he will be in her circumstances." But let anyone else try to say a word against him, and she will scratch his eyes out. I happened to be by one day when my father let something fall. Do you think it was something disrespectful? Not at all. He only remarked to my mother, "Well, what's the news? Has your Hertz arrived yet, or not?" And she gave him such a fare-thee-well that my poor father didn't know whether to stand up or to sit down.

"What do you mean by *my* Hertz? What kind of talk is that? What sort of expression? What do you mean he is mine?"

"Whose is he if not yours? Is he mine?" said my father trying to give battle. But he didn't advance far. My mother attacked him on all sides at once.

"Well, if he is mine, what of it? He is mine, then. You don't like it? His ancestry isn't good enough for you? You had to divide your father's inheritance with him? Is that it? You never got any favors from him? Is that it?"

"Who says I didn't?" my father offered in a milder tone, ready to surrender himself. But it didn't do any good. My mother wasn't ready to make a truce yet.

"You have better brothers than I have? Is that it? Finer men, more important, more prosperous, more respectable ones, is that it?"

"Quiet now. Let there be an end to this. Leave me alone," said my father, pulling his cap over his eyes and running out of the house. My father lost the battle and my mother remained the victor. She is always the victor. She wins every battle, not because she wears the pants in the family, but because of Uncle Hertz. Uncle Hertz is our rich uncle and we are his "poor relations."

What is Uncle Hertz to us? Do we live off him? Or have we received so many favors from him? I cannot tell you, because I don't know. I only know that everyone in our house, from the oldest to the youngest, lives in fear and trembling of Uncle Hertz. *Purim* is two weeks off and we are already getting ready for the Feast at Uncle Hertz's. My older brother, Moses Abraham, a boy with pale, sunken cheeks and sad dark eyes, strokes his earlocks whenever you mention the *Purim* Feast at Uncle Hertz's. As for my two big sisters, Miriam Reizel and Hannah Rachel, it goes without saying that they have been getting ready for a long time. They are having new dresses made in the latest fashion just for the occasion, and they have bought combs and ribbons to put in their hair. They wanted to have their shoes mended too, but my mother put that off for Passover, though it cost her plenty of heartache. She is especially concerned about Miriam Reizel, because Miriam Reizel is engaged, and suppose her young man sees her torn shoes! She has enough trouble with that young man as it is. To begin with, he is a common fellow, a "book-keeper" he calls himself, because he is a clerk in a store. As though that weren't bad enough, he likes to put on airs, and he expects his betrothed to go around dressed in the latest fashion, like a princess.

Every Saturday afternoon this young man comes to our house and he sits by the window with my two sisters and all they talk about is new clothes, stylish costumes, patent leather shoes, galoshes, hats with feathers, pointed parasols. They also talk about embroidered pillow cases, red pillowslips, white sheets, and fine quilts, fluffy and warm, so that it's a pleasure to get under them on a cold winter night. As he talks, I look over at my sister Miriam Reizel and see her go red as a beet. She has a habit of blushing very easily. She hides her feet under the chair, so that her young man won't see the run-down heels and shabby toes if he should look at them.

"Well, are you prepared for the Feast?" my mother asks my father the day after the reading of the *Megilah*.

"Prepared?" says my father. "With what?" And he puts on his Sabbath gabardine. "Where are the children?"

"The children are almost ready," says my mother, though she knows quite well that the children, meaning my two sisters, are far from ready. They are still washing their hair, putting almond oil on it, braiding it for each other, primping, and putting on their new dresses. They have smeared their shoes with fat to make them sparkle like new. But what good is this sparkle when the heels are almost off, and the toes show through in front? How can they keep Miriam Reizel's young man from seeing her shoes? Just then, as if some ill wind blew him in, the young man himself appears, in a new suit with a stiffly starched collar and a bright green tie. From his starched white cuffs dangle his big red hands with the black-rimmed nails. He has just had a haircut and his short hair stands on end. Out of his back pocket he pulls a huge white, starched handkerchief, redolent of spices. The strong scent of cloves and spice is wafted to my nostrils and makes me sneeze suddenly, so that I burst two buttons off my coat. My mother lets fly at me. "Look at the scamp. He can't keep a button on. May you not burst apart altogether." She picks up a needle and thread and sews the buttons back on. Now everyone is ready and we start out all together for Uncle Hertz's house.

In front of the procession walks my father, the skirts of his coat lifted high from the mud. Behind him walks my mother in high men's boots. After her come my sisters tripping daintily with parasols in their hands. (Why anyone needs a parasol at this time of year is beyond me.) After them my older brother Moses Abraham leaps through the mud, holding me by the hand and trying to find a dry spot, but landing each time in the deepest mud and jumping back as though he had been scalded. Alongside of us walks my sister's young man in his new tall galoshes. He is the only one of us who has galoshes and he calls out in a loud voice for everyone to hear, "I hope I don't get my galoshes full of mud."

Though it is still broad daylight, many candles are burning at Uncle Hertz's house. All the lamps have been lighted and sconces burn on the walls. The table has been set. A monstrous *Purim* loaf, as big as the legendary ox reserved for the pious when the Messiah comes, takes up half of the table. All around the table are gathered our relatives, all the uncles and aunts and cousins, poor people all of them, one poorer than the next. They are standing around, whispering among themselves as though they were at a circumcision ceremony waiting for the godparents to bring in the child. Uncle Hertz is nowhere to be seen, and my Aunt, a woman with a string of huge pearls around her neck and a set of false teeth, is bustling around, putting plates on the table, counting us with the left hand, apparently not afraid of the evil eye. . . .

And now the door opens and Uncle Hertz himself appears, dressed in holiday clothes, a shiny black silk coat with wide sleeves, and a fur hat on his head, which he wears only for the *Purim* Feast and the Passover *Seder*. The whole family bows to him and the men smile nervously, rubbing their hands together, and the women wish him a loud good *yom-tev*. We children stand around stiffly, not knowing what to do with our hands. Uncle Hertz gives us all a sweeping glance out of his fierce gray eyes, over the tops of his glasses, coughs and waves his hand at us. "Well, why don't you sit down? Sit down, everybody, here are the chairs."

The whole family sits down. Each one is sitting on the edge of his chair, afraid to touch anything on the table. A terrible silence reigns in the big room. You can hear the candles guttering, everything swims in front of our eyes, and our hearts are heavy. We are hungry, but nobody feels like eating. Our appetites have been taken away as if by magic.

"Why is everybody so quiet? Speak! Let's hear you tell us something," says Uncle Hertz, and he coughs his little cough, shrugs his shoulders, tosses his head and pouts with his lips.

The family is silent. No one dares to utter a word at Uncle Hertz's table. The men smile stupidly as though they would like to speak and don't know what to say. The women exchange frightened glances. We youngsters burn as if in a fever. Miriam Reizel looks over at Hannah Rachel and Hannah Rachel looks back at Miriam Reizel, as though they had never seen each other before. My brother Moses Abraham looks out at the world with a pale scared face. Nobody, nobody dares utter a word at Uncle Hertz's table. Only one person feels at home here, as he does everywhere, and at all times. That is Miriam Reizel's young man, the bookkeeper. He pulls out his huge, starched and strongly perfumed handkerchief from his back pocket, blows his nose with relish, and says, "Did anybody ever see such deep mud at this time of year? I thought sure my galoshes would be filled up."

"Who is this young man?" asks Uncle Hertz, lifting up his silver-rimmed spectacles and giving his little cough.

"He is—my Miriam Reizel's—betrothed," says my father in a low voice like a man confessing to a murder. All of us sit as though turned to stone. And Miriam Reizel, poor Miriam Reizel—her face flames like a straw roof on fire.

Uncle Hertz looks the family over once more with his fierce gray eyes, offers us another cough and a shrug, another toss of his head and pout of his lips and says, "Well, why don't you go and wash? Go on and wash your hands, the water is right here."

After we had washed our hands and said the proper prayer over the little ceremony, we sat down around the table and waited for Uncle Hertz to say grace and to cut the huge *Purim* loaf. We were getting hungry now and would have liked to start eating, but just as if to spite us Uncle Hertz took his time over the grace and the cutting up of the huge ox, prolonging the ceremony and drawing it out as though he were a rabbi in front of his congregation. At last we saw the ox slaughtered and pieces of the loaf were passed to us, but before we had swallowed the first bite Uncle Hertz looked us over with his fierce gray eyes and said, "Well, why don't you sing? Sing somebody. Let's hear a tune in honor of the Feast. The whole world is celebrating today."

The family began exchanging glances among themselves, whispering and arguing and nudging each other. "You sing." "No, you sing." "Why should I? Why not you?" This went on for some time until one of the relations, my young cousin Abraham, Uncle Itzy's son, burst into song. He was a beardless youth with a squeaky voice and blinking eyes and he fancied himself as a singer. What it was that my cousin Abraham wanted to sing, I don't know. He started in his high squeaky voice on a falsetto note that broke in the middle, and the tune was so mournful and the look on his face was so tragic and so comic at once that you had to be God himself or one of His angels to keep from laughing out loud. And especially since right opposite me sat all the boys making faces.

The first burst of laughter came from me, and it was I who caught the first slap from my mother. But the slap did not cool me off. It brought a burst of laughter from the other children, and from me as well. This burst of laughter brought another slap and the slap brought fresh laughter and the laughter another slap and this went on until I was led out of the dining room into the kitchen and from the kitchen outdoors, and then I was brought home, beaten black and blue and drowning in tears.

That night I cursed my own bones and I cursed *Purim* and the *Purim* Feast and my cousin Abraham and more than anyone else I cursed Uncle Hertz, may he forgive me, for he has long since passed on to his reward. On his grave stands a tombstone, the most imposing tombstone in the whole cemetery, and on it in gold letters are engraved the virtues in which he excelled during his life: "Here lies an honest man, kind-hearted, lovable, generous, charitable, good-tempered, devoted and faithful." And so on and so on. . . . "May he rest in peace."

From Passover to Succos

or

THE CHESS PLAYER'S STORY

IT WAS late one winter's night—long past midnight. The guests had finished a late supper and the remains on the table bore witness to the fact that they had done well by themselves. The green card tables were covered with chalk marks and scattered piles of cards from which aces and kings peeped out in profusion as though to say, "Now we are here." The guests would have loved nothing better than to sit down to a game of preference or whist, but somehow it didn't seem proper. It was much too late. So they just sat around, smoked, drank black coffee, and gossiped. The conversation was dying out when someone threw in a word about chess. Another picked it up, then another, and another. It was plain that they were trying to draw out a certain ardent chess player by the name of Rubinstein.

Rubinstein was a rabid chess fiend. He was willing to travel ten miles on foot, to go without food or drink or sleep for a game of chess. It was a passion with him. Many stories made the rounds about his chess playing. It was said: 1. That he played chess with himself all night long. 2. That he had divorced his wife three times already because of chess. 3. That he had once disappeared for three years because of a chess game. In a word, wherever you found Rubinstein, there you found chess. And wherever there was chess, there was Rubinstein.

And Rubinstein loved to talk about chess as a confirmed drunkard loves to talk about liquor.

When you looked at Rubinstein, you were struck first of all by his enormous forehead—it was high and broad, and rounded like a bay window. His eyes also were enormous. They were round and black, but without expression, like two lumps of coal. He was thin and bony in build, but he had a voice like a bell, deep and sonorous. When Rubinstein was among a group of people you heard only Rubinstein and no one else.

When he heard the guests mention chess, Rubinstein wrinkled his already deeply wrinkled forehead, squinted with one eye at the coffee he was drinking as though to determine whether it smelled of soap or of dishwater, and spoke to everyone in general and to no one in particular. His voice rang out like a cathedral bell. "Ladies and gentlemen! If you want to hear a story about a chess player, sit down, all of you, right here near me, and I will tell you a story that happened long ago."

"A story about a chess player? A story of long ago?" The hostess who had been afraid that the gathering was about to break up caught up his words eagerly. "Wonderful! Excellent! Tell Felitchka to shut the piano, and will you please lock the doors and bring in two-three more chairs? Sit down, everybody, please sit down. Mr. Rubinstein is going to tell us a story about a chess player, a story of long ago."

Rubinstein examined the cigar his host had just handed him, from all sides, as though to determine how much it had cost, then he made a grimace and furrowed his enormous brow as though to say, "Maybe it looks like a cigar, but it tastes more like a broom." And he began his story:

"I don't have to explain to you that I am a devoted chess player, ladies and gentlemen, and that our whole family are chess players by nature. The name of Rubinstein is known all over the world. In fact, I would like to have you show me a Rubinstein who is *not* a chess player."

"Why, I know a fellow named Rubinstein who is an insurance salesman. He comes in to see me every week. Aside from life insurance, he knows absolutely nothing. A regular dolt."

This remark was thrown in by one of the guests, a young man with a narrow, pointed head, and gold-rimmed glasses, who considered himself quite a wit. But Rubinstein remained calm. He looked the young man over with his coal-black frigid glance and said in his deep sonorous voice, "He can't be one of our Rubinsteins. A true Rubinstein has to be a chess player. That is as natural as it is natural for a buffoon to crack jokes. My grandfather, Rubin Rubinstein, was a true Rubinstein, for he was, ladies and gentlemen, a born chess player. The world could turn upside down and he wouldn't notice it when he was in the middle of a chess game. People came to play chess with him from all over the world—noblemen, counts, princes. By trade he was only a watchmaker, a poor workingman, but a real craftsman, an artist at his trade. But since the only thing that really mattered in his life was chess, he had difficulty in making a living, and earned barely enough to feed his family.

"And it came to pass, ladies and gentlemen, that one day there rode up to my grandfather's hut a splendid equipage drawn by two pairs of fiery steeds, and a nobleman leaped out of this equipage followed by two men-servants in livery. The nobleman was covered with medals and orders from head to foot, like royalty. He walked into the hut and asked, 'Where is the Jew, Rubin Rubinstein?' At first my grandfather was a little frightened, but he recovered quickly and spoke up, 'I am the Jew, Rubin Rubinstein. How can I be of service to you, your Highness?' The nobleman was pleased with this answer and said to my grandfather, 'If you are the Jew, Rubin Rubinstein, then I am very happy to know you. Have the samovar put on to boil, and bring out your chessboard. I'll play you a game. I've heard it said that you are a very fine chess player and that so far no one has ever checkmated you.'

"Saying this the nobleman sat down (apparently he was a lover of chess) and began playing with my grandfather. They played on and on, one game after another, one game after another. Meanwhile the samovar boiled and tea was served in proper style, on a large tray with preserves and pastries of all sorts. My grandmother saw to that, though she hadn't a *groschen* in her purse. . . .

"Meanwhile a crowd had gathered around the carriage outside my grandfather's door. Everyone was curious to know who it was that had come to see Rubin the Watchmaker. All kinds of rumors flew around the village. It was rumored that the nobleman had come from the capital of the province to carry out an investigation—something about counterfeit money—that it was the work of an informer, a plot of some sort that had been cooked up against Rubinstein. No one dared to walk in and see for himself what was going on. For who would have dreamed that the nobleman and my grandfather were only playing chess?

"And what shall I tell you, ladies and gentlemen? Though the nobleman was a good chess player, a very good chess player indeed, he was checkmated by my grandfather over and over again, and the more he played the more excited he became, and the more excited he became the worse he played. As for my grandfather, do you think he as much as winked an eyelash? Not he. He might as well have been playing with—I don't know whom—for all the emotion he showed. The nobleman must have been pretty much put out by all this. No one likes to be beaten, and to be beaten by whom? By a Jew! But what could he say, when the other was obviously the better player? Ability cannot be denied. And besides, I will have you know, ladies and gentlemen, that a real chess player is more interested in playing the game than in winning or losing. To a real chess player the opponent is nothing, only the game itself counts. I don't know if you will understand this or not."

"We can't swim either, but we understand what swimming is," broke in the witty fellow with the gold-rimmed glasses. Rubinstein the chess player measured him with his chilly glance and said, "Yes, we can see that you know all about swimming." He took a puff of his cigar and went on:

"And since everything in this world must come to an end, ladies and gentlemen, their chess game came to an end too. The nobleman arose, buttoned up the gold buttons on his coat, extended two fingers to my grandfather, and said, 'Listen to me, Rubin Rubinstein, you have beaten me, and I concede that you are the finest chess player not only in my province, but in the whole country, and perhaps in the whole world. I consider myself fortunate to have had the honor and the pleasure of playing with the finest chess player in the whole world. Rest assured that your name will become even more famous than it has been. I shall convey this to the king's ministers. I shall report it in Court.'

"When he heard him mention the king's ministers and reports to the Court, my grandfather asked, 'And who are you, your Highness?'

"The nobleman burst out laughing, puffed out his beribboned and bemedaled chest and said to my grandfather, 'I am the Governor of the Province.'

"My grandfather's heart sank at this. If he had only known with whom he was playing he might have played differently. But it was too late. What was done couldn't be undone. The Governor made his farewells in the friendliest possible manner, went out to his carriage, got in, and rode off.

"It was then that the whole village came flocking around my grandfather wanting to know who the nobleman had been. When they found out that it was the Governor himself, they went on to ask, 'And what did the Governor want with you?' When my grandfather informed them that the Governor had come for a game of chess they spat three times to ward off the evil eye, and each one went on his way. They talked about the affair and talked about it among themselves, but in time it was forgotten. My grandfather forgot about it also. His head was filled with new chess problems and incidentally with the lesser problem of making a living.

"And it came to pass, ladies and gentlemen, a long time after, how long I do not know myself—I only know that it was Passover Eve and my grandfather had nothing with which to celebrate the holiday, not even a piece of *matzo*. He had a houseful of children and this one needed a shirt, that one a pair of shoes. Things were bad. My grandfather, poor soul, was sitting doubled up, a magnifying glass screwed into his eyes, tinkering with a watch that had stopped running and refused to start again, and thinking to himself, 'From whence shall come my help?'

"Suddenly the door opened and in walked two gendarmes and made straight for my grandfather. *'Pazhaluista,'* they said to him, 'If you please.' A thought flashed through my grandfather's head (my grandfather was a man given to strange thoughts), 'Perhaps they have come from the Governor.' Who could tell? Maybe the Governor wanted to reward him, make him wealthy? Hadn't it happened before that through some chance happening, through some little incident, a nobleman had taken a poor Jew and showered him with gold, and endowed his children and his children's children forever and ever?

But it turned out, ladies and gentlemen, to be nothing of the sort. They were only asking him to be so kind as to pick himself up and set out at once, for—guess where—Petersburg! Why, they themselves didn't know. They had just received a paper from Petersburg on which was written: *'Niemedlannia dostavit yevreya Rubina Rubinsteina v Sankt Peterburg.'* This meant that they must this instant deliver the Jew Rubin Rubinstein to St. Petersburg. There must be a reason for this. 'Confess, fellow, what have you done?' My grandfather swore that he was innocent, in all his life he hadn't as much as hurt a fly on the wall. The whole town could vouch for him. They paid no attention to him, but ordered him to come along with them and join the convoy. The order had said to *deliver* the Jew Rubinstein, and what else could that mean except to bring him by convoy and in chains? And *this instant*. Which meant the quicker the better.

"Without wasting any more time, ladies and gentlemen, on unnecessary ceremonies, they took my grandfather, bound chains around his hands and feet, and led him away in a convoy with all the thieves and criminals. And what it meant in those days to 'go by convoy,' I don't have to explain to you. You know yourselves that an ordinary person who was led by convoy seldom reached his destination. There were no trains, no highways. People fell like flies by the roadside. More than half of them died on the way and the rest arrived worn out, sick, and crippled for life.

"But as luck would have it, my grandfather was of the same physical make-up as I am, thin and bony, but with a strong constitution. Besides he was a thinking man, a man with a philosophy of his own. 'A man,' he said, 'dies once, not twice, and if it is fated that he should continue to live, no one can take his life away.' Why did he speak thus of life and death? For it was apparent that this smacked of exile, of Siberia, or maybe even worse. He not only bade his wife and children and the whole village good-bye, he asked for the book of the dying and the dead, and wanted to make his last confession. The whole town turned out to see him off, as though it were his funeral. They mourned for him already as though he were dead, and tears poured like a deluge. . . .

"To describe to you, ladies and gentlemen, what my grandfather went through on his journey, I would have to spend not one night with you, but three nights in a row. And that would be a pity. The time could be much better spent in playing chess. Briefly I can tell you that the journey lasted the whole summer, from Passover to *Succos*. The convoy, ladies and gentlemen, was divided into stations, and at each station the prisoners had to wait a week, or two weeks, or sometimes longer, until new groups of thieves and brigands were assembled. Then they were driven further.

"And when finally after many trials and tribulations they arrived in the great and glorious city of St. Petersburg, do you think that they were through with him? If you think so, you are greatly mistaken. For here at the end of the journey they took my grandfather and locked him up in a stone cell, a tiny dark room in which he could neither sit nor lie, nor move nor even stand upright. . . ."

"Just the place for a game of chess!" broke in the witty young man with the gold-rimmed glasses.

"Or for telling rotten jokes," added Rubinstein the chess player, and went on with his story.

"Here in this stone cell my grandfather prepared himself in earnest for death. He recited the last prayer, beheld the Angel of Death in front of his eyes, and felt his soul leaving his body before sentence could even be passed on him. And to tell the truth, he now wished for death to come. He had only one flicker of hope left. . . . He was certain that his townspeople would intercede for him. There would be mediators, people of good will who would use their influence to set him free. They would go to the various officials, offer bribes if necessary, do everything in order to deliver an innocent man who had been the victim of an ugly frame-up.

"And my grandfather was not wrong, ladies and gentlemen. From the day he had been led away, the town had busied itself about his case. The townspeople consulted lawyers, sought influence in high places, gave money wherever they could. But nothing helped.

"Their money was accepted, but no promises were made. It was impossible, said the officials, to do anything for my grandfather, and here is how they explained it. It is easy to buy the freedom of a thief or a common criminal. Why so? For the simple reason that you knew the thief had stolen a couple of horses, or the criminal had set fire to a house. But a fellow like this Rubinstein who had neither stolen horses nor set anything on fire—who could tell what sort of offender he was? Maybe he was even a 'political'? In those days a 'political' was worse than a murderer who had slaughtered a whole province. To intercede for a 'political' was very dangerous. The very word *'politichesky'* couldn't be spoken out loud, only whispered in the dark. But what did Rubin Rubinstein the Watchmaker have to do with politics? Still, who could tell? Wasn't he a brainy man, a chess player, a philosopher?

"But, ladies and gentlemen, as I have said before, all things come to an end. The day arrived when the doors of the prison opened, and two gendarmes, armed from head to foot, came in, dragged my grandfather out, more dead than alive, put him into a carriage and drove off. Where to? He didn't ask. To the judgment? Let it be to the judgment. To the scaffold? Let it be to the scaffold. Anything to put an end to this. He saw himself standing in front of the Court. 'Rubin Rubinstein,' they said to him. 'Confess your guilt.' And he answered, 'I confess that I am a Jew and a poor watchmaker, and I live by the work of my hands. I have never stolen anything, never swindled anyone, nor insulted anyone. God is my witness. If you want to torture me, do so, but first take away my immortal soul. It is in your hands.'

"As my grandfather argued with the Court in this vein, the carriage drove up to a large building and my grandfather was told to get out. He obeyed. They took him into a room, then into a corridor, then into another room, and told him to take off all his clothes down to his undershirt. He couldn't figure out what this meant, but when an armed gendarme tells you to take off your clothes, you can't very well be impolite and disobey. Then they told him—and I wish to beg your pardon a thousand times for mentioning such a thing, ladies and gentlemen—to take off his undershirt, too. He took off his undershirt, too. Then they took him stark naked into a bathroom and proceeded to give him a bath. And what a bath. They scrubbed him and rubbed him, they scoured him and polished him, rinsed him and dried him. Then they let him get dressed, took him out once more, and drove off. They drove and they drove and they drove. And my grandfather thought to himself, 'Dear Lord, what will become of me now?' He tried to recall all the stories he had ever read of the Spanish Inquisition and he couldn't recall ever having read of a single instance where a condemned man was given a bath before being led to the gallows.

"As he was musing thus, ladies and gentlemen, the carriage drove up to a courtyard surrounded by an iron picket fence; each picket was tipped with gold and on each tip was an eagle. He was led through rows of generals decorated with golden epaulettes and with medals on their chests. He was told that he must not be frightened, he was going to be presented to the King. He was instructed to look straight in front of him, not to say anything unnecessary, not to complain about anything, and only answer the questions put to him with 'yes' or 'no.'

"Before my grandfather could get his bearings he found himself in a magnificent hall hung with paintings and filled with golden furniture. Opposite him stood a tall man with sideburns. The man with the sideburns (it was Tzar Nicholas I) looked my grandfather over and the following conversation took place between them:

The King: What is your name?
Grandfather Rubinstein: Rubin Sholemov Rubinstein.
The King: How old are you?
Grandfather Rubinstein: Fifty-seven.
The King: Where did you learn to play chess?
Grandfather Rubinstein: The knowledge is passed on in my family from father to son.

The King: They tell me that you are the foremost chess player in my kingdom.

"To this my grandfather wanted to say, 'Would that I were not the foremost chess player in your kingdom.' Then the King would surely have asked, 'Why do you say this?' Then my grandfather would have let him know that this was no way to treat an eminent chess player with whom the King wanted to have an audience. Grandfather Rubinstein would have known what to tell the Tzar, you may be sure of that!

"But at this moment the King waved his hand, the generals leaped forward, and the same gendarmes who had brought him in led my grandfather out into the courtyard. There they set him free and ordered him to leave the city instantly, for a Jew had no right to be there. Don't ask how he finally got home. It's enough that he got there alive. He had left home before Passover and he arrived just in time to celebrate *Succos*. Ladies and gentlemen, I have finished. . . ."

Get Thee Out

GREETINGS to you, Mr. Sholom Aleichem, heartiest greetings. I've been expecting you for a long time and wondering why I didn't see you any more. I kept asking, *"Where are you?"* as God once asked of Adam, and I was told that you have been traveling all over the world, visiting faraway countries—*"the one hundred and twenty-seven provinces of Ahasheurus,"* as we say in the *Megilah.*

But you are looking at me strangely. You seem to be hesitating and wondering, "Is it he, or isn't it he?" It is he, Mr. Sholom Aleichem, it is he, your old friend Tevye in person. Tevye the Dairyman, the very same as before, but not a dairyman any longer. Just an ordinary, everyday Jew, and greatly aged, as you can see. And yet I am not so old in years. As we say in the *Hagadah: "I look like a man of seventy.* —I am still far from seventy." Then why should my hair be so white? Believe me, dear friend, it's not from joy. My own sorrows are partly to blame and partly the sorrows of all Israel. For these are difficult times for us Jews—hard, bitter times to live in.

But that isn't what's troubling you, I can see. The shoe pinches on the other foot. You must have remembered that I told you good-bye once, as I was about to leave for Palestine. Now you are thinking, "Here is Tevye, just back from the Holy Land," and you are eager to know what's going on in Palestine—you want to hear about my visit to Mother Rachel's Tomb, to the Cave of Machpelah, and the other holy places. Wait, I will set your mind at rest; I will tell you everything, if you have the time and would like to hear a strange and

645

curious tale. Then listen carefully, as it is written: *"Hear ye!"* And when you have heard me out, you yourself will admit that man is nothing but a fool and that we have a mighty God who rules the Universe.

Well, what portion of the Bible are *you* studying this week in the Synagogue? *Vaikro?* The first portion of Leviticus? I am on a different portion entirely—on *Lech-lecho* or *Get thee out.* I have been told, *"Get thee out*—get a move on you, Tevye—*out of thy country—* leave your own land—*and from thy father's house*—the village where you were born and spent all the years of your life—*to the land which I will show thee*—wherever your two eyes lead you." That's the lesson I am on now. And when was I given this lesson to study? Now that I am old and feeble and all alone in the world, as we say on *Rosh Hashono:* *"Do not cast me off in my old age."*

But I am getting ahead of my story. I haven't told you about the Holy Land yet. What should I tell you, dear friend? It is indeed a *"land flowing with milk and honey,"* as the Bible tells us. The only trouble is that the Holy Land is over there and I am still here— *"outside of the Promised Land."* He who wrote the *Megilah* or Book of Esther must have had Tevye in mind when he had Esther say, *"If I perish, I perish."* I have always been a *shlimazl* and a *shlimazl* I will die. There I stood, as you remember, with one foot practically in the Holy Land. All I had to do was to buy a ticket, get on a ship, and I'm off. But that isn't the way God deals with Tevye. He had something different in store for me. Wait and you will hear.

You may remember my oldest son-in-law Motel Kamzoil the tailor from Anatevka. Well, our Motel goes to sleep one night in the best of health, and never gets up. Though I shouldn't have said he was in the *best* of health. How could he be, a poor workingman, alas, sitting day and night *"absorbed in study and worship of God,"* meaning that he sat in a dark cellar day and night bent over a needle and thread, patching trousers. He did this so long that he got the coughing sickness, and he coughed and coughed until he coughed out his last piece of lung. Doctors couldn't help him, medicines didn't do any good, nor goats' milk nor honey and chocolate. . . . He was a fine boy, the salt of the earth; it's true, he had no learning, but he was an honest fellow, unassuming, and without any false pretensions. He loved my daughter with all his heart, sacrificed himself for the children—and he thought the world of me!

And so we conclude the text with: *"Moses passed away."* In other words, Motel died, and he left me with a millstone around my neck. Who could begin to think about the Holy Land now? I had a Holy Land right here at home. How could I leave my daughter, a widow with small children, and without any means of support? Though if you stop to think, what could I do for her, an old man like me, a sack full of holes? I couldn't bring her husband back to life or return the children's father to them. And besides, I am only human myself. I would like to rest my bones in my old age, take life easy, find out what it feels like to be a human being. I've done enough hustling and bustling in my lifetime. Enough striving after the things of this world. It's time to begin thinking about the next world. I had gotten rid of most of my goods and chattels, sold my cows and let my horse go quite some time ago. And all of a sudden in my old age I have to become a protector of orphans, and provide for a family of small children. But that isn't all. Wait. More is coming. For when troubles descend on Tevye, they never come singly. The first one always brings others trailing after it. For instance, once when a cow of mine died, didn't another one lie down and die the very next day? That's how God created the world and that's how it will remain. There is no help for it.

Do you remember the story of my youngest daughter Beilke and her great good fortune? How she caught the biggest fish in the pond, the contractor Padhatzur who had made a fortune in the war and was looking for a beautiful young bride—how he sent Ephraim the Matchmaker to me, how he met my daughter and fell in love with her, how he begged for her on his knees, threatened to kill himself if he couldn't have her, how he was ready to take her just as she was, without any dowry, and showered her with gifts from head to foot, with gold and diamonds and jewels? It sounds like a fairy tale, doesn't it? The wealthy prince, the poor maiden, the great palace. But what was the end of this beautiful tale? The end was a sorry one. May God have pity on us all! For if God wills it, the wheel of fortune can turn backwards and then everything begins to fall buttered side down as we say in Hallel: *"Who raiseth up the poor out of the dust."* And before you can turn around—Crash! *"That looketh down low upon heaven and upon the earth*—everything is shattered into little pieces."

Thus God likes to play with us human beings. That's how he played with Tevye many times, raising him up, and casting him down, like Jacob ascending and descending the ladder. And that is what happened to Padhatzur. You remember his great riches, his airs and pretensions, the splendor of his mansion in Yehupetz with its dozen servants and thousand clocks and mirrors. What do you think was the outcome of all this? The outcome was that he not only lost everything, and had to sell all his clocks and mirrors and his wife's jewels, but went bankrupt in the bargain, and made such a sorry mess of everything that he had to flee the country and become a fugitive. . . . He went to where the holy Sabbath goes. In other words, he ran off to America. That's where all the unhappy souls go, and that's where they went.

They had a hard time of it in America at first. They used up what little cash they had brought with them, and when there was nothing more to chew on, they had to go to work, both he and she, doing all kinds of back-breaking labor, like our ancestors in Egypt. Now, she writes me, they are doing quite well, God be thanked. Both of them are working in a stocking factory, and they manage to "scrape up a living," as they say in America. Here we call it being one jump ahead of the poorhouse. It's lucky for them, she tells me, that there are just the two of them—they have neither chick nor child. *"That too is for the best."*

And now, I ask you, doesn't he deserve to be cursed with the deadliest curses, I mean Ephraim the Matchmaker, for arranging this happy match? Would she have been any worse off if she had married an honest workingman the way Tzeitl did, or a teacher, like Hodel? You might argue that their luck didn't hold out either, that one was left a young widow, and the other had to go into exile with her husband? But these things are in God's hands. Man cannot provide against everything. If you want to know the truth, the only wise one among us was my wife Golde. She looked about her in good time and decided to leave this miserable world forever. For tell me yourself, rather than to suffer the *"pain of bringing up children,"* the way I have suffered, isn't it better to lie in the earth and be eaten by worms? But how is it said: *"Perforce thou must live.*—Man doesn't take his own life, and if he does, he gets rapped on the knuckles for it." But in the meanwhile we have strayed off the path. *"Let us return to our original subject."*

Where were we? At section *Lech-lecho* or *Get thee out.* But before we go on with section *Lech-lecho* I shall ask you to stop with me for a moment at section *Balak.* It has always been a custom since the world began to study *Lech-lecho* or *Get thee out* first, and *Balak* or the lesson of revenge later, but with me the custom was reversed and I was taught the lesson of *Balak* first and *Lech-lecho* afterward. And I was drilled in *Balak* so thoroughly that I want you to hear about it. The lesson may come in handy some day.

This happened some time ago, right after the war, during the troubles over the Constitution when we were undergoing *"salvations and consolations,"* that is, when reprisals were being carried out against Jews. The pogroms began in the big cities, then spread to the small towns and villages, but they didn't reach me, and I was sure that they never would reach me. Why? Simply for this reason: that I had lived in the village for so many years and had always been on such friendly terms with the peasants. I had become a *"Friend of the Soul and Father of Mercy"* to them—"Brother Tevel" was their best friend. Did they want advice? It was, "do as brother Tevel says." Did one of them need a remedy for fever? It was, "Go to Tevel." A special favor? Also to Tevel. Tell me, why should I worry about pogroms and such nonsense when the peasants themselves had assured me many times that I had nothing to be afraid of? They would never permit such a thing, they told me. *"But it came to pass."*—Listen to my story.

I arrived home from Boiberik one evening. I was still in my prime then—how do you say it?—in high feather. I was still Tevye the Dairyman who sold milk and cheese and butter. I unhitched my horse, threw him some oats and hay and before I had time to wash my hands and say a prayer before eating, I take a look outside and see the yard is full of peasants. The whole village has turned out to see me, from the Mayor, Ivan Poperilo, down to Trochin the Shepherd, and all of them looking stiff and strange in their holiday clothes. My heart turned over at the sight. What holiday was this? Or had they come like Balaam to curse me? But at once I thought, "Shame on you, Tevye, to be so suspicious of these people after all these years you have lived among them as a friend." And I went outside and greeted them warmly, "Welcome, friends, what have you come for? And what good news do you bring?" Then Ivan Poperilo the Mayor stepped forward and said, right out, without any apologies, "We came here, Tevel, because we want to beat you up."

What do you think of such talk? Tactful, wasn't it? It's the same as speaking of a blind man as *sagi nohor* or having too much light. You can imagine how I felt when I heard it. But to show my feelings? Never. That isn't Tevye's way. "*Mazl-tov*," I said, "why did you get around to it at this late date? In other places they've almost forgotten all about it." Then Ivan said very earnestly, "It's like this, Tevel, all this time we've been trying to decide whether to beat you up or not. Everywhere else your people are being massacred, then why should we let you go? So the Village Council decided to punish you too. But we haven't decided what to do to you. We don't know whether to break a few of your windowpanes and rip your featherbeds, or to set fire to your house and barn and entire homestead."

When I heard this, my spirits really sank low. I looked at my guests standing there, leaning on their sticks and whispering among themselves. They looked as though they really meant business. "If so," I said to myself, "it's as David said in the psalm, '*For the waters are come in even into the soul.*' You are in bad trouble, Tevye. '*Do not give Satan an opening.—*You cannot trifle with the Angel of Death.' Something has to be done."

Well, why should I spin out the story any longer? A miracle took place. God sent me courage and I spoke up boldly. "Listen to me, gentlemen. Hear me out, dear friends. Since the Village Council has decreed that I must be punished, so be it. You know best what you do, and perhaps Tevye has merited such treatment at your hands.

But do you know, my friends, that there is a Power even higher than your Village Council? Do you know that there is a God in Heaven? I am not speaking now of *your* God or *my* God, I am speaking of the God who rules over all of us, who looks down from Heaven and sees all the vileness that goes on below. It may be that He has singled me out to be punished through you, my best friends. And it may be just the opposite, that He doesn't want Tevye to be hurt under any circumstances. Who is there among us who knows what God has decreed? Is there one among you who will undertake to find out?"

They must have seen by then that they couldn't get the best of Tevye in an argument. And so the Mayor, Ivan Poperilo, spoke up. "It's like this, Tevel, we have nothing against you yourself. It's true that you are a Jew, but you are not a bad person. But one thing has nothing to do with the other. You have to be punished. The Village Council has decided. We at least have to smash a few of your windowpanes. We don't dare not to. Suppose an official passed through the village and saw that your house hadn't been touched. We would surely have to suffer for it."

That is just what he said, as God is my witness. Now I ask you, Mr. Sholom Aleichem, you are a man who has traveled all over the world. Is Tevye right when he says that we have a great and merciful God?

Well, that's the end of section *Balak*. They came to curse and remained to bless. Now let us turn to section *Lech-lecho* or *Get thee out*. This lesson was taught to me not so long ago and in real earnest. This time fine speeches didn't help me, orations didn't avail me. This is exactly the way it happened. Let me tell it to you in detail, the way you like to have a story told. . . .

It was in the days of Mendel Beiliss, when Mendel Beiliss became our scapegoat and was made to suffer the punishments of the damned. I was sitting on my doorstep one day sunk in thought. It was the middle of summer. The sun was blazing and my head was splitting. "Lord, Lord," I thought, "what times these are! What is the world coming to? And where is God, the ancient God of Israel? Why is He silent? Wherefore does He permit such things to happen?" Wherefore and why and wherefore once more? And when you ask questions of

God you begin to ponder about the universe and go on asking: What is this world? And the next world? And why doesn't the Messiah come? Wouldn't it be clever of him to appear at this very moment riding on his white horse? That would be a master stroke! It seems to me that he has never been so badly needed by our people as now. I don't know about the rich Jews, the Brodskys in Yehupetz for instance, or the Rothschilds in Paris. It may be that they never even give him a thought. But we poor Jews of Kasrilevka and Mazapevka and Zolodoievka, and even of Yehupetz and Odessa, watch and wait and pray for him daily. Our eyes are strained from watching. He is our only hope. All we can do is hope and pray for this miracle— that the Messiah will come.

And while I am sitting there deep in such thoughts, I look up and see someone approaching, riding on a white horse. He comes riding up to my door, gets off, ties the horse to the post, and comes straight up to me. *"Zdrastoi,* Tevel," he says—"Greetings, Tevye." "Greetings to you, your honor," I answer him with a smile, though in my heart I am thinking, *"Haman approacheth.*—When you're waiting for the Messiah, the village constable comes riding." I stand up and say to him, "Welcome, your honor, what goes on in the world? And what good news do you bring?" And all this time I am quaking inside, waiting to hear what he has to say. But he takes his time. First he lights a cigarette, then he blows out the smoke, spits on the ground, and at last he speaks up. "How much time do you need, Tevel," he says, "to sell your house and all your household goods?"

I look at him in astonishment. "Why should I sell my house? In whose way is it?"

"It isn't in anybody's way," he says, "but I came to tell you that you will have to leave the village."

"Is that all?" I asked. "And how did I come to deserve such an honor?"

"I can't tell you," he says, "I am not the one who's sending you away. It's the provincial government."

"And what has the government against me?"

"Against you? Nothing. You aren't the only one. Your people are being driven out of all the villages, out of Zolodoievka and Rabilevka, and Kostolomevka, and all the others. Even Anatevka, which up to now has been a town, has become a village and your people are being driven from there too."

"Even Lazer-Wolf the Butcher?" I asked. "And Naphtali-Gershon the Lame, and the *Shochet* of Anatevka? And the Rabbi?

"Everybody, everybody." And he made a motion with his hand as though he were cutting with a scythe. I felt a little easier at this. How do we say it? *"The troubles of the many are a half-consolation."* But anger at this injustice still burned inside of me. I said to him, "Is your honor aware of the fact that I have lived in this village much longer than you have? Do you know that in this corner of the world lived my father before me, and my grandfather and grandmother before him?" And I began naming all the different members of my family, telling him where each one had lived and where each one died. The Constable heard me out, and when I had finished he said, "You are a clever Jew and you certainly know how to talk, but what good are these tales of your grandfather and grandmother to me? Let them enjoy their rest in Paradise. And you, Tevel, pack up your things and go, go to Berdichev."

That made me good and angry. It wasn't enough that you brought me this glad tidings, you Esau, you have to poke fun at me besides? "Pack up and go, go to Berdichev," he tells me. I couldn't let that pass. I had to tell him a thing or two. "Your honor," I said, "in all the years you have been Constable here, have you ever heard the villagers complaining of Tevye, has anyone ever accused Tevye of stealing from him, or robbing him, or cheating him in any way? Ask any of the peasants if I didn't live alongside them like the best of neighbors? How many times did I come to you yourself, your excellency, to plead in their behalf, to ask you not to ill-treat them?"

I could see that this was not to his taste. He got up, crushed his cigarette between his fingers, threw it away, and said to me, "I have no time to waste on idle chatter. I received a paper and that's all I know. Here, sign right here. They give you three days to sell your household goods and get out of the village."

When I heard this, I said, "You give me three days to get out, do you? For this may you live three years longer *'in honor and in riches.'*

May the Almighty repay you many times over for the good news you brought me today." And I went on, laying it on thick, as only Tevye can do. After all, I thought to myself, what did I have to lose? If I had been twenty years younger and if my Golde had still been alive, if I were the same Tevye the Dairyman as in ancient days, I would have fought to the last drop for my rights. But *"what are we and what is our life?"* What am I today? Only half of my former self, a broken reed, a shattered vessel. "Ah, dear God, our Father," I thought, "why do You always have to pick on Tevye to do Thy will? Why don't You make sport of someone else for a change? A Brodsky, for instance, or a Rothschild? Why don't You expound to them the lesson *Lech-lecho*—Get thee out? It seems to me that it would do them more good than me. In the first place they would find out what it means to be a Jew. In the second place, they would learn that we have a great and mighty God."

But this is all empty talk. You don't argue with God, you don't give Him advice on how to run the world. When He says, *"Mine is the heaven and mine is the earth,"* it means that He is the master and we have to obey Him.

I went into the house and said to my daughter, "Tzeitl," I said, "we are going away. We are moving to town. We've lived in the country long enough. *'He who changes his place changes his luck.'* Start packing right away, get together the pillows and featherbeds, the samovar and the rest. . . . I am going out, to see about selling the house. An order came for us to get out of here in three days and not leave a trace behind us."

When she heard this, my daughter burst into tears. The children took one look at her and burst out crying too. What shall I tell you? There was weeping and wailing and lamentation, just like on *Tish-abov*, the day on which we mourn the destruction of the Temple. I lost my temper and began scolding. I let out all the bitterness that was in my heart to my daughter. "What have you got against me?" I said. "Why did you have to start blubbering all of a sudden like an old cantor at the first *Slichos*? What do you think I am—God's favorite son? Am I the only one chosen for this honor? Aren't other Jews being driven out of the villages too? You should have heard what the Constable had to say. Even your Anatevka which has been a town since the world began has, with God's help, become a village too, all for the sake of the few Jews who live there. Are we any worse off than all the others?"

That is how I tried to comfort her. But after all she is only a woman. She says to me, "Where will we turn, father? Where will we go looking for towns?" "You talk like a fool," I said to her. "When God appeared to our great-great-great-grandfather Abraham and said to him, 'Get thee out of this country,' did Abraham question Him? Did he ask, 'Where shall I turn?' God told him, 'Go unto the land which I will show thee.' Which means, '. . . into the four corners of the earth.' And we too will go wherever our eyes lead us, where all the other Jews are going. Whatever happens to all the children of Israel, that will happen to this son of Israel. And why should you consider yourself luckier than your sister Beilke who was once a millionairess? If 'scraping up a living' in America with her Padhatzur is good enough for her, this is good enough for you. Thank God that we at least have the means with which to go. We have a little saved up from before, a little from the sale of the cows, and I will get something from the house. A dot and a dot make a full pot. *That too is for the best.*' And even if we had nothing at all, we would still be better off than Mendel Beiliss."

And so I persuaded her that we had to go. I gave her to understand that when the Constable brings you a notice to leave, you can't be hoggish and refuse to go. Then I went off to the village to dispose of my house. I went straight to Ivan Poperilo the Mayor because I knew that he'd had his eye on my house for a long time. I didn't give him any reasons or explanations, I am too smart for that. All I said was, "I want you to know, Ivan, my friend, that I am leaving the village." He asked me why. I told him that I was moving to town because I wanted to live among Jews. "I am not so young any more," I said. "Who knows—I might die suddenly." Says Ivan to me, "Why can't you die right here? Who is preventing you?" I thanked him kindly and said, "You'd better do the dying here, instead of me. I will go and die among my own people. I want you to buy my house and land. I wouldn't sell it to anyone else, but to you I will."

"How much do you want for your house?" he asked me. "How much will you give me?" I said. Again he asked, "How much do you want?" And I countered with, "How much will you give?" We bargained and dickered thus until at last we agreed on a price, and I took a substantial down payment from him then and there, so that he wouldn't change his mind. I am too smart for that. And that was how in one day I sold out all my belongings, turning everything into good money, and went off to hire a wagon to move the few odds and ends that were left. And now something else happened to me, something that can happen only to Tevye. Be patient a little longer and I will tell it to you in a few words.

Well, I arrived at home, and found not a house, but a ruin—the walls bare, stripped of everything, almost weeping in their nakedness. The floor was piled with bundles and bundles and bundles. On the empty hearth sat the cat, looking as lonely and forsaken as an orphan. My heart was squeezed tight and tears stood in my eyes. If I weren't ashamed before my daughter, I would have wept. After all, this was my homestead. This village was the nearest thing to a fatherland that I could ever have. Here I had grown up, here I had struggled all my days, and now all of a sudden in my old age, I am told, "Get thee out." Say what you will, it's a heartache. But Tevye is not a weakling. I restrained myself and called out in a cheerful voice, "Tzeitl, where are you, come here." And Tzeitl came out of the other room, her eyes red and her nose swollen with weeping. "Aha," I thought, "my daughter has started wailing again like an old woman on the Day of Atonement. That's women for you—crying at the least excuse. Tears must come cheap to them." "Fool," I told her, "why are you crying again? Aren't you being silly? Just stop and consider the difference between you and Mendel Beiliss." But she wouldn't listen to me. "Father," she said, "you don't know why I'm crying."

"I know very well why you're crying," I told her. "Why shouldn't I know? You are crying because you will miss your home. You were born in this house, this is where you grew up, and your heart aches at having to leave it. Believe me, if I were someone else and not

Tevye, I'd be kissing these bare walls myself and embracing these empty shelves. . . . I would be down on my knees on this earth. For I shall miss every particle of it as much as you. Foolish child! Look, do you see the cat sitting there like an orphan on the hearth? She is nothing but an animal, a dumb creature, and yet she too is to be pitied, left alone and forsaken without a master."

"I want to tell you that there is someone who is more to be pitied," said Tzeitl.

"For instance?" I asked.

"For instance, we are going away and leaving a human being behind us, alone and forsaken."

"What are you talking about?" I said to her. "What's all this gibberish? Which human being? Whom are we forsaking?"

"Father," she said, "I am not talking gibberish. I am speaking of Chava."

When she uttered that name it was just as if she had thrown a red-hot poker at me, or hit me over the head with a club. I began yelling at her, "Why bring Chava up all of a sudden? How many times have I told you that she is dead?"

Do you think she was taken aback by this outburst? Not in the least. Tevye's daughters are made of sterner stuff. "Father," she said, "don't be angry with me. Remember what you yourself told me many times, that it is written that one human being must have pity on another the way a father has pity on his child."

Did you ever hear anything like this before? I grew even more furious with her. "Don't speak to me of pity," I shouted. "Where was her pity when I lay like a dog in front of the priest while she was probably in the next room and no doubt heard every word? Where was her pity when her mother lay covered with black in this very room? Where was she then? And all the sleepless nights I spent? And the heartache I suffered and that I suffer to this day when I remember what she did to me and for whom she forsook me? Where is her pity for me?" My throat went dry, my heart began to hammer, and I couldn't speak any more.

Do you think that Tevye's daughter didn't find an answer to this too? "You yourself have said, father, that God forgives him who repents."

"You speak of repentance, do you? It's too late for that. The limb which has been torn from the tree must wither. The leaf which has fallen to the ground must rot. Don't say another word to me about it. *'Here ends the lesson for the great Sabbath before Passover.'*"

When she saw that she was getting nowhere with talk, and that Tevye was not the person to be won over with words, she fell on my neck and began kissing my hands and pleading with me, "May I suffer some evil, may I die here on the spot, if I let you cast her off as you cast her off that time in the forest when she came to plead with you and you turned your horse around and fled."

"What are you hanging around my neck for? What do you want from me? What have you got against me?" I cried.

But she wouldn't let me go. She clasped my hands in hers and went on, "May I meet with some misfortune, may I drop dead, if you don't forgive her, for she is your daughter the same as I am."

"Let me go. She is not my daughter. My daughter died long ago."

"No, father, she didn't die, and she is your daughter still. The moment she found out that we were being sent away she swore to herself that if we were driven out, she would go too. That's what she told me herself. Our fate is her fate, our exile is her exile. You have the proof right here. This bundle on the floor is hers," said Tzeitl, all in one breath the way we recite the names of the ten sons of Haman in the *Megilah,* and pointed to a bundle tied in a red kerchief. Then she opened the door to the next room and called out, "Chava."

And what shall I tell you, dear friend? There she stood in the doorway, Chava herself in the flesh, tall and beautiful, just as I remembered her, except that her face looked a little drawn and her eyes were somewhat clouded. . . . But she held her head up proudly and looked straight at me. I looked back at her, and then she stretched out both arms to me and said one word—"Father."

Forgive me if tears come to my eyes when I recall these things. But don't think that Tevye weakened and wept in front of his daughters. I have my pride to consider. But you understand that in my heart I felt differently. You are a father yourself and you know how you feel, when a child of yours, no matter how it has erred, looks into your eyes and says, "Father." But then again I remembered the trick she had played on me, running off with that peasant Fyedka Galagan. I remembered the priest, may his name and memory be blotted out, and poor Golde lying dead on the ground. . . . How can you forget such things? How can you forget?

And yet she was still my child. The same old saying came to me: "*A father has mercy on his children.*" How could I be so heartless and drive her away when God Himself has said, "*I am a long-suffering God and slow to anger*"? And especially since she had repented and wanted to return to her father and to her God? Tell me yourself, Mr. Sholom Aleichem, you are a wise man who writes books and gives advice to the whole world. What should Tevye have done? Should he have embraced her and kissed her and said as we do on *Yom Kippur* at *Kol Nidre:* "*I have forgiven thee in accordance with thy prayers.—*Come to me, my child?" Or should I have turned my back on her as I did once before and said, "Get thee out. Go back where you came from"? Try to put yourself in my place and tell me truthfully what would you have done? And if you don't want to tell me right away, I will give you time to think it over. Meanwhile I must go—my grandchildren are waiting for me. And grandchildren, you must know, are a thousand times dearer and more precious than one's own children. *Children and grandchildren—*that's something to reckon with!

Farewell, my friend, and forgive me if I have talked too much. You will have something to write about now. And if God wills it, we shall meet again. For since they taught me the lesson—*Lech-lecho,* Get thee out—I have been wandering about constantly. I have never been able to say to myself, "Here, Tevye, you shall remain." Tevye asks no questions. When he is told to go, he goes. Today you and I meet here on this train, tomorrow we might see each other in Yehupetz, next year I might be swept along to Odessa or to Warsaw or maybe even to America. Unless the Almighty, the Ancient God of Israel, should look about him suddenly and say to us, "Do you know what, my children? I shall send the Messiah down to you." Wouldn't that be a clever trick? In the meanwhile, good-bye, go in good health, and give my greetings to all our friends and tell them not to worry. Our ancient God still lives!

The Passover Expropriation

KASRILEVKA has always been known to ape Odessa. But since the recent disturbances began, Kasrilevka hasn't deviated from Odessa by a hair's breadth. Is there a strike in Odessa? Then there is a strike in Kasrilevka. A Constitution in Odessa? Then there is a Constitution in Kasrilevka. A pogrom in Odessa? Then there is a pogrom in Kasrilevka. Once a certain wag broadcast the news that in Odessa people were beginning to cut off their noses. Right away the people of Kasrilevka began sharpening their knives. Luckily, in Kasrilevka itself, one person apes another, so that each one waited for the next person to cut off his nose first. And they are waiting to this day.

After such an introduction, you won't be surprised to hear that hardly a day passes that you don't read in the papers of some fresh catastrophe taking place in Kasrilevka. You read, for instance, of how a gang of hoodlums broke into a bakery and expropriated all the twists and *beigels*. Or of how a shoemaker who had just finished a pair of shoes—he had only to add the soles and heels—was attacked in broad daylight, told "to lift up his hands and bless the Lord" and the shoes were carried off! Or again of how a poor man was going from house to house begging—this took place on a Thursday—when he was held up in a dark side street, a pistol was stuck in front of his face, and he was cleaned out of everything he had on him. Or listen to the story a woman tells. . . . But a woman's tale is not to be trusted. Women have notoriously weak nerves, the times are unsettled,

and she might have mistaken a stunted cow for a man. I don't want
to be responsible for spreading idle tales.

Suffice it to say that a whole series of expropriations took place in
Kasrilevka, one more terrible than the next. It got so that people
trembled for their very lives. Everyone longed for the good old bygone days when a single police official, who took a bribe now and
then, held the whole town in his grasp. They began to offer up
prayers to God: "Have pity on us, Almighty God, permit us to go
backwards, dear loving Father, renew our days as of old."

But this is still the introduction. The real story begins now.

Benjamin Lastechka is the richest man in Kasrilevka and the most
important. The extent of his wealth—and of his importance—is hard
to estimate. In the first place, he has rich relatives all over the world.
These relatives, it is true, are not as rich as they once were. What
can you expect in these times, with failures and bankruptcies taking
place every day? The wonder is that people still manage to exist, and
especially the people of Kasrilevka who are packed together like
herring in a barrel, in one small spot, devouring each other alive.
It is a lucky thing that there is an America which every year drains
off almost twice as many people as are killed in pogroms or die of
starvation.

And yet you see that in spite of all this, if God wills it, there is
still a rich man left in Kasrilevka, a man by the name of Benjamin
Lastechka, whom everyone envies because he doesn't have to ask
help of anyone except his rich relatives. Asking help of rich relatives
is not the easiest way in the world of earning one's bread, either, for
the majority of rich relatives, if you will pardon my saying so, are
notoriously hoggish by nature. And yet the fact remains that
Benjamin Lastechka is still the richest man in Kasrilevka. When you
need a favor, to whom do you go? To Benjamin Lastechka, of course.
And Benjamin Lastechka listens to your troubles, helps out sometimes
with a piece of advice, sometimes with a word of encouragement, and
once in a while with a groan of sympathy. These are good too, for
without them would it be any better? You'd still have the same pack
of troubles.

What is the difference between a rich man of Kasrilevka and, let us say, a rich man of Yehupetz? The rich people of Yehupetz have such tender hearts that they can't bear to look on at the plight of a poor man. They keep their doors locked and a lackey stationed outside to turn away anyone who is not respectably dressed. And when summer comes, they rise up like swallows and fly off abroad. Just try and follow them. But let a Kasrilevka *nogid* attempt such a thing—he won't get far, I promise you. Whether he likes it or not, Benjamin Lastechka has the honor of being the foremost citizen in our community. In all matters of charity, he has to be the first. He has to be the first not only in giving a donation, but the first to pick up his walking stick and go from door to door collecting charity from the poor to give to the poor.

And especially when it comes to collecting "wheat tithes" or money for *matzos* for the poor before Passover. Then you should see Benjamin Lastechka. I doubt if the greatest welfare worker on earth laboring in the most important cause, has ever sweated as much as Benjamin Lastechka sweats those four weeks before Passover. He swears that between *Purim* and Passover he sleeps every night with his clothes on. We might as well take his word for it, for what does he get for his pains? You might say that he does it for glory. And why not? Everyone likes a little glory, even a king doesn't scorn it. That's only human nature.

The custom of collecting "wheat tithes" before Passover is a very old one. It is an old-fashioned form of philanthropy, and yet I don't think it's as terrible a custom as people nowadays try to make you believe. They tell you that philanthropy is the ruin of Society. I don't care to enter into a philosophical discussion on the subject. I only want to say that according to my lights there is a far worse custom than this—and that is that the rich people aren't willing to give. And a thousand times worse than that is the fact that these noble souls who refuse to give anything try to make you believe that it's a matter of "principle" with them. I advise you to run from such people. They are as dry as a dried fish, and as lonely as a cat. . . .

Thank God that in Kasrilevka "principles" haven't become fashionable as yet. Those who don't give anything, don't give for the simple reason that they have nothing to give. But when it comes to raising "wheat tithes" for Passover, even that is no excuse. There is a common saying in Kasrilevka: "Every man must either give charity for Passover or he must receive it."

Strange people, these Kasrilevkites. Thousands of years have passed since their great-great-great-grandfathers freed themselves from their Egyptian bondage, and they still can't wean themselves away from the habit of eating *matzos* eight days in a row every year. I am afraid that this cardboard-like delicacy won't go out of fashion for a long, long time to come. All year long a Kasrilevkite is allowed to swell up from hunger, but when Passover comes—let the world stand on its head—he must be provided with *matzos*.

And so it has never yet happened in Kasrilevka that a person has died of hunger during Passover. And if by chance such a thing did happen it should have been marked elsewhere on the calendar. For obviously he did not die because he had no *matzos* to eat during the eight days of Passover, but because he had no bread during the remaining three hundred and fifty-seven days of the year. There is, you will admit, quite a difference between the two.

However, there is no rule to which you won't find an exception. The year in which my story takes place was such an exception, something happened that had been unheard of in the annals of Kasrilevka. It turned out that there were more people asking for help than there were people giving it. If it hadn't been for a feeling of pride, almost everyone in Kasrilevka would have applied for aid. It was truly pitiful to watch our *nogid,* Benjamin Lastechka, sitting in the Committee room the day before Passover, turning away people right and left, saying over and over, "There is no more money. It's all gone. I am very sorry."

"May you live until next year," they answered, and muttered under their noses, "and come to us for charity."

One after another the people came out of the Committee room with empty hands and flushed faces, as though they were coming out of a steam bath, and cursed the rich people with every curse known to them.

The last to enter was a band of young fellows, workingmen, who had been going around all winter without a stitch of work. They were banded together like a commune. They had sold everything they had to sell, and shared the proceeds. One of them had just pawned a silver watch and bought cigarettes which they were all smoking to still their hunger pangs.

When they arrived before the Committee, the workingmen put forward as their spokesman a ladies' tailor, by the name of Samuel Abba Fingerhut. But they didn't let Samuel talk alone. They all helped him present their case, talking, pleading, explaining that they were starving, that they were ready to fall down on their faces and pass out any minute. The Chairman of the Committee, Benjamin Lastechka, let them have their say, and when they were through, he spoke to them:

"I am very sorry, but you are all wasting your breath. First of all, none of you is married, and we give money only to married men. Second, you are healthy young men, well able to work and earn money for Passover. Third, we have a plentiful supply of poor people this year, a bumper crop in fact, more takers than givers. Fourth, we are ashamed to admit it, but since early morning we haven't had a crooked *kopek* in the safe. If you don't believe me, just take a look."

Saying this, the Chairman of the Committee turned all his pockets inside out for everyone to see how empty they were. The young men stood gaping, unable to speak. Only their leader Samuel Fingerhut wasn't overawed. He had a tongue in his head, that one, you didn't have to coach him. He addressed himself to the Chairman, half in Yiddish, half in Russian:

"It's a pity that you didn't start at the end, you would have saved yourself gunpowder. But I can give you an answer to all your arguments. In the first place, that we are single. That's to your advantage— you have that many less poor to provide for. In the second place, that we are able to work. *Zdelatie odolzhenie*—do us a favor: Give us work and we will turn the world upside down for you. Third, you speak of the numbers of poor people. Capitalism is to blame for that, *z'odnoi storoni*—on one side—, and the exploitation of the proletariat, *z'drugoi storoni*—on the other side. Fourth, as for your turning your pockets inside out for us, that's no *dokozhatelstvo*—it doesn't prove a thing. I have no doubt, *naprimer*—for instance—that at home your cupboards are bursting with *matzos,* eggs, onions, goose fat, *i tomu podobnoie*—and other such things—as well as wine for the *Seder*. All of you on the Committee are nothing but bourgeois exploiters and men without conscience, and *bolshe nitchevo*—nothing else—*Tovarishchi,* come, let's go!"

I must report that Kasrilevka, which imitates Odessa and other big towns, has not sufficiently progressed to the extent that an exploiter like our *nogid,* Benjamin Lastechka, should throw open his cupboards, divide the *matzos,* eggs, onions, potatoes, goose fat, and wine among the poor, and leave nothing for himself and his family. But I am convinced as surely as two times two makes four that our Kasrilevka exploiters will do it only if Odessa and Yehupetz and other big cities set the example. Kasrilevka, my friends, is not obliged to be the first at the Fair.

With a clear conscience, bathed, and dressed in holiday clothes, Benjamin Lastechka sat down to the *Seder* with his wife and children the first night of Passover. He felt tranquil and at ease, like a monarch who is secure in his kingdom. On his right hand sat his Queen, his wife, Sara-Leah, also dressed in her holiday best, with a new silk kerchief on her head from the folds of which peeped two dangling earrings of genuine 84-carat silver. All around the table sat the children, the princes and princesses, a whole bouquet of newly washed heads, rosy cheeks, and sparkling eyes. Even Zlatka the servant girl, who all year long labors like a donkey harnessed to a yoke, had washed her hair, bathed with perfumed soap, and put on a new cotton dress, fancy boots, and a wide red ribbon on her black hair. They all felt happy, free and unfettered as though they themselves had just escaped from bondage. The youngest boy had just rattled off the four questions with great aplomb, and his father the King, Benjamin Lastechka, was just beginning to deliver in a slow, solemn chant, at the top of his voice, the age-old response: "Because we were slaves unto Pharaoh in Egypt and the Eternal brought us forth with a mighty hand and with many wonders. And he punished Pharaoh with ten plagues. . . ." Benjamin was just beginning to enumerate the plagues when suddenly . . .

Suddenly there was a knock on the door, then another and then two more knocks. Who could it be? To open or not to open? They decided to open, since the knocking was getting louder and more insistent. The King and Queen and the Princes and Princesses all sat very still while Zlatka the maid opened the door and the band of young fellows entered with their leader, Samuel Abba Fingerhut, in front, and greeted the assembled company with a broad, good *yom-tev*. Our *nogid*, Benjamin Lastechka, though his spirits had sunk far down into his boots at the sight, put on a cheerful face and said, "Good *yom-tev*. Good day. Look who's here! And what good news do you bring?"

Samuel Fingerhut, the spokesman, stepped out from the rest of the group and began a speech in mingled Russian and Yiddish as was his custom:

"Here you sit, all of you, in a bright, warm room with the wine glasses in front of you, observing the holy *Seder*, while we poor proletarians are perishing of hunger outside. I consider this a great injustice. I hereby command you to have the dinner served to us instead. And if anyone of you lets out as much as a peep or opens a window, or dares call the police or—*tomu podobniu*—it will be the worse for you. *Tovarisch* Moishe—where is the bomb?"

The last words were enough to turn the family into graven images right where they sat. But when *Tovarisch* Moishe, a swarthy shoe-maker with a black shock of hair falling over his eyes and grimy fingers, approached the table and placed on it a tall, rounded object, covered with a rag, the whole household became as Lot's wife when she turned to see what had become of the cities of Sodom and Gomorrah.

And then Zlatka, the servant girl, her teeth chattering with fright, brought to the table, first the hot, spicy fish, then the soup with dumplings, then the pancakes and other holiday dishes—and the guests went after the food and wine with such appetite you could see they had not eaten for many days. They pledged themselves not to leave a crumb of food or a drop of wine. They even ate up the symbolical foods—the egg and shank-bone, the parsley and the bitter herbs. When they were done, nothing remained of the *Seder* except the prayer books. And while they were eating, the tailor Samuel Fingerhut mocked his host Benjamin Lastechka in these words:

"Every year we recite the *Hagadah* and you eat the dumplings. *Wnastojatcheie wremie*—this time—you recited the *Hagadah* and for once we are eating the dumplings." He raised his wineglass. *"L'chaim* —long life to you—my bourgeois friend, may God grant that you become a proletarian like the rest of us. Next year may we celebrate the Constitution!"

It was long past midnight and the poor *nogid,* Benjamin Lastechka, and all his family still sat around the table. In front of them stood the fearful unknown—the tall, rounded object covered with a rag. The young workingmen had warned them before leaving to remain sitting in their places for two hours—or there would be trouble. That night not one of them slept. They thanked God that they had escaped alive.

Well, and what happened to the tall, rounded object that stood on the table covered with a rag, the anxious reader asks. We are happy to reassure him. A tin container, which once held shoewax, now filled with *matzo* meal is not dangerous. It can stand for a thousand years and it won't blow up anything, except, God forbid—a good *yom-tev.*

The German

I AM as I've told you a Drazhner, that is I come from Drazhne, a tiny, a very tiny town in the Province of Podolia. Nowadays Drazhne has, so to speak, become a big town, with a railway station, a baggage room, a depot. When Drazhne first became a railway town, the whole world envied us. They all thought our fortunes were made. We would be shoveling up money in the streets. The town would become a gold mine. And people began pouring in from the surrounding villages into town. The townspeople began remodeling their houses, putting up new stores. The tax on meat was raised, there was talk of hiring another *shochet,* of building a new synagogue, of buying more land and enlarging the old cemetery. In short, there was great rejoicing. Just think of it. A station, a baggage room, a depot! It's true the town's teamsters rebelled a little, they didn't like the turn of events. But who listened to them? Rails were laid, railway cars brought down, a depot was built, a bell was hung, and a board was nailed up with the words *Stancya Drazhna.* And the deed was done!

When the train began running, my wife said to me, "What do you think you'll be doing now, Jonah?" (That's my name—Jonah.) "What should I be doing? The same thing everybody else is doing. All the citizens of Drazhne are hanging around the train. I'll hang around too." I took my walking stick, strolled over to the depot, and became, with God's help, a station agent—a *pravitel.* What does a station agent do? Well, if a man buys a wagonload of wheat he has to have someone load it on a car and send it off. A *pravitel* does that for him.

But since nearly everybody in Drazhne became a *pravitel,* business was not good. You spent most of your time hanging around, waiting for something to turn up. Sometimes you bought a sack of wheat from a peasant and sold it. You either made a profit on it or you took a loss. Sometimes you picked up a little commission on the side, you tried this, that and the other, anything that came along. But most of the time things were bad. There was nothing to do. You will say that we had nothing to do before either? Yes, but at least we had no railway station then. Now we had a station, with a depot, with a baggage room, with a bell, with trains coming and going, with noise and smoke and confusion—and we weren't any better off!

One day it happened that I was standing at the station in a rather dejected mood seeing off the Potchevo Express. The third bell had sounded, the locomotive had whistled, smoke was pouring out of the chimney. I take a good look, and there on the platform stands a tall, lean individual, an aristocratic-looking fellow in checkered trousers and a tall hat, surrounded by a pile of luggage. He stands there with his long neck stretched out, turning it this way and that way looking for something. "His lordship seems to be in want of something," I think to myself and it's as though something shoved me from behind. "Go up and ask him what he wants." Just as I start out toward him, if he doesn't move right toward me and lift off his tall hat and say to me in German in a sing-song accent, *"Gutt mo-yen, Mein Herr."*

"Good day to you," I answer him, partly in German, partly in Yiddish and the rest with my hands.

I ask him where he hails from. And he asks me if I know of a good inn, that is, a lodging place near by.

"Certainly," I tell him. "Why not?" And to myself I think, "What a pity that I don't own an inn. If only I had an inn I could take him to it myself. He is a fine-looking German, he looks as though he is able to pay." And then a thought flits through my head. "Fool! Is it written on your forehead that you don't own an inn? Just imagine to yourself that you do." And I address myself to him, partly in German, partly in Yiddish and the rest with my hands. "If *Mein Harr* wishes, let *Mein Harr* have me summon a driver and I will lead him, that is, conduct him, to the finest inn, that is, lodging place, immediately."

When he hears this the German is overjoyed and says pointing to his mouth, *"Haben sie vass essen? Shpeizen?"*

"The very best *shpeizen,"* I assure him. "You will feast like a Lord, *Harr* German. For my spouse, that is, my *frau,* is an excellent housekeeper, that is *hausfrau.* Her cooking and her baking are famous in this part of the country. The fish she makes may be eaten by royalty, by Ahasheurus himself."

"Ja wohl," he says joyfully, and his eyes sparkle and his whole face shines like the sun.

"A clever man, this German," I think to myself, and without wasting any more time I hire a wagon and take him straight to my house.

When we arrive I pass the whole story on to my wife—how God has sent me a guest, a German of a very superior sort. But does a woman understand such things? She begins abusing me because I have arrived at the wrong moment, right in the middle of housecleaning. "What's this guest you have there? What's the idea of bringing unexpected guests all of a sudden?"

"Woman," I tell her, "don't converse in our language. This gentleman understands German."

But does she listen to me? She goes on with her cleaning, sweeping her broom right in our faces, muttering angrily. All this time, the German and I are standing in the doorway not knowing whether to back out or to come forward.

At last I convinced her that this was no ordinary guest I was bringing. This guest would pay and pay well for his food and lodging. And we could make something extra from the deal too, lick a bone, as they say. Is that good enough for you? But no, when I finally convinced her, she turns around and says to me, "And where do you want me to put him, in the ground?"

"Be quiet, stupid woman. I told you not to talk, he understands what we are saying."

At last she caught on to what I meant. We showed him to our room, and in no time at all my wife was blowing up the coals under the samovar and getting ready to make supper.

When the German took a look at our room he turned up his nose, as though to say, "It could have been better." But what does a German understand? As soon as the samovar was brought in and tea was brewed, he took out a bottle of rum, poured himself a stiff drink, gave me a little drink too, and all was well. He spread out his suitcases, made himself at home as though he were in his father's vineyard, and we sat down together like old friends.

After we had finished our tea I began a conversation, about this, that and the other. What was he doing in Drazhne? Perhaps he wanted to sell something? Or buy something? It turned out that he was neither buying nor selling. He was expecting some machinery to pass through—some foolishness or other—and in the meanwhile he kept stealing looks into the oven and asking every minute or so when the meal would be ready.

"Apparently, *Mein Harr*," said I, "you believe in taking nourishment." He didn't answer me. But then how can you expect a German to understand when a person is trying to make a joke?

At last the table was set, and supper was brought in—a hot delicious chicken soup with dumplings, a whole chicken with grits and carrots and parsnips and all the other trimmings. (When my wife wants to she knows how!) "A good appetite to you," I said, but he didn't answer. He was going after that chicken as though he'd just been through a fast. "Enjoy your food in good health," I tell him, and he keeps on guzzling the hot soup. Do you think he even said "thank you" to this? Not a word or a nod. "He has no manners and he is a glutton besides," I think to myself.

Well, he finished eating, lit his pipe and sat smoking and smiling to himself. I could see my German friend looking all about him, he was looking for a place to rest his head, his eyes were shutting, and he wanted to go to sleep.

I beckoned to my wife. "Where can we put him to sleep?"

"What do you mean?" she says. "In my bed, of course."

Without any more ado she goes up to the bed and begins getting it ready for him, beating up the featherbed, beating and fluffing up the pillows. (When my wife wants to she knows how!) I look over at the German—he doesn't look very happy, he is probably displeased because feathers are flying. He wrinkles his nose and begins to sneeze violently.

I tell him, *"Gesundheit, Mein Harr,* long may you live." Do you think he says "thank you" to this? "He has no manners," I think to myself. "He isn't even civilized." Well, my wife made up the bed in good style, with featherbeds and pillows as high as the ceiling. A king might rest in such a bed. We wished him a very good night, and then we all turned in.

After I had gone to bed I heard the German snoring in his room, puffing like a locomotive, then gurgling and whistling like a slain ox. Suddenly he wakes up and begins to moan and groan and to scratch himself, to spit and to mutter. Then he turns over on the other side, begins to snore and to puff and to whistle for a while again, and then wakes up once more with a groaning and a moaning and a scratching and a spitting and mumbling. This happened several times over, until I heard him leap out of bed and begin tossing the bedding to the floor, one pillow after another with terrible fury, uttering strange oaths all the time such as, "A thousand devils! Sacramento! *Donner-wetter!"* I ran up and looked through a crack in the door. There stood my German, stark naked, in the middle of the floor, throwing the pillows one after another off the bed and spitting and cursing fearfully in his own language.

"What seems to be the trouble, *Mein Harr?"* I asked, opening the door. When he saw me, he fell on me in a great fury, hitting out with his fists as though he were going to murder me, then he grabbed my hand and led me to the window. He showed me his body, how it had been bitten all over, then chased me out and shut the door behind me.

"That German is crazy," I told my wife. "And much too finicky besides. He imagines he's been bitten by something and you should hear him. It's the end of the world."

"I can't understand it," my wife said. "What could be biting him? I just cleaned all the bedding for Passover, and doused it in kerosene."

The next morning I thought the German would be so insulted that he would run off to where the pepper trees grow. But nothing doing. He greeted us with a cheerful *"gutt mo-yen,"* again puffed on his pipe, again smiled, and again ordered food to be prepared. He wanted soft-boiled eggs with his tea. And how many do you think? Not less than ten eggs. With his meal, he poured himself a stiff drink, poured me a little drink too, and all was well.

Night came and the same thing happened all over again. At first he snored, whistled, puffed and gurgled, then he moaned, groaned, scratched himself and mumbled, leaped out of bed, threw all the bedding on the floor, spat and cursed in his own language: "To the devil! Sacramento! *Donner-wetter!*" And he got up in the morning, again said *"gutt mo-yen,"* again puffed on his pipe and smiled and ate and poured himself a drink and gave me a little drink too. This went on for several days in a row, until the appointed day came, his machines went through, and it was time for him to leave.

When it was time for him to leave, he began to pack his things, and he asked me to figure what he owed me. "What is there to figure?" I said, "It's a short account. *Harr* German, you owe me exactly twenty-five *rubles.*"

He opened his eyes wide as though to say, "I don't understand." So I said to him in my best German, *"Mein Harr,* you will pay me if you please the sum of twenty-five *rubles,* that is five and twenty *rubles.*" And I showed him with my fingers, ten and ten, and then five more. Do you think he appeared shocked at this? Not at all. He merely smiled and puffed on his pipe and then took out a pencil and paper and handed them to me saying that he wanted me to list each item separately.

"You are a clever German," I thought to myself, "but I am cleverer than you. I have more brains in my left heel than you in your whole head."

"Write down, *Harr German,* if you please—For the room, that is for six days' lodging, six times a *ruble* and a half, which makes nine *rubles.* Six times two is twelve samovars, which is twelve *guldens* or ninety *kopeks.* Six times ten eggs in the morning and ten at night is one hundred and twenty eggs, or twice threescore eggs, at a *ruble* a threescore—is two *rubles.* Six chickens at five *guldens* a chicken—aside from the grits and dumplings, the carrots and all the rest—is an even six *rubles.* Six nights—six lamps is sixty *kopeks.* You drank your own schnapps—two *rubles.* You had no sugar or tea—one *ruble,* which makes three *rubles* altogether. You had no wine—one *ruble,* which makes four *rubles* in all. There was no beer—seventy *kopeks.* Five *rubles* altogether. But to make it an even sum, put down five-fifty. Well, Reb German, doesn't that add up to twenty-five *rubles?"* I said this to him in all seriousness, and do you think he disagreed with me? God forbid. He kept on puffing at his pipe and smiling, then he took out a twenty-five *ruble* note and threw it at me the way you might throw a copper coin. We made our farewells, in a most friendly manner, and he went off on the train.

"What do you think of this kind of German, my wife?" said I.

"If God sent us this kind of German every week," she said, "it wouldn't be so bad."

The German left town. Scarcely three days had passed before the mail carrier came and handed me a letter, but first he told me to pay him fourteen *kopeks.* Why fourteen *kopeks?* The sender, he said, forgot to put a stamp on the letter. I paid him fourteen *kopeks* and opened the letter—it's written in German. I can't read a word of it. I began carrying the letter around with me from one end of the town to the other, trying this one and that one. Nobody knew how to read German. What's to be done? I searched the whole town through and at last found one man—the pharmacist at the drugstore— who could read German. He read the letter, then translated it for me. A German was writing to me to thank me for the comfortable and restful lodging he had at my house and for our hospitality and our kind-heartedness which he would never forget.

"Be it so," I think to myself. "If you are happy, I am satisfied." And to my wife I said, "What do you think of our German? Not a little bit of a fool, eh?"

"If God sent us such fools every week," she said, "it wouldn't be so bad."

Another week passed. I come home one day from the railway station and my wife hands me a letter and tells me the mailcarrier told her to pay twenty-eight *kopeks.* "Why twenty-eight *kopeks?"* "Because he wouldn't have it otherwise."

I opened the letter—it's again in German. I ran straight to my pharmacist and asked him to read it to me. The same German, he read, had just crossed the border and since he was on his way to his

Fatherland he wanted to thank me again for the comfortable and restful lodging I had given him and for our hospitality and kind-heartedness which he would never, never forget.

"Let my troubles fall on his head," I thought to myself. When I came home and my wife asked me, "What was in the letter?" I told her, "It's from the German again. He can't forget the favor we did him, the crazy fellow."

"If God sent us crazy fellows like him every week," she said, "it wouldn't be so bad."

Two more weeks passed and a large envelope arrived by mail and I was asked to pay fifty-six *kopeks*. I wouldn't pay it. The mail carrier said, "As you like," and took the letter back. But I had a pang of regret. I was curious to know where the letter was from—maybe it was something important. I paid him the fifty-six *kopeks* and opened the letter. I looked—it's again in German. I went right to my pharmacist and asked him to forgive me for annoying him so often. What else could I do? I was an accursed creature, I couldn't read German. The pharmacist took the letter and read me a long legend. It was the German once more. Since he had just arrived at home, he wrote, and had seen his beloved family, his *"frau"* and his *"kinder,"* he told them the whole story of how he had come to Drazhne, and how he had met me at the station, how I took him to my house, and gave him a most comfortable and restful lodging. Therefore he thanked us over and over for our hospitality and our kind-heartedness which he would never, never forget as long as he lived.

"To the devil with him," I said, wishing him every kind of ill luck. I wouldn't even tell my wife about this letter. I acted as though nothing had happened.

Three more weeks passed and I get a notice from the Post Office for a *ruble* and twelve *kopeks*. "What is this *ruble* and twelve *kopeks*?" my wife asks.

"I haven't the least notion," I told her. "May I know as little of evil." I made straight for the Post Office and began to inquire where I was getting this *ruble* and twelve *kopeks* from. I wasn't getting a *ruble* and twelve *kopeks*, they told me. On the contrary, I had to pay it. "For what?" I asked. "For a letter." "What letter? Maybe it's from the German."

They wouldn't tell me a thing. Would arguing with them have helped? I paid the *ruble* and twelve *kopeks* and got the letter—a large packet this time. I opened it up—it's again in German. I go to my pharmacist. "Forgive me sir, for bothering you again. I have a fresh affliction, a German letter." The pharmacist, not too bright a fellow either, you understand, left all his work in the middle and began reading me another long tale. It was from the same German, may his name be blotted out. What did he write? He wrote that this being a *"Firetag,"* that is a holiday in his country, he had invited all his friends and relatives to his house and when they were all gathered together he told them the whole story from a to z. How he had come to the small town of Drazhne, how he was stranded at the railway station, all alone in a foreign land, unable to speak or understand the language, how he met me and how I took him to my house, in what friendly manner my wife and I received him, gave him a comfortable and restful lodging, let him have the finest room in the house, the best of food and drink and treated him altogether with such honesty and decency, that he couldn't refrain from writing again to thank me for our hospitality and kind-heartedness which he would never, never in the world forget.

"A practical joker, that German," I thought. "I'll never accept another letter, not even if it's stamped with gold."

Another month passed—two months. No more letters. Finished. I was almost beginning to forget about the German. Suddenly there arrives a notice from the railway station that there is a package for me worth twenty-five *rubles*. What kind of package could this be for twenty-five *rubles*? I racked my brain. My wife sat and racked her brain also, and we could think of nothing. Then something occurred to me. We have friends in America—it must be a present from them, a ship's ticket, a lottery ticket, something of the sort. I didn't waste any more time, but went straight to the railway station and asked for my package. They told me to be so kind and please pay two *rubles* and twenty-four *kopeks* first. What could I do—I had to get the two *rubles* and twenty-four *kopeks* and pay it in to get my package.

I got the package—a very handsome little box, carefully wrapped—and ran home with it. I began to unpack the box and what should fall out of it but a portrait? We take a good look. What sort of nightmare or evil visitation is this? The portrait is of him, the *shlimazl,* the German himself with his long scrawny neck, and his tall hat and a pipe in his mouth. With the photograph was a short note written in German, probably the same thing again; he was thanking us for the lodging and our hospitality and our kind-heartedness which he would never, never forget. What a thorn in the flesh this German was getting to be! You can imagine what we both wished him at that moment.

Several more months passed. It's the end. No more German. Thank God we were rid of this affliction. He was as good as buried. My mind was at ease again. I was a happy man. But do you think we were through at last? Listen—it was not the end.

One night without warning there arrived a telegram for me telling me to go to Odessa without fail and to find a certain merchant named Gorgelshtein. This merchant was stopping at the Hotel Victoria and had to see me on very important business. Odessa? Gorgelshtein? Hotel Victoria? Business? "What can it all mean?" I asked my wife. She at once began to urge me to go, for who knows, it might be something important. Maybe a commission, maybe something to do with wheat.

But it's easy to say—go to Odessa. A trip to Odessa costs money. But lack of money is no excuse, when it comes to an important business matter. I borrowed a few *rubles,* got on the train and went off to Odessa. I arrived in Odessa and began inquiring everywhere for the Hotel Victoria. I found the Hotel Victoria, went in, and asked, "Do you have a man here by the name of Gorgelshtein?"

"We have a man by the name of Gorgelshtein," they told me.

"Where is he?"

"He is not in his room right now. Could you please return at ten o'clock in the evening?"

I returned at ten o'clock in the evening. Gorgelshtein was not in. "If you come back at ten in the morning you will find him in."

I came back at ten in the morning. Where was Gorgelshtein? Gorgelshtein had just been there and had left. Before leaving, he had asked them very particularly that if a man from Drazhne should come to see him, they should tell him to be so kind as to return either at three in the afternoon or at ten in the evening.

I returned at three in the afternoon and again at ten in the evening. No Gorgelshtein at either hour.

What more shall I tell you? I wandered around Odessa like a lost soul for six days and six night. I neither ate nor slept. I suffered tortures of body and mind until I finally succeeded in meeting Gorgelshtein.

Gorgelshtein turned out to be a dignified-looking man with a handsome black beard. He greeted me cordially, invited me to be seated.

"You are," he said, half in German, half in Yiddish, "the man from Drazhne."

"I am," I said to him, "the man from Drazhne. What about it?"

"Last winter," he continued, "a certain German lodged at your house."

"Yes," I said. "He did. What about it?"

"Nothing," he said. "This German is a partner of mine in the machinery business." He combed his black beard with his fingers and leaned back in his chair. "I have a letter from him from London. He writes me that when you come to see me in Odessa I must be sure to convey to you his kindest greetings, and to thank you for the comfortable and restful lodging he had at your house and for your hospitality and kind-heartedness. He is indebted to you for your honest and decent treatment of him which he can't possibly forget forever and ever, as long as he lives."

That's the affliction I have to bear. I am planning, with God's help, after the holidays, if God grants me life, to move from Drazhne to some other town. I will run wherever my eyes lead me, wherever my feet carry me, I don't care where, just to get rid of this *shlimazl,* this German, may his name be blotted out from memory forever and ever.

Third Class

THIS, dear reader, is not a story. It is just a few words at parting, a little advice from a good friend.

Before I leave you for good, I should like—out of gratitude for the patience with which you have listened to my tales—to be of some use to you, to leave you with a few last cordial words of advice from a practical person, a traveling salesman. Pay attention to what I tell you and remember it.

If you ever plan to take a trip of any distance at all, and you want to feel that you are really traveling, that is, if you want to get some pleasure out of your trip, don't under any circumstances travel first class or second class.

As far as first class is concerned, there isn't much to say. May Heaven protect you from that! I don't mean the first-class carriage itself. That's comfortable enough. The seats are soft and roomy and rich, with every convenience you can ask for. That much, I'll admit. What I'm talking about is the passengers, the people you have to travel with. The first-class carriage is usually empty, and what's the pleasure in riding all by yourself with no one to talk to? You might even forget *how* to talk. And if once in fifty years you are lucky enough to find another person in the car with you, it turns out to be either a fat aristocrat with puffed-out cheeks like a trombone player blowing on his instrument, or a haughty dame that reminds you of your mother-in-law, or a foreigner in checkered trousers who sits glued to the window so that you couldn't tear him away even if the train caught on fire. If you have to ride with people like that, all sorts of gloomy thoughts begin to crowd into your head, and pretty soon, against your own will, you find yourself thinking about death. And what's the sense of that?

And do you think that second class is any better? Here you sit surrounded by people, people who may look no different from yourself, people with the same desires and the same temptations as yours. They would like to speak to you, they may be dying to know who you are, where you come from and where you're going. But they sit facing each other like dummies in a store window. They have filled their mouths with water and are afraid to open them up. You don't get a word out of them.

Across the aisle from you sits a fashionable gentleman, with long fingernails and a waxed mustache, who looks familiar. You'd swear that you had seen him somewhere before, but you can't remember where. You have a feeling that his pedigree is like yours; his grandfather may have been a count, but much more likely he was a *shammes*. But what can you do when he won't say a word? He twirls his mustache, looks out of the window, and whistles.

If you want to annoy this kind of person, or better still if you want to kill him outright so that he won't even get up on the Day of Resurrection, speak to him in any language you like, but preferably in Russian so that the gentlemen—and even more, the ladies—in the carriage will hear every word: "*Yesli ja nie oshabaius*—if I am not mistaken—didn't I once have the pleasure of meeting you in Berdichev?"

That is a thousand times worse than spitting on his father's grave.

Or if you happen to be somewhere in Poland, you can start talking to him in Polish: "*Pszepraszam pana*—I beg your pardon, sir—but if I am not in error, I think I once had the honor of meeting your father not far from Yarmelinetz. He was a tenant, if I remember correctly, of Count Potocki."

You might argue that this is not such a great insult, but tell me— what does Yarmelinetz and a tenant of Count Potocki smack of? You might as well have come right out and told the whole carriage that this elegant young man is a Jew. But wait! I will tell you something that I actually witnessed and you will see what I mean.

I was traveling in an express train and there was no third-class carriage, so that I had no choice, I had to ride second class. Across the aisle from me sat a young gentleman who might have been either Jewish or Gentile, but he seemed to be more Jewish than Gentile. Still, how could you tell? He was a good-looking young fellow, well-dressed, clean shaven, from all appearances a sportsman, with a black belt on his white trousers, and quite obviously a ladies' man, a gay young blade. Why do I say a blade? Because throughout the trip he was most attentive to a certain young lady, a *fraulein* with an elaborate *chignon* and a pince-nez stuck on a small up-turned nose. They had become acquainted on the train, but they were carrying on like old friends. She offered him chocolates and he, in turn, kept her amused first with Armenian and then with Jewish anecdotes, after which they both rolled with laughter. Especially the Jewish stories, which he told with great gusto, and without paying any attention to the fact that I who sat across from them was a Jew and might feel insulted. . . .

In short, the romance was rolling along, the wheels were well-greased. Before long he was sitting in the same seat with her (at first he had sat across from her) looking deep into her eyes, and she was toying with the chain of his watch. Suddenly at some little station— I have forgotten its name—a man got on, a lame, sallow-faced, perspiring little man with an umbrella. He advanced toward our sportsman, with outstretched hand, and said in a loud voice, in plain, clear Yiddish, "Well, well, how are you? I recognized you through the window. I can give you regards from your uncle Zalman from Menastishtch."

I don't have to tell you that before the train started again our sportsman had disappeared and the young lady was left alone. But that is not the end of the story. A few stations further on the young lady began to get her things together too. Though I sat near her, she didn't even look in my direction. I might as well have not been there. But when she got off, who should meet her on the platform but a fine, patriarchal-looking Jew with a long beard like Father Abraham himself, and a stout woman in a peruke, with diamond earrings. They fell or her neck with tears in their eyes. "Riveleh," they cried, "Riveleh, my daughter."

I don't have to point out the moral of this story. I only wanted to show you the kind of people you meet when you travel second class, and to urge you not to travel that way, because when you travel second class you are bound to feel like a stranger, you're a stranger among your own people.

But if you travel third class, then you're completely at home. If anything, you may feel yourself just a little too much at home. It's true that you won't be as comfortable. If you want a place to sit, you have to fight for it. All around you there is noise and confusion, crowding and pushing. You don't know just where you are and who your neighbors are. But it doesn't take you long to become acquainted with each other. Soon everybody knows who you are, where you are going and what your business is. And you in turn know who they are, where they are going, and what their business is. At night you don't have to worry about sleeping. There is always someone to talk to. And if you don't happen to feel like talking, the others will and you won't get any sleep anyway. But why should anybody want to sleep in a train? There is too much going on all the time. If you talk long enough, you will arrive at something. I have seen perfect strangers close important business deals, find matches for their children, become friends for life in the course of a trip. At the very least you are bound to learn something that will come in handy sometime.

For instance, the conversation will get around to doctors, influenza, toothache, nerves, rest cures, Karlsbad and such things. Sounds like a waste of time, doesn't it? Nevertheless, I once had an experience. . . . I was traveling with a group of men and the talk got around to doctors and medicines and what not. I was suffering at that time from stomach-trouble. One of the men, a salesman from Kamenitz, recommended a powder to me. He had gotten it, not from a doctor of medicine, but from a dentist. It was an excellent remedy, he said, a sort of yellow powder. That is, the powder itself was white like most powders, but it came in a yellow paper. He swore—this salesman from Kamenitz—by his own good health and by his wife and children that if he was still alive today it was due entirely to this yellow powder. If

it hadn't been for this powder he would have been eaten by worms
long ago!

I wouldn't need many of these powders, he told me. Only two or
three and I would be a new man. No more indigestion, no more
doctors; bloodsuckers, liars and quacks, every one of them. I could
tell them all to go to the devil.

"If you like," he said, "I will give you a few of my powders and
you will have something to thank me for the rest of your life."

Well, he gave me the powders. I came home, took one powder, then
another, then a third. I went to sleep, and about midnight I woke up
in such pain I thought my soul was passing out. I was sure that I was
dying. They called a doctor, they called two doctors—they barely saved
my life. And now I know from experience that if a Kamenitzer
salesman offers you a yellow powder that is a sure cure for anything,
you can tell *him* to go to the devil. You see, every bit of knowledge
has its price.

If you are traveling third class and the time comes for morning
prayers and you don't have a *tallis,* a prayer shawl, and *tfillin,* or
phylacteries, with you, don't worry. Someone will see to it that you get
both *tallis* and *tfillin,* and anything else you need. In return, however,
when you are through with your prayers, be so kind please as to open
your suitcase and pass around whatever food you have brought.
Whisky is good, cakes are fine, eggs are always welcome, chicken or
fish are excellent. If you have only an apple or an orange or a piece
of *shtrudel,* don't be ashamed, pass it around. We'll take whatever
you have to offer, nobody will refuse. On the road and in company,
appetites are lively.

If you have a bottle of whisky or wine with you, you will certainly
get plenty of customers. Everyone will taste your wine and give you
his expert opinion of it. One will tell you that it's Bessarabian Muskat,
another that it's imported Akerman. A third will get up and try to
shout them both down: "What do you mean—Akerman? Muskat?
It's a Kovashener Bordeaux." At this, another man will appear from
the farthest corner and with a knowing smile will take the glass
out of your hands as if to say, "Listen to me, friends, when it comes to
wine, ask a real expert." He takes a few sips, his cheeks begin to

flame and he becomes as jolly as a wedding guest. He lifts the glass and announces, "Gentlemen, do you know what this is? I can see quite clearly that you don't. It's plain—simple—pure—clean—kosher home-made Berdichev port."

And everyone agrees with him, that's just what it is, Berdichev port, the kind we make in our own cellars. And everyone takes a few more sips, and everyone's tongue becomes loosened, and he tells you all about himself, and listens while you tell about yourself. We talk, joke, exchange stories, like good friends and comrades. It's a wonderful feeling.

If you are traveling third class to a town you're not familiar with and if you don't know where to stop, ask anyone in the carriage. You will get as many suggestions as there are people. One will tell you that the only place to consider is the Frankfurt Hotel. The Frankfurt, he will tell you, is bright and clean, and warm and cheap. "Frankfurt?" another will break in. "God help you. It's dark and dingy and cold and dear, they'll rob you. If you want to be comfortable, go to the Hotel New Yorker." At this a third man interrupts, "What for? Is he lonesome for bedbugs? Don't listen to them. Frankfurt, New Yorker, bah. You come with me, let me take your suitcase and we'll go to the only good hotel in town, the Rossya. That's where real Jews go."

But be careful about letting him take your suitcase, or you may never see it again. But I ask you, is there any place nowadays in this land of ours where you can be sure that you won't be robbed? After all, being robbed or not being robbed, if you want to know the truth, is no more than a matter of destiny. If it is your fate to be robbed, it will happen to you in broad daylight on the public highway. Police won't save you, neither will a bodyguard. And neither will prayers. If you come out alive, you can bless your lucky stars!

So you might as well travel third class. Take the advice of a good friend and a practical man, a traveling salesman.

Adieu. . . .

Glossary*

Al-ḳein n'Kvach l'cho (Al-ḳen ne Kave lecho): The beginning of the second part of the prayer *Alenu:* "Therefore we hope . . ."

Bar Mitzvah: A thirteen-year-old Jewish boy who is confirmed; the confirmation ceremony itself.

beigel (bagel): Hard circular roll with hole in the center like a doughnut.

blintzes: Cheese or *ḳasha* rolled in thin dough and fried.

borsht: A beet or cabbage soup, of Russian origin.

bris: Circumcision ceremony.

Bubi-Kama (Baba Kama): "First Gate," A Talmudic treatise on compensation for damages.

chad gadyo (Had Gadya): "One Kid," an Aramaic nursery song sung at the conclusion of the *Seder* home service on Passover.

charoses (haroses): A mixture of nuts and apples to symbolize the clay which the children of Israel worked into bricks as slaves in Egypt. Eaten at the *Seder* services on Passover.

Chassidim: Plural of *chassid*; members of a mythical sect founded in the middle of the 18th Century by Rabbi *Bal-Shem.*

cheder: Old-style orthodox Hebrew school.

cholent: Potted meat and vegetables cooked on Friday and simmered overnight for Sabbath eating.

chremzlach: Fried *matzo* pancakes, usually served with jelly or sprinkled with powdered sugar.

datcha: Summer cottage in the country.

dreidel (from the German *drehen,* "to turn"): A small top, spun with the fingers, and played with by children on *Hannuḳah* in East European countries.

*Many of the spellings of Hebrew words used in these stories are rendered phonetically as they occurred in popular usage. In such cases, throughout the glossary, the correct transliterated spelling is given in parentheses.

dybbuk (same as gilgul): A soul condemned to wander for a time in this world. To escape the perpetual torments from evil spirits it seeks refuge in the body of a pious man or woman over whom the demons have no power.

eirev (erub): The law limiting the movements of the pious and the carrying of objects on the Sabbath, hence also the rope used to define the area of free movement.

esrog (ethrog): A large sweet-smelling citrus fruit of the lemon family waved together with palm, myrtle and willow branches in the synagogue procession during the Feast of Tabernacles.

farfel: Doughy preparation cut into small pieces.

fisnoga: Comical combination of the Yiddish *fis* (feet) and the Russian *noga* (feet).

gabai: Synagogue treasurer.

Gamorah (Gemara): the Aramaic name for the *Talmud,* i.e., to learn. (See *Talmud*).

Gehenna: Hell.

gilgul (see *dybbuk*).

gospoda (Russian): Term of address, "Gentlemen!"

gragar: A noisemaking toy used by Jewish children during the *Purim* festival; a rasping chatterbox.

gribbenes: Small crisp pieces left from rendered poultry fat, eaten as a delicacy.

grivnye: Silver coin worth ten *kopeks.*

groschen: Small German silver coin whose old value was about two cents.

gulden: An Austrian silver florin worth about forty-eight cents.

Gymnasia: A secondary school preparing for the university.

Hagadah: The book containing the Passover home service, consisting in large part of the narrative of the Jewish exodus from Egypt.

hamantash: A triangular pocket of dough filled with poppyseed or prunes and eaten on *Purim.*

Hannukah (Channukah): Described variously as "The Festival of Lights," "The Feast of Dedication," and "The Feast of the Maccabees." It is celebrated for eight days from the 25th day of *Kislev* (December). It was instituted by Judas Maccabeus and the elders of Israel in 165 B.C. to commemorate the rout of the invader Antiochus Ephinanes, and the purification of the Temple sanctuary.

Hashono Rabo (Hoshana Rabbah): The seventh day of *Succoth* (Feast of Booths).

Kabala (Cabala): Called "the hidden wisdom," mystical, esoteric knowledge that, beginning with the 13th Century, arose in opposition to the rationalism of the *Talmud.*

kaddish: The mourner's prayer recited in synagogue twice daily for one year by the immediate male relatives, above thirteen years, of the deceased; a son who recites the *kaddish* for a parent.

kasha: Groats.

Kazatsky (Kasatske): A lively Russian dance.

kiddush: Ceremonial blessing said before Sabbath and other holiday meals.

kneidlach: Balls of boiled matzo meal cooked in chicken soup.

knishes: Potato or *kasha* dumpling, fried or baked.

Kol Nidre: The opening prayer of the synagogue liturgy on the eve of *Yom Kippur.*

kopek: A small copper coin; there are 100 *kopeks* in a *ruble.*

kosher: Food that is permitted to be eaten and prepared according to the Jewish dietary laws.

kreplach: Small pockets of dough filled with chopped meat, usually boiled and eaten with chicken soup.

kugel: Noodle or bread suet pudding, frequently cooked with raisins.

luftmensch: Literally "air man," but refers to a person who has neither trade, calling, nor income and is forced to live by improvisation, drawing his livelihood "from the air" as it were.

mah nishtano: Literally, "What is the difference?" The first words in the opening "Four Questions" of the Passover *Hagadah*, traditionally asked by the youngest child in the household at the *Seder* service. (See *Seder*).

matzos: Unleavened bread eaten exclusively during Passover to recall the Jewish Exodus from Egypt.

mazl-tov: Good luck!

mazuza (mezuzah): Small rectangular piece of parchment inscribed with the passages Deut. VI. 4-9 and XI. 13-21, and written in 22 lines. The parchment is rolled up and inserted in a wooden or metal case and nailed in a slanting position to the right-hand doorpost of every orthodox Jewish residence as a talisman against evil.

Medresh (Midrash): A body of exegetical literature, devotional and ethical in character, which attempts to illuminate the literal text of the Bible with its inner meanings. The *Midrash* is constantly cited by pious and learned Jews in Scriptural and Talmudic disputation.

Megila (Megillah): Literally, "a roll," referring to the *Book of Esther* which is read aloud in the synagogue on *Purim.*

melamed: Old style orthodox Hebrew teacher.

Mishnayos (The *Mishna*): A compilation of oral laws and Rabbinic teachings, edited by Judah ha-Nasi in the early 3rd Century A.D., which forms the text of the *Talmud.* It is obligatory for pious Jews to study it constantly.

Mohel: The religious functionary who performs circumcisions.

nogid: A rich man, the leading secular citizen of a community.

nu: Exclamatory question, i.e., "Well? So what?"

Oleinu (Alenu): Literally, "it is our duty," the last prayer in the daily Jewish liturgy.

Pesach: Passover, the festival commemorating the liberation of the Jews from their bondage in Egypt. It lasts seven days, beginning with the 15th of *Nisan* (March-April).

Perek: A chapter of the *Talmud.*

piatekas: Five-*kopek* piece.

Pupik: Navel; a term of teasing endearment.

Purim: Festival of Lots, celebrating the deliverance of the Jews from Haman's plot to exterminate them, as recounted in the *Book of Esther.* It is celebrated on the 14th and 15th of *Adar*, the 12th Jewish lunar month (March).

Rabbiner: A crown rabbi, chosen by election at the requirement of the Czar, to be an official functionary. Generally unpopular in old Russia.

Raboisi (Raboisai): Respectful Hebrew term of address used in Talmudic disputation, saying grace after meals, etc. Literally, "my masters."

Rambam: Popular name for Rabbi Moses ben Maimon (Maimonides) eminent, Spanish-Jewish philosopher and physician (1135-1204).

Reb: Mister.

rebbitzen: The rabbi's wife.

Rosh Hashono (Rosh Hashanah): The Jewish New Year, celebrated on the 1st of *Tishri* (in September), is the most solemn day next to *Yom Kippur* (Day of Atonement).

Rov: Rabbi.

schnorrer: A shameless beggar.

seder: The home service performed on the first two nights of Passover (see *Hagadah*).

Shabbes: Sabbath (Saturday).

shadchan: A matchmaker; a marriage-broker.

Shahu notch shomayem (bastardized Russian-Hebrew): Walk at night under the heavens.

Shalachmones: A friendly offering of food or drinks on *Purim*.

shammes (pl. *shamosim*): A synagogue sexton.

sheigetz (pl. *shkotzim*): A Gentile youth.

sheitel: A wig worn by ultra-orthodox married women.

Shevuos (Shabuot): Variously known as "The Festival of Weeks" and "Pentecost." It originally was a harvest festival and is celebrated seven weeks after Passover.

shi-shi (shishi): Sixth part of the Scriptural portion for the week read aloud on the Sabbath in the synagogue, and regarded as a great honor for the reader.

shkotzim: Plural of *sheigetz*.

shlimazl: An incompetent person, one who has perpetual bad luck. Everything happens to him.

Shma Koleinu (Shema Koleinu): "Hear our voices!" The first words of a Day of Atonement hymn; a popular idiom meaning: "idiot."

Shma Yisroel (Shema Yisroel): The first words in the confession of the Jewish faith: "Hear, O Israel: the Lord our God the Lord is One!"

Shmin-esra (Shemoneh 'Esreh): Eighteen (actually nineteen) benedictions, forming the most important of the daily prayers, recited silently, standing up, by the worshipper.

shochet (pl. *shochtim*): Ritual slaughterer.

shofar: Ram's horn blown in the synagogue at services on *Rosh Hashanah* and *Yom Kippur.*

Sholom Aleichem: Peace be unto you! Equivalent to the more prosaic greeting "Hello!"

shul: Synagogue.

Simchas Torah: "Rejoicing over the Torah," the last day of *Succoth* (Feast of Tabernacles), celebrating the completion of the reading of the Torah.

Slichos: Penitential prayers.

starosta: Village elder or "mayor" in Czarist Russia.

succah: A booth made of fresh green branches in which pious Jews celebrate the Feast of Tabernacles. This is done symbolically to recall the forty years wandering—"that your generations may know that I made the children of Israel to dwell in booths, when I brought them out of the land of Egypt."

Succos (Succoth): The Feast of Tabernacles, survival of the ancient festival on which male Jews were required to go on a pilgrimage to the Temple in Jerusalem. Lasts nine days and begins on the 15th day of the seventh lunar month of *Tishri* (September-October).

sudah: A feast.

tallis (tallith): Prayer-shawl.

tallis-kot'n (tallith katon): "Small *tallis,*" a four-cornered fringed undergarment worn by male orthodox Jews in pursuance of the Biblical commandment to wear a garment with fringes.

Talmud: The Corpus Juris of the Jews, a compilation of the religious, ethical and legal teachings and decisions interpreting the Bible; finished c. A.D. 500.

Talmud Torah: Hebrew school for children.

teigl: A confection.

tfillin: Phylacteries.

T'hilim: Psalms of David.

Tish'abov: Ninth day of the month of *Ab* (August) set aside by Jewish tradition for fasting and mourning to commemorate the destruction of Jerusalem and the Temple, by Nebuchadnezzar in 586 B.C. and by Titus in A.D. 70.

Torah: "Doctrine" or "law"; the name is applied to the five books of Moses (Pentateuch), and in a wider sense to all sacred Jewish literature.

treif: Food forbidden by dietary laws or not prepared according to their regulations.

Troika: A Russian sleigh drawn by three horses.

tzimmes: Dessert made of sweetened carrots or noodles.

vareniki: Fried dough filled with cheese or jelly.

verst: A Russian measure of distance, equal to about ⅔ of an English mile.

vertutin: Cheese or cooked cherries rolled in dough.

Yekum Perkon (Yekum Purkan): Aramaic prayer in the Sabbath service.

yeshiva: Talmudic college.

Yom Kippur: Day of Atonement; the most important Jewish religious holiday; a fast day, spent in solemn prayer, self-searching of heart and confession of sins by the individual in direct communion with God. It takes place on the tenth day of *Tishri*, eight days after Rosh Hashanah (New Year).

yom-tev (yom-tov): Holiday.